Things That Go Bump In The Night

☆   ☆   ☆

He didn't know how long he had slept. At first the bump, bump, bump was part of a dream of a night on the boat, of him and Yvonne. Then he came up out of the dream, slowly, coming to the surface from a great depth. The bump, bump, bump was still there. The dinghy, Kevin thought. The boat had shifted in the current, and now the dinghy was bumping against the side.

No. The dinghy was tied up at the pier. He and Yvonne had decided that, hadn't they? He was coming up from the dream faster now, near the surface of wakefulness.

All he could hear over his heartbeat was the bump, bump, bump against the side of the boat. No dream, no dream.

And the thump of a foot above him, on the deck, and the feel of a boot heeling slightly for a moment with the weight.

It was not a dream.

HELL GATE

HELL GATE

DAVID STOUT
& RUTH FURIE

THE MYSTERIOUS PRESS
New York · Tokyo · Sweden · Milan
Published by Warner Books

A Time Warner Company

MYSTERIOUS PRESS EDITION

Copyright © 1990 by David Stout and Ruth Furie
All rights reserved.

Cover design by Jackie Merri Meyer
Cover illustration by Don Osyczka

The Mysterious Press name and logo are trademarks of Warner Books, Inc.

Mysterious Press books are published by
Warner Books, Inc.
666 Fifth Avenue
New York, New York 10103

A Time Warner Company

Printed in the United States of America

Originally published in hardcover by The Mysterious Press.
First Mysterious Press Paperback Printing: August, 1991

10 9 8 7 6 5 4 3 2 1

For Shelley, Cheryl, Clay, and Craig

We apologize to mapmakers for our geographical revisions of Long Island, New Jersey, and Westchester and Rockland counties, and to the New York Jets football team for giving them yet another new home. This is a work of fiction, and the events herein happened entirely in our imaginations.

We wish to thank Judith Weber, Nat Sobel, and Sara Ann Freed for their careful editing and helpful suggestions.

PROLOGUE

Man and boat blended noiselessly into the gentle darkness of the waves, the oars moving with the silence of an owl in flight. The small rubber dinghy was almost invisible as it moved between the sailboats bobbing on their moorings. Black water, black boat, and black clothing. Although he had done this before, he was sure that the pounding of his heart could be heard over the easy lapping of the tide.

Across the bay the also-rans of the sailboat race were fastening the sail covers, coiling the lines, and closing the hatches. Occasionally a boat horn would sound, signaling that the captain was ready to come ashore. Many of the racers were headed for drinks and backslapping at Chowder's. The man would go there, too, after . . .

He rowed to a sloop at one of the farthest moorings and tied the dinghy to the side facing the bay. As he climbed over the gunwales of the bigger boat, he kept low, almost slithering as he shifted his weight onto the cockpit seat. Squeak! The rubber dinghy rubbed against the hull. He stopped, waiting to see if the noise would repeat, to see if he should retie the small boat to keep it silent. Nothing. Just a soft bump. Good.

He told himself not to hurry, to be careful, but above all

to be silent. He tried to ignore the thumping in his chest that echoed in his head. He told himself that no one else could hear it. He had been on boats for most of his life, felt easy on the water. But tonight his confidence had fled. Terror floated next to him.

It wasn't until he was safely away from the sloop that he felt the evening breeze on his face, that he began to enjoy the summer evening. As he neared the dock, he pulled freely on the oars. Out of danger now. A beer. Maybe a shot, too. At Chowder's.

1

A freshening breeze blew off Long Island Sound, bearing the smells of salt water and fish and the hint of coolness. It was a beautiful August evening, just after dusk, and the running lights of sailboats were visible in the distance through the window behind the bar at Chowder's, where Kevin McNulty was hunched on a stool. He could see the pinpoints of greens and reds as the sloops, ketches, and yawls maneuvered in the dark.

The sea smells came through the open window near the end of the long, curving oak bar where Kevin hunkered over his beer. The smells blended, not unpleasantly, with aromas of gin and beer and fried sole and the spiced fish soup for which Chowder's was famous.

The sounds that skipped across the water were of engines, winches, dinghies bumping against hulls; there were also wisps of voices and laughter. And occasionally, over the bar babble and clinking ice, Kevin could hear the music of halyards jangling against masts.

Kevin McNulty loved that boat music. He thought there must be no better music in the world for a child to go to sleep by, or a man and woman to make love by.

Now the music made him almost want to cry—or, since he couldn't very well do that in public, made him want another beer, his fifth or sixth, whether he needed it or not. The beer would dull his consciousness, or wash out the wound in his soul, or—whatever.

He and Yvonne were selling their boat. Sometimes Kevin wondered if they should have put their own name on it, instead of keeping the name the former owner had christened it with: *Lark IV*. No, it made no difference.

They had already started talking about selling the house as part of the split-up, so it made no sense even to think of the boat as something that was part of what they had been, though it surely was.

Thinking about the boat made Kevin look around the bar for Harvey Green. There he was, thirty feet or so away, talking with a bunch of hard-drinking powerboat types. Harvey was a good mechanic, and he ran a tiny marina that was little more than a garage with a couple of long piers sticking out into the water at the back. His father had started the business, and Harvey had taken it over after the Second World War. Harvey was well off, if you figured the value of his property, though you would never know it to look at him. Word was he had gambled away a lot of money over the years. He was a weird duck, Harvey. But he was a good mechanic.

Kevin and Yvonne had kept their boat at Harvey's. Harvey didn't charge them that much for a mooring, and he was good with the engine. Keeping the boat at Harvey's wasn't quite like belonging to the Port Guinness Yacht Club, but Kevin and Yvonne couldn't have afforded a yacht-club membership even if they had been invited. The closest they had ever got to the club was the weekly sailboat races; they started at the yacht club, even though anybody could race in them. That way, Kevin and Yvonne had had a champagne social life on a beer budget, but that was all over, too.

"Harvey!" Kevin shouted, surprised that his voice sounded a little slurred.

Harvey didn't look his way. Hard-of-hearing, and too dumb to get a hearing aid. Christ, he was past sixty. How much pride does a guy need?

"Harvey!" Kevin tried again. He did not want to go over to him and risk losing his barstool.

Quince, the owner of a forty-foot yacht, was glowering at Harvey, obviously engaging him in some deep conversation. Kevin wondered if Quince was pissed at Harvey for keeping him waiting on some engine job. Quince, tall and dark, with neatly scissored hair, had large eyes that seemed to have no irises because they were so black. His boat had a flying bridge and an enormous array of electronic equipment, evidenced by a battalion of aerials deployed at the top and sides of the boat. Quince was a regular at Chowder's and on race nights bought drinks for the winners, who often had lost their sea legs by the time they went home.

Kevin decided to look for an opening before trying to get Harvey's attention. He watched, sipped his beer, listened with one ear to the talk around him, with another to the exhibition football game on television.

Kevin didn't know what to make of Quince—that was what everyone called him, just Quince. He had an inconspicuous office over on Guinness Boulevard. Trucks, something to do with trucks, Kevin thought. Sometimes Quince drove a van, sometimes a pickup. Sometimes he drove a car. Whatever he drove, it had a phone. Quince usually had a serious, busy expression, especially when he was driving with one hand and holding the phone in the other.

Kevin had heard, variously, that Quince was from Argentina, or Cuba, or Bolivia, or Ecuador, or Colombia. Kevin thought Quince looked like a younger Omar Sharif. Quince definitely had a no-nonsense way about him, and Kevin could imagine him making a lot of money at . . . something.

Sometimes Kevin wished he had more money. But newspapermen didn't make that much. As a sportswriter, Kevin got to travel now and then, but that was getting to be a drag.

Kevin looked over again at Harvey, whose head was bobbing up and down. Quince was smiling now, maybe Harvey had a satisfied customer.

At least three times in as many weeks, Kevin had asked

Harvey to make certain the boat's engine was working right, because he and Yvonne wanted to sell the boat. Harvey had said he would look around for a buyer. He had promised to check the engine every so often and look into the bilge whenever he was on board.

It had felt strange and sad to Kevin not being on the boat all season, not since he had moved out of the house. He supposed Vonnie felt the same way. Well, a lot of things went by the wayside with a marriage.

Now Kevin had his own buyer, a sportswriter friend from *The Bugler,* up in Rockland County. But had Harvey tuned the engine?

"Harvey," Kevin said again, waving. This time, he caught Harvey's attention, so he slid off the stool, hoping the glass of beer in front of it would save his place at the bar.

"Listen, Harv, have you gotten to the engine on the Pearson? We want it right for when we sell it."

"You kidding? Anyhow, the engine's fine. I tuned it up two weeks ago. Running like a top. You don't put no strain on it, the kind of little trips you two take. You ain't been on it all season anyhow."

"Great, Harv. I know you're busy as hell." Kevin had been deliberately vague with Harvey; he hadn't told him, in fact, that he already had a buyer and that they were taking the boat the next morning and never bringing it back.

Kevin wasn't sure just why he had played it so close with Harvey. Yvonne trusted his intuition up to a point, and if she ever asked him he would say that he didn't trust Harvey a hundred percent, even though he liked him some of the time. If Harvey had known they intended to sell to a guy way up in Rockland he might have invented a mechanical problem to keep the boat, saving it as a bargain for some friend of his. Meanwhile, he'd tell Kevin and Yvonne they'd have to take a little less than they wanted, because the boat really had a problem.

Harvey was short and lean, with a leathery face that had been more handsome a lot of sunburns and beers ago and that was still not bad, considering. Although he was a two-fisted drinker, his face never bloated and turned scarlet like most of the Irish drinkers Kevin knew, including some in his family. His hair, what was left of it, probably had been blond once, but now it was the color of old lace curtains.

Kevin went back to his beer. He could drink as much as he wanted to, as long as he was willing to balance it off against a hangover. He wouldn't think about the boat anymore tonight. Getting rid of the boat wouldn't be half as bad as selling the house. . . .

Jesus, the house. He couldn't think about that, couldn't handle it at all.

Bruce the bartender slid the beer to him, and he took a gulp.

"On me, Kevin," Bruce said. Bruce was friendly, and he used his powerful, ham-thick forearm to nudge Kevin's. Or maybe Bruce, who collected Kevin's bets, was just feeling sorry for him.

"Thanks, my man," Kevin said. Kevin figured he must be doing a lot of drinking to get a free beer from Bruce. Or maybe Bruce knew, like everybody else, about his troubles.

"Hear about Tolly from the yacht club?" Bruce asked, leaning over the bar.

"No, what?" Kevin said. Tolly was the club's launch operator and sometime mechanic. He had towed Kevin and Yvonne back to Harvey's once when their engine had conked out on a choppy day, which made Tolly fine forevermore in Kevin's book.

"He bought the locker," Bruce the bartender said. "Found dead this morning, lying on his back in a boat. A big inboard. Monoxide, they think."

"Jesus," Kevin said. Tolly was a nickname; nobody knew his real name, except perhaps Harvey, who had been a drinking buddy of Tolly's. Maybe that's why Harvey was such a jerk just now, Kevin thought.

"Yeah," Bruce went on. "Owner of the boat came on board, and there Tolly was, lying there. Face all bloated. Could be he had some leftover booze in him, too. Could have made him pass out quicker, you know?"

"Damn. He used to come in here sometimes, no?"

"Yeah, sure. Truth is, they didn't want him hanging around the bar over at the club, so he had to come here to do his drinking. Damn shame."

"Yeah. Jesus." Though Kevin had not known Tolly well enough to feel remotely close to him, he did remember the favor. That, plus the simple fact that someone he had known in the world had left it forever, made him feel all the gloomier. Maybe he would say something to Harvey. . . .

The voices and laughter of the racers only deepened Kevin's grief. He tried not to let the noises get to him. Just two and a half weeks to go until Labor Day, so the racers were getting in as much sailing as they could, knowing the summer was winding down. For some sailors, the races were cheerful tests of seamanship, for others they were as serious as the America's Cup.

Once, a couple of summers ago, he and Yvonne had come close to winning a race in their division. They had been having a great sail, even though Kevin had just had a couple of beers. Vonnie was pretty good at reading the ripples coming over the water and sensing how the wind would shift. They had caught the wind just right on a couple of tacks in a row, and suddenly they had the lead.

Then Kevin had screwed it up, failing to cleat the mainsheet properly, so that it came loose and the sail flogged and Yvonne almost went over trying to right things. She had been angry as hell over missing the chance to win the race. No, mostly at him. And Kevin had made the mistake of laughing, just laughing. Because mostly he didn't give a goddamn about the race, it was the sailing he liked, just being out on the water with her, having a few beers. But she hadn't quite understood that, and he couldn't blame her too much. She hadn't forgiven him all that summer, the way he hadn't given a damn.

Now another summer was almost over. The exhibition football game on television, the game Kevin was watching with interest, since he had bet on it, was another sign of that.

The sailboat racing was one of the more lovely things

about Port Guinness, a North Shore village tucked between Port Washington, to the west, and Huntington, just to the east, and less crowded than either. Port Guinness was a little enclave, reachable by a two-lane road off the Long Island Expressway, and most everyone had a boat, or sailed with someone who did, or was about to buy one.

The races were organized more or less along lines of sailing experience and boat length and were almost always followed by beer or gin and tonics at Chowder's. Indeed, there were lithe, suntanned young men and women who had grown up hearing their parents talk about the races. Having heard so much boat talk, they thought everyone lived the way they did.

Kevin hadn't grown up like that, and although Yvonne was a Port Guinness native, her parents had never owned a boat. But Kevin and Yvonne had enjoyed the races, together, for a while. Now, the races and the merriment seemed to Kevin farther away than Montauk, way out at the tip of the Island, or Cape Cod, or Greenland, or anywhere.

Things are bad, he thought. I'm the only one here who cares about that football game and can't enjoy what's left of the summer.

He had always loved football, though he played it only well enough to sit on the bench in high school, and had been happy at first when his newspaper, *Long Island,* assigned him to cover the Jets. After they moved from New Jersey back to Long Island, the Jets were a choice beat for any reporter. But he had covered them for two years, and the novelty was wearing thin. Besides, Yvonne had been bothered by the trips he had to take, by his staying out too late after practices, drinking with some of the players. She had heard the stories of groupies following the pro jocks. Jesus, she flattered me, Kevin thought, taking a big gulp.

Now, as he watched the Jets going through the motions against the Packers on an incongruously steamy evening in Wisconsin, he knew he would be out another twenty bucks.

Shit, betting on an exhibition game was stupid. The Jets had no cornerbacks, and their linebackers weren't putting the pressure on the quarterback, and so the Jets wouldn't cover—cover!—an exhibition game, and he was already thinking about covering spreads!

Yvonne was right; he bet too much. Drank too much, too. And she was a better sailor than he was, with a much better head for detail, more patience, more precision. Which was what you needed on a boat, big or small. Probably would have been a better parent, too.

No, not now for that subject. Not now . . .

Tomorrow might be the last day they would do anything together on the boat, and it probably wouldn't be a lot of fun. They would take it from Port Guinness all the way west on Long Island Sound, into the East River, down to the tip of Manhattan and up the Hudson, way up the Hudson to Haviland, in Rockland County. They were moving the boat themselves, because to have it trucked over to Haviland would cost five hundred bucks or more, and they needed the money. It was as simple as that.

It was a good boat, a damn good boat. A Pearson Ariel, a twenty-six-foot sloop. A classic, some boat people had told him, Pearson didn't make them anymore. Yvonne always called it a boaty boat. Well, they couldn't afford a classic, not now. More to the point, neither could afford it separately.

It would be a long, long trip. All day long. Kevin had told the buyer, Marty Diehl, a young sportswriter whom he sometimes saw at Jets games, that they would try to be there before dark, but that he couldn't promise that. Marty Diehl had agreed to give Kevin and Yvonne a ride down the Palisades Interstate Parkway and across the George Washington Bridge to the bus terminal, where they could get a subway to midtown Manhattan and catch a train back to Long Island.

The more Kevin thought about it, they would be really lucky to make it by dark. Getting there by dark depended not only on getting an early start, but on the engine's running right all the way and nothing else going wrong. And they damn well had to get to Hell Gate for the right tide or they could forget it.

Hell Gate was where the East River turned south and the

Harlem River joined it. Long Island Sound's currents pushed at the river's eastern mouth and the Atlantic pushed at its south end. Hell Gate was where it all swirled together, and depending on the state of the tide the water could be going up to six miles an hour in addition to its cross-currents. A boat the size of their Pearson could only go with the tide.

Between sips, Kevin smiled smugly for a moment, remembering how surprised Yvonne had been (she being the better sailor, and all) to discover that he had been right: They couldn't cut their trip almost in half by going through the Harlem River into the Hudson. That's because there were bridges that were too low for the mast of their Pearson, so they had to go clear to the tip of Manhattan. And they weren't about to pay Harvey to unstep the mast. . . .

Maybe they would have to stay overnight somewhere. Kevin wondered how they would handle that.

He hoped they wouldn't fight too much on the boat.

2

From the deck off the living room, Yvonne watched the racing boats turn at the buoy. Sails puffed and flapped and puffed again as the craft rounded the marker.

The breeze is just right, she thought, an easy turn. Sometimes the best entertainment was watching the boats try to turn when the sailors had misjudged the wind or trimmed the sails wrong. When she wasn't racing herself, Yvonne liked nothing better than playing dockside captain. Kevin often laughed at her as she prompted from her deck chair: "Trim your main, fall off, you're turning too tight." A smile flitted briefly on her lips, replaced almost immediately by the pouting, worried expression that she more often wore these days.

Some of the racers had hailed her as they passed. Then Scotty Durer yelled, "Why don't you get your landlubbing ass out here? Afraid we'll beat you again?"

He had a cheerful voice and knew that it carried like a boat horn. She couldn't pretend she hadn't heard him. She went to the railing, leaned out and forced a smile she didn't feel.

"Didn't you hear? My crew mutinied."

Scotty Durer's white teeth flashed in his tan face. He kept looking at her, waiting for more. His wife, Melba, said something to him that Yvonne didn't and wasn't supposed to hear.

"Watch out," Yvonne shouted. "Your main is luffing."

Scotty lifted his drink from the holder near the helm and raised it, saying, "I luff you too."

At this, Melba brought a Top-Sider up to Scotty's backside and, turning toward Yvonne, she cupped her hands and shouted, "Meet us at Chowder's, we'll buy you a drink. At the rate we're going, we'll get beat by the dinghies."

Scotty, brought up by Melba's assessment, turned his attention to his captain duties and yelled, "Ready about." Melba moved to tend the jenny. Yvonne smiled as she watched Melba's short, plump frame scurry about the deck of the thirty-seven-foot Hunter. A beautiful boat, an expensive boat, and polished like a jewel. Yvonne wondered how much they spent on the boat every year.

If you have to ask, you can't afford it, she thought.

In Port Guinness there were plenty of people who spent more on their boats than on their houses. Scotty spent lavishly on everything. He had never learned to do anything else. His mother had always spoiled him. Always got him the latest toy, whatever clothes he wanted. And yet, Scotty was a nice guy, always had been. Maybe wanting things makes people mean, Yvonne thought.

"Should I go down to Chowder's and let Scotty spend some of his money on me? Or sit around feeling sorry for myself?" Yvonne said aloud. Tess, the Doberman lying on the deck catching the last warmth of the day, opened one eye and wagged her little stump of a tail a few times. "You wouldn't mind if I went, would you, old girl."

The dog's tail thumped on the deck. Ah, Tess was getting old. Gray in the muzzle and a little hard of hearing. Yvonne remembered when she and Kevin had bought her as a puppy, when they had moved into the house. Tess was supposed to protect Yvonne on all those nights when Kevin was out late or out of town covering a game. Well, she was protective. She'd growl when anybody came close to Yvonne, even Kevin sometimes.

Yvonne remembered the first time, when Tess was barely

out of puppyhood, that the dog bared her teeth when Kevin hugged Yvonne. After that, it was a joke. "Don't touch me or I'll call Tess," Yvonne would say. But the dog grew out of growling at Kevin just as she had grown out of chewing Yvonne's shoes. And now, suddenly, she was an old dog, and Kevin and Yvonne would go their separate paths. Yvonne stifled a sob and rubbed a wrist across her eyes.

Cool it on the self-pity, she told herself. Melba's invitation is just what you need. Get up and get out. Chowder's was made for summer evenings. So what if Kevin is there inhaling suds at the bar. That doesn't have to keep you away.

Yvonne couldn't go to Chowder's by herself. Not yet. Not until everybody knew, until people didn't expect that she would be with Kevin, until she didn't have to explain.

The invitation, hollered casually across the water, was perfect. She had someone to be with. But the more she thought about Kevin and Chowder's, the angrier she got. Chowder's was mostly a bar for Kevin, some place for him to curl a foot around the rail and lose himself in a beer glass. Well, she would let him stay draped over the bar. Tonight she would party.

Yvonne lingered on the deck until most of the sails had passed and made their turn to head back into the harbor. The watercolors that she had been dabbling with earlier had dried. She held up one and then another, eyeing them critically. She thought she had improved; she could do with just a few strokes what used to be a labored rendering. She wondered whether suffering really made a difference, somehow made her painting better.

A few other sailors who passed close to shore yelled and Yvonne waved, although the sinking sun behind the boats made it impossible for her to distinguish even the boats, let alone the sailors.

She would give Scotty and Melba plenty of time to get there before her. And she would put on some of that new eye makeup she'd just bought at Bloomie's. She admitted to herself that she wanted Kevin to think she looked great. But why? Spite? Or was there still a spark?

Damn him. She had loved him, but not the person he had become. The drinker, the gambler, the guy who always wanted to be right, who couldn't see his own faults. She tried, most of the time, not to lose the memory of the Kevin she had loved, the sensitive, good-natured, funny, even adventurous Kevin. The friend who could really hold up his end of a conversation, who was right there in the next paragraph.

He had messed it up. Too much drinking, too much betting on stupid games. Too much of God-only-knew-what on the road, and too many lies covering up when he got home. At least, she thought he had told some lies.

The drinking, that had done it. A person should put up with only so much. As though she hadn't felt bad about the baby.

Before she knew it, the tears were there again.

No! Don't go to Chowder's with red eyes. People will think you've been crying or drinking. That's not what you want them to think of you. You're self-sufficient, you're jolly, you're the former cheerleader. You're also too damn proud and an asshole. So put that emotional baggage away for tonight.

Her hot-pink sundress was tied at the nape of her neck. Her shoulders and back were tanned. The soft cotton fabric flowed gently as she paraded in front of the full-length mirror in the bedroom, where the king-size bed looked too big now.

Dressing up lifted her spirits, made her feel like a teenager for a moment. (God, her fifteenth high school reunion was coming up next summer!) Now, looking at herself, liking the way she looked, she giggled and tossed her head.

Ah, what a salve vanity can be, she thought. But maybe it's just a case of arrested development; I'm still a seventeen-year-old cheerleader.

She turned to one side, then the other, and then tried to leap as she used to at the end of a cheer. She muffed it and looked around, grateful then that she was alone.

These days, self-administered pep talks were common. "You have your health and food in the fridge. You have options. . . ."

Losing the baby had been like losing a piece of herself. The baby. She thought of it as that. Even though it hadn't been that far along. But far enough along for the tests to show that it would have had Down's syndrome.

Quite rare before thirty-five, the doctors had said. Not really a person, just a developing mass inside her. A mass that was developing wrong, the tests said. A mass that neither she nor Kevin could deal with. But it had been a baby, hers and Kevin's, planned for, wished for, eagerly awaited. Mongoloid, special care. It might have had other defects, too; they often did, the doctors said. What to do?

They had begun to have long discussions late into the nights. They had called on a couple of support groups. Kevin had even gone to see a priest. But the gods or fate or chance made the decision for them. (Blessing or punishment?) And so the baby—they never knew what sex it was, didn't want to know—had become a mass, a mass that was delivered after the most excruciating pain Yvonne had ever felt. Was childbirth that bad? Her mother had said that when the baby is okay, it's worth it. Yvonne had felt close to her mother during the days her mother had spent with her after she came home from the hospital. Her father had called, but he had stayed in Florida. The beloved chauvinist thought it was women's stuff.

Kevin and Yvonne were told to try again. But now that was unlikely. Their marriage hadn't stood the strain; maybe it was a test that they had somehow failed.

Oh, more than that. At least she was willing to admit that she had felt partly relieved when she miscarried. Kevin hadn't been willing to admit it (he had lied to himself again), and had blamed her. He couldn't admit that, either.

Enough. Stop wallowing. Tonight the lady's not for mourning.

Today, tonight, she was dressed to kill and she was going to have a good time without Kevin. Tomorrow she would have to spend the whole day with him, moving the boat, and for sure there would be more Kevin than she could stand. Probably a hung-over, hangdog Kevin, at that.

Yvonne left a few lights on, set the phone-answering machine, and turned on the radio before she went down the steps to the garage where the roof of the aging Chevy Caprice reflected the overhead light. Yvonne put Tess in the run that opened from the garage. She put down fresh water and gave her a biscuit, a ritual that told the dog she was to stay behind. "Here's your cookie, old girl, now stay and mind the house."

It was only a mile and a half to Chowder's, but in that distance the rocks and marsh grass and sand and sparse housing gave way to the rows of village Cape Cods and then the shops and marinas. Chowder's was one of the few restaurants in town that had their own parking lot. That lot too, in recent years, had become an expensive piece of real estate. Almost too expensive to leave as a parking lot. There had been rumors that the restaurant would be sold to a developer who wanted to put up condos, but no developer had shown up at the planning board yet.

Yvonne had been aware of real estate for as long as she could remember. Her father had owned the office where Yvonne now worked on weekends, the office that Scotty's mother, Rosalie, had purchased when Yvonne's dad decided to retire and go to live in Florida. Her dad had always made a good living, but Rosalie had doubled the business before she'd had it two years. Her dad had liked Rosalie, admired her capacity for work. Yvonne's mother would get kind of quiet when Rosalie was mentioned.

Once, when Rosalie was still working as a real estate salesperson, before she bought the office and became a broker, Yvonne's dad had come into the kitchen to talk to Yvonne and her mother and he started praising Rosalie. A deal she had been working on was turning out to be really big, largely through Rosalie's efforts. Yvonne's mother had slammed down whatever it was she had in her hand and said, "She never does anything the way everybody else does it." Her mother had stormed out of the room, and her father had said, "Your mother thinks women ought to be less aggressive than Rosalie is."

Yvonne parked the car and turned off the engine and the lights, but before she got out she checked her makeup in the rearview mirror and took a few deep breaths because her heart was racing and her stomach felt as if it were turned upside down. "Shit, Kevin, why can't I stop this?" She waited in the darkness for a few minutes, rehearsing what she might say if she saw him, or if he came over to the table, or if she met him on the way in.

When she finally walked into Chowder's, despite all of her resolve, she immediately looked toward the bar, her pulse pounding in her head, and saw Kevin, who looked at her as if he had been waiting for her to arrive.

"Vonnie," he called across the bar.

Yvonne walked toward him, resenting his presumption, wishing she had the nerve to snub him and at the same time longing for the days of the old Kevin and Yvonne perched at Chowder's bar, exchanging jokes with the other regulars.

On the other side of the room, at one of the tables, Melba had been watching for Yvonne. When she saw her, Melba read the pain in her friend's face. Before Yvonne reached Kevin, Melba was at her heels, chattering a busy greeting full of words and empty of meaning. Yvonne and Kevin exchanged wide-eyed looks of hurt and recrimination, but he said only, "How's Tess?" and she answered, "She's fine. I took her for her rabies shot."

Melba stepped into the awkwardness. "Kevin, you old sot, Yvonne is joining us for a few drinks, and maybe we'll even persuade her to dine with us. When you're through here, why don't you stop by our table for a few minutes. Scotty would like to say hello, I'm sure."

She's a genius, Yvonne thought with some relief; she's friendly but she's obviously not including Kevin in the evening's festivities.

Kevin looked toward the table where Scotty, Rosalie, and a young guy who looked like a tennis star were in an animated, good-natured exchange. "Scotty seems to be all taken up in conversation right now, Melba, but thanks. I'll be leaving soon. I'll stop by before I go," he said.

His lips were drawn tight across his teeth in what passed for a smile with everyone but Yvonne. His glass was full, but Yvonne did not call attention to it; it was probably high time he went home. Yvonne recognized the signs: Kevin's eyes slightly out of focus, his lips pursed ever so slightly when he talked so that he wouldn't slur. She could also tell by the way his trousers were wrinkled at the crotch that he had been sitting at the bar for a couple of hours.

Kevin turned to Yvonne and said, "I'll meet you at Harvey's at eight, unless you want me to pick you up."

"Harvey's at eight is fine," Yvonne said, not wanting to continue the conversation in which a decision would have to be made. Let her make it now and be done with it.

"Is . . . is that a new dress?"

She had bought it the week after Kevin left, but this was only the second time she had worn it. "Not really," she said.

"It's smashing," Kevin said. "Isn't it smashing, Melba?"

"You're absolutely right," said Melba. "Now I think I will whisk her away and show off that smashing dress to the rest of the bar. Maybe you'll even be on one of the videos." Melba nodded toward a corner, where a captain and his crew, red-faced and beaming behind a trophy surrounded by empty beer cans, were being videotaped and photographed.

As Melba guided Yvonne away, Yvonne gave her arm a little squeeze and said, "Thanks for getting me through that."

"I didn't know he'd be here when I invited you. I know you two are having it tough. But what the hell are you doing with him tomorrow?"

"We're taking the boat to its new owner. We can't afford to keep it and it's too big for one person to sail alone, at least the way it's rigged. And whenever I miss sailing, I'll offer to crew."

"You can crew for us anytime, if you can put up with a sloppy captain. And I'll just sit back and watch."

"You've got yourself a deal. I love the way your Hunter

sails. Hi, Scotty, thanks for the invitation. Hello, Rosalie, how's the Millridge deal going? Did they get their mortgage?"

"Yes," answered Rosalie. "Your commission should be rolling in about a month from now." Rosalie was a smaller, more compact version of her son. The same deeply tanned and lustrous skin, the same large sherry-brown eyes ringed with thick black lashes that matched the hair. Their clothing was always neat and well-tailored—excessively neat, Yvonne sometimes thought. Rosalie was flashier, though. She had flair and an eye for color.

Tonight she was wearing a powder-blue blouse with matching trousers. Yvonne thought the trousers were linen and the blouse silk. Over them she wore a lavender coat-length, sleeveless cashmere cardigan. Yvonne was certain that Rosalie had crocheted it herself; it had a little drama to it that store-bought things couldn't match. Yvonne noticed that Rosalie's eye makeup was the same as hers and wondered how many others had been sold that combination this week at Bloomie's.

"Good, I'll be able to use the money," Yvonne said.

"You ought to give up teaching and work with us full-time," Rosalie said. "It's in your blood, you know."

"So's teaching. I've never been able to choose." It was true. Yvonne's mother and several of her aunts had been elementary school teachers, and she had been raised with funny stories about the antics of little children. Her father's conversation was more often than not about what house sold for what, who was asking too much for a house, which neighborhood was appreciating. . . . So Yvonne had studied art at Bennington and worked in the real estate office during vacations.

"That's a great sweater," Yvonne said. "Another original?"

"Not exactly. I borrowed the idea from an old drawing."

"It's still great."

"Thank you."

"I bought that computer you recommended," Yvonne

said as she slid in beside Rosalie. Rosalie shifted a bag of yarn to her other side.

"So soon," said Rosalie. "Well, the sooner, the better. Keeping the listings on the computer is so much easier. And being able to work from home will be even better. You'll see."

"I'm ready to go as soon as you can get me hooked up. I have a modem and I've copied the office programs. I may need some help getting my machine set up at home, though."

"You won't need all the office programs. I have one program I use to plug into a network where I get crochet lessons."

"You don't need lessons. You could be giving the lessons."

"There's always more to learn. Just the other day . . ."

Rosalie was interrupted by Scotty at this point, complaining, "You girls are always talking shop. Besides, Yvonne, I haven't introduced you to Erik Walters. He's working with me now."

Scotty's work, which didn't seem to occupy much of his time, was running a travel agency in a storefront office adjoining his mother's real estate agency. Yvonne suspected that Rosalie paid most of Scotty's bills.

"Hi, Erik," Yvonne said. "Don't let Scotty work you too hard."

"No danger," Erik said, grinning beautifully with his wide mouth and big, even teeth. "I'm your basic sloth."

"The only things busy in that office are the spiders," Melba said, "spinning webs between you and Scotty."

While this exchange was going on, Rosalie nudged Yvonne and said, "I'll come over some night soon and get you started on the office programs."

Kevin stopped by on his way out and said to Yvonne, "I'll meet you at Harvey's at eight. Unless you want me to pick you up."

"Eight is fine," Yvonne said. "That should get us through Hell Gate at the right time." She wondered if he was drinking so much that he blacked out. They had already settled the arrangements about meeting at Harvey's.

Rosalie got up to leave the group shortly after cocktails and hors d'oeuvres, enough hors d'oeuvres to make a meal. Yvonne felt sated after sampling the trays that Scotty had ordered: a platter of shrimp, a bucket of steamers, another platter of oysters a la Chowder's (oysters with bread crumbs and Dijon mustard, baked in the shell), and several servings of fried mozzarella.

"You young folks have a nice evening," Rosalie said. "I have to go back to the office and then I'm going home. I have to get my beauty sleep. If I told my nutritionist what I ate tonight, he'd be apoplectic."

"What's that guy supposed to be doing for you anyway?" Scotty, always the diplomat, asked.

"Haven't you noticed how much more energy I have lately? And I think my skin is better, too."

"So now you can work sixteen hours a day instead of fourteen. Terrific. And there was nothing wrong with your skin, Ma."

"I'll consider those remarks as compliments and quit while I'm ahead. When you get back, Yvonne, I'll show you which programs you need. And I'll stop by to check on Tess."

"Terrific," Yvonne said.

Scotty continued to order huge amounts of food and drink, and the conversation stayed pleasant and gossipy. Erik fawned over Yvonne all evening but wasn't so pushy as to ask to take her home. He was younger than Yvonne, intelligent, polite, and dressed in very expensive casual clothes. Yvonne thought she remembered seeing the same grayed mauve sweater in an ad for a very chichi Italian designer.

When, during a trip to the powder room, Yvonne accused Melba of matchmaking, Melba laughed.

"Just window dressing, my dear, and ego nourishment. Erik is as gay as a fruit fly, which he will tell you if you try to get fresh with him."

This sent Yvonne into a fit of giggling that infected

Melba as well and delayed their return to the table and had them wiping tears from their eyes when they joined Scotty and Erik.

"Are you going to let us in on the joke?" Scotty asked.

"It's just women talk, I'm afraid," Melba answered.

"You had to be there," said Yvonne.

"You girls have all the fun," Erik said, igniting the hilarity once more.

"We don't tell you guys everything," Melba said, a remark that successfully unfurled Erik's brow.

That started a whole round of jokes. Erik told gay jokes. Scotty, whose maternal grandfather's last name was Bernardo until the officers on Ellis Island changed it to Bernard, told Italian jokes.

Yvonne and Melba told knock-knock jokes as the foursome dropped all pretense at adult behavior.

When the waiters started to yawn and count their tips, Melba suggested that they continue the festivities at Scotty and Melba's place.

"I'm tempted, Melba. This has been such fun. But tomorrow is another day. I've got to go up the river."

"It sounds like a sentence," Scotty slurred.

"It is," Yvonne said. "It's got a perfectly good subject and predicate."

"Smart ass," Scotty said, his pronunciation of the letter s not improving.

Scotty, Melba, and Erik saw Yvonne to her car and asked whether she was all right to drive. Yvonne told them that she was only tipsy with enjoyment and thanked them all for the wonderful evening. Yvonne hummed and smiled as she drove home, realizing that it was the first time since the miscarriage that so many hours had passed without thought of her grief. She promised herself that she would do something nice for Melba and Scotty.

Though he was still smarting from the encounter with Yvonne, Kevin was glad he had stopped drinking when he did. He was sure he would have stopped when he did anyhow, even without seeing her, but he was glad just the same. The Port Guinness cops knew him from his days on the police beat, and he could probably call in a favor if he had to, but he didn't want a DWI charge.

Melba frustrated him sometimes. Like tonight. Oh, hell, there was no getting away from the frustration. Not when all he wanted to do was punch her in the mouth, so hard that she'd fall backward over the booth in Chowder's, right through the window and into the street. . . .

She had cut him out of it, the bitch. . . .

Jesus, good thing he had stopped drinking when he had. Fucking Jets . . .

What he should do, he told himself, was drive straight by the turnoff to Duck Point Lane, without even looking, and go straight to his apartment and straight to bed. He should not even think about . . .

He slowed down as he neared Duck Point Lane. Suddenly, he was almost blinded by the high beams from a car behind him. The light shone off the dirt and film on his own rear window and windshield.

Cop, Kevin thought. Jesus, if the guy wanted to be a prick Kevin had no chance at all. Especially since his newspaper had recently run a series investigating how drunk-driving laws were enforced.

Dazzled by the reflected light, Kevin felt a panic both deep and childlike. Squinting into the rearview mirror as he slowed to a near-stop, he waited to see the whirling red gumball he knew would appear any second.

Self-disgust and fear washed over him. God, he was in deep shit. You couldn't fix up a DWI charge anymore by pleading down to reckless driving and paying a traffic fine. Drunk driving was a misdemeanor, a crime.

He flicked on his turning signal, saw in the mirror that the cop had done the same. He was almost to the Duck Point Lane turnoff.

Kevin didn't know what to do. He was afraid that if he pulled all the way over and stopped just before the turnoff, the cop car would rear-end him and blame him for it. Jesus, the cop would hang all the paper he could on him; it might even make a funny story for the TV reporters. But if he pulled over too slowly, in the cop's judgment, it would be just as bad. Cops were always sizing people up, checking out their attitudes.

He decided to turn onto Duck Point Lane, then pull over immediately. Tell him I wanted to get off the main road, Kevin thought. Act humble.

He turned, and the car followed close behind. The cop can wreck my life if he wants to, Kevin thought. Lose my license, get in trouble with the paper, pay hundreds of dollars, maybe a couple thousand, in fines and for the lawyer. . . .

Go to jail, go to jail . . . Vonnie would really be through with him for good.

He squinted in the mirror. Still no red gumball. Suddenly, the car pulled around him and sped by.

No cop.

Kevin sucked in the cleansing night air, essence of salt water and trees and grass. Better than mints. He offered a prayer of thanks. This time, *this* time, he really meant it. He would not lie to God by swearing he would never drink again, but he sure as hell would never *drive* like this again.

The car that had passed him slowed a few hundred feet ahead, the flash of its brake lights somehow conveying confusion and tentativeness. The vehicle turned slowly, hesitantly, onto a side road—a path, really—that Kevin knew was a short cul-de-sac. Lost, Kevin thought. Easiest thing in the world, getting lost in Port Guinness, with all the side roads that followed the shoreline. Well, they could get directions without much trouble.

Port Guinness was a friendly place; he and Vonnie had always thought that. They hadn't known how lucky they were when they found the house. No, not lucky. Blessed. They hadn't known it, at least he hadn't. But that was when they were younger. . . .

You had to be rich to have a house on or near the water nowadays. They had stumbled onto the house almost by pure luck. Decades before, it had been the servants' shack for the Blair Estate, and it still sat incongruously, almost comically, amid the mansions of the wealthy on Duck Point Lane.

When they had first moved in, Kevin and Yvonne had been embarrassed when their far-from-new, middle-class cars had encountered the BMWs and Cadillacs along the lane. Then they had learned to laugh about it, and the people in the BMWs and Cadillacs smiled and waved more often than not.

Tonight, driving slowly down the lane, Kevin hoped he would meet nobody. He knew he had a while to spare before Yvonne came back, and he just wanted to be alone near the house.

He stopped the car and turned off the lights and the engine a couple hundred feet away. Maybe if he was real quiet and the wind was blowing right, Tess wouldn't start barking right away. She was a little hard of hearing. Good old dog. God, he loved her.

Kevin figured he wasn't too drunk, because he was able to walk pretty quietly on the gravel. Then he guessed he must have figured wrong because he was overcome by sadness. The sound and smell of the water, the soughing of the trees, the sound of frogs and crickets were too much for him.

Kevin heard the old Doberman stir in the run by the house. She growled and was about to bark.

"Tessie, girl. It's just me. Your daddy."

He knelt down unsteadily, feeling the wet grass soak through the knees of his trousers, and put his face near the fence. The dog's tongue came through the links, flicked off his ear, again and again. Kevin laughed, and the dog licked some more.

"You good old girl, I hope you live forever. How the hell you get so old so fast, huh?"

The dog licked harder still. That was one of the nice things about dogs: You could say almost anything to them, and if you said it in a pleasant tone, they were happy.

"Missed you, old girl. Had to come by and visit." He hoped Yvonne would remember to leave the dog plenty of water while they were moving the boat. Sure, she would.

That was one thing they were together on; they both loved the dog.

Kevin stood up, not knowing whether he should savor the night all he could, trying to take some of it with him, or try to forget it entirely.

Fat chance.

"People like us . . . people like me, we get one chance at a house like this. . . ."

The grass and trees and water would belong to someone else.

"Bye, Tess. Take care. Tell her to water the plants."

He turned and walked quickly back to the car, looking straight ahead all the while.

As Yvonne's car entered the garage, Tess started her hello bark, and Yvonne hurried to let the dog out of the run to quiet her. Even though the neighbors were not close, they weren't far enough away not to hear Tess. The Doberman rubbed her head and then her side against Yvonne's legs, her short tail quivering and her nose stopping at Yvonne's skirt and then at her shoes, hands, and purse.

"Would I come home without a treat for you, old girl?" Yvonne patted the dog's head and started up the stairs from the garage to the kitchen. She expected the dog to follow her up the stairs, but Tess was standing by the closed garage door and growling a low, soft growl.

A chill ran through Yvonne, draining away all the warmth of the evening's camaraderie. Her breathing quickened and became shallow as she stood on the stairs listening. Usually the dog barked at strange noises or strangers, but this menacing growl was different, frightening.

Tess stood with her nose to the floor next to the overhead door. The hair on her back was up and her tail was still. Yvonne felt vulnerable standing on the stairs in the lighted garage. If there was someone outside, she was clearly visible through the panes of the garage door.

She turned and ran up the steps, calling to the dog in a loud whisper, "Tess, come." The dog, always obedient, followed. Yvonne wanted to see if she could catch whoever or whatever it was. She left the house lights as they were when she left, and, once the door was relocked, she hit the light switches that turned on the outdoor lights.

She ran to the window in the big bedroom, which was over the garage. Tess followed her and growled again. Yvonne sucked in her breath. The bushes had moved. Someone, something was there. She stood staring at the spot where the bushes had swayed and the wind moved among the leaves. Was it the wind?

"What was it, girl? I know you're trying to tell me," Yvonne said, rubbing Tess behind the ears. The dog growled again.

After searching the house, keeping the dog at her side, and scanning the yard several more times, Yvonne decided that some strange animal must have been nearby. Tess had stopped growling by the time Yvonne was making her second pass at the windows.

Yvonne had been planning to sit on the deck for a while before she went to bed. She had always felt so safe in the house, in the neighborhood. Maybe the dog was getting senile. But she didn't sit on the deck. Instead she locked up all the windows except for the high ones. And when she slipped into bed, the dog, wise as old dogs get, nonchalantly hopped up next to Yvonne.

"You're about as senile as a fox," she said, patting the dog. Tess grunted happily.

3

The gate on the chain-link fence was locked when Kevin got to Harvey's Boatyard the next morning. God, he hoped Harvey was in by now. Sometimes, early in the morning, Harvey would go inside, then relock the gate for an hour or so. Like he was doing something real mysterious. Kevin felt pretty sure he didn't have a woman in there. At least he had never seen one. . . .

"Yo, Harv," Kevin shouted. "Yo, Harv."

Kevin felt a little satisfaction having beaten Yvonne to the yard. He just hoped he didn't look too green around the gills. Good thing he'd stopped when he did; another glass and he might not have made it. As it was, the coffee and toast sloshed uneasily inside him.

The goddamn Jets. No cornerbacks. Couldn't cover against the Packers. He hoped Yvonne wouldn't ask him if he had bet.

Well, Kevin had kept his part of the deal: He had rolled out of bed early, even done a little weight lifting to sweat out some of the beer before showering and jumping into cutoffs and Top-Siders. Now, if Harvey would just open the gate and Vonnie would just get her ass here, they might make it to Hell Gate on time. . . .

"Yo, Harv."

Nothing yet.

Vonnie . . . He had thought of her just then as Vonnie, his affectionate name for her. Then he thought of Chowder's the night before and got pissed off again. Goddamn her, too. Goddamn it . . .

Kevin's head started to ache a little. Always did when he was hung over and mad both. . . .

A car door slammed. There, there was Vonnie. Cutoffs and a T-shirt, and no denying she looked good in them. And her hair was wet. Probably had been to the pool and swum a mile already. She was carrying a couple of bags. He had packed some things in case they didn't make it all the way in one day. He hoped she had brought overnight provisions, too, but didn't want to ask. He wondered what would happen if they had to sleep on the boat.

"Morning," he said.

"Where's Harvey?"

Ah, that's my Yvonne, Kevin thought. Never mind saying hello, just get right to the point. Like it's my fault the gate is closed.

"Morning," Kevin tried again.

"Did you tell him we were leaving?"

You had to hand it to her, she could really be stubborn. "No. But he's supposed to open at seven-thirty. You know how he is."

"Har-veeeey!" Yvonne shouted, loud enough to scatter several nearby gulls.

"Yo, Harv!"

Finally, Harvey emerged from behind a small shed a couple hundred feet inside the fence and shuffled toward them, unsmiling.

"What is it with him?" Yvonne asked.

"Maybe he curls up in the shed with a *Playboy* magazine."

"What brings you here so early?" Harvey asked, smiling a little bit but not concealing . . . what? He seemed not just annoyed but uneasy. "You ain't sailed all summer, and now you show up with the sun."

"Gotta get an early start, Harv," Kevin said.

Harvey unlocked the gate and swung it open, his face still puzzled and—what? "The good breezes usually don't come up this time of day," he said.

"This ain't a sailing day, Harv." Hey, might as well tell him now, Kevin thought. "We got a buyer. Way up in Rockland. Kind of sudden, like." That was a lie, but what the hell. "So we gotta say good-bye, Harv."

"Jesus, you mean you're leaving for keeps?"

"You got it, Harv," Kevin said. "Listen, we appreciate everything. This just came up." More lies, but he was on a roll, and he had no more time for Harvey.

"Jesus," Harvey muttered. "Talk about short notice."

"You said the engine was okay," Kevin said.

"We have to get going," Yvonne said. "The tide won't wait."

"Well, oh Jesus, at least let me look at the engine one last time," Harvey said. "I mean, Jesus, a long trip like that. We gotta be sure we're square on the money, too."

"Kevin said you said the engine was okay," Yvonne said. "And if you didn't do anything to the engine, then we're paid up."

"You're paid up if I say you're paid up," Harvey said. He stood in their way and seemed to shiver.

What is it with him? Kevin thought. The DTs?

"You know where to find us, Harvey," Yvonne said. "You know we always pay our bills, too. Let's go, Kevin. Hell Gate won't wait."

Yvonne stepped around Harvey, who put his hand on her arm for a moment as if to halt her. He thought better of it and had pulled his hand back even before the look of revulsion came over her face.

"Enough," Kevin said, stepping up to Harvey so that Harvey had to step back. "You keep your goddamn hands . . ."

"Never mind, Kevin. Drop it."

Kevin looked into Harvey's eyes, bewildered. He could smell the booze, but that was nothing new. What *was* new was the cornered look in his eyes.

"The tide, Kevin."

Kevin stepped past Harvey and started down the dock. Harvey followed them, causing the dock to rock up and down with the footsteps, making soft slurping sounds in the water.

What the hell is it with him? Kevin thought. Maybe he's drinking even more than I am. Affecting his brain or something . . .

"You check this guy out?" Harvey said. "I mean, you sure he's good for the money? Jesus, you don't want to let just anybody have your boat. Once they got your boat and the check bounces, I mean . . ."

"So now you're worried about us, Harvey? A minute ago you were talking like we were trying to screw you."

"I seen a lot of friendships ruined by sales like this. I mean, I can sell it for you. Forget the commission, I'd sell your boat. . . ."

Yvonne stopped, so sharply that the dock made a louder slurping noise with the sudden shift. "Enough is enough, Harvey. It has nothing to do with you or with the commission. And we thank you for the things you've done for us. . . ."

"Like towing us off the sandbar that time," Kevin said, trying for a laugh and missing. He owed Harvey that much.

"This has been a good place for us to keep our boat," Yvonne went on smoothly, not unkindly. "We're leaving and we're selling." Yvonne had already started walking again toward the end of the dock, where their dinghy was.

Harvey bumped Kevin as he trotted after Yvonne, who turned in alarm.

"Yvonne, talk sense to him, for Chrissake. Let me keep it and get a fair price."

Kevin was furious that Harvey would try to undercut him in front of Yvonne—no, *through* Yvonne—and about something Kevin was sensitive about just then: money.

"Not that it's any of your damn business, Harvey, but we got a good price. Seven thousand, which isn't bad at all. And I've known the guy for years. Marty Diehl. He covers the Jets for *The Bugler*. Now back off. All right?"

Kevin looked into Harvey's face, saw him move his lips silently. Sauce on the brain, Kevin thought.

"I need some time," Harvey stammered. "I mean, you might still owe me for the mooring, I can't keep everything straight all the time for you kids. Now you're up and leaving."

Harvey's eyes were dark—piglike, Kevin thought—and drops of spittle from the shouting had flown into Kevin's face.

"I don't owe you shit, Harvey," he said. "Don't owe you fucking shit!"

Kevin's voice had risen to a near-scream, enough to hurt his throat.

"Kevin!" Yvonne yelled, dismayed at Kevin's temper. When would he learn that he didn't have to counter stupidity with a tantrum? Nevertheless, she felt she ought to show she was on his side in this.

"Harvey, back off," she said. "You can't hold us back, whether we owe you or not. I want an itemized bill of all the charges you say we owe, and if I don't get an apology from you for this, I'll tell everyone in town how you treat the people who rent space from you."

Kevin brushed by Harvey and grabbed the front of their dinghy, which was lying upside down on the end of the pier. He flipped it over and slid it into the water.

Yvonne stowed her bags, stepped lightly into the dinghy, then held on to the pier to steady the small boat so that Kevin could step in.

"As for owing you," Kevin said, still in high dudgeon, "we always paid, and we know you let other people use our dinghy, which wasn't kosher. So we are damn well square."

"Kevin, let's go!" She hoped he wouldn't get into a fistfight.

Kevin hurled his bag into the dinghy and stepped in hard enough to rock the boat. He slammed the oars in the oarlocks and churned the water furiously, making more splashing than progress until he got control of his stroke. He felt sick, spent, disgusted by his anger. For the thousandth time?

"Harvey," Kevin called hoarsely.

"Just row, Kevin. Let it be."

"Harvey, if we owe you, we can talk at Chowder's some night. Buy you a gin."

But Harvey was out of earshot, walking away from them down the pier.

"Do we owe him anything?" Yvonne asked.

"No, goddammit!"

"Don't shout at me. It's not an unreasonable question. It wouldn't be the first time you forgot—"

"Oh, hey, spare me this crap—"

"Maybe I should have let you vent your spleen on Harvey. Then I wouldn't have to put up with it."

"Look, Harvey's a jerk. I don't owe him diddley-squat. He's just a drunk who sees a boat commission sailing out of his yard. You always run into morons in boatyards. Anyhow . . . I shouldn't have shouted."

When they reached their boat, Kevin tied the dinghy to the stern and Yvonne started the engine, which turned over like a top and purred as smoothly as a teakettle, making little bubbles and ripples in the water.

Engine couldn't be better, Kevin thought.

Yvonne had the drill down cold: God, she was a sailor, Kevin thought. She loosened the bowline and cast off from the mooring. Now she walked smoothly back along the gunwale, stepped into the cockpit, took the rudder (as if Kevin weren't even there, that always pissed him off).

Yes, she had the drill down, still had it down, and so did he. Yvonne let the boat drift back from the mooring ball a few feet, then said, "Okay."

And Kevin pushed the gearshift into forward, gunned the throttle slightly, and they were off. Just like old times.

The confrontation, especially his own outburst, had left him depressed—as though all the friendly exchanges with Harvey, the occasional favors he had done for them and their thanks, had been wiped out.

He would look Harvey up at Chowder's, soon, buy him a drink, smooth it all out.

* * *

Yvonne watched Kevin's face register remorse, then sadness, then the hopeful resolve of a child coming out of a confessional, or, more likely, she thought, the endless starting all over of the alcoholic, who expects an apology to erase an offense. She couldn't blame him for getting mad at the way Harvey acted, but Kevin should have had more control.

"Harvey was way out of line," she said. "He would have pissed off the Pope. But of course, when the Pope gets pissed, he prays. He doesn't say the f-word and all the other four-letter words he can think of."

Kevin sensed that Yvonne was trying to lighten the gloom, and appreciated it. "Yeah, well, I see your point. About the Pope, I mean. I guess it wasn't all my fault. I don't know. Maybe Harvey's mad because we're leaving him."

Enough, Kevin thought. They had many nautical miles to go, and promises to keep. Kevin fiddled with the throttle, finally getting it where he wanted it, about three-quarter speed.

"That's good," Yvonne said. "Just right."

Her voice was soft, not like before, and Kevin looked up and nodded. God, she looked good in cutoffs.

"Let me know when you want me to steer," Kevin said. He thought he saw her nod. He pulled his legs onto the bench and rested his back against the outside of the cabin so that he was looking toward the stern.

To his great relief, the water smell and the motion were perking him up, helping to dissolve his hangover. Sometimes he thought the water smelled like a big gin and tonic.

"We picked a good day for it," Yvonne said.

"Hmmm . . ."

Vonnie must still be jogging, Kevin thought. Her legs looked so firm and tan, even the tops, near the frayed edges of the cutoffs. He remembered when they had jogged together, usually in the morning and near the water. On the best days, the salt on their skin afterward had been part sweat, part sea spray. Showering together had been fun too. Sometimes a lot of fun.

Suddenly, without meaning to at all, Kevin remembered how she had looked when she got pregnant, her belly just starting to swell. That reminded him of all the rest, especially the tests, and the doctor seeming to say, without coming right out and saying, that it might be just as well if the pregnancy didn't go all the way.

Kevin swung his legs off the bench and stood up, facing the bow. He sucked in the air and the smell of the water. Then he clenched his teeth. Goddamn you, Vonnie, it's not just my fault we lost it. Goddamn me too. Goddamn everything.

After a while, he took the tiller and she sat near the throttle. She pulled a Thermos of iced tea out of her deep purse and gave a cup to Kevin. It tasted like it was from heaven, and he loved her again, not even minding very much when she gave little hand motions, wordlessly, to correct his course.

He wanted to tell her then that he still loved her, and hoped they could try again, boat or not, house or not. He really loved the way her hair licked around her face in the breeze. He remembered all the times on the boat, how her eyes had looked, intent on the tightness of the sails, the direction of the telltales, the surface of the water. Her pupils would shrink to tiny black flints in a field of cornflower blue. God, what a sailor . . .

All he could say was, "Really is a good day for it."

Near the Throgs Neck Bridge, they slowed down to let a freighter go by. And when the big steel hulk had slid off the horizon, Kevin saw a boat bobbing near one of the bridge towers. Funny place for a boat to be, he thought. When Kevin first spotted it, the boat was a few hundred yards away. As they drew closer to the bridge, Kevin thought it looked like one of Harvey's boats, a knockabout that Harvey used sometimes for fishing and sometimes for beer outings with his cronies. He would have sworn that the guy on the boat was looking at them through binoculars. Then the boat started up, spurted away from the bridge and headed back toward the open Sound.

Going under the bridge, Kevin heard the hum of the cars above.

"Did you see that boat?" Kevin asked. But Yvonne had her timetable on her mind. "Goddamn, freighter held us up," she said. "We don't want to fart around getting to Hell Gate." So she put the throttle on full, the stern dipped more into the water as the bow came up. When Kevin looked back for a moment, he would have sworn he saw the speedboat again, far in the distance and reversing course. But he wasn't sure.

Past the Throgs Neck, they were in a big calm basin that marked the start of the East River. The Bronx-Whitestone Bridge was at the other end of the basin and seemed very close. It took them twenty minutes to get to it. Another rumble-hum far overhead as they passed under the Bronx-Whitestone.

He's slacking off on the jogging, she thought. Probably drinking too much, not getting outdoors enough, eating a lot of hamburgers and heros and pizzas.

"Did you bring any sunscreen?" she asked.

"Nah. Real men don't wear sunscreen." It was one of their old routines about what real men and real woman do, and he had meant it to be light-hearted.

Yvonne didn't laugh. Health was an important item on her agenda. "Real men get skin cancer," she said. "I have some in my bag, but I'm not sure it will be enough for you."

"Thanks, Vonnie, really. It'll be better than nothing. I didn't think of it. But," he said, reaching into the cabin for his duffel bag, "I did remember to pack"—and he lifted each item with a flourish—"pickles, and apple juice, and turkey-and-cheese sandwiches."

Yvonne smiled in spite of herself, touched that he had remembered her favorites. She, too, had packed a lunch with things she liked, but she thought she would wait until later to tell him that she had packed roast-beef sandwiches with mustard, lettuce, and mayonnaise, and some V-8 for his hangover. She used to feel sorry for him when he woke in the morning with eyes cracked with red lines; she had even shared some bleary mornings with him early in their marriage, both of them bedbound till noon wearing cold washcloths across their foreheads and eyes. She had resented his drinking after she became more health-conscious, especially when she was pregnant. Then she hadn't drunk, had taken her vitamins, gone to bed early, had become a blooming incubator. And for what?

There were advantages to an aborted pregnancy: no stretch marks, and then there was the freedom. She had been willing, though, to give up the freedom, twenty years of it, for the next in line on earth. And stretched skin was a small price to pay to have a child that is part of you, that you made, that wouldn't be on earth except for you.

She was staring out across the wake, watching the churning greens and blues and grays darken as they receded. The colors claimed her attention and she found herself wishing she had brought along her watercolors. She had painted on the boat before, but usually at anchor or at the mooring. She felt the waves toss the boat slightly and thought that she would produce a sloppy watercolor while they were motoring. She would try to remember the colors and the way they changed.

"I think we'll hit Hell Gate in plenty of time," Kevin said.

His voice snapped the reverie. "Oh, let's see." Yvonne pulled out the charts and tables, which were marked with the arrival times on the route. She checked her watch and then the chart and then looked toward shore. "That's College Point. Yes, we have time to spare. Good."

An oil tanker with a Spanish or Portuguese name passed them on its way toward the ocean. Several suntanned crewmen waved to them from among the clusters of pipes and valves high above. Kevin and Yvonne waved back.

"Look at her," Yvonne said as the first waves from the tanker slapped at their boat. "A lot longer than a football field."

"Yep, easy. And she's nothing compared to the big

supertankers. What do you say we let the engine slack off a bit?"

"Aye, aye," said Yvonne, with a little salute. That was another of their games. Whoever was at the tiller was the captain. She pushed back the throttle.

"Hey, that's better," said Kevin. "I can see over the bow sitting down now."

"Captains shouldn't be slothful," she said, looking back again over the wake, which now left small ridges in the surface.

Now they were crossing the landing path for LaGuardia Airport. One after another, it seemed like every minute, jetliners appeared as dots on the horizon, grew bigger, then roared overhead, drowning out the sound of the boat engine.

They were passing Rikers Island, the city prison, when it occurred to her that she had been seeing a small speedboat behind them for some distance. "Kevin," she said, "am I imagining that the boat back there is following us?"

"Where? I thought I saw a boat that looked like Harvey's back by the Throgs Neck."

"Harvey? What the hell is going on? I thought you said we don't owe him any money."

Kevin bit his lip; she still had the touch to piss him off. "No, we don't. The only bill we could have is the latest one for engine work, but he said it was okay. Remember?" Kevin paused to cool himself down. "To tell you the truth, I half-imagined I saw something myself."

"Okay, okay, I'm sorry. Why don't you kind of sneaky-like get the binoculars and peek out from the cabin. I'll take the tiller back."

Kevin climbed down the steps into the galley and pulled the binoculars from one of the cabin drawers. "We have to clean out these drawers, Vonnie, I don't think we need to leave all this stuff for Marty Diehl. Hey, there's some good stuff here. Cribbage board, that extra compass you got me last Christmas. . . ." Kevin stopped. There was a lump in his throat. He thought he saw sadness flash over Yvonne's face, too.

Yvonne indeed had felt a sharp pang when she thought how happy they had been at Christmastime, at least before the big fight about the Jets party. She recovered her composure, yelling, "Are you taking inventory or are you **going** to check on that speedboat?"

Kevin braced himself on the hatch and kept low as he focused the glasses. They were passing between the North Brother and South Brother islands, and he scanned the river bank past Rikers toward the Bronx-Whitestone.

There. Yes, it looked like Harvey's boat, but he couldn't be sure. Lots of boats looked like that. Gray, or blue, or silver, or silver-gray, or silver-blue.

"Well?" she said.

"No way I can tell."

"You're sure?"

"I'm sure I can't be sure. How's that?" I'm not sure of anything anymore, he thought.

4

As the sound of the Pearson's engine faded, Harvey walked back along the pier toward the big garage and storage shed, a tiny corner of which served as his office. The pier bobbed only slightly with his steps, but Harvey felt that his world was turning upside down. He had to swallow to keep from losing the contents of his stomach from the nausea stirred by his hangover, self-disgust—and fear.

"Goddammit and Jesus Christ to hell and back!" How could he have been so goddamn stupid, not to have picked up on what those kids were pulling. Jesus. All summer they don't go out on the boat, then that snot nose Kevin nags him about the engine. Easiest thing in the world to see that they were going to take the boat away. Jesus Christ!

Harvey got to the end of the pier, gave one last hard swallow, and leaned his back against the garage, savoring the shade. All right, all right. If he could just think straight.

"Jesus Christ almighty."

Was he being punished somehow by God, or the gods of chance, for not being a hundred percent sorry his old friend Tolly had gone to the great big bilge? Well, shit, it had been Tolly's own fault and no one else's, doing what he did.

41

Drinking so much he passed out the next day working on an engine. Plain common sense should have told him better. He, Harvey, had never done anything that stupid, not since he was a kid anyhow.

For a moment, Harvey felt naked in his guilty knowledge. Yes, after first feeling sorry about Tolly he had been glad that Tolly was out of the way. All right, sure, it was true. Harvey had been glad. Well, no wonder. Tolly had started to get careless, greedy, trying to take over what had been Harvey's idea in the first place. Wanting more of a split than he deserved, too.

Harvey left the shade of the building, went around the corner and into a side door. He sat in the old wooden chair that served as the main piece of furniture in his "office," actually an area bounded by shelves and boxes packed with various cans and bottles of boat paint, marine oil, varnish, grease, and God knew what else.

Again, for a moment, his mind wandered. This time, he thought way back, if not in time then certainly in circumstance, to how things had been before they came to him offering a business deal. The deal had changed everything, and there was no canceling it.

Sitting there, waiting for his heart to slow down, Harvey breathed deeply, taking small comfort in the smells of tar and rope, varnish and canvas that had been part of the garage since his father had run it. Good, warm, timeless boat smells. Comfortable and uncomplicated.

Damn, Harvey thought, I had the world by the ass *before* the deal.

Harvey picked up a work rag that wasn't too dirty, wiped his sweating face, tossed the rag in the corner.

He picked up the phone and dialed. "It's me," he said. "We got a problem. . . . Just listen. Them two kids with the boat. Well, they came here this morning and took the goddamn thing away. . . . Of course they don't know. You think I'm crazy, for Christ's sake? . . . Because I didn't have time, that's why. . . . Just calm down and listen to me. . . ."

After a few minutes, Harvey hung up. He felt better, having taken some action.

He really didn't have anything against Kevin and Yvonne, kind of liked them, in fact. Especially her, with them legs of hers.

Maybe it could be undone so no one got hurt. Then again, maybe not. Got nothing against those kids at all, Harvey thought, but first things first. Anything can happen, not my fault. They shouldn't have surprised me like that.

Harvey breathed deeply, wondering if he could retrace his steps.

The money had been so tempting, so easy, even before. . . .

He shook his head, swallowed hard, again and again. He had to keep his head, no matter what. If only things hadn't got so complicated.

He didn't know how long he sat there before he heard the phone. Long enough to be startled by the ring. But not so long, he realized with alarm, for the call to be a response to his own.

He picked up on the third ring, concentrated on making his voice matter-of-face, bored.

"Harvey's Boatyard," he said. No, he had not quite pulled it off.

"Harvey," the familiar voice said. "It's that time again. Why don't you drop by for something cold."

Harvey pulled into the lot behind Quince's building and parked next to one of the rental vans. As he reached the door of the building, he was surprised that it was pulled open from the inside.

"Harvey," the door opener said as Harvey stepped in.

"Whaddya say," Harvey responded.

Harvey knew the man only casually. His name was Chuck, and he worked for Quince. He had a thick back and shoulders, heavy, with slabs of muscle that were perfect for heavy lifting or . . .

"He here?" Harvey asked hoarsely.

"Waitin' for you."

"Good. Hope he's got a cold one handy."

But Harvey's little stab at camaraderie was met with silence, leaving him embarrassed, edgy.

Harvey went down a dark corridor and knocked on a door at the end.

"Come," said the familiar voice inside.

Harvey entered and instantly was aware of globs on his face as the chill from the air conditioner bathed his skin.

"Say, Quince," Harvey said, trying his best friendly voice.

"Harvey. Sit down, please." Quince's voice was soft, businesslike, controlled.

Harvey sat in a Naugahyde chair facing Quince's barge-sized desk. Quince sat down at his desk, leaned back a little, crossed his legs.

"How are you anyhow?" he said. Then he smiled, but his eyes were flinty.

Harvey expected Quince to offer him a cold beer any moment. As a hint, he said, "I'm about the same as I was last night at Chowder's. Feel like I had maybe one too many. Getting too old to learn—"

"Tell me, do you have any problems at your yard? You know, with stealing? That kind of thing?"

"Well, no, I'm careful all the time." Harvey tried to sound casual, but his blood had gone to ice.

"How about with unauthorized use of equipment from your yard?"

"You mean . . ."

"I mean boats, say. Anyone ever use a boat from your yard without your say-so?"

"Well, no. Hell, no. Not that I know of." The chair arms were slippery now from perspiration.

"And it's just you at the yard, isn't it? You have no associates. . . ."

"No. Just me."

"Although at one time, I think I remember, you did do

business with that fellow who breathed the wrong stuff. Tolly."

"Tolly? Oh, yeah, we go back a ways. Told you that. Shame what happened to him."

"A shame. But that's what comes from carelessness."

"Mmmm." The sweat was running down Harvey's face and arms. He thirsted for the cold beer he hoped to be offered any moment, and for the easy friendship Quince had shown toward him only the night before.

"I myself know about carelessness," Quince went on solemnly. "Back a while, when I was first getting started in trucking, I learned the hard way that I couldn't trust everyone. Petty thievery from the docks, employees filling their own gas tanks, that kind of thing."

"Right. Gotta be careful."

"But you've managed to prevent theft at your yard. Tell me," Quince went on, baring his teeth in a smile, "how do you do it?"

Harvey squirmed in the slippery chair. "Just me," he said, almost stammering. "Just me in the yard, so I know everything that goes on."

"Ah. Then you know why one of your boats is chasing those two who left a while ago with that Pearson sloop."

"Chasing . . . ?" Harvey's voice almost died in a croak.

"Chasing, following, whatever. You know, surely. You just told me—"

"No, not chasing. I mean, not really. I know where . . . See, I figure they might still owe me for . . . for engine work I did."

"Well, you could just bill them."

"Well, sure, but once the boat's gone—"

A flashing red light from above and off to his left had caught the corner of Harvey's eye. He looked at the ceiling corner closest to him and saw that a television security camera was trained directly on him. The red bulb light on top of the camera blinked regularly.

"You could just bill them. Unless there's something else."

"Something else? Well . . ." Harvey was dizzy with fear. The blinking red light . . .

"Tell me, confidentially and man-to-man. Do you think there's even a remote chance they found out about . . . you know. And that, having found out, they took advantage of your trust?"

"Well, I hope not. I mean . . ." Harvey was confused as well as afraid; he couldn't figure what Quince was driving at.

"He gambles, I hear at Chowder's. On football. And the lovebirds are flying their separate ways, so perhaps they have a money problem. Or perhaps *separate* money problems." ·

"Well, could be, I guess. About them and money."

"So you did have them followed so that . . . so that . . . well, *why* exactly?" Quince seemed both puzzled and annoyed.

"Well, like I said . . ." Harvey slipped and slid in the moist chair. "I mean . . ." The blinking red light atop the camera seemed like a laser beam drilling into his brain. "Say, that light is driving me nuts. Could you turn it off?" Harvey wanted more than anything in the world to have Quince break a gut-splitting laugh and hand him a cold one.

"It's just a camera," Quince said incredulously. "Like they have in banks. They have their money to look after, and we have ours."

"I was only . . ."

"I know this is a little unsettling for you. Please forgive me. But we all have our orders."

"Orders?"

"Mine are to check into what we think has been some, you know, pilferage."

Harvey's mind was racing in terror. He tried to remember how long the corridor was, whether he had any chance of running out of the office and . . . but where would he go?

"As I said, we have been concerned about pilferage."

"Mmm . . ." No use even thinking about trying to get

away, Harvey knew. He would never get outside the building, and even if he did . . .

"You're bothered by that camera?" Quince had changed his tone. Suddenly he was friendly, smiling, jovial.

"Ain't that. I just take shitty pictures." Harvey managed a small laugh.

"Me too. I have some pictures of myself that you'll just have to see . . . I'm sorry. I forgot. Can I get you something?"

Harvey felt as if a stone had been lifted from his chest. "Just a beer, Quince."

"Please, let me join you in a gin and tonic. Please."

"Sure. Gin and tonic it is."

Quince walked to a near wall, opened a dark oak cupboard, took out glasses and gin. Then he opened a small refrigerator within the cupboard and fetched tonic water, ice cubes, wedges of lime. His back to Harvey, Quince went on talking as he mixed drinks.

"Everybody has a boss. Isn't that the truth? Years ago, when I was just getting started on my own, I thought I was my own boss. . . . Here, drink this and you'll feel better than you have all day."

Quince handed Harvey a big glass and sat down at the desk holding a glass of his own.

"Everybody has a boss," Quince went on. "So I was on my own. My own boss, I thought. No. My customers were my boss. My employees were my boss, in a sense, because they made me do things I would otherwise not have done. Do you see?"

Harvey wasn't sure he did, but he nodded just the same.

"Cheers," Quince said, raising his glass in Harvey's direction and sipping.

Harvey took a gulp; a stiff drink, he thought.

"What I mean," Quince went on, "is that I wanted to be a trusting person. But I found I couldn't be. So I used to set little traps for the dishonest ones. I would arrange to have stray items left where they could be stolen by those so inclined. A TV set left in a dark corner of a semitrailer, even a basket of fruit behind a forklift on a dock . . ."

Quince paused, smiled, waited for Harvey to show he understood.

Harvey nodded and drank. He was starting to relax now. His arms, no longer wet with sweat, were settling into the chair.

"And I—we—have done the same thing with our goods recently. I mean the items we have been leaving with you, for safekeeping in your yard before transfer. Do you follow?"

Harvey nodded. He still felt uneasy, but Quince's voice was smooth, soothing, and Harvey was reassured because Quince was confiding in him. Harvey started to take another gulp from his drink, but he held off. Better to pace himself; he was feeling it already.

"Some time ago, we thought we detected the tiniest bit of pilferage. Of course, even a little bit here and there adds up when we're dealing with something this valuable."

"Mmmm." Harvey was grateful for the way the drink had taken the edge off his nerves, but the slight dulling of his senses had made it harder to follow Quince. Harvey was aware of the red light still blinking at the edge of his vision.

"We—I mean myself and my real boss—we have discussed this problem at length. At first, we suspected . . ." Quince paused and looked at Harvey, smiled. "You."

Harvey sat up with a jolt; some of his gin and tonic sloshed out, running in a cool rivulet from his wrist to his elbow.

Quince chuckled and his eyes brightened. "I said *at first* we suspected you. Then, after we talked it over, we realized how little sense that made. I mean, you have always been so careful and reliable. We have paid you well. And you and I have toasted each other at Chowder's, as friends."

"Friends . . ." Harvey felt a great relief from what Quince had just said. And he was becoming more and more relaxed.

"And if it wasn't you, then who? We asked ourselves that, over and over. Then we wondered—as crazy as it sounds—could it be those two young people?"

Again Harvey was startled. "You mean . . ."

"Yes, those two with the Pearson. Kevin and Yvonne. Their behavior has changed lately. They're supposed to be splitting up, yet when they bump into each other—such a small town—they seem to be in love. Surely you've noticed."

"Mmmm."

"What if that is all a charade? we asked ourselves. I mean, suppose they are faking their estrangement. She's a quick study; we know that. He's a newspaperman, smarter than he acts. Do you see?"

Harvey's mind was racing, yet it dare not trip between what Quince was saying and what Harvey knew to be true.

"Do you see? It's brilliant, really. There could hardly be a safer storage place, a safer means of transport."

"I do see." Harvey took another sip. The gin and lime was deliciously cool and slaking.

"And we know they hung around your yard, your shop, a lot when they were using the boat. Always needing to talk about the engine, needing line—needing to pay you for pulling them free of a sandbar. Remember?"

"I remember."

"And we concluded that they had seen something in your garage, probably while you were on the dock. Oh, we don't blame you for that. They saw something they shouldn't have. And then they enlisted someone's help."

Harvey sat upright again, as if jolted by an electric current. An ice cube slipped out of the glass and plopped onto his chair.

"And if it wasn't your help," Quince went on solemnly, "it had to be Tolly's."

"Tolly?" Harvey was bewildered.

"Don't you see it? He is an old friend of yours, an old associate. Yes? If anyone would know how to get into the yard easily, move around the garage easily at night, it would be Tolly. Don't you see?"

"Tolly . . ."

"A lowlife. Forgive me, Harvey. A lowlife, your friendship notwithstanding. He abused your friendship, stole from you. From us. With the help of those two lovebirds. It's so clear."

Harvey fought off the gin haze, thinking as nimbly as he could. Salvation lay just ahead if he didn't stumble. "I'll be damned," he said at last. "Tolly."

"Fortunately, he did himself in with his carelessness and stupidity, saving us a problem."

"Damn."

"And you doubtless meant to head off another problem by following the lovebirds, yes?"

"Yes! Yes!"

"And you were just about to tell us that?"

"Yes! Damn straight." Harvey took a second to think. "I was just gonna call you, when you called me." Harvey took another gulp; the gin and tonic was one of the best he had ever tasted. He felt like he'd had a couple already. Maybe three.

"Good. That only leaves the problem of what to do with them. After we get our goods back, of course."

"You think you'll have to . . ." Harvey couldn't finish the thought. That kind of thing was way beyond what he had bargained for.

"We'll see," Quince said softly. "That will depend."

On what? Harvey was tempted to ask. But he thought better of it. He was not home free yet, and he had to worry about himself before thinking about Kevin and Yvonne.

Suddenly, Harvey remembered the phone call he'd made. Jesus; he would have to get to a phone, somehow. He had to cancel . . . Damn. Could he do that? Would it be better to tell Quince? No.

Harvey was really feeling the gin now. He shifted the glass from one hand to another; it almost slipped from his grasp. He put his free hand up to support his head.

"We'll talk some more," Quince said.

Harvey thought Quince sounded very far away. In a distant corner of his vision, Harvey again caught the red camera light, blinking, blinking, blinking, blinking. . . .

Harvey's eyes closed. The gin glass dropped from his hand, bounced off the edge of the chair, fell to the floor. By the time he was lifted out of the chair and carried to the van he was in a deep sleep.

5

At the Astoria Consolidated Edison Plant the river turned south and narrowed into a sluiceway toward Hell Gate. Yvonne and Kevin had timed their arrival perfectly, but Hell Gate was still no pushover. The water had just a light chop, like shallow rapids dashing over stones, or a mass of snakes writhing under satin, but beneath the surface the treacherous tides ripped at one another and wrenched the boat off course one way, then another. The water eddied and glistened in the sun, almost like quicksilver.

They went under the black steel bow of the railroad bridge. A few minutes later, the Triborough Bridge roared with traffic high above them. They looked up, but only for a moment: Hell Gate had tricked better sailors than they, scuttled bigger boats than theirs since long before the Triborough was built, long before the men who built it were born. Although the big buildings had been visible on the skyline during the whole trip, when Kevin and Yvonne came out from under the Triborough, the city looked like a wall of concrete.

They were in the current, the Pearson hurtling through the water as though it were skidding on ice. Except that they were in control. Kevin kept his hand on the throttle, ready to adjust it if need be. Yvonne had the tiller and her face and body were taut with attention. Damn, Kevin thought, she looks like she was born holding a tiller.

The bow dipped into a wave, came riding up again, then splashed down, causing spray to fly into the cockpit.

"Yes!" Kevin shouted. "All right! Anyone doesn't like this feeling doesn't deserve to be loved by a good boat."

For a moment, she felt the same thrill, and they were together on their boat.

"Hi, Gracie," Kevin said, smiling, as they passed the mayor's mansion on its bluff overlooking the river.

Then they were past Hell Gate and the south-rushing tide gave them new speed. Only a couple of hundred feet away, a constant flow of traffic buzzed along the FDR Drive. It was moving, free of its rush-hour clot.

"There's the Animal Medical Center," Yvonne said. "Hello, all you good people who saved our Tess."

Kevin saluted the hospital. "Good work, folks."

They both remembered how they had worried together all one night while the doctors battled to save Tess from an infection. And the joy of the next day when the battle had been won. Together, then.

Neither of them said any more.

A helicopter dropped down onto the pad next to the Fifty-ninth Street Bridge, churning the air. Yvonne pushed her hair back in place after the copter had passed.

"A lot of new buildings on Roosevelt Island," Kevin said.

"New subway stop," Yvonne said.

Kevin had to think a minute to realize she had answered him. The new subway stop had made the island more accessible.

"Anyhow, she'll make Marty a damn good boat," Kevin said, trying again. But it had only made things worse. He attempted a graceful exit. "Thanks again for the V-8, Vonnie. I mean, that was above and beyond . . ."

"You're welcome, again." Yvonne wanted to tell him to shut his mouth unless he had something new to say; at the same time, part of her wanted to hear him say the old tired things. Sick, sick, sick, she told herself.

This day, the East River was as rocky as a child's bathtub. It took only a few powerboats and a barge or two to churn up the water, because the wave action had no place to go. It slammed against the wall of the FDR Drive on one side and onto Roosevelt Island on the other, not that far away, and the unspent forces rolled back through the water toward the middle.

"Those old ruins, what the hell are they?" Kevin said, pointing to the end of Roosevelt Island. "Looks like an old fort."

"That's what's left of an old sanitarium. Every so often the city talks about tearing it down."

When they had passed the end of Roosevelt Island Yvonne looked east toward Brooklyn. "Look, Kevin," she said. "You can see church steeples towering over the buildings."

"Yeah, and in Manhattan they're walled in."

"Funny, isn't it. So different on one side of the river from the other."

"You want funny? Wait till we get to the Hudson and you can see New Jersey."

"But that's another state."

"That's another world."

"You sound like a New York chauvinist."

"Is that better or worse than a male chauvinist?"

"Either way it means you've got a head like a boulder."

Yvonne liked the tiller, liked the control, the response of the boat to her touch.

Kevin was just as happy to let her steer, and he squinted as his eyes scanned the sun-dazzled water, trying to discern the chop.

"Vonnie, want to steer into that?" He pointed toward a big wave, probably left by a barge and coming at an angle. It wouldn't have come close to swamping them, but the tiller adjustment let them meet it head-on, so that the bow dipped gently and there was no yawing at all.

Yvonne pushed the tiller back, the bow came around, and they headed straight downriver again. "Good eye," she said.

"How's the real estate business this summer?" Kevin asked.

"Okay. Pretty good, actually."

"Think it'll ever get good enough to make you want to give up teaching?"

"Uh-uh. I miss the kids when school's out." Kevin had asked her that before.

"The office run pretty much the same as ever?"

"It seems busier. We do more for the customers. Get them mortgages even. Rosalie's computer system makes it a snap to find houses. That machine could double her business."

"She seems to be doing all right now."

"She is. Look at her cars, the house, not to mention Scotty's. She's a workaholic, but she's always pleasant. She knows what's going on and she praises you to high heaven when something good happens. She's really great."

"Wonder why your mom doesn't like her."

"Mother told me about some gossip once that Mr. Durer wasn't really Scotty's father. That Rosalie had had a long affair with some shady but very wealthy man. Mother thought that the money to buy Dad's agency hadn't really come from the insurance when Mr. Durer died, but from Rosalie's inamorato."

Kevin chuckled. "Glad to hear your mom hasn't mellowed on her world view. What does your dad say about the rumor?"

"Dad doesn't like hearing bad things about people he likes. He sticks his head in the sand and waits for things to blow over."

"I can relate to that."

"Right."

He caught the edge in her voice, but ignored it. "And I'm glad you like real estate."

After a few seconds she said, "Your job is all right?"

"Yeah. I still think now and then—you remember—

about transferring out of sports to the regular news side. Maybe someday I'll get off my ass and really do it. Then again . . ."

"Then again . . ."

"This is a good time of year to be covering football," he said. "Wonderful mix of new players coming in, old guys trying to hang on to their jobs, some of them not being able to."

"It sounds heartless."

"In a way it is. But it's . . . what . . . rich. In emotion, nostalgia. At least it can be, if you find the right stories and handle them with some, you know . . ."

"Restraint."

"Bingo. You always were my best editor."

She smiled at the compliment, but if he was dangling bait for an intimate conversation she wouldn't bite.

They had talked God knew how many times about whether he should switch jobs. Kevin kept up with current events (at least he had before his beer intake went up after the split, Yvonne thought) and read history, biography, and politics in his spare time. At least she hoped he was still doing some serious reading.

She remembered that he had liked covering the police beat early in his career, before he switched to sports. And she thought she knew better than he did the deeper reasons he dragged his feet on switching back to regular news.

"I gotta admit," Kevin said, "you were right about my enjoying the role—you know, Mister Inside Football whenever the big-shot editors want to hear sports gossip."

"Told you." She said it lightly, but she hadn't forgotten how he had taken offense before when that subject came up.

"At least the Jets don't play on Thanksgiving this year."

Yvonne knew what that meant. Kevin loved Thanksgiving and Christmas, was always desperate, even if they were fighting, for them to do something special as a couple. *He's already angling for an old-fashioned Thanksgiving of stuffing and drumsticks,* she thought. *He's not getting it from me.*

"Hello, Citibank," Kevin said as the distinctive, slant-roofed skyscraper in midtown came into view. "How come you never asked us to be in your TV commercials?"

"We're not rich, that's why."

That exchange left a momentary brittleness in the air, and they tacitly agreed to keep quiet for a while until it dissolved.

They passed the United Nations Building on their right, a power plant with three huge stacks on their left.

"Is that big Pepsi-Cola sign in Queens or Brooklyn?" Kevin said.

"I don't remember."

They passed the ancient sailing ships berthed at the South Street Seaport, passed the cluster of fabric-covered tennis courts, the "bubbles" where some of the city's privileged played. A while later, they saw the buildings where some of the privileged made their fortunes: the towering skyscrapers of Wall Street.

"I keep forgetting," Kevin said. "I think of the big buildings being uptown, except for the World Trade Center. Then I saw the Wall Street buildings from the water. . . ."

"Plenty of yuppies left in the world," Yvonne said. "Don't let anyone tell you otherwise."

"Who was it said, 'Behind every great fortune there is a crime'? Or something like that. You believe it?"

"No. Not entirely, anyhow."

"There, Vonnie!" Kevin said, chuckling as he pointed to a low yellow building squatting near the water's edge. "I almost worked in that building. Remember?"

And so he had: as they went under the Manhattan Bridge, the New York Post Building came into view.

"Oh, right," Yvonne said, warming to the memory despite herself. Early in their marriage, Kevin had tried for a job at the *New York Post*, been disappointed when he didn't get it, and she had been disappointed with him. Then he had got the job with the newspaper on Long Island, and everything seemed to fall into place. For better and worse.

They went between the massive stone supports of the Brooklyn Bridge, heard the whining of tires on the metal grating above. They had been on the boat for several hours and were nearing the tip of Manhattan.

"There she is," Yvonne said. "I still get goose bumps."

"Nothing wrong with that."

Off to their left in the distance was the Statue of Liberty.

"I wonder if I could ever capture that opaque pale green with my watercolors," Yvonne said.

At the tip of Manhattan, they gave a respectful distance to a Coast Guard cutter and a Staten Island ferry so as not to get caught in their wakes. Then they scooted around the Battery and started north on the Hudson.

"According to the charts, the tide should turn soon and push up the Hudson." She smiled smugly.

"A star for the navigator."

"Very funny."

Just north of the Battery, on an unused concrete support abandoned from the heyday of commercial shipping in New York, several dozen nude men lounged, their skin bronze and shiny in the hot midday sun.

"I'll get the binoculars," Kevin said.

Yvonne turned away. "Bastard," she said. She raised her foot in a playful kick aimed at his midsection, then arrested the move halfway through. The moment of mirth had been only that—a moment.

Kevin glanced once more toward the pier, just long enough to see a fully clothed man standing near the edge, looking out at the water. Toward their boat? Kevin couldn't tell.

He felt uneasy. "See that guy?"

"What guy?"

"There. The one with the clothes on."

"I was trying not to look," she said, turning toward the pier. "Okay, I see him. Why?"

"Is he watching us?"

"Why would somebody be watching us?"

"I don't know. Why the hell did Harvey go bonkers?"

"I still don't know, Kevin." She was annoyed that he had brought that up again. "Maybe the guy on the pier was following us in that boat you saw. He's part of Harvey's army of bill collectors."

But Yvonne felt something squirming in her gut. Maybe it was just the incongruity of a man with clothes on amid the nude sunbathers. Why would he be there, at the end of the pier, if not to watch something on the water?

At that point, a speedboat cut rudely across their bow not fifty feet ahead. "Macho bastard," Yvonne said. She turned the boat so the wake wouldn't hit them broadside.

After they rode the chop, they looked at the pier. The man was gone.

"I'm hungry," she said.

Although they were getting help from the tide, they had no time to waste.

"Think we'll make it before tonight?" he said.

"Yes, if the engine doesn't break. Should have just enough daylight to see what we're doing, once we're there. I did some figuring on our speed and the sunset and so on."

"Suppose we have to lay over?"

She thought she detected a little-boy-lost tone in his voice. "There's a place up near Edgecliff. A little marina with a restaurant. I called before we left."

"I don't remember your telling me that." He was hurt.

"I didn't."

Her curtness puzzled him, but only for a moment.

"In case we weren't going to have enough time, I called a friend of mine to see if I could stay overnight while you slept on the boat," she said.

"Oh." He turned his face to keep her from seeing the jealousy he knew was written all over it.

"DeeDee Lockwood," she said, enjoying his discomfort.

A mutual friend. He hid his face to hide his relief.

He ate his lunch slowly, then filled the time with his own sadness as he spelled her at the tiller and watched her lean against the outside of the cabin and close her eyes. She would nap, he knew. He stared with lonely fondness at the gently snoring woman who could hurt him so much, the woman he had hurt so much.

Tonight he would drink nothing. Nothing. That would deny her the pleasure of sulking at him (for that, anyhow), and would make it easier to say good-bye to the boat.

Damn, they had got so used to the boat. They could steer up to the gas pumps as easily as handling a car, usually him at the tiller and her at the bow, because she was quicker with knots. Damn, how Vonnie looked good stepping onto the pier, cleating two lines faster than a lot of sailors could fasten one.

Vonnie was still snoring. When they were first married, she had denied that she snored. Vonnie, I used to love your snoring. Still do . . .

He thought of the time—they had only had the boat a few days—when they had pulled up to refuel for the first time and made fools of themselves in front of everyone within sight. He had had trouble steering, then had come up to the dock way too fast. "We don't have brakes, you stupid bastard," she had shouted, loud enough for fifty or two hundred or a thousand people to hear. Then she had stepped onto the dock and fallen on her ass, and he had laughed at both of them, but only after he knew she wasn't hurt. Then they had both laughed, and told the story a hundred times after that, and laughed again. . . .

Part of the problem was that they had stopped laughing.

A little while later, with Kevin at the tiller, Yvonne woke and went below to use the head. About the time she was due to come topside, Kevin heard her shout, "Damn!" Hand still on the tiller, he stood up and saw a fountain of water spurting into the galley.

"What the hell . . . Jesus, Vonnie . . ."

"It's the sink hose. It's broken," she said. She slipped on the floorboards, just barely righting herself.

"You okay?" he shouted.

"The fitting, it's rotted through. This is serious."

She groped into the jet of water, trying to ignore the gushes of dirty river that soaked her face and hair and T-shirt and cutoffs. There, there was the hole. She grabbed the hose to try to stop the rush, but the hose broke away from the base of the sink. So much water coming in. She pushed her thumb into the tube, but her thumb was not big enough. Then she thought to bend the tube like a garden hose.

"Kevin, throw rags down here. Every damn one we have on board. And head toward shore."

He flipped open a cockpit hatch, pulling out an old sailbag full of discarded underwear and shirts.

"Toss the whole thing down here."

The bag landed next to her, splashing water onto her legs. Yvonne tied a couple of small rags around the bend and hoped that the rubber was not so rotten that it would burst somewhere else.

"Throw down that bucket, too. I'm going to pump the bilge. The damn thing must have been leaking slowly before it started to gush. Water's over the floorboards. I think the bandage will keep us afloat until we can get it fixed," she said. "No way we can go all the way today."

"Goddamn."

"Head for Edgecliff. We'll get it fixed there."

He turned sharply toward shore.

"Here," Yvonne said, hoisting the bucket.

"Why don't . . ." He stopped himself so he didn't sound totally stupid, but not before Yvonne realized what he had been about to say. They had always pumped the bilge into the sink in the galley.

At the marina, they pulled in as close as they could get to a building that looked like a combination storage shed and garage. As soon as they were fast, Yvonne trotted down the pier. Kevin watched her disappear into the garage; he was both annoyed and grateful that she had taken charge, as usual. In no time she reappeared, accompanied by two burly, earnest-looking men in grease-stained work clothes.

Yes, the men said, they had hose to fix the sink, but they wouldn't be able to do the permanent repair until the next morning. Meantime, they could plug the leak securely. For sure, it would hold overnight, as long as they didn't go anywhere.

"We can use one of the moorings out in the river," Yvonne said. "They're cheaper than the slips."

"Save a few bucks," Kevin said.

Yvonne took her overnight bag, went to the women's room and cleaned up. When she was done, she went to a pay phone.

"I called DeeDee," she said, rejoining Kevin. "She's coming over."

Kevin was glad enough to have DeeDee Lockwood join them; he had always liked her—and she was sexy. And having a third person with them for a while might smooth some bumps.

"They did a patch job on the sink," he said.

"The dockmaster said we can tie the dinghy near the end of the pier," she said. "You'll be all right on the boat. I'll probably be up before you anyhow."

"So you can row me out?"

"Right. And I guess you should call your friend and tell him we're not going to make it today. So he's not waiting there all night to buy a boat and we never show up. . . ."

"Yeah, I'll do that." She was taking charge. Again. He was annoyed at her need to super-explain everything to him.

6

I'll take the cheesecake," Yvonne told the waitress. The restaurant was built over some of the slips and had a view of the Hudson River and New York City.

"Speaking of cheesecake," Kevin said, looking over Yvonne's shoulder.

Yvonne turned. What she saw made her feel dirty and unkempt from her day on the boat. "Wow," she said, dusting crumbs from her lap.

Deirdre Lockwood was wearing tennis whites. Everyone noticed her arrival except for a child begging for ice cream and an old woman who was cutting her meat into very small pieces. DeeDee was a long-legged blonde, very much like Yvonne. In high school people even had mistaken one for the other, and sometimes Yvonne and DeeDee would go along with the mistake as a joke. Now, however, DeeDee had lightened her hair to a Nordic platinum and, while Yvonne was lean and slim from exercise, DeeDee was voluptuous, with tan, tight flesh. Her shirt was loose-fitting and cut low over her breasts. The lower curve of her buttocks peeked from under a pleated skirt.

Yvonne waved and she and Kevin stood up to greet her. DeeDee bussed each of them on the cheek.

"Excuse the outfit," DeeDee said. "I just came from a

tennis lesson. Yvonne, you should see the instructor. What a hunk."

"You look wonderful," Yvonne said. Inhaling her perfume, Yvonne wondered whether she really had been playing tennis.

"Yeah, you look great," Kevin said.

Yvonne felt a twinge of jealousy as she saw his eyes race up and down. "We're just having dessert," she said. "Do you want some cheesecake, coffee?"

"I could use a diet soda. Dessert is not on my diet. I joined the new diet club Regimes."

"I've heard that's expensive," Yvonne said.

"Yes, but I'm worth it," DeeDee said with a giggle.

Kevin shook his head and smiled, a sort of fawning smile, Yvonne thought as the twinge returned.

The waitress, a chubby teenager, had been gaping at DeeDee. "A Diet Coke?" she said.

When the waitress left, Kevin said, "Wanna bet she screws it up?"

Yvonne turned to DeeDee. "She gave me french fries and I ordered rice, and Kevin had no cheese on his cheeseburger."

"She's probably having trouble with her boyfriend," said DeeDee, flashing a smile that pushed her eyes into little curves and made her look like Marilyn Monroe.

"There you go again," said Yvonne. "Always psychoanalyzing."

"Remember when I was teaching in Port Guinness, you used to call me the shit-house analyst?" DeeDee tossed her head back and laughed a round, full guffaw.

Yvonne thought, that's the DeeDee I know. The natural, fun-loving, raucous friend still lives under this sexpot exterior. I wonder what's happening with her love life.

Just as DeeDee's guffaw had reopened the camaraderie between the two women, it had broken the spell for Kevin. "You still seeing that stiff from Fort Lee? I couldn't stand the way he used to close his eyes when he talked." DeeDee had dated an English teacher whom Kevin considered priggish.

"You mean Josh? I still see him, but he's a bit too tepid for me. Like a tea bag in lukewarm water."

"You always said that tea needed water that was boiling passionately," Yvonne said. That had been one of DeeDee's quirks in Port Guinness. Whenever the kettle in the teachers' room was left to whistle, someone would say, "Where's DeeDee?" because she wouldn't use the water until the kettle was screeching.

"They made fun of me for that at Leonia High too. What an epitaph that would make: She made her tea with passionately boiling water."

"How do you like Leonia schools?" Yvonne asked. "Are you still glad that you left Port Guinness?"

"My unhappiness with Port Guinness, I realize now, was manufactured. What I really wanted was to be near Josh. Why else would I have looked for a job only near him? But I'm glad I took the plunge. It has worked out rather well, professionally anyhow. My love life is another story, but I'm not alone in being alone. It's the complaint of the nineties."

Yvonne and Kevin looked at each other and then down at their place mats.

"What's with you two?" DeeDee said.

"We're splitting," Yvonne said.

DeeDee's face drained. "No. You two? The perfect couple? I mean, teenagers in Port Guinness wanted to grow up and be like you. You guys, you had everything," DeeDee protested.

"Times change, people change," said Kevin, hoping to end the conversation by retreating to aphorism.

The waitress returned with a Diet Coke for DeeDee, a cup of water and an envelope of decaf for Yvonne, and a cup of coffee and a saucer of coffee for Kevin. "The last piece of cheesecake is all mushed up. I don't think you'd want it," she said. "And we're all out of the pecan pie. Do you want the ice cream?"

She had got the order right after all.

"I'll have some ice cream," Kevin said.

"Me, too," said Yvonne.

"Make that three," said DeeDee. "I'll run a lap around the tennis court to work it off."

"Diet soda goes great with ice cream," Yvonne said, laughing.

They managed to avoid the uncomfortable until the check came and Yvonne slid fifteen dollars to Kevin. DeeDee, seeing her, began to fish in her purse, but Yvonne put a hand on her arm and shook her head.

"It's okay, I'll get it," said Kevin, pushing the bills toward Yvonne. "I'll let you treat me tomorrow."

He managed that gracefully, Yvonne thought. Then Kevin flashed his great Irish smile, and Yvonne felt her insides melting.

The sun had dropped behind the Palisades when the women rowed Kevin out to the boat. Yvonne couldn't help noticing the way Kevin watched DeeDee climb into the dinghy. Would he call her for a date? she thought. God, I couldn't take that. But I don't own him; I don't have any claim on him. Let go. Let go.

As soon as Kevin was dropped off and the dinghy was out of earshot of the boat, DeeDee looked at Yvonne and said, "I wouldn't. I've been used like that before."

"Mind-reading again," said Yvonne, her smile downcast. "Used?"

"Husbands try to hurt their ex-wives by dating their friends. And women are so keyed in to men's desires that they think the guy was lusting after them all the while. I've been there, Yvonne, and I spent a lot of money on a shrink to learn how to stay out of those messes."

"Really?" Yvonne thought that DeeDee's appearance belied her depth. She wanted to ask her how she could dress like a temptress and think like a sage. She tried. "You look like you're in the dating game. I mean, very soigné— alluring, even."

"You know what Lil says about that? Lil's my shrink. She says this kind of outfit is a power play within the bounds of socially acceptable power."

"No shit," said Yvonne.

"She's good. I think she's wise. You'd like her. But now that I've got you alone, tell me what the hell happened to you and Kev."

DeeDee was easy to talk to, and somehow this time the telling was less painful. The pregnancy, the miscarriage, the bitterness, the blaming, the feeling of being betrayed.

Only when they walked down the pier was the conversation interrupted. There some rough-looking men gaped and pointed at them, and Yvonne thought the men followed them as they walked to DeeDee's car. Damn jackrabbits, Yvonne thought.

An Edgecliff police car drove by and the men disappeared, much to Yvonne's relief. DeeDee was less bothered by the men, probably because she got a lot of attention when she was power-dressing, Yvonne thought.

DeeDee's condo was all art deco, light and airy and furnished with blissful disregard for child- or pet-rearing. Best of all was her balcony, which had a wide-angle view of New York City and a southern exposure. Yvonne could see the Pearson rocking at its anchor, facing northward toward the current now that the tide had changed.

Yvonne and DeeDee sat inside the doors to the balcony sipping white wine and catching up. They hadn't seen each other for a year, the longest they'd been separated. They figured this out by retracing their lives since they first met in kindergarten. The second-longest time had been when they were juniors in college. DeeDee had spent that summer on campus at Northwestern, avoiding her hometown where her parents were at the plate-throwing stage of separating. That was the year that Yvonne had started to work in her father's office.

"I think you were responsible for my going into real estate," Yvonne said.

"You were headed that way anyway. You were father-fixated," DeeDee said. "Don't blame it on me."

"Shit-house analyst," Yvonne said, and they laughed again. "Let's not lose touch this time. Let's get together regularly, okay?"

"It should be easier now that Kevin and Josh are not taking up so much of our time. We could go hunting together."

"I don't know about that. Seeing you get all the attention wouldn't do much for my ego. We could just do what we're doing now."

"Well, what do you say if I lose a little weight, you gain a little and we both start wearing our hair the same. We could start confusing people again." DeeDee had leaned forward and her face had taken on the expression of a child playing make-believe.

Yvonne knew that DeeDee wasn't going to lose weight, but was surer still that she herself could not stop her own jogging and exercise. But she answered, "What will it be? Platinum or mousy blond?"

"Mousy with platinum highlights."

"Where do I get an outfit like that?"

"You buy it off the rack and then spend hours taking tucks here and there until it falls carelessly in just the right way, hiding the uglies, showing the good stuff."

"It doesn't look like you're hiding anything," Yvonne said.

"You alley cat. But I am, I'm hiding my waistline. It's bulgy. But in this outfit my bust and my derriere distract from it. But if you breathe a word of this to anyone, I'll tell everybody that you used to wet your bed."

"You bitch. At least you made me laugh. I haven't laughed so much in years."

"Neither have I," said DeeDee. "It's good therapy."

They dissolved into more laughter, followed by tears and hiccups.

The moon crept up from behind the New York skyline and lit the balcony and the marina below. They had been sitting in semidarkness, almost talked out, tired and content when Yvonne noticed a small boat sliding up next to their Pearson. At least she thought it was the Pearson.

"DeeDee, look. Is that our boat? Where that little boat is next to the bigger one? Out there on the moorings?"

DeeDee looked toward the spot where Yvonne pointed.

"I don't remember. Your boat was in that area. But there's frequently some activity out there at odd hours."

Yvonne decided that one of the other boats must be the Pearson. She hugged her arms, realizing that she was chilled. "Do you have a sweater or a cotton blanket?"

"Let's close the doors and go raid the icebox," DeeDee said. "Then I'm afraid we'll have to go to bed. What time do you want to get up? Shall I set the alarm?"

"I never sleep later than eight no matter what time I go to bed. Kevin certainly won't be up before I get to the boatyard, even if he doesn't have anything to drink tonight. Hmmmm, I'll bet I know why those two guys were out by the Pearson, if it was the Pearson."

"Huh? Why?"

"I'll bet Kevin ordered some booze from the kid who runs the tender. Or maybe Kevin had already gone back to the bar and he brought back a drinking buddy to the boat."

"Why didn't he just stay at the bar?"

"You know how budding alcoholics are. They make promises to themselves that they can't keep."

"Do you really think Kevin's an alcoholic?"

"Not yet, but getting close. Frankly, I don't want to be there when he goes over the line."

"What are you going to do? I mean without Kevin?"

"Oh, I've got my health and my work. I'm getting good on the computers, actually."

"When did you get converted to computers? You used to think they would undermine civilization as we know it."

"Being around Rosalie and seeing how much she gets done is contagious. She's an electronic whiz kid. She keeps her books, does her business, and belongs to a couple of computer networks. She even gets crochet lessons from one of the bulletin boards."

"I never could figure how she did all that needlework and yet kept a flawless manicure. Is she crocheting any little things for Scotty and Melba's progeny yet?" DeeDee smirked as she asked the question.

"Ha. Melba and Scotty? No way. Can you imagine the

two of them . . . no. No. And I've never heard Rosalie say anything about grandchildren either."

"It does seem rather bizarre to think of Scotty and Melba as parents. But just think of all the new things Rosalie could make. Anyhow, you sound happy when you talk about the computer." DeeDee yawned. "It's probably a good distraction at this point in your life."

Yvonne suddenly realized that she had had a conversation about babies and hadn't thought about her own pain. She was getting better. Grief doesn't last forever.

They had been nibbling Vermont cheddar and rice crackers and drinking soda water at the kitchen snack bar. The blue numbers on the digital clock over the sink had all just blinked from 2:59 to 3:00.

"I'll try to be quiet when I get up tomorrow. You don't have to get up and show me out."

"I'll give you a lift to the marina."

"You'll be a zombie in the morning. It's not that far. I'll walk. Just show me where the towels are and I'll shower tonight. I'll call you next week, and we'll get together again soon. Thanks for everything, really. I missed you."

DeeDee smiled and yawned again. "I missed you, too. Good night."

Yvonne watched DeeDee in her tennis outfit scuffing sleepily toward the bedroom, looking more like the little girl she had known in kindergarten than the centerfold she had become.

7

The ache inside Harvey's head made him afraid to open his eyes—as though the stab of light would make him sick at once. He was waking, much against his will, to a hangover. What he really wanted to do was go to sleep again; he imagined himself slipping down into a deep, blue, cool tunnel of bliss. If he could just go back to sleep, he would stay there until—until?

But the ache in his head would not let him sink into the tunnel. Jesus, maybe he really was drinking too much. His memory had blacked out. He had been drinking with Quince, in Quince's office. He remembered the blinking red light.

The memory roused him instantly. How many drinks had he had? Just the one; that was all he could remember. He hadn't even finished . . .

Bits of recollection darted through his mind like silver minnows, appearing, then vanishing, impossible to hold.

Were his eyes open now? All around him was pitch-black. Was he dreaming?

The last sure thing he could remember was drinking with Quince. Yes, that had really happened; Quince had called him right after—

Oh, Jesus. Holy Christ!

Panic tumbled over panic as Harvey recalled the fear he'd felt while drinking with Quince. No, he had not seemed friendly at all. Wait! Hadn't Quince changed later, become more friendly?

Sure, he had. Quince must have given him a ride home too. Sure, Harvey thought. That must be it. I passed out, and Quince . . .

But suddenly Harvey knew his eyes were wide open and seeing nothing. He was not home. He was not dreaming! Fear filled him, a beast in his chest.

He listened, caught a pulsing sound. His own heart? No, an engine! He was on a boat! He tried to swing his legs out so he could stand up and explore, but he couldn't move. He was tied! His arms were held close to his body, his ankles bound together.

The darkness was heavy with the smells of oil and tar and rope. In a hold, he thought, on a big boat. He tried to get comfortable, but something stung the end of his nose. Rope, he thought. I have a coil of rope for a pillow, for Chrissake. As he moved, a bristle from the line stuck into his nostril. He shifted his head again. Not a good idea; a barnacle cut the edge of his nose.

Was he dreaming all this? He wished he were, but the smell of the hold, the rumble of the engine, the heave of the boat were too real.

Night, it must be night. They were on the Sound, probably. Or the ocean? How long had he been out? Jesus, where was he going? Why was he tied up? Were they going to . . .? Oh, God. No, don't think about that.

He had learned years ago to keep calm in an emergency. He could postpone pain if he had to. A good sailor learned to do that. Plenty of times, with a purple squall coming up, he had done things right, done them quickly and correctly. He had picked up cuts and bruises—he thought of the time he had gashed his palm open years before, couldn't remember how—but he had been in control then. Now someone else was in control.

Quince! Maybe Quince was near. He almost shouted for him, then changed his mind. Harvey sobbed for a moment, then choked it back. A tear ran down his nose and fell onto the coil of rope in the dark.

His feet were cold. Oh, there was nothing on his feet except his socks. Where were his shoes?

He wondered what time it was. Maybe Chowder's was still open. How happy they must be there, not to be worrying about what was going to happen to them. . . .

No, no. He had to fight the fear, had to keep his head. He had some things going for him. They must need to talk to him, or else they would have already . . . Maybe they would believe him. Quince! Quince had said he understood. Quince would stick up for him.

Over the rumble of the engine he could hear voices. Closer. There was a bang of a door, a sound of metal scraping on metal as it was pushed open wide. Heavy feet now, near his head, and a flashlight in his face, blinding him.

"Up, up," a thick voice said. Huge, strong hands, a pair of them clamped around each of Harvey's biceps, yanked him to his feet.

"C'mon, c'mon," the same thick voice said. The voice belonged to Chuck, the big guy who worked for Quince. Harvey was being dragged now, toward the open door. His right big toe caught on a coil of line; it hurt, but he was afraid to complain.

Out of the hold and into a brightly lit white metal corridor. The boat he was on must be a sixty-five, seventy-footer, he thought.

Into a small cabin the rough hands dragged him. Harvey was set down hard in a gray metal folding chair. The chair was out of place in the cabin, which was carpeted, wood-paneled, and lit softly by lamps next to the portholes on both sides. Quickly and efficiently, Harvey was untied. He felt the circulation pick up in his hands and feet.

He was facing a large dark wood desk whose top held a small lamp and a telephone. Fancy boat, big businessman's boat, Harvey thought. Maybe it belongs to the guy who runs everything.

A noise from behind him. Someone coming into the cabin on soft feet.

"Harvey," the familiar voice said. "I'm truly sorry about all this."

Quince sat down in the chair behind the desk. He wore a dark turtleneck, and a soft smile slightly turned up the ends of his mustache.

"Take it easy, my friend," Quince said. His voice sounded almost . . . sad.

"Quince, I . . . Jesus. What happened?"

"Just relax," Quince said quietly.

The desktop phone rang. Quince put the receiver to his ear but said nothing. Then he nodded. Harvey thought he saw his forehead wrinkle, thought he saw Quince's eyes change, and change again, but he was not sure.

"Right," Quince said. "I'll ask him. Yes, right in front of me now. Right . . . Let you know as soon . . ."

Quince's voice trailed off, and Harvey was bewildered as well as afraid. Quince nodded some more as he listened. After a minute or so he cradled the receiver.

Quince pressed a button on the desk, bent low and whispered into a microphone Harvey couldn't see. A moment later, Chuck entered wordlessly and set a big mug on the desk close to Harvey.

"It's just coffee," Quince said, chuckling. "No tricks this time. Go on, drink."

Harvey picked up the mug, blew the steam away, sipped. The coffee was strong, but even the aroma seemed to help his headache.

"That was some gin and tonic," Harvey said.

Quince smiled, but his eyes remained serious. "And now that you're here, we want you to be alert. Do you remember? We were talking about how those two youngsters were not to be trusted."

"Right. Right."

"And how your friend Tolly was also not to be trusted."

"Right."

"We were talking also about how you were following the youngsters, or having them followed."

"Right . . ."

"Helping us."

"Right, right!" Harvey was afraid, wanted desperately not to be afraid.

"And you want very much for me to believe you."

Harvey opened his mouth but could not speak.

Quince stood up, opened a sliding door to reveal a television set with a videocassette recorder. He took out a box labeled "Port Guinness Sailing Races," took out a videotape and put it in the VCR.

"Watch now," Quince said. A command, Harvey recognized.

The television screen lit up, and Harvey saw himself, sitting in Quince's office.

"Watch closely," Quince ordered. In his hand was a small remote control for the VCR.

Harvey heard Quince's voice coming from the television set:

"Some time ago, we thought we detected the tiniest bit of pilferage. . . ."

"Mmmmm."

Harvey saw himself slumped in the chair, looking uneasy.

The tape went on:

"We—I mean myself and my real boss—we have discussed this problem at length. At first we suspected . . . you."

"There!" Quince said, pressing the remote control to freeze the picture. "See how that question jolted you? See how you splash gin on yourself."

"I was . . . I was nervous, is all." Harvey's throat had gone dry.

Quince smiled with his lips; his eyes were cold. Then he let the tape play.

Harvey saw himself on the screen, listened to his pathetic lies.

"See," Quince said, pausing the tape. "See your eyes

there? The facial twitching? See how you are almost jolted upright?"

"I was nervous, afraid . . ."

"With reason."

"Oh, my God . . ."

"Afraid because you weren't telling the truth."

"Oh, dear Jesus."

"Let's watch some more. . . ."

The tape rolled, and Harvey relived the lies about Kevin and Yvonne and Tolly. Watching himself, he saw how childish had been his attempts at deception.

Quince stopped the tape. "Tell me," he said, "did you think we would buy such a fairy tale, even for an instant?"

"Quince, you said—"

"No, *you* said. I gave you bait and you took it. How silly."

"Oh, Jesus. Quince . . ."

But Quince waved his hand, shook his head in disgust. "What kind of man are you, that you would lie about others, put them in danger . . ."

Quince paused, his contempt filling the silence. "Whose idea?" he said at length. "Yours or Tolly's?"

"Tolly's! Tolly's! I mean, oh, Jesus . . ."

"And those kids—they don't have any idea what they're carrying?"

"No, no, I swear. I even tried to get it back—" Harvey realized with horror that he had gone way too far.

"So. We thought there were others. You sent them to try to retrieve what you had planted on the boat for safekeeping. Is that it?"

Harvey was shaking; he put his face in his hands.

"These others? Where did you find them?"

"From Tolly! From Tolly!"

"Ah," Quince said softly.

"Where on the boat is it?" Quince said.

Harvey was wild with fear. He knew, having planted the stuff himself, but he dare not say, because that would be confessing his guilt. "I . . . Tolly, he did it. I mean, he . . . I never . . . Tolly told me he put it on the boat. . . ."

"You're saying this was Tolly's idea?"

"Tolly's! Oh, Tolly's! Tolly's!"

Again Quince shook his head with disgust. Then he got up and changed the tape in the VCR.

At first Harvey thought it was the same tape. The scene was in Quince's office, same wall, same chair. But in the chair where Harvey had sat was Tolly. Tolly alive. Tolly having a drink with Quince. Tolly talking in his Irish brogue, smiling.

On the tape, Quince and Tolly talked in low, lazy tones—about the Mets, about the yacht club where Tolly ran the launch, about boat engines.

Then Quince shifted the conversation, so gradually that Tolly—at least to judge by his face on the tape—did not notice at first. But Harvey, knowing what he knew now, knowing that the Tolly he was watching on the tape was soon to die, felt his skin crawl as Quince kept Tolly talking about boats and engines, then about who was the better mechanic: Tolly or Harvey?

Tolly made a joke, but he looked uneasy in the chair.

Quince's voice on the tape changed to a lower, more serious tone. "Do you think Harvey is sometimes a little careless?" he asked.

Tolly sat up straighter in the chair. "Careless?"

"Careless. You know, not attentive enough about details. Little things."

"Little things . . ." The light in Tolly's eyes changed. He didn't like the way the talk was going.

"Yes. I've been wondering if he's careful enough about things entrusted to him. You know?"

On the screen, Tolly looked up, wide-eyed. He was looking right into the camera, and Harvey saw that he was startled, just the way he himself had been.

Quince went on: "You and Harvey have been very helpful, but lately we've been wondering a little about Harvey. Whether he's getting careless. Or . . ."

Tolly raised his glass to drink, but the glass was empty

and his hand shook and the ice cubes rattled in the glass. Tolly coughed, but he couldn't cover the sound of the clinking ice.

"Am I on candid camera?" Tolly said, laughing in a wooden cackle.

Quince let the joke lie like a stone.

Tolly looked confounded, still fighting the plunge into fear.

"Come on," Quince said to Tolly. "You're a friend of Harvey's, but haven't you noticed how careless he's become?"

"Yeah, yeah, I have." Squirming now.

"But you haven't become . . . careless?"

"No. No."

"But Harvey has?"

"He . . . maybe. Oh, Jesus."

"Harvey said you're the one who's become careless. Or even—"

"No! Harvey's a liar. It was his . . . Oh, Jesus."

"You see?" Quince said to Harvey. "I didn't tape Tolly soiling himself in his fear. That would have been degrading. And I erased the later tape, the one in which he says you were the one. The tape that shows Tolly sucking booze and engine fumes."

Harvey's jaw dropped. "You were there. You . . ."

Quince pressed "rewind," then "erase." For a long time, the whir of the tape was the only sound.

"Quince, please. You gotta believe." Harvey sobbed.

"Believe? Who to believe? And if one doesn't know who . . . ?"

"Quince, listen. We've been friends. 'Member all the times I fixed your engine for nothing? Remember the Mets game we went to? You gotta help me this once." Tears and snot ran down Harvey's face, but he was beyond humiliation.

Quince's eyes seemed to soften for a moment. "I can help you," he said quietly. "I can."

"Quince, I won't forget."

Quince took a pint bottle of gin from the desk, took off the top, gave it to Harvey. "Drink," Quince said.

Harvey took a long, hot gulp, then a deep breath. If he got out of this, he would never, ever . . .

"Of course," Quince said, "you must tell us the names of the others."

"Ernesto and Felipe. You know them two—"

"Ah," Quince said. "And they followed the two young people?"

"They followed. I can get in touch with them, get them to see you—"

"That won't be necessary. Drink some more."

"Quince, you said you could help me. You promised."

"Drink."

Harvey took another gulp. "Please. You said—"

"I am helping you, amigo. Drink."

"Quince!" Harvey took a swallow.

The desktop phone rang. Quince put the receiver to his ear and listened for several seconds. "Yes," he said finally. "Yes . . . No, we're sure. . . . Yes, as soon as possible. Ernesto and Felipe next. Yes."

Quince cradled the phone and looked at Harvey. "We're going to put you back on your boat," Quince said. "We've got it in tow."

"*Annabelle?* So I can take my own boat home?"

"Yes, you're going home in your own boat."

"Quince, I don't know how—"

"Save it."

The door to the cabin opened and three men came in: Chuck; another big man whom Harvey had seen from time to time around Quince's trucks; and a third, smaller man. Harvey thought his bowels might give.

"Quince! You said—"

Big, strong hands grabbed Harvey by the biceps and dragged him out to the corridor. They shoved him roughly to the floor, one big man stretching Harvey's arms up over his head. Then Harvey saw the other big man holding Harvey's own pair of chest-high waders, the ones with the suspenders. They had been taken off *Annabelle*, he thought.

The corridor was all white, and Harvey could feel the gin.

Quince knelt down next to him. "Open wide and drink, amigo," he said. "Drink as much as you want. It's the only choice you have left."

Quince held the bottle to Harvey's mouth. Harvey opened and took a swallow; the gin was warm. He wanted to ask Quince if Quince could please, please fix things up just one time, for the sake of friendship. Harvey started to plead, but another dose of gin went down his throat, some of it the wrong way. Harvey coughed.

Harvey continued to cough as one big man held his arms back over his head and the other began to jam the waders onto his legs. The man forcing the waders on was rough, Harvey could feel his toes being twisted and pinched by the rubber. He tried to ask the man to be more careful, but he wasn't done coughing. The man strained and puffed; he had the waders on up to Harvey's knees now.

"Please. Please, Quince," Harvey managed to say before coughing again.

The man who had forced the waders onto Harvey's legs said something to the other big man, who reached over Harvey's body and pulled the waders up the rest of the way, pulling the suspenders into place across the shoulders. One of the suspenders snapped across Harvey's face, stinging his nose. The men hadn't done that on purpose, but they didn't care either.

The big men pulled Harvey roughly to his feet. Now Harvey wasn't sure he could stand on his own, there in the white corridor. He could feel the gin. . . .

The men held him there. If he could just talk to Quince alone, as a friend. Quince was still holding the gin bottle.

"Quince . . . Quince . . ." Harvey's words did not come out right.

"Shhh, amigo," Quince said softly. He held the bottle to Harvey's mouth again. "Take some more. Please."

Quince put the neck of the bottle in Harvey's mouth, and he took a gulp of hot gin. He was getting drunk. No, he couldn't get drunk; he had to make Quince understand, had to make him remember all the times they had been friends.

"More." Quince put the bottle into Harvey's mouth again, but this time Harvey shook his head violently. He spit out the gin. He had to make Quince listen to him.

One man was chewing gum, harder and harder, as if he were watching a porno movie, Harvey thought.

"Aaargh . . ." Harvey could not believe he had made that sound. It didn't even sound like Quince's name.

The door to the outside was opened. Harvey could smell the water and salt air. As the big man steered him through the door, Harvey saw that they were on the Sound, which shone with moonlight. They led him to the stern, where Harvey saw that his *Annabelle* was tied alongside. *Annabelle*'s engine was running softly, at trolling speed.

Quince stood on *Annabelle*'s deck, still holding the bottle of gin. The big men half lifted, half pushed Harvey over the gunwales of the bigger boat, onto *Annabelle*. Then the big men themselves stepped nimbly onto Harvey's boat.

"Do you want some more gin, amigo?" Quince said.

Harvey screamed. He wanted to beg, but the sound that came from his throat was not human. He would tell! He would! He tried to make the sound come out right, but his tongue was dead.

"Put him over," Quince said.

The big men lifted Harvey and dropped his legs into the water. They let him down slowly, allowing him to claw for the gunwale of *Annabelle*. Harvey felt the water, cold and heavy, filling his waders. He could feel the weight on the suspenders. Why couldn't he make Quince hear him?

Harvey was barely able to hold on to *Annabelle*, his waders were so heavy.

"All set," Quince said. Harvey saw him step back onto the bigger boat, saw that the big men were holding *Annabelle* close to the bigger boat with a hooked pole, saw them lift the pole away, felt Annabelle slowly pull away, at trolling speed.

Harvey could not hold on, he knew it. His only chance was to keep cool, keep cool, keep cool. Get out of the waders, out of the waders, and stay afloat. . . .

A light was trained on him from the bigger boat. They were still close enough. Maybe Quince would hear, would change his mind. . . .

Harvey could not believe the sound that came from his throat, an animal growl that rolled across the water.

His fingers came loose and he fell into the water. Harvey thrashed, wanting to stay up long enough to plead to Quince one last time.

Harvey screamed across the widening expanse between the boats. It wasn't agonized vocal cords that made him stop screaming—Harvey had enough terror to scream forever, despite the pain—but the water that rushed into his nose and throat.

He was under now, sinking, still able to see the light playing on the water, but sinking. He clawed at the suspenders, got them loose, and tried to roll over to get the waders above him. He had to cough; bubbles jetted from his mouth, and then the water rushed down his throat. He couldn't roll over, but he knew it didn't matter.

Harvey was in total blackness, no longer able to see any light. He tried to remember the prayers from his childhood. He had a long way to go before he hit bottom.

8

As always when he slept on the boat, it took Kevin a while to settle down. With the tight quarters, the low headroom, plus the gentle motion of the Hudson as it crept beneath his feet toward New York Bay, the whole task took about twice as long as it would have on land.

He arranged the cushions on the port side of the V-berth (Yvonne had always slept on the starboard side), propped the hatch open an inch or so, and opened the tiny starboard porthole halfway. That way, he figured, he would get a gentle breeze through the V-berth without a draft blowing right over his head.

Then he shut the door between the V-berth and galley (Yvonne had always preferred to have it open, liking the feeling of openness, but the door sometimes swung back and forth, which usually woke him up); took off his shoes, slacks, and shirt; and tried to get comfortable. For starters, he pulled a sheet over himself.

God, he was tired. No wonder: Starting the day with a hangover, then the thing with Harvey—what the hell had that been about, anyhow?—then the trip itself.

At least he felt good about not having had anything to drink. Zip, zero, nada. Nothing. Good. Maybe Yvonne would respect him more in the morning.

The drinking was no small thing to Kevin. He could stand the thought—no, the fact—that he drank too much sometimes, even the fact that the sometimes were too often lately. What he couldn't stand was the notion that he was hooked. He had to be able to go a whole day without a drop. Well, today he had. Call it penance, he thought. No, call it not being a drunk.

He got his head comfortable on the pillow and breathed deeply. The sails, the anchor line, faint aroma of bilge, brine. A good smell, a boat smell.

He shifted his arms and head. One of the wrists smelled like Yvonne's skin lotion. He had always liked the smell, the way it blended with the smell of Yvonne.

Then he thought of how DeeDee had smelled. He had picked up a wisp of her perfume, found it interesting—no, arousing. Not that it took much to make her attractive to him. God, she was sexy.

Yvonne's smell on his wrist made him fight off the fantasies about DeeDee. Vonnie, the things I do for you.

He wondered if his sense of smell was keener without alcohol in his blood.

His father had never been able to face up to himself about the booze. Jesus, the Irish. It was true what they said about the Irish, at least in his family. Poor old bastard. Always the red face, and for the longest time the boy Kevin had thought it was because his father worked near the furnace in the mill, worked real hard to buy him shoes and braces and ice cream. Or maybe his face had got redder as the years went by. Probably.

The Hudson slid along under him, its timeless rhythm rocking the boat up and down, up and down, gently.

So many things were clearer, looking back. On Sundays, after church, Kevin's father often poured himself a glass of wine. Years later, Kevin understood why his mother frowned and turned away when he did that.

Later, it was whiskey in the morning on Sundays. There, that was the big sign. When his father switched to whiskey instead of wine on Sunday mornings. A gradual thing. As

Kevin recalled it, his father preferred whiskey on cold winter Sunday mornings. And his father loved Christmas, which was always like a Sunday no matter what day it fell on. And Christmas was cold. Perfect for celebrating with whiskey. . . .

And the fireplace. His father had loved that. A glass of whiskey in his hand, he'd sit in his easy chair in front of the fireplace. Kevin remembered the reflections in his spectacles: flame from the fireplace, lights from the Christmas tree.

The river went by underneath, sometimes slapping gently on the boat. Funny, but the sound of the river and the hiss of the fireplace on Christmas morning seemed to be one. . . .

Kevin started. Had he been asleep? Yes, but not for long. One arm was a little numb. Okay, it would not take him long to doze off again. He was tired, tired. He pulled the sheet up to his shoulders, gave himself up to the motion of the river.

Probably the saddest thing was that his father wasn't sharing when he sat by the fireplace, sipping whiskey. Never just one whiskey . . .

He was shutting people out, that was the thing. It had taken Kevin a long time to figure that out, and he still didn't have it all straight. And never would. His mother had died before he could talk to her about it. If he ever would have.

The river rocked him up and down, the river that had flowed by for thousands of years, millions of years. . . .

Kevin sifted out some of the bad stuff, thought of a house full of Christmas smells, sausage and bacon and pancakes and warm whiskey and the fireplace, all the way from Christmas Eve to late on Christmas Day, and sitting in front of the fireplace, waiting patiently for a standing rib roast. . . .

He and Yvonne had had some things like that. Kevin reached out to touch her, touched only emptiness. He started awake again. Not there, she was not there. He had started to dream.

Christmas had ended in disaster. He'd gone to the Jets party, telling Vonnie and himself that it went with the job. All right, he'd come home with more than a few drinks on his breath and some lipstick on his face. The lipstick had been from holiday kisses, nothing more. Well, only a little more: any man would have enjoyed getting kissed by that girl in the ticket office. But it had never been like Yvonne suspected.

He and Yvonne had had a terrible fight, a watershed kind of fight, looking back on it. Okay, he should have stayed home, especially with her pregnant and worried. But she had been wrong to suspect him.

Maybe they would lie near each other, next to each other, again. Maybe, maybe not. He couldn't do anything about it tonight, so he might as well shake off the sadness and go to sleep.

He shifted his arms again, put the wrist with her smell on it right next to his face. He could almost feel her arm over him as the eternal river cradled the boat gently up and down, up and down. . . .

He zeroed in on a good memory and held it, caressed it. A memory of a night just a few years ago. They had been so happy.

Beautiful memory of a beautiful summer evening. No races that night. He had come home early from the Jets' practice, it had been a light day, and they had just packed a bottle of chilled white wine and some crackers and fruit and cheese and gone sailing.

Some sailors swore that late summer was the best time on the Sound, that that was when the breezes came in just right in the late afternoon, filling the sails and bearing the smell of the sea but not stirring up the water.

What a beautiful sail they had that day, that evening. God, if he could have known how precious that would become, he would have savored it so much it couldn't get away. . . .

Ah, but it would have. Had he started to dream? No, no, he was remembering what had really happened. . . .

Oh, right, they had taken Tess along on the sail. He had always worried she would jump overboard or something, and Yvonne had always dismissed that worry, saying the dog wasn't dumb, and anyway, she could swim better than he could.

That night, Tess had lain down between them in the cockpit, utterly content, putting her head first on one set of feet, then on the other. And Kevin and Yvonne had sailed, leisurely, leisurely, not bothering to tack very often, and hardly ever jibbing because it took more work. They had sipped wine and eaten fruit and cheese and crackers, tossing a cracker to Tess once in a while, and watched the sun dapple off the purple water. And sailed back in time to get the boat moored before dark, and gone home sober enough to make love. . . .

Kevin tried to focus on how things had changed, thinking if there were any steps he could just retrace to fix things.

Kevin fell asleep, thinking about Yvonne, imagining that the smell on his wrist was really Yvonne herself, sleeping on the starboard side of the V-berth. He could almost hear her snoring.

He didn't know how long he had slept. At first the bump, bump, bump was part of a dream of a night on the boat, of him and Yvonne. Then he came up out of the dream, slowly, coming to the surface from a great depth. The bump, bump, bump was still there. The dinghy, Kevin thought. The boat had shifted in the current, and now the dinghy was bumping against the side.

No. The dinghy was tied up at the pier. He and Yvonne had decided that, hadn't they? He was coming up from the dream faster now, near the surface of wakefulness. Bump, bump, bump.

Kevin thought as hard as he could. Yes, the dinghy had been left at the pier. Yes, that was absolutely real, that had happened, no dream. And he was awake now, no dream, the sweat pouring off his chest, his heart pounding in his ears like a hammer.

All he could hear over his heartbeat was the bump, bump, bump against the side of the boat. No dream, no dream.

And the thump of a foot above him, on the deck, and the feel of the boat heeling slightly for a moment with the weight.

It was not a dream.

Still in the bunk, he propped himself up on one arm, the arm shaking from the strain and his fear. Footsteps above him. No, he was not dreaming this.

He blinked, hard, hoping to see that it was daylight, hoping that the steps were just Yvonne's, that she had come back to the boat.

No, no. Pitch-dark outside, still deep in the night. Not Yvonne's footsteps (he knew her footsteps), but a man's. No, more than one man. Above him, a pant leg had brushed against the partly opened hatch.

Kevin thought he should try to pull his pants on. No, he could swim better without them. . . . But he might need his shoes if he had to move around the boat at all, if he struggled.

But he was afraid to move. He lay there, breathing as quietly as he could, listening to the footsteps. His arm was getting tired of supporting his body. Slowly, he let his body back down on the bunk. He lay there, trying to control his breathing, trying to hear over the thunder of his heart.

Voices. From above, in whispers. Speaking Spanish. Whispering.

Jesus, were they whispering because they knew he was on board? No, no, that made no sense. They had to be whispering because they didn't want to arouse anyone else nearby. How near? Probably no one within a few hundred feet, at least no one who could help him. No one who could come in time to stop the men from braining Kevin, or cutting his throat.

As much as anything, Kevin feared the thought of his throat being cut. Years before, covering the police beat, he had known firsthand of throat cuttings, and they had chilled his stomach like nothing else.

The footsteps went aft, stopping about where the galley hatch was. Spanish voices again. Kevin wished he had studied Spanish. No, maybe it was better if he didn't know what they were saying. . . .

There, the sound of the galley hatch being slowly opened. A thump as a foot came inside the galley, landing on the first step, then a louder thump as both feet landed inside. The water around the boat sloshed slightly, and there was a bump against the side again. Must be their dinghy. Another thump, another foot landing on the first galley step, then a louder thump as two more feet landed inside. The water sloshed again, the dinghy bumped the side.

If Tess were with him, she would have barked by now, maybe scared them away. Or maybe they would have killed her. Jesus.

Muffled whispers in Spanish, shuffling feet, tapping and banging. They were right out there, just a few feet away. Kevin pushed up on his arm again; through the crack at the bottom of the door between the galley and V-berth he could see flickers from a flashlight.

If they were looking for something, they would come into the V-berth. Kevin forced himself to sit up. He slowed his breathing and, still looking at the crack at the bottom of the door, he reached behind him. On the shelf, right next to the porthole, he found a foot-long winch handle. It was for trimming the big jenny, which he and Yvonne had almost never used, and it was steel. Yes, a good weapon. He would crack someone's cheekbone or wrist or knee before he would let his throat be cut. . . .

He strained to hear their whispers, even though he understood no Spanish.

"Key . . . key . . ." one of them said. English now, Kevin thought. A key for the ignition? Jesus Christ, they want to steal the goddamn boat. The ignition key, with the tiny red plastic buoy attached, was in a drawer in the galley, along with some miscellaneous junk. They could find it if they looked hard enough.

Kevin strained to hear, strained to keep his own breathing

quiet. He tried to put himself into the minds of the intruders: If they started the boat, would they come into the V-berth? Maybe not, maybe there would be no reason.

He might have a good chance of getting away, once they started up. Even in broad daylight, the mast partly cut off the view from the cockpit. At night, he might be able to climb out of the hatch and slip over the side without their seeing him.

He waited for the sound of the drawer being pulled open, expected at any moment to hear them dump the contents, looking for the key. They did not seem to be moving around too much.

Maybe they just wanted to steal some of the equipment. A lot of sailors lost their fenders to thieves. No, if that was all they wanted, they would look in the hatches up in the cockpit, the logical place for fenders, and in fact where the fenders were. . . .

Kevin heard one of the men breathing hard, cursing. There was the sound of wood scraping against wood. Jesus, they were trying to take out the steps that led to the galley, the steps that also served as the engine cover.

Yvonne would be furious with him for letting someone come and steal the battery, or maybe steal the whole engine. . . . Maybe they wouldn't come into the V-berth. Oh! Maybe they had been watching, had seen them go ashore together and had not seen him come back. So they figured the boat was empty, with no dinghy tied alongside.

He gripped the winch handle tight. The first guy to come into the V-berth would get smacked real good—on the wrist, on his face, in the balls.

He heard the puffing and wood scraping and cursing. They were having just as tough a time as he always did getting the steps pulled off.

More muttering in Spanish.

From outside, getting closer, sounds of a powerboat, maybe a thirty-five-footer. It was a few hundred feet away, but Kevin could hear voices and laughter.

"Hey, you asshole, you fucking asshole . . ."

A splash, from about wherever the powerboat was. A bottle thrown into the river?

"Eat it. . . ."

They were drunk, whoever they were. Kids, maybe. In their twenties, at the most. Great help . . .

Silence in the galley; the Spanish guys were listening too. Jesus. For a moment Kevin wondered whether he should just stand up, pop his head through the hatch and holler as loud as he could for help. No. He had a better chance trying to defend himself. At least he was sober.

Another voice, older, not drunk, from over where the powerboat was: "All right, shut the fuck up, unless you want to be in deep shit."

Oh! A flickering blue light; Kevin could see it reflected on the water. Police boat, a police boat! Stopping a bunch of drunks. Now, now he should stand up and holler like hell. No bullshit, no worry about whether it was macho.

Only, before he could decide to do that, Kevin felt the boat rock as the intruders scrambled topside, rock some more as they scrambled into the dinghy, one of them cursing as he cracked a knee or an ankle, as he and Yvonne had each done a hundred times. Whispers in Spanish, the slopping sound of water around the boat as they paddled away in the dinghy, away from the sight of the police boat, Kevin thought—but how far away?

"You take the wheel and take this goddamn thing home right now," he heard a policeman say to someone in the powerboat. "Rest of you, shut up and stay shut up till you're home. Got it?"

The silence was broken after only a moment as the powerboat, its passengers quiet and chastened, chugged by.

At last, Kevin had the courage to look up through the hatch. He caught a glimpse of a white T-shirt in a dinghy just before the dinghy disappeared into the darkness.

Should he shout for the police? A "Yo!" started to form in his chest, but before it could reach his throat the police boat's engines roared.

He was alone again, still standing up in the hatch. He

stared a long time into the darkness, praying he would not see the dinghy reappear. Everything was quiet. At last, he went below again.

Kevin was still in a praying mood. He prayed that God would tell him who the people on the powerboat were, so that he could send them a case of beer. Make it two. . . .

Then he prayed some more, this time that God would lead him to the intruders, in broad daylight, so that he, Kevin, could smash their skulls with the winch he still clutched in his fist. The intruders had made him feel less of a man.

Slowly, the feeling of violation ebbed, leaving him with questions: Who were they? What the hell did they want?

Since his boyhood, the deep of night had always been a time for feeling afraid and helpless, either after nightmares or if he couldn't sleep at all. Now, after the day with Harvey and the strange boat and the man on the pier, his night fears had him staring into an abyss.

He longed for Vonnie, and a drink.

He wasn't sure if he slept for the rest of the night. Maybe he did: he would suddenly find his mind wandering, and not be able to recall what he had been thinking about, or trying to think about. Mostly, Kevin just lay in the V-berth, still gripping the winch handle tight, just in case.

His mind churned with dread, relief, elation, bewilderment, shame at the terror he had felt. He could sort the feelings out later. All he wanted was to get through the night.

He heard the birds start up while the sky was still blue-black. By the time it was dawn, the birds were doing a raucous chorus. Then it was full daylight, though still a long way to go before most people got up. Kevin's back ached, and his hand was sore from clutching the winch handle.

At last, he heard people stirring nearby, in boats and on the pier. Then there was the sound of a dinghy—them!

No, Yvonne. It was Yvonne.

"Kevin?" she called, bumping the dinghy gently against the boat.

He stood up and looked through the hatch.

Disgust in her face. "You look like hell," she said. "I thought you weren't going to drink last night."

9

After Kevin told Yvonne that he hadn't had anything to drink the night before, that his life might have been in danger because of a boarding party, she said she was sorry.

"Last night I did think I saw men around the boat," she said. "Then I thought I must have mixed up our boat for someone else's. Or else . . ."

"Or else I must have been taking on a cargo of beer."

"It did cross my mind."

Kevin took a deep breath. "I can understand how you might have thought that."

They ate the bagels and oranges and drank the coffee Yvonne had brought.

Kevin thought the bagel tasted fine going down, but it sat like a sinker in the cold mist of his stomach.

Yvonne thought that she had made an honest mistake. She had often seen that bedraggled face in the morning. But this morning, when she got a whiff of his breath and smelled only the vapors of morning dragon and not the overworked-liver exhaust, she believed him. She wanted to start the day all over again and hear again about the intruders.

"Nice morning," she said.

"Hmmm."

It was. The river was slow and calm and there was no traffic yet. Across the water, they could see cars crawling along the West Side Highway.

"I called Rosalie last night and reminded her about Tess. Just to make sure that automatic feeder and water dispenser are working. You did tell me you got hold of your friend last night?"

"I got Marty's answering machine. He checks it all the time. I told him we'd be along today."

"Maybe we should report it. Those men boarding the boat last night."

"Hmmm. Well, what can we tell the cops?"

"Just that. They were trespassing. What did they want? And why was Harvey . . . ? Oh, I don't know, but we should tell someone."

"Well, they were scared off. So what could we say?"

"Tell me what you're really thinking."

Her bullshit detector's working again, he thought. "Well, under those new Coast Guard regs, I think we have an illegal head. . . ."

"Kevin, the police don't give a shit. Why don't you want to report it?"

"Okay, if you want to. But I'm not sure on the registration, exactly. . . ."

"What does that mean?"

"I don't think we're up to date. I guess I didn't renew it last time. I might have let it slide. . . ."

"You might have? You mean you did." She knew the feeling; she had let some things slide too. They'd been over that ground, left so many footprints in it, that she couldn't tell for sure how things went.

"Suppose we'd been stopped in a routine check. They do that, you know."

"Well, I figured the odds were against it."

"Right, you know all about odds. . . ."

He sipped his coffee and said nothing.

She hadn't meant to say that. "Okay, I know what you mean."

"We can talk about it some more. We've got a ways to go."

"Did you lose on the Jets game?"

"Twenty. Just a friendly bet."

"Jackass Jets . . . they should have stayed in New Jersey."

He was grateful for her friendly allusion to the game and his betting, and she was pleased that he had picked up on it.

They motored to the pier and checked in with the repairmen. The sink would be done in about an hour.

"I showered at DeeDee's," Yvonne said. "I'll wait for you in the coffee shop. You'll need quarters for the shower."

"Tell me the truth, Vonnie. You must miss me. Who do you have to boss around?"

Yvonne shot him a stern look. "I should have let you get to the shower, stand there naked, and realize you didn't have any quarters."

"There are worse things that could happen to a man."

"Yeah. Being bossed around," she said.

"Or not being bossed around."

"Go wash the stink off." She was smiling.

"Yes, dearest." Kevin saluted.

Yvonne decided to call Rosalie again. Rosalie would have checked on Tess by now on her way to the office. Yvonne wanted to hear something about Tess, how the dog missed her or whatever.

"Yes?" Rosalie answered.

"It's Yvonne. Sorry to bother you again, but I just wanted to check on my doggy."

"Yvonne! We're fine here. Tess was sleeping when I arrived at your place. Did you tell me last night that you were staying in Edgecliff?"

"Yes, at DeeDee Lockwood's. Do you remember her from Port Guinness?"

"No. I don't think so. A friend of yours?"

"You'd remember her if you saw her." Yvonne thought Rosalie sounded preoccupied. "We almost sank yesterday."

"Sank?" Rosalie said, sounding more interested.

"A stupid sink fitting gave out. Anyhow, uh, did the food and water dispensers work okay?"

"Like a charm. I may get them for my little Peon." Peon was Rosalie's little Shih Tzu.

"And will you look in on Tess on your way home tonight? Or if you can't, will you ask Melba? I think we should make it back today, but it may be late."

"Of course. I'll peek in on Tess."

"I'll bore you with our adventures when we get back."

"Adventures? I can't wait."

Yvonne was about to say good-bye, but she had an impulse to vent some anger. "You know, that damn Harvey thinks he's so terrific with engines. If you see him before I do, tell him he should look at sink fittings, too."

"No telling when that'll be, hon. Listen, I gotta run. Take care."

"Time to get going, I guess," Yvonne said, taking the bowline off the pier cleat. The repairmen had finished, and Yvonne had picked up the scores of little clippings and snippets they'd left behind.

Kevin had the engine going. He swung the boat out into the river, feeling the tide fighting them a little. It would slow them up a bit before it turned.

"I'll take the tiller if you want to take a nap," Yvonne said.

That sounded good to him, though he was far too wound up to sleep. He stretched out, getting his back as comfortable as he could against the cabin. "Vonnie?"

"Hmmm."

"I was scared out of my mind."

"You were right to be. Funny they didn't look in the V-berth."

"I figure they just wanted to steal the boat. I heard them muttering and swearing, looking for a key to start the engine."

"Lucky you took it out of the ignition."

"Jesus, suppose . . ."

"The really lucky thing was that the police boat came by. I still think we ought to report it."

"A few hours from now, the boat won't be ours anyhow."

"What about Harvey? Could he have sent them to steal it?"

"I was just thinking about that. Doesn't sound like him, does it?"

"He wasn't himself yesterday morning, either. And what about that boat we thought was following us?"

"I don't know. Hell, maybe Marty Diehl talked about the boat, and someone decided to steal it. It is a classic."

"We're getting paranoid, Kevin. Let's stick to what we know. Somebody was on the boat last night, and we should tell the police."

Kevin recognized her tone. It was the one she used when she was sure she was right.

"Well?" she persisted.

"You're tough. Steel and ice."

"What?"

"You. You're steel and ice."

"No, Kevin. Not steel and ice, just common sense." She wondered if he'd ever really known her. The cringing, frightened child that she became after the baby was gone. She hadn't even known herself. How could he know?

"Okay, we'll report it."

"Call the New Jersey State Police," she said.

"Hey, Yvonne, maybe you should call. You know what you want to say."

"You were the one on board. You talk to the cops. You're the ex-police reporter."

"And you're the one who wants to report it."

"Yes, and is this some kind of blackmail? If I want it reported, I have to do it myself?"

"I give up. You win, I'll report it."

"Good. Is that all the fight I'm getting out of you?"

He looked in her face. There was a smile playing at the corner of her mouth.

"Bitch," he said, laughing.

* * *

Several miles north of the George Washington Bridge they saw a marine-supply place on the Jersey side of the river. Actually, it was nothing more than a wooden pier on which rested a small shack, a couple of gasoline tanks—and a telephone booth. Yvonne told the attendant, who was clad only in cutoffs, that he could top off their fuel tank.

The inside of the phone booth was decorated with obscene graffiti. The phone book had been partly shredded, so it ran from *C* to *Y*, but Kevin was able to look up the Jersey State Police. The Hudson River station answered after a single ring. The officer asked for a description of the boat, took down the hull number, and to Kevin's relief asked nothing about the registration date.

Kevin told him about the men coming on board, explaining that he had been sleeping in the V-berth and had stayed hidden until a police boat scared off the intruders.

"You did the right thing," the officer said. "No sense confronting them. You can always buy a new boat."

"Right."

"We have had some electronic equipment stolen off boats recently. But you say yours doesn't have any fancy stuff?"

"No. Too much money."

"Hmmm. If you do find anything missing, just let us know. Then you can report it on your insurance."

"Thanks."

Kevin told Yvonne what the officer had said.

"Did he say any boats had been stolen?"

"No, just electronic gear."

"Well, at least we reported it."

Kevin shook his head. "Goddamn Harvey anyway. All the money we paid him over the years, and he couldn't even check out the sink fitting."

"Goddamn Harvey is right. We know we're not terrific mechanics. That's why we pay him."

"Suppose the sink fitting had waited until we were way upriver, when it was almost dark."

"Blub, blub, blub."

"We'd still be holding onto the mast."

The image made her laugh.

But Kevin was still boiling. "I'm gonna call Harvey and ream him out."

"Give him a jab for me."

Kevin got quarters from the pier attendant and went back to the phone booth. He expected the phone to ring five, six, seven times, which it often did when he called the boatyard. It meant Harvey was down by the pier, or fussing on a boat. Kevin hoped Harvey was as far from the phone as possible; let him get pissed.

Kevin's pleasure at imagining Harvey's annoyance gave way to frustration when no one answered. He let it ring a few more times, finally stopped counting and hung up.

"Figures," Yvonne said. "He probably doesn't get enough of Chowder's at night. Needs his beer in the daytime now, too."

"Yeah, well, I'm not even that bad."

She smiled at the little joke.

"I almost feel like calling Chowder's," Kevin said.

"We can tell him off later. If we want to bother."

"Yeah, and if we ever get another boat, we're not gonna keep it at Harvey's."

Kevin wished he hadn't said that, but Yvonne ignored it. She had the engine running and motioned for him to uncleat the bowline.

Yvonne pulled away from the pier, then gunned the engine. Some spray splashed into the cockpit. Kevin liked the feel of it on his face, liked the look of it on Yvonne's shirt.

It was coming closer, Kevin thought sadly. The time when they would no longer have the boat. When they weren't even "they."

Kevin propped himself up, his back against the cabin. Maybe now he could nap. The pier with the shack and phone booth grew smaller. Kevin saw the pier attendant talking to two men. Was it his imagination, or did the attendant point at the boat?

"Vonnie, look. Those guys back there."

"What?"

"I think they just pointed at us."

"It couldn't be that the whole world's after us, Kevin."

"They pointed. I saw them."

Yvonne studied the pier. The men were just standing there now. Then her eyes followed the line from the dock past their boat, looking for something else that the men could have pointed at. A buoy? An apartment building on the opposite shore? "I don't know, Kevin."

Kevin felt stressed out; nerves and lack of sleep could do that, not to mention the whole thing with Vonnie. If it hadn't been for the guys on the boat last night, the world wouldn't seem dangerous at all. Would it?

A sensation came over him like a chill—as cold as ice, or the edge of a razor.

"Kevin, look."

Yvonne's voice startled him. Still at the tiller, she pointed upriver. Kevin swung around and saw, in plain view but still a good distance away, a dozen or so sailboats—no, two dozen. Maybe more.

"Racing," Yvonne said.

The sun was poised to start its slow descent and reflected dazzlingly on the whites and reds and blues of the sails.

"Neat," Kevin said.

"We'll have to be careful we don't get in their way," she said.

"We're just about at the widest point of the river. We can give them plenty of room."

"I hope your friend is there to meet us."

"Well, if he isn't, I'll just call him again. Marty doesn't live that far away." Besides, Kevin thought, Marty was the one he owed the twenty bucks to because the Jets hadn't covered.

"Want to take her for a while?" Yvonne said.

"Sure."

He slipped into the rearmost part of the cockpit and took the tiller. Instead of sliding over, Yvonne went forward, feet skipping nimbly along the gunwale and her hands grasping the rails along the top of the cabin, to the bow. She sat down, just aft of the pulpit, pulled her knees almost up to her chin and wrapped her arms around her legs. When spray hit her face, she realized her skin was hot. Tension. As if there weren't enough just being with Kevin.

Just a few days before, he had suggested they get back together. How could he think, after all that's happened, that we could just start over? she thought. He's living in a dream, a childish dream, as if he could go confess to a priest, say a few Hail Marys, and all the sins would be erased. She felt a little sorry for him, though, baring himself, asking for another chance. But children did that too, to get what they want.

She had to manage her own separate life, tend to her own wants and needs. She didn't want to be half of a relationship; she wanted to be whole, not swallowed up.

She took a few deep breaths, stomach-breathing, trying to relax, to refocus. Work, the office, working with the young couple who were planning to have a child and wanted to buy a house in Port Guinness even though they only had enough money for half a house. Handyman special, they said they wanted.

Rosalie had advised Yvonne to stop wasting time on them. Impossible, she said. Rosalie kept an eye on the bottom line. But the search had made Yvonne something of a guru of low-priced houses in Port Guinness. Another extra had been getting to know the computer listing system. Many of the other sales people, especially the older ones, were paper-bound.

Funny, Yvonne thought, about her conversion to electronic record keeping; how tentative she had been at first, how afraid, every time the screen went black. She hadn't told Kevin that she had borrowed money from Rosalie for the computer. Well, she wasn't obligated to tell him. It was her business.

She felt the anger creeping up again, but now it was cooler, like resentment. So who's childish now? Children and the powerless feel resentment. Then she remembered something her father used to say: "He cannot do what seems right to you, only what seems right to him." Something like that, only it was about children. Her father had said that Shaw, George Bernard Shaw, had said it somewhere or other. Well, he was right. Her father, and Shaw, if that's who said it first.

Kevin can't do what seems right to me. And I can't do what seems right to him. The best we can do is communicate.

I'll try, she thought. After all, he was one of three people on earth with whom she had been closest. Her mother was first. Then in her teens and early twenties, it was her dad, who lost favor periodically as boyfriends popped in and out of her life.

But Kevin had been different from the others; he even got along with her dad. Her mother liked him, too. Kevin did, does still, probably, have a certain Irish charm about him.

Where had all that good feeling gone?

They went under the Tappan Zee Bridge; car tires hummed overhead. They were close enough now to hear the sounds of the racers—sails flogging, rigging twanging through the tack, curses and laughs.

Kevin looked at Yvonne. He had always liked watching her on the bow, wind and spray in her face, as if she ruled the water and the air and the sky.

Snap out of it, he told himself. What are you going to do when you see her out with somebody else?

He pushed the tiller to the right a little, aiming the Pearson more toward the west bank.

"Hi!" The shout had come from the nearest boat, the voice filled with joy and not a little beer. Yvonne waved back; so did Kevin. He and Yvonne had been like those people. That hadn't been that long ago. Had it?

"Join us!" someone shouted. "No skill necessary."

"Good thing," another strange voice said.

"Eat shit . . ."

They've got the world by the ass and don't even know it, Kevin thought.

Now they were passing two stragglers, small, beat-up sloops loaded to the gunwales with wisecracking sailors and, apparently, cold beer.

"Join ush," a member of one crew shouted, just before he stumbled. A crewmate saved him from cracking his head.

"Gonna lash you guys to the mast. . . ." The raucous voices were muffled as a mainsail swung gracelessly through a tack. Then Kevin and Yvonne were past them.

"Damn," Kevin whispered. "I wish I could be that happy again."

Not too much later, they passed a red can buoy in the middle of the Hudson.

"See that?" he shouted. "It means the turn into the Haviland marina is just a little farther. Marty said to look for an old coal chute right near the water."

"I thought you just got his machine," she shouted from her perch on the bow.

"I mean he told me that way back when, when we first agreed."

"I hope he's there."

Kevin recognized the coal chute from several hundred yards away. He was relieved; it was still broad daylight, and there was no chance now that they would get lost.

So now it's down to this, he thought, as he saw the entrance sign for the marina. A few minutes to go a few hundred feet down a channel, and that's it for the boat. Jesus, when I let things slip away from me, I don't mess around, do I.

But he refused to dwell on it. For one thing, he was steering a boat into a strange harbor. And he was bone-tired; the lack of sleep had caught up with him.

He hoped that Marty Diehl would need no more than ten minutes to show them where to park the boat, then take them to his car for the ride down to the city. If Marty could do that, Kevin wouldn't even mind paying the twenty for the side bet they'd had on the Jets. Throw in a beer, too. . . .

A couple of boats heading out to the river passed them in the channel. Now Yvonne was standing, looking back at him questioningly. He shrugged. They were nearing the end of the channel and coming to a large basinlike area of water at least as big as a football field, the piers lined with boats.

"Vonnie, hang a couple of fenders off the port side."

She scrambled back to the cockpit, got a pair of the rubber bumpers out of a hatch and in no time had them dangling over the side, protecting the widest part of the boat.

Not seeing Marty Diehl anywhere, Kevin pulled into an empty area of the pier. They could tie up there for a few minutes and not be in anybody's way. There were no boats within a couple hundred feet.

As they drew near, Kevin threw the engine into reverse and the Pearson nestled to the pier as gently as if he'd used brakes. Yvonne stepped out and tied a line onto a piling, fore and aft.

"Well?" she said.

"No Marty."

"Why don't you call him, and I'll stay here."

"Okay. Right. Let me just rest a minute, okay?"

"Okay."

He leaned back, either too tired to be sad or too sad to be tired, he wasn't sure which. Jesus, the least Marty could have done is send someone. . . .

Kevin could see all the way up the pier, to where it intersected with a wide walkway where eight or ten piers connected. Big marina, Kevin thought.

He started to stand up, brushed his knee against the gearshift sticking up from the cockpit floor, reached down to pull the shaft out, then thought the hell with it. God, he was tired.

Three men were walking toward their boat from the other end of the pier. Marty's friends? Kevin wondered. One was Kevin's size, although more muscled; one was smaller; and one was much bigger, taller. Sunglasses, dark hair, jeans and T-shirts.

Yvonne's back was to them; she was looking at Kevin now, puzzled that he wasn't getting out of the boat to call Marty Diehl.

"Vonnie, I think we have company."

She turned and looked down the pier, and when the three men saw both Kevin and Yvonne looking at them, they smiled and waved. Most boaters wear cutoff pants on a day like this, Kevin thought.

"Maybe they're friends of your friend," Yvonne said.

"Maybe."

Yvonne caught the uncertainty in his voice, looked into his face with alarm, stood up to face the approaching strangers. Kevin stood up too. His legs felt rubbery.

"Hi," the tall one said. Phony attempt at heartiness, Kevin thought. They were at the end of the pier now; no room for Kevin and Yvonne to get off the boat, no other boaters nearby.

"Hello," Kevin said. He tried to sound casual, at ease, but knew his voice hadn't made it.

"Nice boat," he said. "You're looking to sell, right?"

"How'd you know?"

Yvonne spoke up. "Did Marty Diehl send you?"

"That's right, Martin Diehl sent us."

No, Kevin thought. Marty is never anything but Marty.

"He asked us to look over the boat and be sure it was okay," the big one continued. "He couldn't make it himself."

No, Kevin thought. Marty had seen the boat; he didn't need to have it inspected again. And no way he would have missed the meeting, not when we're friends, not when I owe him twenty bucks from the Jets game. . . .

For a moment, Kevin wished the three strangers weren't wearing sunglasses, so that he could study their eyes. Then he thought it was just as well he couldn't see their eyes, and just as well he was wearing sunglasses too. Because they could have read the fear.

"He couldn't make it himself?" Kevin said. He couldn't keep the fear out of his voice.

Without bothering to answer, the big stranger stepped onto the boat—heavily, clumsily, and without waiting for an invitation—and his unsmiling companions stepped aboard after him, causing the Pearson to slosh and bob. Kevin wondered if two of them were the men who had boarded the night before. How did they know where to meet them?

"Let's all sit down," the big stranger said.

Kevin didn't like the way they sat on the side closer to the pier; he felt like a prisoner. He was.

He and Yvonne sat down. She slid close to him.

"Friends of Marty?" Kevin said, his voice a frightened croak.

"Take a look below, Tony," the big stranger said.

The man named Tony went below clumsily. Kevin and Yvonne heard him open the door to the V-berth with a bang. Thump, thump, clang, thump as cushions, life jackets, and winches were tossed unceremoniously into the galley.

"Kevin," Yvonne whispered, sliding closer.

"You're not really friends of Marty Diehl," Kevin heard himself say.

"No shit."

From below, the thumps and clunks continued.

"Tell your friend that gear's expensive," Yvonne said.

Kevin couldn't believe his ears. He had always admired her courage, knew how it would usually get the best of her fear, but this was ridiculous.

"Tell him yourself," the big stranger said.

Before Kevin could stop her, Yvonne stood up, planted her hands on either side of the opening to the galley, swung her legs up and over the threshold and dropped below—gracefully, as always.

"Stop that, goddammit!" she shouted.

"Tough bitch," the big one said, chuckling softly.

From below, more thumps and clunks, and voices:

"I said, stop that."

"Fuck off, lady."

"I'll scream bloody hell."

"Better not," the man below said, "unless you want your dickhead husband all cut up."

As if on cue, the small man sitting next to the big one pulled up a pant leg and took something from a leather sheath on his calf. Kevin heard a click, saw the blade gleam in the sun. Long, silver blade. Cut a man's throat as easily as a lamb's. Kevin felt sick in the stomach. He thought he might faint.

"We can cut you, cut both of you, and be out of here before anybody knows," the big stranger said.

"Want to see if we're right?" the man with the knife said, chewing his gum with a fierce energy.

Kevin did not want to see if they were right, especially when he saw Yvonne's face looking up from the galley, her face contorted in pain.

"Kevin, he's got my arm. . . ."

"Don't," Kevin said—a plea, not a command. God, please don't let this happen. "Please."

"Tell us where, or we tear this fuckin' boat apart," the big guy said.

"Tear you apart too," the man with the knife said, his chewing gum snapping.

Kevin looked around; they were a galaxy away from people who might help.

"Where?" the big stranger said.

"Where what?" Kevin said. He could not bear Yvonne's face.

"Ow . . ." Yvonne said.

"Where is it?"

"Ow . . ."

Vonnie, his Vonnie, was being hurt. Could this really be happening? As if in a nightmare, Kevin saw the man step across the cockpit to the galley hatch, pull a roll of wide adhesive tape from a pocket and wrap a couple of strips roughly around Yvonne's mouth. Hurting her, Kevin thought. Hurting Vonnie. Her eyes were wide with fear and pain.

"Take her to the bunk and have some fun," the big stranger said. "Me next."

Yvonne's face disappeared as she was spun around and shoved toward the bow.

"Please," Kevin said. "Just tell us what you want. Please." He would give them anything, anything, if only—

From below came the sounds of scuffling. The V-berth door banged once, twice. Yvonne was fighting him off.

"Don't," Kevin said. "Tell him don't. Please . . ."

"Where?"

"Where what, for Jesus's sake?"

"Go ahead, Tony. Think up something new."

Louder scuffling from below. "Mmmm . . ." Yvonne was trying to scream through the tape; Kevin couldn't bear the sound. He stood up; the big stranger and the knife-holder stood up too. The blade flashed near Kevin's face.

"Wanna bet we can cut your neck open before you can holler?"

"No . . ."

Kevin moved slightly, trying to get away from the blade. His leg brushed against the gearshift handle still sticking up from the cockpit floor. The big stranger and the man with the knife were looking below, their eyes momentarily diverted from Kevin, wanting to see what their friend was doing to Vonnie, his Vonnie.

From below, more scuffling, louder. Yvonne still fighting. How much longer could she fight? "Mmmm . . ."

Kevin bent slightly at the knees, grasped the handle of the gearshift and pulled it free. Good, heavy metal, about the length and weight of a tire iron.

Yvonne and the third man twisted and struggled in the V-berth. He had tried to pin her arms, to hold her down, but she had struggled free. Whenever he seemed to have her under control and reached to unzip his trousers, she would lunge again. He kept looking over his shoulder as if he were wondering whether the other two were watching. Yvonne's head was pounding with exertion and something else, an animal response, a closing off of the usual channels of thought. She kicked and scratched and pummeled, ripped at the man's clothing. Her rage was unstoppable, but he was stronger than she and she was tiring. She couldn't get her breath with the tape over her mouth. She started to tear at the tape, and he had her, her arms pinned behind her back.

The men were still looking below; the man with the knife was resting his right arm—his blade arm!—on the roof of the galley.

Kevin started his swing from as far back as he could, bringing the metal shaft down in a long, smooth arc that ended on the hand that held the knife. The crunch was followed instantly by a shriek of surprise and pain and a second later by a metallic clatter as the wicked knife fell to the floor of the galley below. The man who had lost his knife and the use of his hand in the same moment crumpled to the floor of the cockpit, whimpering.

The other one came at Kevin, knocking him back against the gunwale with his weight, then sprawling on top of him as Kevin lay on the bench of the cockpit. Kevin held on to the gear handle as hard as he could, but he could get no room to swing. Kevin kept squirming with his arms and legs; he knew he had to keep the big man from getting steady on top of him, because if that happened the man would smash his face with a single punch, crushing his mouth and breaking his teeth or driving the bone in his nose deep into his brain.

The man whose hand Kevin had smashed stood up clumsily, still whimpering, then he collapsed again, his movement tilting the boat just enough to send Kevin and the big man sprawling to the floor of the cockpit. Kevin rolled over, got to his feet, still holding the gear handle.

The man who had dragged Yvonne forward started to climb up, his face bewildered. Kevin saw his hands. No knife, no knife. He hadn't picked up the knife from below. Before the man could climb up, Yvonne appeared behind him (her face wild with anger, like Kevin had never seen, not even in their worst fights!), the masking tape dangling from her cheek, a winch handle in her hand.

The winch handle was almost as long as a hammer, and about the same weight. Kevin wondered if she would have the stomach to use it. He only wondered for a moment, because Yvonne brought the winch handle down on the man's head, not hard enough to knock him cold but hard enough to gash his scalp open, so that when the man stumbled up from the galley he was dripping blood all over the cockpit and holding his head with both hands.

The man whose hand Kevin had smashed lurched to his feet, stumbled from the boat onto the pier, almost falling into the water and tilting the boat enough so that the biggest stranger lost his balance for a second as he came at Kevin.

He started to get up again, but the boat tilted yet again as the man with the head wound followed his companion to the pier, and the biggest stranger was down on his hands and knees, coming at Kevin like a crab and growling in fury.

Kevin had no time to think, but didn't need it. He still remembered *"Take her to the bunk and have some fun. . . . Think up something new. . . ."* He remembered Yvonne's pain and his anguish, his shame at not being able to help her.

Kevin brought the metal shaft down again. It glanced off the side of the big man's head, splashing more blood into the cockpit, then spent the rest of its force on the man's upper back. The man groaned, and Kevin stepped to the farthest corner of the cockpit.

"Kevin?" Yvonne said softly.

Kevin didn't think his legs would hold him. He could smell his own sweat. Like an animal . . . The big man was getting to his feet again. God, he's strong, Kevin thought. Have to hit him again. Bleeding all over the place.

"C'mon, Chuck," the gum-chewer said, still holding his hand.

The big man stood up, stepped onto the gunwale and scrambled up onto the pier. There he took off his shirt and pressed it against his head, as the man Yvonne had hit was doing. The man with the smashed hand pressed it against his chest with his other forearm.

A couple of hundred feet away near the other end of the pier, a knot of boaters had gathered. They watched, not knowing what to do. The three bleeding men backed away as Kevin waved the gearshift handle. Yvonne stood behind him, holding the winch.

"Get away from us," Kevin said. "Get away. . . ."

"You're as good as dead," the big man shouted back.

Kevin's heartbeat pounded in his ears; he breathed in great gulps. He felt exhilaration from the victory, rage over what they had planned to do to Vonnie, his Vonnie, who sobbed even as she started the engine and untied the lines from the dock—clumsily, her hands trembling.

"Come on, Kevin. Put the gearshift in. We're getting out

of here." She had pushed the boat a couple of feet away from the dock.

The three strangers had recovered, even the one with the broken hand, and started toward them again. The two with the head cuts were still stanching the blood with their T-shirts. Now Kevin was waving the winch handle.

"We're going to kill you next time," the big stranger said.

"First we cut you like bait," said the one who had had the knife.

The knife! Kevin jumped below, picked the knife off the galley floor, scrambled topside. "With what, creep?" Kevin screamed, holding the knife in the air.

"Kevin, stop it, for God's sake."

"With *what?*" Kevin tossed the knife into the water. It splashed like a fish and sank.

"You should have kept it to show the police," Yvonne said.

Several from the crowd of boaters started uncertainly toward the three bleeding men. The three turned their heads toward the crowd. "Help us!" Chuck shouted to the crowd. "He's crazy! Attacked us for no reason. Must be on drugs. Look what he did. . . ."

"He's a liar!" Kevin yelled. "They came after us!"

Chuck was cooler now. Still holding his T-shirt to his head, he turned to the onlookers. "That guy's drunk."

Someone in the crowd spoke up. "Do you want us to call an ambulance?"

"There, you see?" Yvonne said to Kevin. "Those people believe them. They're the ones who are bleeding."

Another voice in the crowd: "Harbor patrol. Someone call the harbor patrol."

"What the hell are they doing?" someone else said. "Get the number of their boat."

Yvonne backed the boat into the channel, hoping that she wouldn't hit a high spot and run aground. The dinghy bumped against the side.

It's in the way, she thought; the dinghy will slow us down. Get rid of it.

One hand on the tiller, she untied the dinghy and let it drift.

"They'd believe us. We have the proof that this is our boat—" Kevin stopped, remembering that the registration had expired. Did that matter?

Yvonne shifted into forward and gunned the engine. She steered toward the river. She could hardly hear the engine over the pounding in her head. Escape. Please let us escape.

Kevin looked over his shoulder. The three were watching. They said they would hunt us down. Jesus, why?

But for now, he and Vonnie, his Vonnie, had beaten them. "I love you, Vonnie."

"Get up on the bow," she said through her teeth. "Make sure we don't hit any rocks."

He stumbled forward. He did feel love for her. But he felt something else too. He felt savage, triumphant.

"Ha!" he shouted as loud as he could. Jesus help me, he thought. It was almost worth it, worth the pain and fear, just to swing the gear handle and draw blood.

10

Yvonne cried and cursed as they reached the Hudson, steering across the chop left by a freshening breeze, the kind of breeze that would have elated them if it had been another time, another place.

Kevin's heartbeat had slowed, and he looked back toward the channel entrance. Nothing. He scanned the bank, the trees, the shadows. They were there. He was sure. He knew they were watching.

Speedboat! The noise of the churning screws came up suddenly, from rear port side. Kevin could see two men; the third must be crouched down—waiting to blast them with a shotgun? Jesus . . .

"Vonnie."

"Oh, Kevin. God."

He pulled the gearshift handle out of its hole again. He wished he had not thrown the knife away, they would have a better chance with the knife. God, please, don't let this happen. . . .

As the speedboat came near, it suddenly slowed—out of pure courtesy, it turned out. The driver smiled and nodded and his companion waved as they passed, then sped up.

Yvonne let out her breath.

Kevin was so relieved that he vowed never to say, or think, an unkind word about speedboaters again.

"Kevin, look. Back there."

Another speedboat had appeared at the channel mouth. It was just a speck, but getting bigger, aiming for them as if drawn by a laser beam on the Pearson's stern. The speedboat was gray, low to the water line, sinister. This time, Kevin had no doubts.

"Vonnie, maybe we just want to head for the Westchester shore in a straight line."

"No way we outrun a speedboat."

"Jesus, then what . . . ?"

"Get below, fast. Bring up the jib." Her voice was controlled, the way Kevin remembered it when she was sure what to do. "We can't outrun them, so we won't try," she said. "We're going to be part of the sailboat race. They're all about our size. We'll blend in. Stay out here all day if we have to."

Kevin jumped below, stepped through the pile of cushions, life jackets, winches, and other gear left by the goons, and scrambled up topside with the sailbag.

"We can do it," he said, more with hope than conviction.

"Hurry, Kevin."

"You got it, kid." He would not let her down this time. Kevin went to the bow, banging his knees as always, to rig the jib.

The racers were between them and the speedboat. Now they were close to one end of the racecourse. As he knelt on the bow his knees rested on part of the sailbag to keep it from rolling overboard; that had happened once, and she had hollered at him as she fished the sailbag out of the water with a boat hook. . . .

As he fastened the jib hanks to the forestay, he could hear the luffing sails of the race boats as they tacked around the marker.

Yvonne had taken the engine out of gear to let the boat drift as she hoisted the mainsail and let it luff in the wind.

"Yo!"

Kevin looked up and recognized the boat and its cargo of drunks from before.

"Yooo!" Kevin hollered back. "Yoo! Yes, this time, yes!"

"Yoooo!"

"Kevin, goddammit. Don't act crazy, just hurry up!"

"You got it, kid."

He did not feel as cool as he tried to sound, not nearly. As he finished hooking the hanks, he was surprised to see that his hands were bleeding from scratches that he couldn't remember getting. Yvonne was back at the tiller now, trimming the main. Kevin stepped up next to the mast to hoist the jib.

"Get on the windward side, Kevin, or the sail will blow you overboard," she said.

"Shit," he said.

The speedboat was a hundred yards or so away, closing fast, sleek and menacing as a serpent.

Kevin hoisted the jib, willing his hands not to fumble with the halyard. The sail luffed momentarily, then filled with a thump as Yvonne pulled in the sheet. Kevin scrambled back to the cockpit.

Under sail.

"Hey, mister. You can't just barge into a race. . . ." A sober voice, serious sailor, from a small sloop just rounding the marker. Kevin and Yvonne had just blocked their wind.

"Sorry," Kevin said. "Buy you a beer later."

"Yooo, fuck him. He's not drinking." The inebriate again—a sailor more like Kevin.

"Kevin."

He looked to where Yvonne had pointed with her head, off to the starboard. A hundred yards or so away, the gray speedboat idled, riding the chop.

"Watching us," Kevin said.

"I'm not sure it's them."

Kevin had to squint; the speedboat was between them and the sun. He blinked hard but it didn't help. One moment he could see the speedboat, the next moment gray spots danced in front of his eyes.

"Jesus," he said.

The speedboat looked like the one he had seen yesterday, near the Throgs Neck. But he couldn't be sure. He squinted again; the men in the speedboat looked dark-haired, dark-faced. Or was it just the sun behind them that made them look like that?

"I can only see two guys," Kevin said.

"That doesn't mean anything. They might've left the one with the bad hand. Or one of them might be below. And even if it's not them, it could be part of the same gang."

"Damn."

"Hey, you racing or not, you people? Either get out of my wind or fall off, okay?"

"Sorry."

"I don't know why you want to cut in late anyhow. It won't mean anything."

"Actually," Yvonne said to the sailor, "it could mean a lot." Then she turned to Kevin. "Here," she said. She tossed him a fresh orange T-shirt to replace the sweat-soaked gray one he'd worn all day.

"Do I smell that bad?"

"Yes, but I don't care. Crouch down and change your shirt. Make it harder to spot us."

Kevin did so. God, she was sharp.

Without taking off her own pale-blue top, Yvonne pulled a yellow one over it. Then she put on a floppy boat hat, tucking her hair up in it.

Then she began to cry again. "Those bastards."

Now they were not just one boat on the water but one of a score or so of sloops racing, more or less, around a triangular course. A couple of the boats had distinctive traits—a hull of firecracker red or royal blue, say—but most, like theirs, were silver or gray or somewhere in between. Anyone following them could easily lose track.

"Vonnie." He put his hand on her shoulder.

He could not tell if he was any comfort to her. It was the same helpless feeling he had had when she lost the baby.

"Anything I can say?" he asked hoarsely.

"No."

There was no rebuke in her voice. He moved away from her and pulled in the jib sheet.

The boat heeled a little and picked up speed.

"Kevin?"

"Yeah?"

She nodded toward where the speedboat had been. It was gone now. Gone where? And did it matter at all?

They caught a good cross-river breeze and let it take them down the course on a starboard tack, close-hauled. They had always liked sailing close-hauled, feeling the wind coming at them and the boat heeled over.

"Yoo!" It was the drunk hailing them again. But this time the elation had gone out of Kevin. The feeling had been triggered by fear and adrenaline anyhow, and had been closer to horror than he cared to think about just yet.

"Yooo . . ."

Kevin waved at him halfheartedly and looked back at Yvonne. She had stopped crying, but her face was swollen and her lower lip was trembling. Kevin bent over to put his head in his hands and saw that they were shaking violently. He put his right hand against the gearshift and squeezed as hard as he could. He remembered what the men had said, about hurting Vonnie, and the sounds of her scuffling with the man below, and he wished for all the world that he could swing the gearshift at them again. The man who had been below with Vonnie was the only one he hadn't hit. God, if you don't do anything else for me, just give me the chance to splatter his brains. Okay?

Jesus, Kevin thought. What the hell kind of prayer is that?

"Ready about," Yvonne ordered.

"Ready." Damn, she was a sailor to her marrow.

Yvonne swung the Pearson smoothly around the marker and let the boom swing across the cockpit and out over the port gunwale. Kevin trimmed the jib, and they were heading back up course.

"Look at all the boats," Kevin said. "Pretty."

Yvonne said nothing.

The boat with the serious sailor, the one whose wind they

had blocked out, passed them without so much as a wave. Serious sailor, Kevin thought. Fuck him.

"I don't see the speedboat anywhere," Yvonne said.

"Good. I've had enough for a day. Or a life."

"The leading boats are heading downriver a little and cutting over to the Westchester side. We'll follow along and tie up wherever we can."

"Do you believe this shit, Vonnie?"

"I don't know what it means, but I know we can't handle it. And I told you I never trusted Harvey."

"That's right, you didn't."

"And what about your friend?"

"No, Marty's okay. Just a sportswriter, like me. He can't be in on all this. But what's it all mean?"

"They were looking for something. On this boat."

"What? And where? No place to hide anything. We're not the *Queen Elizabeth,* for Christ's sake. Maybe they wanted the boat itself."

"No. Something else. Soon as we tie up, we call the police."

"I'm gonna call that goddamn Harvey—"

"The police. First thing. We tell them everything we can remember. Everything."

They were downriver now, on the other side of the Tappan Zee. The leading boats were passing under a banner strung across the entrance to a channel on the Westchester side. "Tansytown Boat Club Annual Late-Summer Sailing Races," the banner read.

Kevin saw a gray speedboat bobbing up and down near the channel entrance. Them! He was about to say something to Yvonne when he took another look and saw that a man standing up in the speedboat was holding a clipboard and writing something down. Oh, a race official. Of course, for God's sake.

"For a second I thought that boat there—"

"Me too," she said.

The man with the clipboard wore a straw hat, dark glasses, and a T-shirt that said "Tansytown Yacht Club." As the Pearson passed near him, he smiled like Bert Parks and said, "Race number?"

"We're not racers, not officially," Kevin said. "We just want to put up here for a while if that's all right."

The man with the clipboard stiffened and his smile took on an edge, as though he were dealing with social inferiors. "Keep to your right down the channel," he said. "You can tie up at the pier that says 'Guests.' We have reciprocal privileges with some clubs in the area. You'll have to talk to the dockmaster." The man said that as though he was absolutely certain they couldn't possibly belong to any decent club in the area, or anywhere else.

Kevin dearly wanted to tell him to fuck off, but he thought the better of it. They had barged into a race, and they looked like a couple of bums. At least he did.

They tied up at the guest pier between a couple of ketches that were worth fifty or a hundred thousand dollars more than their boat. Kevin got a bucket, filled it with water from a faucet on the pier, and rinsed the blood out of the cockpit. Yvonne took a sponge and finished the cleanup, then had second thoughts.

"Should we have left the blood alone?" she asked. "We're throwing all the evidence into the Hudson. The blood, the knife."

"Maybe. I don't know." Now he half wished he hadn't thrown the knife away.

Kevin and Yvonne agreed that maybe it was good to be parked in such exclusive company: security would be tighter with these expensive boats around. Wouldn't it?

Then how come two men with mean hard looks were walking down the pier, each carrying a satchel, coming right for their boat? They were about Kevin's size, sun-burned, with muscles in the arms and shoulders like he only dreamed about. . . . Eyes like lasers, mean. Jesus.

"Vonnie." He grasped the gearshift handle again, but his arm felt weak.

The men stopped in front of their boat. No one around to help, the whoops and laughter of the racers far away . . .

Kevin and Yvonne looked up at them. Kevin started to

pray, hoped that it still counted because he hadn't been to church for so long. The men were tough-looking; sun blisters around their lips, no doubt used to pain, used to dishing out pain. . . .

Still frowning, the men unzipped their satchels. This can't be happening, Kevin thought. Our Father Who Art in Heaven . . .

One man took a metal canister out of his satchel and tossed it in a graceful arc toward Kevin. Kevin brought his hand up just in time to catch the can of beer as it bounced off his chest. It was cold, with bits of ice clinging to the metal.

"You catch better than you sail," one man said, breaking into an ear-to-ear grin. "Welcome to the Tansytown Boat Club."

"How about you, ma'am?" the other man said.

"I can use one," Yvonne said, smiling.

One of the men, it turned out, was the dockmaster, the other a race organizer. They came on board, spoke admiringly of the Pearson Ariel, looked puzzled when Kevin and Yvonne said they were planning to sell it, but didn't press the subject. About halfway through the beer (which tasted so good Kevin knew he could never give it up completely), Kevin and Yvonne began to tell about the boarding party and being followed.

"Cops. You wanna talk to the cops," the dockmaster said. "Drink up, and I'll take you up to the office. By the way, my name's Mel."

"Kevin."

"I'm Steve."

"Yvonne."

Then still another voice, a woman's, from the stern of one of the ketches: "I love your boat. We used to have a Pearson."

"Thank you," Yvonne said.

"Aw gee, never forget her. Great boat." The voice belonged to the husband of the woman on the ketch. Both had come up from the galley and were sipping gin and tonics and smiling.

"We've had a good time on her," Kevin said. He figured the man to be ten or twelve years older than he was, the woman that much older than Vonnie.

A little girl appeared from the galley of the ketch. About nine or ten years old, face like both her parents, freckles and braces.

That should be us not so far down the road, Kevin thought, and he wondered if Yvonne was thinking the same thing.

She was.

The people on the ketch exchanged pleasantries with Mel and Steve about the race and the weather and sailmakers. Then the woman said, "Have fun with that Pearson, you two."

Treating us like a couple, Kevin thought. That doesn't make it so.

Mel and Steve led them up the pier to a small office crammed with charts and boat equipment. They had felt safe leaving the Pearson untended; the people on the ketch promised to keep an eye on things, and Mel and Steve said they would watch it. As they sat in the office, Kevin and Yvonne felt safe for the first time in hours.

Kevin dialed the State Police, told them the bare bones of what had happened. The officer on the phone said he and Yvonne should stop at the office and fill out a report, and Kevin said there was no way they could do that because they didn't have a car with them. Then Kevin gave him a few more details—about the knife, Yvonne's near rape, how they'd fought off the men with gearshift handles and winches, cracking heads and hands, and the officer's voice changed. Now he takes us seriously, Kevin thought.

The officer told Kevin they should stay at the boat club, stay out of sight, and he would send an investigator pronto.

Next, Kevin dialed Marty Diehl and was relieved when the man and not his machine answered.

"Marty, what the hell happened?"

"Damn, Kevin, I thought the deal was off; I mean, there was a message on my machine."

"A strange, Spanish-sounding voice?" Kevin asked.

"How did you know?"

"A long story. Do you still have that voice on your answering-machine tape?"

"Uh, no, it's already erased. Funny thing is, when I got the message I was relieved, because I was having second thoughts about buying a boat this late in the season. . . . Um, you still want to sell it?"

" 'S okay, Marty," Kevin said. "We can talk about it later."

Yvonne understood enough just from Kevin's end of the conversation to know what was going on. They shook their heads, swore together and laughed.

"Can't afford to keep the boat and can't get rid of it," Yvonne said.

"Maybe we're not supposed to sell it," he said. But he didn't want to go any further with that line.

"We don't have a ride either," she said.

"We'll rent a limo," he said.

They shared a laugh over that.

"I was impressed with you back there," she said.

"Yeah, well, ditto. Double ditto."

They talked about calling Harvey but decided not to until their tempers had cooled.

They got up to leave the office and go back to their boat when it occurred to Yvonne to call the police in New Jersey again, to tell them about the boarding party and ask if they had any leads.

Kevin dialed and got the same man he'd talked to earlier. The man said Kevin's and Yvonne's recollections might be very important, and that the New Jersey police would be comparing notes not only with the police in New York State but with the local police in Edgecliff as well.

"Why is that?" Kevin asked.

"Because an Edgecliff woman was beaten and tortured and her apartment was ransacked earlier today," the officer said.

"A woman tortured? Her apartment in Edgecliff ransacked?" Kevin said, thinking he sounded like Donald Duck.

Yvonne felt the blood drain out of her face.

"You know the name?" Kevin asked.

"Not being released at this time," the officer said.

"Deirdre Lockwood," Kevin said, telling him rather than asking.

"You know her?" the officer said.

"We know her," Kevin said.

Yvonne's knees buckled and she sank to the floor. Who would do that to DeeDee? A boyfriend? A jilted lover? The tennis instructor? Then Yvonne knew. "I should never have stayed there. It's my fault." Yvonne sobbed. "Poor DeeDee."

11

Kevin sat in the cockpit, listening to the sobbed curses, shuffling and thumps in the galley.

Thump, thump, thwack as life preservers, winches and charts flew onto the galley floor.

"Something . . . something . . ." Yvonne said between sobs.

"Vonnie . . ."

"Shut-UPPP!" she screamed.

"Let's wait for the police, Vonnie."

"The hell with the police." Sob and choke. "My friend is lying mangled in the hospital. And there's something someone wants on this boat."

"Please, Vonnie."

"Please what? Please don't make you feel uncomfortable? Please don't cry about DeeDee? Please just be quiet and don't disturb you or anyone else? Please be reasonable in the face of violence? Please what? Please who? Don't PLEASE me, goddamn you. If we weren't splitting up, if we didn't have to move the boat ourselves . . . It's the boat. Something on this boat."

"It's just a boat. Just a boat." Kevin felt a hundred years old.

"Then why did those animals threaten us? Why did that gorilla drag me into the V-berth . . . ?"

Almost suddenly, Yvonne sat down on one of the galley benches, gave one last, racking sob, and began to cry more quietly. He sat stiffly, wishing that he could cry, could wash out some of the pain the way she did.

Kevin peeked below. Over Yvonne's heaving shoulders he could see into the V-berth. She had emptied it out, right down to the triangular cushions. As he watched, Yvonne took a deep breath, went up into the V-berth as far as she could and knelt on the bare fiberglass, feeling with her fingers along the edges, right up to where the anchor lay in the bow.

"Nothing," Yvonne mumbled. "Men on the boat in the middle of the night. Boats following us. Leaking sink hose. Rapist. Men on the boat with a knife. Asking us where. Where. DeeDee hurt. What's happening? Why us? Why me? Oh, poor DeeDee. Why her?"

Yvonne went back into the galley and sat down again. "Kevin." A change in her voice now.

Kevin looked down into the cabin and was taken back in time to the day he saw Yvonne in the hospital right after the miscarriage. Her face was the same, full of pain, swollen with tears, and infused with a strange expression, more than grief and pain. It radiated betrayal, defeat, distrust and loss, maybe a loss of hope.

The police would arrive soon, Kevin knew. God, he hoped he and Yvonne didn't have to talk to them a long time. All he wanted was to go home. Home? He caught himself thinking of the house he and Yvonne had shared. No, no time for that.

"I'm sorry, Vonnie. Can I do anything for you?" He realized those were the same words he had used that day. That day when she had looked this way. Everything had gone wrong from that day on. Could he do better this time?

"Kevin," Yvonne said again, "tell me about last night when the boat was boarded."

Kevin was about to protest. Why go over the same

ground? But maybe it would help her. Hadn't he just asked if there was anything he could do?

"The goons looked below," he said. "They didn't find anything, but that's where they looked. And a key. They were looking for a key. Maybe they didn't want a key to the ignition but a key to the topside hatches."

Kevin went below, stepped around Yvonne's legs and opened the drawer near the V-berth. He took out the keys, then went topside again. Kneeling, he opened the port and starboard cockpit hatches, then the stern hatch. Each side hatch had about as much space as an old-fashioned steamer trunk, the stern hatch about half that. The side hatches held fenders; the port one also held sponges, brushes, a spare plastic bucket. The starboard hatch had coils of extra line. The stern hatch held spare life preservers (one, for a child, they had left there for someday) and a hose.

Kevin took out each fender, felt the rubber cylinders one at a time. He half expected to find that one or more had been slit open, then resealed. Of course, a perfect hiding place. A boat that hasn't been used all summer, sitting out in the water. Harvey, you prick, I gotta hand it to you. I didn't think you had it in you.

The fenders were untouched, as were the life jackets.

Yvonne watched as Kevin searched, following his hands. He had nice hands, strong broad palms and long squared fingers. He had a capable way of moving them.

A key? "Kevin, didn't you say they were speaking Spanish?"

"Yes, most of the time."

"'*Aquí*,' they were saying, not a key, A-Q-U-I, it means 'here' in Spanish."

"Here? That means, Jesus, that means they knew where they were supposed to look."

"And that's why they didn't look in the V-berth. It wasn't in the V-berth. Where did they mean when they said 'here'?"

"Shit, I don't know."

"What about the mechanics who fixed the sink fitting? Maybe they found something and kept it."

They looked at one another and shook their heads.

"Too . . ." said Yvonne.

"Farfetched," Kevin added.

"Something still . . ."

"Doesn't make sense," said Kevin.

"You're finishing my sentences," Yvonne said, almost smiling.

"Maybe that means we're back on the same wavelength," Kevin said.

Yvonne looked away as they heard the sound of street shoes on the pier. They looked up to see two men: one tall, young, and uniformed; the other a little older, heavy, wearing a rumpled suit.

"I'm Detective Guardino," the man in the suit said, perfunctorily showing his credentials. He looked into the boat, frowned when he saw the debris in the galley.

"My wife was looking for . . . whatever."

The detective nodded, almost imperceptibly, to the trooper, then said, "He'll stay with the boat. Why don't we go inside."

The detective sat them down in the boat-club office, took out a notepad. "You saw Miss Lockwood when you were in Edgecliff?"

"Just me, not him," Yvonne answered. "I left her this morning around seven."

The detective looked puzzled for a moment and wrote in a notebook. "You weren't together, the two of you?"

"Kevin stayed with the boat," Yvonne said, irritated that her life was this man's business.

"We were taking the boat up the Hudson to sell it," Kevin said.

"Two men came on board the boat at Edgecliff," Yvonne said. "While Kevin was on it."

"At night," Kevin said.

"Then three men boarded the boat over at the Haviland marina," Yvonne said.

"Forced their way on," Kevin said. "One guy had a knife. They tried to beat us up—"

"What do you mean, *tried,*" Yvonne said angrily. "We had to fight them off. One of them tried—"

"Whoa, whoa," the detective said. "My circuits are getting overloaded."

"Well, ex-CUSE me," Yvonne hissed.

The detective put his notebook down, sat back in his chair and smiled. "I know this is tough," he said gently. "I've got to take you through this, believe me."

And he did take them through it, all of it, starting with their departure from Harvey's the morning of the day before. The detective at first seemed plodding, dull, but before long they realized he was just being absolutely meticulous and thorough.

They told him how they had timed their departure to give them time to get to Hell Gate. A non-sailor, the detective was interested in hearing how the timing of the current had to be considered. The detective asked them what kind of unusual things had happened.

Yvonne listened as the investigator asked questions and Kevin answered most of them. Maybe the detective was an old-fashioned male chauvinist (like most cops, she thought), or maybe he was just more comfortable interviewing a man (which maybe amounted to the same thing), but most of the detective's questions were directed at Kevin.

Yvonne didn't feel like making an issue of it. For one thing, she thought she was a bit more strung out than Kevin who, after all, hadn't had to fight off a sexual attack. (Not that she could resent Kevin too much, after the way he had smacked that bastard on the hand. . . .) Then, too, Kevin had been on the boat when the two men had come on board during the night.

Something about that still didn't sit quite right with her. What the hell was it?

Yvonne found herself taken up with the puzzle of what had happened to them in the last day and a half. She was glad for the mental exercise.

As a girl, she had been good with jigsaw puzzles. She could look at a tiny piece of a puzzle and see how it might fit into a larger whole; sometimes she had seemed able to see the bigger picture from the hints in the fragments. Sometimes, two pieces that seemed to belong very far apart, or to have no connection whatever, were joined by one piece. Then all the other pieces fell into place.

She let Kevin go on—his reporter's recollection was pretty good, in all fairness—but she interrupted from time to time to add something. She especially wanted to make it clear that DeeDee wasn't a hot number. She thought she had noticed a leer when the cops talked about DeeDee. The cops seemed to want to connect DeeDee to all that had happened to Kevin and Yvonne.

"She's a good person, DeeDee," Yvonne said. "A teacher. You can check all you want to and you won't find her involved in drugs or anything like that."

Some things Kevin and Yvonne agreed on: Harvey had acted strange when they took the boat; they had had the feeling—no, more than that—of being followed, once, twice, or three times. Of being watched.

"Chowder's," Yvonne said.

The detective looked at her uncomprehendingly.

"We were at Chowder's the night before last," Yvonne said.

"A well-known seafood restaurant and bar in Port Guinness," Kevin explained.

The detective nodded and kept his eyes on Yvonne.

"We were there—and so was Harvey!" Yvonne said. "So was half the town, for God's sake. I mean, there were a bunch of people who knew we were moving the boat."

"They thought there was something on the boat," Kevin said. "I mean, the guys in Haviland, the ones who tried to . . . well, one of the first things they said when they climbed on the boat was, 'Where is it?' Or something like that."

At that point, Yvonne told the detective that what Kevin had heard as "key" might have been Spanish for "here." The detective wrote something in his notebook.

"We don't know where 'here' is," Kevin said.

"Wait a minute, Kevin," Yvonne said, waving for everyone else to shut up. "If the guys on the boat last night were saying 'here' in Spanish and the bastards at Haviland were saying 'where' in English . . ."

"Then there's five guys who're after us because of something on our boat," Kevin finished.

"Five . . . that we know of," Yvonne said, swallowing hard.

The door to the office opened just then and the uniformed trooper stuck his head in. "Nothing yet," he said. "Maybe we'll have to haul it out of the water and look at the bottom."

"I guess we shouldn't complain too much," Kevin said, "but you never asked us if you could search our boat."

Detective Guardino smiled and spoke softly. "You gave me every reason," he said. "I checked your boat number through the computer. Registration's expired, so officially I had every reason."

"Goddammit, Kevin," Yvonne said.

"Pardon my French," Detective Guardino said, "but I don't give a shit about the registration. I'd like to find out why someone beat up on your friend."

Kevin realized he had only glanced at the detective's badge. "Who're you with?" Kevin asked.

"Bergen County, New Jersey, prosecutor's office. I wasn't just interested in searching your boat for . . . whatever. If you had had any of Miss Lockwood's belongings . . ." The detective raised his eyebrows suggestively and shrugged his shoulders.

"Look," Kevin said. "I'm a newspaper reporter, for *Long Island*. I, we, don't need any special treatment, but if you'll just check us out . . ."

"We will. But I wouldn't worry. I can tell what kind of people you are."

"Chowder's," Yvonne said. "A lot of it starts, somehow, with Chowder's. And Harvey, he was there the other night, and yesterday morning he acted really weird."

"We'll definitely talk to him," the detective said.

The door to the office opened again and the uniformed officer entered. "Nothing yet," he said. "Looked in all the hatches. There seems to be some recent repair work under the sink . . ."

"A fitting broke," Kevin said. "Yesterday, near Edge-cliff. That's why we stopped, in fact—all the water gushing in."

"If it hadn't been for that, maybe . . ." Yvonne said.

"What about the steps that lead down to the inside?" the trooper said. "They seem to wiggle. That storage space under there, or what?"

"Just the engine," Kevin said. "Matter of fact, the guys that came on last night, I think they were trying to pry the steps up when a police boat came by."

The two investigators looked at Kevin for more explanation.

"See, they were looking around the back, sort of whispering. I think they were yanking at the steps when a police boat came by to quiet down a boatload of drunks."

"And they left right after that without looking under the steps?" the detective asked.

"Yeah, and I'm sure of that, because they would have made a lot more noise if they'd pulled the steps out. We never look under there because we aren't mechanical at all. . . ."

Kevin stopped and looked at Yvonne. Something clicked between them.

"That's where 'here' is," Kevin said quietly. "Under the steps, near the engine. We can't even get the steps up ourselves most of the time without scraping our fingers."

"Harvey has done all the engine work for us," Yvonne said. "I mean, all of it."

"And we haven't used the boat this summer at all," Kevin said. "Because we haven't been together."

"Have a look," the detective said to the trooper, who hurried off.

Through the small office window, Kevin could see that it was getting dark. He was exhausted, hungry, depressed. Needed a shower. "What happens now?" he asked.

"We'll figure out how to take care of you for the night," the detective said.

"We don't have a way to get back to Long Island," Yvonne said. "Oh, Tessie!"

"The dog," Kevin explained.

"It might be a good idea if you didn't go home tonight. You got on the wrong side of some bad people. You know that. I think you should stay up here tonight."

"In Westchester?" Yvonne said.

"I know a place," the detective said. "Small and clean. Out of the way but not far from the New York State police. They've used it to put up witnesses. They keep a good eye on it. You couldn't be safer. I'll see that you're looked after."

The door to the office opened, and the trooper came in, holding up a plastic-wrapped package the size of a large sandwich bag. "White powder," he said. "Not talcum."

"Afraid we'll have to impound the boat," the detective said. "The New York cops are taking statements at the marina. They'll work with us on this. And the feds will want to know about it too. You got any overnight stuff on board, better get it. I'll see about the motel."

"We'll have to call about the dog," Yvonne said, thinking how much she missed Tess.

"We'll have one of the Port Guinness officers look in on your dog, Mrs. McNulty. We'd rather you didn't call anybody tonight. We don't want anyone to know where you are."

Later, when Yvonne was in the shower at the motel, she wondered why she hadn't asked the trooper to give them separate rooms . . . adjoining rooms. Then they could each have a bed. She didn't intend to share a bed with Kevin, but she wanted him to be nearby. Then she thought of DeeDee. She wanted to see her and explain what had happened, to tell her how sorry . . . DeeDee. Beaten. Left in a puddle of blood. Her lovely white rug. Bloody. Yvonne wondered if she would be able to sleep, and if she did, what horrible dreams would run riot through her head all night.

Kevin sat slumped in a plastic chair, listening to the

shower running. A couple of times he thought he heard sobbing sounds. He would not intrude on Vonnie's pain, but he would share if she asked him.

Suddenly he remembered: He was supposed to work the next day, covering whatever news came out of the Jets' practice.

No way. He dialed the newsroom switchboard of *Long Island* and told the clerk he wouldn't be in the next day because he was sick (not far off, considering how he felt). He was surprised that his call had gotten through, and wondered how thorough the cops were, since they hadn't made sure no calls could be made from the room.

Yvonne emerged from the bathroom, trailing steam and fragrance of skin lotion. Her eyes were moist and her hair was wrapped in a towel.

"Me next," he said, grabbing clean cutoffs, underwear, and T-shirt. In no time, he was under the shower. The hot water made his bruises feel better and lessened his tension, if not his melancholy.

Yvonne was lying on the bed, her hair still wrapped, watching television when he came out.

A knock at the door made Yvonne sit up; the towel fell off her head.

Kevin went to the door, looked through the peephole and saw the strong, protective face of the trooper.

"It's him," Kevin said. Kevin opened the door, and the trooper entered with a cardboard box that contained several large bags and one small one.

"Provisions," the policeman said. He unpacked two loaf shapes wrapped in foil ("steak-and-cheese sandwiches, best I ever ate"), two containers of salad, a large bag of french fries—and a six-pack.

"I'll get some ice," the trooper said.

Kevin and Yvonne unpacked their food hungrily.

The trooper put some ice in the sink, added water and submerged the six-pack like a guy who had done it before. "You're all set," he said.

"Thank you," Yvonne said.

"You've got a friend in the press from now on," Kevin said. "What do we owe you?"

"You're dining courtesy of the great Empire State," the policeman said. "Don't open your door to strangers, and dial this number if there's any trouble. We'll be checking on you every hour or so all night."

That's why the phone is working, Kevin thought. "Will you want to talk to us tomorrow?" he asked.

"Probably. Detective Guardino will call you. We'll pick you up in the morning."

The trooper smiled, waved good-bye and left.

"I think he likes us," Kevin said. "Thinks we're lost, or something."

"He's not wrong."

Kevin took two cans of beer from the sink, opened them and handed one to Yvonne, who did not protest. He took a huge gulp. Then he opened the small bag the trooper had brought, opened the bottle of iodine and, with unsteady fingers, dabbed some on the scratches that crisscrossed his hands, elbows, and knees. There were more than he had realized. One of his shoulders ached; he had noticed it only after squirming as he applied the iodine.

He opened the rubbing alcohol, got a washcloth and slapped some on his shoulder. Instantly, he yelped with pain.

"Take your shirt all the way off," Yvonne said, getting up from the bed. Standing over him, she said, "You have a dirty, nasty scratch there—look, blood on your shirt—in the middle of a big bruise. Hold still. . . ."

For a moment, the sting of the iodine was more than he could handle. He felt nauseous from the pain and from the mingling smells of food and medicine. He thought he was going to faint.

"Thanks for fighting so hard," she said.

"You're welcome. Let's not do it again for a while. . . ."

She took the iodine and alcohol to the bed and began dabbing methodically. Kevin was about to offer to help, but he thought it might sound too much like a come-on.

"I called the paper. Told them I wasn't coming in

tomorrow. I didn't tell them where we were. I figured that would be okay with the cops."

"What about DeeDee? We've got to go see her." That was as far as she could get without choking up.

"They didn't even tell us what hospital she was in."

"Oh, God. I hope they didn't do any . . . anything permanent."

"We can't do anything tonight."

Yvonne looked at him sharply but said nothing.

They went back to their meals; in no time, they had each drained a beer and wolfed down half their sandwiches and most of the salad and french fries.

Kevin fetched two more beers. He took his time on his second, but he was still done before Yvonne had taken more than a few sips. He would hold off on his third; maybe wait until Yvonne was asleep.

In fact, Yvonne was feeling drowsy. "Kevin?"

"Yeah, Vonnie?"

"Is it okay if I take the bed?"

"Sure, Vonnie. Sleep well."

Kevin saw that Yvonne had put her head back on the pillow. Her mouth was open slightly. Sleeping, he thought. He went over and picked up the beer can resting against her thigh. Still some left. He drained it.

He went to the window, pulled the curtain just enough to see into the parking lot. Nothing. He checked the lock on the window, secured the chain, checked the door. Finally, he took another beer from the sink.

Kevin turned off the light and lay down on the plastic sofa, which wasn't quite long enough to accommodate him comfortably. Then he began to think night thoughts. He thought about what had happened since yesterday and even more about how he had messed things up.

Yvonne felt herself falling. That feeling of falling, an endless fall . . . What's at the bottom? Nothing . . . No, DeeDee's there to catch me. . . . It's not DeeDee; it's a man with a knife. I can't get away.

"Help," she tried to say. But it came out as a groan as she edged her way toward consciousness. It was a dream. Where was Kevin? In the bathroom. In the bathroom with the baby. No, no baby. She opened her eyes and stared at the unfamiliar walls.

"Where . . . ?"

"You were dreaming," Kevin said.

"Uh." She mumbled, thinking she was telling Kevin about the dream.

"We're in a motel in Westchester."

Yvonne blinked and looked toward Kevin. His feet rested on one arm of the couch and his head was tilted up at the other end. She patted the bed next to her. "You can sleep here," she said. "Stay on your own side."

His pride told him to stay where he was, but comfort won out. He slid under the covers near the edge and breathed a deep sigh. "This is better," he said.

She turned on her side away from him. Wide awake now, she thought. She wondered how she would get back to sleep, tried a few deep breaths, remembering her Yoga class. Before she had finished the third breath she was asleep. Deep in the abyss, this time.

Kevin looked at the space between them and took a little of it. Maybe they could try once more, if the ground rules were different. He would go to a shrink, therapist, whatever, if Vonnie wanted him to. He would do it. "I still love you, Vonnie," he whispered into the dark.

12

Yvonne started to wake up first, comforted by Kevin's arm draped over her shoulder. Then she blinked. What was he doing? Then she realized she had flung one of her legs over his. Had they made love? No, she didn't think so. She didn't know whether that made her relieved or sad.

As she started to move away, Kevin stirred. Still half asleep, he patted her shoulder as he always had. Then he opened his eyes wide.

"Uh, sorry," he said. "I tried to stay on my own side."

"So did I," she said, pulling her leg the rest of the way back.

An embarrassed quiet settled over both of them. They were relieved when the phone rang.

"Good morning. It's Detective Guardino. How're you doing?"

"We've both been better, thanks," Kevin said.

"I don't doubt it. Listen, we arrested three men last night. Or I should say the police in Fort Lee did. We think they're the three who messed you up."

"All right!" Kevin said. Then, covering the phone, he said to Yvonne, "It's Detective Guardino. They think they got the three guys."

"Do the police think they're the ones who beat up DeeDee?" Yvonne asked.

"Tell me more," Kevin said into the phone.

"There was a traffic jam at the George Washington Bridge," Guardino began.

"Do they think they're the ones who beat up DeeDee?" Yvonne asked again.

". . . just a usual traffic jam at the bridge this time of year," Guardino went on. "Some people had taken enough notice of the big tussle at the marina to get the license number of the van the three left in . . ."

"Kevin."

". . . after they saw the blood on the guys. . . ."

"Just a second," Kevin said. Then, to Yvonne. "I'll give you the phone, I won't let him hang up."

"Some witnesses called the police at Haviland and they put out a bulletin, and there we were. They're not charged in the assault on your friend, but we're looking at that."

"Do you think we're safe now?" Kevin asked.

"We'll need your cooperation," the detective went on, in an evasion Kevin would have picked up at once even if he hadn't got used to talking to cops from his days on the police beat. "As I said, we're pretty sure they're the three who messed you up. One of them has a badly injured hand. . . ."

"Yeah, well, I'm not sorry."

"Right. Anyhow, I'll pick you up in a little while. Don't go out of the room till I get there."

"Tell him we haven't had breakfast," Yvonne said.

"We haven't had breakfast yet," Kevin said, this time glad Yvonne had butted in.

"I'll swing by with coffee and juice."

"Then what?"

"Then down to Hackensack, where my office is. Also where the Bergen County Prosecutor's office and jail is. Some more questions to ask you, then we can see about sending you home to Long Island. After you look at a lineup, of course."

"Just a minute, Yvonne wants to talk to you," Kevin said.

"Do you think these are the guys who broke into DeeDee's place?" Yvonne asked.

"As I told your husband, Mrs. McNulty, we're looking into that possibility, checking your friend's apartment for prints. Is there anything special that you'd like for breakfast? I don't want you to leave the room till we get there."

"You mean we're not safe yet?"

"We don't want to take any chances."

"Okay, but we want you to take us to see DeeDee," Yvonne said.

Detective Guardino sat on the edge of the sofa, smiling between his clumsy stabs at small talk and trying to show concern for their feelings. But his impatience was so transparent that Kevin and Yvonne hurried through the coffee and juice.

They tossed their meager baggage into the rear seat of the police car, where it acted as a divider.

They rode in near silence through the near perfect late-summer morning. Guardino took them across the Tappan Zee Bridge, from which they could see dozens of boats on the gleaming Hudson.

Once into New Jersey, Guardino took several serpentine roads with easy familiarity.

"I live not too far from here," he said, seeming to read their thoughts.

They passed comfortable middle-class homes with tidy lawns and flowers and children playing out front.

Kevin and Yvonne looked at each other.

"Do you believe this shit?" Kevin said quietly.

Understanding at once, she shook her head no. Yesterday, they had shared fear and danger. Today, they envied the people they passed, people who weren't being chased and menaced. People who were still together.

The hospital was a huge, sprawling complex of buildings built in stages over the decades as northern New Jersey's population grew. It took Kevin and Yvonne almost five minutes to go from the reception desk to the wing that housed DeeDee's room, where a nurse sat outside a closed door marked "I.C.U."

The nurse, who looked barely out of her teens, was sandy-haired and freckled. "May I ask who you're here to see?" she said, looking at Kevin.

"We're here to see our friend DeeDee Lockwood," Yvonne said.

"All right. Since this is an intensive-care section, I'll have to ask you to put on gowns and to please limit your stay to fifteen minutes. She is under sedation right now."

They helped each other into the pale-yellow gowns that tied in the back. The nurse put Yvonne's bag on a shelf and asked them to scrub their hands. "If you have a cold, we'd like you to wear a mask," the nurse said, pointing to a binful of plastic bags.

"No colds," Yvonne said.

"Then you can go in now."

Inside the room, another nurse sat at a desk crowded with clipboards, folders, a telephone, and a copy of a women's magazine. The nurse sipped a diet soft drink through a straw, looked up and smiled.

Kevin and Yvonne recoiled for a moment at the sights: a teenage boy lying flat on his back, his head wrapped in a cocoon of white bandages, his arms in casts by his side; an old woman, tiny and bird-thin on her pillows, apparently unaware of a much younger woman sitting by her side, gently stroking her hand; a girl of five or six, eyes closed and mouth open in sleep, her entire torso swathed in bandages.

And over to the side, DeeDee.

Kevin pulled the curtains on either side of the bed; then he and Yvonne sat in metal folding chairs next to her.

"Jesus Christ," Kevin whispered.

"I think she's asleep. How could anyone do—" Yvonne's voice broke.

DeeDee Lockwood's head lay nestled in pillows. Around the edge of the bandages they could see that some of her hair was missing; they could see that part of her head had been shaved so the doctors could stitch the deep cuts, and in some places her head looked raw, as if some of her hair had been yanked out.

DeeDee's eyes, the lids swollen and purple, were closed. A thick white pad covered her entire forehead, and gauze two inches deep was taped over her nose. Thick pads were also taped to her cheeks. Her lips were swollen and cracked. As she breathed in and out, the thin transparent tube that led from the nose gauze to a bottle by the bedside moved ever so slightly.

Kevin wanted to say something but couldn't.

Tears formed in Yvonne's eyes. "I don't know whether to wake her or not," she said quietly. She shook her head slowly. "She's alive, at least."

"Hmmmm. I'm alive. I am." DeeDee had opened her eyes, which were red where they should have been white.

"DeeDee, it's Yvonne and Kevin. You're safe. We love you." Yvonne squeezed her friend's hand.

"Hi, DeeDee," Kevin said.

"My nooose," DeeDee said with a wheeze. "They broke it. . . . It hurt a lot when they broke it. . . ."

"Oh, DeeDee," Yvonne said.

"Cut me . . . too. But the nose hurt so bad . . . cuts didn't hurt so much."

"Animals!" Yvonne said.

"No. Animals are nice." DeeDee's swollen lips turned up at the corners.

Yvonne squeezed her hand harder and felt DeeDee squeeze back.

"Cheeks cut . . . bad. I had a dream about . . . about the knife . . . silver knife. . . ."

"Don't worry, DeeDee," Kevin said, glad that he'd smashed the hand that had wielded the knife.

"You're safe now. Safe here," Yvonne said.

"Safe . . ." The purple lids closed, and Yvonne felt DeeDee's hand relax.

"Asleep," Kevin said.

"That's okay. We'll sit here for a while and let the cops wait."

"Not . . . asleep." DeeDee's eyes opened again.

"You fooled us," Yvonne said.

"Fooled you. . . . The men . . . thought I had something . . . thought you . . ."

Yvonne and Kevin looked at each other and shared a realization. "I'm sorry, DeeDee. I didn't know they were following us. . . ."

"Kept asking me . . . hitting me . . . 'Where's the stuff . . .?' Coc-aine stuff . . . How I know? I never, ever . . . You know where stuff is?"

"I didn't know yesterday, but I do now." Yvonne gripped her friend's hand tight again. "But don't worry. The cops got those guys."

Huge tears oozed from under the purple eyelids.

"Dirty bastards," Kevin whispered.

"Know . . . what?" The puffed-up mouth formed a smile again.

"What?"

"Finally gonna get . . . that nose job I wanted. . . ."

Yvonne and Kevin laughed out loud at that. The form on the bed shook with laughter too.

"Good for you, DeeDee," Yvonne said.

"Maybe a face-lift . . . no more wrinkles . . . Good?"

"Good," Yvonne said.

"Did me a . . . favor." DeeDee's mouth turned up even more in a smile. Then in an instant it turned all the way down again, and tears streamed down her cheeks.

"Goddamn Pollyanna," Yvonne said, crying too.

" 'Nother good thing."

"What's that?" Yvonne said.

"They make good tea here."

Yvonne and Kevin laughed again and the nurse came over to the bed. She checked DeeDee's tube and held her wrist for a few seconds. "We can probably put you in your own room tonight," she said, patting DeeDee on the arm.

DeeDee winced.

"Sorry," the nurse said. "I didn't know they got you

there, too. I'll check it after your friends go." The nurse turned to Kevin and Yvonne again. "Her mother is asleep on a couch down the hall. Do you want to see her?"

"No. Just say hello for us, would you?" Yvonne said.

"Sure thing," the nurse said, glancing at her watch.

"Our time up?" Kevin asked.

" 'Fraid so," the nurse said. "I'd let you stay longer, but the cops want to talk to her later and I don't want to tire her."

"I'll talk . . . to cops," DeeDee said.

"They'll be here later," the nurse said. "After you rest."

"We've got to go now," Yvonne said.

"Bye," DeeDee said. Her eyes closed and her head rolled to one side and she fell into a deep, peaceful slumber.

"Welcome to Hackensack," Detective Guardino said.

He opened the car door to let them out. "Follow me," he said.

Without thinking Kevin took Yvonne's hand and she welcomed the clasp for a moment. Then they both realized what had happened and let go.

They followed the detective down a cold cement corridor. Near the end, he steered them into a room with two rows of theaterlike chairs and a wall almost totally filled by a window that revealed a lighted stage.

"Just like on the TV cop shows," Detective Guardino said. "We can see them, but they can't see us. Now, you folks are gonna have to view separately."

"Huh?" Yvonne demanded. Though not afraid, she liked the idea of having Kevin next to her for this.

"So a defense lawyer can't claim the identification was tainted in any way," Kevin said.

"You got it."

"I'll go first," Kevin said.

"Mrs. McNulty, could you step outside just for a moment."

Yvonne stood outside the door. Far away, down the end of the cold corridor, were sounds of office machines, telephones, and bureaucratic mumblings. People sounds. They made her feel safer.

The detective pressed a button on the wall and spoke into a screened microphone. Kevin heard the muffled sound of a door opening and closing. Four sullen men shuffled onto the silent stage from the right, stopped, turned and faced the window.

"Second from right," Kevin said. "He was the one with the knife."

"Take your time and be sure," Guardino said.

"It's him. End of discussion."

Kevin saw that the man had a graying bandage on his right hand, and that he seemed to be trying to hold his hand behind him. For a moment, Kevin was sorry he had crushed his hand.

"I'll have them turn to their left and right, one by one," Guardino said.

"Suit yourself. It'll still be him."

Kevin smiled reassuringly at Yvonne as he came out, and she smiled back as she went inside.

"Just relax," Guardino said. Yvonne thought he had a good protective manner.

Yvonne heard the faint sound of shuffling steps. There, on the stage, was the man who had had the knife.

"Second from left," she said. "Where are the others?"

"We have two more groups."

When the second group came on stage, Kevin felt a rush of anger that made his head throb. There, the very first one, was the one who had hurt Vonnie.

"Number one. He's the one who . . . you know, my wife . . ."

"Be sure."

"Number one, goddamn it."

Yvonne had to bite her lip. "That's the one who . . . the one I had to fight off."

"Number three, step forward, please," Detective Guardino said.

"I know who he is," Yvonne said, barely keeping control.

"Turn to your left, please, number three." To Yvonne, the detective said gently, "Take your time."

"Never mind," Yvonne said, steel back in her voice. "Let's do this right."

When the man stepped forward and turned to his left, a blood-crusted gauze pad was visible just below the top of his head.

"That's where I hit him," she said. For a moment she felt, not guilt, but . . . sorrow, as though the act of wounding the man—justified or not—had tainted her soul.

"Second from right is the leader," Kevin said as the third group came on stage.

Kevin tuned out Detective Guardino's words as the man Kevin had picked out stepped forward, turned left and right, then stepped back.

It was him, no doubt about it. What bothered Kevin was that, while the two men he had picked out in the earlier lineups had seemed sullen and defiant, their leader looked scared.

"Pardon the filth," Detective Guardino said, ushering them into his small one-window office and nodding toward an overflowing wastebasket and a desktop full of files.

"We've already seen the real filth," Yvonne said.

"Did we pass?" Kevin asked.

"Flying colors, both of you. Of course, we switched the order of the men in each lineup. . . ."

"In case we were comparing notes, you mean?" Yvonne snapped.

"Have to do it that way," Guardino said.

"Who were the other men in the lineup?" Yvonne asked.

"The usual catch of drunk and disorderlies," Guardino said. "Plus a couple of our undercover officers."

"Tell them they fit right in," Kevin said.

"So . . . we'll give you a ride to the GW Bridge. Nassau County will give you a ride from there."

"Well, we could take the subway to the LIRR," Kevin said, not sure whether he welcomed the ride in a police car.

"You've been through a lot," Guardino insisted. "Least we can do is give you a ride."

Guardino flashed a small smile, but Kevin's arm hairs told him it was partly for show.

"We, uh, want you to watch out for yourselves," Guardino went on, eyes downcast in embarrassment. "Depending on the progress of the investigation, we might need you."

"Depend on it." It was a new, officious voice, belonging to a man in a gray suit and pale-blue shirt. He was linebacker-tall and strong, clean-shaven, close-cut hair, handsome, grim.

A fed, Kevin figured at once.

"Special agent Bleucher, Drug Enforcement Administration," the newcomer said.

Kevin was about to extend his hand, but something in special agent Bleucher's manner stopped him. "I'm Kevin McNulty," he said.

"I'm Yvonne." She, too, was put off.

"I need to go over your story with you, step by step," Bleucher said. His voice was cold and infuriating.

"How long will this take?" Kevin said, voice rising in annoyance.

"As long as I need," the federal agent said.

Screw you, Kevin thought.

"We have needs, too," Yvonne said. "Like getting home to Port Guinness and getting our lives back to some kind of normal."

"I understood you were separated," the fed said.

"So?" Kevin challenged. He looked at Guardino, who stood near a window, posture and expression apologetic.

Sure, Kevin thought. Guardino believes us, and this guy isn't sure, and Guardino told him everything he could about us and feels bad about it. Which he should, because we trusted him. Ah, we're the ones who should feel bad, Vonnie and me. For trusting.

"So," the fed said, picking up the challenge, "I'll ask what I need to ask, and if I need to ask again, and again and again, either because I don't like your answers or I need more information, I will. Understand?"

Kevin was furious. He felt as if he'd been slapped. He knew if he tried to put his rage into words he'd blow it by sputtering.

Yvonne had always been able to articulate her anger better, which had given her a big advantage in their fights. This time, Kevin was grateful to her.

"Agent Belcher . . . Bilker . . .?" she began.

"Bleucher," the Fed corrected pompously.

I love you, Vonnie, Kevin thought, knowing her mispronunciation had been deliberate.

"Whatever," Yvonne went on contemptuously. "I'd like to say 'Fuck you,' but I'm a woman, even a lady sometimes, so I won't. I'll just say let's cut right through all this horseshit. We've been threatened, been beaten up, and I was almost—"

"So you say."

"Let me finish. Almost raped. And a friend of ours was badly beaten. We're victims, and you're hassling us. Now, that pisses me off, I can't tell you how much, and if you don't like what I'm saying, I don't really give a goddamn."

I love you, Vonnie, Kevin thought.

"You always kept your boat at the same place on Long Island," the fed went on, like a robot. "Then you suddenly move it. How come?"

"We told the cops that," Kevin said. "We have to sell it. We thought we had a buyer, up in Rockland County. Moving a boat the size of ours would cost five hundred bucks at least by truck."

The federal agent said nothing, and Kevin could tell nothing from his eyes. Kevin looked at Guardino and said, "Didn't you tell him what happened?"

"Sure, he did," Yvonne said. "Mister Federal Agent here is just sizing us up, trying to trip us up, because he's trained not to trust people. If he knew what he was doing, he'd interview Harvey. He acted—"

"We can't find Harvey," Guardino said. "We don't know if he—"

The federal agent's eyes flashed at Detective Guardino, who pursed his lips and looked at the floor. Having lost his secret, the fed went on: "His boat was found circling in the Sound. No Harvey."

"We don't know where he is. Period," Yvonne said.

Kevin felt a chill crawl over his skin. "You have a theory?" he asked.

"We thought you might help," the agent said.

"Why? How?" Kevin said.

The fed said nothing, but Yvonne thought she knew. "They think we might be partners with Harvey," she said. "Partners in crime."

"What bullshit," Kevin said.

"All the same, we can't find Harvey." For the first time, the federal agent had allowed some humanity to soften his voice—too late, Kevin and Yvonne thought.

"We can't help," Kevin said.

"The police told you, I suppose, how weird, belligerent, he was the other morning, when we took our boat away—" Yvonne stopped. Had it only been the other morning?

"You do have a theory," Kevin said. "About Harvey."

"We think he collected a bundle and skipped the country," the fed said, then he shrugged. "So far as we know, you were the last people to see him."

"Shit," Kevin said. "How much more trouble can we get into?"

"You cops better get your act together and look for the real source of the trouble," Yvonne said. "You have one missing, an innocent bystander beat up, and we're just lucky we're not corpses." She was flaming.

"Come on," Guardino said in a gentle, slightly embarrassed voice. "Your ride is waiting."

"Stay in touch," the fed said.

Yvonne shot him a scorching glare.

* * *

They were on the Long Island Expressway. Almost subconsciously, Kevin reached across the back seat of the police car and put his hand on Yvonne's. "I remember something you told me once," Kevin said.

"What?"

"That people don't really change. Deep down."

Damn him, Yvonne thought. She had welcomed his hand as a friendly, comforting gesture. Now, she figured it was a come-on. It was just like him, she thought, to remember one hurtful remark and forget more important things. She had said that thing about people not really changing when he had promised (for the tenth or hundredth time) to cut down on his drinking and cut out his betting.

"I don't suppose you recall anything else from that conversation," she said.

But Kevin was thinking of something altogether different. "I meant Harvey," he said.

"What about Harvey?"

"That fed's theory about him going to another country? It's all bullshit."

Yvonne sat up straighter. She had misread him; now she told him with her silence to go on, for she had never stopped believing in his hunches.

"Harvey's set in his ways."

"Yes?"

"You know. Fart around the boats all day, do just enough work to keep his yard going. Then gin and beer at Chowder's."

"Okay."

The cop-driver picked up his microphone and responded to a radio message. Kevin went on: "That's his life, see? He wouldn't change that much. He wouldn't leave his boat and his boatyard—and Chowder's; he wouldn't leave his social life at Chowder's to go off to another country. Forever and ever. He just wouldn't."

Yvonne let that sink in. Probe, she told herself. "Then why was he acting so crazy? And what happened to us? And him?"

"He was doing something cute. Not planning to run to another country, not that cute. But still something too cute for him. And one thing I know for sure. Harvey is not the boss. There are bigger fish. And I think the cops know that."

Yvonne calculated quickly. "And we upset Harvey's plans, his routine, by taking our boat away. We screwed up his cute little side deal with the drugs. Just by doing something unexpected."

Kevin nodded.

The cop pulled off the highway, stopping behind a car emitting clouds of steam from under the hood. The cop got out and went to talk to the motorist.

Kevin thought about Harvey. He tried to put himself in Harvey's place, tried to imagine what Harvey would *feel*.

Suddenly, Kevin felt a wave of pity. "Harvey was afraid," he said. "He was just so afraid . . . what he needed more than anything was to stop us, somehow. . . ."

"Because once the boat changed hands . . ."

"Good-bye drugs," he said.

"So he followed us—or sent somebody to follow us."

"Harvey was out of luck anyhow, once we left with the drugs. I mean . . ."

"No, no. Listen," she said. "Maybe Harvey was just so afraid that he lied to . . . whoever. And blamed us! Told them we had stolen the drugs."

"Right! That's what I was getting at. If Harvey was really afraid, he'd make up some story to tell the higher-ups he was working for and to cover up his own double-cross. . . ."

"He would tell them he'd found out that we were stealing some drugs and taking them somewhere to sell," Yvonne said, seeing it now with great, sad clarity. "Even if they didn't believe him, they'd follow us and—"

"Board the boat to look for the drugs. And they followed you to DeeDee's, and you left before they got there. . . ."

"They thought I'd delivered drugs to her."

"Yes," Kevin said. "Harvey would say anything if he was desperate. If he was afraid for his life." He paused, felt a chill, remembered his own fear when he had seen the knife. "Who wouldn't?"

"Yes, that fits," Yvonne said.

"A little double-cross would have been Harvey's style, all right," Kevin went on. "Always looking for the short-cut, the easy way. He was just small potatoes to the organization. They used him to run errands, maybe to store stuff in his yard—"

"Of course. A million places to hide things there, and who would look?"

"Then he thought up his little scam. And then he had to lie to save his skin. . . ." Kevin let the thought trail off. He still felt a chill.

The cop was walking back to the car now.

"But . . . who are the people he lied to?" Yvonne asked. "We're not out of the woods yet. Those guys on the boat weren't the bosses either."

"Maybe not."

"If we hadn't upset things by having to take our boat away to sell it . . ."

"See," Kevin said. "I told you we shouldn't have split up."

That joke didn't go over with Yvonne, who was still thinking. "Harvey wasn't figuring on fleeing the country or anything like that," she said. "He was just doing a small-time rip-off. So where is he now?"

Kevin and Yvonne looked into each other's tired eyes. They said nothing, and didn't have to. They remembered DeeDee's face, the struggle in the boat, the gleaming knife.

The answer hung in the silence.

13

Yvonne fell in love with the house all over again when the car drove into the driveway. There it was, hunkered down among the old pines on its narrow slice of land between a couple of four-acre waterfront garden spots.

A plain house, bereft of any artistic aspirations, a functional house. Really a garage and a basement with rooms over them, a rectangle with a deck overlooking the water.

That it was *hers* now, not theirs, and that it was soon to be someone else's didn't keep her from enjoying the moment.

She was remembering some of the parties that she and Kevin had had on summer evenings, parties that had sprawled from the open space that served as kitchen, living room, and dining room down the stairs and onto the rocky beach and into the Sound.

Yvonne was about to mention one rowdy party in particular, when Kevin said, "Remember that party when Scotty went swimming with his clothes on?"

Yvonne giggled, recalling Scotty holding his drink aloft and wading into the Sound. "He didn't go swimming. Don't you remember? He said he was just washing off the gin that he'd spilled on his clothes."

"And then Rosalie called from the shore: 'Gin doesn't stain, Scotty dear.'"

"The look on Scotty's face. 'Mother! Now you tell me!'"

"Then he spent the rest of the evening dressed in an old muumuu."

Their musing was interrupted by the dog's frantic joyful barking.

"I'm going in to see Tess before she has a stroke," Kevin said.

"Ah," Yvonne said, smiling.

Kevin and Yvonne squatted beside the old Doberman as she bumped against them, wagging from her tail to her nose.

"Well, there's one thing we agree on," Kevin said.

"Absolutely." Yvonne smiled, turning her mouth away from the dog to escape the flapping tongue. The dog happily licked on, catching ear, neck, cheek, and hair, then moving on to Kevin.

"Let's give her some canned food, she's been living on the dry stuff for three days. Then I'm going to get out of these clothes. What about you? Do you want to go to your apartment and pick up some clothes and then come back?" Yvonne paused. "I think I'd feel better if you stayed over."

"I would, too."

The cop who had dropped them off had told them to call if they saw anything unusual. He was quick to tell them that the law-enforcement agencies thought they had a handle on what was happening, but just to be on the safe side, there would be a detail patrolling Duck Point Lane for a while.

"Do you still have those old sweatshirts and khaki trousers that I left here?" Kevin said.

"Oh, yes. They're on the shelf in your closet. . . . What used to be your closet."

That remark, the licorice-sweet night, and the Irish in him gave rise to sentimental longings again. "Do you think we could keep the place, Vonnie? I mean, I really liked living here."

"How would we manage that once the divorce is final?"

"Maybe it won't be. And I could live in the basement."

"I'll bet that would impress your girlfriends—living in the basement of the house your ex-wife lives in. Very classy."

No girlfriends, so far, Kevin wanted to say. But that would make him too vulnerable, so instead he laughed. "I guess it would take someone very understanding."

"How about crazy?"

"Anyway. I wish we could think of a way to keep it."

"Maybe we could rent it. I think we could get more than enough to pay the mortgage and make the repairs. But you wouldn't get a chunk of cash now to buy anything else."

"Hmmm. But I wouldn't be living here. That's what I want."

"Maybe you want to buy my half then. But I'm not going to sell out cheap. You'll have to pay the going rate."

"Well, I guess it'll have to be the cellar and I'll give up dating." Kevin laughed again.

"There is the possibility—I know it's remote, but I may have a date at some time in the future. Who's going to want to come to my house with my ex living in the basement?"

"Well, you could go to his place." Kevin was enjoying the joke now, or trying to. "That is, until you got serious. Then you'd have to confess, I guess. But by then he wouldn't be able to live without you no matter what."

"And . . .?" Yvonne was smiling.

"And I could just go on living downstairs and you and your new husband could live upstairs."

"Upstairs, downstairs, eh? . . . Well, there is one advantage that you haven't mentioned yet. We'd both get to see Tess, and we'd have a built-in dog-sitter for vacations."

"That's settled. Now let's map out the showering strategies, for tonight, I mean. You can go first and I'll feed the dog and wash the lettuce, if you have any."

"No lettuce, but some tomatoes and cucumbers. And some red onion. I think they're still edible. I have some

Italian sausage in the freezer, and I can make some pasta in the machine."

"Great. I'll make the garlic and oil for the pasta, if you have those. . . ."

"Of course. You start on the cutting. I'll pick up where you leave off."

Yvonne started toward the bathroom, but turned back toward the living room. Kevin watched her happily, wondering what she was doing. When she returned to the kitchen area, she was carrying something behind her back.

"Here. Open this and let it breathe."

"Right! . . . Jesus! It's that great Chianti! Yahoo!"

"Don't shake the wine!" Yvonne said, turning again toward the bathroom. "And try to make this enough, instead of having five beers afterward."

"Four, then."

They had finished eating and were cleaning up the kitchen when the phone rang. Kevin gathered from the one side of the conversation that he heard that it was Rosalie and she was coming over. He would rather have had Yvonne to himself, Rosalie's dog-sitting and all the help she gave Vonnie notwithstanding.

"Rosalie wants to hear our adventures. She said she'll give me a brief computer lesson, too. Just enough to get me started while she has the time. Maybe I could use a dose of everyday life just now." Pause. "But I hope she doesn't stay too long. I'm starting to feel whipped."

"Me, too," Kevin said, meaning that he hoped she didn't stay too long.

"The computer is still in the box it came in. I guess I'd better start unpacking it."

"Wait for Rosalie. She'll probably know what to unpack first and save you a few steps."

"True. Okay. I won't desert you in the kitchen."

"That wasn't why—"

"Just kidding."

Rosalie drove in the driveway before the cleaning up was finished.

"What did she do? Call from her car?" Kevin said.

"She only lives down the road."

"She couldn't walk from her bedroom to her garage in the time she took to get here," Kevin said.

"I'll grant you that—in that big house of hers. But maybe she called from the kitchen."

"The car. I'll bet you."

"Never mind betting," Yvonne said.

Kevin stopped speculating on where Rosalie had called from and started wishing that there weren't little buzz words like "bet" that could open the doors on so much bad feeling.

Rosalie swept in, trailing chiffon and preceded by bundles.

"This is for Tess," she said, putting down a bag on the dining-room table, "and this is for you two. Tell me that you haven't had dessert yet." She watched Kevin and Yvonne shake their heads. "Wonderful. I've brought profiteroles. Just zap this in your microwave for a minute and a half," she said, giving Yvonne a jarful of chocolate sauce.

"Will you join us?" Yvonne said.

"Is the Pope Catholic?" Rosalie laughed. "Just don't remind me of all the money I pay my nutritionist . . . until after I'm done eating."

"What is this dessert?" Kevin asked.

"Profiteroles," Rosalie said in her best French accent.

"Oh, well, now that you say it in French . . ." Kevin said.

"You remember . . . we had them at Chez Susanne," Yvonne said.

"Am I in heaven, or what?" said Kevin.

"Not heaven, must be what," Rosalie said. "But tell me about your adventures."

As she said that, Kevin felt Rosalie's hand on his forearm. As he looked into her eyes, which were clear and wise, measuring him, she squeezed his arm and smiled slightly.

Yvonne had put the sauce in the microwave and was getting out three dessert bowls when she heard Tess bark.

"She wants to come in again, Kevin. Besides, Tess hasn't had the treat Rosalie brought."

"I'll get her as soon as we finish dessert," Kevin said.

Yvonne looked impatient, exasperated. "Dish out the dessert, I'll get the dog. Then we'll fill Rosalie in on everything."

"Okay," Kevin said. There were some commands he felt didn't need obeying. Sometimes Yvonne was just plain bossy. "Rosalie, you can pour on the sauce."

Yvonne was already on her way down the stairs, wondering why she was so pissed. Was it such a big deal? Did the dog have to come up right away? "Coming, Tess." Yvonne thought she heard the dog whine. She opened the door to the run, but the dog was not at the opening. Yvonne opened the door wider, and to her horror the dog was lying on her side, still.

"Tess! Tess! Oh, Tess!" No, God, not this too. Yvonne started toward the animal, afraid of what she would find, when she was caught from behind roughly and pulled back out of the pen.

She wheeled around and felt her dinner pressing up against her lungs as she was confronted by two figures. Bright ski masks, one yellow, one fire-engine red. Goggles around the eyes. They pointed guns at her.

"Shut up. Get up the stairs," one of them said in a thick whisper.

This time, we'll die, we can't be lucky enough to live through something like this again. I'm going to go through what DeeDee did, Yvonne thought. She decided she had nothing to lose by screaming. But the bigger of the two was ready for her and had covered her mouth before the scream could form. He had big arms and smelled of musk under the detergent smell of a bright-yellow jacket. It's washable, she thought. Yvonne briefly wondered why she was taking note of all this. It would be futile this time, she was sure. His hand smelled of something she had smelled before. Somewhere. What was it?

* * *

Kevin was startled to hear so many footsteps coming into the house—two people? three? Where was Vonnie? There was Vonnie, her face pale and pleading, shoved roughly through the kitchen and into the living room by two creatures from a nightmare.

"They killed Tess," Yvonne said, starting to cry.

"They what?" Kevin said, talking a half-step toward them. But his courage was gone, replaced only by childlike terror, even before he saw the guns, before a gun butt smashed into the side of his face.

He went down hard, toppling a standing lamp as he fell, the glass crashing into pieces as it struck the wall. He knew the kick that went into his ribs was a hard one, but he already had too much pain to feel the difference.

From way above him, far away, he heard the sounds of slaps, then screams that were quickly muffled. Vonnie had screamed, then Rosalie. Then Kevin heard only the muffled gagging sounds the women made as they tried to scream.

Another slap, then another, and Kevin recognized somehow that it was Rosalie who was trying to breathe her pleas for mercy through some kind of cloth gag.

Then other slaps, one, two, three, closer—Vonnie!—and Kevin prayed. Don't let them kill Vonnie.

Unable to get off the floor, worried that he would choke to death on the food that threatened to rush into his throat from his stomach, Kevin turned his head and managed to look up. All he wanted to do was plead, to tell them that they could have anything they wanted, but they already knew that.

It was a mistake for Kevin to look, because the next moment he saw a shoe grow large, blotting out all the light, as the tip of it rammed into his nose. Kevin heard a loud sob, as near to a scream as Vonnie could get, before everything went dark for him.

Yvonne had been pushed down roughly onto the couch and had scrambled to an upright position. A yellow kerchief had been tied across her mouth, cutting the corners. It, too, had the familiar smell. It made her retch.

Her arm ached where the bigger man had twisted it behind her back. Her faced burned where it had been slapped repeatedly. Her head was pounding with fear and the tourniquet-tightness of her kerchief.

Why haven't they killed us yet? she thought, and at the same moment thought of the dog. Oh, Tess. Poor innocent baby.

And then she saw the shoe crash into Kevin's face and saw his eyes roll back and the blood gush onto the carpet. And she gasped, sobbed, choked.

Poor Kevin. He's as much an innocent baby as Tess. Have they killed him? Oh, Kevin. Live, please. She stared at the blood. So much blood. Will he bleed to death? Let it clot; oh, let it stop. Could she clot it by staring at it? Could she will the blood to stop? Was he still breathing? Will he choke to death on all the blood?

As she stared she felt her left eye closing. She could not keep it open. Then there was more blood. Hers. Dripping onto her shirt. And the big horrid face was looking into her other eye. The moment seemed to last forever. Yvonne could no longer hear what was said. Only the pounding, pounding, rushing blood. And then the room began to spin and she fell, spinning, down, down.

When Kevin regained consciousness, it was like coming to the surface through a hundred fathoms of pain. At first, he heard the faraway sounds of furniture being shifted and bumped, of heavy feet trodding carelessly through the house.

Vonnie's gone and sold the house, Kevin told himself. The movers are here and they're taking everything away.

No, that wasn't right.

He tried to breathe deeply, to wake himself up, but the blood going into the back of his throat made him gag and cough. Then he remembered.

Kevin opened his eyes, saw a saucer-size bloodstain on the carpet near his face. My blood, he thought, mine.

He listened carefully, tried to think through the pain. The heavy footsteps were far away, in another room. Slowly, he raised his head. There was Rosalie, tied to a chair, a towel around her mouth. Her eyes met his: Be still, they told him, be still and pray that they go away.

Kevin shifted his head, every little movement filling his face with pain. He wondered if his nose had been broken.

There, there was Vonnie! Tied to the sofa, her head rolled to one side. Oh, Jesus, is she dead? They had hit her. One eye was swollen shut. Her puffed, reddened cheeks glistened with tears.

Kevin's lights went out again.

Yvonne heard a voice pierce the darkness. A man said, "They're both out."

Another voice whispered, "Can it."

"They can't hear." The voice shifted to a whisper. "You got it, boss."

Yvonne decided to play possum and maybe groan a little. No sense giving them any more reason to hurt her, she thought. She remembered Kevin and all the blood pouring from his nose and wanted to open her eyes again. "Aannhh," she moaned, then listened. Footsteps, going away from her. More steps—in the bedroom, in the kitchen, then down the stairs. Heavy footfalls going down the stairs. A few seconds later footsteps coming up, lighter steps. Yvonne groaned again and lifted her head, trying to open both eyes and having only one respond.

The smaller intruder, wearing a pink jacket, was carrying the TV through the kitchen and heading toward the stairs. Thieves. Here. After all the other—drug dealers, thugs— now thieves. Why here? With all the fancy neighbors. Why us? She was about to protest with a grunt through the gag, but she caught Rosalie's eye.

Rosalie shook her head slightly and knitted her brows, as if to say, "Hush."

When Kevin started to come to again, the footsteps were much louder, more rapid. Just like the movers, he thought. When they're near the end of a job and a place is almost empty, they can move around faster and there's less to absorb the sound.

Wait. These aren't the movers.

"Couple of TVs, a camera with a long lens . . ."

"A microwave. Cheap model, but what the hell. Niggers in Queens will love it. Hear that?"

Was the voice talking to him? Kevin wondered. It didn't matter; he couldn't answer, could barely open his eyes into slits that saw only the carpet fiber, close up, with his blood on it.

Heavy steps from the small bedroom. "Bingo!" a voice said. Sounds of heavy cardboard being ripped open. "Lookit. A computer. Brand new!"

"We'll find a Wall Streeter who wants a bargain. Get a thou for it, I bet."

As he drifted in and out of awareness, sometimes stopping in the station of half-consciousness with the noises that seemed to come from a dream, Kevin felt profoundly sorry. He had heard a lot of stories about burglaries in the posh communities of Long Island. He had even reported about them for his newspaper. Some of the bigger houses in the better neighborhoods—their owners were often the ones hardest hit. There had been cases of men and women tied up, beaten, abused, forced to watch as their homes were emptied. Sometimes even . . .

Kevin felt profoundly sorry for those people; he was one with them now.

"Hell of a computer," he thought he heard a voice say. "Never been used, still in the box."

Good, Kevin thought. Maybe that will make them happy and they'll leave. He was beyond wishing for anything else: just let them leave, he prayed.

The heavy footsteps were close now. He was afraid they would kick him some more as he lay on the carpet. If they kick me again, I'm probably going to die, he thought. This is what it's like.

"How you feeling?" a voice from above him called. "Want some more?"

Kevin tried to say no, tried to plead, but all he could

manage was a moan. Should he try to crawl toward the wall to gain some protection? No, if they wanted to, they could just drag him back into the middle of the floor and break every bone in his body.

Besides, Kevin realized, his hands were tied behind him. Something seemed to be cutting into his wrists; a belt, perhaps.

"We're going now," said a cackling whisper above Kevin.

"Are you happy we're going? Are you happy?"

Kevin moaned.

"Good. Now you won't have so much furniture to worry about if you move."

"Let's go," the other voice said.

"Should we work them over again, just for the hell of it?"

"No. We did enough. C'mon."

And then, quickly, they stomped out the back door, slammed it loudly and were gone.

Kevin sent up a prayer of thanksgiving. He was alive, Yvonne was alive. He wasn't crippled; he knew that because he could move his arms and legs.

He didn't know how much time went by. He was awakened by the motion of someone loosening the belt that bound his hands behind his back.

"Kevin . . . oh, Kevin, Jesus . . . Kevin . . ." Vonnie's voice, right behind him and above. Oh, she was the one, she was the one loosening the belt. "Oh, Kevin . . ."

His hands were free. Something wet and cold on his forehead, and on the back of his neck. Cold and good. Something wet and cold on his face now, being rubbed gingerly around his nose. Now he could focus on the carpet fibers just in front of his eyes.

Kevin raised his head, put it down again in dizziness. "Vonnie," he said.

"Kevin, oh God. Kevin."

The police, Kevin thought. Got to call them. He pushed up with an arm; yes, he could make it through the pain now, nothing broken. Vonnie held his other arm; she was already standing, and she was helping him to his feet.

Kevin looked at her face, bruised and swollen. "Oh, Vonnie, Vonnie. Jesus Christ."

"They're gone. They're gone."

"The police! Goddamn them, I gotta call—"

"They're on their way," Rosalie said. She was standing in the doorway to the living room. One side of her face was reddened, but she had fared better than Kevin and Yvonne.

"Rosalie got loose first, then she undid me," Yvonne said.

Kevin put his arm over Yvonne's shoulders, and she put her arm around his waist. Together they stood, sharing a sense of violation.

"After all we've been through," Kevin hissed through bloody lips. "Fight off a bunch of drug dealers, a friend of ours gets beat up, and the police back home can't even keep us safe. . . ."

He had to stop, because he was close to tears. Yvonne was already crying, her head resting on Kevin's shoulder. Kevin fished out his handkerchief, thought of offering it to Yvonne, then thought he had better use it to dab his bloody nostrils.

"Thank God we're alive," Rosalie said.

They looked at her. Her eyes, even after what they had all been through, were cool and wise. Never had she seemed so formidable to them.

Yvonne remembered the sight of their Doberman, lying on her side. "They killed Tess," she said.

Those words almost made Kevin's knees buckle. In his terror and pain, he had forgotten. "I loved her. I did," he said.

Kevin stumbled toward the back door. After all the dog had meant, he had to see her, had to bear witness to her suffering, had to tell her how much she had meant. Even if she couldn't hear.

He had tears in his eyes by the time he walked out the door into the sweet-smelling night. The tears blurred the light from the moon and stars, making it hard for him to focus on the backyard. He bit into his already sore lip to keep from crying too much (he didn't care if Yvonne saw him, but he didn't want Rosalie or the police to see him). He tried to steel himself for the sight of the dog's body by breathing deeply, but that hurt his ribs.

And then he heard Tess's gentle, friendly whine.

"Tessie, Jesus! Tessie."

She limped toward him from the end of the run, favoring a rear leg. But her tail was wagging, her tongue flicking at his face as he knelt. She was alive, alive, alive.

Kevin turned his head. "Vonnie!" he shouted toward the back door. "Tess is okay!"

But Yvonne had already seen. She was rushing toward the dog, feeling no shame at all in her joyful crying as she knelt.

The dog scrambled to lick one face, then the other, its tail wagging furiously. Then the dog began to lick tentatively at Kevin's shirt, where some blood had caked.

Yvonne grinned. "She's not sure she's supposed to like that."

"Blood is blood, isn't it, old girl," Kevin said, rubbing the dog behind her ear. "She was limping. Something's the matter with one of her back legs."

Yvonne and Kevin examined the dog's hind quarters and found a small puncture. The dog shied when they touched her near the wound.

"Did they shoot her? Is that a bullet wound?" Yvonne asked.

"Easy, girl," Kevin said, pressing the flesh on the dog's flank. "There's something sticking out of here. A tranquilizer dart."

"Bastards."

"Hey, you two," Rosalie called from the back door. "The police are here."

14

It was barely light and the birds had set up their usual morning chorus when Yvonne opened her eyes. Her left one was open today, the swelling having subsided. Another day . . . She sighed, thinking that she was lucky to be alive and hearing the birds. And in the next moment, she was angry and resentful and wondering why Providence had picked her to dump misfortune on.

The police had treated the robbery as if it were an isolated incident, but she was not convinced of that. Too much of a coincidence, she thought. Especially with so many bigger houses nearby. The cops had an answer for that, too: "But they all have security systems, Mrs. McNulty." As if it's my fault that my house was robbed, because I don't have a security system. And then that crack about Kevin and me being split: "They may have been watching the house and knew you were living alone."

To hell with that. Anybody could see I wasn't alone yesterday. Rosalie's car was in the driveway; they couldn't come up with an answer to that. And then all the rigmarole filling in this law-enforcement agency with this piece of information and that bunch of cops with this other item that they didn't know about. You'd think we were the crooks. They ask a million questions and then ask them all over again. "Who's DeeDee Lockwood?" "What's her connection to the drugs that were found in your boat?" "Why were you motoring to Haviland Marina?" "What were you doing in Edgecliff?" "How long have you known Harvey?" "When was the last time you saw Harvey?" "Did you know Tolly?"

Tolly. I wonder why they were asking about Tolly. His death was an accident. He was a marina gofer all the years I knew him. It seems he was around the water forever. Even when I was a kid, when we'd go down to Chowder's for supper, Tolly was around. He always looked the same. So did Harvey. Harvey. They say he's missing. That no one has seen him since we left in our boat. Yvonne was wrenched from her thoughts by a noise in the kitchen. Her heart started to pound, and Tess, who had been sleeping at the foot of the bed, lifted her head, sniffed, and wagged her tail. "Oh, it's Kevin," she said, relieved. He had roused himself early from the sofa where he'd spent the night, and she was thankful for his presence.

She dragged herself up, feeling pain in her arm and in her back, neck, and legs as well. "They really did a job on me."

By now, Tess was whining at the bedroom door. She wants to see Kevin, she thought. She misses him.

Yvonne slipped her feet into an old pair of scuffs and pulled on a cotton robe. When she opened the door, Kevin was standing there, about to knock. "The dog wants to see you, but don't get her too excited or she'll pee on the floor."

"Good morning to you, too, Attila," Kevin said. "I'll put her right out. C'mon, Tessie girl."

While Yvonne brushed her teeth, she giggled. "Attila," she said, remembering that Kevin used to call her hon, and then later Attila the hun.

She looked in the mirror at her battered face as she washed her hands. Her eye was still puffed and was turning black. A shiner, great. She tried to remember where she had put her dark glasses. The rest of her face seemed to have come through without much bruising. Not so her arms, though. They were splotched with blue, red, and some yellow. Then she looked at her legs, which were somewhat less marked than her arms, and she thought back to the rough handling the men had given her.

When she got to the kitchen, she saw that Kevin had been up for a while. The coffee was perked, peaches were sliced for cereal, and bread, butter, and jam were at the ready next to the toaster. She smiled at Kevin, who looked as if he had been waiting for just such a smile. "It's nice to have you here. I feel spoiled," she said.

"I think you could use a little spoiling right about now," he said.

"Tell you what. I'll spoil you a little. How would you like some Newburg tonight?"

"You've made my day. It's almost worth all the trials."

"Not really."

"No. Not really. What the hell has been happening? Have you got any ideas?"

"I was wondering this morning why those guys put on such elaborate disguises."

"Maybe we would have recognized them without the masks."

"As I was coming to, I heard one of them talking in a normal voice. He said, 'They're both out.' But he rolled his *r* a little. Then the other one told him to can it. Then he went back to his whisper and he called the other one 'boss.'"

"Boss? Hmmm. Do you remember anybody built like one of those guys? You're always good at checking out the way people are built. Your old figure-study classes may come in handy now."

"It's hard to remember anything except the bright colors. I remember that the big one smelled of musk and something that I've smelled before, but I can't remember where."

"Musk is everywhere. But what was the other smell? Lighter fluid? Cleaning fluid? Weed killer?"

"I don't know. I'll remember when I smell it again."

"Those jackets were beauts, too. Hot pink and canary yellow. You'd think the cops would have noticed a couple of people decked out like that. The cops said they were right at the turn into Duck Point Lane until they got the call to come to our house after the robbery. If they went by, the cops should have seen them."

"If they went by? If they didn't pass the cops, they came from another house on Duck Point Lane or from a boat or from a plane. And where's our stuff? Where's their car? And why us? I don't buy the cops' explanation that they picked this house because there's no security system, and because I live alone."

"They arrested the three who worked us over at Haviland. Maybe these two were the guys that got on the boat that night in Edgecliff." He corrected himself at once. "No. The guys in Edgecliff spoke Spanish. All I can remember from last night is the bright colors. And the pain."

"Yes, but was there anything about—are you sure these were different guys? Is there anything at all you remember? A voice print in your brain, perhaps."

"All I got was a footprint on my face."

"Well, if the ones last night were different from the ones on the boat at Edgecliff . . ."

"Then we've got two more guys to watch out for. Terrific . . ."

They nibbled at their food halfheartedly, each chewing carefully to avoid the sore spots.

"At least if we have Newburg tonight, we don't have to chew too hard," Kevin said.

"How is your poor face this morning? All things considered, you look pretty good."

"All things considered is right. I did look in the mirror this morning, so you can cool it with that blarney. You're not the Irishman."

"Well, you are recognizable."

Kevin laughed. " 'Recognizable' is not the same as 'pretty good.' Ouch."

"Don't tell me. It only hurts when you laugh, right?"

"Right. I guess I'm lucky that nothing is broken. Not even my nose, which used to break at every football practice."

The police had given them a ride to North Shore Hospital the night before, where the doctors and nurses in the emergency room had greeted them with inquisitive looks and professional sympathy. Rosalie had declined the policemen's offer, saying she would go to her own doctor.

"What happened? What happened?" Kevin and Yvonne had been asked several times by the ER people.

"Burglars," Kevin said finally, just wanting them to shut up.

"Really?" a middle-aged nurse said.

Suddenly, Yvonne understood. "We didn't beat each other up," she said. "This isn't domestic violence, okay?"

Kevin and Yvonne winced as their wounds were cleaned and bandaged. Then they had X rays. The best news was that Kevin had no broken ribs.

A young doctor studied Kevin's face, pressed around his eyes, managed to hit all the sore spots with his fingers. He told Kevin to put his head back and shined a pen-sized flashlight up his nose.

"Well," the doctor said cheerily, "it's not broken. But you did sustain some trauma to the nostril tissues."

"No shit," Kevin said.

The police had driven them home. With painkillers from the hospital, Kevin and Yvonne had even managed to sleep fairly well. They had had their nightmare before closing their eyes.

"Kevin. If that was not a regular robbery, what was it? And what were they after?"

"If it wasn't a regular robbery, I guess it was an irregular robbery."

"Be serious."

"Okay. Hey, do you realize that they didn't take the VCR? Our friends in law enforcement didn't notice that last night."

"What?" Yvonne got up and went into the living room. There, on the shelf under where the TV used to be, was the VCR. "They had to unplug the TV from it to take the TV. And yet they didn't take the VCR. Strange." Yvonne put her hands on her hips and stretched her back. "Oooh. I am so stiff. What I need is three days in a hot tub."

"When we make up the list for the cops and the insurance

company, we'll mention the fact that the thieves didn't take the VCR," Kevin said. "You know, they didn't bother with any of the kitchen appliances except for the microwave. Do you think that's strange, too?"

"I don't know. Maybe kitchen stuff is harder to fence. But we can tell the cops that, too. Let's see, there's the toaster, the mixer, the food processor, the blender, the pasta maker, the ice-cream maker."

"They mustn't have spent much time in the kitchen at all. Some of this stuff should be fenceable. They took fairly cheap stuff from the bedroom. The clock radio, for instance, and the little TV, and your Walkman, for Chrissake."

"You're right. They were pretty selective. Maybe their fence gave them a list. Maybe they were after something that they knew was in the bedroom. Jesus! Suppose someone stashed drugs here, too!"

"Who? Nobody's been in the house but you and me. Even Rosalie didn't have a key when she was feeding the dog."

"Okay. No drugs stashed. But what then?" Yvonne walked back into the bedroom and came out again. "You're right. They did a pretty thorough job on the bedroom. They got my new computer before I even took it out of the box. There must have been four or five boxes of stuff with the computer."

"Could the cops be right? That the burglary was unrelated . . ."

"I hope they're watching Duck Point Lane better than they were yesterday," Yvonne said, agitated. "Look, the guys on the boat are in custody. When they boarded, they were looking for drugs. They were looking for drugs at DeeDee's too."

"If these guys are part of the same gang, what are they looking for? And why didn't they question us?"

"Where are the cops today?" Yvonne said, getting up again and going to the bedroom window, which looked over the driveway and toward the road.

"Do you see them?" Kevin hollered from his perch at the

kitchen table. It hurt him to move despite the fact that he had no broken bones.

"Not yet. Oh yes, there they are. Parked right next to the driveway." Yvonne was on her way back to the kitchen. "Maybe we should tell them it's all right to use the conveniences . . . offer them some coffee."

"Do you mind if I just sit here?"

"You hurt, don't you? Do you want me to get you some of the pain pills?"

Kevin nodded. The pain really was closing in. His chest felt as if it were in a vise. "Would you mind if I took over the bed for a little while?"

"Be my guest."

Kevin got up slowly, grimacing. "Well, I am sort of your guest." He felt terribly old and feeble as he made his way painfully toward the bed. Once he was lying down, though, the pain left him and he felt the tension in his limbs uncoil. The bed felt good. His bed. His and Vonnie's bed.

Two hours later, when Kevin opened his eyes, he thought that he had just closed them a moment before. But then he noticed that the light was brighter and lifted his head to see the clock. But the clock was gone. He seemed to ache less and remembered what he had heard about the curative powers of sleep, thinking that maybe he would nod off again.

No. There were things to do. Got to help Vonnie get the list ready. No clock. What time was it? He sat up gingerly, expecting the pain to pounce on him again, and was relieved to find it much less intense. He felt almost cheerful.

"I called the insurance company," Yvonne said as he entered the living room. "They're sending an adjuster out today."

"Were they nice?"

"Pretty much. They asked if we'd called the police, and I told them we had. The woman was sympathetic when I told her a little of what happened."

"Good," said Kevin, heading toward the coffeepot. He noticed as he pulled a cup from the cupboard that he couldn't keep his hand from shaking. By the time he had made himself some toast and poured the coffee, the shaking had subsided somewhat. But he held on to the toast plate and the coffee cup carefully as he walked back across the living room and planted himself on the couch. He saw that Yvonne had swept away the broken glass and had sprayed carpet cleaner where his nose had bled. "Thanks for cleaning up," he said.

Yvonne nodded, smiled a "you're welcome" and sat down across from him. "We're alive," she said.

"Barely," he said. Then he felt a nose nudge his elbow. "Tessie, baby, I bet you came by for a treat."

Kevin held a toast end in his mouth, bent forward and let the Doberman take the toast gently, if somewhat wetly.

"You two," Yvonne said in mock rebuke. "You keep doing that, and the next time we have dinner guests Tess will—"

She stopped, realizing the implications of what she was saying.

Kevin knew why she stopped, but he let her off the hook by continuing to fuss over the dog. "Good old Doberman, you even smell good. At least, I think you do."

"She was limping just a little this morning, but I think she's okay. I called Port Guinness Animal Hospital. They said to watch her for a day or two, but as long as she got through last night, she should be fine . . ."

"Weird," Kevin said.

". . . that it was most likely a regular animal tranquilizer dart. What's weird?"

"Those bastards last night. They pound the shit out of us, take everything we own. Mean, right? But they spare the dog."

"There's no figuring. Just be thankful. . . . But wait! They had to come prepared with an animal tranquilizer. They knew there was a dog here. They must have been watching the house. Oh, it gives me the creeps to think of someone watching the house."

"But—" Kevin was getting agitated. "Those mugs on the boat would have killed Tess without a second thought.

These guys were just playing at violence. But I can't believe it's not connected."

"Tell the cops that. See if they'll listen."

"They're not the greatest listeners, are they? For them, crime unfolds in a certain way. It's like the newspaper business, you know the old line, 'We've always done it that way.'"

And then the phone rang. Yvonne answered it. It was Detective Guardino.

"Wait a minute," she said. "We both want to hear this."

Yvonne handed the phone to Kevin and went to the bedroom to pick up the other extension.

"I've got some news for you," Guardino said. "You know someone named Quince?"

"Yeah," Kevin said.

"We just picked him up."

"For what?" Yvonne said.

"The three guys we arrested at the George Washington Bridge told us a lot about him. First one broke, and now they've all found their voices. Quince ran a cocaine warehouse. He was a big distributor for a lot of Long Island."

"I never liked him," Yvonne said.

That's right, Kevin thought. She always thought he was creepy.

"Our boys tell us Quince made Harvey disappear."

"Well, where is he?" Kevin said.

"We think we know about where to look, and we're dragging the Sound for him," Guardino said.

Yvonne felt a twist in her stomach. "How do you know what happened to him?"

"The three guys were there when he was dumped over with his waders on," the cop said.

"Oh, Lord," Yvonne said.

"Jesus," Kevin said. "We weren't great friends or anything, but he used to take care of our boat."

"Yeah," Yvonne said. "We were pissed at him, but we never would have wished this on him."

"Mmmm. At least you're in the clear now. And the DEA guy won't be bothering you anymore."

"The prick," Kevin said.

"You mean agent Belcher? Bilker?" Yvonne said.

"Bleucher," Guardino said, chuckling. "I was wondering if you mangled his name on purpose."

"What about our boat?" Kevin asked.

"It'll be released before too much longer."

"Is that real time, or federal-government time?" Yvonne asked.

"It won't be tomorrow. A month, maybe. Meantime, the Port Guinness people say they have some good leads on your house burglary."

"Terrific," Kevin said without enthusiasm, for he knew from his newspaper experience that the police were usually closer to solving a crime when they had *one* lead, not several, and that when they had a good lead they didn't talk about it.

"Uh, just one other thing," Guardino said.

"Yeah?"

"The Port Guinness police would, uh, appreciate it if you and your wife wouldn't, you know, say too much about what happened. I mean about the whole thing in general, but especially . . ."

"Especially the part about how we had the shit beat out of us and our house trashed while they were guarding us."

"Uh, yes. They're pretty upset over this. I mean, really upset. They'd hate to read . . ."

"Don't worry," Kevin said. "I just write about pro football this time of year. Nothing about violence and drugs."

15

The sports department was in the far corner of the newsroom. As Kevin walked around the perimeter of the battleship-sized floor, he looked straight ahead so that his eyes would meet as few eyes as possible. He longed for the days when the news floor reverberated with the staccato of typewriters. The noise created shields of privacy. Two people could talk without being overheard ten feet away, and a person could walk through the newsroom almost unnoticed.

But the typewriters had been replaced by green-glowing terminals and the soft clickety-click of their keyboards and their gentle hum.

Kevin felt almost naked. He was scarcely halfway to his desk when he heard the voice.

"Jeez, Kevin, what happened to you?" The voice belonged to Carol (Kevin didn't remember her last name), a clerk who Kevin thought was cute (though too young for him) and always greeted cheerfully.

"Long story," he said. "Tell you soon. Honest." He was brusque, and when he saw her feelings had been hurt he added, "Had a little boating accident."

Kevin kept walking. He reached the safety island of his desk, scanned the morning paper, read his messages. Good;

they were all routine. He was not in the mood for surprises.

Kevin saw a reporter colleague walking across the room toward him, curiosity all over his face. Kevin picked up the phone, pressed it against a sore ear, pretended to take notes as he listened to the dial tone. He was psychologically strung out, and he wasn't ready for questions about how his skin had got to be all puffy and scratched and bruised and where had he been the early part of the week.

The insurance adjuster had been sympathetic and helpful and told them they would get a check within a couple of weeks. But Kevin and Yvonne had to figure out what to buy with the money, now that they had two households. Which was in itself depressing for Kevin.

Marty Diehl was still waffling on whether to buy the boat, once it was out of impoundment.

Yvonne was still upset about DeeDee Lockwood; she was unable to forget the image of her in the hospital. Neither could Kevin.

Worst of all, Kevin was going to go back to his own apartment tonight, an apartment that was adequate for his needs and was not that uncomfortable. Except that it had no dog, no style. No Vonnie.

He put the phone down and opened a brown interoffice envelope; the message inside was from Bruce Dunning, the competent but unflamboyant sports editor: "Kevin, welcome back. Hope you had a nice vacation."

Kevin paused, laughed ruefully to himself. He had told his editor he needed the time off for some urgent personal business, not a vacation. It was Wednesday, five days since they had taken their boat out of Port Guinness. God, that was a long time ago. Kevin had told his editor originally that he needed extra time because he had to sell his boat. The editor had looked puzzled, and Kevin had told him quietly that he and his wife were splitting and he just had to have the time. The sports editor had said, "Sorry to hear that; take all the time you need." There was hardly a newspaper editor alive who wasn't familiar with marriage problems.

Kevin read on: "Joe B. is honcho today. I told him

you could do a story on what's wrong with the Jets's secondary—other than the fact they can't stop a passing attack."

Kevin knew at once which one of his sources to tap. He would call Chili Wilkins.

Chili Wilkins was a retired, now legendary defensive back of the Jets, one of the few in football who had managed to star in what were almost two different eras. He had been great several years back, when the defensive backs were allowed to bump the receivers quite a bit, and had starred after the bumping rules were tightened.

The more recent rules placed a higher premium on speed and finesse. Chili Wilkins had made the transition, had been a perennial all-pro, would no doubt be in the Hall of Fame.

"God gave me speed and grace as well as strength and courage," he had said. "Why shouldn't I be able to change my style?"

After retiring, Chili Wilkins had settled in Great Neck, a few miles west of Port Guinness, and opened a Chevy dealership. He was hard not to like, partly because the NFL's public-relations machine regularly featured him on its nostalgia films at halftime, partly because he treated people right.

Kevin thought he was one of the nicest people he had ever met in sports, and he was that way without being either arrogant or self-conscious about being black. Or so Kevin thought, having filtered it all through the prism of his Irish, quasi-Catholic prejudice.

He shook the depressing thoughts out of his head, or tried to. And he dialed.

"Chili Wilkins Chevrolet."

"Kevin McNulty from the *Long Island* sports department. Is Chili in?"

"Please hold."

"Chili Wilkins speaking."

"Hi. I have a sixty-five Corvair with dogshit on the tires and I'd like to trade it in for a new Pimpmobile with bucket seats."

"Kev-IN, you dumb honkie! How are you, my man?"

"Surviving." Kevin was glad that the racial humor was out of the way; his heart wasn't really in it, but Chili always expected it of him.

"What can I do for you, my man?"

"Got a few minutes to talk about pass coverage?"

"Why not."

Kevin asked a few questions, told Chili that he had bet and lost on the Packer game. Chili chuckled, then started to talk, smoothly and easily.

Chili had always been great with the quotes, and Kevin took down his words (or at least the ones he was sure he'd want to use) on his computer. His fingers flew in easy clicks, and the lines piled up on Kevin's green screen.

"Hold one sec, Chili." Kevin pressed the "store" button, so that everything he had taken down to that point would not vanish if there was a power failure or a thunderstorm, or if the computer coughed just for the hell of it. "Okay. You were saying?"

"I was saying there's no substitute for the great speed. You have it or you don't, man. The great speed. You can't really coach somebody to do forty yards in four point three if God wants him to do it in four and a half."

"Okay, I already know, but say it for the reader. Two-tenths of a second can mean something?"

"Man, *one*-tenth of a second can mean something. Can mean *everything*. Say I let myself get a little flabby. Say I let myself get *old*; it happens, man. So I lose a tenth—a half-step. That's the difference between my body being next to the receiver's, with my hands pretty level with his but still all legal, and my being that little bit farther away from him, enough so he can get his hands higher than mine. You dig?"

"I dig."

"Put it simple, man. At that level of competition, that fraction is everything. God gave some of us the great speed, but it never lasts. Just like youth. You know anyone who's faster at thirty than he was at twenty-five, all other things being equal?"

"No."

"Course not. Trick is to hold on to your speed and quickness as long as you can. You do that by conditioning and discipline."

"Right." Then Kevin felt his instincts kick in, and with it a question he had not planned to ask. "Do you think any of the Jets might have, you know, another kind of problem?"

Pause. "This is on deep background, man. Okay? I mean, file it away to use another time."

"Right."

"Good. So far, from what I hear, the Jets are clean. There's ways to get around the drug-testing, but I don't think they have to. They're clean."

"Good. I didn't lose my bet on somebody's high."

"Right. Only white stuff they use is foot powder. I know some guys on other teams ain't gonna hold on to their God-given gifts too long. But far as I know, the only thing wrong with the Jets is they're too slow."

"Too slow. Okay."

There was a silence on the phone; Chili's choosing his words carefully, Kevin thought.

"Trades are more complicated now than they used to be. I mean, the coaches won't say that, except way off the record. You think a coach is gonna say, 'We'd like to have so-and-so, he's got the speed, loves to hit, but we hear he snorts a line every chance he gets'? Shit, no."

Kevin sensed that Chili Wilkins had more to say. He waited.

"See, I hear a lot 'cuz of who I am and where I am. I mean, Great Neck is close enough to Queens so I know plenty about what goes on. With some of the brothers. And not just the brothers. And I hear things from people, once they trust me, you know? From addicts and users. Because of the work I do in United Way, counseling and all that."

"Right."

"Ummm, Kevin. I'll tell you something if you don't press me on it. Okay?"

"Okay."

"There was a guy, not with the Jets, a big-name star who

retired at the end of last season. Said he wanted to go out while he was still on top."

Kevin had a file-card memory for retirements, trades, the waiver list and such. "I count three, maybe four guys who fit that description."

Chili Wilkins chuckled. "Good. I'll let you guess which one I'm gonna tell you about. Anyhow, he gave some bullshit about not wanting to wait until his knees went."

Kevin's mind raced: the part about the knees made it likely Chili Wilkins was talking about a running back or wide receiver. Kevin almost said something, but he stopped himself, remembering his pledge not to press.

"You listening, Kevin? It wasn't his knees at all. It was his nose. Next time you hear about this guy, it'll be when he's in drug rehab. Or in the slammer for dealing coke big-time. Or . . ."

"Or on a slab in a morgue."

"You're not hearing this from me. When the drug tycoons in Colombia declared war on the government down there, that should have opened everybody's eyes. Finally."

"To what?"

"That the drug business is like a separate nation. With its own army, its own treasury, its own foreign relations."

Kevin longed to tell Chili about his and Yvonne's ordeal, to share something with him, but the police had advised him to say as little as possible. Now he wondered how much he dared say, to anybody.

"The police arrest a few people and grab a basement full of cocaine, but so what? The whole thing is like wild berries."

"Wild berries?"

"I can tell you weren't raised in the country. You pull up a plant, chop out some shallow roots, but there's still a root growing down there, real deep. And it springs up somewhere else."

"Hmmm."

"The cops can grab up everything that shows, but it doesn't help in the long run. Because what *doesn't* show is still there. And it starts the bramble all over again."

"You know anybody like that?"

"I don't know who they are. I just know they are. I've said enough, Kevin. Just don't bet on the Jets till they get a couple of cornerbacks who're about two-tenths faster over forty yards than the ones they got. Simple as that. Listen, I gotta sell some cars. Take care."

Kevin thanked Chili Wilkins and said good-bye. After hanging up, he shivered for a moment. Wild berries?

"Kevin, how are you?"

Kevin looked up to the easygoing face of Joe Boles, the assistant sports editor. "Hi, Joe."

"What happened?" Joe Boles said.

Kevin took a deep breath; tell him and be done with it, Kevin decided. "A couple of guys invaded our house the other night. They beat the living shit out of us and ransacked the place." Kevin's voice almost broke.

"Oh, God. Is Yvonne all right?"

"Yeah. She's banged up too, but we're all right."

"Did the cops get 'em?"

"Not yet."

"Is there anything I can do?"

"No. Thanks." Kevin appreciated the kindness, but he wanted to change the subject. "I just got done talking to Chili Wilkins. Some pretty decent stuff. Nothing world-shaking but okay."

"Five or six hundred words?"

"That's about right."

"Good. You don't have to hang around too long today."

Before walking away, Joe Boles brushed Kevin's shoulder lightly with his hand, and for a moment Kevin was more full of emotion than he wanted to be.

Needing a break before he started writing, Kevin walked to a corner where there were machines for sandwiches, coffee and soft drinks, a small table and a few chairs. He bought a root beer and sat down at the table.

"How's it going?" a voice over his shoulder said.

Jesus no, Kevin thought. But he said, "Hi, Landon."

Landon Brice was the paper's Pulitzer Prize–winning investigative reporter. He was—there was no denying it—a gifted journalist: a brilliant writer as well as a tireless, ingenious fact-finder. He was highly intelligent, widely read, deeply knowledgeable about the inner workings of governments and courts from the village to the national level. He spoke a couple of languages and was an excellent cook. And he had enormous confidence in his abilities.

Kevin admired him grudgingly, but couldn't feel warm toward him. They had never socialized, even though Brice's house was just a few miles from Kevin and Yvonne's.

"Wow! You got the license number, I hope." Landon Brice chuckled.

Kevin felt the heat rush to his face. He was annoyed but said nothing; he could not match Brice's repartee even when he was in top form.

"You okay?" Brice said more seriously, as he sat down with his coffee.

"Surviving."

Landon Brice nodded solemnly and locked laser-bright eyes on Kevin's. "What happened?" he asked.

"Some guys beat us up the other night. After drugging our dog."

"Us?"

"Me and Yvonne. And a friend."

"Where?"

"Our house."

"Robbery?"

"They cleaned us out. Almost."

Brice whistled and shook his head. "And they worked you over while they were doing it."

"Sure did."

"Did they have guns?"

"Yep."

"Cops ask you a lot of questions?"

"I guess. I don't know. They're gonna talk to us again tomorrow."

Suddenly, Kevin realized he was being interviewed. That was Landon Brice's way: he had to know everything, and he had an uncanny way of making people open up.

Brice frowned. "It's puzzling, in a way. No offense,

Kevin, but isn't your house one of the smaller ones around Duck Point?"

"The smallest."

"So what were they doing in your place?"

"I didn't ask."

"What did the cops say?"

"They gave us some shit about not having a burglar alarm. The other thing is, I haven't been living there lately. They might've figured Vonnie was there alone."

"Ah. But you happened to be there the other night. With a friend."

"Yeah. You ask more questions than the cops." At first, Kevin had found the telling cathartic, but now he was tired of being interviewed.

"You're lucky you're alive," Brice said quietly.

"I'm really strung out," Kevin said, pausing to sip his root beer.

"Is there more?" Brice said, sounding like a confessor.

Kevin took a deep breath, let the air out slowly and began again to talk. He told about waking up to the sounds of men on the boat that night while he was in the V-berth and how terrified he was, about DeeDee Lockwood, about the struggle at the Haviland Marina and how he was both thrilled and sickened when he hit the thug's hand with the gearshift, about the discovery of the cocaine.

Brice nodded, stopping Kevin now and then with a question, and he listened. He listened.

"This guy Harvey. He's still missing?"

"Bottom of the Sound, the cops think."

"Why do they think that?"

"Because the guys arrested in New Jersey told them."

"Good. Somebody's talking."

"Enough so the cops picked up a guy in Port Guinness. Guy named Quince."

"Quince? Mmmmm. Trucking outfit?"

"Something like that. You know him?"

"No, but I think I remember rumors of some tax problems a few years back."

"Well, he seemed to do all right. Big fancy boat. Owns

a lot of commercial property. Hung around Chowder's a lot. I knew him just to nod to. Kept his boat at Harvey's yard."

"Instead of at the club? That's interesting."

"We kept our boat at Harvey's too."

"You did it because it was cheap," Brice said good-naturedly. "I bet Quince had other reasons."

"I guess."

"Anyhow, sounds like you and your wife are pretty goddamn tough." A soft, respectful chuckle.

"No. We were scared to death. I'm still scared. Being scared made us strong. And maybe we had a little luck. I don't know. . . ."

"Did the cops tell you you're safe now?"

"Well, they said they thought so, with Quince and those guys arrested in New Jersey."

Landon Brice's expression reminded Kevin of a doctor about to give a patient some bad news. "Hmmmm. That doesn't guarantee anything. They didn't catch the guys who trashed you and your house. Did the cops think the whole thing was connected? The burglary, what happened to you on the boat trip?"

"Cops just told us to be careful. They didn't seem to see any connection."

Brice frowned and shook his head. "Coincidences do happen but . . ."

"Yeah, but."

"Just be careful. You and your wife stumbled into something, and who knows how far it goes, who you're stepping on. You never suspected Quince, or Harvey. Hell, I never even heard anything about them."

"Are you looking into drugs?"

"Could be. I don't like to say too much about what I'm doing. I prefer to ask questions."

"Yeah, I noticed."

Brice chuckled. "Anyhow, watch yourself. Most of us have never been involved with people like this. The pressure's on like never before, and the stakes are higher. The people who stay in the game are, if you'll excuse the expression, the best and the brightest. And the most vicious. I know mob people—physical, enforcer types—who are scared to death of drug people."

"Yeah, include me in that."

"And the people at the top are harder to catch than ever. They've got the best brains and the latest technology. All paid for in cash. They arrange their drop-offs and pay-offs at the last minute and make it all go like clockwork. Very high-tech. They do their business right next door to the supermarket or the shoe store, while some cops are still staking out warehouses at night."

Brice was making Kevin very uncomfortable. "So Quince . . . ?"

"Quince? From what you've told me, he's probably somewhere in the middle. Anyhow, they're dealing coke all over the Island. When my dad had a boat, he kept a jug of Chivas on board. Now, a good host offers his guests a snort."

Landon Brice stopped, shook his head and chuckled softly. "Don't get me wrong, I got nothing but contempt for these people. They're scum. Still, I have a grudging respect for them. Or for their ingenuity. They've forced the cops to rethink their tactics. I've been with them on lots of the usual stakeouts—dark corners, abandoned buildings, Greyhound-terminal lockers, that stuff. But now, with the distribution moving out east as well, the cops have to use their imaginations a lot more. There aren't many abandoned buildings out east, only new ones. And the traffickers use marinas, yachts, the wide-open parking lot of the new shopping malls."

Kevin sipped his root beer, directing the cool liquid over a sore spot in his mouth. He didn't feel safe at all. And Vonnie! Sometimes on her job she drove to out-of-the-way spots near the water. Isolated, winding roads near the shore. Alone. Should he call her?

What was it Brice had said? Or was it something Chili Wilkins had said?

"The winners make big, big bucks," Brice went on in his quiet, authoritative tone. "The losers, they end up like

Harvey. Or like the two guys in the story the city desk is working."

"Huh?"

"Couple guys found dead in a car on a side road just off the Expressway this morning."

"Murdered?"

Brice nodded and smiled—grimly, this time. "Unless they decided to chain themselves in the car and then set fire to it."

"Jesus. Who were they?"

"Don't know yet. Cityside is trying to find out. They were pretty well barbecued. The plates were phony, it turns out. Cops were waiting for the car to cool off so they could lift the vehicle ID number. If it's not filed off."

"Damn. Oh, damn."

"Listen," Brice said, getting up to leave. "I know you've been through a lot of shit. If I can help at all, let me know."

Kevin felt slightly guilty for all the times he'd found Landon Brice insufferably pompous.

"Take care, Kevin." Brice grabbed Kevin's hand, shook it warmly, and departed.

Damn, Kevin thought, standing up. Damn. Do I know who my friends are?

On the way back to his desk Kevin passed a young reporter who was wearing a telephone headset and typing furiously. "And you don't know if they were alive or dead when the car was torched. . . . Was there an explosion? Not that you know of. . . . Car was registered to first name Ernesto? Last name . . . spell, please . . . L-U-N-E-S . . . Was he one of the victims? Checking, okay. . . . Some of the chain links were fused by the heat. Oh, gross!"

Kevin felt weak, sick. He was afraid, afraid of what could happen to him and Vonnie.

He got back to his desk and sat down.

"You okay, Kevin? You look kinda white and wobbly." Joe Boles's face was wrinkled in concern.

"I'm okay. I think."

"Feel up to writing?"

God, he had to do the Chili Wilkins story. "Sure, no sweat."

Kevin was thankful the story was an easy one to write; if he had had to *think* he might have lost it. Like a robot, he typed:

"Chili Wilkins, who starred in the Jets's secondary in an era when most defensive backs were pit bulls and later when they were greyhounds, thinks he knows what's wrong with the team's pass coverage."

No, Kevin thought. That's too corny, and not quite accurate. Some of the old defensive backs were fast as well as tough, and some of the new, fast ones could hit.

Screw it. Usually, he made his lead paragraph as grabby as he could, but now he didn't have the stomach to tinker. After typing a few more paragraphs he picked up the phone. Got to tell Vonnie what Landon Brice had said, got to tell her to be careful.

The line was busy. Damn, oh, damn. Vonnie's got to be the only one there, and she's on the phone.

What if someone tried to trick her, telling her to meet them at a house. She wouldn't go. . . . Sure, she would! Real estate people do that all the time. The call she's on right now might be a trick.

Kevin typed a couple more paragraphs, sucked in air to calm himself, hit the "store" button on his computer.

Something Brice had said, or Chili . . .

Kevin dialed again. Busy. He put the phone down, typed some more. Six hundred words was not a lot (Kevin was a fast, facile writer), and he was done before long.

Please, he prayed as he picked up the phone again. Please let her answer this time.

Ringing. Kevin breathed more easily. Okay, Vonnie, pick up. Ringing, ringing, ringing. Where the hell are you, Vonnie? In the john or what? Ringing, ringing, ringing.

"Kevin, you sure you're okay?" Joe Boles said. "You look awful. You never take sick days. Want one now?"

"Yeah, yeah. Thanks. Story's done. Want to check it out?"

Boles called up the story and scrolled through it while Kevin dialed Vonnie's office again. Busy.

"The story's fine. Get out of here."

Kevin almost trotted toward the exit. One last time he stopped, picking up a phone at a corner desk. He dialed. Please, God.

Busy.

Kevin would drive to her office, would stay with Vonnie and protect her. He would get some more time off from work, quit if he had to, and he would take Vonnie away where she would be safe. Where *they* would be safe. Vonnie and he, and Tess.

The last thing he heard as he ran out the door was the busy clickety-click of the keyboards (reporters reducing agony and death to electronic impulses on green screens) and the impersonal hum of the computers.

Dear God, just let me do this right.

16

Yvonne was looking forward to getting back to the office, back to where she would meet people whose worst aggressive behavior would be to try to steal her customer. She wondered whether she would ever stop looking over her shoulder. Even yesterday when she had gone to the supermarket, she had looked at perfectly harmless people and suspected that they were the thugs who had broken into her house or were behind the men who had boarded the boat at Edgecliff.

Perhaps she would be back to normal by the time school started in a couple of weeks. Maybe seeing the kids again would snap her out of it.

The kids. Would they seem more precious and fragile to her now that she had lost one of her own? Would she be more appreciative of the stories about the things they had done during the summer, more tolerant when they misbehaved?

And they'd all have new clothes, pristine notebooks, sharpened pencils. She remembered how it felt to go back to school, with new dresses, new shoes, a new bookbag, and . . .

Suddenly her thoughts were full of DeeDee, who had been there on all those first days of school every September, and who wouldn't be back in front of her own classes for a while.

Yvonne was thankful that DeeDee wasn't blaming Kevin and her for what Quince's men had done. Yvonne had gone to DeeDee's place with DeeDee's mother to clean up and had been nauseated by the sight of so much blood. Mrs. Lockwood had ended up comforting Yvonne. Yvonne could think only how close her friend had come to death.

Yvonne wished that she could believe in a heaven. She thought death would seem less awful if she could look forward to seeing people again whom she had lost. In a heaven, maybe the baby would eternally goo and ga.

She envied those who were certain in their faith, who were sure that death was just a door to another world. Somewhere in the Bible she had read about people who think too much. Could she put all the thoughts away and just blindly believe? How do you get faith? Pray for it?

She wondered if she would get another chance at motherhood. Maybe a little girl to name after DeeDee.

Her head was starting to ache. Too many things that she couldn't do anything about.

She'd put those thoughts away and pick out the clothes she would wear to the office. Tangibles were easier to deal with.

Yvonne chose light clothing, short sleeves, and to heck with the bruises showing. But she would take a sweater, because the office air-conditioning was always churning. Rosalie kept the office below seventy-five because, she said, it was better for the electronic equipment not to get overheated. However, Yvonne knew that Rosalie hated to sweat. Her house was kept as cold as the office, and so were the cars, for that matter.

Rosalie was just leaving when Yvonne arrived, and Yvonne asked her how she felt. It upset Yvonne that Rosalie had been beaten on her visit to her house.

"A little achy, but not too bad," Rosalie answered.

"You look wonderful. I would never know they laid a glove on you," Yvonne said, smiling.

"Makeup," Rosalie said. "Those bastards. How are you doing? And how is Kevin? And Tess?"

"We're all recovering. Kevin creaks a lot, though. I'm afraid he got the worst of it."

"Poor thing."

"You know, I was playing possum and heard one of them talk in a normal voice."

"Good for you. Did you recognize the voice?"

"No. But the police are coming to the house again tomorrow to pick our brains anyhow. Cripes, I am sick of this. What more do they think we can tell them?"

"I thought they had wrapped it up when they arrested Quince."

"I guess they want to be sure that the robbery isn't related to the drug ring. They're inclined to think it's just your plain-vanilla robbery. But Kevin and I don't think so."

"Ah. Why's that?"

"Well, for one thing, they didn't take the VCR."

Rosalie laughed. "That is odd."

"And they left a lot of the little kitchen appliances, too. It was like they were after something specific. Maybe looking for drugs there, too. I don't know. It makes my head ache to start thinking about it."

"You've been through hell," Rosalie said, patting Yvonne on her arm right where there was a big bruise.

Yvonne pulled her arm back. "Ooh. You got a sore spot."

"Oh, dear. I'm sorry. Oh, how clumsy! Listen, are you going to be in the office for a while? I'll be back late this afternoon. I'd like to talk to you then. You haven't changed your mind about going back to teaching, have you?"

"No, no," Yvonne said. A conversation with Rosalie frequently took some sharp turns.

"Too bad. See you later."

Yvonne watched her walk quickly across the sidewalk in front of the office and get into the back of her car, already cooled and waiting at the curb. Carlo, who worked in many capacities for Rosalie, today was driving a stretch limo.

Business must be good, Yvonne thought, entertaining briefly thoughts about real estate as a full-time venture.

There were two other salespeople in the office today: Merle Bentsen, a sixtyish man who specialized in commercial rentals; and Betty Cavendish, whose face was in a perpetual smile from numerous face-lifts, whose blond hair was always poufed and sprayed and windproof, and who flirted with every man who walked in the office, regardless of age. Betty rarely sold anything, but she took a lot of floor time and was good at answering phones, otherwise Rosalie would have sent her packing long ago. But real estate people don't get salaries, so Rosalie had an extra secretary, gratis. And Betty actually seemed flattered whenever Rosalie asked her to do something. Yvonne almost never talked at length to either Merle or Betty, but since they were very solicitous about Yvonne's injuries and the robbery, Yvonne felt obliged to talk to them about it for a little while. She also wanted to dispel the rumors, which Melba had told her about, that Kevin and Yvonne were all banged up because they had come to blows in their marital discord. Yvonne wondered where the story had started, and suspected one of the nurses in the emergency room of being the source.

When Yvonne got to her desk, she returned the more pressing phone calls. A psychiatrist was interested in one of the houses she had listed, but he wanted to hold therapy sessions in his basement. Yvonne told the saleswoman from another office that the zoning was okay for that, but that he might have a problem if there were too many cars parked outside all the time. The saleswoman was excited, Yvonne thought. She smelled a sale. Yvonne remembered when a sale would do that to her, but that thrill had gone now. It was only money, after all, for the salesperson; but for the people it was their house, their investment. For some, it was all they had. She couldn't think about customers as sources of money anymore. Maybe that meant that she wasn't a good saleswoman. Money drives the real estate machine. "You have to apportion your day to maximize your income," the teacher of the real estate course had said way back when Yvonne had first started.

No. I can't be that way, Yvonne thought. It wasn't the first time that she found herself going one way, and the crowd, the other.

Yvonne was eager to get to work on the computer. She would be able to buy a new one, the insurance adjuster had said, because she would get full coverage on the one the thieves had taken. After all, there was nothing to depreciate; it had been brand new, still in the box. Actually, she thought the insurance adjuster had been quite liberal in the allowances he had made for their losses. She had expected him to be a lot tougher.

Before she started work on the computer, Yvonne had one more item on her agenda. Melba had called to ask Yvonne to crew for Thursday's race, and Yvonne had said she would be delighted, but her arm was still bothering her and she thought she might be slow on the winches and lose the race for Scotty. Yvonne went next door to Scotty's office and found Scotty and Erik hunched over a computer terminal.

"My God, you're working," Yvonne said in mock horror.

Scotty turned a cheerful face toward Yvonne. "Hello, beautiful. Oh, you poor baby," he said, pointing to the bruised arm. "Come sit on Scotty's lap and let him console you," he said.

Yvonne laughed. "I came to tell you that my arm is bothering me and I don't want to lose the race for you if I'm too slow."

"You wouldn't lose the race for us. We do that for ourselves every week. Besides, Erik will do all the hard work. I want you to navigate."

Yvonne was flattered and said so. "I hope I can come up to your expectations," she said.

"He has the expectations of a dirty old man," Erik said. "But don't worry, I'll protect you."

"You two. . . . Hey, what have you got there? A new computer?" Yvonne was curious about new equipment in an office that seemed so quiet. Since it was the same brand as Rosalie's—and Yvonne's stolen machine—Yvonne wondered if hers had been fenced already.

"We ordered it last week and it just arrived," Scotty said.

Yvonne berated herself silently for her suspicions.

"Big R has been nagging me forever to hook into the twentieth century before it's the twenty-first," Scotty said. "We really can do wonders with it. We were just getting Cunard and the *Queen Elizabeth II* sailings on the screen. Wanna watch?"

"No, thanks. I've got to get to the green screen on the other side of the wall. I've got work to do. I'll be happy to navigate tomorrow. What time do you want me to show, Captain?"

"We can't sail on an empty stomach. We'll have an early dinner or late lunch at Chowder's at four-thirty. The race starts at six. You have to dine with the captain so that he can supervise your diet."

Yvonne laughed. "See you at four-thirty," she said and gave a little salute before she turned to go. She turned back, remembering that the police were coming tomorrow. "Listen, Scotty, I may be late. The cops are coming over to talk to us again."

"You people with criminal tendencies . . ." Scotty said.

"Rosalie told us the cops had it all wrapped up. What do they want with you guys now?" Erik said.

"That's what we thought. But they want to go through the whole thing again, in case the burglary at our house has any connection to the other stuff. I hope they get through it fast. Anyway, I'll meet you at the boat at six even if I have to bounce the cops out of my house bodily. If I get loose earlier, I'll meet you at Chowder's."

"Tell the cops that you have to discuss strategy with the captain," Scotty said.

"I'm sure they'll understand," Erik said.

"I'm beginning to wonder if they understand anything. At least so far as Kevin and I are concerned. They tell us to be careful, they say they are watching over us, and two guys come in and beat us up and clean us out."

"Yeah," said Scotty. "Big R says they really bashed Kevin."

"Yeah, they did. Me too. And your mother, although not quite as bad."

"Rosalie said they had on bright ski masks and jackets," Erik said.

"Yeah, and they mostly whispered," Yvonne said. "But I heard one talk in a normal voice when he thought I was unconscious."

"Good thing you didn't let him know you heard him," Scotty said. "They might have . . . well, they sound like bad guys."

"The worst," she said. "And one of them was very trim and wiry. He moved like a cat, even when he was carrying the big computer box."

"Oh, say, I was sorry to hear about your computer," Scotty said. "Big R said you hadn't even unpacked it. What a shame."

"The insurance will pay for most of it, but I won't have it set up and be working at home until September—if I'm lucky. Soooo I guess I'd better get next door and get to work. At least I did one thing right. I left the discs that I had copied Rosalie's office programs onto here in my desk, so I still have them."

"You're lucky Rosalie let you copy hers. When we told her we were getting our computer, she wouldn't let us use any of her systems," Erik said.

"She's probably got them refined so that they work specifically for real estate," Yvonne said.

"She's got some bookkeeping systems that would be useful," Erik said. He was pouting.

"Well, maybe she'll relent after a while," Yvonne said. "Gotta go."

Yvonne returned to her desk and started to run the programs for updating the listings. There hadn't been many sales during the summer, leaving a bumper crop of listings. That means a buyer's market, Yvonne thought, and when the sellers figure it out, they won't want to list their houses, because in a buyer's market you have to sell cheap. After she checked for the closing date for her listing that had sold, she started to research neighborhoods and price ranges that were selling.

After about an hour of slow going, wading through the electronic files and digging into the paper files that the rest of the staff used, Yvonne remembered that Rosalie had a program for this type of research.

Yvonne tried to remember which disc it was on and what the program was called. She started to search through the directories, trying to find the right file. She remembered that when she watched Rosalie use it, Rosalie had called up the file and then had just followed the instructions that were in it. Rosalie had set up a number of files that way, so that they would be easy for the office staff to use. "I have to set it up so that even Betty can use it," Rosalie had said.

Merle left the office at two and Betty left about a half hour later, leaving Yvonne alone. Yvonne was interrupted by the phones frequently, taking messages, making notations of who borrowed what key, who was showing what house. A couple of times she didn't get to answer a phone before whoever it was gave up. Finally the phones quieted down and Yvonne was able to concentrate on finding the program she wanted.

The office seemed colder than ever and when Yvonne looked outside, she saw that the sky was getting dark. Rain, she thought. It's probably getting colder outside, so in here it's like a refrigerator. She buttoned her sweater but shivered anyway.

She decided to turn down the air conditioner despite Rosalie's orders to the contrary. But the thermostat was in Rosalie's office, and the door was locked. When Yvonne looked through the glass panel that separated Rosalie's office from the rest of the room, she saw that Rosalie's computer terminal was on and hooked up to the phone.

Yvonne knew that the multiple-listing service sent out their updates early in the day, so what was the computer doing? Another crochet lesson, maybe. A bag of yarn was on the desk next to the terminal.

Yvonne could see why Rosalie would lock the door. Now that Scotty had his own computer, he might walk in and meddle with hers. Scotty had a mischievous streak, and he wasn't always considerate of things other people thought were important. He was capable of butting in on a crochet lesson and tripling the number of stitches in a sweater just for the fun of it.

Short of breaking into Rosalie's office, there was nothing Yvonne could do about the temperature. She considered going next door to borrow another sweater, but she really wanted to get on with what she was doing. So she went back to her search.

When she had gone through all of the discs but two, she hit a malfunction. At least, she thought that it was a malfunction. When she called up the directory on a disc labeled "East End," she got a list of supermarkets and malls that all seemed to be located on the eastern end of Long Island. When she tried to call up one of the files, none of the office programs worked. She tried file after file, but she could not get the computer to do anything except show the directory of the disc. Yvonne decided to ask Rosalie about the disc and go on to the last one.

Strange, though, Yvonne thought. This office has never done commercial real estate and never had any properties way out in Suffolk County.

Yvonne decided to have one more go at the East End disc. Perhaps she had copied the original incorrectly. She went to the cabinet where Rosalie kept the office working discs and took the box of discs over to her desk. She went through them one by one to make sure that everything she had copied coincided. But there was no East End disc in the office file.

Well, another question for Rosalie, she thought, and put back the office discs and began searching the last disc for the research program, which, of course, was right at the top of the directory, clearly labeled SERCHUS. Eureka! Yvonne thought, and slipped a disc of sales into the second disc drive.

In seconds the computer was racing through the lists and collecting the information she wanted. Yvonne was delighted and decided to print out her data. She could take that home to study. She hit another glitch in the system, though, when she tried to engage the printer. No dice. Then she remembered that Rosalie was using the modem and wondered whether that would interfere with the printer. She thought that Rosalie had mentioned something about needing more capability. Another question for Rosalie. Well, Big R would be along soon, Yvonne thought, remembering that Rosalie had something to talk to her about. Meanwhile, I can watch to see if that program that's running in Rosalie's office will shut down. Maybe then I'll be able to use the printer.

Yvonne would be able to tell when the program was done, because the light on the phone extension would go off. She picked up the phone and pushed the button next to the light. The phone was whistling and whining.

Yvonne wondered if she could tap into Rosalie's crochet lessons if she plugged her terminal into the phone. Would it show the same thing on this screen that it was showing on Rosalie's? I'm as bad as Scotty. Sticking my nose into someone else's business.

Her curiosity overcame her sense of propriety, and she hooked into the phone with her computer. The data on her disc began to get scrambled and she quickly disconnected.

She scolded herself for not realizing that the office programs wouldn't work with the East End disk. Yvonne realized that she had lost a good part of her research in her experiment and told herself about curiosity and the cat.

She intended to pick up the SERCHUS program and repair her data, but having picked up the East End disc in error and having called up the directory, she thought she'd try that disc with the modem, logic telling her that if the office programs didn't work, perhaps this odd disc would key into Rosalie's crochet lesson. Besides, she thought, the disc is missing from the office file. Maybe Rosalie is using it.

Yvonne congratulated herself on finding her way through the electronic thicket. The East End disc clicked into the modem and began spewing numbers and abbreviations across the screen. Yvonne took them to be the shorthand that crochet lessons are given in. But there were slashes and colons mixed in. An intricate pattern, Yvonne thought. But then it would have to be.

It certainly was a long crochet lesson. But why would a crochet lesson be coming in on a disc labeled "East End"? Yvonne couldn't very well ask Rosalie that question without admitting that she had been nosy.

Yvonne had corrected her research at about the time the light on the phone went out. She had just finished printing her information when Rosalie returned, looking harried and rushed.

"I have to talk to you," Rosalie said, after greeting Yvonne perfunctorily. Rosalie went directly to her office, where she reclosed the door and began to work at the terminal. Yvonne saw Rosalie talking angrily into the phone and then reattach the receiver to the computer modem.

Yvonne packed up her papers and tried to get Rosalie's attention to tell her that she was leaving. When Rosalie finally looked through the glass, her face bore an uncharacteristic worried expression, which was washed over by her habitual cheerful mask as soon as Yvonne caught her eye. Rosalie signaled Yvonne to wait and held up two fingers.

Yvonne waited, but more than two minutes, flipping through the research that she had printed. In the section of houses priced at half a million, Yvonne saw about a half page that looked like the crochet lessons.

Oh, God! I guess those discs aren't completely incompatible after all, she thought. Yvonne flipped to the next page—and hoped she didn't look too guilty—when she realized that Rosalie was coming out of her office.

"Sorry to keep you waiting, Yvonne dear. But some days I can't seem to shake loose from my list of shoulds. I feel I'm neglecting you. I had promised to get you started on your computer and then those yeggs walked off with it. I can give you more instruction here in the office, but of course this is all set up and all I can tell you is how we did it."

"I didn't do too badly today. I'm rather proud of myself," Yvonne said. "Although I have a long way to go to get in your league. I got all my discs to work except for the one marked 'East End.' That one doesn't respond to the same commands as the others. All it does is give the directory."

"Your discs? Where are they?"

"Lucky for me, and maybe for the office, too, the robbers didn't get the ones I programmed. I remember just before I went to Chowder's last Thursday I was thinking that I ought to stop in at the office to pick them up. With all the upheaval with Kevin I had just forgotten to take them home. I guess some things happen for the best," Yvonne said, but she was thinking again about DeeDee and resenting any divine plan that could countenance the terrible assault.

Rosalie smiled. "Oh, yes, lucky. I'd hate to have them fall into the wrong hands."

Yvonne returned the grin. "Does that include Erik and Scotty? Erik was complaining that you wouldn't lend him your software."

Yvonne thought Rosalie looked annoyed.

"Scotty, although I love him dearly, is like a bull in a china shop in all respects. I wouldn't lend him anything but the simplest electronic equipment. Something with one button that says, 'Push here.' As for Erik, he's too nosy. He'd be checking my bank balance before I even taught him how to log on."

Yvonne hoped her guilt didn't show when Rosalie mentioned nosiness.

"By the way," Yvonne said, "the East End disc isn't in the office file. I looked for it when I couldn't get mine to work. I thought maybe I'd made an error when I copied it."

"Ah yes, the East End disc. I was coming to that. It's in my office, but it seems to be malfunctioning. I wanted to ask you about that."

Yvonne was sure Rosalie knew about her electronic eavesdropping.

But Rosalie said, "Remember this morning I said I wanted to talk to you?" Rosalie's mood had shifted. She was talking excitedly, happily now. Without waiting for Yvonne to answer, she said, "We're invited to a little get-together on the East End. I have been so busy, and what with all your adventures, I didn't get around to telling you. Anyway, that rich client that I introduced you to a couple of weeks ago says he wants to work with you. Tonight he's having a cocktail party and he particularly asked me to bring you. It should be a good party. He has a great spot on a little peninsula that juts into the Sound."

"But I'll have to go home and change," Yvonne said.

"Oh no. You look fine. And it is getting late. Just because we'll be drinking champagne doesn't mean we have to dress formal. You will come, won't you. Especially if I apologize for not telling you sooner?"

Rosalie rattled on about how wealthy the guy was and how much he wanted to buy a place in Port Guinness, all the while packing up to leave and putting the office systems in their overnight mode. Yvonne realized that Rosalie had not waited for an answer; she had just assumed that Yvonne would comply.

Oh well, she is good to me, Yvonne thought. Sits with my dog. Lends me money. Listens to my troubles. Although I haven't really bent her ear about Kevin and me. Wonder why. Probably because I haven't seen her as much this summer. I stayed home and sulked too much. But she's been busy, too. She hasn't been in the office when I've been here.

"Carlo is waiting out back with the limo," Rosalie said.

"Uh, I could drive my own car."

"No, no. Carlo won't be drinking. You won't have to worry about driving under the influence. Come on. We'll have a wonderful time." Rosalie seemed ecstatic.

Yvonne gathered up her files and put the discs in her top drawer.

"Is that where you kept the discs to foil the thieves?"

"They've been there since I copied them."

"Did you use the East End disc at all today?"

Yvonne squirmed and was sure her face had reddened. "I tried to," she said. "It doesn't work the way the others do, though."

"No," Rosalie said. "It's not supposed to."

Yvonne wanted to blurt out the truth, but she was too embarrassed and uneasy. She hoped that Rosalie would explain the way the disc worked, would show her the crochet lessons. Then Yvonne wouldn't have to worry about letting anything slip. Yvonne regretted the mischief now. It was getting to be too big a thing.

17

Kevin cheated on four or five traffic lights, honked his horn when any car delayed him more than two seconds, drove more recklessly than he had since he was a teenager. When he was held up he shouted curses to himself. He followed the curses immediately with prayers: Dear God, just let me get there and see Vonnie's car in the parking lot, then find her safe in the office. Do that, and I'll make everything else up later.

At last, he was in the outskirts of the village of Port Guinness, driving by the pizza place where they had been regulars, past the hardware store, past the video-rental place. Finally, he turned a corner, one of the busiest and slowest in Port Guinness, and he could see the real estate office and the parking lot behind it.

And there was Vonnie's car. Thank you, God.

Kevin swung into the lot, steered into the space next to her car, saw a limousine parked at the end of the lot near the building. Probably for Rosalie, Kevin thought.

He got out and started walking toward the building, then saw Yvonne and Rosalie coming out of the office into the parking lot.

Rosalie saw him first and said something to Yvonne, who waved awkwardly.

Kevin waved back. What would he say to her? What the hell, Kevin thought. Try the truth.

"Kevin, what are you . . . ?" Yvonne began.

"What brings you here?" Rosalie said, smiling and poised.

"Hi, Rosalie, how are you? Vonnie . . ."

Yvonne cocked her head, as she often did when she was puzzled, and waited for him to go on. "We were just leaving, Kevin," she said.

"That's okay, I mean . . ." Don't lose it now, he told himself.

"We're taking a trip, Rosalie and I."

"On our way to Suffolk. A rich prospect invited me for a little gathering at his summer place on Smithtown Bay."

"He could be a really big prospect, Kevin. Rosalie says it could really help if he feels comfortable with me, too. In a business sense, I mean. You don't have to—"

"Yeah. Well, great. I guess. Uh, Vonnie, can we talk?"

"I'll wait in the limo," Rosalie said.

"Kevin, can this wait?"

"No. I had this feeling at work. Not just a feeling; I was talking to Landon Brice."

"And?"

"He knows everything that's going on. And he told me we had to be really careful. But I already felt that. I came over, praying you'd be okay. I tried to call."

"Well, the police are coming again tomorrow. We can go over it again with them. All of it." He's really wound up tight, Yvonne thought, feeling some of the same tension herself.

Kevin felt a gentle hand on his arm, turned and looked into Rosalie's face. Her smile was bright and inviting, despite the slight discoloration around her cheek.

"Rosalie, you too. You've got to watch. Look what they did to you the other night. . . ."

"Listen to me, both of you," Rosalie said. "I couldn't help but overhear." Rosalie gently pushed Kevin and Yvonne toward each other, kept her hands on their shoulders. "You two broke my heart when you separated, you want to know the truth. I know, I know, it's none of my business, but I love both of you. Well, we're not going to stop living, no matter what. Kevin, are you through with work for the rest of the day?"

"Yeah. I was so out of it, my editor sent me home."

"Excellent. Then it's settled. For old time's sake, tomorrow's sake, you're coming along."

"I hate to invite myself," Kevin said. In fact, he liked the idea of spending another evening close to Yvonne.

"You're not inviting yourself," Rosalie said. "I'm inviting you. Have to keep good relations with my close friends in the press. This guy is a terrific football fan. He'll love talking to you."

"Well, am I dressed okay?"

"Are you kidding?" Rosalie said. "He and his rich buddies wear cutoffs and Top-Siders all summer."

"Come on, Kevin," Yvonne said. "It'll help you unwind." For some reason, the idea of having Kevin along was appealing.

"No more arguments," Rosalie said. "Get in the limo. We're going the last leg of the trip on my boat. With any luck, there'll be a few interesting people there. I know there'll be plenty of booze and food."

Kevin was trying to work up to the idea of gulping champagne and devouring stuffed mushrooms and making totally harmless small talk about pro football. At least Vonnie would be close. "I never met a party I didn't like," he said, though this time he would have preferred just to be with Yvonne. On the other hand, he had fond memories of get-togethers with Rosalie and her rich clients.

"Carlo, if you please!" Rosalie said to the chauffeur in her social-organizing voice.

The chauffeur, Carlo, a lean, wiry man who looked as if he could have been a welterweight boxer, smiled and opened the door wide. Yvonne got in the back, followed by Kevin. The chauffeur, businesslike behind dark glasses, nodded and smiled.

The limo seats were deep and comfortable. Kevin and

Yvonne touched hands for a moment, smiled and settled back.

"This is all right," Kevin said, feeling some of the tension drain out of him.

"So what got you so strung out?" Yvonne asked.

Before he could answer, Rosalie settled into the front seat, turned to them and said, "Excuse me. Let me give you a little privacy, and I'll make a few phone calls." She smiled as a transparent plastic shield slid up into place between the front and rear seats. Then Carlo got in and the limo took off.

"Strung out," Kevin said. "The other night, those guys. There's gotta be a connection. Landon was sure Quince isn't the end of it. Like today . . ." He started to tell her about the two men who had been burned in the car but decided it wouldn't help. "Anyhow, I got worried about you."

"Well, I'm here and I'm okay, and I'm going to be careful. Just don't act too hyper, okay? There might be some people there who are important to Rosalie."

"I promise not to get drunk."

"You've said that before."

"Yeah, well, I guess you have a point. A small one. Maybe I'll get drunk tonight anyhow."

"Well, if you want to loosen up a bit tonight I guess we both deserve it. And we're not driving."

They tried to relax in the quiet, cool isolation.

"I could learn to travel like this," Yvonne said. "How did they treat you at work your first day back?"

"Okay. Couple people gave me funny looks, because of my face. I was vague when they asked questions. Talked to Chili Wilkins about the Jets's pass coverage."

"He's the one in the United Way commercials."

"He got me started worrying. He hears a lot."

"What?"

"When we were talking he told me rooting out drugs is like chopping wild berries—"

"Kevin, look!"

The limo had stopped. Kevin leaned over to see a couple of dozen geese waddling lazily across the road. Duck and

geese crossings were so commonplace around Port Guinness that the village fathers had erected diamond yellow
crossing signs like those near schools, except that the signs
pictured ducks and geese.

"Cute," Kevin said.

"Oh, they are so darling . . ."

After a minute or so, Carlo shook his head impatiently
and honked his horn. Several of the last geese jumped for a
moment, then proceeded indignantly.

Kevin and Yvonne saw Rosalie scold her chauffeur.

"Good for her," Kevin whispered. "I like people who
watch out for animals."

"That's why she's such a wonderful dog-sitter. Next to
us, Tess loves her more than anyone."

"I'm really glad we still have Tess with us." Something
stirred in Kevin's mind, then was gone.

"You were telling me about your talk with Chili
Wilkins," Yvonne said. She was trying to make conversation; actually, she had much, much less interest in football
than Kevin.

"We started out talking football, and he told me there's at
least one big star who retired last year because he's a coke
head. Not that that's so startling in itself, it's just . . ."

"You thought you heard everything like that."

"Well, yeah. I guess really I know I don't hear every
single thing. But it made me wonder what else I don't know.
So I got worried."

Through the transparent divider, they heard a gentle,
regular beep. Rosalie picked up the phone. Kevin and
Yvonne could make out a few words: ". . . yes, she has a
binder. . . . Stove stays and refrigerator goes. . . ."

"She's always working," Yvonne said. "That's how she
got where she is."

"She really bounced back from getting punched around,"
Kevin said.

Yvonne put her hand on his: a friendly gesture.

"I'm glad you don't mind my coming along," Kevin
said.

"I'm glad for your company."

They saw Rosalie nod and hang up. A minute later, they came to a stop sign. Carlo slid open the divider, looked at Kevin and smiled understandingly. "How about them dog-ass Jets," the chauffeur said. "Looks like a long season."

"Dog-ass Jets!" Kevin said, delighted that someone else had heard that old nickname. "Yeah, they're hurting."

"You hear anybody who wants to buy tickets, you send them to me," Carlo said. "I'll sell mine."

"You got it."

"Dog-ass Jets," Carlo said again, closing the divider.

The sky looked threatening. Kevin said he almost hoped it would storm, because there were few things more thrilling than being on the water in thunder and lightning. Yvonne told him (only half kidding) to shut up, because he shouldn't tempt fate. Rosalie's boat was big enough to hold up under any weather. But still . . .

"Oh, I meant to tell you about my day with the computer," Yvonne whispered. She felt like crowing a bit about her electronic success. She also told Kevin about the East End disk and how she had butted in on Rosalie's crochet lesson.

"I even got a printout of her lesson in the middle of my listing data. I wish I understood more about the way the computer works."

"Damn. Makes me feel old sometimes. There's people in my office who never worked on a typewriter. They've never seen a printer handling trays of type, reading them upside down and backward. I still remember the first week we had computers in our office. . . ."

Yvonne had heard the story before, but it would be a long trip to the party.

"Saturday afternoon, early October. Lots of college-football and baseball play-offs. And lots of political stories. And then it rained. Thunder and lightning."

"Tell me what happened next, Kevin," Yvonne said, teasing.

He laughed. "Zap, is what happened. Big lightning bolt, blank screens. All the computer wizards running around with worried looks, their pants filling up with—"

"Shhh!"

"Right. After an hour they said, 'All fixed.' Then the end of a political story showed up in the Notre Dame–Purdue game. I love it, how the computers have their own logic."

"That's like what happened to me today. The computer had its own logic. I bet Rosalie could tell me. If I had the nerve to ask her."

"Why can't you ask her?"

"I was in an unauthorized file, I think."

"You mean you were being nosy?"

"It was sort of accidental. I just put in the wrong disk. While it was in the computer, I tried to use it. I butted into Rosalie's crochet lesson, and I think she knows it."

"So? What's the big deal?"

"I got the feeling she had to start the lesson all over again. Anyhow, she asked me what I'd been doing."

"And you told her. So?" Kevin was as interested in crochet as Yvonne was in professional football.

"I didn't tell her everything. The computer spewed part of her lesson into my research. I hope I didn't do any damage."

"Probably not. Computers are tougher than that."

"I want the insurance check to come. So I can get a new computer."

"And a TV set. At least they left the VCR."

"Pretty selective burglars. When they took the computer they took the box of discs too." Yvonne felt a slight, inexplicable shiver go through her. Before she could pin her thoughts down, the limo swung into a service station. It stopped at a row of pumps, and Rosalie slid back the screen.

"We'll just be a minute," Rosalie said.

Just before Rosalie swung the screen into the closed position again, Carlo opened his door to get out. A tiny breeze blew in, past Yvonne's face, just enough breeze to carry a familiar smell. Yes, of course. Musk! And that other smell. Cedar! Of course, cedar! That's what I smelled the other night.

"Maybe I'll go to the john," Kevin said.

Before Yvonne could stop him, Kevin was out of the

limo. Yvonne looked out the left side and saw Carlo chatting with the teenager pumping gas. Carlo was graceful. Though Yvonne tried not to make too many comparisons, most men moved more gracefully than Kevin. Still, Carlo was something else altogether. Quick and catlike. And strong: Yvonne could see that easily. Had she imagined recognizing the smell? No, she didn't think so.

God in heaven, Carlo was built like one of the men from the other night. Think, Yvonne told herself. Think. You're the logical one. Pretend you're talking to the police, and you're remembering everything you can. Damn it, I wish Kevin would hurry. I need to filter this through him. He doesn't always let logic get in his way. . . .

Of course. The insurance man had noticed it. The burglars hadn't bothered to take the VCR, but they had taken the computer. More than that: They had taken the box of discs, which weren't all that expensive. There was nothing special about them, except . . .

What had Kevin said? Something about the computers in his office going bonkers and a lot of unexpected stuff coming out. . . .

Yvonne watched Carlo get back into the car.

She managed a faint smile as Carlo's eyes in the mirror met hers. Carlo looked away, then his eyes darted back to the mirror, catching her stare again. Was he measuring her reactions? She had to say something. . . .

"Did you pay already?" She managed not to stammer.

"Rosalie's gonna pay," Carlo said matter-of-factly. "As soon as she's done on the phone."

On the phone? "But . . ." Yvonne started to say, *There's a phone right here in the car*.

Kevin moistened a paper towel and wiped his face. He studied himself in the mirror. Well, he didn't look too bad to go to a party; maybe he would tell people he'd fallen on his boat or something if they asked about his bruises.

Kevin was feeling less enthusiastic about the evening. What he really wanted to do now was go home—home to the house, not his apartment—and have one or two beers. Maybe bring Tessie up on the sofa with him.

Kevin felt his memory stir. It was like the feeling he'd had at the goose crossing. He would have to talk to Vonnie about it.

The hum from the fluorescent light over the sink sounded like a computer.

Computers, computers. The computer in Vonnie's office. Vonnie's own computer, stolen. By people who beat the hell out of us and trashed our house. First they put the dog out of commission. They had to know the dog was there. They came prepared with a tranquilizer. She was knocked out quietly.

I have to run this by Vonnie. Breathe deep and think.

He walked back to the limo. Carlo got out to open the door for him, then stood outside.

"Where's Rosalie?" Kevin said.

"Making a phone call. Something's wrong."

"I know, I feel it."

"Carlo smells like one of the men from the other night. Cedar. That's what the other smell was. He moves the same."

"Can that be?"

"How many men do you think I've smelled, for God's sake?"

"Oh, Jesus. We have to tell Rosalie."

"Here she comes. Don't tell her yet."

Carlo opened the door, closed it when Rosalie was seated. Rosalie slid the screen open. "We'll have a good time," she said. "I'm glad Kevin could make it."

"Me too," Kevin said.

Kevin's and Yvonne's hands met in the middle of the seat.

"Did you tell me how many people will be there?" Yvonne said.

"A few dozen maybe." Rosalie kept smiling.

Kevin tried to smile back at Rosalie, but she saw something in his face, and her expression changed.

"I'm still a little sore from the other night," Kevin said. "Inside of my mouth was cut."

"Ah. I was a lot luckier."

"Well, a drink will make me feel better," Kevin said.

Rosalie slid the screen shut.

Rain had begun to lash the windows. The drops and the rhythm of the windshield wipers created enough noise that Kevin and Yvonne dared to speak to each other quietly.

"Something's wrong," Kevin whispered.

"I know. Tell me your feelings, and don't waste any words."

"Somebody knew we had a dog."

"Carlo."

"Would Carlo . . . ? Would he beat up Rosalie? Wouldn't she know him? You recognize him now. Your computer, Vonnie . . ."

"The burglars wanted my computer, and the discs. Look." Yvonne slid a page of her printout toward Kevin. "The East End disc has a list of shopping malls and plazas," she whispered. "It was running all afternoon. I butted in, and this is what came out."

Kevin looked down at the sheet and frowned. "Numbers and letters. Do you know what they mean?"

"Looks like crochet abbreviations. SC for single crochet, DC for double, CH for chain. But Rosalie is much more advanced than that, and I don't understand all of it. The symbols and numbers."

Kevin studied the colons and slashes. "Dates and times?"

"In a crochet lesson? In a disc about malls on the East End?"

"Not a crochet lesson. What did you tell her about your discs?"

"That I put them in the drawer. I had them in the office all the while. That the men the other night didn't get them."

"You snooped in her computer. You intercepted something."

"Intercepted?"

"You loused up her transmission. That's how drug

deliveries are set up. By computer, at the last minute. That's how they move it so fast."

"You're saying Rosalie . . ."

Through the plastic screen, as Rosalie talked business with Carlo, Kevin saw the familiar tough set of her jaw. Yes, Rosalie was a tough one, all right, and she had bounced back so quickly from getting beaten up. . . .

"Rosalie never got hit as bad as we did," Kevin said.

"No. We went to the hospital. She didn't."

"What about tonight? This rich guy's place on the water?"

"I was only invited after I asked about the East End disc."

"There isn't any party," Kevin said. "She just wants to get us on her boat. She must be the next layer. Quince's boss."

"The first chance we get, we run. Anywhere. Keep smiling. Just keep smiling."

The limo turned off the highway onto a two-lane road toward a boatyard. Rosalie slid the partition open. "Almost there," she said.

Kevin and Yvonne had always boarded Rosalie's boat at the Port Guinness Yacht Club. They didn't know the road they were on now, didn't know the boatyard they were entering.

The limo stopped. Carlo got out and opened the door for Rosalie. "Come right down to the dock," she said, smiling.

Carlo opened the door for Yvonne, who got out and stood on shaking knees. Kevin slid across the seat, got out slowly and saw something in Carlo's expression and stance that revealed a second's worth of carelessness.

In that second, Kevin pushed the door into Carlo, who was knocked back against the side of the limo before falling to the ground.

"Run," Kevin said.

They did, heedless of the gravel that seemed to stab at the bottoms of their feet. They fled toward a jungle of boats, putting themselves farther from the road.

Yvonne stumbled, felt a sick emptiness in her stomach but righted herself before her knees touched the ground.

"Jesus, Vonnie." He was not angry with her, only alarmed. Now he wondered—insanely—if he should tell her he was not mad, before it was too late to tell her anything.

"I love you," he said. His voice sounded crazy in his ears.

"Run," she said, so breathless she thought she might faint. To herself she said: God, just give us another chance at life, and I promise . . .

Shouts, other feet on the gravel behind them.

Just ahead lay a long gray metal building. To its right, as they approached it, lay an area mostly open except for a few boat cradles. They ran toward the building's left, where there was a virtual forest of cradled boats—old, new, plastic, wood, power, sail.

They sprinted into the maze of boats, less clumsily now because the ground surface was more hard sand than gravel.

Shouts again, behind them, slightly farther away.

"*Aquí! Aquí!*" a pursuer shouted. (Here, here, Kevin remembered.)

"Hide. We have to hide," Yvonne breathed. "Can't run away. Can't surprise them. Not anymore . . ."

"There," Kevin said. He pointed to an ancient wooden sloop that rested atop a tar-stained cradle. Boat and cradle looked forgotten, forlorn. Around the base of the cradle, directly under the hull that showed chalklike stains from barnacles long gone, weeds grew knee-high.

Kevin and Yvonne crawled under the boat, Kevin banging his right knee on something metallic as they knelt. "Oh, damn . . ." His knee hurt.

Yvonne saw that he had bumped into an old half-gallon paint can. She picked it up; someone had left paint in it. A weapon? It was heavy enough to do some damage.

Rubbing his knee as he crawled low, Kevin peered through the weed tops, scanning the boatyard, as much as he could see of it.

"Aquí, aquí." The voices were farther away now, but still between their hiding place and escape.

And where was Rosalie?

The voice again. Still distant.

"I haven't heard her voice," Yvonne whispered.

"No. She could be anywhere. Maybe waiting for us to head back to the road."

The air was getting colder and it smelled of rain. Thunder rolled across the sky like a barrel.

"If it storms, they won't be able to hear us. Maybe we can hide longer."

"But not forever." Kevin didn't finish his thought: that a storm could also drown out the sounds of guns—or screams.

Kevin was scanning the yard through the weeds. Deeper into the maze, about fifty feet away, a gleaming white-and-blue twenty-six-foot O'Day sloop rested in a pristine cradle. The boat had a "For Sale" sign hanging from one side. In late summer, every yard had a couple of spanking-new boats put on the market by first-time owners lured by the romance of the water but turned off by the reality of maintenance.

A shiny aluminum stepladder stood next to the boat. If they could get there, they could climb into the cockpit and pull the ladder up after them and be out of sight.

"There, Vonnie. That's where we want to be."

Yvonne agreed.

The voices were still on the other side of the long gray building. Thunder rolled over the Sound, closer this time.

"Maybe we should try now," Kevin said.

It was almost a question, Yvonne thought, hearing the fear in his voice, and knowing (how many times had this happened before?) that she must help him be braver than he imagined he could be.

"Right now. Quick and quiet," she said. It was not that she was braver, just that she saw the truth.

Kevin stood up and peered as far as he could down the aisles of cradles. Nothing in sight.

"Let's go," Yvonne said.

Kevin saw Yvonne pick up the paint can. "Good," he said, thinking she meant to bring it as a weapon.

Yvonne had another idea, had figured the odds were against their being able to get to the boat, get up the ladder, and pull the ladder up after them without being seen. Unless . . .

She took a deep breath, remembering her days of playing softball, and flung the can as hard as she could in the opposite direction from their route to the boat.

Kevin could hardly believe his eyes as he watched the can hurtle through the air, over the near corner of the long gray building, landing with a clatter out of sight.

It worked. As Kevin and Yvonne moved across the open space to the foot of the ladder, they heard the voices move toward the noise of the can. Kevin steadied the ladder as Yvonne scrambled up. He shook with fright as he climbed, and for a moment thought the ladder would topple. Then he was in the boat and he and Yvonne were hauling the ladder into the cockpit out of sight. They folded it quietly and let it come to rest on the floor where they hunkered down as the thunder rolled in closer. The sky had turned purple and the air was sharp and cold.

The voices were still distant.

"Where's Rosalie?" Kevin whispered.

"Somewhere waiting for us to make a mistake."

More thunder, the voices closer.

Kevin took Yvonne's hand. "I'm sorry I screwed up so much," he said. "I'm sorry I chased you away."

I'm the one living in the house, she thought, not him. But she knew what he meant. But now's not the time to dredge it up. Or is it? Maybe it's the only time we have left. A chill shook her. She pulled her hand away, but brushed his arm as she did so. "Let's think of ways to stay alive," she said.

They looked around the cockpit. It still had the plastic new-boat smell. There were lockers on both sides, under the seats, but they were all secured by tough bronze marine locks.

"Maybe there's something below, in the galley, something we can use," Yvonne said. "A radio. Maybe a radio."

Kevin thought that was unlikely but didn't say so.

The entrance to the galley was covered with three interlocking boards. A sliding panel was fastened to the top board by a hasp with a lock on it, a typical arrangement for a boat this size.

"Stay quiet," Yvonne said. "Just stay quiet."

The voices, shouts, and swearing in Spanish seemed closer. They heard wood thumping on the ground, then wood against wood, a sawhorse being moved, maybe, and not that far away.

Kevin tried to think straight. There were dozens of boats in the yard. How long would it take to check every one? A long time. But not forever. The pursuers had the time—no one else was likely to come into the yard, not with the sky darkening and the thunder growling closer.

From a couple of hundred feet away came a noise that brought Kevin and Yvonne face-to-face, eyes and mouths agape: the metallic rattle followed by a plastic thunk.

It told them their pursuers had found another ladder.

Oh, think, Yvonne pleaded with herself. Block out your heartbeat.

"We have a chance below in the galley," she said, sounding cooler than she felt. "Even if they get to this part and look into the cockpit."

"But how do we get in?" Then he noticed the small unlocked hatch at the stern. Even before he opened it, he knew some of the things he'd find: a few old rags, a sponge, a coffee can, pieces of line.

An old screwdriver! "Lucky," Kevin said. It was rusted, a foot long, and as thick as a man's little finger.

Out in the yard, closer, another metallic clatter, then footfalls on a ladder. *"Nada."*

Louder thunder.

They could shout for help, but no one would hear. Except for their pursuers, they were alone in a sprawling boatyard. It was late in the season, late on a workday, and a storm was coming.

Yvonne looked at Kevin and nodded.

"If they come here, stick the screwdriver through the first

hand you see," Yvonne said. "Then we'll try to jump out the other side and . . ."

But Kevin had another use for the screwdriver. He knelt next to the galley hatchway and jammed the screwdriver under the hasp and pried.

Another ladder noise, closer.

"Kevin . . ." she whispered.

"Our Father . . ." he breathed. The wood made a soft ripping sound, and the hasp screws pulled loose.

"Good," Yvonne said. "It won't be that easy to see when we slide the panel back."

Kevin started to pull up the boards so that they could climb down, but Yvonne slithered over the top and dropped into the galley. Kevin followed and slid the top panel back, holding the torn-away hasp till it cleared the top board.

"I hope they don't notice that the hasp is just hanging there," Kevin said.

"At the rate they're going from boat to boat . . . maybe they won't."

The cabin smelled of new upholstery and a trace of mildew.

"I don't see a radio," Yvonne said.

Kevin looked through one of the long, shallow windows, seeing only cradles and boats and a flash as lightning danced over the Sound. Thunder crashed overhead, then silence, then tap, tap . . .

"Here it comes," said Yvonne, as raindrops hit, heavy as coins.

Kevin opened the door to the V-berth in the bow of the boat. Just what he expected: the anchor nestled far forward on coils of line, a plastic paddle, winches along the shelves, a life preserver, a couple of full sailbags, a sparkling white ring buoy—all of it spread on bright cushions.

Thunk. Over the sound of the rain, a ladder hitting the side of a boat. Closer now. The voices again. Men's voices.

The paddle could be a weapon, Kevin thought. Then he saw it, partly concealed by a sailbag. It was an orange plastic cylinder about a foot and a half long: a standard Coast Guard–approved distress kit.

"Flares," Kevin said.

Kevin pulled it open and dumped the contents onto the cushions: a pistol and a packet of cartridges. He picked up the pistol, broke it open with trembling hands.

"Oh, Kevin . . ." Yvonne took the packet and bit through the plastic wrap holding the cartridges. They were red, thumb-thick, like shotgun shells.

Kevin took one cartridge from Yvonne, plunged it into the chamber, snapped the pistol shut.

"What's to lose?" he said. The scraping of the ladder was only a few yards away now.

"Go for it," she said. "They're over there, so shoot it out the starboard porthole."

Kevin opened the porthole, pointed the pistol at the purple sky and squeezed the trigger.

He felt Yvonne's face next to his as they watched the tiny rocket hurtle through the rain with a pop-pop-pop, trailing sparks.

Several hundred feet up, the shell burst like a firecracker, a huge hissing orange light leaving behind it a plume of bright smoke as it fell slowly earthward.

Voices from the ground, closer.

"Fire another, Kevin."

He broke open the pistol, chucked the smoking empty shell onto the cabin floor, plunged home another flare cartridge, closed the pistol, put his arm through the porthole and fired again into the rain. This time, the shell did not go straight up, angling off instead toward the road before it burst.

"Again, Kevin. Someone has to see."

"We only have two shells left." He loaded one into the gun.

Then Kevin spotted a propeller peeking out from a narrow storage space. "There's an outboard motor," he said.

"So?"

"If the guy's got a spare motor, he might have a gas can on board."

Kevin scrambled into the galley, banging his head on the

V-berth door. "Son of a bitch," he said, rubbing his scalp. "They're getting closer."

He flung aside the cushion over the starboard bench to get at the storage hold below. He opened the hold, but all he found was a couple of charts and a few yachting magazines.

By that time, Yvonne had got to the storage hold on the port side. She opened the hatch and saw the red can.

"Here, Kevin, but it's almost empty."

Kevin saw a smaller can in the hold and picked it up. Almost full. It was alcohol fuel for a galley stove.

Voices closer outside, and the sound of a stepladder clanging against a nearby boat.

"A fire," Kevin said. "We're going to set a fire if those bastards come on the boat. Come on."

They went into the V-berth, and Kevin latched the door that separated it from the galley. The latch could stand one or two hard shoves from a strong man, but no more than that.

Kevin took one sailbag and set it against the door. He poured some of the alcohol on the bag, then he set the gasoline can on top of the bag. He emptied the small can so that some of the alcohol splashed over the gasoline can.

"What are you doing?"

"Fumes," he said. "We can set off the fumes in the gas can."

Kevin knew the small brass screw on top of the gas can was meant to ventilate vapors that always build up inside a gasoline container, even a nearly empty one. He turned the ventilating screw slightly. A high-pitched whistle filled the V-berth.

"Okay," he said, retightening the screw.

A ladder slammed against the side of the boat.

The V-berth smelled of alcohol and gasoline fumes and fear sweat.

Kevin stuck the last flare cartridge in his pocket. "We go up through the hatch when we hear them in the galley. We don't want to cut it too close."

The boat shook as the pursuers climbed the ladder and landed in the cockpit. Curses and shouts as they pulled out the hatch cover. Loud thumps as the men jumped into the galley. "Here! Here!"

Yvonne opened the hatch, stood up so that her head was exposed to the wind and rain and her hands were resting on the outside of the boat. She hoisted herself up and out and stood up on the deck. She looked toward the ground, directly into the face of Carlo, who was waiting next to the boat with another man. Carlo and his friend (they were the pair from the other night, Yvonne knew) stared at her. A blade gleamed in Carlo's hand. Their clothes were soaked and their skin glistened in the rain.

"Kevin!"

"Here I come!"

He stood up, feeling raindrops on his face. As he was climbing out, he heard the slam against the V-berth door, once, twice. He banged his left leg but still managed to get it up and out. As he hauled himself up, right leg still dangling in the boat, the V-berth door burst open.

The sailbag fell softly on its side, the gas tank clattered to the floor and hands grabbed his right leg. Kevin kicked furiously, freeing his leg for a moment, and before the hands could get a good grip again he pointed the flare pistol below and pulled the trigger.

A light as bright as a welder's torch flashed in the V-berth. Then several things happened nearly at once. There was a loud metallic whump as the whole boat shook. The red gas tank flew up and slammed into the ceiling of the V-berth, just missing Kevin's dangling leg. Kevin managed to get his leg up and out of the boat, an instant ahead of the red-orange flame tongues that hissed out of the opening. Kevin lost his balance, and he expected to fall onto the bow. Instead, a moment after his shoulder came down hard on the boat, he found himself looking at the sand.

"Kevin!"

The thud knocked the wind out of him. The next thing he knew, he was lying on his back, staring up at the flames that flicked higher and higher into the rain. He heard shouts of rage and pain from inside the boat. As if in a dream he thought, someone's on fire. An odd sort of peace came over him; he knew that, even if he could get up, he couldn't run fast enough to get away. No, he couldn't. He hoped Vonnie would understand.

A pair of feet landed in the sand a couple of feet from Kevin's head, and then he was looking up into Vonnie's face. He thought she looked very beautiful in a way he had never seen before and surely never would again: hair and skin wet, catching points of light from the flames, her mouth and eyes set in determination despite the fear. . . .

"Kevin, the flare!"

Oh, yes. "Pocket," he heard himself say. He raised himself up a little, and Vonnie pulled the flare out. Then he felt his fingers being twisted as she pulled the gun out of his grasp.

"Stay away! I mean it, goddamn you!"

As she reloaded the flare gun, she faced Carlo and another man whose tattered shirt had singe marks. Another man knelt several yards away, holding out his bare burned arms to the cooling rain.

"Stay away!"

She backed away from the boat. She was aware of the smell of burning plastic and burned hair. The flames from the boat hissed in the rain.

Kevin started to crawl toward Yvonne, tried to get up, but one knee buckled.

"We're all going for a boat ride," Carlo said.

"No, we are not," Yvonne said. She backed up another step, but the three men were not coming after her. They stood behind Kevin, and Carlo knelt down next to him.

Carlo held up his knife. "End of argument," he said to Yvonne. "You and your shit-for-brains husband can come with us on the boat, or we can leave him here with an extra hole in his throat and just bring you along."

"Where's Rosalie? We were friends. She wouldn't let you—"

"Look, you stupid bitch. Make up your mind."

In the distance a siren. No, more than one. Yvonne read urgency on Carlo's face.

"You decide right now," Carlo said.

Kevin had regained a little strength, and he knew he could push up with the leg that had buckled under him only a moment ago. They were not going on any boat ride, and no one was going to cut his throat. . . .

Carlo reached around Kevin with his free arm, started to bring the knife in for the cut.

Kevin lashed out with one elbow, pushed up with one leg, rolled onto the wet sand, out of the way.

Carlo started to go after Kevin again, but before he could get close with the knife, Yvonne stepped forward.

"No!" she shouted.

All the pain and fear she and Kevin had endured, all the guilt she had felt over the slashing of DeeDee Lockwood crystallized for Yvonne. The feeling was enough to make her point the flare pistol at Carlo and pull the trigger.

Carlo shrieked as the flare buried itself in his shoulder. He went on screaming as he flopped like a fish on the wet sand, grabbing at the flare that sizzled yellow, hissing in the rain as it cooked his flesh.

And Yvonne screamed, because she could not bear Carlo's agony, could not bear the thought of what she had done. She screamed again, her scream caught up now in the sirens from the fire truck and police cars that were racing into the boatyard.

Carlo's companions had run into the thicket of boat cradles, toward the water and the boat where Rosalie must have fled.

Carlo's shrieks subsided to moans as the flare burned itself out. His head lolled to one side and his eyes closed.

Kevin had stood up, and he put his arm around Yvonne.

"Look," Kevin said.

A big powerboat, a sixty-footer at least, was backing away from the pier in a hurry. The sides scraped against pilings, sending the vessel's rubber fenders into the water with splash after splash. Kevin and Yvonne heard the sound of other boats' rigging and trim being ripped away as the big boat swung around to head for open water.

"Rosalie," Yvonne said. "Rosalie."

Now there were other sirens, from the water. Kevin and

Yvonne recognized the blue-and-orange trim on the Nassau County Police boats. Several men carrying rifles and shotguns stood on the bows as they blocked the big boat's exit.

Shivering in the rain, Kevin and Yvonne saw two ambulance attendants put Carlo on a stretcher, cover him with a blanket and take him away.

A man in a raincoat stood behind Kevin and Yvonne, placed his gentle hands on their shoulders. Could this be? Yes. "Let me take you inside somewhere," federal agent Bleucher said gently.

18

The Hudson was a choppy glistening silver. They were glad for the sunshine, because without it the wind would have made for a chilly day. Even with the sun, they wore sweatshirts.

"Feel the autumn," Kevin said as they walked down the pier at the Tansytown Yacht Club.

"I feel it," Yvonne said.

"Hello, boat," Kevin said, stepping on board. The boat had been returned almost to the very spot where they had left it weeks ago.

"You have the keys, I hope," Yvonne said.

"Hey, have I ever forgotten them?" He had, once.

Kevin unlocked the hatch entry and went below. Kneeling, he pulled up the floorboard that covered the bilge. "We got a little water here," he said.

It took them not quite five minutes to pump out the bilge.

"I think the boat's glad to see us," he said.

"How can you tell?"

"Oh, I just feel it."

"Well, I'm glad to see it too. Even though it's almost time to put it up for the season."

Something obvious, but until then overlooked, flashed in Kevin's mind. "Hey . . ."

"I know. We have to make arrangements with another boatyard for winter storage. The next owner of Harvey's yard will probably go upscale anyhow."

"Damn. We may not find anyone as cheap. . . ."

What would next season be like? he mused. Next season. They had not even had *this* season.

Kevin had shared a bottle of wine with Vonnie the previous night as they had dinner and a long talk. He still felt a glow, more from the talk than the wine.

Kevin struck the gearshift into place (trying not to remember the time he had used the metal shaft to crush someone's hand), and turned the ignition.

The Pearson's engine came to life at once. Harvey had been a good mechanic.

Vonnie uncleated the forward line and pushed the bow out.

"Ready on the engine?" Yvonne said.

"Ready."

Yvonne loosened the stern line, pushing the stern out as she stepped from the pier to the cockpit.

Kevin backed clear of the pier. Then he swung the bow around and they started down the short channel that led to the Hudson.

"I hereby pronounce you free of impoundment," Kevin said.

"It's good to have her back," Yvonne said.

"Nice of Bleucher to give us a ride over here."

"Maybe he's trying to make up for how he acted in Hackensack."

"I got that impression."

When it was all over that day in the Long Island boatyard, Bleucher had driven them to the police station, sat them down in an office, and brought them coffee.

"So, this time we're not suspects?" Yvonne said acidly.

"Of course not," Bleucher said. "We thought you'd like to know what happened."

"What we really need is dry clothes and a stiff drink," Kevin said.

"No, I want to hear this," Yvonne said.

"We'll get you some blankets from the cellblock," Bleucher said.

"Terrific," Kevin said.

"Well . . . after we started questioning Quince and the guys who were arrested over in Jersey, things started to come together.

"I have to admit, we couldn't figure you two out at first. Then that poor woman was beaten and slashed in Jersey. We didn't think you had done it. The Edgecliff police interviewed her neighbors and found one who remembered her saying she was meeting a couple of old friends and one of them was staying overnight."

Kevin and Yvonne nodded.

"As I said, we didn't think you had hurt her; it made no sense. Kevin, you mentioned two men boarding the boat while you were sleeping, how they rooted around in the galley area."

"And jumped off when a police boat came by to shut up a bunch of drunks," Kevin said.

"Yes. Well, we checked, and sure enough, a marine patrol unit recalled a minor incident with some partygoers. So we asked ourselves, how come those guys didn't look through the entire boat? The answer is, they didn't have to look through the boat. Because Harvey sent them.

"We know who the people working with Harvey were," Bleucher went on. "Ernesto Lunes and Felipe de Leon."

"The roasts on the LIE," Kevin said.

"Roasts?" Yvonne said.

"Yes, burned in a car," Bleucher said. "We think that when they couldn't contact Harvey, they went into hiding. But they couldn't hide from Rosalie. They didn't even know who she was."

Kevin recalled what Chili Wilkins had said: "I don't know who they are. I just know they are."

"What about the guys who roughed us up at the marina?" Kevin said.

"Quince sent them," Bleucher said. "They were there when Harvey was deep-sixed. Harvey told Quince you two didn't know anything about the stuff on the boat. But by that time Harvey had told so many lies—"

"To save his life," Yvonne said.

"To save his life," Bleucher said. "He told so many lies, Quince didn't know if you were in on it or not."

"Neither did you," Kevin said. "But if Quince had already talked to Harvey, how come Quince's men at the Haviland Marina didn't know where the stuff was?"

"Harvey never told where it was," Bleucher said. "He kept saying he didn't know, because if he had told—"

"He would have been admitting he'd put it there," Yvonne said.

"Exactly. So he waffled back and forth, digging himself in that much deeper, until Quince was done with him."

Kevin and Yvonne sipped their coffee and wrapped themselves in the blankets a deputy brought.

"As for Miss Lockwood . . ."

"Poor DeeDee," Yvonne said.

"They thought you had delivered the drugs there. Obviously they didn't find them, so they continued to tail you."

"I'll always feel guilty about dragging her into this," Yvonne said.

Kevin shook his head.

Bleucher spoke quietly. "None of this was your fault. A broken sink fitting? If Harvey hadn't put the drugs on your boat, that's all it would have been. Who's to say Harvey didn't weaken the sink fitting himself? Accidentally, I mean, lying on his back to jam the cocaine way back out of sight. His shoulder might have bumped the fitting."

The agent went on in a consoling tone. "You might be dead if you hadn't stopped where you did. Quince's men might have been watching you at Edgecliff that night and been scared off when *they* saw that police boat. They might have been told by Quince that you were working with Harvey. Who knows? Mrs. McNulty—"

"Yvonne."

"Yvonne. You just missed the bunch that hurt your friend. She opened the door to them after you'd gone. She had no reason to be suspicious."

"My life might have been saved just because I get up early," Yvonne said.

"Harvey and his people were in way over their heads, second-stringers," Bleucher said. "Quince and his people—and Rosalie, of course—they were the varsity."

"And we beat the varsity," Kevin said. But his heart was as empty as his voice.

"God may have been on your side."

Kevin and Yvonne studied the agent's face for a sign of cynicism. There wasn't any.

"Of course, there were more earthly reasons. Quince's people were never quite able to get you two alone for any length of time, where they could . . . well . . ."

"They came close enough at the marina," Yvonne said.

"By that time, we figure, they not only wanted their cocaine back. . . ."

"But Rosalie might have told them not to kill us because she needed to find out where my copies of her programs were." Yvonne shivered. "The night I told her I had copied the discs . . . that night when I came home from Chowder's, Tess was growling at something outside."

"You never told me about that, Vonnie," Kevin said.

"I thought it was an animal. I . . . all this other crap hadn't happened yet. Even after she knew where the discs were, she needed to know how much I knew . . . and who else knew."

"Very likely." Bleucher looked very tired as he rubbed his eyes with his fingertips. "I hope I wasn't too rough on you before. I probably was. This kind of work, it can consume you. The business in Colombia, it's been worse than most people know."

They waited for Bleucher to go on.

"This is off the record, please. Not so long ago, I had a colleague. An anti-drug agent for the Colombian government. Total courage, total integrity. A family man. We became good friends, actually. Anyhow, they managed to kidnap him."

"What happened?" Yvonne asked.

"They cut off his hands and feet. Even after that, they

weren't done cutting him. . . ." The agent stopped, shook his head.

"You mean he was still . . . ?" Kevin's voice tailed off.

"He wouldn't talk, you see," Bleucher went on. "Wouldn't give them what they wanted. His body was found by a country road with, well, something in his mouth. I try not to dwell. I just throw myself into the job, saving as much as I can for my wife and daughter."

Bleucher's face changed; an emotional curtain had come down.

"I'll drive you home," the agent said. "We can talk some more in the car, if you'd like."

As Kevin and Yvonne stood up to leave, Kevin put an arm across her back and hugged her to him. She didn't resist.

Sitting in the back of the government car while Bleucher drove wasn't as luxurious as riding in a limo, but they preferred it.

The rain fell steadily, but more gently, and there was no more thunder crashing overhead. The sound of the windshield wipers was oddly comforting.

"Are you still going to sell the boat?" Bleucher said.

"We'll see if we still have a buyer when you guys release it," Kevin said.

"It's a good boat," Yvonne said. "I always liked the way it looked in the water. But I guess we'll have to sell it. Probably . . ."

Kevin saw the agent look in the rearview mirror. "We think Harvey's scheme started to unravel even before you took the boat away."

"How so?" Yvonne said.

"Well, that friend of Harvey's, the one they called Tolly?"

"The guy who found that booze and carbon monoxide don't mix."

"Stop trying to be a hard-ass, Kevin."

"You hit it on the head, Kevin. Medical examiner's office

is taking a closer look. At first it looked pretty cut and dried. Guy with a reputation for liking his booze works on an engine in close quarters, gets too much exhaust. Ingenious, really."

"Somebody killed him?" Yvonne said.

"The pathologist noticed what looked like a freshly chipped tooth, and that just under the gum line he found a tiny, tiny chip of glass. Do you see?"

"He was force-fed the booze," Kevin said.

"That's our theory. I'm betting the tests on the tissue samples are going to show an abnormally high level of both alcohol *and* carbon monoxide, and that they both entered his system around the same time."

"Jesus," Kevin said. "Meaning he was force-fed the gas too."

"Now you can see how Harvey was in way over his head."

About a hundred feet over, Kevin thought. He kept that sick joke to himself.

"You tell me where to turn off, okay?" Bleucher said. "Are you, uh, both going to the same place?"

"Our cars are in the parking lot at Rosalie's office," Yvonne said. "But we'll probably both stay at Duck Point Lane tonight."

Kevin realized he didn't want to be anywhere in the world but there on this night, even if he slept on the sofa.

"This is just all so sad and terrible and way too much to digest," Yvonne said.

"If they'd got us on that boat, Rosalie and Carlo, what then?" Kevin said.

"I don't want to think about that," Yvonne said.

"I can guess," the agent said, "but I'd rather not. Of course, they had to have you alive until they were sure what you knew about her computer program—"

"Which made it easier to fight them off, because they couldn't kill us right away," Kevin said.

"—but on the boat, and Mrs. McNulty—I mean Yvonne—with your relationship with Rosalie she would have had ideas on how to get the information."

"She was nice to our dog," Kevin said. "That's one of the things that dawned on us. Isn't that crazy? Didn't have the heart to kill our dog."

"I can understand that," Bleucher said. "I have a dog."

Something dawned on Kevin. "Wait a minute," he said. "How did you know we were in trouble, and how did you know where to find us?"

"A combination of good police work and outside help. Once the Port Guinness police got over their embarrassment at having let your house be raided that night—that was a setup, by the way, because Rosalie—"

"We knew that already," Yvonne said.

"It took us awhile," Kevin said.

"And us," the agent said. "Anyhow, once the Port Guinness police started to look at things objectively, with some help from us, the only thing that made sense was that the thugs had never come down Duck Point Lane."

"Because they'd come from Rosalie's," Yvonne said. "Maybe by boat first, to Rosalie's place, and from there to our place."

"Right," the agent said.

"Turn down here," Kevin said.

"I still don't know how you found us exactly," Yvonne said.

"For one thing, we traced some of Quince's phone calls to Rosalie."

Yvonne remembered the computer-telephone hookup in the office. "And you saw a bunch of long calls that made you suspicious. The ones where the computer was running."

"Yes. She was scheduling deliveries."

"The computer calls were supposed to look like crochet lessons," Yvonne said. "She kept a bag of yarn next to the phone."

"Crochet?" Bleucher said. "My wife . . . well, anyhow. Besides checking on the phones, there were other things that made us wonder about her. Some I can't talk about, at least right now. And Kevin, you've got a good friend in your office."

* * *

The Hudson was still restless, but by midday, with the George Washington Bridge just ahead of them, Kevin and Yvonne were warm enough to take off their sweatshirts.

"The sun feels good on my arms," Yvonne said. "I'm a little surprised there aren't many people out."

"This is the time of year people start thinking more of football. At least those people who give a damn about football."

"Just the same. By the way, I hope your friend Marty Diehl finds another boat."

"Yeah, well, if he wants one bad enough, he will."

"I'm sure."

A grim joke, but not too grim, occurred to Kevin. "You know, maybe he can pick up that one on Long Island for a bargain. I mean the one we set fire to in the boatyard."

Yvonne chuckled a little. Sometimes (not often) Kevin hit a bull's-eye with his humor. Well, that one was in the inner ring anyhow. She would take a laugh wherever she found it.

"Funny how boat people get about boats, isn't it?" Kevin said.

"Meaning?"

"Well, like this Pearson is *our* boat, and meant to be our boat. I mean, we've filled up this boat with memories and . . . and . . . all that sentimental shit."

"And you use words for a living?"

"Still," he said, "we ought to give the boat a name, our name for it, not the previous owner's.

"You're right. *Lark IV* doesn't seem to suit it."

Kevin laughed. "How about *Narc IV?*"

"Not funny."

"I've got it. Really. How about *Happy Ours?*"

Yvonne started to protest.

"Without the *h* on 'ours.' "

"Mmmm, not bad," Yvonne said.

Kevin was making resolutions silently. He would drink less. He would try harder. There would be no more betting on football, at least not with money. A cup of coffee at most.

"I'm going to work at us, Vonnie. I mean, I'm gonna hold on to what's important and—"

"Right now, the most important thing you have a hold of is the tiller. Just keep your eye on the river."

"Yes, dearest."

Good, Yvonne thought. He had taken her remark just as she had intended it. "Sentimental Irish windbag," she whispered, loud enough for him to hear. Lucky he was used to that quirk in her, that need to sound tough, she thought.

The George Washington Bridge thrummed with traffic high above him. Looking up, Kevin thought of the last time they had gone under the span, going the other way.

Shooting the flare into Carlo that day in the boatyard had affected Vonnie. She had been relieved to find out that Carlo would recover, though he would always have a nasty scar.

"What the hell," Kevin said, "a scar will make him look real macho to the other convicts." But Kevin had liked his joke not much more than Vonnie had.

They were near Edgecliff now, about to pass within sight of DeeDee's balcony. She would use it again, one day.

They had agreed that, if they needed to refuel, they would not do it at Edgecliff. Not matter what.

"We have to remember this, Kevin. All of it. If we're ever in a position to make a difference, to, to . . ."

She stopped, out of words but with her composure intact, and welcomed his arm across her shoulders.

"I think I'm done with violence," he said. "For life. In movies, books, whatever. Except for football."

For a little while, they flowed along with the river and the silence. Then Yvonne had an inspiration.

"You know," she said, "we should have Landon Brice and his wife over for dinner."

"You think so?"

"You know we'll find things to talk about."

"Yeah, it's just that he's so shy and withdrawn."

She elbowed him gently. "We really should."

"Okay."

Kevin remembered the last time he had seen Landon Brice. After the mess in the boatyard and Rosalie's arrest, he had asked for time off from work yet again. But he had had to stop in the office to see Landon Brice.

Brice was one of a very few reporters to have his own office. His was a tiny corner cubicle jammed with gray metal file cabinets on which rested stacks of notebooks and old newspapers.

Kevin saw that Brice was on the phone (he wore a headset that was hooked up to a tape recorder). Kevin turned to walk away but stopped when Brice looked up and motioned for him to come in.

Brice nodded, smiled, pointed to a chair. *"Oui, oui, je comprends,"* Brice said into the phone and conversed for several more minutes in what sounded to Kevin like perfect French.

"Au revoir," he said finally.

He took off the headset and turned to face Kevin. "A mob source from Montreal," Brice said. "Calls me every few months just to shoot the *merde*. That's French for—"

"I know. *Merci*, Landon."

"Encore?"

"Thanks. You know, for maybe saving our lives."

"Ah, that. Well, it sounds like you saved your own lives. How did you guys know enough to run?"

Kevin told him how they'd compared notes in the limo and things had fallen into place.

"Yeah," Brice said, "Rosalie was running the whole East End operation."

"And Yvonne recognized Carlo from the way he walked. And from the cedar smell."

Brice chuckled. "Some of the traffickers pack coke in cedar chips. They think it fools the dogs."

"Does it?"

Brice chuckled again and shrugged. "How would I know?"

"Anyhow," Kevin said, "it might not have done us any good, shooting the flares like that, if the cops hadn't been on their way already."

Brice smiled in an "aw shucks" way. "I happened to see you on the phone, just before you left the office. Dialing, then slamming the receiver down, like you were all upset. I knew what a tough time you'd had. So I was worried about you, and I decided to call your home to tell your wife."

"And she wasn't home," Kevin said.

"No. So I checked the city desk Rolodex and got your wife's work number. But I dialed a couple of times and couldn't get through. So I began to think that's where you'd been calling and you couldn't get through either."

"So then you called the cops."

"Not right away. Then my scalp started itching, like it does when I have a hunch. I didn't buy that theory that the robbery was unrelated, and I decided I had to call the cops."

"So you steered them to Yvonne's office."

"They were already pretty sure you were clean. I mean, when you got the crap beat out of you in your house, what else could they think?"

"That we were drug dealers who'd been beaten up by other drug dealers. You know, a double-cross . . ."

At that, Brice threw back his head and guffawed. "Naw, Kevin. Not you. Not your wife. What's your big vice? A six-pack?"

"Or two. And betting on football."

"Anyhow," Brice went on, "I told the cops to find you, find your wife. Fast."

Kevin realized that Brice, sitting back now in his chair with his feet on the desk, had reverted to his customary I-know-more-than-you-do manner. A shield, Kevin thought.

"Besides," Brice said, "what I told 'em dovetailed with what they were piecing together on their own."

"So things were starting to point to Rosalie?"

"Yeah."

"So why the hell didn't the cops move faster and save us a lot of grief?"

"Couldn't. Not enough to go on, for one thing. If they'd

moved in too fast on Rosalie, they wouldn't have had a case at all. See, Quince started to talk when the cops connected him to the break-in at your house."

"How'd they do that?"

"They found pink and canary jackets on Quince's boat. They knew the robbers hadn't passed the stakeout on Duck Point Lane. So they figured the robbers came by boat. And only Quince knew about Rosalie, and he was coming around slowly."

"So the cops weren't just using us as bait?"

"Not at all. See, that thing at your house, that was smart thinking by Rosalie, but you know what her mistake was?"

"What?"

"Not having those guys hit *her* as hard as they hit you and your wife."

"Well, Vonnie and I finally figured it out. Then there was the dog tranquilizer . . ."

Landon chuckled. "Dumb of her."

"Well, I'm glad she was soft on our dog."

Brice told him how puzzled the police were at first that only Kevin and Yvonne, not Rosalie, had gone to the emergency room after the house was trashed. "Not only that, the cops couldn't find any doctor who had treated her."

"How would they know where to look?"

"They have their ways." Brice's eyes sparkled, a signal that he was debating with himself how much to tell his naive listener.

Kevin found the familiar Cheshire-cat grin momentarily irritating. "Cast a flickering torch into the vast caves of my ignorance," he said.

Brice laughed. "Plastic surgeons! A handsome, wealthy woman with a face that's messed up is gonna see a plastic surgeon. Only, the cops couldn't find any plastic surgeon who'd treated Rosalie. So they were on to Rosalie, and after I talked to them they raced over to your wife's office—"

"And saw both our cars in the lot."

"So they decided to check the marinas and boatyards along the North Shore, partly because of what happened to

Harvey. They were working on the water as well as on land."

"There's a lot of marinas, though."

"But the cops knew about what time you and your wife had left her office. They asked Rosalie's son and the other guy in his office, and then they double-checked on the limo, just in case Scotty was in on the deal."

"The limo . . . ?"

"The phone in the limo."

"Bugged?"

"You see? That narrowed it down. They did their best, put a lot of manpower into it, figuring they'd let you down once already. They got lucky. That's how it goes sometimes."

"Well, thanks anyhow."

"Hey, all in a day's work. . . . And one more thing . . ."

Kevin could tell that Brice was savoring the moment. "Okay, Landon. Hit me with it."

"Your motel room up in Tansytown?"

"Yeah?"

"I've got a real close source in the DEA. I hear your room was bugged."

"Bugged . . ." Of course, Kevin thought. No wonder the cops were so thoughtful: fixing us up with a room, bringing us food. And beer, bringing us beer, for God's sake. Hey! What if Vonnie and I hadn't been technically separated, what if we . . . ? "Any more surprises, Landon?"

"Well, the cops did look through your house just before you got back from the boat trip."

"Why, those dirty . . . I never gave them permission. . . . Goddamn!"

Landon chuckled softly. "Hey, Kevin, the cops offered to check in on your dog. I'm sure one of the officers thought he might have heard something in the house. Just doing their jobs."

Kevin had wanted to say more to Landon Brice that day, to suggest that maybe they could have a beer or two or three. But Brice's phone had rung, and the reporter had put on his headset and waved good-bye.

* * *

"We will have Landon over," Kevin said. "Do me good to talk to someone like him. It's not his fault he's a genuis."

"From what you told me, I think he's a little shy."

Kevin kept his skepticism about that to himself.

"Besides," Yvonne said, "we have to build a new social life."

Kevin heard her voice catch, did not ask her why she went forward to sit on the bow.

When Bleucher had given Yvonne a message from Rosalie, Yvonne had felt repelled.

She remembered playing possum the night of the burglary and hearing one of the thugs say in a normal voice. "They're both out." But the "both" meant the thug was referring to Kevin and Yvonne and talking *to* Rosalie. "Boss," one thug had called her.

One of the intruders had mentioned that Yvonne and Kevin would be moving: another clue that pointed to someone who knew them.

It was all so clear now. There was no more denying, and the sense of betrayal was almost immobilizing.

Then Bleucher had brought a message from Judas herself. The feds were setting her up with a new identity. She was going to testify against Quince and the others, and there were even bigger fish.

"She wanted me to tell you that she would never have hurt you or Kevin or Miss Lockwood," Bleucher said. "She puts the blame for all the violence on Quince. We think she might have got into the business by inheritance."

"By inheritance?" Yvonne had asked.

"We think Rosalie's father might have been a gofer for the mob years ago, and that she herself started running errands for them."

"You say you just think that?"

"We've done a lot of background research on Rosalie," Bleucher said. "Her tracks are pretty well covered. Even some of the stuff she told her son wasn't true."

"My mother told me she'd heard Scotty's father wasn't

Mr. Durer," Yvonne said. "There was some rich shady guy who showed up now and then."

"We traced that," Bleucher said. "We couldn't find anything. In fact, beyond a certain point in the past, Rosalie doesn't exist."

Doesn't exist, Yvonne thought. "Where are Scotty and Melba?"

"They had to leave Port Guinness for their own safety. Also to make Rosalie more useful to us. If someone kidnapped Scotty or Melba—"

"That would shut Rosalie up as a witness," Yvonne said.

"Scotty and Melba didn't have the faintest idea where most of the money was coming from," Bleucher said. "They were innocents."

"Extravagant ones at that," Yvonne said. "I wonder what they'll do now."

"We'll take care of them for a while. And that brings me to a job we have for you, Mrs. McNulty. Yvonne, I mean. Rosalie wants us to let you see to the sale of the family assets. Hers, Scotty's, and Melba's. The commission is very good."

Bleucher went on: "The government will take most of the money, but there'll be many personal items we won't care anything about. Those things will be yours for the taking. We'll be glad to have someone see to the details.

"You'll need to keep good records. Rosalie says Program Add-Up on Disc D will work fine. You have a copy of that, Rosalie says."

Yvonne asked, "What I want to know is, is she trying to bribe me with this bit about selling her assets?"

"That may have crossed her mind. She is a devious person. But we got the okay and you can do it if you want. One of our legal people will contact you and he or she will get the signatures you need."

"I don't want anything of hers," Yvonne said. "I'll sell everything and give the money to some organization that takes care of children."

"Rosalie told us that you'd say something like that," Bleucher said.

"She's good at reading people," Yvonne said, lowering her chin so that her tearing eyes would not be so obvious.

"We'll have to watch her or she'll be setting up new enterprises," Bleucher said.

Yvonne came back into the cockpit. Kevin recognized the look on her face; it was the one she got when she had put something behind her and was ready to move on.

"We'll have a little more money," she said. "And you won't be paying rent on an apartment."

"You thinking of some projects?"

She laughed. "Your guard is always up. As a matter of fact, the living room could stand painting. So could the boat."

"Hey, painting the boat! That idea I like. Seems right, somehow. Maybe we can hire someone to paint the living room and do the boat ourselves."

"I didn't think painting the living room would be such a big deal, work-wise."

Kevin caught on: Before they separated, Yvonne had liked to share projects with him. "Okay. A deal. Next time I get two days off in a row, we'll do it. How about a nice purple?"

"Gag, puke. How about a nice eggshell white?"

"You win again. But of course it'll have to wait until after football season."

"No dice. Football season is never over." Yvonne smiled and punched his arm playfully. She would work him into the painting gradually. Once the living room was done, they would think about a color for the corner room. That room was to be the nursery before. Who knows? Maybe they would try again. But not yet.

"We do have some work ahead of us, don't we?" she said.

"Yeah, we do. We both do."

"Well, I'll do my best."

"You always do. So will I."

It was time for lunch. "Turkey or tuna?" she asked.

"Tuna sounds good."

She handed him half a sandwich, then took out one of the cans of beer she had surreptitiously stowed. "Here," she said. "A small celebration."

"All, *RIGHT!*" Kevin had been drinking a lot less and enjoying it a lot more. Right now seemed like a good time for a beer.

"Maybe pizza tonight?"

"That sounds good too."

They rounded the Battery. This time there were no Staten Island ferries or barges in their way. Yvonne took note of the wooden pilings in front of the ferry slips. The pilings were short, meaning the tide was high. That bothered her, but she didn't know why just yet.

"There's no one I'd rather have a beer with, Vonnie."

"Well, that's a good sign."

"You know what I mean."

"No." But she did.

"It means I love you, for God's sake."

"Well, that's as it should be. Because I love you too."

They motored in silence for a while—an easy silence this time, with sightseeing and beer-sipping.

As they neared Hell Gate, Yvonne thought the snake-like ripples were coming at them instead of going with them.

"Uh, Kevin, you did check the tide chart?"

"Of course I did."

Now she knew what had bothered her about the pilings at the ferry slips. She had a sudden troubling thought and went below. She found the tide chart and checked it. She came back topside.

"Kevin, I could tell by the pilings at the Battery that it was past high water back there."

"Yeah?"

"Have you noticed that we're not making as much headway? Seems like the Triborough has been the same size for a long time."

"Hmmm."

"The Hell Gate tide is coming right at us. Will be for quite a while."

Kevin took the tide chart from her. The arrows and

numbers confirmed that she was right. He couldn't remember where he'd made his mistake. Damn, he thought. She's still a better sailor. Always will be.

"Okay, I see it now. But let's just go full speed ahead. We have plenty of gas. We can make a little headway . . ."

The engine was going full speed.

"We're gonna do it," Kevin said. "Got plenty of gas, and the engine is fine."

Yes, that's Kevin, she thought. Exactly the wrong perspective. Exactly the right perspective.

"Know what, Kevin? Eventually the tide will go our way."

MORE MYSTERIOUS PLEASURES

Order #	Titles	Price
	HAROLD ADAMS	*The Carl Wilcox series*
501	MURDER	$3.95
601	PAINT THE TOWN RED	$3.95
602	THE MISSING MOON	$3.95
420	THE NAKED LIAR	$3.95
502	THE FOURTH WIDOW	$3.50
603	THE BARBED WIRE NOOSE	$3.95
901	THE MAN WHO MISSED THE PARTY	$4.95
	THOMAS ADCOCK	
902	SEA OF GREEN	$4.95
	TED ALLBEURY	
604	THE SEEDS OF TREASON	$3.95
802	THE JUDAS FACTOR	$4.50
903	THE LANTERN NETWORK	$4.95
904	ALL OUR TOMORROWS	$4.95
	ERIC AMBLER	
701	HERE LIES: AN AUTOBIOGRAPHY	$8.95
	KINGSLEY AMIS	
905	THE CRIME OF THE CENTURY	$4.95
	ROBERT BARNARD	
702	A TALENT TO DECEIVE: AN APPRECIATION OF AGATHA CHRISTIE	$8.95

Order #	Titles	Price

THOMAS MAXWELL

523	KISS ME ONCE	$4.95
822	KISS ME TWICE	$4.95
628	THE SABERDENE VARIATIONS	$4.95

RIC MEYERS

| 725 | MURDER ON THE AIR: TELEVISION'S GREAT MYSTERY SERIES | $12.95 |

MARCIA MULLER   *The Sharon McCone series*

930	EDWIN OF THE IRON SHOES	$3.95
931	ASK THE CARDS A QUESTION	$3.95
932	THE CHESHIRE CAT'S EYE	$3.95
933	GAMES TO KEEP THE DARK AWAY	$3.95
934	LEAVE A MESSAGE FOR WILLIE	$4.95
935	THERE'S NOTHING TO BE AFRAID OF	$4.95
823	EYE OF THE STORM	$3.95
936	THERE'S SOMETHING IN A SUNDAY	$3.95
937	THE SHAPE OF DREAD	$4.95

FREDERICK NEBEL

| 712 | THE ADVENTURES OF CARDIGAN | $9.95 |

SUSAN OLEKSIW

| 728 | A READER'S GUIDE TO THE CLASSIC BRITISH MYSTERY | $19.95 |

ELIZABETH PETERS   *The Amelia Peabody series*

| 209 | CROCODILE ON THE SANDBANK | $3.95 |
| 210 | THE CURSE OF THE PHARAOHS | $3.95 |

The Jacqueline Kirby series

| 411 | THE SEVENTH SINNER | $3.95 |
| 412 | THE MURDERS OF RICHARD III | $3.95 |

ELLIS PETERS   *The Brother Cadfael series*

| 824 | THE HERMIT OF EYTON FOREST | $4.50 |
| 808 | THE CONFESSION OF BROTHER HALUIN | $3.95 |

Order #	Titles	Price
	DAVID WILLIAMS	*The Mark Treasure series*
112	UNHOLY WRIT	$3.95
113	TREASURE BY DEGREES	$3.95
	GAHAN WILSON	
843	EVERYBODY'S FAVORITE DUCK	$4.95
	CORNELL WOOLRICH/LAWRENCE BLOCK	
646	INTO THE NIGHT	$3.95

- -

AVAILABLE AT YOUR BOOKSTORE OR DIRECT FROM THE PUBLISHER

Mysterious Press Mail Order
129 West 56th Street
New York, NY 10019

Please send me the MYSTERIOUS PRESS paperback titles below:

Order #	Title	Price

Please add another page for additional titles.

Shipping

CREDIT CARD #

Circle One: AM EX, VISA, MC   Exp. Date   TOTAL

I am enclosing $_____ (please add $3.00 postage and handling for the first book, and 50¢ for each additional book.) Send check, money order or credit card only—no cash or COD please. Allow 4 weeks for delivery.

NAME _____

ADDRESS _____

CITY _____ STATE _____ ZIP CODE _____

New York State residents please add appropriate sales tax.

BATTLE FLAG

BERNARD CORNWELL was born in London and raised in Essex, and now lives mainly in the USA, with his wife. In addition to the hugely successful Sharpe novels, Bernard Cornwell is the author of the highly praised Starbuck Chronicles, the acclaimed Warlord trilogy, and the recent bestsellers *Harlequin* and *Gallows Thief*.

For more information, visit:
www.bernardcornwell.net

BERNARD CORNWALL

Battle Flag

HARPER

HarperCollins*Publishers*
77–85 Fulham Palace Road,
Hammersmith, London W6 8JB

www.harpercollins.co.uk

Special overseas edition 1995
This paperback edition 1996
1

First published in Great Britain by
HarperCollins*Publishers* 1995

ISBN 978-0-00-783379-5

Set in Goudy

Printed and bound in Great Britain by
Clays Ltd, St Ives plc

Battle Flag
is for my father, with love

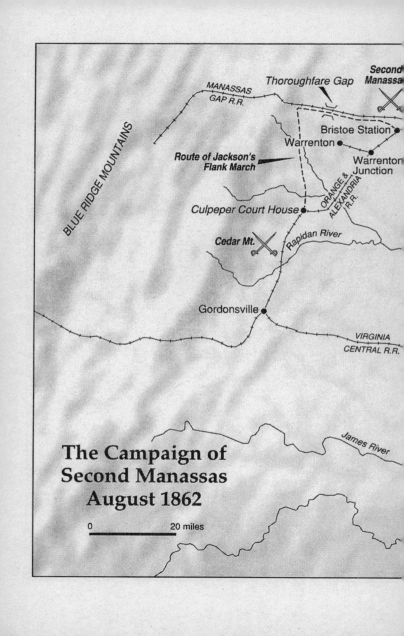

MANASSAS GAP R.R.

Thoroughfare Gap

Second Manassa

BLUE RIDGE MOUNTAINS

Bristoe Station

Warrenton

Route of Jackson's Flank March

Warrenton Junction

ORANGE & ALEXANDRIA R.R.

Culpeper Court House

Rapidan River

Cedar Mt.

Gordonsville

VIRGINIA CENTRAL R.R.

James River

The Campaign of Second Manassas August 1862

0   20 miles

PART ONE

PART ONE

CAPTAIN NATHANIEL STARBUCK first saw his new commanding general when the Faulconer Legion forded the Rapidan. Thomas Jackson was on the river's northern bank, where he appeared to be in a trance, for he was motionless in his saddle with his left hand held high in the air while his eyes, blue and resentful, stared into the river's vacant and murky depths. His glum stillness was so uncanny that the marching column edged to the far margin of the ford rather than pass near a man whose stance so presaged death. The General's physical appearance was equally disturbing. Jackson had a ragged beard, a plain coat, and a dirty cap, while his horse looked as if it should have been taken to a slaughterhouse long before. It was hard to credit that this was the South's most controversial general, the man who gave the North sleepless nights and nervous days, but Lieutenant Franklin Coffman, sixteen years old and newly arrived in the Faulconer Legion, asserted that the odd-looking figure was indeed the famous Stonewall Jackson. Coffman had once been taught by Professor Thomas Jackson. "Mind you," Lieutenant Coffman confided in Starbuck, "I don't believe generals make any real difference to battles."

"Such wisdom in one so young," said Starbuck, who was twenty-two years old.

"It's the men who win battles, not generals," Coffman said, ignoring his Captain's sarcasm. Lieutenant

Coffman had received one year's schooling at the Virginia Military Institute, where Thomas Jackson had ineffectively lectured him in artillery drill and Natural Philosophy. Now Coffman looked at the rigid figure sitting motionless in the shabby saddle. "I can't imagine old Square Box as a general," Coffman said scornfully. "He couldn't keep a schoolroom in order, let alone an army."

"Square Box?" Starbuck asked. General Jackson had many nicknames. The newspapers called him Stonewall, his soldiers called him Old Jack or even Old Mad Jack, while many of Old Jack's former students liked to refer to him as Tom Fool Jack, but Square Box was a name new to Starbuck.

"He's got the biggest feet in the world," Coffman explained. "Really huge! And the only shoes that ever fitted him were like boxes."

"What a fount of useful information you are, Lieutenant," Starbuck said casually. The Legion was still too far from the river for Starbuck to see the General's feet, but he made a mental note to look at these prodigies when he did finally reach the Rapidan. The Legion was presently not moving at all, its progress halted by the reluctance of the men ahead to march straight through the ford without first removing their tattered boots. Mad Jack Stonewall Square Box Jackson was reputed to detest such delays, but he seemed oblivious to this holdup. Instead he just sat, hand in the air and eyes on the river, while right in front of him the column bunched and halted. The men behind the obstruction were grateful for the enforced halt, for the day was blistering hot, the air motionless, and the heat as damp as steam. "You were remarking, Coffman, on the ineffectiveness of generals?" Starbuck prompted his new junior officer.

"If you think about it, sir," Coffman said with a youthful passion, "we haven't got any real generals, not like the

4

Yankees, but we still win battles. I reckon that's because the Southerner is unbeatable."

"What about Robert Lee?" Starbuck asked. "Isn't he a real general?"

"Lee's old! He's antediluvian!" Coffman said, shocked that Starbuck should even have suggested the name of the new commander of the Army of Northern Virginia. "He must be fifty-five, at least!"

"Jackson's not old," Starbuck pointed out. "He isn't even forty yet."

"But he's mad, sir. Honest! We used to call him Tom Fool."

"He must be mad then," Starbuck teased Coffman. "So why do we win battles despite having mad generals, ancient generals, or no generals at all?"

"Because fighting is in the Southern blood, sir. It really is." Coffman was an eager young man who was determined to be a hero. His father had died of consumption, leaving his mother with four young sons and two small daughters. His father's death had forced Coffman to leave the Virginia Military Institute after his first year, but that one year's military schooling had equipped him with a wealth of martial theories. "Northerners," he now explained to Starbuck, "have diluted blood. There are too many immigrants in the North, sir. But the South has pure blood, sir. Real American blood."

"You mean the Yankees are an inferior race?"

"It's an acknowledged fact, sir. They've lost the thoroughbred strain, sir."

"You do know I'm a Yankee, Coffman, don't you?" Starbuck asked.

Coffman immediately looked confused, though before he could frame any response he was interrupted by Colonel Thaddeus Bird, the Faulconer Legion's commanding officer,

5

who came striding long-legged from the rear of the stalled column. "Is that really Jackson?" Bird asked, gazing across the river.

"Lieutenant Coffman informs me that the General's real name is Old Mad Tom Fool Square Box Jackson, and that is indeed the man himself," Starbuck answered.

"Ah, Coffman," Bird said, peering down at the small Lieutenant as though Coffman was some curious specimen of scientific interest, "I remember when you were nothing but a chirruping infant imbibing the lesser jewels of my glittering wisdom." Bird, before he became a soldier, had been the schoolmaster in Faulconer Court House, where Coffman's family lived.

"Lieutenant Coffman has not ceased to imbibe wisdom," Starbuck solemnly informed Colonel Bird, "nor indeed to impart it, for he has just informed me that we Yankees are an inferior breed, our blood being soured, tainted, and thinned by the immigrant strain."

"Quite right, too!" Bird said energetically; then the Colonel draped a thin arm around the diminutive Coffman's shoulders. "I could a tale unfold, young Coffman, whose lightest word would harrow up thy soul, freeze thy young blood, and make thy two eyes, like stars, start from their spheres." He spoke even more closely into the ear of the astonished Lieutenant. "Did you know, Coffman, that the very moment an immigrant boat docks in Boston all the Beacon Hill families send their wives down to the harbor to be impregnated? Is that not the undeniable truth, Starbuck?"

"Indeed it is, sir, and they send their daughters as well if the boat arrives on the Sabbath."

"Boston is a libidinous town, Coffman," Bird said very sternly as he stepped away from the wide-eyed Lieutenant, "and if I am to give you just one piece of advice in this sad

6

bad world, then let it be to avoid the place. Shun it, Coffman! Regard Boston as you might regard Sodom or Gomorrah. Remove it from your catalog of destinations. Do you understand me, Coffman?"

"Yes, sir," Coffman said very seriously.

Starbuck laughed at the look on his Lieutenant's face. Coffman had arrived the day before with a draft of conscripted men to replace the casualties of Gaines' Mill and Malvern Hill. The conscripts had mostly been culled from the alleys of Richmond and, to Starbuck, appeared to be a scrawny, unhealthy, and shifty-looking crew of dubious reliability, but Franklin Coffman, like the original members of the Legion, was a volunteer from Faulconer County and full of enthusiasm for the Southern cause.

Colonel Bird now abandoned his teasing of the Lieutenant and plucked at Starbuck's sleeve. "Nate," he said, "a word." The two men walked away from the road, crossing a shallow ditch into a meadow that was wan and brown from the summer's heat wave. Starbuck limped, not because he was wounded, but because the sole of his right boot was becoming detached from its uppers. "Is it me?" Bird asked as the two men paced across the dry grass. "Am I getting wiser or is it that the young are becoming progressively more stupid? And young Coffman, believe it if you will, was brighter than most of the infants it was my misfortune to teach. I remember he mastered the theory of gerunds in a single morning!"

"I'm not sure I ever mastered gerunds," Starbuck said.

"Hardly difficult," Bird said, "so long as you remember that they are nouns which provide—"

"And I'm not sure I ever want to master the damn things," Starbuck interrupted.

"Wallow in your ignorance, then," Bird said grandly. "But you're also to look after young Coffman. I couldn't bear to

7

write to his mother and tell her he's dead, and I have a horrid feeling that he's likely to prove stupidly brave. He's like a puppy. Tail up, nose wet, and can't wait to play battles with Yankees."

"I'll look after him, Pecker."

"But you're also to look after yourself," Bird said meaningfully. He stopped and looked into Starbuck's eyes. "There's a rumor, only a rumor, and God knows I do not like passing on rumors, but this one has an unpleasant ring to it. Swynyard was heard to say that you won't survive the next battle."

Starbuck dismissed the prediction with a grin. "Swynyard's a drunk, not a prophet." Nevertheless he felt a shudder of fear. He had been a soldier long enough to become inordinately superstitious, and no man liked to hear a presentiment of his own death.

"Suppose," Bird said, taking two cigars from inside his hatband, "that Swynyard has decided to arrange it?"

Starbuck stared incredulously at his Colonel. "Arrange my death?" he finally asked.

Bird scratched a lucifer match alight and stooped over its flame. "Colonel Swynyard," he announced dramatically when his cigar was drawing properly, "is a drunken swine, a beast, a cream-faced loon, a slave of nature, and a son of hell, but he is also, Nate, a most cunning rogue, and when he is not in his cups he must realize that he is losing the confidence of our great and revered leader. Which is why he must now try to do something which will please our esteemed lord and master. Get rid of you." The last four words were delivered brutally.

Starbuck laughed them off. "You think Swynyard will shoot me in the back?"

Bird gave Starbuck the lit cigar. "I don't know how he'll kill you. All I know is that he'd like to kill you, and that

8

Faulconer would like him to kill you, and for all I know our esteemed General is prepared to award Swynyard a healthy cash bonus if he succeeds in killing you. So be careful, Nate, or else join another regiment."

"No," Starbuck said immediately. The Faulconer Legion was his home. He was a Bostonian, a Northerner, a stranger in a strange land who had found in the Legion a refuge from his exile. The Legion provided Starbuck with casual kindnesses and a hive of friends, and those bonds of affection were far stronger than the distant enmity of Washington Faulconer. That enmity had grown worse when Faulconer's son Adam had deserted from the Southern army to fight for the Yankees, a defection for which Brigadier General Faulconer blamed Captain Starbuck, but not even the disparity in their ranks could persuade Starbuck to abandon his fight against the man who had founded the Legion and who now commanded the five regiments, including the Legion, that made up the Faulconer Brigade. "I've got no need to run away," he now told Bird. "Faulconer won't last any longer than Swynyard. Faulconer's a coward and Swynyard's a drunk, and before this summer's out, Pecker, you'll be Brigade commander and I'll be in command of the Legion."

Bird hooted with delight. "You are incorrigibly conceited, Nate. You! Commanding the Legion? I imagine Major Hinton and the dozen other men senior to you might have a different opinion."

"They might be senior, but I'm the best."

"Ah, you still suffer from the delusion that merit is rewarded in this world? I suppose you contracted that opinion with all the other nonsense they crammed into you when Yale was failing to give you mastery of the gerund?" Bird, achieving this lick at Starbuck's *alma mater*, laughed gleefully. His head jerked back and forth as he laughed, the odd jerking motion explaining his nickname: Pecker.

Starbuck joined in the laughter, for he, like just about everyone else in the Legion, liked Bird enormously. The schoolmaster was eccentric, opinionated, contrary, and one of the kindest men alive. He had also proved to possess an unexpected talent for soldiering. "We move at last," Bird now said, gesturing at the stalled column that had begun edging toward the ford where the solitary, strange figure of Jackson waited motionless on his mangy horse. "You owe me two dollars," Bird suddenly remarked as he led Starbuck back to the road.

"Two dollars!"

"Major Hinton's fiftieth birthday approaches. Lieutenant Pine assures me he can procure a ham, and I shall prevail on our beloved leader for some wine. We are paying for a feast."

"Is Hinton really that old?" Starbuck asked.

"He is indeed, and if you live that long we shall doubtless give you a drunken dinner as a reward. Have you got two bucks?"

"I haven't got two cents," Starbuck said. He had some money in Richmond, but that money represented his cushion against disaster and was not for frittering away on ham and wine.

"I shall lend you the money," Bird said with a rather despairing sigh. Most of the Legion's officers had private means, but Colonel Bird, like Starbuck, was forced to live on the small wages of a Confederate officer.

The men of Company H stood as Starbuck and Bird approached the road, though one of the newly arrived conscripts stayed prone on the grass verge and complained he could not march another step. His reward was a kick in the ribs from Sergeant Truslow. "You can't do that to me!" the man protested, scrabbling sideways to escape the Sergeant.

Truslow grabbed the man's jacket and pulled his face close in to his own. "Listen, you son of a poxed bitch, I can

10

slit your slumbelly guts wide open and sell them to the Yankees for hog food if I want, and not because I'm a sergeant and you're a private, but because I'm a mean son of a bitch and you're a lily-livered louse. Now get the hell up and march."

"What comfortable words the good Sergeant speaks," Bird said as he jumped back across the dry ditch. He drew on his cigar. "So I can't persuade you to join another regiment, Nate?"

"No, sir."

Pecker Bird shook his head ruefully. "I think you're a fool, Nate, but for God's sake be a careful fool. For some odd reason I'd be sorry to lose you."

"Fall in!" Truslow shouted.

"I'll take care," Starbuck promised as he rejoined his company. His thirty-six veterans were lean, tanned, and ragged. Their boots were falling to pieces, their gray jackets were patched with common brown cloth, and their worldly possessions reduced to what a man could carry suspended from his rope belt or sling in a rolled blanket across his shoulder. The twenty conscripts made an awkward contrast in their new uniforms, clumsy leather brogans, and stiff knapsacks. Their faces were pale and their rifle muzzles unblackened by firing. They knew this northward march through the central counties of Virginia probably meant an imminent battle, but what that battle would bring was a mystery, while the veterans knew only too well that a fight would mean screaming and blood and hurt and pain and thirst, but maybe, too, a cache of plundered Yankee dollars or a bag of real coffee taken from a festering, maggot-riddled Northern corpse. "March on!" Starbuck shouted, and fell in beside Lieutenant Franklin Coffman at the head of the company.

"You see if I'm not right, sir," Coffman said. "Old Mad Jack's got feet bigger than a plowhorse."

As Starbuck marched into the ford, he looked at the General's feet. They were indeed enormous. So were Jackson's hands. But what was most extraordinary of all was why the General still held his left hand in midair like a child begging permission to leave a schoolroom. Starbuck was about to ask Coffman for an explanation when, astonishingly, the General stirred. He looked up from the water, and his gaze focused on Starbuck's company. "Coffman!" he called in an abrupt, high-pitched voice. "Come here, boy."

Coffman stumbled out of the ford and half ran to the General's side. "Sir?"

The ragged-bearded Jackson frowned down from his saddle. "Do you remember me, Coffman?"

"Yes, sir, of course I do, sir."

Jackson lowered his left hand very gently, as though he feared he might damage the arm if he moved it fast. "I was sorry you had to leave the Institute early, Coffman. It was after your plebe year, was it not?"

"Yes, sir. It was, sir."

"Because your father died?"

"Yes, sir."

"And your mother, Coffman? She's well?"

"Indeed, sir. Yes, sir, thank you, sir."

"Bereavement is a terrible affliction, Coffman," the General observed, then slowly unbent his rigid posture to lean toward the slim, fair-haired Lieutenant, "especially for those who are not in a state of grace. Are you in a state of grace, Coffman?"

Coffman blushed, frowned, then managed to nod. "Yes, sir. I think I am, sir."

Jackson straightened again into his poker-backed stance and, as slowly as he had lowered his left hand, raised it once more into midair. He lifted his eyes from Coffman to stare into the heat-hazed distance. "You will find it a very hard

12

thing to meet your Maker if you are unsure of His grace," the General said in a kindly voice, "so study your scriptures and recite your prayers, boy."

"Yes, sir, I will, sir," Coffman said. He stood awkward and uncertain, waiting for the General to speak further, but Jackson seemed in his trance once again, and so the Lieutenant turned and walked back to Starbuck's side. The Legion marched on, and the Lieutenant remained silent as the road climbed between small pastures and straggling woods and beside modest farms. It was a good two miles before Coffman at last broke his silence. "He's a great man," the Lieutenant said, "isn't he, sir? Isn't he a great man?"

"Tom Fool?" Starbuck teased Coffman.

"A great man, sir," Coffman chided Starbuck.

"If you say so," Starbuck said, though all he knew about Jackson was that Old Mad Jack had a great reputation for marching, and that when Old Mad Jack went marching, men died. And they were marching now, marching north, and going north meant one thing only: Yankees ahead. Which meant there would be a battle soon, and a field of graves after the battle, and this time, if Pecker was right, Starbuck's enemies would not just be in front of him but behind as well. Starbuck marched on. A fool going to battle.

The midday train stopped at Manassas Junction amidst a clash of cars, the hissing of steam, and the clangor of the locomotive's bell. Sergeants' voices rose over the mechanical din, urging troops out of the cars and onto the strip of dirt that lay between the rails and the warehouses. The soldiers jumped down, glad to be free of the cramped cars and excited to be in Virginia. Manassas Junction might not be the fighting front, but it was still a part of a rebel state, and so they peered about themselves as though the landscape

13

was as wondrous and strange as the misty hills of mysterious Japan or far Cathay.

The arriving troops were mostly seventeen- and eighteen-year-old boys come from New Jersey and Wisconsin, from Maine and Illinois, from Rhode Island and Vermont. They were volunteers, newly uniformed and eager to join this latest assault on the Confederacy. They boasted of hanging Jeff Davis from an apple tree, and bragged of how they would march through Richmond and roust the rebels out of their nests like rats from a granary. They were young and indestructible, full of confidence, but also awed by the savagery of this strange destination.

For Manassas Junction was not an inviting place. It had been sacked once by Northern troops, destroyed again by retreating Confederates, then hastily rebuilt by Northern contractors, so that now there were acres of gaunt, raw-timbered warehouses standing between rail sidings and weed-filled meadows that were crammed with guns and limbers and caissons and portable forges and ambulances and wagons. More stores and weapons arrived every hour, for this was the supply depot that would fuel the summer campaign of 1862 that would end the rebellion and so restore a United States of America. The great spread of buildings was shadowed by an ever-present pall of greasy smoke that came from blacksmiths' shops and locomotive repair sheds and the fireboxes of the locomotives that dragged in their goods wagons and passenger cars.

Two cavalry officers waited at the depot. They had clearly gone to some considerable effort to make themselves presentable, for their uniform coats were brushed spotless, their spurred boots were shining, and their leather belts polished. The older man was middle-aged and balding, with a pleasant face and thick muttonchop whiskers. His name was Major Joseph Galloway, and he clutched a plumed hat in his nervous hands. His companion was a much younger man, handsome and fair-haired, with a square beard and wide shoulders and an open face that inspired trust. His coat showed a captain's bars.

Both men were Virginians, yet both fought for the North. Joseph Galloway owned property just outside Manassas itself, and that farm was now the depot for a regiment of Northern cavalry exclusively recruited from Southerners loyal to the government in Washington. Most of the troopers for Galloway's Horse were volunteers from the border states, the disputed lands of Maryland, and the western counties of Virginia, but a good number were refugees from the Confederate States themselves. Galloway had no doubt that some of his men were fugitives from Southern justice, but the majority were idealists who fought to preserve the Union, and it had been Major Galloway's notion to recruit such men for reconnaissance work deep behind the rebel lines. Northern horsemen were solid and brave, but they rode the Virginian countryside as strangers, and in consequence they were timid compared to the rakehell Southerners who knew that every Virginian village and hamlet contained sympathizers prepared to hide and feed them. It had been Galloway's inspiration to raise a regiment that could ride the rebel states like native Southerners, yet the idea had received only lukewarm support from Washington. Raise the regiment, the government's bureaucrats had told Major Galloway, and we might deign to employ it, but only if it came properly equipped with weapons, horses, and uniforms.

Which was why Major Galloway and Captain Adam Faulconer now waited for a passenger who was supposed to have arrived on the midday train that had just steamed into Manassas. The two cavalry officers worked their way against the flood of excited soldiers toward the train's last car, which

15

had been reserved for passengers more exalted than mere cannon fodder. A porter lowered the carriage steps, and two ladies, their hooped skirts scarce able to squeeze through the car's narrow doorway, were handed down. After the ladies came a group of senior officers, their mustaches trimmed, their uniforms brushed, and their faces flush from the day's heat and from their consumption of the railroad's whiskey. One officer, younger than the rest, broke away and shouted at some orderlies to bring horses. "Chop, chop now! Horses for the General!" the aide shouted. The ladies' twin parasols bobbed white and lacy through the mist of tobacco smoke and the crush of dark military hats.

The last man to alight from the passenger car was a thin, tall, and elderly civilian with white hair and beard, fierce eyes, and a gaunt, stern face. He had sunken cheeks, a Roman nose as imperious as his gaze, a black frock coat, a top hat, and despite the heat, a high-buttoned vest over which a pair of starched Geneva bands hung white. He carried a dark maroon carpetbag and an ebony stick that he used to push aside a black servant who was lifting the ladies' cabin trunks onto a handcart. The gesture was peremptory and unthinking, the act of a man accustomed to authority.

"That's him," Adam said, recognizing the minister whom he had heard preach in Boston just before the war began.

Major Galloway pushed through the crowd toward the white-haired man. "Sir?" he called to the newly arrived preacher. "Doctor Starbuck, sir?"

The Reverend Elial Joseph Starbuck, Doctor of Divinity, pamphleteer, and the most famous of all the North's abolitionist preachers, scowled at his welcomers. "You must be Galloway. And you're Faulconer? Good! My bag." He thrust the carpetbag into Adam's hand, which had been stretched out for a handshake.

16

"You had a pleasant journey, I trust, sir?" Major Galloway inquired as he ushered his guest toward the roadway.

"It became successively less pleasant, Galloway, as I journeyed south. I am forced to conclude that engineering has reached its apotheosis in New England and that the further one journeys from Boston the less comfortable the conveyance." The Reverend Starbuck delivered these judgments in a voice trained to reach the deepest recesses of the largest churches and lecture halls in America. "The Southern rails, I must say, are distinctly lumpy. The degraded product, no doubt, of a Slavocracy. Am I expected to walk to my destination?" the Reverend Starbuck demanded, suddenly stopping dead in his tracks.

"No, sir. I have a buggy." Galloway was about to request that Adam go fetch the carriage, then realized Adam was too encumbered with the preacher's heavy carpetbag. "I'll fetch it directly, sir. It isn't far."

The Reverend Starbuck waved Galloway on his way, then peered with a fierce inquisitiveness at a group of civilians waiting for the mail to be unloaded from the newly arrived caboose. "Have you read Spurzheim on phrenology?" he demanded of Adam.

"No, sir," Adam responded, surprised by the fiercely abrupt question.

"Science has much to teach us," the Reverend Doctor Starbuck declaimed, "so long as we remember that its conclusions are ever subject to the approval and emendations of Almighty God, but I am interested to observe these proofs of Spurzheim's treatise." He waved his stick toward the waiting civilians. "The New Englander generally possesses a noble brow shape. He displays cranial contours that denote intelligence, benevolence, wisdom, and adhesiveness, but even in these upper regions of the South I notice how the shape of men's skulls betrays depravity, combativeness,

17

destructiveness, and a distinct tendency toward cretinism."

Adam's torturing conscience, like his ingrained patriotism, might have driven him to fight against his father's land, yet he was still a native son of Virginia, and the Northern preacher's criticism made him bridle. "Was not George Washington a Southerner, sir?" he demanded stiffly.

But the Reverend Starbuck was too old a controversialist to be trapped into recantation. "George Washington, young man, like yourself, was a product of the gentry. My observations are confined solely to the common ruck of people. The general there, you see him?" The peremptory stick, narrowly missing an artillery sergeant, pointed at a plump officer who had shared the passenger car with the Reverend Starbuck.

"I see him, sir," Adam said, wondering what characteristics the general's skull shape revealed.

But the Reverend Starbuck had abandoned the subject of phrenology. "That is Pope," the preacher announced. "He was good enough to pay me his respects during the journey. A fine-looking man, indeed."

Adam looked with interest at this new commander of the North's Army of Virginia. General John Pope was a high-colored and confident-looking man with intelligent eyes and a bushy beard. If phrenology did provide an accurate guide to a man's character, then Pope's broad forehead and solid, square appearance suggested that he might indeed be the savior that the North had been seeking ever since the war's sad beginning. John Pope had distinguished himself in the fighting on the Mississippi and had now been brought east to work his magic in the intransigent Virginian countryside where Northern general after Northern general had first been bamboozled and then beaten by the ragged rebel armies.

"Pope has the right ideas," the Reverend Starbuck went on enthusiastically. "It's no good being kind to rebels.

18

Disobedience calls for punishment, and defiance demands retribution. The Slavocracy must be smitten, Faulconer, and its lands laid waste. Pope won't stay his hand, he assures me of that. He is a man for the Lord's work." And indeed, General Pope, almost as soon as he had been appointed commander of the Army of Virginia, had declared that the old policy of treating Southern civilians with respect was finished. Northern soldiers would henceforth take what they needed from the Southern population, and any Southerner who resisted such depredations would be punished. The Reverend Elial Starbuck applauded Pope's zeal. "The Southerner," the preacher now lectured Adam, "understands only one language. Brute force. It is the language he has used to oppress the Negro, and it is the language that must now be used to oppress him. You agree?"

"I think, sir," Adam said tactfully, "that the North must gain victory very soon."

"Quite so, quite so," the Reverend Starbuck said, not certain whether he had received agreement or not. He certainly deserved agreement, for it was upon the Reverend Starbuck's generosity that both the future of Adam and of Galloway's Horse depended. Adam had been penniless when he deserted the South, but it had been his good fortune to know Major James Starbuck, the preacher's eldest son, and it had been James who had informed Adam about Galloway's Horse and who had suggested that his famous father might be able to provide Adam with the necessary funds to join the regiment.

The Reverend Doctor Starbuck had proved more than willing to advance the money. Too old to fight, yet too passionate to abstain from fighting, he had watched, impotent, as the North suffered defeat after defeat in Virginia. The defeats had stirred the Reverend Starbuck into contributing his own and his church's money to the raising and equipping of Massachusetts regiments, only to see those regiments led to disaster. Other men, lesser men, might have abandoned their efforts, but the disasters only fed the preacher's zeal, which was why, given the chance to contribute to the establishment of Galloway's Horse, the Reverend Starbuck had been quick to agree. He was not only supporting Adam but donating fifteen thousand dollars' worth of weaponry and ammunition to Galloway's regiment. The money was not the Reverend Starbuck's own but had been raised by God-fearing New England abolitionists. "In the past," he told Galloway and Adam as they journeyed westward from Manassas in the buggy, "we used such charitable donations for our work in the South: distributing tracts, establishing Sabbath schools for blacks, and, of course, conducting investigations into the evils of the Slavocracy, but now, cut off from those activities, our charities need other outlets for their expenditure."

"There's surely much to be spent on the welfare of escaped slaves?" Adam asked, hoping at the same time that he was not talking Galloway and himself out of their funding.

"The contrabands are amply provided for. Amply!" The Reverend Starbuck's disapproving tone suggested that those slaves who had managed to escape to the North were living in pampered luxury rather than struggling for insanitary survival in makeshift camps. "We need to strike a blow at the root of slavery, not pluck a few diseased leaves from its topmost branches." Adam, hearing the anger behind the preacher's words, suspected that the Reverend Elial Starbuck was much keener to punish the slaveholders than actually free the slaves.

The buggy climbed the shallow hill from New Market, passed between deep woods, then plunged downhill toward the Warrenton Turnpike. As Major Galloway drove, he pointed out landmarks made famous in the battle that had been fought the previous summer across this same ground. There were the ruins of the house where Surgeon Henry's widow had died in the shell fire, and there the Matthews house, which had been used as a hospital. As the buggy rattled down the Sudley road north of the turnpike, Galloway pointed to where the Northern flank attack had come from the river's far side, but as he talked he became aware that the Boston preacher was hardly enthusiastic in his responses. The Reverend Doctor Starbuck did not want a guided tour of the place where the North had met its first defeat; he only wanted to hear promises of victory, and so the conversation died away as Galloway steered the buggy onto the track leading to the farm he had inherited from his father.

Major Galloway, a kindly man, was nervous around the famous abolitionist and relieved when the Reverend Starbuck announced that he had no intention of staying overnight at the comfortable farm, but instead intended to take the evening train south to Culpeper Court House. "My friend Banks did the courtesy of inviting me," the preacher said, referring to General Nathaniel Banks, who had once been Governor of Massachusetts and was now a Union general who believed that a visit from his old friend would serve to encourage his troops' flagging spirits. The invitation had certainly done wonders for the preacher's spirits. He had been chafing in Boston, taking his war news from newspapers and letters, but now he could learn for himself exactly what was happening in Virginia, to which end he had arranged to be absent from his pulpit for the whole month of August. He was fervently praying that a month would be long enough to allow him to be the first Northern minister to preach the gospel from a Richmond pulpit.

But before joining Banks the preacher had agreed to this meeting with Major Galloway and his men. He spoke to Galloway's regiment in the meadow behind the house, where he encouraged them to fight the good fight, but his brusque manner made it plain that he was in a hurry to conclude the day's business and continue his journey. Major Galloway tactfully abandoned the planned display of saber fighting and instead conducted his guest toward the farmhouse, which was an impressive building shaded by great oaks and lapped by wide lawns. "My father prospered in the law," Galloway said, explaining the luxurious house.

"A slave owner, too?" the preacher demanded fiercely, pointing with his ebony cane at the small cabins that lay to the north of the house.

"I freed all the people," Galloway said hastily. "If I'd sold them, sir," he went on, "I wouldn't be needing to beg money for the regiment. I mortgaged the farm to raise funds, sir, and used all the money to buy the horses and weapons you've just seen, but frankly, sir, I've no resources left. I've made myself penniless in the cause of liberty."

"In which cause we must all be prepared to suffer, Galloway," the Reverend Starbuck exclaimed as he followed the Major up the veranda steps and into the hallway. The house echoed like an empty building, which it very nearly was, for with the exception of a few essential pieces of furniture Galloway had sent all his books and pictures and drapes and ornaments north into storage so that his rebellious neighbors could not take revenge on his allegiance by stealing his valuables. And if his neighbors did not steal the goods, he explained, his own brother would. "My brother fights for the South, alas," Major Galloway told the preacher, "and he'd like nothing more than to take the house and its contents from me." He paused for an instant. "There's nothing sadder, sir, is there, than family members fighting on opposite sides?" The Reverend Starbuck offered a belligerent grunt as answer, and that ill-tempered noise should have warned Major Galloway against proceeding further with the conversation, but the Major was a guileless man. "Am I right, sir," Galloway asked, "in believing you have a son who fights with the rebels?"

"I know of no such person," the preacher said, stiffening perceptibly.

"But Nate, surely—" Adam began, only to be fiercely interrupted.

"I have no son called Nathaniel," the preacher snapped. "I recognize no person called Nathaniel Starbuck. He is doomed, he is cast out, not only from my family, but also from the loving congregation of Christ! He is a reprobate!" This last condemnation was trumpeted in a voice that might have carried a half-mile into a mighty wind.

Galloway realized he had been tactless and so hurried on, talking inconsequentially about the house and its amenities until he reached the doors of the library, where a tall, heavyset Captain waited. The Captain had a ready smile and a quick, friendly manner. "May I introduce my second-in-command?" Galloway said to the preacher. "Captain William Blythe."

"Sure glad to meet you, Reverend." Blythe extended a hand.

"Captain Blythe was a horse trader before the war," Galloway said.

"You should never have told the minister that, Joe!" Blythe said with a smile. "Everyone knows that us horse traders are the crookedest folks this side of tarnation, but God bless me, sir"—he had turned back to the preacher—"I tried to be as honest a trader as a Christian man could."

"I'm glad to hear it," the Reverend Starbuck said stiffly.

"A hundred cents to an honest dollar, sir, that was always my way," Blythe said cheerfully, "and if I ever rooked a man, sir, why it was never on purpose. And I'll tell you another thing, sir." Blythe dropped his voice confidingly. "If ever a man of the cloth wanted a horse, why sir, I swallowed the profit and sometimes a good bit more besides. I confess I was never a churchgoing man myself, sir, to my regret, but my pa always contended that a bucketful of prayer never hurt no one and my dear ma, God bless her dear soul, fair wore out her knees on the church planking. And she sure would have liked to hear you speaking, sir, for they all say you do a mighty sermon!"

The Reverend Starbuck seemed pleased by Blythe's forthright and friendly manner, so pleased that he did not even show a sign of distaste when the tall Captain draped an arm around his shoulders to conduct him into the bare-shelved library. "You say you're not a churchgoing man," the preacher inquired, "but I trust you are saved, Captain?"

Blythe released his grip so that he could turn an astonished face to the Reverend Starbuck. "Washed white in the blood of the lamb, Reverend," Blythe said in a voice that suggested shock that anyone might have taken him for a heathen. "In fact I'm fair swilled in that precious blood, sir. My dear ma made sure of that before she died, praise the Lord and God rest her dear soul."

"And your mother, Captain, would approve of your allegiance in this war?" the Reverend Starbuck asked.

Captain William Blythe frowned to show his sincerity. "My dear mother, God bless her simple soul, sir, always said that in the eyes of God a nigra's soul was the same as any white man's. So long as that nigra's a Christian, of course. Then come heaven time, she said, we'd all be white as snow, even the blackest nigra, praise the Lord for His goodness." Blythe raised his eyes to the ceiling, then, over the unsuspecting preacher's head, offered Major Galloway an outrageous wink.

24

Galloway cut short his second-in-command's blarney by seating his guest at the library's large table, which was heaped with account books. Galloway, Adam, and Blythe sat opposite the preacher, and the Major described his ambitions for his regiment of cavalry; how they would ride the Southern paths with a confidence and local knowledge that no Northern horseman could hope to match. The Major spoke modestly, stressing the army's need for good reconnaissance and his own ambitions for a tightly disciplined regiment of horsemen, yet his words were plainly disappointing the Boston preacher. The Reverend Starbuck wanted swift results and dramatic victories, and it was the bombastic William Blythe who first sensed that desire. Blythe intervened with a chuckle. "You have to forgive the Major, Reverend," he said, "for not talking us up overmuch, but the real truth is we're going to twist Jeff Davis's tail, then we're going to scald the skin straight off that tail, and dang me if we won't then cut the thing clean off! I promise you, Reverend, that we're going to make the rebels squeal, and you'll hear that squeal all the way to Boston Common. Ain't that so, Major?"

Galloway merely looked surprised, while Adam stared at the table's scarred top, but the Reverend Starbuck was delighted by the implications of Blythe's promise. "You have specific plans?" he asked eagerly.

Blythe looked momentarily shocked. "We couldn't say a danged thing about specifics, sir, it would be downright unsoldierlike of us, but I do promise you, Reverend, that in the weeks to come it won't be Jeb Stuart you'll be reading about in the Boston newspapers, no sir, it'll be Major Joseph Galloway and his gallant regiment of troopers! Ain't that a fact, Joe?"

Galloway, taken aback, nodded. "We shall do our best, certainly."

"But there ain't nothing we can do, sir"—Blythe leaned forward with an earnest expression—"if we don't have the guns, the sabers, and the horses. As my sainted mother always said, sir, promises fill no bellies. You have to add a lick of hard work and a peck of money if you want to fill a Southern boy's belly, and sir, believe me, sir, it hurts me, it hurts me hard, to see these fine Southern patriots standing idle for want of a dollar or two."

"But what will you do with the money?" the Reverend Starbuck asked.

"What can't we do?" Blythe demanded. "With God on our side, Reverend, we can turn the South upside down and inside out. Why, sir, I shouldn't say it to you, but I guess you're a closemouthed man so I'll take the risk, but there's a map of Richmond up in my sleeping room, and why would a man like me need a map of Richmond? Well, I ain't going to tell you, sir, only because it would be downright unsoldierly of me to tell you, but I guess a clever man like you can work out which end of a snake has the bite."

Adam looked up astonished at this implication that the regiment was planning to raid the rebel capital, and Galloway seemed about to make a firm demurral, but the Reverend Starbuck was gripped by Blythe's promised coup. "You'll go to Richmond?" he asked Blythe.

"The very city, sir. That den of evil and lair of the serpent. I wish I could tell you how I loathe the place, sir, but with God's help we'll scour it and burn it and cleanse it anew!"

The horse trader was now speaking a language the Reverend Starbuck longed to hear. The Boston preacher wanted promises of rebel humiliation and of dazzling Union victories, of exploits to rival the insolent achievements of the rebel Jeb Stuart. He did not want to hear of patient reconnaissance duties faithfully performed, but wild

26

promises of Northern victories, and no amount of caution from Major Galloway would convince the preacher that Blythe's promises were exaggerated. The Reverend Starbuck heard what he longed to hear, and to make it a reality he drew from his frock coat's inner pocket a check. He borrowed a pen and an inkwell from the Major and then signed the check with a due solemnity.

"Praise the Lord," William Blythe said when the check was signed.

"Praise Him indeed," the preacher echoed piously, thrusting the check across the table toward Galloway. "That money comes, Major, from a consortium of New England abolitionist churches. It represents the hard-earned dollars of simple honest working folk, given gladly in a sacred cause. Use it well."

"We shall do our utmost, sir," Galloway said, then fell momentarily silent as he saw the check was not for the fifteen thousand dollars he had expected, but for twenty thousand. Blythe's oratory had worked a small miracle. "And thank you, sir," Galloway managed to say.

"And I ask only one thing in return," the preacher said.

"Anything, sir!" Blythe said, spreading his big hands as though to encompass the whole wide world. "Anything at all!"

The preacher glanced at the wall over the wide garden doors, where a polished staff tipped with a lance head and a faded cavalry guidon was the room's sole remaining decoration. "A flag," the preacher said, "is important to a soldier, is it not?"

"It is, sir," Galloway answered. The small guidon over the door had been the banner he had carried in the Mexican war.

"Sacred, you might say," Blythe added.

"Then I should esteem it an honor if you would provide

27

me with a rebel banner," the preacher said, "that I can display in Boston as proof that our donations are doing God's work."

"You shall have your flag, sir!" Blythe promised swiftly. "I'll make it my business to see you have one. When are you returning to Boston, sir?"

"At month's end, Captain."

"You'll not go empty-handed, sir, not if my name's Billy Blythe. I promise you, on my dear mother's grave, sir, that you'll have your rebel battle flag."

Galloway shook his head, but the preacher did not see the gesture. He only saw a hated enemy battle flag hanging in the chancel of his church as an object of derision. The Reverend Starbuck pushed back his chair and consulted his fob watch. "I must be returning to the depot," he said.

"Adam will drive you, sir," Major Galloway said. The Major waited until the preacher was gone, then shook his head sadly. "You made a deal of promises, Billy."

"And there was a deal of money at stake," Blythe said carelessly, "and hell, I never did mind making promises."

Galloway crossed to the open garden door, where he stared out at the sun-bleached lawn. "I don't mind a man making promises, Billy, but I sure mind that he keeps them."

"I always keep my promises, sure I do. I keep 'em in mind while I'm working out how to break them." Blythe laughed. "Now are you going to give me aggravation for having fetched you your money? Hell, Joe, I get enough piety from young Faulconer."

"Adam's a good man."

"I never said he weren't a good man. I just said he's a pious son of a righteous bitch and God only knows why you appointed him Captain."

"Because he's a good man," Galloway said firmly, "and because his family is famous in Virginia, and because I like him. And I like you too, Billy, but not if you're going to argue with Adam all the time. Now why don't you go and get busy? You've got a flag to capture."

Blythe scorned such a duty. "Have I? Hell! There's plenty enough red, white, and blue cloth about, so we'll just have your house niggers run up a quick rebel flag."

Galloway sighed. "They're my servants, Billy, servants."

"Still niggers, ain't they? And the girl can use a needle, can't she? And the Reverend'll never know the difference. She can make us a flag and I'll tear it and dirty it a bit and that old fool will think we snatched it clean out of Jeff Davis's own hands." Blythe grinned at the idea, then picked up the check. He whistled appreciatively. "Reckon I talked us into a tidy profit, Joe."

"I reckon you did too. So now you'll go and spend it, Billy." Galloway needed to equip Adam's troop with horses and most of his men with sabers and firearms, but now, thanks to the generosity of the Reverend Starbuck's abolitionists, the Galloway Horse would be as well equipped and mounted as any other cavalry regiment in the Northern army. "Spend half on horses and half on weapons and saddlery," Galloway suggested.

"Horses are expensive, Joe," Blythe warned. "The war's made them scarce."

"You're a horse dealer, Billy, so go and work some horse-dealing magic. Unless you'd rather I let Adam go? He wants to buy his own horses."

"Never let a boy do a man's work, Joe," Blythe said. He touched the preacher's check to his lips and gave it an exaggerated kiss. "Praise the Lord," Billy Blythe said, "just praise His holy name, amen."

The Faulconer Legion made camp just a few miles north of the river where they had first glimpsed the baleful figure of their new commanding general. No one in the Legion knew where they were or where they were going or why they were marching there, but a passing artillery major who was a veteran of Jackson's campaigns said that was the usual way of Old Jack. "You'll know you've arrived just as soon as the enemy does and no sooner," the Major said, then begged a bucket of water for his horse.

The Brigade headquarters erected tents, but none of the regiments bothered with such luxuries. The Faulconer Legion had started the war with three wagonloads of tents but now had only two tents left, both reserved for Doctor Danson. The men had become adept at manufacturing shelters from branches and sod, though on this warm evening no one needed protection from the weather. Work parties fetched wood for campfires while others carried water from a stream a mile away. Some of the men sat with their bare feet dangling in the stream, trying to wash away the blisters and blood of the day's march. The four men on the Legion's punishment detail watered the draft horses that hauled the ammunition wagons, then paraded round the campsite with newly felled logs on their shoulders. The men staggered under the weight as they made the ten circuits of the Legion's lines that constituted their nightly punishment. "What have they done?" Lieutenant Coffman asked Starbuck.

Starbuck glanced up at the miserable procession. "Lem Pierce got drunk. Matthews sold cartridges for a pint of whiskey, and Evans threatened to hit Captain Medlicott."

"Pity he didn't," Sergeant Truslow interjected. Daniel Medlicott had been the miller at Faulconer Court House, where he had earned a reputation as a hard man with money, though in the spring elections for field officers he had distributed enough promises and whiskey to have himself promoted from sergeant to captain.

"And I don't know what Trent did," Starbuck finished.

"Abram Trent's just a poxed son of a whore," Truslow said to Coffman. "He stole some food from Sergeant Major Tolliver, but that ain't why he's being punished. He's being punished, lad, because he got caught."

"You are listening to the gospel according to Sergeant Thomas Truslow," Starbuck told the Lieutenant. "Thou shalt steal all thou can, but thou shalt not get caught." Starbuck grinned, then hissed with pain as he jabbed his thumb with a needle. He was struggling to sew the sole of his right boot back onto its uppers, for which task he had borrowed one of the three precious needles possessed by the company.

Sergeant Truslow, sitting on the far side of the fire from the two officers, mocked his Captain's efforts. "You're a lousy cobbler."

"I never pretended to be otherwise."

"You'll break the goddamn needle, pushing like that."

"You want to do it?" Starbuck asked, offering the half-finished work to the Sergeant.

"Hell no, I ain't paid to patch your boots."

"Then shut the hell up," Starbuck said, trying to work the needle through one of the old stitching holes in the sole.

"It'll only break first thing in the morning," Truslow said after a moment's silence.

"Not if I do it properly."

"No chance of that," Truslow said. He broke off a piece of tobacco and put it in his cheek. "You've got to protect the thread, see? So it don't chafe on the road."

"That's what I'm doing."

"No, you ain't. You're just lashing the boot together. There are blind men without fingers who could make a better job than you."

31

Lieutenant Coffman listened nervously to the conversation. He had been told that the Captain and Sergeant were friends—indeed, that they had been friends ever since the Yankee Starbuck had been sent to persuade the Yankee-hating Truslow to leave his high-mountain farm and join Faulconer's Legion—but to Coffman it seemed an odd sort of friendship if it was expressed with such mutual scorn. Now the intimidating Sergeant turned to the nervous Lieutenant. "A proper officer," Truslow confided to Coffman, "would have a darkie to do his sewing."

"A proper officer," Starbuck said, "would kick your rotten teeth down your gullet."

"Anytime, Captain," Truslow said, laughing.

Starbuck tied off the thread and peered critically at his handiwork. "It ain't perfect," he allowed, "but it'll do."

"It'll do," Truslow agreed, "so long as you don't walk on it."

Starbuck laughed. "Hell, we'll be fighting a battle in a day or two, then I'll get myself a pair of brand-new Yankee boots." He gingerly pulled the repaired boot onto his foot and was pleasantly surprised that the sole did not immediately peel away. "Good as new," he said, then flinched, not because of the boot, but because a sudden scream sounded across the campsite. The scream was cut abruptly short; there was a pause, then a sad wailing sound sobbed briefly.

Coffman looked aghast, for the noise had sounded like it came from a creature being tortured, which indeed it had. "Colonel Swynyard," Sergeant Truslow explained to the new Lieutenant, "is beating one of his niggers."

"The Colonel drinks," Starbuck added.

"The Colonel is a drunk," Truslow amended.

"And it's anyone's guess whether the liquor will kill him before one of his slaves does," Starbuck said, "or one of us,

32

for that matter." He spat into the fire. "I'd kill the bastard willingly enough."

"Welcome to the Faulconer Brigade," Truslow said to Coffman.

The Lieutenant did not know how to respond to such cynicism, so he just sat looking troubled and nervous, then flinched as a thought crossed his mind. "Will we really be fighting in a day or two?" he asked.

"Probably tomorrow." Truslow jerked his head toward the northern sky, which was being reddened by the reflected glow of an army's fires. "It's what you're paid to do, son," Truslow added when he saw Coffman's nervousness.

"I'm not paid," Coffman said and immediately blushed for the admission.

Truslow and Starbuck were both silent for a few seconds; then Starbuck frowned. "What the hell do you mean?" he asked.

"Well, I do get paid," Coffman said, "but I don't get the money, see?"

"No, I don't see."

The Lieutenant was embarrassed. "It's my mother."

"She gets the money, you mean?" Starbuck asked.

"She owes General Faulconer money," Coffman explained, "because we rent one of his houses on the Rosskill road and Mother fell behind with the rent, so Faulconer keeps my salary."

There was another long pause. "Christ on his cross." Truslow's blasphemy broke the silence. "You mean that miserable rich bastard is taking your three lousy bucks a week for his own?"

"It's only fair, isn't it?" Coffman asked.

"No, it damn well ain't," Starbuck said. "If you want to send your mother the money, that's fair, but it ain't fair for you to fight for nothing! Shit!" He swore angrily.

33

"I don't really need any money." Coffman nervously defended the arrangement.

"'Course you do, boy," Truslow said. "How else are you going to buy whores and whiskey?"

"Have you talked to Pecker about this?" Starbuck demanded.

Coffman shook his head. "No."

"Hell, then I will," Starbuck said. "Ain't going to have you being shot at for free." He climbed to his feet. "I'll be back in a half hour. Oh, shit!" This last imprecation was not in anger for Washington Faulconer's greed but because his right sole had come loose on his first proper step. "Goddamn shit!" he said angrily, then stalked off to find Colonel Bird.

Truslow grinned at Starbuck's inept cobbling, then spat tobacco juice into the fire's margin. "He'll get your cash, son," he said.

"He will?"

"Faulconer's scared of Starbuck."

"Scared? The General's scared of the Captain?" Coffman found that hard to believe.

"Starbuck's a proper soldier. He's a fighter while Faulconer's just a pretty uniform on an expensive horse. In the long run, son, the fighter will always win." Truslow picked a shred of tobacco from between his teeth. "Unless he's killed, of course."

"Killed?"

"You're going to meet the Yankees tomorrow, son," Truslow said, "and some of us are going to get killed, but I'll do my best to keep you from getting slaughtered. Starting now." He leaned over and ripped the bars off the Lieutenant's collar, then tossed the cloth scraps into the fire. "Sharpshooters put telescopes on their rifles, son, just look-ing for officers to kill, and the Yankees don't care that you're not full-grown. See a pair of bars like that, they shoot, and you're two feet underground with a shovelful of dirt in your eyes." Truslow spat more tobacco juice. "Or worse," he added darkly.

"Worse?" Coffman asked nervously.

"You could be wounded, boy, and screaming like a stuck pig while a half-drunken doctor rummages through your innards. Or sobbing like a baby while you lie out in the field with your guts being eaten by rodents and no one knowing where the hell you are. It ain't pretty, and there's only one way to keep it from being even uglier and that's to hurt the bastards before they hurt you." He looked at Coffman, recognizing how the boy was trying to hide his fear. "You'll be all right," Truslow said. "The worst bit is the waiting. Now sleep, boy. You've got a man's job to do tomorrow."

High overhead a shooting star whipped white fire across the darkening sky. Somewhere a man sang of a love left behind while another played a sad tune on a violin. Colonel Swynyard's flogged slave tried to keep from whimpering, Truslow snored, and Coffman shivered, thinking of the morrow.

THE YANKEE CAVALRY PATROL reached General Banks's headquarters late at night. The patrol had come under fire at the Rapidan River, and the loss of one of their horses had slowed their journey back to Culpeper Court House, as had the necessity to look after two wounded men. A New Hampshire corporal had been struck by a bullet in his lower belly and would surely die, while the patrol's commander, a captain, had suffered a glancing hit on the ribs. The Captain's wound was hardly serious, but he had scratched and prodded at the graze until a satisfactory amount of blood heroically stained his shirt.

Major General Nathaniel Banks, commander of General Pope's Second Corps, was smoking a last cigar on the veranda of his commandeered house when he heard that the patrol had returned with ominous news of enemy forces crossing the Rapidan. "Let's have the man here! Let's hear him. Lively now!" Banks was a fussy man who, despite all the contrary evidence, was convinced of his own military genius. He certainly looked the part of a successful soldier, for there were few men who wore the uniform of the United States with more assurance. He was trim, brusque, and confident, yet until the war began he had never been a soldier, merely a politician. He had risen to be Speaker of the House of Representatives, though it had taken 133 ballots to achieve that honor, and afterward Governor of Massachusetts, a state so rich in men willing to be taxed that the federal government had deemed it necessary to offer its governor the chance of immortal martial glory as a token of its thanks. Governor Banks, who was as passionate in his love for his country as in his hatred of the slave trade, had leaped at the chance.

Now he waited, ramrod straight, as the cavalry Captain, wearing his jacket like a cloak so that his bloody shirt showed clearly, climbed the veranda steps and offered a salute, which he dramatically cut short with a wince as though the pain in his chest had suddenly struck hard.

"Your name?" Banks demanded peremptorily.

"Thompson, General. John Hannibal Thompson. From Ithaca, New York. Reckon you might have met my uncle, Michael Fane Thompson, when you were a congressman. He sat for New York back in—"

"You found the enemy, Thompson?" Banks asked in a very icy voice.

Thompson, offended at being so rudely cut off, shrugged. "We sure found someone hostile, General."

"Who?"

"Damned if I know. We got shot at." Thompson touched the crusted blood on his shirt, which looked brown rather than red in the lamplight.

"You shot back?" Banks asked.

"Hell, General, no one shoots at me without getting retaliation, and I reckon me and my boys laid a few of the bastards low."

"Where was this?" the aide accompanying General Banks asked.

Captain Thompson crossed to a wicker table on which the aide had spread a map of northern Virginia illuminated by two flickering candle-lanterns. Moths beat frantically around the three men's heads as they leaned over the map. Thompson used one of the lanterns to light himself a cigar, then tapped a finger on the map. "It was a ford just around there, General." He had tapped the map well west of the main road that led due south from Culpeper Court House to Gordonsville.

"You crossed to the south bank of the river?" Banks asked.

"Couldn't rightly do that, General, on account of there being a pack of rebs already occupying the ford."

"There's no ford marked there," the aide interjected. Sweat dripped from his face to stain the Blue Ridge Mountains, which lay well to the west of the rivers. The night had brought no relief from the sweltering heat.

"A local nigger guided us," Thompson explained. "He said the ford weren't well known, being nothing but a summer back road to a gristmill, and some of us reckoned he just might be lying to us, but there sure was a ford after all. Seems the nigger was truthful."

"The word, Thompson, is Negro," Banks said very coldly, then looked down at the map again. Other patrols had spoken of rebel infantry marching north on the Gordonsville road, and this new report suggested that the Confederates were advancing on a broad front and in considerable strength. What were they doing? A reconnaissance in force, or a full-scale attack aimed at destroying his corps?

"So how many men fired at you?" Banks resumed his questioning of the flippant Thompson.

"Wasn't exactly counting the minny balls, General, on account of being too busy firing back. But I reckon there was at least one regiment north of the river and more of the devils coming on."

Banks stared at the cavalryman, wondering just why responsibility always seemed to devolve onto fools. "Did you try to take a prisoner?"

"I guess I was too busy making sure I didn't end up six feet underground, General." Thompson laughed. "Hell, there were only a dozen of us and more than a thousand of them. Maybe two thousand."

"Did you ascertain the identity of the regiment which fired on you?" Banks asked with an icy pedantry.

"I sure ascertained that it was a rebel regiment, General," Thompson answered. "They were carrying that new flag, the one with the cross on it."

Banks shuddered at the man's obtuse stupidity and wondered why the North's horsemen were so inept at gathering intelligence. Probably, he thought, because they had none themselves. So who were these rebels marching north? There was a rumor that Stonewall Jackson had come to Gordonsville, and Banks winced at the thought of that bearded, ragged man whose troops marched at the speed of wildfire and fought like fiends.

Banks dismissed the cavalryman. "Useless," he said as the man paced off down Culpeper Court House's main street, where sentries stood guard on the taverns. In the town's small wooden houses yellow lights burned behind the muslin curtains used as insect screens. An undertaker's wagon, its shafts tilted up to the sky, stood outside a church where, Banks remembered, the famous Boston preacher Elial Starbuck was due to speak on Sunday morning. The town's population was not anticipating the abolitionist's sermon with any pleasure, but Banks, an old friend of the preacher, was looking forward to Starbuck's peroration and had demanded that as many of his officers as possible should be present. Nathaniel Banks had a noble vision of God and country marching hand in hand to victory.

Now, with a frown on his face, Banks looked back to the map, on which his sweat dripped monotonously. Suppose the enemy move was a bluff? Suppose that a handful of rebels were merely trying to frighten him? The rebels had surely guessed that he had his eyes on Gordonsville, because if

39

he captured that town, then he would cut the railroad that connected Richmond with the rich farmland in the Shenandoah Valley. Sever those rails, and the enemy's armies would starve, and that thought reignited the glimmer of promised martial glory in Nathaniel Banks's mind. He saw a statue in Boston, envisaged streets and towns all across New England named after him, and even dreamed that a whole new state might be fashioned from the savage western territories and given his name. Banks Street, Banksville, the state of Banks.

Those inspired visions were fed by more than mere ambition. They were fed by a burning need for revenge. Earlier in the year Nathaniel Banks had led a fine army down the Shenandoah Valley, where he had been tricked and trounced by Thomas Jackson. Even the Northern newspapers had admitted that Jackson had cut Banks to pieces—indeed, the rebels had taken so many guns and supplies from Banks that they had nicknamed him "Commissary Banks." They had mocked him, ridiculed him, and their scorn still hurt Nathaniel Banks. He wanted revenge.

"The prudent course, sir, would be a withdrawal behind the Rappahannock," the aide murmured. The aide was a graduate of West Point and supposed to provide the politician-general with sound military advice.

"It may be nothing but a reconnaissance," Banks said, thinking of vengeance.

"Maybe so, sir," the aide said suavely, "but what do we gain by fighting? Why hold ground we can easily retake in a week's time? Why not just let the enemy wear himself out by marching?"

Banks brushed cigar ash off the map. Retreat now? In a week when Boston's most famous preacher was coming to visit the army? What would Massachusetts say if they heard that Commissary Banks had run away from a few rebels?

40

"We stay," Banks said. He stabbed his finger down at the contours of a ridge that barred the road just south of Culpeper Court House. If Jackson was marching north in the hope of resupplying his army at the expense of Commissary Banks, then he would have to cross that ridge that lay behind the small protection of a stream. The stream was called Cedar Run, and it lay at the foot of Cedar Mountain. "We'll meet him there," Banks said, "and beat him there."

The aide said nothing. He was a handsome, clever young man who thought he deserved better than to be harnessed to this stubborn bantam-cock. The aide was trying to frame a response, some persuasive words that would deflect Banks from rashness, but the words would not come. Instead, from the lamplit street, there sounded men's voices singing about loved ones left behind, of sweethearts waiting, of home.

"We'll meet him there," Banks said again, ramming his finger onto the sweat-stained map, "and beat him there."

At Cedar Mountain.

The Legion did not march far on the day they crossed the Rapidan. There was a curious lack of urgency about the expedition, almost as though they were merely changing base rather than advancing on the Northerners who had invaded Virginia. And next morning, though they were woken long before dawn and were ready to march even before the sun had risen above the tall eastern trees, they still waited three hours while a succession of other regiments trailed slowly by on the dusty road. A battery of small six-pounders and short-barreled howitzers was dragged past, followed by a column of Virginia infantry, who good-naturedly jeered the Faulconer Legion for its pretentious name. The day was hot and promised to get hotter still, yet still they waited as the sun climbed higher. More troops passed until, just short of midday, the Legion at last led the Faulconer Brigade out onto the dusty road.

Just moments later the guns started to sound. The noise came from far ahead, a grumble that could have been mistaken for thunder if the sky had not been cloudless. The air was sullen, moist, and windless, and the faces of Starbuck's men were pale with road dust through which their sweat ran in dark lines. Soon, Starbuck thought, some of those rivulets would be blood red, fly-coated, and twitching, and that premonition of battle turned his belly sour and caused the muscles in his right thigh to tremble. He tried to anticipate the sound of bullets as he coached himself to display courage and not the fear that was liquefying his bowels, and all the while the distant cannons hammered their flat, soulless noise across the land. "Goddamned artillery," Truslow said in a sour tone. "Some poor bastards are catching hell."

Lieutenant Coffman seemed about to say something, then decided to keep quiet. One of the conscripts broke ranks to pull down his pants and squat beside the road. Normally he would have been good-naturedly jeered, but the muffled thump of the guns made every man nervous.

In the early afternoon the Legion halted in a shallow valley. The road ahead was blocked by a Georgia battalion beyond which lay a ridgeline crested by dark trees beneath a sky whitened by gunsmoke. Some of the Georgians lay asleep on the road, looking like corpses. Others were penciling their names and hometowns on scraps of paper that they either pinned to their coats or stuck into buttonholes so that, should they die, their bodies would be recognized and their families informed. Some of Starbuck's men began to take the same gloomy precaution, using the blank end pages of Bibles as their labels.

"Culpeper Court House," George Finney announced suddenly.

Starbuck, sitting beside the road, glanced at him, waiting.

"Billy Sutton says this is the road to Culpeper Court House," George Finney explained. "Says his daddy brought him on this road two years back."

"We came to bury my grandmother, Captain," Billy Sutton intervened. Sutton was a corporal in G Company. He had once been in J Company, but a year of battles had shrunk the Faulconer Legion from ten to eight companies, and even those companies were now understrength. At the war's beginning the Legion had marched to battle as one of the biggest regiments in the rebel army, but after a year of battle it would scarcely have filled the pews of a backcountry church.

Three horsemen galloped southward through the brittle stubble of a harvested cornfield, their horses' hooves kicking up puffs of dust from the parched dirt. Starbuck guessed they were staff officers bringing orders. Truslow glanced at the three men, then shook his head. "Goddam Yankees in Culpeper Court House," Truslow said, affronted. "Got no damned business in Culpeper Court House."

"If it is Culpeper Court House," Starbuck said dubiously. Culpeper County had to be at least sixty miles from the Legion's home in Faulconer County, and few of the men in the Legion had traveled more than twenty miles from home in all their lives. Or not until this war had marched them up to Manassas and across to Richmond to kill Yankees. They had become good at that. They had become good at dying, too.

The gunfire suddenly swelled into one of those frenetic passages when, for no apparent reason, every cannon on a battlefield spoke at once. Starbuck cocked an ear, listening for the slighter crackle of musketry, but he could hear nothing except the unending thunder of artillery. "Poor bastards," he said.

"Our turn soon," Truslow answered unhelpfully.

"This rate they'll run out of ammunition," Starbuck said hopefully.

Truslow spat in comment on his Captain's optimism, then turned as hoofbeats sounded. "God damn Swynyard," he said tonelessly.

Every man in the company now either feigned sleep or kept his eyes fixed on the dusty road. Colonel Griffin Swynyard was a professional soldier whose talents had long been dissolved by alcohol but whose career had been rescued by General Washington Faulconer. Swynyard's cousin edited Richmond's most influential newspaper, and Washington Faulconer, well aware that reputation was more easily bought than won, was paying for the support of the *Richmond Examiner* by employing Swynyard. For a second Starbuck wondered if Swynyard was coming to see him, but the Colonel, closely followed by Captain Moxey, galloped past H Company and on up the slope toward the sound of battle. Starbuck's heart gave an acid beat as he guessed Swynyard was going to mark the place where the Legion would deploy, which meant that at any second the orders would come to advance into the guns.

Ahead, where the road vanished across the shallow ridge, the Georgian troops were already struggling to their feet and pulling on bedrolls and weapons. The cannon fire had momentarily abated, but the snapping sound of rifle cartridges now crackled across the dry landscape. The sound increased Starbuck's nervousness. It had been a month since the Legion last fought, but a single month was not nearly long enough to allay the terrors of the battlefield. Starbuck had been secretly hoping that the Legion might sit this skirmish out, but the Georgia battalion was already trudging north to leave a haze of dust over the road.

"Up, Nate!" Captain Murphy relayed Bird's orders to Starbuck.

Truslow bellowed at H Company to stand up. The men hitched their bedrolls over their shoulders and dusted off their rifles. Behind H Company the men of Captain Medlicott's G Company stood slowly, their lapels and belt loops dotted with the scraps of white paper on which they had written their names.

"Look for Swynyard on the road," Captain Murphy told Starbuck.

Starbuck wondered where Washington Faulconer was, then assumed the General would be leading his Brigade from behind. Swynyard, whatever his other faults, was no coward. "Forward!" Starbuck shouted; then, rifle and bedroll slung, he took his place at the head of the column. Dust thrown up by the boots of the Georgians stung his throat and eyes. The road was daubed with dark stains of tobacco juice that looked uncannily like blood spattered from wounds. The sound of rifle fire was more intense.

That sound swelled even further as Starbuck led the Legion through the woods at the crest of the ridge that had served to disguise and diminish the sound of fighting, which now spread across Starbuck's front in a furious cacophony. For a mile beyond the trees there was nothing but gunsmoke, flame, and chaos. The fields to the left of the road were filled with wounded men and surgeons hacking at broken flesh, to the right was a hill rimmed with artillery smoke, while ahead lay a second belt of woodland that concealed the actual fighting but could not hide the pall of smoke that boiled up either side of the road nor disguise the sound of the guns.

"By golly," Coffman said. He was excited and nervous.

"Stay near Truslow," Starbuck warned the young Lieutenant.

45

"I'll be all right, sir."

"Every damned man who's died in this war said that, Coffman," Starbuck reacted angrily, "and I want you to shave before you're shot. So stay close to Truslow."

"Yes, sir," Coffman said meekly.

An artillery bolt smacked through pine tops to the right of the road, leaving the branches whipping back and forth above the spray of needles that sifted down to the dust. Wounded men, all rebels, were lying on both verges. Some had already died. A man staggered back from the fighting. He was barechested and his suspenders were hanging loose beside his legs. He was clutching his belly, trying to keep his guts from spilling into the dust. His forearms were soaked in blood. "Oh, golly," Coffman said again and went pale. The blood on the dusty road looked blacker than the tobacco stains. The sound of rifle fire was splintering the afternoon that smelt of pine resin, sulfur, and blood. The shadows were long, long enough to give Starbuck an instant's wild hope that night might fall before he needed to fight.

Starbuck led the company on across the open land and into the cover of the second belt of timber. The leaves here flicked with the strike of bullets, and fresh scars of yellow wood showed where artillery bolts had sheared limbs off trees. An ammunition wagon with one wheel smashed was canted at the side of the road. A black teamster with a bloody scalp sat leaning against the abandoned wagon and watched Starbuck's men pass.

The trees ended not far ahead, and beyond, in the smoky open, Starbuck knew the battle was waiting for him. Common sense told him to slow down and thus delay his entry onto that bullet-riven stage, but pride made him hurry. He could see the gunsmoke sifting through the last green branches like a spring fog blowing out of Boston Harbor. He could smell the smoke's foul stench, and he knew it was

46

almost time for the Legion to deploy. His mouth was powder dry, his heart erratic, and his bladder full. He passed a man whose body lay splayed open from the strike of an artillery shell. He heard Coffman retch dryly. Flies buzzed in the close air. One of his men laughed at the eviscerated corpse. Starbuck unslung his rifle and felt with a finger to check that the percussion cap was in place. He was a captain, but he bore no signs of rank and carried a rifle just like his men, and now, like them, he pulled his cartridge box around to the front of his rope belt, where it would be handy for reloading. His broken right boot almost tripped him as he left the shadow of the trees to see ahead a shallow valley scarred and littered by battle. The low land was rifted with smoke and loud with gunfire. Beside the road a horse lay dead in a dry ditch. Coffman was white-faced but trying hard to look unconcerned and not to duck whenever a missile howled or whipped overhead. Bullets were whickering through the humid air. There was no sign of any enemy—indeed, hardly any men were in view except for some rebel gunners and Colonel Swynyard, who, with Moxey beside him, was sitting his horse in a field to the left of the road.

"Starbuck!" Colonel Swynyard shouted. "Over here!" Starbuck led the company across the brittle corn stubble. "Form there!" Swynyard called, pointing to a spot close behind his horse; then he turned in his saddle to stare northward through a pair of binoculars. Captain Moxey was fussily ordering H Company to align themselves on his marker, so Starbuck left him to it and walked forward to join Swynyard. The Colonel lowered his glasses to watch the battery of rebel six-pounders that was deployed just a hundred yards ahead. The smoke from the small guns was obscuring the fighting beyond, but every now and then a Yankee shell would explode near the battery, making Swynyard grin in appreciation. "Oh, well done! Good shooting!" Swynyard called aloud when an enemy shell eviscerated a team horse picketed fifty paces behind the guns. The horse screamed as it flailed bloodily on the ground, panicking the other tethered horses, which reared frantically as they tried to drag their iron picket stakes out of the ground. "Chaos!" Swynyard said happily, then glanced down at Starbuck. "Yankees are damned lively this afternoon."

"Guess they were waiting for us," Starbuck said. "Knew we were coming."

"Guess someone told on us. A traitor, eh?" Swynyard offered the suggestion slyly. The Colonel was a man of startling ugliness, much of it the result of wounds honorably taken in the service of the old United States, but some of it caused by the whiskey that generally left him comatose by early evening. He had a coarse black beard streaked with gray and crusted with dried tobacco juice, sunken eyes, and a tic in his scarred right cheek. His left hand was missing three fingers, and his mouth was filled with rotting, stinking teeth. "Maybe the traitor was a Northerner, eh?" Swynyard hinted clumsily.

Starbuck smiled. "More likely to be some poor drunken son of a bitch needing cash for his whiskey . . ."—he paused—"Colonel."

Swynyard's only response was his cackling laugh, which hinted at madness. Remarkably, despite the lateness of the day, he was still sober, either because Washington Faulconer had hidden his whiskey or else because Swynyard's small remaining shred of self-protection had convinced him that he had to function efficiently on a day of battle or else lose his job altogether. Swynyard glanced up at the gunsmoke, then looked back to the notebook in which he was writing. On his right sleeve he wore a square patch of white cloth embroidered with a red crescent. The symbol was from Washington Faulconer's coat of arms, and the General had dreamed up the happy idea of issuing the badges to every man in his Brigade, though the idea had not been wholly successful. Some men refused to wear the patch, and generally it was possible to tell Faulconer's supporters from his detractors by the badge's presence or absence. Starbuck, naturally, had never worn the crescent badge, though some of his men had patched their pants' seats with the convenient square of cloth.

Swynyard tore the page out of his notebook, put the book itself away, and then drew out his revolver. He began slipping percussion caps over the firing nipples of the loaded chambers. The barrel of the gun was pointed directly at Starbuck's chest. "I could have an accident," Swynyard said slyly. "No one could blame me. I'm three fingers short of a hand so no wonder I fumble sometimes. One shot, Starbuck, and you'd be buzzard meat on the grass. I reckon General Faulconer would like that." Swynyard began to thumb the hammer back.

Then a click sounded behind Starbuck, and the Colonel's thumb relaxed. Sergeant Truslow lowered the hammer of his rifle. "I can have an accident, too," Truslow said.

Swynyard said nothing but just grinned and turned away. The nearby battery had ceased firing, and the gunners were hitching their weapons to limbers. The smoke of the battery dissipated slowly in the still air. The rebel guns had been fighting a duel with a Northern battery, a duel that the Northerners had won. "The Yankees will be raising their sights," Swynyard remarked, staring through his glasses. "They've got four-and-a-half-inch rifles. Can't fight four-and-a-half-inch rifles with six-pounder guns. We might as well throw rocks at the bastards."

Starbuck watched the Southern guns wheel fast away to the rear and wondered if he was now supposed to fight four-and-a-half-inch rifled cannon with rifles. His heart seemed to be beating too loudly, filling his chest with its drumbeats. He tried to lick his lips, but his mouth was too dry.

The sound of musketry slackened, to be replaced by Northern cheers. Yankee cheering was much deeper in tone than the blood-chilling yelp of attacking rebels. The cannon smoke had thinned sufficiently to let Starbuck see a belt of woodland a half-mile ahead, and then to see a sight he had never dreamed of witnessing on one of Thomas Jackson's battlefields.

He saw panic.

Ahead and to the left of Starbuck a horde of Southern soldiers were pouring out of the woodland and fleeing southward across the shallow valley. All discipline was gone. Shells exploded among the gray-jacketed soldiers, adding to their desperation. A rebel flag went down, was snatched up again, then disappeared in another flame-filled burst of shell smoke. Horsemen were galloping through the fleeing mass in an attempt to turn the men around, and here and there among the panic a few men did try to form a line, but such small groups stood no chance against the flood of fear that swept the majority away.

Swynyard might be a drunkard and a foul-tempered brute, but he had been a professional soldier long enough to recognize disaster. He turned to see that Captain Medlicott's G Company had formed alongside Starbuck's men. "Medlicott!" Swynyard shouted. "Take these two companies forward! You're in charge!" Medlicott, though much older than Starbuck, had less seniority as a captain, but Swynyard had given him the command of the two companies as a way of insulting Starbuck. "See that broken limber?" The Colonel pointed toward a shattered vehicle that lay two hundred paces ahead, where a strip of grass marked a divide between a patch of harvested corn and a wider field of wheat. "Form your skirmish line there! I'll bring the Legion

50

up in support." Swynyard turned back to Starbuck. "Take this," he said and leaned down from the saddle to hold out a folded scrap of paper.

Starbuck snatched the piece of paper, then shouted at his men to advance alongside G Company. A shell screamed overhead. It was odd, Starbuck thought, how the debilitating nervousness that afflicted a man before battle could be banished by the proximity of danger. Even the day's stifling heat seemed bearable now that he was under fire. He licked his lips, then unfolded the scrap of paper that Swynyard had given him. He had supposed it would be written orders, but instead he saw it was a label for a dead man. *Starbuck*, the paper read, *Boston, Massachusetts*. Starbuck threw it angrily away. Behind, where the rest of the Legion hurried into ranks, Swynyard saw the gesture and cackled.

"This is madness!" Truslow protested to Starbuck. Two companies of skirmishers could not stand against the tide of fear that was retreating from the Yankee guns.

"The rest of the Legion will help," Starbuck said.

"They'd better," Truslow said, "or we're vulture meat."

Company G was advancing to Starbuck's right. Medlicott seemed unworried by the odds, but just stumped ahead of his men with a rifle in his hands. Or maybe, Starbuck thought, the miller just did not display his fear. "Keep the ranks straight!" Starbuck called to Coffman. "I want them steady." He felt in his pocket and found the stub of a cigar he had been saving for battle. He borrowed a lit cigar from a man in the ranks, lit his own, and drew the bitter smoke deep into his lungs.

Lieutenant Coffman had drawn ahead of H Company and was holding a brass-handled bayonet like a sword.

"Get back, Mr. Coffman!" Starbuck called.

"But, sir—"

"Your place is behind the company, Lieutenant! Go there! And throw away that toy sword!"

The first Northern soldiers suddenly appeared at the tree line on the valley's far crest, which blossomed with the small puffs of white rifle smoke. A shell exploded ahead of Starbuck, and pieces of its casing whipped past him. To his left the field had been partly harvested, so that some of the wheat was standing but most was drying in stooks. Small fires flickered where the shell fire had set the dry crops alight. There were patches of corn stubble among the wheat and two rows of standing corn, where a group of rebel soldiers had taken cover. The tasseled corn shivered whenever a bullet or shell whipped through the stalks. A Northern flag appeared at the far trees. The standard-bearer was waving it to and fro, making the stripes flutter brightly. A bugle was sounding, and off to the west the rebel infantry was still running. Rebel officers still galloped among the fugitives, trying to stem their flight and turn them round. General Jackson was among them, flailing with his scabbarded saber at the panicked men. More Northerners were at the tree line, some of them directly ahead of Starbuck now.

Another shell landed close to Company H, and Starbuck wondered why Medlicott did not order the two companies into skirmish order. Then he decided to hell with military etiquette and shouted the order himself. Medlicott echoed the order, thus shaking the two companies into a loose and scattered formation. Their job now was to fight the enemy skirmishers who would be advancing ahead of the main Yankee attack. "Make sure you're loaded!" Starbuck called. The Northern line had halted momentarily, perhaps to align itself after advancing through the trees. The Southern fugitives had disappeared behind Starbuck's left flank, and it suddenly seemed very quiet and lonely on the battlefield.

It also seemed very dangerous. Captain Medlicott crossed to Starbuck. "Is this right, do you think?" he asked, gesturing at the scatter of isolated skirmishers who were alone in the wide field. Medlicott had never liked Starbuck, and the red crescent patch on the shoulder of his uniform coat marked him for a loyal supporter of General Faulconer, but nervousness now made Medlicott seek reassurance from Faulconer's bitterest enemy. Close to, Starbuck could see that Medlicott was not hiding his fear at all; one cheek was quivering uncontrollably, and the sweat was pouring off his face and dripping from his beard. He took off his brimmed hat to fan his face, and Starbuck saw that even the miller's smooth, bald, chalk white pate was beaded with sweat. "We shouldn't be here!" Medlicott exclaimed petulantly.

"God knows what's happening," Starbuck said. A Northern battery had appeared where the road vanished among the farther trees. Starbuck saw the guns slew round in a shower of dirt. In a moment, he thought, that artillery will have us in their open sights. Dear God, he thought, but let it be a clean death, quick as a thought, with no agonized lingering under a surgeon's knife or dying of the sweated fever in some rat-infested hospital. He turned to look behind and saw the Faulconer Brigade streaming off the road and forming into ranks. "Swynyard's coming soon," he tried to reassure Medlicott.

The Northern infantry started forward again. A half-dozen flags showed above the dark ranks. Three of the flags were Old Glories, the others were regimental flags carrying state badges or martial insignias. Six flags translated into three regiments that were now attacking two light companies. Captain Medlicott went back to his own men, and Sergeant Truslow joined Starbuck. "Just us and them?" he asked, nodding at the Yankees.

"Swynyard's bringing the rest of the Brigade forward," Starbuck said. Shells from the newly deployed battery screeched overhead, aimed at the Faulconer Brigade. "Better them than us, eh?" Starbuck said with the callous indifference of a man spared the gunners' attentions. He saw George Finney aim his rifle. "Hold your fire, George! Wait till the bastards are in range."

The Northern skirmishers ran ahead of the attacking line. Their job was to brush Starbuck's men aside, but soon, Starbuck thought, the rest of the Faulconer Brigade's skirmishers would advance to reinforce him. Another salvo of shells thundered above him, the cracks of their explosions sounding a second after the percussive thump of the guns themselves. Starbuck began looking for enemy officers among the approaching skirmishers. Yankee officers seemed more reluctant than Southerners to abandon their swords and glinting rank badges and bright epaulettes.

A second Northern battery on the crest opened fire. A shell screamed just inches over Starbuck's head. *For what we are about to receive,* he thought, *may the Lord make us truly thankful.* He could hear the beat of drums sounding from the Yankee infantry. Was this to be the breakthrough battle for the North? Were they at last to batter the Confederacy into surrender? Most of the rebel forces in Virginia were seventy miles away on the far side of Richmond with Robert Lee, but it was here that the Northerners were attacking, and if they broke through here, then what was to stop them marching south, ever south, until Richmond was cut off and the whole upper South split from the Confederacy? "Hold still now!" Starbuck called to his men as he walked slowly along his scattered skirmish line. Another minute, he thought, and the Yankee skirmishers would be in range. "You see that red-haired son of a bitch with the hooked sword, Will?" Starbuck called to Tolby, one of the Legion's finest marksmen. "He's yours. Kill the bastard."

"I'll take care of him, Captain!" Tolby eased back the hammer of his rifle.

Starbuck saw the enemy cannons disappear behind a

blossom of gray-white smoke, and he anticipated another flight of shells overhead, but instead the missiles slammed into the field all around Starbuck's men. One of Medlicott's sergeants was flung backward, his blood momentarily misting the hot air. A shell splinter whipped into the broken limber, which carried a stenciled legend announcing that the vehicle belonged to the 4th U.S. Artillery, evidence that the rebels had pushed the Yankees back across the valley before being routed in the far woods. Or perhaps, Starbuck thought, the limber had been captured earlier in the war, for it seemed that at least half of the rebels' equipment was of Northern origin. A solid shot landed close beside Starbuck, then ricocheted up and back. The nearness of the shot made him wonder why the Yankee gunners were aiming at a scattered skirmish line when they could be firing at the massed ranks of the Faulconer Brigade, and that curiosity made him turn to look for Swynyard's promised reinforcements.

But Swynyard had vanished, and with him the whole Faulconer Brigade, leaving Starbuck and Medlicott alone in the field. Starbuck turned back. The Northern skirmishers were close now, close enough for Starbuck to see that their uniforms were smart, not patched brown and gray like the rebels'. The Northerners were advancing in good style, the sun reflecting off their belt buckles and brass buttons. Behind the skirmish line a battalion trampled down a row of standing corn. There were a half-dozen mounted officers at the rear of the Yankee formation, evidence that at least one of the attacking regiments was new to the war. Experienced officers did not invite the attention of sharpshooters by riding high in saddles. But nor did two companies of skirmishers stand to fight against a whole Yankee brigade.

"Fire!" Truslow shouted, and the Legion's skirmishers began their battle. The men were in pairs. One man would fire, then reload while his companion looked for danger. The red-haired Yankee was already down, clutching his chest.

Truslow ran across to Starbuck. "I was never a religious man," the Sergeant said as he rammed a bullet down his rifle's barrel, "but ain't there a story in the Bible about some son of a bitch king sending a man to die in battle just so he could riddle the man's wife?"

Starbuck peered through the veil of rifle smoke, saw a Yankee go onto one knee to take aim, and fired at the man. A Northern bullet whipsawed the air a few inches to his left. Behind their skirmish line the Northern brigade advanced stolidly beneath their bright flags. He could hear their boots crushing cornstalks, and he knew that as soon as the marching line reached the further edge of the wheat field, they would stop to take aim, and then a killing volley would scream over the field, with every bullet aimed at the two stranded companies of the Legion. There was nothing to check the Yankees out here in the open. No rebel guns were firing, there were no bursting shells or clawing sprays of canister to fleck the wheat field red. Tom Petty, an eighteen-year-old in Starbuck's company, turned round with his mouth open and his eyes wide. He shook his head in disbelief, then sank to his knees. He saw Starbuck's eyes on him and forced a brave smile. "I'm all right, sir! Just bruised!" He managed to stand and face the enemy.

"King David," Starbuck said aloud. King David had sent Uriah the Hittite into the front line of the battle so that Bathsheba would become a widow. "Set ye Uriah in the forefront of the hottest battle"—the verse came back to Starbuck—"and retire ye from him, that he may be smitten, and die." Well, damn Faulconer, who had made Swynyard set Starbuck in the forefront of the hottest battle that he might be smitten and die. "We're getting out of here!" Starbuck shouted across to Captain Medlicott.

Medlicott, though officially in command, was grateful for

the younger man's leadership. "Back!" he shouted at G Company.

The Yankees cheered and jeered as they saw the handful of skirmishers retreat. "Enjoying your licking, boys!" one Northerner shouted. "Keep on running! We'll be right after you!" called another, while a third shouted to give his respects to Stonewall Jackson, "And tell him we'll hang him real gentle now!"

"Steady now!" Starbuck called to his men. He kept his back to the enemy, concentrating on his company. "Back to the trees! Steady, don't run!" No one else from the Brigade was in sight. Swynyard or Faulconer must have taken the whole Brigade back into the woods, abandoning Starbuck and Medlicott to the enemy. But why had Bird not protested? A shell landed just behind Starbuck, buffeting him with its hot punch of air. He turned and saw the Yankee skirmishers running toward him. "Double back to the woods!" he shouted, so releasing his men from their slow, steady withdrawal. "Muster them by the road, Sergeant!" he called to Truslow.

More Northern jeers and a handful of bullets followed the skirmishers' hurried retreat. The Yankees were in high spirits. They had waited a long time to give Stonewall Jackson a whipping, and now they were laying the lash on thick and hard. Back among the trees beside the turnpike Starbuck's men panted as they crouched and looked nervously at their officer, who, in turn, was watching the shadows lengthen across the wheat field. He was also watching the far tree line, where still more guns and infantry had appeared. The Yankees were triumphant and the rebels beaten. "If we stay here"—Medlicott had joined Starbuck again—"we'll like as not be prisoners."

"Swynyard put you in command," Starbuck said pointedly.

Medlicott hesitated, unhappy to take responsibility, then diffidently suggested that the two companies should retreat further through the trees. To the east of the turnpike a furious artillery battle was deafening the evening air. Smoke poured off the hillside where rebel guns were emplaced, but those cannon were of no use to the beaten men west of the turnpike, where the Yankee line had crushed the standing corn to drive Jackson's infantry back into the timber on the valley's southern crest. The Northern guns had the range of those trees now, and the green summer woods were filled with the whistling menace of shrapnel. Starbuck wondered where the Georgia regiment had gone and where the rest of the Brigade was hidden.

"I can't see the Brigade!" Medlicott said despairingly. A salvo of shells cracked ahead of the skirmishers, filling the trees with whistling shards of hot metal. The men leading the retreat had followed the twisting path into a small hollow, and now they instinctively crouched rather than leave their scanty cover to walk into that zone of fire. The perplexed and frightened Captain Medlicott seemed content to let them rest. "Maybe we should send a patrol to look for the Brigade?" he suggested to Starbuck.

"While the rest of us wait here to be captured?" Starbuck asked sarcastically.

"I don't know," Medlicott said. The miller was suddenly bereft of confidence and initiative. His doughy face looked hurt, like that of a child struck for an offense it had not committed.

"Yankees!" Truslow called warningly, pointing west to where blue uniforms had appeared in the woods.

"Stay still!" Medlicott shouted in sudden panic. "Get down!"

Starbuck would have gone on retreating, hoping to join up with the rebel reserve, but Medlicott had been panicked into making a decision, and the men crouched gratefully in the shadows. Two of Starbuck's company lowered a body they had been carrying. "Shall we bury him?" one of the two men asked Starbuck.

"Who is it?" It was dark under the trees, and the evening was drawing in.

"Tom Petty."

"Oh, dear God," Starbuck said. He had seen Petty wounded but had thought he would live, and surely Petty had deserved to live, for he had been a boy, not a man. He had used to shave each morning, but the blade had made no difference to his cheeks. He had only used the razor to explain his lack of beard, but he had been a good soldier, cheerful and willing. Starbuck had planned to make him up to corporal, but now it would have to be Mellors, who was not nearly so quick on the uptake. "Scratch him a grave," he said, "and get Corporal Waggoner to say a prayer for him."

All around them the shouts of the Yankees grew louder. The woodland was filled with screaming shells, so many that at times the torn leaves looked like a green snow drifting through the warm evening air. The trees echoed with the pathetic cries of dying men. Lieutenant Coffman hunkered down beside Starbuck, his small face showing bewilderment because his beloved Southerners were being whipped, because the North was winning, and because nothing in his world made sense.

The Reverend Elial Starbuck shared in the joy as the realization of victory dawned on the Yankee headquarters. And what a victory it was proving! Prisoners had confirmed that the enemy commander was indeed the notorious Stonewall Jackson. "The wretch won't be fetching his supper from my supply wagons tonight!" General Banks exulted. It was true that the enemy was still holding firm on the slopes of Cedar

Mountain, but Banks's staff brought message after message that told how the Federal right wing under General Crawford was driving the rebels clean across the valley and into the woods beyond. "Now we'll turn their flank!" Banks exclaimed, gesturing extravagantly to show how he meant to hook the right wing of his army around the backside of Cedar Mountain and thus surround the remnants of the Confederate army. "Maybe we'll have Jackson as our supper guest tonight!"

"I doubt he'll have much appetite after this drubbing," an artillery major observed.

"Fellow's reputed to eat damned strangely anyway," an aide responded, then blushed for having sworn in front of the Reverend Starbuck. "Nothing but stale bread and chopped cabbage, I hear."

"You and I could chop the rogue some cabbage, eh, Starbuck?" General Banks thus drew his distinguished guest into the jubilant conversation.

"I would make him eat what the slaves eat!" the Reverend Starbuck said.

"I think he eats worse than any slave!" Banks jested. "Force a slave to eat what Jackson dines on and the whole world would revile our inhumanity. Maybe we should punish the man by giving him a proper meal? Oysters and pheasant, you think?"

Banks's aides laughed, and their master turned his gaze back to the battle smoke that was already touched with a faint pink tinge of evening sunlight. In the slanting light Banks looked quite superb: straight-backed, stern-faced, the very image of a soldier, and suddenly, after months of disappointment, the politician did at last feel like a soldier. He had, Banks modestly admitted to himself, grown into the job and was now ready for the battles to come. For despite this day's splendid victory, there would be more battles. With

Stonewall Jackson defeated, General Robert Lee, who was protecting Richmond from McClellan's army, would be forced north even if such a move did open the rebel capital to McClellan's forces. McClellan would dutifully overwhelm the Richmond defenses, Pope would crush Lee, and then, bar some mopping up on the Mississippi and skull-breaking in the deep South, the war would be over. Better, it would be won. All that remained was a few battles, a rebel surrender, a Federal victory parade, and most important of all, the absolute necessity for President Lincoln and the dunderheads in the United States Congress to realize that it had been Nathaniel Prentiss Banks who had precipitated the whole process. My God, Banks thought, but others would try to steal his glory now! John Pope would doubtless make the attempt, and George McClellan would certainly write to every newspaper editor in creation, which made it all the more important for this night's victory dispatch to be written firmly and clearly. Tonight's dispatch, Banks knew, would fashion history books for years to come, but more important, the words he wrote tonight would garner votes for the remainder of his career.

Federal officers gathered round to offer the General their congratulations. The commander of Banks's bodyguard, a tall Pennsylvanian *Zouave*, handed the General a silver stirrup cup of brandy. "A toast to your triumph, sir," the *Zouave* proclaimed. A ragged line of disconsolate prisoners trudged past the group of horsemen. One or two of the captured seceshers glanced sullenly at the Northern General, and one rogue spat in his direction, but tonight, Banks thought, he would have the most valuable prisoner as his dinner guest. He would treat General Jackson with courtesy, as a gallant soldier should, and the world would wonder at the victor's modesty. Then Banks imagined himself at another dinner table, a much grander table in Washington that would gleam with massive presidential silver, and in his mind's eye he saw the foreign diplomats and their admiring bejeweled wives bend forward to catch his words. President Banks! And why not? George Washington might have made this country, but it had needed Nathaniel Prentiss Banks to save it.

A mile south of Banks, in a belt of woodland where fires started by shell fire tortured the wounded, men screamed and fought and died. The Yankee counterattack was being slowed by the undergrowth and by the stubborn defiance of Southern riflemen, whose muzzle flames stabbed bright in the smoky shadows. Shells slashed through the treetops, thrashing the branches and hammering the sky with their explosions. Blood and smoke reeked, a man called for his mother in the voice of a child, another cursed God, but still the North pushed on, yard by hard yard, going through hell in search of peace.

"Nothing is served," General Washington Faulconer said icily, "by breaking the Brigade into small detachments. We shall go into battle united."

"If there's any battle left," Swynyard said with a manic glee. He seemed to be enjoying the panic that had infected the western side of Jackson's battle.

"Watch your tongue, Colonel," Faulconer snapped. He was more than usually displeased with his second-in-command, who had already lost a quarter of the Legion instead of just Starbuck's company, and what was left of the Brigade must be husbanded, not frittered away by being committed to the battle in dribs and drabs. Faulconer edged his horse away from Swynyard and gazed at the woods, which were filled with smoke and thrashing from the passage of Northern shells and bolts. God only knew what had happened in the wide valley beyond those woods, but even here, far behind where the fighting had taken place, the evidence of impending disaster was awesome and obvious. Wounded men staggered back from the trees; some of the injured were being helped by friends, others crawled or limped painfully back to where the surgeons hacked and sawed and probed. Many of the fugitives were not wounded at all but were merely frightened men who were trying to escape the Yankee advance.

Faulconer had no intention of allowing that advance to enmesh his Brigade. "I want the 65th on the right," Faulconer called to Swynyard, referring to the 65th Virginia, which was the second largest regiment after the Legion in Faulconer's Brigade, "the Arkansas men in the center, and the 12th Florida on the left. Everyone else in reserve two hundred paces behind." That meant that the remaining six companies of the Legion, who were presently the foremost battalion in the Brigade, would now become Faulconer's rearmost line. The redeployment was hardly necessary, but moving the front line to the rear killed some precious moments while Faulconer tried to determine just what disasters were happening beyond the woods. "And, Colonel!" Faulconer called after Swynyard, "send Bird to reconnoiter the ground. Tell him to report to me within a half hour!"

"Colonel Bird's already gone," Swynyard said. "Went to fetch his skirmishers back."

"Without orders?" Faulconer asked angrily. "Then tell him to explain himself to me the instant he returns. Now go!"

"Sir?" Captain Thomas Pryor, one of Washington Faulconer's new aides, interjected nervously.

"Captain?" Faulconer acknowledged.

"General Jackson's orders were explicit, sir. We should advance quick, sir, with whatever units are available. Into the trees, sir." Pryor gestured nervously toward the woods.

But Faulconer had no wish to advance quick. The woods seemed to be alive with smoke and flame, almost as though the earth itself was heaving in the throes of some mythic struggle. Rifle fire cracked, men screamed, and cannons pumped their percussive explosions through the humid air, and Faulconer had no desire to plunge into that maelstrom. He wanted order and sense, and a measure of safety. "General Jackson," he told Pryor, "is panicking. We serve no purpose by committing ourselves piecemeal. We shall advance in good order or not at all." He turned away from the battle and rode back to where his second line would be formed. That reserve line consisted of the six remaining companies of the Legion and the whole of the 13th Florida, two regiments that Faulconer had every intention of holding back until his first line was fully committed to the fight. Only if the first line broke and ran would the second line fight, and then merely to serve as a rear guard for the fugitive first line. Washington Faulconer told himself he was being prudent, and that such prudence might well save a defeat from being a rout.

He wondered where Starbuck was and felt the familiar flare of hatred. Faulconer blamed Starbuck for all his ills. It was Starbuck who had humiliated him at Manassas, Starbuck who had suborned Adam, and Starbuck who had defied him by remaining in the Legion. Faulconer was convinced that if he could just rid himself of Starbuck, then he could make the Brigade into the most efficient unit of the Confederate army, which was why he had ordered Swynyard to place a company of skirmishers far ahead of the Brigade's position. He had trusted Swynyard to know precisely which company of skirmishers was to be thus sacrificed, but he had hardly expected the drunken fool to throw away both companies. Yet even that loss might be worthwhile, Faulconer reflected, if Starbuck was among the casualties.

On Faulconer's left a column of rebel troops advanced at the double, while another, marching just as quickly, headed for the woods to the right of his Brigade. Reinforcements were clearly reaching the fighting, which meant, Faulconer decided, that he had no need to hurl his own men forward in a desperate panic. Slow and steady would win this fight, and that natural caution was reinforced by the sight of a riderless horse, its flank a sheet of crimson, limping southward down the turnpike with its reins trailing in the dust and its stirrups dripping with blood.

The Faulconer Brigade laboriously formed its new battle lines. In the first rank were the 65th Virginia, Haxall's men from Arkansas, and the 12th Florida. The three regiments raised their dusty flags, the banners' bright colors already faded from too much sun and shredded by too many bullets. The standards hung limp in the windless air. Colonel Swynyard gave his horse to one of his two cowed slaves, then took his place at the center of the forward line, where lust at last overcame caution and made him take a flask from a pouch on his belt. "I see our gallant Colonel is inoculating himself against the risks of battle," General Faulconer remarked sardonically to Captain Pryor.

"By drinking water, sir?" Pryor asked in puzzlement. Thomas Pryor was new to the Brigade. He was the younger son of a Richmond banker who did much business with Washington Faulconer, and the banker had pleaded with Faulconer to take on his son. "Thomas is a good-natured fellow," the banker had written, "too good, probably, so maybe a season of war will teach him that mankind is not inherently honest?"

A second's silence greeted Pryor's naive assumption that Swynyard was drinking water, then a gale of laughter swept the Brigade headquarters. "Swynyard's water," Faulconer informed Pryor, "is the kind that provides the Dutch with

courage, puts men to sleep, and wakes them sore-headed."
The General smiled at his own wit, then turned indignantly
as a mounted man galloped toward him from the turnpike.

"You're to advance, sir!" the officer shouted. The man
had a drawn sword in his right hand.

Faulconer did not move. Instead he waited as the officer
curbed his horse. The beast tossed its head and stamped nervously. It was flecked with sweat and rolling its eyes white.
"You have orders for me?" Faulconer asked the excited
officer.

"From General Jackson, sir. You're to advance with the
other brigades, sir." The aide gestured toward the woods, but
Faulconer still made no move other than to hold out a hand.
The aide gaped at him. No one else on this field had
demanded written orders, for surely no one could doubt the
urgency of the cause. If the Yankees won here, then there
was nothing to stop them crossing the Rapidan and breaking
Richmond's rail links with the Shenandoah Valley, and
nothing, indeed, to stop them advancing on the rebel capital. This was not a time for written orders but for Southern
men to fight like heroes to protect their country. "General
Jackson's compliments, sir," the aide said in a tone that
barely managed to stay on the civil side of insolence, "and
his regrets that he has no time to put his orders into writing,
but he would be most obliged if you were to advance your
Brigade into the trees and help dislodge the enemy."

Faulconer looked at the woods. Fugitives still emerged
from the shadows, but most were now men wounded by the
fighting rather than frightened men seeking safety. Nearer to
the Brigade two small guns were being unlimbered by the
road, but the cannons looked a pitiable force to withstand
the noisy Northern onslaught that churned among the shadowed woods. Those shadows were long, cast by a sun that
reddened in the west. Flames started by shell fire flickered

deep among the trees where rifles snapped angrily. "Am I to tell General Jackson that you won't advance, sir?" the mounted officer asked in a voice cracked with near despair. He had not given his name nor announced his authority, but the urgency in his tone and the drawn sword in his hand were all the authority he needed.

Faulconer drew his sword. He did not want to advance, but he knew there was no choice now. Reputation and honor depended on going into the awful woods. "Colonel Swynyard!" he called, and the words were hardly more than a croak. "Colonel!" he shouted again, louder this time.

"Sir!" Swynyard pushed the flask of whiskey back into his pouch.

"Advance the Brigade!" Faulconer called.

Swynyard drew his own sword, the blade scraping into the day's dying light. Ahead of him fires burned in the wood, their flames bright in the dark shadows where men fought and died. "Forward!" Swynyard shouted.

Forward into the maelstrom where the woods burned.

Into battle.

"IT'S GOD'S WILL, BANKS! God's will!" The Reverend Elial Starbuck was beside himself with joy. The smell of battle was in his nostrils and inflaming him like an infusion of the Holy Spirit. The preacher was fifty-two years old and had never known an exultation quite like this thrill of victory. He was witnessing God's hand at work and seeing the triumph of righteousness over the Slavocracy. "On, on!" he shouted encouragingly to a fresh battery of Northern artillery that traveled toward the smoke of battle. The Reverend Starbuck had come to Culpeper Court House to preach to the troops, but instead found himself cheering them on to glory.

The Reverend Elial Starbuck's jubilation matched General Banks's excitement. The politician turned general was realizing he had won! He was actually trouncing the wretched and infamous Jackson who had given him such misery earlier in the year. The bells of Boston would ring for this success of a native son, and suddenly the realization of the Governor's most daring ambitions seemed so dazzlingly close. Nathaniel Prentiss Banks, seventeenth President of the United States of America. He said the phrase under his breath, relishing it, but then the glory of that triumph dizzied Banks in his saddle, and to steady himself he turned back to the Reverend Starbuck. "How's that son of yours, Starbuck?" Banks asked, trying to give the impression of a man humble and confident enough to make small talk at the moment of glory.

"James is well, thank you, Governor," the preacher responded. "He's with McClellan's forces in front of Richmond. He suffered a touch of fever a month ago, but writes to say he is fully recovered."

"I meant the young man you named after me," Banks said. "How is he?"

"Nathaniel's well, so far as I know," the Reverend Starbuck said curtly, then was saved from any further queries about his traitor son by the arrival of an aide on a horse that had a mane paled by dust and flanks foaming with sweat. The aide gave Banks a swift salute and a note from Brigadier General Crawford. The note had been hastily scribbled in the saddle, and Banks found it hard to decipher the penciled letters.

"News of victory, I hope?" Banks suggested to the newly arrived aide.

"The General's requesting reinforcements, sir," the aide said respectfully. His horse trembled as a rebel shell wailed overhead.

"Reinforcements?" Banks asked. In the pause after his question the rebel shell exploded harmlessly behind, scattering dirt across the road. "Reinforcements?" Banks said again, frowning as though he found the word incomprehensible. Then he straightened his already immaculate uniform. "Reinforcements?" he asked a third time. "But I thought he was driving the enemy from the field?"

"We need to break them, sir." The aide sounded enthusiastic. "One more brigade will rout them utterly."

"I hoped they were finished already," Banks said, crumpling Crawford's message in his hand.

"They're skulking in some woods, sir. Our fellows are pressing hard, but they'll need help."

"There isn't any help!" Banks said indignantly, as though

the aide were spoiling his moment of glory. "I sent him Gordon's brigade; isn't that enough?"

The aide glanced at the gaudily uniformed Pennsylvania *Zouaves* who formed General Banks's personal bodyguard. "Maybe we should send every man available, sir, to destroy them before they're saved by nightfall?" He spoke very respectfully, as befitted a captain offering tactical advice to a major general.

"We have no reserves, Captain," Banks said in a peevish voice. "We are fully committed! So press on. Press hard. Tell Crawford it's his responsibility now. I won't have men calling for help, not when we're on the verge of victory. Go back and tell him to push on hard, you hear me? Push on hard and no stopping till nightfall." The long speech had restored Banks's confidence. He was winning; it was God's will that the vaunted Stonewall Jackson should be humbled. "It's nervousness, plain nervousness," Banks explained General Crawford's request to the men who surrounded him. "A fellow finds himself on the winning side and can't believe his luck so he asks for help at the last moment!"

"I hope you'll be kind to Crawford in your memoirs, sir," the *Zouave* commander observed.

"To be sure, to be sure," Banks said, who had not considered his memoirs till this moment, but now found himself dreaming of a three-volume work, provisionally entitled *Banks's War*. He decided he would depict his early defeats as necessary deceptions that had lured the cabbage-eating Jackson on to destruction at Cedar Mountain. "I might have been reviled"—the General rehearsed a sentence in his head—"but I was playing a longer hand than my critics knew, especially those journalistic curs who dared to offer me advice even though not one of them could tell a Parrott gun from a bird's beak."

The Reverend Elial Starbuck broke this pleasant reverie

by begging Banks's permission to ride forward so he could observe the pursuit and final humiliation of the enemy. "Your triumph is an answer to my prayers, Governor," the preacher said, "and I would dearly like to witness its full fruits."

"My dear Starbuck, of course you must ride forward. Captain Hetherington?" Banks summoned one of his junior aides to accompany the preacher, though he also cautioned the aide not to expose the Reverend Starbuck to any danger. The caution was given to make certain that the Reverend Starbuck survived to preach Banks's fame from his influential pulpit. "A wounded cur can still bite," Banks warned the preacher, "so you must stay well clear of the dying beast's jaws."

"God will preserve me, Governor," the Reverend Starbuck averred. "He is my strong shield and protector."

Thus guarded, the Reverend Starbuck set off across the fields with Hetherington, first threading a path between rows of army wagons with white canvas hoods, then passing a field hospital where the Reverend Starbuck paused to inspect the faces of the wounded Southern prisoners who lay after surgery on the grass outside the tents. Some were still comatose from the effects of chloroform, a few slept from sheer weariness, but the majority lay pale and frightened. A few crudely bandaged casualties lay waiting for the surgeons' knives, and to anyone unaccustomed to battle the sight of such grievously hurt men might have proved more than the strongest stomach could abide, but the Reverend Starbuck seemed positively enlivened by the horrid spectacle. Indeed, he leaned out of his saddle for a closer look at one man's mangled limbs and bloodied scalp. "You note the low cranial gap and the pronounced teeth?" he observed to Hetherington.

"Sir?" Hetherington asked in puzzlement.

"Look at his face, man! Look at any of their faces! Can't

you see the pronounced difference between them and the Northern visage?"

Captain Hetherington thought that the Southerners did not look very much different from Northerners, except that they were generally thinner and a good deal more raggedly uniformed, but he did not want to contradict the eminent preacher, and so he agreed that the captured rebels did indeed display low foreheads and feral teeth.

"Such features are the classic symptoms of feebleminded-ness and moral degradation," the Reverend Starbuck announced happily, then remembered the Christian duty that was owed even to such fallen souls as these rebel prison-ers. "Though your sins be as scarlet," he called down to them, "yet you may be washed whiter than snow. You must repent! You must repent!" He had come equipped with copies of his tract, *Freeing the Oppressed*, which explained why Christian men should be prepared to die for the sacred cause of abolishing slavery, and now the Reverend Starbuck dropped a few copies among the wounded men. "Something to read during your imprisonment," he told them, "some-thing to explain your errors." He spurred on, cheered by this chance to have spread the good word. "We have been remiss, Captain," the preacher declared to Hetherington as the two men left the hospital behind, "in restricting our mis-sion work to heathen lands and Southern slaves. We should have sent more good men into the rebellious states to tussle with the demons that dwell in the white man's soul."

"There are plenty of churches, are there not, in the seces-sionist states?" Captain Hetherington inquired respectfully after leading the preacher around a tangle of telegraph wire that had been dumped beside a ditch.

"There are indeed churches in the South," the Reverend Starbuck said in a tone of distaste, "and pastors, too, I dare say, yet their existence should not deceive us. The scriptures warn us against those false prophets who shall inhabit the latter days. And such prophets have no difficulty in persuading the feebleminded to adopt the devil's ways. But the Second Epistle of Peter promises us that the false prophets shall bring upon themselves a swift destruction. I think we are witnessing the beginnings of that providence. For this is the Lord's doing," the Reverend Doctor Starbuck declaimed happily, gesturing toward two dogs that fought over a dead man's intestines close to a smoking shell crater, "and we should rejoice and be glad in it!" A less pious impulse made the Reverend wonder whether the money he had just expended on Galloway's Horse was going to be wasted. Maybe the war would be won without Galloway's men? Then he thrust that concern away and let this day's good news fill him with joy instead.

Captain Hetherington wanted to drive the two dogs away from their offal, but the Reverend Starbuck was spurring ahead, and the aide's duty was to stay with the preacher, so he galloped to catch up. "Are you saying, sir," Hetherington asked respectfully, "that none of the rebels are Christians?"

"How can they be?" the Boston preacher responded. "Our faith has never preached rebellion against the lawful and godly authority of the state, so at best the South is in grievous error and thus in desperate need of repentance and forgiveness. And at worst?" The Reverend Starbuck shook his head rather than even consider such a question, yet the very asking of it made him think of his second son and how Nate was even now irretrievably committed to the fires of hell. Nate would burn in everlasting flames, tormented through all eternity by agonies unimaginable. "And he deserves it!" the Reverend Starbuck protested aloud.

"I'm sorry, sir?" Hetherington asked, thinking he had misheard a comment addressed to him.

"Nothing, Captain, nothing. You are saved yourself?"

"Indeed, sir. I came to Christ three years ago, and have praised God for His mercies ever since."

"Praise Him indeed," the Reverend Starbuck responded, though in truth he was secretly disappointed that his escort should thus prove to be a born-again Christian, for there were few things Elial Starbuck enjoyed so much as having what he called a tussle with a sinner. He could boast of having left many a strong man in tears after an hour's good argument.

The two men arrived at a Northern battery of twelve-pounder Napoleons. The four guns were silent, their shirt-sleeved gunners leaning on their weapons' wheels and staring across the valley to where a long-shadowed stand of trees was crowned with gunsmoke. "No targets, sir," the battery commander answered when the Reverend Starbuck asked why he was not firing. "Our fellows are inside those woods, sir, or maybe a half-mile beyond, which means our job's done for the day." He took a pull of his flask, which contained brandy. "Those shell bursts are rebel guns firing long, sir," he added, gesturing at the white explosions that blossomed intermittently on the far crest. The sound of each explosion followed a few seconds later like a small rumble of thunder. "Just their rear guard," the artilleryman said confidently, "and we can leave the peasantry to look after them."

"The peasantry?" the Reverend Starbuck inquired.

"The infantry, sir. Lowest of the low, see what I mean, sir?"

The Reverend Starbuck did not see at all, but decided not to make an issue of his puzzlement. "And the rebels?" he asked instead. "Where are they?"

The gunner Major took note of the older man's Geneva bands and straightened himself respectfully. "You can see

74

some of the dead ones, sir, excuse my callousness, and the rest are probably halfway to Richmond by now. I've waited over a year to see the rascals skedaddle, sir, and it's a fine sight. Our young ladies saw them off in fine style." The Major slapped the still warm barrel of the closest gun, which, like the rest of the Napoleons in the battery, had a girl's name painted on its trail. This gun was Maud, while its companions were named Eliza, Louise, and Anna.

"It is the Lord's doing, the Lord's doing!" the Reverend Starbuck murmured happily.

"The seceshers are still lively over there." Captain Hetherington gestured to far-off Cedar Mountain, where gunsmoke still jetted from the rebel batteries.

"But not for long." The artillery Major spoke confidently. "We'll hook behind their rear and take every man jack of them prisoner. As long as nightfall doesn't come first," he added. The sun was very low and the light reddening.

The Reverend Starbuck took a small telescope from his pocket and trained it on the woods ahead. He could see very little except for smoke, leaves, and burning shell craters, though in the nearer open land he could make out the humped shapes of the dead lying in the remnants of the wheat field. "We shall go to the woods," he announced to his companion.

"I'm not sure we should, sir," Captain Hetherington demurred politely. "There are still shells falling."

"We shall come to no harm, Captain. Though we walk through the valley of the shadow of death we shall fear no evil. Come!" In truth the Reverend Starbuck wanted to ride closer to those bursting shells. He had decided that his exhilaration was symptomatic of a natural taste for battle, that maybe he was discovering a God-given talent for warfare, and it was suddenly no wonder to him that the Lord of Hosts had so frequently exhorted Israel to the fight. This blood and slaughter was the way to see God's work accomplished! Sermonizing and mission work were all very well, and doubtless God listened to the prayers of all those wilting women with faded silk bookmarks in their well-thumbed Bibles, but this hammer of battle was a more certain method of bringing about His kingdom. The sinners were being scourged by the holy flail of sword, steel, and gunpowder, and the Reverend Doctor Starbuck exulted in the process. "Onwards, Captain," he encouraged Hetherington. "The enemy is beaten, there's nothing to fear!"

Hetherington paused, but the artillery Major was in full agreement with the preacher. "They're well beaten, sir, and amen," the Major declared, and that encouragement was enough to make the Reverend Starbuck hand down some copies of *Freeing the Oppressed* for the weary gunners. Then, spirits soaring, he spurred his horse past the quartet of fan-shaped swathes of scorched stubble that marked where Eliza, Louise, Maud, and Anna had belched flame and smoke at the enemy.

Captain Hetherington followed unhappily. "We don't know that the rebels are yet cleared from the woods, sir."

"Then we shall find out, Captain!" the Reverend Starbuck said happily. He trotted past the remains of a Northerner who had been blown apart by the direct hit of a rebel shell, and who was now nothing but a fly-crawling mess of jagged-ended bones, blue guts, torn flesh, and uniform scraps. The Reverend felt no anguish at the sight, merely the satisfaction that the dead man was a hero who had gone to his Maker by virtue of having died for a cause as noble as any that had ever driven man onto the battlefield. A few paces beyond the dead Federal was the corpse of a Southerner, his throat cut to the bone by a fragment of shell casing. The wretch was dressed in gaping shoes, torn pants, and a threadbare coat of pale gray patched with brown, but the corpse's most repellent aspect was the grasping look on his face. The preacher reckoned he saw that same depraved physiognomy on most of the rebel dead and on the faces of the rebel wounded who cried for help as the two horsemen rode by. These rebels, the Reverend Starbuck decided, were demonstrably feebleminded and doubtless morally infantile. The doctors in Boston were convinced that such mental weaknesses were inherited traits, and the more the Reverend Elial Starbuck saw of these Southerners, the more persuaded he was of that medical truth. Had there been miscegenation? Had the white race so disgraced itself with its own slaves that it was now paying the hereditary price? That thought so disgusted the Reverend that he flinched, but then an even more terrible thought occurred to him. Was his son Nathaniel's moral degradation inherited? The Reverend Starbuck cast that suspicion out. Nathaniel was a backslider and so doubly guilty. Nathaniel's sins could not be laid at his parents' door, but only at his own wicked feet.

The Reverend Elial Starbuck thus ruminated about heredity, slavery, and feeblemindedness as he rode across the hot battlefield, yet he did not entirely ignore the cries that came from the parched, hurting men left helpless by the fighting. The wounded rebels were pleading for water, for a doctor, or for help in reaching the field hospitals, and the Reverend Starbuck offered them what comfort was in his power by assuring them that salvation could be theirs after a true repentance. One dark-bearded man, sheltering under a bullet-scarred tree and with his leg half severed and a rifle sling serving as a tourniquet about his thigh, cursed the preacher and demanded brandy instead of a sermon, but the Reverend Starbuck merely let a tract fall toward the man and then spurred sadly on. "Once this rebellion is ended, Captain," he observed, "we shall be faced with a mighty task in the South. We shall needs preach the pure gospel to a people led into error by false teachers."

Hetherington was about to agree with that pious observation but was checked from speaking by a sudden sound coming from the west. To the Reverend Starbuck, unused to the noise of battle, the sound was exactly like gigantic sheets of stiff canvas being ripped across, or perhaps like the noise caused by the wretched urchins who liked to run down Beacon Hill dragging sticks along the iron palings. The noise was so sudden and intrusive that he instinctively checked his horse, but then, assuming that the weird sound presaged the end of rebellion, he urged the beast on again and muttered a prayer of thanks for God's providence in giving the North victory. Captain Hetherington, less sanguine, checked the preacher's horse. "I didn't think the rebs were that far west," he said, apparently speaking to himself.

"West?" the preacher asked, confused.

"Rifle volleys, sir," Hetherington answered, explaining the strange noise. The Captain stared toward the dying sun, where a trembling veil of smoke was starting to show above the trees.

"That noise!" the Reverend Starbuck exclaimed. "Listen! You hear that noise? What is it?" His excitement was caused by a new sound that was suddenly added to the rifle volleys. It was a high-pitched noise infused with a yelping triumph and thrilled through with a ululating and gleeful quality that suggested that the creatures who made such a sound were come willingly and even gladly to this field of slaughter. "You know what you're hearing?" The Reverend Starbuck asked the question with enthusiasm. "It's the *paean*! I never thought I should live to hear it!"

Hetherington glanced at the preacher. "The *peon*, sir?" he asked, puzzled.

"You've read Aristophanes, surely?" the preacher

demanded impatiently. "You remember how he describes the war cry of the Greek infantry? The *paean?*" Maybe, the preacher thought, some classically minded officer from Yale or Harvard had fostered the pleasant fancy of teaching his Northern soldiers that ancient war cry. "Listen, man," he said excitedly, "it's the sound of the phalanx! The sound of the Spartans! The sound of Homer's heroes!"

Captain Hetherington could hear the sound only too clearly. "That's not the *paean*, sir. It's the rebel yell."

"You mean . . ." the Reverend Starbuck began, then fell abruptly silent. He had read about the rebel yell in the Boston newspapers, but now he was hearing it for himself, and the sound of it suddenly seemed anything but classical. Instead it was infused with the purest evil; a noise to chill the blood like a scrabble of wild beasts howling or like the baying of a horde of demons begging to be released from the smoking gates of hell. "Why are they yelling?" the preacher asked.

"Because they're not beaten, sir, that's why," Hetherington said, and he reached for the preacher's reins and pulled his horse around. The Reverend Starbuck protested the about turn, for he was already very close to the woods and he wanted to see what lay beyond the trees, but the Captain could not be persuaded to continue. "The battle's not won, sir," he said quietly, "it might even be lost."

For a rebel yell meant only one thing: a rebel attack.

Because the wretches weren't beaten at all.

Captain Nathaniel Starbuck, crouched in the woods close by the turnpike, heard the screaming of a rebel counterattack. "About goddamned time," he murmured to no one in particular. The gunfire in the trees had been sporadic for the last few minutes, and Starbuck had begun to fear that the Legion's stranded skirmishers would be trapped far behind a victorious Northern army. So far the only resistance to the Northern attack had seemed haphazard and futile, but now the rifle fire swelled into the full intensity of battle, to which the screams of the attacking Southerners added an unearthly descant. The battle was all sound to Starbuck, for he could see nothing through the smoky, deep-shadowed undergrowth, but the sounds indicated that the attacking Northerners were being checked and even counterattacked. "I reckon we should join in," Starbuck said to Captain Medlicott.

"No," Medlicott said. "Absolutely not!" The reply was too vehement, betraying Medlicott's fear. The miller turned soldier was as white-faced as though he had just come from a hard shift at his old grindstones. Sweat dripped and glistened in his beard, while his eyes flicked nervously around the sanctuary his men had fortuitously discovered among the trees. The sanctuary was a shallow scrape that would have been flooded by the smallest fall of rain, yet was so surrounded by undergrowth that an army could have marched on the road behind and not seen the men hidden just paces away. "We'll just wait here till things calm down," Medlicott insisted.

Starbuck did not like the thought of skulking in the shadows. So far the two companies had avoided any Northerners, but that luck might not last, yet Medlicott would not listen to the younger man's ideas. Medlicott had been happy enough to accept Starbuck's guidance when they were exposed to the enemy's fire, but now that he was in a seemingly safe refuge, Medlicott was rediscovering the authority that Colonel Swynyard had conferred on him. "We stay here," he insisted again, "and that's an order, Starbuck."

Starbuck went back to his company. He stretched himself at the edge of the shallow hollow and stared through the foliage toward the sounds of battle. The branches of the wood made a dark lacework against an evening sky that was layered with red-tinted bands of gunsmoke. The rebel yell swelled and faded, hinting at surges as regiments advanced and went to ground before advancing again. Volleys crashed among the trees, then footsteps trampled the undergrowth close by, but the leaves grew so thick that Starbuck could see no one. Nevertheless he feared the sudden irruption of a company of nervous Yankees, and so he twisted around and hissed at his men to fix their bayonets. If the Yankees did come, then Starbuck would be ready for them.

He pulled out his own blade and slotted it into place. Squirrels chattered unhappily in the branches overhead, and a flash of red feathers showed where a cardinal flew among the trunks. Behind Starbuck, beyond the deserted turnpike, gunsmoke lay like layers of mist above a patchwork of wheat and cornfields. There was no infantry visible there. It was almost as if the road divided the battlefield into two discrete halves, the one filled with cannon smoke and the other with struggling men.

Truslow, his rifle tipped with steel, dropped beside Starbuck. "What's wrong with Medlicott?"

"Frightened."

"Never was any damned good. His father was the same." Truslow spat a viscous gob of tobacco juice into the leaf mould. "I once saw old John Medlicott run from a pair of horse thieves who weren't a day over fifteen."

"Were you one of them?" Starbuck asked shrewdly.

Truslow grinned, but before he could answer there was a sudden panicked rush of feet, and a single Northern soldier burst through the bushes ahead. The Yankee was oblivious of the two rebel companies until he was just paces away, then his eyes widened and he slid to a panicked halt. His mouth dropped open. He turned, seemingly to shout a warning to his comrades, but Starbuck had climbed to his feet and now hammered the side of the Northerner's skull with the brass butt of his rifle just a split second before Truslow pulled the man's feet out from beneath him. The Yankee fell like a poleaxed steer. Truslow and Starbuck dragged him back to the company and disarmed him. "Shut your god-damned mouth," Starbuck hissed at the man, who had begun to stir.

"I'm not . . ."

"The officer told you to shut the hell up, you son of a whore, so shut the hell up or I'll rip your damned tongue out," Truslow growled, and the Northerner went utterly quiet. The buckle on his leather belt showed he was a Pennsylvanian. A trickle of blood showed among the roots of his fair hair above his ear. "You'll have a peach of a bruise there, you bastard," Truslow said happily. He was rifling the man's pockets and pouches. He tossed the Pennsylvanian's rifle cartridges back among the company, then found a pale brown package marked with the trademark of John Anderson's Honeydew Fine-Cut Tobacco of New York. "It ain't Virginia, but someone will smoke it," Truslow said, pushing it into his pouch.

"Leave me some," the Pennsylvanian pleaded. "I ain't had a smoke in hours."

"Then you should have stayed in Pennsylvania, you son of a whore, instead of trampling our corn. You're not wanted here. If you got what you deserved you'd be breathing through a hole in your ribs by now." Truslow eased a wad of folded Northern dollar bills from the man's top pocket. "Lucky at cards, are you?"

"And with women." The Pennsylvanian had a snub-nosed and cheeky charm.

"Lie still and be quiet, boy, or your luck will end here." Truslow unlooped the boy's canteen and found it still held a half-inch of water, which he offered to Starbuck. Starbuck, despite his thirst, refused, so Truslow drained the canteen himself.

Starbuck stood to give himself a view over the surrounding brush. Captain Medlicott hissed at him to get his head down, but Starbuck ignored the miller. Another burst of screaming announced a renewed rebel charge, and this time a group of some two dozen Yankees appeared just twenty paces beyond Starbuck's hiding place. A handful of the Northerners knelt and fired into the trees before retreating again. Two of the Yankees fell as they went back, driven down by rebel bullets, and the rest of the men would doubtless have kept on running had not the color party come through the trees to rally them. A tall, white-haired officer waved a sword toward the rebels. *"Vorwärts! Vorwärts!"* the officer cried, and the retreating men turned, cheered, and delivered a splintering volley toward their pursuers. The two flags were bright squares of silk in the smoke-riven shadows. One was Old Glory, battle-torn and stained, while the second was a purple flag embroidered with an eagle and a legend Starbuck could not decipher. *"Vorwärts!"* the white-haired officer called again.

"Are they goddamned Germans?" Truslow asked. The Sergeant had an irrational dislike of German immigrants, blaming them for many of the rules and regulations that had begun to infest his former country. "Americans used to be free men," he often declared. "Then the damned Prussians came to organize us."

"We're Pennsylvania *Deutsch*," the prisoner answered.

"Then you're godforsaken son of a bitch bastards," Truslow said. Starbuck could read the Gothic-lettered legend on the second flag now: *"Gott und die Vereinigten Staaten,"* it said, and it struck Starbuck that such a flag would make a handsome trophy.

"Feuer!" the white-haired officer shouted, and another

83

Northern volley ripped into the attacking rebels. The Germans cheered, sensing that their sudden resistance had taken the attackers by surprise.

"We can take those bastards," Starbuck said to Truslow.

The Sergeant glanced toward Captain Medlicott. "Not with that yellow bastard's help."

"Then we'll do it without the yellow bastard's help," Starbuck said. He felt the elation of a soldier given the inestimable advantage of surprise; this was a fight he could not lose, and so he cocked his rifle and twisted around to look at his company. "We're going to put one volley into those German sons of bitches and then run them off our land. Hard and fast, boys, scare the daylights out of the sumbitches. Ready?" The men grinned at him, letting him know that they were good and ready. Starbuck grinned back. There were times when he wondered if anything ever again in all eternity would ever taste as good as these moments in battle. The nervousness of anticipation was utterly gone, replaced by a feral excitement. He glanced at the prisoner. "You stay here, Yankee."

"I won't move an inch!" the prisoner promised, though in truth he intended to run just as soon as he was left unattended.

"Stand!" Starbuck shouted. The heady mix of fear and excitement swirled through him. He understood the temptation of following Medlicott's lead and staying hidden and safe, yet he also wanted to humiliate Medlicott. Starbuck wanted to show that he was the best man on a battlefield, and no one demonstrated such arrogance by cowering in the bushes. "Take aim!" he called, and a handful of the rallying Yankees heard the shouted order and looked around fearfully, but they were already too late. Starbuck's men were on their feet, rifles at their shoulders.

Then it began to go wrong.

"Stop!" Medlicott shouted. "Get down! I order you! Down!" The miller had panicked. He was running up the shallow scrape and shouting at Starbuck's men, even thrusting some of them back down to the ground. Other men crouched, and all were confused.

"Fire!" Starbuck shouted, and a puny scatter of rifle flames studded the shadows.

"Down!" Medlicott waved a hand frantically.

"Get up and fire!" Starbuck's yell was ferocious. "Up! Fire!" The men stood again and pulled their triggers, so that a stuttering mistimed volley flamed in the dusk. "Charge!" Starbuck shouted, drawing the word out like a war cry.

The white-haired officer had turned the Pennsylvanians to face the unexpected threat to their flank. Medlicott's interference had bought the Yankees a few seconds of precious time, long enough for a half-company to form a ragged firing line at right angles to the rest of their battalion. That half-company now faced Starbuck's confused assault, and as he watched the Yankees lift their rifles to their shoulders, he sensed the disaster that was about to strike. Even a half-company volley at such short distance would tear the heart from his assault. Panic whipped through him. He felt the temptation to break right and dive into the underbrush for cover, indeed a temptation to just run away, but then salvation arrived as the rebel regiment that was assaulting the Pennsylvanians from the south fired an overwhelming volley. The hastily formed Northern line crumpled. The fusillade that should have destroyed Starbuck was never fired. Instead the two Union flags faltered and fell as the overpowered Yankees began to retreat.

Sheer relief made Starbuck's war cry into a chilling and incoherent screech as he led his men into the clearing. A blue-coated soldier swung a rifle butt at him, but Starbuck easily parried the wild blow and used his own rifle's stock to hammer the man down to the leaf mould. A rifle shot half deafened him; the Northerner who had fired it was retreating backward and tripped on a fallen branch. Robert Decker jumped on the man, screaming as loudly as his terrified victim. Truslow alone advanced without screaming; instead, he was watching for places where the enemy might recover the initiative. He saw one of the Legion's new conscripts, Isaiah Clarke, being beaten to the ground by a huge Pennsylvanian. Truslow had his bowie knife drawn. He slashed it twice, then kicked the dying Pennsylvanian so that his body would not fall across Clarke. "Get up, boy," he told Clarke. "You ain't hurt bad. Nothing that a swallow of whiskey won't cure."

The Pennsylvanians were running now. The stripes of Old Glory had disappeared northward to safety, but the blue eagle flag with its ornate German legend was being carried by a limping sergeant. Starbuck ran for the man, shouting at him to surrender. A Yankee corporal saw Starbuck and leveled a revolver that he had plucked from the body of a fallen rebel officer, but the chambers were not primed, and the revolver just clicked in his hand. The corporal swore in German and tried to duck aside, but Starbuck's bayonet took him in the belly; then Esau Washbrook's rifle butt slammed onto his skull and the man went down. A great tide of screaming rebels was coming from the south. The white-haired officer snatched the blue eagle flag from the limping sergeant and swung its staff like a clumsy poleax. The sergeant fell and covered his head with his hands, and the officer, shouting defiance in German, tripped over the man's prostrate body. The fallen officer fumbled at his waist for a holstered revolver, but Starbuck was astride him now and ramming his bayonet down into the man's ribs. Starbuck screamed, and his scream, half relief and half visceral, drowned the cry of the dying Pennsylvanian. Starbuck forced the blade down until the steel would go no farther, then rested on the gun's stock as Truslow pulled the eagle flag away from the hooked, scrabbling, and suddenly enfeebled hands of the dying man whose long white hair was now blood red in the day's last light.

Starbuck, his instincts as primitive as any savage, took the flag from Truslow and shook it in the air, spraying drops of blood from its fringe. "We did it!" he said to Truslow. "We did it!"

"Just us," Truslow said meaningfully, turning to where Medlicott was still hidden.

"I'm going to kick the belly out of that bastard," Starbuck said. He rolled the bloodied flag around its varnished pole. "Coffman!" he shouted, wanting the Lieutenant to take charge of the captured flag. "Coffman! Where the hell are you, Coffman?"

"Here, sir." The Lieutenant's voice sounded weakly from behind a fallen tree.

"Oh, Christ!" Starbuck blasphemed. Coffman's voice had been feeble, like that of a man clinging to consciousness. Starbuck ran over the clearing, jumped the tree, and found the young Lieutenant kneeling wide-eyed and pale-faced, but it was not Coffman who was wounded. Coffman was fine, just shocked. Instead it was Thaddeus Bird, kind Colonel Bird, who lay death white and bleeding beside the fallen trunk.

"Oh God, Nate, it hurts." Bird spoke with difficulty. "I came to fetch you home, but they shot me. Took my revolver, too." He tried to smile. "Wasn't even loaded, Nate. I keep forgetting to load it."

"Not you, sir, not you!" Starbuck dropped to his knees, the captured flag and Medlicott's cowardice both forgotten as his eyes suddenly blurred. "Not you, Pecker, not you!"

Because the best man in the Brigade was down.

*

All across the field, from the slopes of Cedar Mountain to the ragged corn patches west of the turnpike, the rebels were advancing by the light of a sinking sun that was now a swollen ball of fading red fire suspended in a skein of shifting cannon smoke. A small evening wind had at last sprung up to drift the gunsmoke above the wounded and the dead.

The four guns named Eliza, Louise, Maud, and Anna suddenly found employment again as gray infantry appeared like wolf packs at the timberline. The gunners fired over the heads of their own retreating infantry, lobbing shells that cracked pale smoke against the dark-shadowed woods. "Bring up the limbers! Jump to it!" The Major, who a moment before had been tilting the pages of the battery's much-thumbed copy of *Reveries of a Bachelor* to the last rays of sunlight, saw that he would have to move his guns smartly northward if the battery were not to be captured. "Bring my horse!" he shouted.

The four guns went on firing while the teams were fetched. A lieutenant, fresh from West Point, noticed a group of mounted rebel officers at the wood's margin. "Slew left!" he called, and his team levered with a handspike to turn Eliza's white-oak trail. "Hold there! Elevate her a turn. Load shell!" The powder bag was thrust down the swabbed-out barrel, and the gunner sergeant rammed a spike down the touchhole to pierce the canvas bag.

"No shell left, sir!" one of the artillerymen called from the pile of ready ammunition.

"Load solid shot. Load anything, but for Christ's sake, hurry!" The Lieutenant still watched the tempting target.

A round of solid shot was rammed down onto the canvas bag. The Sergeant pushed his friction primer into the touchhole, then stood aside with the lanyard in his hand. "Gun ready," he shouted.

Eliza's limber, drawn by six horses, galloped up behind to take the gun away. "Fire!" the Lieutenant shouted.

The Sergeant whipped the lanyard toward him, thus scraping the friction rod across the primer-filled tube. The fire leaped down to the canvas bag, the powder exploded, and the four-and-a-half-inch iron ball screamed away across the smoke-layered field. The gun itself recoiled with the force of a runaway locomotive, jarring backward a full ten paces to mangle the legs of the two leading horses of the limber team. Those lead horses went down, screaming. The other horses reared and kicked in terror. One horse shattered a splinter bar, another broke a leg on the limber, and suddenly the battery's well-ordered retreat had turned into a horror of screaming, panicked horses.

A gunner tried to cut the unwounded horses free, but could not get close because the injured horses were thrashing in agony. "Shoot them, for Christ's sake!" the Major shouted from his saddle. A rifle bullet whistled overhead. The rebel yell sounded unearthly in the lurid evening light. The gunner trying to disentangle the horses was kicked in the thigh. He screamed and fell, his leg broken. Then a rebel artillery shell thumped into the dirt a few paces away, and the broken fragments of its casing whistled into the screaming, terror-stricken mass of men and horses. The other three guns had already been attached to their limbers.

"Go!" the Major said, "go, go, go!" and the black-muzzled Louise, Maud, and Anna were dragged quickly away, their crews hanging for dear life to the metal handles of the limbers while the drivers cracked whips over the frightened horses. The gun called Eliza stood smoking and abandoned as a second rebel shell landed plum in the mess of blood, broken harness, and struggling horses. Eliza's lieutenant vomited at the sudden eruption of blood that gushed outward, then began limping north.

Captain Hetherington led the Reverend Doctor Starbuck past the abandoned gun and the bloody twitching mess that remained of its team. The preacher had lost his top hat and was constantly turning in the saddle to watch the dark gray line of men who advanced beneath their foul banners. One of the advancing rebels was wearing the Bostonian's top hat, but it was not that insult that caused the preacher to frown but rather the conundrum of why God had allowed this latest defeat. Why was a righteous cause, fought by God's chosen nation, attended by such constant disaster? Surely, if God favored the United States, then the country must prosper, yet it was palpably not prospering, which could only mean that the country's cause, however good, was not good enough. The nation's leaders might be committed to the political cause of preserving the Union, but they were lukewarm about emancipating the slaves, and until that step was taken, God would surely punish the nation. The cause of abolition was thus made more explicit and urgent than ever. Thus reassured about the nobility of his mission, the Reverend Starbuck, his white hair streaming, galloped to safety.

A mile behind the Reverend Elial Starbuck, at the wooded ridge where the North's attack had surged, crested, and then been repulsed, General Washington Faulconer and his staff sat on their horses and surveyed the battlefield. Two brigades of Yankee infantry were retreating across the wide wheat field, their progress hastened by some newly arrived rebel cannon that fired shell and shot into the hurrying ranks. Only one Northern battery was replying to the gunfire. "No point in making ourselves targets," Faulconer announced to his aides, then trotted back into the trees to hide from the gunners.

Swynyard alone remained in the open. He was on foot, ready to lead the Brigade's first line down the long slope. Other rebel troops were already a quarter-mile beyond the woods, but the Faulconer Brigade had started its advance late and had yet to clear the trees. Swynyard saw that Faulconer had disappeared into the trees, so he pulled out his flask of whiskey and tipped it to his mouth. He finished the flask, then turned to shout at the advancing line to hurry up, but just as he turned so a blow like the beat of a mighty rushing wind bellowed about him. The air was sucked clean from his chest. He tried to call out, but he could not speak, let alone cry. The whiskey was suddenly sour in his throat as his legs gave way. He collapsed a second before something cracked like the awesome clangor of the gates of hell behind him, and then it seemed to Swynyard that a bright light, brighter than a dozen noonday suns, was filling and suffusing and drowning his vision. He lay on his back, unable to move, scarce able to breathe, and the brilliant light flickered around his vision for a few golden seconds before, blessedly, his drink-befuddled brain gave up its attempts to understand what had happened.

He fell into insensibility, and his sword slipped from his nerveless hand. The solid shot that had been fired from the doomed Eliza had missed his skull by inches and cracked into a live oak growing just behind. The tree's trunk had been riven by the cannonball, splaying outward like a letter Y with its inner faces cut as clean and bright as fresh-minted gold.

The Faulconer Brigade advanced past the prostrate Colonel. No one paused to help him, no one even stooped to see if the Colonel lived or was dead. A few men spat at him, and some would have tried to rifle his pockets, but the officers kept the lines moving, and so the Brigade marched on through the wheat field in laggard pursuit of the retreating enemy.

It was Captain Starbuck and Sergeant Truslow who eventually found Colonel Swynyard. They had carried

Colonel Bird to Doctor Danson's aid post, where they had pretended to believe Doc Billy's reassurance that the Colonel's chest wound might not prove fatal. "I've seen others live with worse," Danson said, bending in his blood-stiffened apron over the pale, shallow-breathing Bird. "And Pecker's a tough old fowl," Danson insisted, "so he stands a good chance." For a time Starbuck and Truslow had waited while Danson probed the wound, but then, realizing there was no help they could offer and that waiting only made their suspense worse, they had walked away to follow the footsteps of the advancing Brigade. Thus they came upon the prostrate Swynyard. The sun had gone down, and the whole battlefield was suffused by a pearly evening light dissipated by the smoke that was still sun-tinged on its upper edges. Carrion birds, ragged-winged and stark black, flapped down to the dirt, where they ripped at the dead with sharp-hooked beaks.

"The bastard's dead," Truslow said, looking down at Swynyard.

"Or drunk," Starbuck said. "I think he's drunk."

"Someone sure gave the bastard a hell of a good kicking," Truslow observed, pointing to a bruise that swelled yellow and brown across the side of the Colonel's skull. "Are you sure he ain't dead?"

Starbuck crouched. "Bastard's breathing."

Truslow stared out across the field, which was pitted with shell craters and littered with the black-humped shapes of the dead. "So what are you going to do with him?" he asked. "The son of a bitch tried to have us all killed," he added, just in case Starbuck might be moved toward a gesture of mercy.

Starbuck straightened. Swynyard lay helpless, his head back and his beard jutting skyward. The beard was crusted with dried tobacco juice and streams of spittle. The Colonel was breathing slow, a slight rattle sounding in his throat with every indrawn sigh. Starbuck picked up Swynyard's fallen sword and held its slender tip beneath Swynyard's beard as though he was about to plunge the steel into the Colonel's scrawny throat. Swynyard did not stir at the steel's touch. Starbuck felt the temptation to thrust home; then he flicked the sword blade aside. "He's not worth killing," he said, and then he rammed the sword down to skewer a pamphlet that had been blown by the small new wind to lodge against the Colonel's bruised skull. "Let the bastard suffer his headache," he said, and the two men walked away.

Back on the turnpike the Federals made one final effort to save the lost day. The retreating infantry were trading volleys with the advancing rebels, who were also under the fire of one last stubborn Yankee artillery battery that had stayed to cover the North's retreat. Now it seemed that the guns of that last battery must be captured, for the gunners were almost in range of the Southern rifles that threatened to kill the team horses before they could be harnessed to the cannons.

So, to save the guns, the 1st Pennsylvania Cavalry was ordered forward. The men rode fresh corn-fed horses in three lines, fifty troopers to a line. A bugle sounded the advance, and the horses dipped their heads so that their manes tossed in the evening light as the first rank of horsemen trotted out past the guns.

The second line advanced, then the third, each leaving a sufficient space between themselves and the line ahead so that the troopers could swerve around a dead or dying horse. Sabers scraped out of scabbards and glittered in the blood red light of dying day. Some men left their sabers sheathed and carried revolvers instead. A swallow-tailed guidon, blue and white, was carried on a lance head in the front rank.

The cannon were hitched to limbers, and the gunners' paraphernalia was stowed in boxes or hung from the trail hooks. The gunners hurried, knowing that the cavalry was buying them a few precious moments in which to escape. The cavalry horses were going at a fast trot now, leaving tiny spurts of dust behind their hooves. The three lines stretched onto the fields either side of the turnpike, which here ran between open fields that had been harvested of wheat and corn. Curb chains and scabbard links jingled as the horsemen advanced.

Ahead of the horsemen the Confederate infantry halted. There was a metallic rattle as ramrods thrust bullets hard down onto powder charges. Fingers stained black with gunpowder pushed brass percussion caps onto fire-darkened cones. "Wait till they're close, boys! Wait! Wait!" an officer shouted.

"Aim for the horses, lads!" a sergeant called.

"Wait!" the officer shouted. Men shuffled into line, and more men ran to join the rebel ranks.

The Northern bugle called again, this time raggedly, and the horses were spurred into a canter. The guidon was lowered so that the lance point was aimed straight at the waiting infantry, who looked like a ragged gray-black line stretched across the turnpike. Fires burned on the far ridge, their smoke rising slow to make grim palls in the darkening sky, where the evening star was already a cold and brilliant point of light above the smoke-clad slopes of Cedar Mountain. A waxing moon, bright and sharp as a blade, rose beyond those smoky southern woods. More infantry hurried toward the turnpike to add their fire to the volley that threatened the approaching horsemen.

The bugle called a last defiant time. "Charge!" an officer shouted, and the troopers screamed their challenge and slashed back their spurs to drive their big horses into a full gallop. They were farm boys, come from the good lands of Pennsylvania. Their ancestors had ridden horses in the wars of old Europe and in the wars to free America, and now their descendants lowered their sabers so that the blade points would rip like spears into the ribcages of the rebel line. The dry fields on either flank of the turnpike shuddered to the thunder of the pounding hooves. "Charge!" the cavalry officer shouted again, drawing out the word like a war cry into the night.

"Fire!" the rebel cry answered.

Five hundred rifles slashed flame in the dusk. Horses screamed, fell, died.

"Reload!"

Ramrods rattled and scraped in hot rifle barrels. Unhorsed men staggered away from the carnage on the turnpike. Not one single trooper in the front rank had stayed in his saddle, and not one horse was still on its legs. The second line had been hit hard, too, but enough men survived to gallop on, mouths open and sabers bright as they galloped toward the remnants of the first rank, where horses screamed, hooves thrashed, and viscous blood sprayed from the twitching, dying beasts. A horseman of the second line leaped a bloody mound of writhing bodies only to be hit by two bullets. The rebels were screaming their own challenge now as they edged forward, loading and firing. An unhorsed cavalryman ran back a few paces, then doubled over to vomit blood. Horses screamed pathetically, their blood trickling in black rivulets to make thick puddles on the dusty road.

The third line checked behind the milling remnants of the second line. Some cavalrymen fired revolvers over the gory barricade, which was all that remained of their leading ranks, but then another volley flamed and smoked from the advancing rebel ranks, and the surviving horsemen pulled their reins hard around and so turned away. Their retreat brought jeers from their enemy. More rifles cracked and more saddles were emptied. A horse limped away, another fell among the wheat stooks, while a third raced riderless toward the west. The surviving troopers galloped north in the wake of the rescued guns that were being whipped back toward Culpeper Court House.

A hundred and sixty-four troopers had charged an army. Seventy returned.

And now, at last, under a warm wind reeking of blood, night fell.

In the fields at the foot of Cedar Mountain the battleground lay dark beneath the banded layers of smoke that shrouded the sky. High clouds had spread to hide the moon, though still a great wash of eye-bright stars arced across the northern portion of the sky.

The wounded cried and called for water. Some of the battle's survivors searched the woods and cornfields for injured men and gave them what help they could while other men looted the dead and robbed the wounded. Raccoons foraged among the bodies, and a skunk, disturbed by a wounded horse blundering through the woods, released its stench to add to the already reeking battlefield.

The new rebel front line was where the Yankees had started the day, while the Yankees themselves had withdrawn northward and made a new defensive line across the road to Culpeper Court House. Messengers brought General Banks news of more Northern troops hurrying south from Manassas in case the rebel attack presaged a full-scale thrust northward. Culpeper Court House must be held, General Pope ordered, though that command did not stop some panicked Yankees loading wagons with plunder taken from abandoned houses and starting northward in case the feared rebel cavalry was already sweeping east and west of the town to cut off General Banks's army.

Other wagons brought the first wounded from the battle-field. The town's courthouse, a fine arcaded building with a belfry and steeple, was turned into a hospital, where the sur-geons worked all night by the smoky light of candles and oil lamps. They knew the morning light would bring them far more broken bodies, and maybe it would bring vengeful rebels, too. The sound of bone saws rasped in the darkness, where men gasped and sobbed and prayed.

General Banks wrote his dispatch in a commandeered farmhouse that had been looted by Northern soldiers who had taken General Pope's orders to live off the land as per-mission to plunder all Southern homes. Banks sat on an empty powder barrel and used two more such barrels as his table. He dipped his steel nib into ink and wrote that he had won a victory. It was not, he allowed privately, the great vic-tory that he had hoped for, but it was a victory nonetheless, and his words described how his small force had faced and fought and checked a mighty rebel thrust northward. Like a good politician he wrote with one eye on history, making of his battle a tale of stubborn defiance fit to stand alongside the Spartans who had defended Greece against the Persian hordes.

Six miles to the south his opponent also claimed victory. The battle had decided nothing, but Jackson had been left master of the field, and so the General knelt in prayer to give thanks to Almighty God for this new evidence of His mercies. When the General's prayers were finished, he gave curt orders for the morning: The wounded must be col-lected, the dead buried, and the battleground searched for weapons that would help the Confederate cause. And then, wrapped in a threadbare blanket, Jackson slept on the ground beneath the thinning smoke.

Nervous sentries disturbed the sleep of both armies with sporadic outbreaks of rifle fire, while every now and then an apprehensive Northern gunner sent a shell spinning south toward the smear of fires that marked where the Southerners tried to rest amidst the horrors of a field after battle. Campfires flickered red, dying as the night wore on until at last an uneasy peace fell across the wounded fields.

And in that fretful dark a patrol of soldiers moved quietly.

The patrol was composed of four men, each wearing a white cloth patch embroidered with a red crescent. The patrol's leader was Captain Moxey, Faulconer's favorite aide, while the men themselves came from Captain Medlicott's company, the one most loyal to Faulconer. Medlicott had gladly loaned the three men, though he had not sought the permission of Major Paul Hinton, who had taken command of the Legion from the wounded Thaddeus Bird. Hinton, like Moxey and Medlicott, wore the red crescent badge, but he was so ambivalent about his loyalty that he had deliberately dirtied and frayed his patch until it could hardly be recognized as the Faulconer crest, and had Hinton known of Moxey's mission, he would undoubtedly have stopped the nonsense before it began.

The four men carried rifles, none of them loaded. The three privates had each been promised a reward of five dollars, in coins rather than bills, if their mission was successful. "You might have to break a few heads," Faulconer had warned Moxey, "but I don't want any bloodshed. I don't want any courts-martial, you understand?"

"Of course, sir."

Yet, as it turned out, the whole mission was ridiculously easy. The patrol crept through the Legion's lines well inside the ring of sentries whose job was to look outward, not inward. Moxey led the way between sleeping bodies, skirting the dying fires, going to where Starbuck's Company H slept beneath the stars. Coming close, and wary lest one of the company's dogs should wake and start barking, Moxey held up his hand.

The problem that had made this mission necessary had begun earlier in the evening when the men of Faulconer's Brigade were making what supper they could from the scraps of food they had either plundered or discovered in their knapsacks. Captain Pryor, General Washington Faulconer's new aide, had come to Starbuck and requested that the captured Pennsylvanian flag be handed over.

"Why?" Starbuck had asked.

"The General wants it," Pryor answered innocently. Thomas Pryor was far too new to the Brigade to comprehend the full enmity that existed between Starbuck and Faulconer. "I'm to take it to him."

"You mean Faulconer wants to claim that he captured it?" Starbuck demanded.

Pryor colored at such an ignoble accusation. "I'm sure the General would do no such thing," he said.

Starbuck laughed at the aide's naïveté. "Go and tell General Faulconer, with my compliments, that he can come here and ask for the flag himself."

Pryor had wanted to insist, but he found Nathaniel Starbuck a somewhat daunting figure, even a frightening figure, and so he had carried the unhelpful message back to the General who, surprisingly, showed no indignation at Starbuck's insolence. Pryor ascribed the General's reaction to magnanimity, but in truth Washington Faulconer was furious and merely hiding that fury. He wanted the flag, and even felt entitled to the flag, for had it not been captured by men under his command? He thus considered the flag to be his property, and he planned to hang the trophy in the hall- way of his house just outside Faulconer Court House, which was why, at quarter past three in the morning, Captain

Moxey and three men were poised just outside the area where Starbuck's men slept.

"There," one of Moxey's men whispered and pointed to where Lieutenant Coffman lay curled under a blanket.

"Are you sure he's got it?" Moxey whispered back.

"Certain."

"Stay here," Moxey said, then tiptoed across the dry grass until he reached the sleeping Lieutenant and could see the rolled-up flag lying half concealed beneath Coffman's blanket. Moxey stooped and put a hand on Coffman's throat. The grip woke the boy. "One word," Moxey hissed, "and I'll cut your damned throat."

Coffman started up, but was thrust hard down by Moxey's left hand. Moxey seized the flag in his other hand and started to edge it free. "Keep quiet," he hissed at Coffman, "or I'll have your sisters given the pox."

"Moxey?" Coffman had grown up in the same town as Moxey. "Is that you?"

"Shut up, boy," Moxey said. The flag was at last free, and he backed away, half regretting his failure to give a sleeping Starbuck a beating, but also relieved that he would not have to risk waking the Northerner. Starbuck had a belligerent reputation, just like his company, which was considered the most reckless in the Legion, but the men of Company H had all slept through Moxey's raid. "Let's go!" Moxey told his own men, and so they slipped safely away, the trophy captured.

Coffman shivered in the dark. He wondered if he should wake Starbuck or Truslow, but he was scared. He did not understand why Moxey should need to steal the flag, and he could not bear the thought of having let Starbuck down. It had been Captain Starbuck who had shamed General Washington Faulconer into paying his salary, and Coffman was terrified that Starbuck would now be angry with him,

100

and so he just lay motionless and frightened as he listened to the far-off whimpers and cries that came from the taper-lit tents where the tired doctors sawed at limbs and prised misshapen bullets from bruised and bloodied flesh. Thaddeus Bird was in one of Doctor Danson's tents, still breathing, but with a face as pale as the canvas under which he slept.

The plight of the men still on the battlefield was far worse. They drifted in and out of their painful sleep, sometimes waking to the voices of other men calling feebly for help or to the sound of wounded horses spending a long night dying. The night's small wind blew north to where the frightened Yankees waited for another rebel attack. Every now and then a nervous artilleryman fired a shell from the Yankee lines, and the round would thump into the trampled corn and explode. Clods of earth would patter down, and a small thick cloud of bitter smoke would drift north as a chorus of frightened voices momentarily sounded loud before fading again. Here and there a lantern showed where men looked for friends or tried to rescue the wounded, but there were too many men lying in blood and not enough men to help, and so the abandoned men suffered and died in the small wicked hours.

Colonel Griffin Swynyard neither died nor called for help. Instead the Colonel lay sleeping, and in the dawn, when the sun's first rays lanced over the crest of Cedar Mountain to gild the field where the dead lay rotting and the wounded lay whimpering, he opened his eyes to brightness.

Thirty miles north, where train after train steamed into Manassas Junction to fill the night with the clash of cars, the hiss of valves, and the stench of smoke, Adam Faulconer watched the horses purchased with the Reverend Elial Starbuck's money come down from the boxcars. The beasts were frightened by the noises and the pungent smells of this strange place, and so they pricked their ears, rolled their eyes white, and whinnied pitifully as they were driven between two lines of men into a makeshift corral formed from empty army wagons. Captain Billy Blythe, who had purchased the horses and shipped them to Manassas, sat long-legged on a wagon driver's high box and watched to see how Adam liked his animals. "Real special horses, Faulconer," Blythe called. "Picked 'em myself. I know they don't look much, but there ain't nothing wrong that a few days in a feedlot won't set straight." Blythe lit a cigar and waited for Adam's judgment.

Adam hardly dared say a word in case that word provoked a fight with Blythe. The horses were dreadful beasts. Adam had seen better animals penned at slaughter yards.

Tom Huxtable was Adam's troop sergeant. He came from Louisiana but had chosen to fight for the North rather than strain the loyalty of his New York wife. Huxtable spat in derision of the newly arrived horses. "These ain't horses, sir," he said to Adam. "Hell, these ain't no horses. Broken-down mules is all they is." He spat again. "Swaybacked, spavined, and wormy. I reckon Blythe just pocketed half the money."

"You say something, Tom Huxtable?" a grinning Billy Blythe called from his perch.

For answer Sergeant Huxtable just spat again. Adam curbed his own anger as he inspected the twenty frightened horses and tried to find some redeeming feature among them, but in the lanterns' meager light the animals did indeed look a sorry bunch. They had capped hocks and sloping pasterns, swaybacks and, most troubling of all, too many running noses. A horse with bad lungs was a horse that needed to be butchered, yet these were the horses being given to the men under Adam's command. Adam cursed himself for not buying the horses himself, but Major

Galloway had insisted that Blythe's experience in horse dealing was one of the regiment's valuable assets.

"So what do you think, Faulconer?" Blythe asked mockingly.

"What did you pay for them?"

Blythe waved the cigar insouciantly. "I paid plenty, boy, just plenty."

"Then you were cheated." Adam could not hide his bitterness.

"There just ain't that many horses available, boy." Blythe deliberately taunted Adam with the word "boy" in hopes of provoking a show of temper. Blythe had been content to be Galloway's second-in-command and saw no need for the Major to have fetched a third officer into the regiment. "The army's already bought all the decent horses, so we late-comers have to make do with the leavings. Are you telling me you can't manage with those there horses?"

"I reckon this gray has distemper," Corporal Kemp said. Harlan Kemp, like Adam, was a Virginian who could not shake his loyalty to the United States. He and his whole family had abandoned their farm to come north.

"Better shoot the beast, then," Blythe said happily.

"Not with one of your guns," Adam snapped back. "Not if they're as good as your horses."

Blythe laughed, pleased at having goaded the display of temper out of Adam. "I got you some right proper guns, Faulconer. Colt repeaters, brand-new, still in their Connecticut packing cases." The Colt repeater was little more than a revolver elongated into a long-arm, but its revolving cylinder gave a man the chance to fire six shots in the same time an enemy rifleman needed to fire just one. The weapon was not famed for its accuracy, but Major Galloway reckoned a small group of horsemen needed volume of fire rather than accuracy and claimed that forty horsemen firing six shots were worth over two hundred men with single-shot rifles.

"It ain't a reliable gun," Sergeant Huxtable murmured to Adam. "I've seen the whole cylinder explode and take off a man's hand."

"And it's too long in the barrel," Harlan Kemp added. "Real hard to carry on horseback."

"You spoke, Harlan Kemp?" Blythe challenged.

"I'm saying the Colt ain't a horse soldier's weapon," Kemp responded. "We should have carbines."

Blythe chuckled. "You're lucky to have any guns at all. So far as guns and horses go, we're on the hindmost teat. So you'll just have to clamp down and suck hard."

Huxtable ignored Blythe's crudity. "What do you reckon, sir?" he asked Adam. "These horses can't be ridden. They ain't nothing but worm meat." Adam did not answer, and Tom Huxtable shook his head. "Major Galloway won't let us ride on nags like these, sir."

"I guess not," Adam said. Tonight Major Galloway was fetching orders from General Pope, and those orders were supposed to initiate the first offensive patrols of Galloway's Horse, but Adam knew he could do nothing on these broken-backed animals.

"So what will we do?" Harlan Kemp asked, and the other men of Adam's troop gathered round to hear their Captain's answer.

Adam looked at the sorry, shivering, diseased horses. Their ribs showed and their pelts were mangy. For a moment he felt a temptation to give way to despair, and he wondered why every human endeavor had to be soured by jealousy and spite, but then he glanced up into Billy Blythe's grinning face, and Adam's incipient despair was overtaken by a surge of resolution. "We'll exchange the horses," Adam told his anxious men. "We'll take these nags south and we'll exchange them for the best horses in Virginia. We'll change them for horses swift as the wind and strong as the hills." He laughed as he saw the incomprehension on Blythe's face. Adam would not be beaten, for he knew just where to find those horses, the best horses, and once he had found his horses, he would sow havoc among his enemies. Billy Blythe or no, Adam Faulconer would fight.

SATURDAY MORNING, the day after battle, again dawned hot and humid. Leaden clouds covered the sky and added to the air's oppression, which was made even fouler by a miasmic smell that clung to the folds of the battlefield like the morning mist. At first light, when the troops were stirring reluctantly from their makeshift beds, Major Hinton sought out Starbuck. "I'm sorry about last night, Nate," Hinton said.

Starbuck offered the Legion's new commanding officer a curt and dismissive judgment of Washington Faulconer's raid to snatch the captured flag. The Bostonian was stripped to the waist and had his chin and cheeks lathered with shaving soap plundered from a captured artillery limber. Starbuck stropped his razor on his belt, leaned close to his scrap of mirror, then stroked the long blade down his cheek.

"So what will you do?" Hinton asked, plainly nervous that Starbuck would be provoked into some rash act.

"The bastard can keep the rag," Starbuck said. He had not really known what to do with the captured standard; he had thought that perhaps he might give it to Thaddeus Bird or else send it to Sally Truslow in Richmond. "What I really wanted was the Stars and Stripes," he confessed to Hinton, "and that eagle flag was only ever second-best, so I reckon that son of a bitch Faulconer can keep it."

"It was a stupid thing for Moxey to do, all the same," Hinton said, unable to conceal his relief that Starbuck did not intend to inflate the night's stupidity into an excuse for revenge. He watched as Starbuck squinted into a broken fragment of shaving mirror. "Why don't you grow a beard?" he asked.

"Because everyone else does," Starbuck said, although in truth it was because a girl had once told him he looked better clean-shaven. He scraped at his upper lip. "I'm going to murder goddamn Medlicott."

"No, you're not."

"Slowly. So it hurts."

Major Hinton sighed. "He panicked, Nate. It can happen to anyone. Next time it might be me."

"Son of a bitch damn nearly had me killed by panicking."

Major Hinton picked up the plundered jar of Roussel's Shaving Cream, fidgeted with its lid, then watched Starbuck clean the razor blade. "For my sake," he finally pleaded, "will you just forget about it? The boys are unhappy enough because of Pecker and they don't need their captains fighting among themselves. Please, Nate? For me?"

Starbuck mopped his face clean on a strip of sacking. "Give me a cigar, Paul, and I'll forget that bald-headed lily-livered gutless shadbelly bastard even exists."

Hinton surrendered the cigar. "Pecker's doing well," he said, his tone brightening as he changed the subject, "or as well as can be expected. Doc Billy even reckons he might survive a wagon ride to the rail depot." Hinton was deeply worried about replacing the popular Colonel even though he was a popular enough officer himself. He was an easy-going, heavyset man who had been a farmer by trade, a churchman by conviction, and a soldier by accident of history. Hinton had hoped to live out his years in the easy, rich countryside of Faulconer County, enjoying his family, his acres, and his foxhunting, but the war had threatened Virginia, and so Paul Hinton had shouldered his weapons

107

out of patriotic duty. Yet he did not much enjoy soldiering and reckoned his main duty was to bring safely home as many of the Faulconer Legion as he possibly could, and the men in the Legion recognized that ambition and liked Hinton for it. "We're to stay where we are today," Hinton now told Starbuck. "I've got to detach a company to collect small arms off the battlefield and another to bring in the wounded. And talking of the wounded," he added after a second's hesitation, "did you see Swynyard yesterday? He's missing."

Starbuck also hesitated, then told the truth. "Truslow and I saw him last night." He gestured with the cigar toward the woods where his company had fought against the Pennsylvanians. "He was lying just this side of the trees. Truslow and I didn't reckon there was anything to be done for him, so we just left him."

Hinton was shrewd enough to guess that Starbuck had abandoned Swynyard to die. "I'll send someone to look for him," he said. "He ought to be given a burial."

"Why?" Starbuck demanded belligerently.

"To cheer the Brigade up, of course," Hinton said, then blushed for having uttered such a thing. He turned to look at the great smear of smoke that rose from the Northern cooking fires beyond the woods. "Keep a good eye on the Yankees, Nate. They ain't beaten yet."

But the Yankees made little hostile movement that morning. Their pickets probed forward but stopped obediently when the rebel outposts opened fire, and so the two armies settled into an uneasy proximity. Then it began to rain, slowly at first, but with an increasing vehemence after midday. Starbuck's company made shelters at the edge of the woods with frameworks of branches covered in sod. Then they lay under cover and just watched the gray, rain-lashed landscape.

In midafternoon, when the rain eased to a drizzle, Corporal Waggoner sought Hinton's permission for a prayer meeting. There had been no chance for such a service since the battle's ending, and many soldiers in the Legion wanted to give thanks. Hinton gladly gave his permission, and fifty or more Legionnaires gathered beneath some gun-battered cedars. Other men from the Brigade soon joined them, so that by the time the drizzle stopped, there were almost a hundred men sitting beneath the trees and listening as Corporal Waggoner read from the Book of Job. Waggoner's twin brother had died in the battles on the far side of Richmond, and ever since that death Peter Waggoner had become more and more fatalist. Starbuck was not sure that Waggoner's gloomy piety was good for the Legion's morale, but many of the men seemed to like the Corporal's spontaneous sessions of prayer and Bible study. Starbuck did not join the circle, but rested nearby, watching northward to where the Yankee defense line showed between the distant woodlands as a newly dug strip of earthworks broken by hastily erected cannon emplacements. Starbuck would have been hard put to admit it, but the familiar sounds of prayer and Bible reading were oddly comforting.

That comfort was broken by a blasphemous oath from Sergeant Truslow. "Christ Almighty!" the Sergeant swore.

"What is it?" Starbuck asked. He had been half dozing but now sat up fully awake. Then he saw what had provoked Truslow to blasphemy. "Oh, Jesus," he said, and spat.

For Colonel Swynyard was not dead. Indeed, the Colonel hardly appeared to be wounded. His face was bruised, but the bruise was covered and shadowed by a wide-brimmed hat that Swynyard must have plucked from among the battlefield litter, and now the Colonel was walking through the Brigade's lines with his familiar wolfish smile. "He's drunk," Truslow said. "We should have shot the bastard yesterday."

Peter Waggoner's voice faltered as the Colonel walked up to the makeshift prayer meeting. Swynyard stopped at the edge of the meeting, saying nothing, just staring at the men with their open Bibles and bare heads, and every single man seemed cowed by the baleful eyes. The Colonel had always been a mocker of these homespun devotions, though until now he had kept his scorn at a distance. Now his malevolence killed the prayerful atmosphere stone dead. Waggoner made one or two brave efforts to keep reading, but then stopped altogether.

"Go on," Swynyard said in his hoarse voice.

Waggoner closed his Bible instead. Sergeant Phillips, who was one of Major Haxall's shrinking Arkansas battalion, stood to head off any trouble. "Maybe you'd like to join us at prayer, Colonel?" the Sergeant suggested nervously.

The tic in Swynyard's cheek twitched as he considered his answer. Sergeant Phillips licked his lips while others of the men closed their eyes in silent prayer. Then, to the amazement of everyone who watched, Colonel Swynyard pulled off his hat and nodded to Phillips. "I would like that, Sergeant, I would indeed." Sergeant Phillips was so taken aback by the Colonel's agreement that he said nothing. A murmur went through the Bible study group, but no one spoke aloud. Swynyard, the bruise on his face visible now, was embarrassed by the silence. "If you'll have me, that is," he added in an unnaturally humble voice.

"Anyone is welcome," Sergeant Phillips managed to say. One or two of the officers in the group muttered their agreement, but no one looked happy at welcoming Swynyard. Everyone in the prayer group believed the Colonel was playing a subtle game of mockery, but they did not understand his game, nor did anyone know how to stop it, and so they offered him a reluctant welcome instead.

"Maybe you'll let me say a word or two?" Swynyard suggested to Phillips, who seemed to have assumed leadership of the prayer meeting. Phillips nodded, and the Colonel fidgeted with the hat in his hands as he looked around the frightened gathering. The Colonel tried to speak, but the words would not come. He cleared his throat, took a deep breath, and tried again. "I have seen the light," he explained.

Another murmur went through the circle of seated men. "Amen," Phillips said.

Swynyard twisted the hat in his nervous hands. "I have been a great sinner, Sergeant," he said, then stopped. He still wore the same hated smile, but some of the men nearer to Swynyard could sense that it was now a smile of embarrassment rather than sarcasm. The same men could even see tears in the Colonel's eyes.

"Drunk as a bitch on the Fourth of July," Truslow said in a tone of wonder.

"I'm not sure," Starbuck said. "I think he might be sober."

"Then he's lost his damn wits," Truslow opined.

Sergeant Phillips was more generous. "We have all been sinners, Colonel," the Sergeant said, "and fallen short of the glory of God."

"I more than most." Swynyard, it seemed, was determined to make a public confession of his sins and of his rediscovered faith. He was blinking back tears and fidgeting with the hat so frenetically that it fell from his hands. He let it lie. "I was raised a Christian by my dear mother," he said, "and I received the Lord into my heart at a camp meeting when I was a youth, but I have been a sinner ever since. A great sinner."

"We've all sinned," Sergeant Phillips averred again.

"But yesterday," Swynyard said, "I came to my senses. I was near killed, and I felt the very wings of the angel of death beat about me. I could smell the sulfur of the

111

bottomless pit and I could feel the heat of its flames, and I knew, as I lay on the field, that I deserved nothing less than that terrible punishment." He paused, almost overcome by the memory. "But then, praise Him, I was pulled back from the pit and drawn into the light."

A chorus of amens and hallelujahs sounded among the circle of men. They were all sincere Christians, and though they might have hated this man with an intense hatred, the more honest among them had also prayed for the Colonel's soul, and now that their prayers were being answered, they were willing to give thanks to God for His mercies to a sinner.

Swynyard had tears on his cheeks now. "I also know, Sergeant, that in the past I have been unfair in my dealings with many men here. To those men I offer my regrets and seek their forgiveness." The apology was handsomely spoken, and the men in the group took it just as handsomely. Then Swynyard turned away from the circle and looked among the shelters for Starbuck. "I owe another man an even greater apology," the Colonel said.

"Oh, Jesus," Starbuck swore and wriggled back into the shadow of his shelter.

"Bastard's touched in the head," Truslow said. "He'll be foaming at the mouth next and pissing himself. We'll have to take him away and put him out of his misery."

"We should have shot the bastard when we had the chance," Starbuck said, then fell silent because Swynyard had left the Bible circle and was walking toward his shelter.

"Captain Starbuck?" Swynyard said.

Starbuck looked up into his enemy's face. "I can hear you, Colonel," Starbuck said flatly. He could see now that the Colonel had made an attempt to improve his appearance. His beard was washed, his hair combed, and his uniform brushed. The tic in his cheek still quivered, and his hands

112

shook, but he was plainly making a great effort to hold himself straight and steady.

"Can I talk with you, Starbuck," the Colonel asked, then, after a moment's silence, "please?"

"Are you drunk?" Starbuck asked brutally.

Swynyard offered his rotting, yellow-toothed smile. "Only on God's grace, Starbuck, only on His divine grace. And with His help I shall never touch ardent spirits again."

Truslow spat to show his disbelief. Swynyard ignored the insult, gesturing instead to indicate that he would like to take a walk with Starbuck.

Starbuck climbed reluctantly out of his turf shelter, shouldered his rifle, and followed the Colonel. Starbuck was wearing new boots that he had taken from a dead Pennsylvanian. The boots were new and stiff, but Starbuck was convinced they would wear in well enough after a day or two. Now, though, he felt the makings of a blister as he walked self-consciously beside Swynyard. News of the Colonel's conversion had spread through the Brigade, and men were drifting toward the picket line to see the proof for themselves. Some evidently believed that the Colonel's religious experience was just another inebriated escapade, and they grinned in anticipation of a display of drunken idiocy, but Swynyard seemed oblivious to the attention he was receiving. "You know why I sent your company forward yesterday?" he asked Starbuck.

"Uriah the Hittite," Starbuck said shortly.

Swynyard thought for a second; then the story of David and Bathsheba came back from his dusty memories of childhood Sunday schools. "Yes," he said. "And I intended for you to be killed. I am sorry, truly."

Starbuck wondered how long Swynyard's manifestation of honesty would last and reckoned that it would be only until the Colonel's thirst overcame his piety, but he kept that skepticism to himself. "I guess you were just obeying someone else's orders," he said instead.

"It was still a sinful action," Swynyard said very earnestly, thus obliquely confirming that it had indeed been Washington Faulconer who had ordered Starbuck's company into the place of danger, "and I ask your forgiveness." Swynyard concluded his confession by holding out his hand.

Starbuck, excruciated with embarrassment, shook the offered hand. "Say no more about it, Colonel," he said.

"You're a good soldier, Starbuck, a good soldier, and I haven't made life easy for you. Not for anyone, really." Swynyard made the admission in a gruff voice. The Colonel had been weeping when he gave his halting testimony at the prayer meeting, but now he seemed in a more rueful mood. He turned and gazed north to where groups of Yankees could be seen in the far fields beyond the nearer stands of trees. No man on either side seemed inclined to belligerence this day; even the sharpshooters who delighted to kill at long range were keeping their rifle barrels cold. "Do you have a Bible?" Swynyard asked Starbuck suddenly.

"Sure I do." Starbuck felt in his breast pocket where he kept the small Bible that his brother had sent him. James had intended the Bible to spark Starbuck into a repentance like the one that was transforming Swynyard, but Starbuck had kept the scriptures out of habit rather than need. "You want it?" he asked, offering the book to the Colonel.

"I shall find another," Swynyard said. "I just wanted to be certain you have a Bible because I'm sure you're going to need one." Swynyard smiled at the suspicious look on Starbuck's face. The Colonel doubtless intended the smile to be friendly, but the resulting foul-toothed leer uncomfortably recalled the Colonel's usual malevolence. "I wish I could describe what happened to me last night and this morning," he now told Starbuck. "It was as though I was struck by a great light. There was no pain. There's still no pain." He touched the livid bruise on his right temple. "I remember lying on the earth and hearing voices. I couldn't move, couldn't speak. The voices were debating my death, and I knew I had come to the judgment seat and I felt a fear, a most terrible fear, that I was being consigned to hell. I wanted to weep, Starbuck, and in my terror I called out to the Lord. I remembered my mother's teaching, my childhood lessons, and I called on the Lord and He heard me."

Starbuck had heard too many testimonies of repentant sinners to be either moved or even convinced by the Colonel's change of heart. Doubtless Swynyard had received a shock, and doubtless he intended to reform his life, but Starbuck was equally convinced that Swynyard's conversion would prove soluble in alcohol before the sun went down. "I wish you well," he muttered grudgingly.

"No, no, you don't understand." Swynyard spoke with some of his old savage force and laid his maimed left hand on Starbuck's elbow to prevent the younger man from turning away. "When I recovered my senses, Starbuck, I found my sword stuck into the turf beside my head and there was a message impaled on the sword. This message." The Colonel took from his pocket a crumpled and torn pamphlet, which he pushed into Starbuck's hand.

Starbuck smoothed the tract to see that it was called *Freeing the Oppressed* and had been printed in Anne Street, Boston. The cover showed a picture of a half-naked black man springing free from broken manacles toward a cross that was infused with a heavenly light. The shattered manacles were attached to great iron weights labeled "Slavocracy," "Ignorance," and "Wickedness," and beneath those iron weights was written the name of the pamphlet's author: the Reverend Doctor Elial Starbuck. Starbuck felt his usual tremor of distaste at any reminder of his father's existence, then handed the tract back to the Colonel. "So what was your message?" he asked sourly. "That slavery is a sin against God? That America's blacks have to be returned to Africa? Is that what you're going to do with your pair? Set them free?" And never, Starbuck reflected, had two slaves more deserved freedom.

Swynyard shook his head to show that Starbuck was still misunderstanding him. "I don't know what to believe about slavery. Dear God, Starbuck, but everything in my life has to be changed, can't you understand that? Slavery, too, but that wasn't the reason God left the tract beside me last night. Don't you see? He left it there to give me a task!"

"No," Starbuck said, "I don't see."

"My dear Starbuck," Swynyard said very earnestly. "I have been brought back from the path of sin at the very last moment. At that very instant when I was poised on the edge of hell's fire, I was saved. The road to hell is a terrible path, Starbuck, yet at its beginning the journey was enjoyable. Do you understand now what I'm saying?"

"No," Starbuck said, who feared that he understood exactly what the Colonel was saying.

"I think you do," Swynyard said fervently. "Because I think that you are on the first easy steps of that downward path. I look at you, Starbuck, and I see myself thirty years ago, which is why God sent me a pamphlet with your name on it. It's a sign telling me to save you from sin and from the agonies of eternal punishment. I'm going to do that, Starbuck. Instead of killing you as Faulconer wanted I am going to bring you to eternal life."

Starbuck paused to light a cigar he had plundered from the white-haired Pennsylvanian officer who had tried so hard to protect his flags. Then he sighed as he blew smoke past Swynyard's bruised face. "You know, Colonel? I think I really preferred you as a sinner."

116

Swynyard grimaced. "How long have I known you?"

Starbuck shrugged. "Six months."

"And in all that time, Captain Starbuck, have you ever called me 'sir'?"

Starbuck looked into the Colonel's eyes. "No, and I don't intend to either."

Swynyard smiled. "You will, Starbuck, you will. We're going to be friends, you and I, and I shall draw you back from the paths of sin."

Starbuck blew another plume of smoke into the damp wind. "I never did understand, Colonel, just why some son of a bitch can have a lifetime of sin and then, the moment he gets scared, turn around and try to stop other folks from enjoying themselves."

"Are you telling me the path of righteousness is not enjoyable?"

"I'm telling you I've got to get back to my company," Starbuck said. "I'll see you, Colonel." He touched his hat with a deliberate air of insolence, then walked back to his men.

"So?" Sergeant Truslow greeted Starbuck, the inflection of the word inviting news of the Colonel.

"You were right," Starbuck said. "He's gibbering mad."

"So what's changed?"

"He's got drunk on God," Starbuck said, "that's what's changed." He was trying to sound dismissive of Swynyard, but a part of him was sensing the same fires of hell that had brought the Colonel to God. "But I'll give him till sundown," he went on. "Then he'll be tight on whiskey instead."

"Whiskey works faster than God," Truslow said, but he heard something wistful in his Captain's voice, and so he thrust a pewter flask at him. "Drink some of this," the Sergeant ordered.

117

"What is it?"

"The best spill-skull. Five cents a quart. Tom Canby made it two weeks back."

Starbuck took the flask. "Don't you know it's against army regulations to drink homemade whiskey?"

"It's probably against army regulations to go caterwauling with the wives of serving officers," Truslow said, "but that ain't ever stopped you yet."

"Too true, Sergeant, too true," Starbuck said. He drank, and the fierce liquor momentarily doused the fear of hellfire, and then, beneath a lowering sky, he slept.

The federal government's bureaucrats might have been reluctant to fund Major Galloway's Horse, but General Pope immediately saw the value of having Southern horsemen scouting behind Southern lines, and so he gave the Major such a slew of tasks that a cavalry force ten times larger would have been hard-pressed to fulfill them inside a month, let alone the one week that General Pope offered Galloway.

The chief task was to determine whether General Robert Lee was moving his troops from Richmond. The Northern headquarters in Washington had ordered Lee's opponent, McClellan, to withdraw his army from its camps close to the rebel capital, and Pope feared that Lee, hearing of that order, might already be marching north to reinforce Jackson. He also feared that the rebels could be building up troops in the Shenandoah Valley and had asked Galloway to make a reconnaissance across the Blue Ridge Mountains. And, as if those two tasks were not sufficient, Pope also wanted to know more about Jackson's dispositions, and so Galloway found himself under pressure to send horsemen south, east, and west. He compromised as best he could, taking his own troop south toward Richmond while Billy Blythe was ordered to cross the Blue Ridge Mountains and sniff out the rebel dispositions in the valley of the Shenandoah.

Adam, meanwhile, needed to replace the horses Blythe had wished on him. Major Galloway tried to reassure Adam that Blythe had meant no harm in buying such spavined hacks. "I'm sure he did his best," the Major said, trying to knit the unity of his squadron.

"I'm sure he did, too," Adam agreed, "and that's what worries me." But Adam at least knew where his troop could acquire more horses, and Galloway had given Adam permission to make his raid on condition that on Adam's way back he reconnoitred the western flank of Jackson's army. Adam left to perform both tasks three days after the far-off sound of the battle at Cedar Mountain had bruised the summer's heavy air.

Two miles beyond the Manassas farmhouse that was Galloway's headquarters Adam found Billy Blythe's troop waiting. "Thought we'd ride with you, Faulconer," Blythe said, "seeing as how you and I are going in the same direction."

"Are we?" Adam asked coldly.

"Hell, why not?" Blythe said.

"The Shenandoah Valley's that way," Adam said, pointing west, "while we're going south."

"Well now," Blythe said with his lazy smile, "where I come from a gentleman doesn't go around teaching other gentlemen how to suck a tit. I'll choose my own route to the valley, if that's all right with you."

Adam had little choice but to accept Blythe's company. Sergeant Huxtable whispered his suspicion that Blythe merely wanted to follow Adam and take whatever horses Adam found for his own profit, but Adam could hardly stop his fellow cavalry officer from riding in convoy. Nor, on his dreadful horses, could Adam outrun Blythe, and so, for two days, the forty cavalrymen crept slowly southward. Blythe showed no sense of urgency and no desire to turn toward one of the high passes that led through the Blue Ridge Mountains. He ignored the Chester Gap, then Thornton's Gap, and finally Powell's Gap, hinting all the while that he knew of a better route across the mountains further south. "You're a fool if you use Rockfish Gap," Adam said. "I know for a fact the rebels will guard that pass."

Blythe smiled. "Maybe I won't use any gap at all."

"You won't get horses over the mountains otherwise."

"Maybe I don't need to cross the mountains."

"You'd disobey Galloway's orders?" Adam asked.

Blythe frowned as though he was disappointed in Adam's obtuseness. "I reckon our first duty, Faulconer, is to look after our men, specially when you reckon that the Southern army ain't going to take too kindly to Southern boys riding in Yankee blue, so it ain't my aim to take any real bad risks. That's why Abe Lincoln's got all those boys from Massachusetts and Pennsylvania; if anyone's going to beat ten types of hell out of the Confederates, it'll be them, not us. The important thing for us to do, Faulconer, is just survive the war intact." Blythe paused in this long peroration to light a cigar. Ahead of the cavalrymen was a gentle valley crossed by snake fences and with a prosperous-looking farm at the southern end. "What Joe Galloway ordered me to do, Faulconer," Blythe went on, "is discover how many rebels are skulking in the Shenandoah Valley, and I reckon I can do that well enough without crossing any damned mountain. I can do it by stopping a train coming out of the Rockfish Gap and questioning the passengers. Ain't that right?"

"Suppose the passengers lie?" Adam asked.

"Hell, there ain't a woman alive who'd tell me lies," Blythe said with a smile. He chuckled, then turned in his saddle. "Seth?"

"Billy?" Sergeant Seth Kelley answered.

"Reckon we should make sure no rebel vermin are hanging around that farmhouse. Take a couple of men. Go look."

Seth Kelley shouted at two Marylanders to follow him, then led them south through the trees that bordered the valley. "Reckon we'll just wait here," Blythe said to the other men. "Make yourselves at home now."

"You say our most important duty is to survive the war?" Adam asked Blythe when the troopers had made themselves comfortable in the shade of the broad-leaved trees.

"Because I reckon that the war's ending is when our proper work begins, Faulconer," Blythe said happily. "I even reckon that surviving the war is our Christian duty. The North's going to win. That's plain as the nose on a pelican's face. Hell, the North's got the men, the guns, the ships, the factories, the railroads, and the money, while all the South's got is a heap of cotton, a pile of rice, a stack of tobacco, and more damn lazy niggers than half Africa. The North's got a whole heap of stuff and the South ain't got a besotted hope! So sooner or later, Faulconer, we're going to have an ass-whipped South and a mighty pleased North, and when that day comes we want to make sure that we loyal Southerners get our just rewards. We are going to be the good Southerners, Faulconer, and we'll be the ones who take over down south. We are going to be hogs in clover. Rolling in milk and honey, and getting the pick of the girls and making dollars like a dog makes spit." Blythe turned to stare at the farm. "Now you don't want to risk all that by getting a bullet in your belly, do you?"

Adam heard the chuckles of those men who agreed with Blythe. Others looked grim, and Adam decided he would speak for those idealists. "We've got a job to do. That's what we volunteered for."

Blythe nodded as though Adam had made a wonderfully

121

cogent point. "Hell now, Faulconer, no one agrees with you more than me! Hell, if I could reconnoitre clean down to the Rappahannock, then no one would be as happy as Billy Blythe. Hell, I'd reconnoitre down to the Pee Dee if I could, down as far as the Swanee! Hell, I'd reconnoitre to the last gol-darned river on earth for my country, so I would, but I can't do it! Just plumb can't do it, Faulconer, and you know why?" And here Blythe laid a confiding hand on Adam's elbow and leaned so close that his cigar smell wreathed Adam's head. "We can't do nothing, Faulconer, and that's the plain sad truth of it. We can't even ride to the brothel and back on account of our horses being razor-backed pieces of four-legged hogshit. What's the first duty of a cavalryman?"

"To look after his horse, Billy," one of his men answered.

"Ain't that God's blessed truth?" Blythe responded. "So I reckon that for the horses' sake we just has to go gentle and keep ourselves unpunctured for the rest of the war. Hell now, what in tarnation was that?" The question was Blythe's response to a pair of gunshots that had sounded from somewhere near the farmhouse. For a man who had just preached a gospel of staying well clear of trouble, he seemed remarkably untroubled by the gunfire. "Reckon we'd best ride to see if old Seth's in one piece, boys," he called, and the men of his troop slowly pulled themselves into their saddles and loosened the Colt repeating rifles in their holsters.

"Reckon your troop should stay and keep watch," Blythe told Adam. "I ain't saying we expects any trouble, but you can never tell. These woods are full of bushwhackers and every man jack of them is as mean as a snake and twice as treacherous. So you watch out for partisans while the rest of us make certain old Seth ain't gone to meet his Maker."

Adam watched from the trees as Blythe took his troop down to the farmhouse, which was typical of so many homesteads in the Virginia Piedmont. Adam had often dreamed of settling in just such a farm, miles away from his father's pretensions and wealth. The two-story house was weatherboarded with white-painted planks and handsomely surrounded by a deep veranda, which, in turn, was circled by a straggling but colorful flower garden. A wide vegetable garden stretched between the house and the largest of a pair of barns that formed two sides of a yard that was completed by a rail fence. Orchards ran downhill from the house to where a stream glinted in the distance. The sight of the homestead gave Adam a pang of remorse and nostalgia. It seemed wicked that war should inflict itself on such a place.

At the farm itself Sergeant Seth Kelley waited on the veranda for Captain Blythe. Kelley was a long thin man with a narrow black beard and dark eyes, who now lounged in a wicker chair with his spurred boots propped on the veranda's rail and a cigar in his mouth. His two men were leaning against the posts that flanked the short flight of veranda steps. Kelley took the cigar from his mouth as Captain Blythe dismounted on the parched lawn. "We was fired on, Billy," Kelley said with a grin. "Two shots that came from the top floor. Came damn close to killing me, so they did."

Blythe shook his head and tutted. "But you're all right, Seth? You ain't wounded now?"

"They missed, Billy, they missed. But the rascals had this piece of bunting flying from the house, so they did." Kelley held up a small rebel flag.

"Bad business, Seth, bad business," Blythe said, grinning as broadly as his Sergeant.

"Sure is, Billy. 'Bout as bad as it can be." Kelley put the cigar back in his mouth.

Blythe led his horse across the flower bed and tied its reins to a rail of the porch. His men dismounted as Blythe climbed the veranda steps and used Kelley's cigar to light one of his own. "Any folks inside?" Blythe asked the Sergeant.

"Two women and a passel of brats," Sergeant Kelley said.

Blythe pushed into the house. The hall floor was made of dark wood on which lay a pair of hooked rugs. A long case clock stood by the staircase, its face proclaiming that it had been made in Baltimore. There was a pair of antlers serving as a coatrack, a portrait of George Washington, another of Andrew Jackson, and a pokerwork plaque proclaiming that God was The Unseen Listener to Every Conversation in This House. Blythe gave the clock an appreciative pat as Seth Kelley and two men followed him through the hall and into the kitchen, where three children clung to the skirts of two women. One woman was white-haired, the other young and defiant.

"Well now, well," Blythe said, pausing in the kitchen doorway. "What do we have here?"

"You ain't got no business here," the younger woman said. She was in her thirties and evidently the mother of the three small children. She was carrying a heavy cleaver, which she hefted nervously as Blythe walked into the kitchen.

"The business we got here, ma'am, is the business of the United States of America," Billy Blythe said happily. He strolled past an ancient dresser and picked an apple from a china bowl. He bit a chunk from the apple, then smiled at the younger woman. "Real sweet, ma'am. Just like yourself." The woman was dark-haired with good features and challenging eyes. "I like a woman with spirit," Blythe said, "ain't that so, Seth?"

"You always did have a right taste for such women, Billy." Kelley leaned his lanky form against the kitchen doorpost.

"You leave us alone!" the older woman said, scenting trouble.

"Nothing in this world I'd rather do, ma'am," Blythe said.

124

He took another bite from the apple. Two of the children had started to cry, prompting Blythe to slam the remnants of the apple hard onto the scrubbed kitchen table. Scraps of the shattered fruit skittered across the kitchen. "I would be obliged if you kept your sniveling infants silent, ma'am!" Blythe snapped. "I cannot abide a sniveling child, no sir! Sniveling children should be whipped. Whipped!" The last word was bellowed so loud that both children stopped crying in sheer fright. Blythe smiled at their mother, displaying scraps of apple between his teeth. "So where's the man of the house, ma'am?"

"He ain't here," the younger woman said defiantly.

"Is that because he's carrying arms against his lawful government?" Blythe asked in a teasing voice.

"He ain't here," the woman said again, and then, after a pause, "There's only us women and children here. You ain't got no quarrel with women and children."

"My quarrels are my business," Blythe said, "and my business is to discover just why one of you two ladies fired a couple of shots at my nice Sergeant here."

"No one fired at him!" the older woman said scornfully. "He fired his own revolver. I saw him do it!"

Blythe shook his head disbelievingly. "That's not what Mr. Kelley says, ma'am, and he wouldn't tell me a lie. Hell, he's a sergeant in the army of the United States of America! Are you telling me that a sergeant of the army of the United States of America would tell a lie?" Blythe asked the question with feigned horror. "Are you really trying to suggest such a thing?"

"No one fired!" the younger woman insisted. The children were almost buried in her skirts. Blythe took a step closer to the woman, who raised the cleaver threateningly.

"You use that, ma'am," Blythe said equably, "and you'll be hanged for murder. What's your name?"

"My name's none of your business."

"So I'll tell you what is my business, ma'am," Blythe said, and he reached out for the cleaver and plucked it from the woman's unresisting grasp. He raised it, then slashed it hard down to bury its blade tip in the table. He smiled at the younger woman, then blew cigar smoke toward the bunches of herbs hanging from a beam. "My business, ma'am," he said, "is with General Order Number Five, issued by Major General John Pope of the United States Army, which General Order gives me the legal right and solemn duty to feed and equip my men with any food or goods we find in this house that might be necessary to our well-being. That is an order, given me by the General in command of my army, and like a good Christian soldier, ma'am, I am duty-bound to obey it." Blythe turned and jabbed a finger toward Sergeant Kelley. "Start searching, Seth! Outhouses, upstairs, cellars, barns. Give the place a good shaking now! You stay here, Corporal," he added to one of the other men who had come into the kitchen.

"We ain't got nothing!" the old woman protested.

"We'll be the judge of that, ma'am," Blythe said. "Start searching, Seth! Do it thorough now!"

"You damned thieves," the younger woman said.

"On the contrary, ma'am, on the contrary." Blythe smiled at her, then sat at the head of the kitchen table and took a preprinted form from a leather pouch at his belt. He found a pencil stub in a pocket. The pencil was blunt, but he tried its lead on the tabletop and was satisfied with the mark it made. "No, ma'am," he went on, "we ain't thieves. We are just trying to put God's own country back into one piece, and we need your help to do it. But it ain't thieving, ma'am, because our Uncle Sam is a kind uncle, a good uncle, and he'll pay you folks real well for everything you give us today." He

126

smoothed out the form, licked the pencil, and looked up expectantly at the younger woman. "Your name, honey?"

"I ain't telling you."

Blythe looked at the older woman. "Can't pay the family without a name, Grandma. So tell us your name."

"Don't tell him, Mother!" the younger woman cried.

The older woman hesitated, then decided that giving the family's name would not cause much harm. "Rothwell," she said reluctantly.

"A mighty fine name," Blythe said as he wrote it on the form. "I knew a family of Rothwells down home in Blytheville. Fine Baptists, they were, and fine neighbors too. Now, ma'am, you happen to know what today's date is?" The house echoed with men's laughter and the heavy sound of boots thumping up the staircase; then a burst of cheering erupted as some treasure was discovered in one of the front rooms. More feet clattered on the stairs. The young woman looked at the ceiling, and a frown of distress crossed her face. "Today's date, ma'am?" Blythe insisted.

The older woman thought for a second. "Yesterday was the Lord's Day," she said, "so today must be the eleventh."

"My, how this summer is just flying by! August the eleventh already." Blythe wrote the date as he spoke, "in the year of Our Lord, eighteen hundred and sixty-two. This danged pencil is scratchy as hell." He finished the date, then leaned back in the chair. Sweat was pouring down his plump face and staining the collar of his uniform coat. "Well now, ladies, this here piece of paper confirms that me and my men are about to commandeer just about any gol-darned thing we take a fancy to in this property. Anything at all! And when we've got it, you're going to tell me the value of all that food and all those chattels, and I'm going to write that value down on this piece of paper and then I'm going to sign it with my God-given name. And what you're going to do, ladies, is keep ahold of this piece of paper like it was the sacred word in the good Lord's own handwriting, and at the end of the war, when the rebels are well beaten and kind Uncle Sam is welcoming you all back into the bosom of his family, you're going to present this piece of paper to the government and the government, in its mercy and goodness, is going to give you all the money. Every red cent. There's just one small thing you ought to know first, though." He paused to draw on his cigar, then smiled at the frightened women. "When you present this piece of paper you'll have to prove that you've stayed loyal to the United States of America from the date on this form until the day the war ends. Just one little piece of evidence that anyone in the Rothwell family might have borne arms or, God help us, even a grudge against the United States of America will make this piece of paper worthless. And that means you'll get no money, honey!" He laughed.

"You damned thief," the younger woman said.

"If you're a good girl," Blythe said mockingly, "then you'll get the money. That's what General Order Number Five says, and we shall obey General Order Number Five, so help us God." He stood. He was a tall man, and the feather in his hat brushed the kitchen's beams as he walked toward the frightened family. "But there's also General Order Number Seven. Have you folks ever heard of General Order Number Seven? No? Well General Order Number Seven decrees what punishment must be given to any household that fires on troops of the United States of America, and a shot was fired at my men from this house!"

"That's a lie!" the older woman insisted, and her vehemence made the three children start to cry again.

"Quiet!" Blythe shouted. The children whimpered and shivered but managed to keep silent. Blythe smiled. "By orders of Major General Pope, who is duly authorized by the

President and by the Congress of the United States of America, it is my duty to burn this house down so that no more shots can be fired from it."

"No!" the younger woman protested.

"Yes," Blythe said, still smiling.

"We didn't fire any shots!" the young woman said.

"But I say you did, and when it comes right down to the scratch, ma'am, whose word do you think the President and the Congress will believe? My word, which is the word of a commissioned officer of the United States Army, or your word, which is the caviling whine of a secessionist bitch? Now which of us, ma'am, is going to be believed?" He took a silver case from his pocket and clicked open the lid to reveal the white phosphorus heads of lucifer matches.

"No!" The younger woman had started to cry.

"Corporal Kemble!" Blythe snapped, and Kemble pushed himself off the kitchen wall. "Take her to the barn," Blythe ordered, pointing to the younger woman.

The woman lunged for the cleaver that was still stuck in the table, but Blythe was much too fast for her. He knocked the cleaver out of her reach, then drew his revolver and pointed it at the woman's head. "I'm not a hard-hearted man, ma'am, just a simple horse trader turned soldier, and like any good horse trader I do sure appreciate a bargain. So why don't you and I go and discuss matters in the barn, ma'am, and see if we can't work out an accommodation?"

"You're worse than a thief," the woman said, "you're a traitor."

"Sir?" Kemble was worried by Blythe's order.

"Take her, Kemble," Blythe insisted. "But no liberties! She's mine to deal with, not yours." Blythe smiled at the woman and her children. "I do so love war, ma'am. I do so love the pursuit of war. I reckon war is in my blood, my hot blood."

Kemble took the woman away, leaving her children crying while Billy Blythe went to reserve the pick of the house's plunder before snatching the real pleasure of his day.

On the Saturday after the battle Captain Anthony Murphy opened a book on how long it would take for Colonel Swynyard to begin drinking again. It had been a miracle, the whole Legion agreed, that the Colonel had lasted two nights, even if he had been concussed for much of the first, but no one believed he could last another two nights without the succor of raw spirits. Ever since his alleged conversion the Colonel had been shaking visibly, such was the strain he endured, and on the Friday night he was heard moaning inside his tent, yet he endured that night, and the next, so that on Sunday he appeared at the Brigade's church parade with his once-ragged beard trimmed and clean, his boots polished, and a determined smile on his haggard face. His was the most earnest voice in prayer, the most enthusiastic to shout amen, and the loudest in singing hymns. Indeed, when the Reverend Moss led the Legion in singing "Depth of mercy, can there be mercy still reserved for me? Can my God His wrath forbear? Me the chief of sinners spare?" Swynyard looked directly at Starbuck and smiled confidingly as he sang.

General Washington Faulconer took his second-in-command to one side after the open-air service. "You're making a damned fool of yourself, Swynyard. Stop it."

"The Lord is making a fool of me, sir, and I praise Him for it."

"I'll cashier you," Faulconer threatened.

"I'm sure General Jackson would like to hear of an officer being cashiered for loving the Lord, sir," Swynyard said with a touch of his old cunning.

"Just stop making a fool of yourself," Faulconer growled, then walked away.

Swynyard himself sought out Captain Murphy. "I hear you have a book on me, Murphy?"

The Irishman reddened but confessed it was so. "But I'm not sure I can let you have a wager yourself, Colonel, if that's what you'll be wanting," Murphy said, "seeing as how you might be considered partial in the matter, sir, if you follow my meaning?"

"I wouldn't have a wager," Swynyard said. "Wagering is a sin, Murphy."

"Is it now, sir?" Murphy asked innocently. "Then it must be a Protestant sin, sir, and more's the pity for you."

"But you should be warned that God is on my side, so not a drop of ardent spirits will pass my lips ever again."

"I'm overjoyed to hear that, sir. A living saint, you are." The Irishman smiled and backed away.

That night, after the Colonel had testified at the Legion's voluntary prayer meeting, he was heard praying aloud in his tent. The man was in plain agony. He was lusting after drink, fighting it, and calling on God to help him in the fight. Starbuck and Truslow listened to the pathetic struggle, then went to Murphy's shelter. "One more day, Murph'." Starbuck proffered the last two dollars of his recent salary. "Two bucks says he'll be sodden tight by this time tomorrow night," Starbuck offered.

"I'll take two bucks for tomorrow night as well," Truslow added, offering his money.

"You and a score of others are saying the exact same thing," Murphy said dubiously, then showed the two men a valise stuffed with Confederate banknotes. "Half of that money is saying he won't last this night, and the other half is only giving him till tomorrow sundown. I can't give you decent odds, Nate. I'll be hurting myself if I offered

131

you anything better than two to one against. It's hardly worth risking your money at those odds."

"Listen," Starbuck said. In the silence the three men could hear the Colonel sobbing. There was a light in Swynyard's tent, and the Colonel's monstrous shadow was rocking back and forth as he prayed for help. His two slaves, who had been utterly taken aback by the change in their master's demeanor, crouched helplessly outside.

"The poor bastard," Murphy said. "It's almost enough to stop you from drinking in the first place."

"Two to one on?" Starbuck asked. "For tomorrow night?"

"Are you sure you don't want to put your money on tonight?" Murphy asked.

"He's survived this far," Truslow said. "He'll be asleep soon."

"For tomorrow night, then," Murphy said and took Starbuck's two dollars and then the two dollars that Sergeant Truslow had offered. When the wagers were recorded in Murphy's book, Starbuck walked back past the Colonel's tent and saw Lieutenant Davies on his knees beside the entrance.

"What the . . ." Starbuck began, but Davies turned with his finger to his lips. Starbuck peered closer and saw that the Lieutenant was pushing a half-full bottle of whiskey under the flap.

Davies backed away. "I've got thirty bucks riding on tonight, Nate," he whispered as he climbed to his feet, "so I thought I'd help the money."

"Thirty bucks?"

"Even odds," Davies said, then dusted the dirt off his pants. "Reckon I'm onto a sure thing. Listen to the bastard!"

"It's not fair to do that to a man," Starbuck said sternly. "You should be ashamed of yourself!" He strode to the tent, reached under the flap, and took out the whiskey.

"Put it back!" Davies insisted.

"Lieutenant Davies," Starbuck said, "I will personally pull your belly out of your goddamned throat and shove it up your stinking backside if I ever find you or anyone else trying to sabotage that man's repentance. Do you understand me?" He took a step closer to the tall, pale, and bespectacled Lieutenant. "I'm not goddamn joking, Davies. That man's trying to redeem himself, and all you can do is mock him! Christ Almighty, but that makes me angry!"

"All right! All right!" Davies said, frightened by Starbuck's vehemence.

"I'm serious, Davies," Starbuck said, although the Lieutenant had never actually doubted Starbuck's sincerity. "I'll goddamn kill you if you try this again," Starbuck said. "Now go away." Starbuck watched the Lieutenant vanish into the night, then let out a long sigh of relief. "We'll keep this for tomorrow night, Sergeant," he told Truslow, flourishing the whiskey that Davies had abandoned.

"Then put it into Swynyard's tent?"

"Exactly. God damn Davies's thirty bucks. I need money far more than he does."

Truslow walked on beside his Captain. "What that suffering bastard Swynyard really likes is good brandy."

"Then maybe we can find some on the battlefield tomorrow," Starbuck said, and that discovery seemed a distinct possibility, for although three days had passed since the battle, there were still wounded men lying in the woods or hidden in the broken stands of corn. Indeed, there were so many dead and wounded that the rebels alone could not retrieve all the casualties, and so a truce had been arranged and troops from General Banks's army had been invited to rescue their own men.

The day of the truce dawned hot and sultry. Most of the Legion had been ordered to help search the undergrowth in the belt of trees where the Yankee attack had stalled, but Starbuck's company was set to tree-felling and the construction of a massive pyre on which the dead horses of the Pennsylvanian cavalry were to be burned. On the turnpike behind the pyre a succession of light-sprung Northern ambulances carried away the Yankee wounded. The Northern vehicles, specially constructed for their purpose, were in stark contrast to the farm carts and captured army wagons that the rebels used as ambulances, just as the uniformed and well-equipped Northern soldiers looked so much smarter than the rebel troops. A Pennsylvanian captain in charge of the detail loading the ambulances sauntered down to Starbuck's men and had to ask which of the ragamuffins was their officer. "Dick Levergood," he introduced himself to Starbuck.

"Nate Starbuck."

Levergood companionably offered Starbuck a cigar and a drink of lemonade. "It's crystallized essence," he said, apologizing for the lemonade that was reconstituted from a powder mix, "but it doesn't taste bad. My mother sends it."

"You'd rather have whiskey?" Starbuck offered Levergood a bottle. "It's good Northern liquor," Starbuck added mischievously.

Other Pennsylvanians joined the Legionnaires. Newspapers were exchanged and twists of tobacco swapped for coffee, though the briskest trade was in Confederate dollars. Every Northerner wanted to buy Southern scrip to send home as a souvenir, and the price of the ill-printed Southern money was rising by the minute. The men made their trades beside the great pyre that was a sixty-foot-long mound of newly cut pine logs on which a company of Confederate gunners was now piling the horses. The artillerymen were using a sling-cart that had a lifting frame bolted to its bed. The wagon's real purpose was rescuing dismounted cannon barrels, but now its crane jib hoisted the rotting horse carcasses six feet in the air, then swung them onto the logs, where a team of men with their mouths and nostrils scarfed against the stink levered the swollen corpses into place with handspikes. Another two masked men splashed kerosene on the pyre.

Captain Levergood peered at the sling-cart. "That's one of ours."

"Captured." Starbuck confirmed the cart's Northern origins; indeed the sling-cart still had the letters USA stenciled on its backboard.

"No, no," Levergood said. "One of my family's carts. We manufacture them in Pittsburgh. We used to make sulkies, buggies, Deerborns, and horsecars, now we mostly make army wagons. A hundred wagons a month and the government pays whatever we ask. I tell you, Starbuck, if you want to make a fortune, then work for the government. They pay more for a seven-ton wagon than we ever dared charge for an eight-horse coach with leather seats, stove, silk drapes, turkey carpets, and silver-gilt lamps."

Starbuck drew on his cigar. "So why are you being shot at here instead of building carts in Pittsburgh?"

Levergood shrugged. "Wanted to fight for my country." He sounded embarrassed at making the confession. "Mind you, I never dreamed the war would last more than a summer."

"Nor did we," Starbuck said. "We reckoned one good battle to teach you a lesson and that would be the sum of it."

"Reckon we must be slow learners," Levergood said affably. "Mind you, it won't be long now."

"It won't?" Starbuck asked, amused.

"McClellan's leaving the peninsula, that's what we hear. His men are sailing north and in another couple of weeks his army will be alongside ours and then we'll be down on you

135

like a pack of wolves. Pope's army and McClellan's combined. You'll be crushed like a soft grape. I just hope there are enough beds in Richmond to take care of us all."

"There are plenty of prison beds there," Starbuck said, "but their mattresses ain't too soft."

Levergood laughed, then turned as a voice boomed from the road. "Read it! Read it! Let the word of God work its grace on your sinful souls. Here! Take and read, take and read." An older man dressed in preacher's garb was distributing tracts from horseback, scattering the leaflets down to the rebel soldiers beside the road.

"Jesus!" Starbuck said in astonishment.

"The Reverend Elial Starbuck," Levergood said with evident pride that such a famous man was present. "He preached to us yesterday. My, but he's got a rare tongue in him. It seems he's close to our high command and they've promised him the honor of preaching the very first sermon in liberated Richmond." Levergood paused, then frowned. "You're called Starbuck, too. Are you related?"

"Just a coincidence," Starbuck said. He edged around the end of the pyre. He had faced battle with evident courage, but he could not face his father. He went to where Esau Washbrook was mounting a solitary guard over the company's stacked weapons. "Give me your rifle, Washbrook," he said.

Washbrook, the company's best marksman, had equipped himself with a European-made sniper's rifle: a heavy long-range killing machine with a telescopic sight running alongside the barrel. "You're not going to kill the man, are you?" Levergood asked. The Pennsylvanian had followed Starbuck from the road.

"No." Starbuck aimed the rifle at his father, inspecting him through the telescopic sight. The gunners had set fire to the horses' funeral pyre, and the smoke was beginning to whip across Starbuck's vision while the heat of the fire was quivering the image held in the gun's crosshairs. His father, astonishingly, looked happier than Starbuck had ever seen him. He was evidently exulting in the stench of death and the remnants of battle.

"The flames of hell will burn brighter than these fires!" the preacher called to the rebels. "They will burn for all eternity and lap you with insufferable pain! That is your certain fate unless you repent now! God is reaching His hand out for you! Repent and you will be saved!"

Starbuck lightly touched the trigger, then felt ashamed of the impulse and immediately lowered the gun. For a second it seemed that his father had stared straight at him, but doubtless the preacher's own vision had been smeared by the shimmer of smoky heat, for he had looked away without recognition before riding back toward the Federal lines.

The flames of the pyre leaped higher as fat from the carcasses ran down to sizzle among the logs. The last ambulances were gone north and with them the final wagons carrying the Yankee dead. Bugles now called the Yankee living back to their own lines, and Captain Levergood held out his hand. "Guess we'll meet again, Nate."

"I'd like that." Starbuck shook the Northerner's hand.

"Kind of crazy, really," Levergood said in half-articulated regret at meeting an enemy he so liked; then he shrugged. "But watch out next time we meet. McClellan will be leading us, and McClellan's a regular tiger. He'll have you beat soon enough."

Starbuck had met the tiger once and had watched him being beaten, too, but he said nothing of that meeting nor of the beating. "Be safe," he told Levergood.

"You too, friend."

The Northerners marched away pursued by the evil-smelling smoke of the burning carcasses. "Did you know your father was here?" Colonel Swynyard's harsh voice suddenly sounded behind Starbuck.

Starbuck turned. "I saw him, yes."

"I spoke with him," Swynyard said. "I told him I had the honor to command his son. You know what he said?" Swynyard paused to dramatize the moment, then grinned. "He said he had no son called Nathaniel. You do not exist, he said. You have been written out from his life; expunged, condemned, disinherited. I said I would pray that you would be reconciled."

Starbuck shrugged. "My father ain't the reconciling kind, Colonel."

"Then you will have to forgive him instead," Swynyard said. "But first get your fellows ready to march. We're pulling back over the Rapidan."

"Tonight?"

"Before first light tomorrow. It'll be a fast march, so tell your boys not to carry unnecessary baggage. Can't have them laden down with things like this, eh, Starbuck?" Swynyard took a bottle of brandy from his pocket. "Found this in my tent, Starbuck. Just after you took that whiskey away. I heard you reprove Davies, and I'm grateful that you did, but a dozen other people brought me liquor anyway."

Starbuck felt a twinge of shame at having planned to place Davies's whiskey back in Swynyard's tent this very night. "Were you tempted?" he asked the Colonel.

"Of course I was tempted. The devil has not relinquished me yet, Starbuck, but I shall beat him." Swynyard gauged the distance to the funeral pyre, then heaved the brandy at the flames. The bottle scored a direct hit, breaking to splash a pale blue light in the heart of the fire. "I'm saved, Starbuck," Swynyard said, "so tell Murphy's friends to keep their liquor to themselves."

"Yes, Colonel. I'll do that," Starbuck said, then walked back to Sergeant Truslow. "He's saved and we're poor, Sergeant," Starbuck said. "I reckon we've just lost our damned money."

Truslow spat in the dust. "Bugger may not last the night," he said.

"Two bucks says he will."

Truslow thought about it for a second. "What two bucks?" he finally asked.

"The two bucks I'll win from you tomorrow morning if Swynyard lasts the night."

"Forget it."

The smoke blew north, there to meld with dark clouds that heaped in the summer sky. Somewhere beneath those clouds the armies of the United States were gathering to march south, and Jackson's men, outnumbered, could only retreat.

Adam waited with his troop at a place where he had a view toward the distant Blue Ridge Mountains. He was watching for partisans, but Sergeant Tom Huxtable kept glancing back toward the farmhouse. "Tidy place," he finally commented.

"Kind of house a man could live in forever," Adam agreed.

"But not after Billy Blythe's finished searching it." Huxtable could no longer keep his concern silent. "Our job's to hunt down rebels," he said, "not persecute womenfolk."

Adam was acutely uncomfortable with this direct criticism of his fellow officer. He suspected the criticism might be justified, but Adam always tried to give all men the benefit of the doubt, and now he tried to find some saving grace in Blythe's character. "The Captain's simply investigating gunfire, Sergeant. I didn't hear anything said of womenfolk."

"Gunfire that Seth Kelley shot," Huxtable said, "like as not."

Adam kept silent while he examined the woods and fields to the south. The trees lay still in the windless air as he turned the field glasses back to the mountains.

"A man should have beliefs, you see," Sergeant Huxtable said. "A man without beliefs, Captain, is a man without purpose. Like a ship without a compass."

Adam still said nothing. He turned the glasses northward. He watched an empty track, then slid the lenses across a wooded ridge.

Huxtable shifted his lump of chewing tobacco from one cheek to the other. He had been a cooper in his native Louisiana and then apprenticed to a cabinetmaker in his wife's village in upstate New York. When the war had broken out, Tom Huxtable had visited the white-spired village church, knelt in prayer for twenty minutes, then gone home and taken his rifle from its hooks over the fireplace, a Bible from the drawer in the kitchen table, and a knife from his workshop. Then he had told his wife to keep the squash well watered and gone to join the Northern army. His grandfather had been killed by the British to establish the United States of America, and Tom Huxtable was not minded to let that sacrifice go for nothing.

"It mayn't be my place to say it," Huxtable now went remorselessly on, "but Captain Blythe don't have a belief in his body, sir. He'd fight for the devil if the pay was right." Adam's men were of a like mind with their Sergeant and murmured agreement. "Mr. Blythe's not in the North by choice, Captain," Huxtable continued doggedly. "He says he's fighting for the Union, but we hear he left his hometown a pace ahead of a lynching party. There's talk of a girl, Captain. A white girl of good family. She says Mr. Blythe wrestled her down and—"

140

"I don't want to know!" Adam said abruptly. Then, thinking he had spoken too fiercely, he turned apologetically to his Sergeant. "I'm sure Major Galloway has considered all this."

"Major Galloway's like yourself, sir. A decent man who doesn't believe in evil."

"And you do?" Adam asked.

"You've seen the plantations in the deep South, sir?" Huxtable asked. "Yes, sir, I believe in evil."

"Sir!" The conversation was interrupted by one of Adam's men, who pointed northward. Adam turned and raised the field glasses. For a second his view was of nothing but blurred leaves; then he focused the lenses to see mounted men on a crestline. He counted a dozen riders, but guessed there were more. They were not in uniform but carried rifles slung from their shoulders or thrust into saddle holsters. A second group of horsemen came into view. They had to be partisans: the Southern horsemen who rode Virginia's secret paths to harass the Northern armies.

Huxtable stared at the distant horsemen. "Captain Blythe will run away," he said disgustedly.

"He needs to be warned. Come on." Adam led his troop down from the hilltop. They spurred east, and Adam wished their horses were not so decrepit.

The parched lawn in front of the farmhouse was now a bizarre array of furniture and household goods, which Blythe's men were picking through in search of plunder. There were buckets, spittoons, pictures, lamps, and rush-bottom chairs. There was a sewing machine, a long case clock, two butter churns, a chamber pot, and meal sifters. Some men were trying on suits of clothes while two more were swathed in women's scarves. A man threw a bolt of cloth from an upstairs window, and the bright cloth cascaded across the veranda roof and down to where the horses

141

were picketed in the flower beds. "Where's Captain Blythe?" Adam demanded of one of the scarfed men.

"In the barn, Cap'n, but he won't thank you for finding him there," the man answered. Children screamed in the house. Adam threw his reins to Sergeant Huxtable, then ran to the barn, where Corporal Kemble was standing guard. "You can't go in, sir," the Corporal said unhappily.

Adam just pushed past the Corporal, unlatched the door, and pushed into the barn. Two empty horse stalls were on the right, an oat cutter stood in the floor's center, while a mound of hay filled the barn's farther end. Blythe was in the hay, struggling with a crying woman.

"Bitch!" Blythe said, slapping her. "Goddamned bitch!" There was the sound of cloth ripping; then Blythe realized the door had been thrown open, and he turned angrily around. "What the hell do you want?" He could not recognize the intruder who was silhouetted against the light outside.

"Leave her alone, Blythe!" Adam said.

"Faulconer? You son of a bitch!" Blythe scrambled to his feet and brushed scraps of hay from his hands. "I'm just questioning this lady, and what I do here is none of your damned business."

The woman clutched the remnants of her dress to her breasts and pushed herself across the floor. "He was attacking me, mister!" she called to Adam. "He was going to —"

"Get out!" Blythe shouted at Adam.

But Adam knew the time had come to make his stand. He drew his revolver, cocked it, then aimed the weapon at Blythe's head. "Just leave her alone."

Blythe smiled and shook his head. "You're a boy, Faulconer. I ain't attacking her! She's a rebel! She fired on us!"

"I never!" the woman called.

"Step away from her!" Adam said. He could sense his

142

heart pounding and recognized his own fear, but he knew Blythe had to be confronted.

"Shoot the interfering son of a bitch, Kemble!" Blythe shouted past Adam to the Corporal.

"Touch the trigger, Corporal, and I'll kill you." Sergeant Huxtable spoke from beyond the door.

Blythe seemed to find the impasse amusing, for he still grinned as he brushed scraps of hay from his uniform. "She's a traitor, Faulconer. A damned rebel. You know what the penalty is for firing on a Northern soldier? You've read General Order Number Seven, ain't you?" He had taken the silver case of lucifers from his pocket.

"Just step away from her!" Adam repeated.

"I never wanted to be near her!" Blythe said. "But the bitch kept trying to stop me from doing my job. And my job, Faulconer, is to burn this property down like Major General John Pope ordered." He began to strike the lucifers, then to drop the burning matches into the hay. He laughed as the woman tried to beat the flames out with her bare hands. Her torn dress dropped open and Blythe gestured at her. "Nice titties, Faulconer. Or can't you make a comparison on account of never having seen none?" Blythe chuckled as he dropped more matches and started more fires. "So why don't you shoot me, Faulconer? Lost your nerve."

"Because I don't want to tell the partisans we're here. There's a group of them a mile north of here. And coming this way."

Blythe stared at Adam for a heartbeat, then smiled. "Nice try, boy."

"Maybe two dozen of them," Sergeant Huxtable said flatly from the barn door.

Behind Blythe the hay had started to burn fiercely. The woman retreated from the heat, crying. Her hair had come loose to hang either side of her face. She clasped her bodice, then spat at Blythe before running out of the barn. "Thank you, mister," she said as she passed Adam.

Blythe watched her go, then looked back to Adam. "Are you lying to me, Faulconer?" he asked.

"You want to stay here and find out?" Adam asked. "You want to run the risk of meeting that woman's husband?"

"Goddamn partisans!" Sergeant Seth Kelley shouted his sudden warning from the sunlight outside. "'Bout a mile away, Billy!"

"Jesus hollering Christ!" Blythe swore, then ran past Adam and shouted for his horse. "Come on, boys! Get out of here! Take what you can, leave the rest! Hurry now! Hurry!"

The hay was well alight, the smoke churning out the barn door. "Where to?" Sergeant Kelley asked.

"South! Come on!" Blythe was desperate to escape the farm before the partisans arrived. He snatched a bag of plunder, rammed his spurs back, and galloped south toward the woods.

His men followed in ragged order. Adam and his troop were the last to go. They found Blythe a half-mile inside the woods, hesitating over a track leading west and another going south. There were men's voices in the distant air, and that was enough to make Blythe choose the southward track that promised a faster escape because it went downhill. Adam's horses were tired, their lungs wheezing asthmatically and their flanks wet with white sweat, yet still Blythe pressed the pace, not stopping until they had ridden a good six or seven miles from the farmhouse. There was no evidence of any pursuit. "Bastards probably stopped to put out that fire, Billy," Seth Kelley opined.

"Can't tell with partisans," Blythe said. "Cunning as serpents. Could be anywhere." He looked nervously around the green woods.

144

The horsemen had stopped beside a stream that flowed eastward through sunlit woodlands. The horses were all winded, and a couple of the beasts were lamed. If the partisans had followed, Adam knew, then every man in Blythe's command would either be killed or captured. "What do we do now?" one of the men asked Blythe.

"We find out where the hell we are," Blythe snapped irritably.

"I know where we are," Adam said, "and I know where we're going."

Blythe, panting hard and with his red face covered in sweat, looked at his fellow officer. "Where?" he asked curtly.

"We're going to get some decent horses," Adam said, "and then we're going to fight like we're supposed to."

"Amen," Sergeant Huxtable said.

Blythe straightened up in his saddle. "Are you saying I don't want to fight, Faulconer?"

For a second Adam was tempted to accept the challenge and make Blythe either fight him or back down in front of his men. Then he remembered the partisans and knew he could not afford the luxury of fighting a duel so deep behind the enemy's lines.

Blythe saw Adam's hesitation and translated it as cowardice. He grinned. "Lost your tongue?"

"I'm going south, Blythe, and I don't care if you come or stay."

"I'll let you go, boy," Blythe said, then pulled his horse around and spurred westward. He planned to take his men to the foothills of the Blue Ridge, then follow the mountains north until he came to the Federal lines.

Adam watched Blythe go and knew he had merely postponed their confrontation. Then, after dusk, when his horses and men were rested, Adam led the troop south to where he planned a victory.

PART TWO

JACKSON, LIKE A SNAKE THAT HAD STRUCK, hurt, but not killed its prey, retreated sullenly back across the Rapidan River, thus abandoning the battlefield at the foot of Cedar Mountain with its blackened swathes of scorched turf and long raw mounds of newly turned graves where turkey vultures gorged on bodies uncovered by dogs.

The Yankees were left in possession of Culpeper County and counted its possession as a victory, though no one really believed Jackson was defeated. The snake still had fangs, which meant that the Northern generals must try to scotch it again. Yankee troops poured southward and spread their camps along the Rapidan's northern bank while, south of the river in Gordonsville, the railcars brought fresh rebel troops from Richmond.

On both banks of the river there was a nervous sense of great events waiting to happen, and inevitably rumors fed that apprehension. The rebels feared that McClellan's Army of the Potomac had joined forces with Pope's Army of Virginia, and if that prospect was not frightening enough, a Northern newspaper hinted that the Yankees had emptied every jail between Washington and the Canadian border and put the convicts in uniform, handed them guns, and sent them to lay Virginia waste. Another tale insisted that the North was recruiting mercenaries in Europe, Germans mostly, and that each foreigner had been promised an acre of Indian territory for every rebel killed. "I knew we'd end up fighting Hessians," Truslow remarked, "but we beat the sumbitches in '76 so we'll beat the sumbitches in '62 as well." Yet the most persistent rumor of all was that Abe Lincoln was enlisting freed slaves into his army. "Because he can't find anyone else willing to fight against us," Lieutenant Coffman averred patriotically.

Most men dismissed the rumor of armed slaves as unthinkable, but a week after the Legion retreated from Cedar Mountain, Captain Murphy found confirmation of the story in a two-week-old copy of the *Hartford Evening Press* that had somehow found its way into the rebel lines. "See!" Murphy exclaimed to the officers sharing a jug of whiskey around a fire. "It is true!" He tilted the newspaper toward the campfire. "'Congress has extended permission for the President to enrol colored men into the army,'" Murphy read aloud. "'Congressman Matteson of New Jersey claims that the sable brethren of America are fervent in their desire to contribute their blood toward the great crusade and that, so long as their childlike and excitable nature proves tractable to military discipline, there is no reason why they should not fight at least as well as any treasonable rebel.'" A chorus of jeers greeted the last two words. Afterward there was much discussion of the newspaper's report, and Starbuck sensed a nervousness among the officers. There was something very nightmarish in the thought of black troops coming to take vengeance on their old masters.

"Though how many of us ever owned a slave?" Lieutenant Davies asked resentfully.

"I own some," Murphy said mildly and then, after a pause, "Mind you, I pay the buggers well enough. I don't think we Irish are very good at slaveholding."

"Major Hinton owns a dozen," Lieutenant Pine of Murphy's D Company added.

"And Swynyard's owned plenty enough in his lifetime," Starbuck said.

"Though not any longer," Lieutenant Davies observed in wonderment, and indeed, to everyone's astonishment, the Colonel had manumitted his two slaves when Jackson pulled the army back across the river. The Colonel, despite coming from one of Virginia's most prominent slave-trading families, had set free at least a thousand dollars' worth of prime Negroes by sending the two men north to the Federal lines. Somehow it was that sacrifice, even more than the Colonel's astonishing achievement of staying away from liquor, that had impressed on the whole Brigade that their second-in-command truly was a converted man. "He's even given up cigars," Davies added.

Murphy took the stone jug from Starbuck. "God knows why you Protestants have such an unpleasant religion."

"Because it's the true religion," Lieutenant Ezra Pine averred, "and our reward will be in heaven."

"And heaven," Murphy insisted to his Lieutenant, "is a place of all pleasures, is it not? Which means that there'll be rivers running brimful with the tastiest of whiskeys and boxes of the choicest cigars waiting ready lit at every corner, and if those pleasures are good enough for the angels they're good enough for me. God's blessing on you, Pine," Murphy added and lifted the stone jug to his lips.

Ezra Pine wanted to start a theological argument about the nature of heaven, but he was shouted down. Out in the darkness a man sang a love ballad, and the sound of it made the officers silent. Starbuck guessed they were all thinking about that horde of convicts, Hessian mercenaries, and vengeful freed slaves that was supposedly massing on the Rapidan's far bank.

"If Lee was here," Murphy broke the silence, "he'd have us all digging trenches. It'd be sore hands, so it would."

151

Everyone agreed that Robert Lee would have fought a defensive battle, but no one understood what Thomas Jackson might do. "I wish Lee would come," Murphy said wistfully, "for there's nothing on God's earth so good for stopping a bullet as a yard or two of good clean dirt."

The next day Starbuck heard the first rumor that confirmed that Lee was indeed coming to take command of the rebel forces on the Rapidan. Starbuck heard the rumor from an old friend who rode into the Legion's encampment brandishing two bottles of fine French wine. "We took ten cases off the Yankees three miles beyond the Rappahannock!" The jubilant speaker was a Frenchman, Colonel Lassan, who was ostensibly a foreign military observer, but who actually rode with the rebel cavalry for the sheer delight of fighting. He had just come back from a raid deep behind the Yankee lines and brought news of the enemy's preparations. "There are lines of wagons as far as the eye can see, Nate! Mile after mile of them, and every one crammed full with food, powder, and shot."

"Is that McClellan's army?" Starbuck asked.

Lassan shook his head. "That's Pope's army, but McClellan's coming." The Frenchman sounded happy at such a gathering of armies with its implicit promise of fighting.

"And if McClellan comes," Starbuck said, "Lee will come, and that'll mean digging mile after mile of trenches."

The Frenchman gave Starbuck a look of surprise. "Dear Lord, no. Lee can't afford to wait. He dug trenches to protect Richmond, but trenches won't help here"—he waved at the open country—"and Lee has to break the Yankees before they join their armies together. Lee's no fool, Nate. He knows which end of a pig makes the mess."

Starbuck laughed at the quaint phrase. Lassan spoke perfect English, the legacy of a British father, but at times he transposed a Norman peasant's language into his father's tongue. Lassan himself was no peasant but a professional soldier who had fought in Italy, the Crimea, and North Africa, and who bore the scars of those wars across his eye-patched face. They were terrible scars, scars to terrify a child to nightmare, yet Lassan himself was an easygoing man whose besetting sins were warfare and women. "Both dangerous pursuits," he liked to tell Starbuck, "but why settle for dullness in this sad, bad world?"

Now, with his horse picketed, the Frenchman strolled with Starbuck through the Legion's camp lines. The weather was such that none of the men had bothered to make turf shelters, preferring instead to sleep on the open ground, and so the lines were little more than piles of belongings interrupted by the remnants of cooking fires. The Legion's new draftees were being drilled by Sergeant Major Tolliver while the veterans not on picket duty were either sleeping, playing cards, or reading.

Lassan, who seemed to have taken it on himself to educate Starbuck in matters military, was explaining why Lee could not afford a defensive strategy. "Dig trenches and gun emplacements behind this river, my friend, and how are you to stop the Yankees simply strolling round the end of your earthworks? You don't have enough men to guard a trench dug from the Chesapeake Bay to the Blue Ridge Mountains, so instead of digging you will have to march and tip the enemy off balance. It will be a war of maneuver, a cavalry-man's war! Naturally you infantrymen will have to do the real fighting and dying, that's why God made infantrymen, but we cavalrymen will do your scouting for you." Lassan scratched beneath his mildewed eye patch. "You'll know things are getting warm, Nate, when Lee arrives."

"Or when the Yankees attack," Starbuck said.

"They won't. They're too sluggish. The North is like a

153

man who has grown so fat he is unable to move fast. He just wants to roll over you and so crush you to death, while you have to slice him up into little pieces."

Starbuck walked a few paces in silence. The two men had left the Brigade lines behind and were now walking toward a stand of trees that screened the south bank of the Rapidan. "Can we win this war?" Starbuck finally asked the Frenchman.

"Oh, yes," Lassan said without hesitation, "but it will be expensive. If you kill enough Yankees, then they may think the game isn't worth the candle. You'll also need luck." The Frenchman had sounded confident, but it nevertheless struck Starbuck as a gloomy prescription. "Of course," Lassan went on, "if you could get European support, then everything changes."

"Can we?" Starbuck asked, as if the question had not been debated endlessly in the Confederacy.

Lassan shook his head. "France won't do anything unless Britain leads the way, and Britain has been burned too badly by its past American adventures, so Britain won't intervene unless the South looks capable of winning the war by itself, in which case you wouldn't need their help anyway, which all means, *mon ami*, that it is up to the South to fight and win its own war." They had reached the edge of the trees now, a place made ragged by the axes of men seeking firewood, and Starbuck hesitated to go further, but Lassan gestured him on. "I wanted to talk to you in private," the Frenchman said, and so he led Starbuck down a vague path that zigzagged erratically through the underbrush. Pigeons clattered through the upper leaves while a woodpecker's staccato rattle sounded sudden and close. "I have to tell you"—Lassan half turned to Starbuck as he spoke—"that I have set myself up in an establishment in Richmond."

It seemed an oddly unnecessary confession to Starbuck,

perhaps because he was not entirely sure what the Frenchman meant by an "establishment." "A business, you mean?" he asked.

"Dear Lord God, no!" Lassan laughed at the very thought. "I've no head for commerce, none! No, I mean I have established a household. It's on Grace Street. You know it?"

"Very well." Starbuck was amused by the thought of Lassan fussing with domestic arrangements.

"It's an apartment," Lassan said. "We have five rooms above a tailor's shop on the corner of Fourth Street. Then we have slave quarters downstairs at the back where there's a kitchen, a small garden for herbs, a peach tree, and a wooden stable. It's rented, of course, and the kitchen chimney smokes when the wind's in the west, but otherwise it's really very comfortable." The middle-aged Lassan had never counted comfort as one of life's priorities, and he gave the word an ironic twist.

"You've got slaves?" Starbuck asked, surprised.

Lassan shrugged. "When in Rome, *mon ami*." He took a cigar from his pouch, lit it, and handed it to Starbuck before lighting one for himself. "I can't say that I'm comfortable with the arrangement," he went on, "but I convince myself that the slaves are better off with me than with anyone else. I have a stable boy, there are two kitchen girls who clean as well, and of course an upstairs girl who looks after clothes and all the rest of the flummery."

He sounded embarrassed again. The two men had reached an old cart track that was much overgrown but was wide enough to let them walk side by side. "You sound as if you've taken a wife," Starbuck said lightly.

Lassan stopped and faced his friend. "I have taken a companion," he said very seriously. "We are not married, nor shall we marry, but for the moment, at least, we suit

155

each other." Lassan paused. "You introduced me to her."

"Oh," Starbuck said, coloring slightly and remembering how, when Lassan had first crossed the lines to attach himself to the rebel forces, he had asked Starbuck for an introduction to a house of pleasure in Richmond. Starbuck had sent Lassan to the best of all such houses, the most exclusive house, the house where Sally Truslow worked. "It's Sally?" Starbuck asked.

"Indeed," Lassan said. His one eye examined Starbuck anxiously.

Starbuck was quiet for a moment. Sally was the rebellious daughter of Sergeant Truslow and a girl with whom Starbuck sometimes thought he was in love himself. He had asked Sally to marry him earlier in the year, and at times Starbuck was still convinced that they could have made such a marriage work. He had been delighted when she had abandoned the brothel for the more lucrative job of being a spiritual medium, and Sally's séances were now famous in Richmond, a town obsessed with supernatural phenomena, but there was no doubt that her success had more than a little to do with the fact that the darkened shrine of Madame Royall, as Sally now called herself, was attached to Richmond's most notorious house of assignation, a proximity that added the spice of wickedness to her clients' visits. Starbuck had half dared to hope that Sally might want to complete her conversion to respectability by taking a husband, but instead she had taken a lover, and Starbuck understood that, in the gentlest possible way, he was now being warned away from Sally's bed. "Good for you," he told Lassan.

"She wanted to tell you herself," Lassan said, "but I insisted."

"Thank you," Starbuck said, wondering why he was suddenly so damned jealous. He had no call for jealousy. Indeed, if he was so in love with Sally, why did he sneak out of the

156

Brigade's lines at night to visit the crude tavern just south of the camp? McComb's Tavern had been put out of bounds, but there was a red-haired girl working one of the upstairs rooms, and Starbuck was happy to risk Washington Faulconer's punishment to visit her. He had no call for jealousy, he told himself again, then began walking north along the cart track. "You're a lucky man, Lassan."

"Yes, I am."

"And Sally's lucky, too," Starbuck said gallantly, even though he could not help feeling betrayed.

"I think so," the Frenchman said lightly. "I am teaching her French."

Starbuck forced a smile at the thought of Sally Truslow, a girl from a hardscrabble farm in the Blue Ridge Mountains, learning to speak French, except it was not so strange, for Sally had journeyed a long way from her father's comfortless house. She had learned society's manners, and how to dress and how to talk, and yet again Starbuck felt a pang of jealousy at the memory of Sally's exquisite beauty; then he again thought how unfair it was for him to be envious, for as often as he thought of Sally he also thought of Julia Gordon, Adam Faulconer's abandoned fiancée, and he did not know which girl he preferred, or whether, in truth, he was simply a fool for any woman, even for a red-haired whore in a country tavern. "I am glad for you, Lassan," he said with forced generosity, "truly."

"Thank you," Lassan said simply, and then stopped beside Starbuck where the cart track left the trees to run down to the river. A house had once stood on the nearer bank, but all that was left of the house now was a stub of broken brick chimney and the outlines of a stone foundation within which grew a thick and entangling clump of bushes. The farther bank of the river was a forest of shade trees that hung over the swirling water, though immediately opposite the house a cart track led between two willows into the far woods. Lassan stared at that distant cart track, then frowned. "Do you see what I see, Nate?"

Starbuck had been thinking of Sally's startling beauty and of Julia Gordon's graver face, but now, sensing that he was being tested, he stared at the landscape and tried to see whatever was significant in it. A ruined house, a river, a far bank of thick trees, and then he saw the anomaly just as clearly as Lassan's trained eye had seen it.

The track that he and Lassan had followed to this spot did not end at the river but rather continued on the farther bank. Which meant there was a ford here. Which was strange because every crossing of the Rapidan was supposedly guarded to prevent a surprise Northern attack, yet here was a ford standing empty and unwatched. "Because no one knows the ford's here," Starbuck said. "Or maybe the roadbed is washed away?" he added.

"There's an easy way to find out," Lassan said. He had the instinctive caution of any soldier coming to a river, especially a river that divided two armies, but he had stared hard at the further bank through a small glass and was satisfied that no Yankees waited in ambush, and so he now walked into the sunlight, where he took off his spurred boots and hitched up his saber. Starbuck followed the Frenchman, wading into the river, which flowed fast, clear, and shallow across a bed of fine gravel. Long weeds trailed upstream, and a few fish darted in the shadows downstream, but nothing obstructed Lassan and Starbuck's progress; indeed, the water scarce reached either man's knees. At the far bank the road reared steeply up from the water, but not so steeply that a horse team could not have pulled a heavy gun and limber out of the river. "If the Yankees knew about this ford," Lassan said, "they could be round your backside in a trice."

"I thought you said they weren't going to attack us,"

158

Starbuck commented as he pulled himself up onto the northern bank.

"And I've also told you a hundred times that you must always expect the unexpected from your enemy," Lassan said as he sat in the shade of a willow and stared back across the river. He gestured upstream with the cigar. "What units are that way?"

"None," Starbuck said. "We're the westernmost brigade of the army."

"So the Yankees really could hook round your backside," Lassan said softly. He smoked in silence for a few seconds, then abruptly changed the subject back to his new household. "Sally hopes you'll visit us when you're in Richmond. I hope so, too."

"Thank you," Starbuck said awkwardly.

Lassan grinned. "I am becoming domesticated. My mother would be most amused. Poor Mama. I am an adventurer, while my sister lives in England, so Mama is rather alone these days."

"You've a sister?"

"The Countess of Benfleet." Lassan gave a half-mocking grimace at the grand-sounding title. "Dominique married an English nobleman, so now she has a castle, five grown children, and probably twice as many lovers. I hope she does, anyway." He tossed the stub of his cigar into the water. "One of Dominique's sons wants to join this war and she asked me which side he should fight for. I said the North if he wants to be respectable and the South if he wants adventure." Lassan shrugged as if to suggest he did not much care either way. "I wonder if this ford's got a name," he said idly.

"Dead Mary's Ford." A man spoke suddenly from the far side of the track, and the voice so startled Starbuck that he reached for his revolver. "It's all right, massa! Silas is just plain harmless." The unseen speaker chuckled; then the bushes stirred and Starbuck saw that an old Negro had been hiding in the trees just a few feet away. The old man must have been watching them for a long time. "Silas is a free man!" the Negro said as he sidled onto the track and drew from his filthy clothes a scrap of paper that had long lost any legibility. "Free! Massa Kemp gave Silas freedom." He waved the disintegrating scrap of greasy paper. "God bless Massa Kemp."

"You're Silas?" Lassan asked.

"Silas." The old man confirmed his identity with a nod. "Mad Silas," he added as though the qualification might prove useful. He was staring keenly at the stub of Starbuck's cigar.

Lassan took out a new cigar, lit it, and gave it to the old man, who was now squatting in the road. "Do you live here, Silas?"

"Over there, massa." Silas pointed to the ruined house. "Silas has a lair in there." He chuckled, then found the internal rhyme even funnier and almost rolled backward as he laughed at himself.

"How old are you, Silas?" Lassan asked.

"Silas is older than you, massa!" Silas laughed again. "But Silas's daddy now, he saw the redcoats!"

"Why Dead Mary's Ford, Silas?" Lassan asked.

The old man shuffled a few inches nearer. His clothes looked as old as himself, and his hair was white and matted with dirt, while his face was deep lined. Lassan's question had swept the humor from that face, replacing it with suspicion. "'Cos Mary died," he said at last.

"Here?" Starbuck asked gently.

"The white folks came. Looking for Silas, but Silas wasn't here. Mistress Pearce's baby gone, see? They thought Silas took it, so they came and burned Silas's house. And burned Silas's wife." The old man looked very

160

close to tears as he stared at the house, where, Starbuck now saw, a kind of hollowed den was scooped in the bushes under the brick chimney. "But the baby was never gone after all." Silas sighed as he finished the story. "She grown up now. But Silas's Mary, she's still here too."

Lassan lit himself another cigar and smoked in companionable silence for a few moments before giving the old man a smile. "Listen, Silas. More white folk are coming here. They're going to dig trenches along the edge of the trees over there, at the top of your meadow. They don't mean you any harm, but if there's anything in your house that's valuable to you, take it away and hide it. You understand me?"

"Silas understands you, massa," Silas said very intensely.

Lassan gave the old man two more cigars, then clapped Starbuck on the shoulder. "Time to get back, Nate." The two men waded the ford, pulled on their boots, then walked back through the woods. Starbuck wanted to find Major Hinton, but the Major was out of the lines, and so, accompanied by Lassan, Starbuck went to the big farmhouse that Washington Faulconer had commandeered for his headquarters.

Washington Faulconer had gone to Gordonsville, leaving Colonel Swynyard in command of the Brigade. The Colonel was in the farmhouse parlor, sitting beneath the crossed flags of the Faulconer Legion that Faulconer kept unfurled and draped across the parlor wall. One of the two flags was the Faulconer Legion's own banner derived from the Faulconer family's coat of arms. It showed three red crescents on a white field and had the family's motto, "Forever Ardent," wreathed around the lower crescent. The flag measured thirty-six square feet and had a yellow fringe, just as did its companion flag, which was the new battle flag of the Confederate States of America.

The original flag of the Confederacy had carried three

stripes, two red and one white, with a star-spangled blue field in its upper corner, but when the wind dropped and the flag hung limp, it had resembled the Stars and Stripes, and so a new flag had been designed, a scarlet banner blazoned with a blue cross of Saint Andrew, and on that diagonal, white-edged cross were thirteen white stars. The old flag with its stars and three stripes was still the official flag of the Confederacy, but when the Confederacy's soldiers marched into battle, they now marched under their new battle flag.

The Confederate War Department had decreed that infantry regiments should carry a battle flag four feet square, but such a flag was not nearly grand enough for Brigadier General Washington Faulconer, who had insisted on having a banner six feet by six feet made of the finest silk and edged with a tasseled fringe of golden threads. The General had intended that his Legion's two flags should be the finest war banners in all the Confederacy, and so he had commissioned them from the same expensive French factory that had manufactured his ill-fated crescent-badged shoulder patches.

"Which means," Colonel Griffin Swynyard said when he saw the Frenchman admiring the lavish flags, "that every marksman in the Northern army will be aiming for them."

"Maybe you could persuade Faulconer to stand beneath them?" Starbuck suggested sweetly.

"Now, Nate. Let us be charitable," Swynyard said. The Colonel had been busily trying to reconcile the Brigade's accounts and seemed glad to be interrupted by visitors. He stood and shook hands with Colonel Lassan, apologized that General Faulconer was away from the headquarters, and insisted on hearing what circumstances had brought the scarred French cavalry officer to the Confederate army. "You're welcome to a lemonade, Colonel," Swynyard said when the story was told, indicating a jug of pale yellow liquid that was protected from wasps by a beaded cover of fine muslin.

"I have wine, Colonel." Lassan produced one of his captured bottles.

Swynyard grimaced. "Captain Starbuck will tell you that I have forsworn all ardent liquor, Colonel. For over two weeks now!" he added proudly, and it was astonishing what a change the abstinence had wrought in the Colonel. The sallow cast of his skin had vanished, his sweating fits had faded, and the twitch in his cheek that had once convulsed his face into a grotesque rictus had subsided to a faint tic. His eyes were clear and alert, he stood straighter, and he was dressed each day in clean linen. "I am a new man," he boasted, "though alas, my rebirth has not given me a facility for mathematics." He gestured at the Brigade's ledgers. "I need someone who can understand accounts, someone with an education; someone like you, Starbuck."

"Not me, Colonel," Starbuck said, "I was at Yale."

"That must make you good for something," Swynyard insisted.

"Not one whole hell of a lot," Starbuck said, "except maybe discovering unmapped fords." He crossed to a hand-drawn map of the area that lay on a claw-footed table. "Just here," he said, "not a long rifle shot away from the lines."

For a moment Swynyard thought Starbuck was being jocular; then he crossed to the map table. "Truly?" he asked.

"Truly," Lassan confirmed.

"Right there." Starbuck pointed on the pencil-drawn map. "It's called Dead Mary's Ford."

"We waded across it, Colonel," Lassan said, picking up the tale, "knee deep, passable by artillery, and as wide open as a barrack-town whorehouse on a Saturday night."

Swynyard shouted for his horse. Now that he had released his slaves, he was using Hiram Ketley, Colonel

Bird's half-witted orderly, as his servant. Bird himself was on his way home to Faulconer Court House and was expected to survive so long as his wound stayed clean. "You don't have a horse, Starbuck?" Swynyard asked as his own mare was brought to the front of the house.

"No, Colonel. Can't afford one."

Swynyard ordered another horse saddled, and then the three men rode north through the woods to where the ruined house stood beside the river. Swynyard rode across the ford, then back again. "Our lord and master," he said to Starbuck, "ordered me not to change the Brigade's dispositions without his permission, but even Faulconer, I suspect, would agree that we have to put a guard here." He stopped talking, distracted by the stooped, ragged figure of Mad Silas, who had suddenly appeared out of the bushes in his ruined house like a beast scuttling out of a burrow. "Who's that?" Swynyard asked.

"Some poor, old, mad black," Lassan said. "He lives there."

"Is that a skull he's carrying?" Swynyard asked in a tone of horror.

Starbuck stared and felt a sudden shock as he realized that the object in Silas's hands was indeed an old yellow skull. "Jesus," he said faintly.

"It's more likely to belong to Dead Mary," Lassan said dryly.

"I suppose he knows what he's doing," Swynyard said as Silas crossed the river and disappeared into the far woods, "which is more than we do." He returned his attention to the ford. "If we've not heard of this crossing, then I can't believe the Yankees know about it, but even so we can't take a chance. Why don't you bring your company here, Starbuck, with B and E as well? I'll make you a separate command, which means you'll bivouac here. You'll have to dig in, of course, and I'll inspect your earthworks at sunset tonight."

For a second Starbuck did not quite understand the implications of the Colonel's words. "Does that mean I'll be in command?" he asked.

"Who else? The tooth fairy?" Swynyard's conversion had not entirely robbed him of savagery. "Of course you're in command. B and E Companies are commanded by lieutenants, in case you hadn't noticed. But, of course," he added, "if you don't feel equal to the responsibility of command?" He left the question dangling.

"I'm up to it, sir, and thank you," Starbuck said, and then he saw Swynyard's triumphant grin and realized that he had actually called the Colonel "sir." But then this was a special occasion, the first time that Captain Nathaniel Starbuck had been given the responsibility of an independent command.

"I suspect the ford is in safe hands now," Swynyard said, pleased with himself. "So, Colonel"—he turned to Lassan—"you've plainly seen more adventure than most. Like me!" He held up his left hand with its missing fingers. "So let us exchange stories of scars. Off you go, Starbuck! Fetch your men. Leave the horse with Ketley."

"Yes, sir," Starbuck said and felt his spirits soar. He had a ford to guard.

Priscilla Bird had taken over her husband's responsibilities in the small schoolroom of Faulconer Court House where, day by day, she taught fifty-three children whose ages ranged from five to sixteen. She was a good teacher, patient with the slow, demanding of the quick, and firm in her discipline, yet since the war had begun, there were two sounds that were guaranteed to erode all order in her schoolroom. One was the noise of marching feet, and the other the clatter of massed hoofbeats on the road outside, and despite all Priscilla's strictures the older children would always respond to those sounds by first sidling along their benches to see out of the windows, and if they saw soldiers passing, they would then ignore her protests and insist on hanging over the sills to cheer their passing heroes.

Yet as the August temperatures rose to record levels, Priscilla became as sensitive to the sound of horses as any of the children. She expected her wounded husband's return, and that expectation was shot through with apprehension, love, relief, and fear, which was why she no longer protested when the children crowded at the windows, for she was as keen as they to investigate every odd sound in the street. Not that troops passed very often, for, since the Faulconer Legion had marched away a year before, the town had seen precious few soldiers in its streets. The townsfolk read about the battles in the *Faulconer County Gazette*, but the tides of war had ebbed and flowed far from the streets of Faulconer Court House. Indeed, in the summer of 1862, hardly a uniform was seen in the town at all until, on an August day as hot as any in memory, the sound of cavalry drew the children to the schoolroom windows. Priscilla joined them, scanning the street for the sight of a wagon that might be carrying her husband, but all she saw was a tired group of horsemen with weapons on their shoulders. The schoolchildren cheered while Priscilla, her heart aching, felt sorry for the weary-looking men and their poor swaybacked horses.

One or two of the troopers smiled at the cheering children, but most stayed grim-faced as they passed the school. There were only twenty of the horse soldiers, but their arrival was stirring the town with excitement and the expectation of news. "Are you with Jeb Stuart?" one boy called repeatedly from the schoolhouse. The Confederacy still buzzed with the remembered pleasure of Stuart's mocking ride clean around the whole of George McClellan's army. "Are you Jeb Stuart's men, mister?" the boy called again.

"Damn Stuart, you black-assed bastard," one of the dusty troopers called back.

Priscilla frowned, stared, and hardly dared to believe the suspicion that suddenly crossed her thoughts. These men wore blue coats, not gray or brown, and the leader of the troop was suddenly familiar beneath the mask of dust on his suntanned face. The man had a square, golden beard and blue eyes that looked up to meet Priscilla's gaze. He half smiled, then courteously touched the brim of his hat. It was Adam Faulconer.

"Get back!" Priscilla shouted at the children, and such was the fear and anger in her voice that all but the most rebellious of her pupils obeyed.

For there were Yankees in Faulconer Court House.

Adam had known it was imprudent to take his men through the very center of his hometown, but once he had thought of the notion, he could not shake it free. He wanted to flaunt his new allegiance in front of his father's neighbors, and the very hurtfulness of that disloyal act made it all the more appealing. He suddenly felt free of both his father and of his father's money, and that liberation had made him cast all caution to the wind and bring his blue troopers into the heart of his hometown. "Sergeant Huxtable!" he shouted when he saw Priscilla Bird pull back from the open school-room window.

"Sir?" Huxtable called.

"Let the banner fly, Huxtable. Let's not be coy!"

"Yes, sir." Huxtable grinned, then ordered Corporal Kemp to pull the cloth cover off the Stars and Stripes. Kemp unrolled the banner, then raised it high on its lance shaft-pole. A last child had been cheering from the schoolroom but fell abruptly silent as the old flag unfurled to the bright Virginia sun. Adam, looking at that flag, felt the familiar catch in his throat.

It was a sweet moment for Adam as he rode through Faulconer Court House beneath his proper flag. He rode proud in a strange uniform, and he enjoyed the astonishment on the townspeople's faces. "Good morning, Mrs. Cobb!" he called happily. "Your husband's well? You'll doubtless be hoping for some rain for your vegetables." He waved to Grandmother Mallory, who was on the steps of the bank, then greeted the blacksmith, Matthew Tunney, who was one of a group of drinkers who had crowded out of Greeley's Tavern to watch the strange horsemen pass. "Keep your hand off your gun, Southerly!" Adam warned an elderly man whose face displayed a livid outrage. Adam's own men had unslung their Colt rifles.

"Traitor!" Southerly called, but kept his hands in clear sight as the dusty, hard-faced horsemen passed by. The horses, some of the townsfolk noted, were mangy and ill-kept. "Should be ashamed of himself, a Faulconer, riding nags like that," Matthew Tunney observed.

Adam led the nags past Sparrow's Dry Goods Store, then by the Episcopal church and the Baptist church, the courthouse and the livery stable. Sleeping dogs were startled awake and slunk out of the road as the horses clattered by. Adam paused by the livery stable to touch his hat to a wan, thin woman. "I was so sorry to hear about Joseph, Mrs. May," he said, "sincerely sorry." Mrs. May just stared in apparent shock. Some townsfolk followed the horsemen, but once Adam had passed Medlicott's water-mill, which marked the eastern extremity of Faulconer Court House, he quickened his troop's pace and so left the curious townspeople behind. "They'll be sending for help," Sergeant Huxtable warned Adam.

"There's no help nearer than Rosskill," Adam reassured the Sergeant, "and we'll be well gone before anyone can get there and back. And no one in Rosskill will hear that noise!" he added as someone in the town began to tug the rope of the courthouse bell. The bell was still tolling its alarm as Adam turned his troop into a white-gated entrance that opened into an avenue edged by mature live oaks. Beyond the oaks were deep, well-watered pastures, where cows stood to their bellies in cool ponds, while at the end of the avenue was a wide, comfortable house clad in creepers that smothered the house's weatherboards and encroached on its steep-gabled roofs. A weathervane shaped like a galloping horse surmounted a clock tower above the stable entrance. The only warlike aspect of the house was a pair of bronze six-pounder cannons that flanked the main entrance. The twin guns had been purchased by Washington Faulconer at the war's beginning in the expectation that the Faulconer Legion needed to have its own artillery, yet in the rush to reach the first battle the weapons had been left behind and Faulconer had found it simpler to appropriate the two cannons as garden ornaments.

Adam pointed Huxtable toward the stable. "You'll probably find a half-dozen decent horses in there," he said, "and the rest will be in the bottom fields. I'll take you there when I've finished in the house."

Huxtable paused before swerving away. "A nice place," he said, staring up at the house.

"Home," Adam said with a grin, "sweet home."

Home was Seven Springs, Adam's father's country house where Washington Faulconer kept the Faulconer stud that was reputed to breed the finest horses in all Virginia. It was here that Adam would find the remounts for his cavalrymen, and not just any remounts, but horses sprung from the best Arab blood crossed and strengthened with sturdier

American strains to breed a fast, willing, and enduring horse that could hunt a long cold winter's day among the short hills and wooded valleys of Virginia, or else be spurred into a winning gallop in the last furlongs of a lung-breaking, sweat-streaked steeplechase. Adam had risked coming this far south to equip his men with the best horses in America—horses that could outrun and outlast the best of the South's famed cavalry. Indeed, they were horses that should have belonged to the Southern cavalry, for the Richmond government had ordered that all saddle horses should be surrendered to the army, but Adam knew his father had chosen to ignore the command. Faulconer horses, according to Washington Faulconer, were too valuable to be wasted on war, and so the stud still existed.

Adam let himself into the house. He did not know whether or not his mother would want to see him, but he intended to pay his respects anyway, though as he walked into the front hall with its four portraits of Washington, Jefferson, Madison, and Washington Faulconer, the first person he met was Nelson, his father's personal servant. Adam stopped in surprise. "Is my father here?" He asked the question with some trepidation, for though he felt he was making a fine and defiant gesture in stealing a score of horses from Seven Springs, he did not particularly want to meet his father while he made it.

Nelson shook his head, then put a finger to his lips and gave a glance upstairs as though warning Adam of some danger. Then Nelson beckoned Adam along the corridor that led to Washington Faulconer's study. Adam followed the black man. "The mistress sent John to Rockville, Mr. Adam," Nelson said when he was certain that no one in the household could overhear him. "Young Master Finney ran here from the town, saying how you'd arrived with the soldiers, so Mistress sent young John to fetch help."

Adam smiled. "Then no one will be here for at least an hour and a half."

"Maybe," Nelson agreed, "but the mistress says you're to be held here. She says you're mind-sick, Mr. Adam. She says you're to be locked up till the doctors can see you." The two men had reached the study, and Nelson now closed the door to give them privacy. "They say you've clear gone plumb mad crazy, Mr. Adam," the servant said.

"They would say that," Adam admitted sadly. He knew his parents could not stomach his betrayal of Virginia, nor would they ever accept Adam's conviction that Virginia was best served by adherence to the Union. He looked out of a window and saw some of the stable boys running in panic from Sergeant Huxtable's men. "What are you doing here, Nelson?" he asked the servant.

"The General sent me to deliver something," Nelson said evasively. He was a trusted servant, much older than his master, and in charge of three younger black men who served the General as valets and cooks. Nelson, like all Washington Faulconer's servants, was a free man, though freedom, in Adam's experience, rarely lifted a Negro out of poverty or released him from the need to show an obsequious respect to all white men, and Adam suspected that the outwardly servile Nelson still harbored the secret resentments of most slaves. Washington Faulconer, on the other hand, believed utterly in Nelson's loyalty and had provided him with a pass enabling him to travel freely throughout Confederate-held Virginia.

Adam crossed to the giant map of Virginia that hung on a wall of the study. "Do you think I'm mad, Nelson?"

"You know I don't, Mr. Adam."

"Do you think I'm wrong?"

Nelson paused, then shrugged. Somewhere deep in the house a woman's voice called in sharp reproof and a

171

bell rang. "The mistress will be wanting me," Nelson said.

"Where is my father?" Adam asked. "Here?" He stabbed a finger at the peninsula east of Richmond, where he had last seen the Legion.

Again Nelson paused, then seemed to cross whatever Rubicon of loyalty had been restraining him and walked to Adam's side. "The General's here," he said, placing a finger on the banks of the Rapidan River to the west of the road going north from Gordonsville to Culpeper Court House. "They fought against General Banks up here"—Nelson's finger moved up the Culpeper road—"then they went back again. I guess they're just waiting."

"For what? For the North to attack?"

"Don't know, sir. But on my way here, sir, I saw ever so many troops marching north. I reckon there'll be fighting soon."

Adam stared at the map. "How's my friend Starbuck?" he asked, half ironically, yet also interested in the fate of the man who had once been his closest friend.

"That's why the General sent me here, sir," Nelson said mysteriously, and then, when Adam frowned in puzzlement, the servant gestured across the study to where a flag lay draped across the General's desk. "Mr. Starbuck captured that flag, sir, from the Yankees. The General took it from Mr. Starbuck and made me bring it back here to be kept safe. It's a Pennsylvania flag, sir."

Adam crossed the study and picked up the powder-stained, scorched, bullet-torn flag of purple cloth. He smoothed out the embroidered eagle with its long talons above the German motto: *Gott und die Vereinigten Staaten.* "God and the United States," Adam murmured aloud, and the sight of the captured Northern banner gave him a sudden and exciting idea. He went back to the map and asked Nelson to describe the Faulconer Brigade's deploy-

172

ment, and as he listened Adam found his idea becoming ever more practicable. He was remembering the Reverend Elial Starbuck's fervent wish to be presented with a rebel battle flag, and Adam suddenly saw how he might be able to fulfill that desire.

For the moment, however, he contented himself with confiscating the Pennsylvanian banner. "I'll return it to its rightful owners," he told Nelson, "but first I should visit Mother."

"And your sister," Nelson said, "she's upstairs, too. But don't be long, master. Young John can ride fast."

"I won't be long." Outside the study window Sergeant Huxtable's men were busy saddling their wonderful new horses. Adam smiled at the sight, then crossed to the study door. God willing, he thought, those horses would carry him to a coup that would make the North ring with triumph and the South cringe with shame.

Then, his mother's bell clanging loud, he climbed the stairs and nerved himself for combat.

By sunset Dead Mary's Ford was properly protected. At the edge of the woodland Starbuck had dug a line of fifteen rifle pits that were invisible from the river's far bank. The red excavated earth had all been thrown back into the undergrowth, and the pits' parapets disguised with brush and dead logs so that if an enemy did try to cross the river, they would be met with a blast of rifle fire from an apparently deserted tree line. The advance picket was hidden inside Silas's ruined house, where four men could keep a close watch on the far woods, but the majority of Starbuck's 130 men were bivouacked two hundred yards behind the rifle pits. There they had made their encampment, and there they would wait in case they were needed to reinforce the men serving their turn of duty in the ruins or in the rifle pits.

Colonel Swynyard approved all he saw. "Have you sent anyone over the river?" he asked.

"Sergeant Truslow!" Starbuck called, and Truslow came and told the Colonel what he had found on the far bank.

"Nothing," Truslow said. He spat tobacco juice, hitched his pants higher, then told how he had led a dozen men up the far track until the trees ended. "That's a fair ways, 'bout a long mile. Beyond that's a farm. Family called Kemp lived there, but they're gone." He spat again. "Yankee lovers," he explained both his expectoration and the absence of the Kemp family. "Saw a neighbor at the farm. She lives another half-mile north and says she ain't seen a live Yankee in weeks."

"So you're probably in for a restful time, Captain," Swynyard said. "Did you consider putting pickets on the far bank?"

"I'd rather not," Starbuck said. "I don't want anyone shooting one of our own men by mistake."

"I told the woman at the Kemp farm to stay away from the river," Truslow said. "And the Captain said the same to the old nigger."

"But a sentry post a hundred yards up that track would give you more time to rouse your reserves," Swynyard pointed out.

Truslow answered for his Captain. "I laid a dozen felled trees over the track, Colonel. There ain't a Yankee born who can come down that road without waking the dead."

Swynyard nodded his approval, then turned and gazed westward, where another track followed the riverbank. "Where does that lead?" he asked.

"To Lieutenant Davies and twelve men," Starbuck answered. "There's a ruined barn just out of sight. That's our western picket."

"You seem to have thought of everything!" Swynyard said

174

approvingly. "Including, I hope, the need to provide me with supper? And after that, Captain, you'll doubtless allow me to lead a small prayer group for those men who care about their souls?"

Starbuck shrugged. "We're pretty short of food, Colonel. Not that you ain't welcome, but supper's nothing but rough rice, stewed squirrel, and pea coffee if you're lucky. But I'm staying here." He wanted to see the night fall across the river so he would know what to expect when he took the late sentry watch.

"Don't get too tired," Swynyard advised; then he strode back to where the cooking fires sifted their smoke into the leaves. Starbuck stayed at the tree line and watched as darkness fell and as the moon climbed above the far trees to silver the shallow water hurrying across its gravel bed. He walked along the rifle pits and was filled with pride because this was his first independent command. If a Yankee cavalry patrol should come south and prove foolish enough to force its way past the felled trees, then Starbuck would fight his very own battle, and if he recognized the truth, he wanted to fight that battle because he knew he would win. He would turn the silver ford bloody and add a pack of Yankee ghosts to join the unquiet spirit of poor Dead Mary.

The river ran quick, the moon threw black shadows, and Starbuck prayed that God would send him his own, his very own, small battle.

THERE WERE TIMES WHEN General Washington Faulconer needed to leave the problems of the Brigade behind him. Such times, he said, gave him an opportunity to assess his Brigade from what he called the distant perspective, though most of his officers suspected that the distant perspective merely served to relieve the General's distaste for the discomforts of campaigning. Washington Faulconer had been raised to luxury and had never lost his taste for cosseted living, and a month of bivouacs and army food inevitably drove him to discover a hotel where clean sheets were smoothed onto a properly stuffed mattress, where hot water was available at the pull of a bell rope, and where the food was not hardtack, worm-ridden, or rancid. The General even believed he deserved such trifling luxuries, for had he not raised the Legion with his own money? Other men had marched enthusiastically to war, but Washington Faulconer had added an open wallet to mere enthusiasm. Indeed, few men in all the Confederacy had spent as much on a regiment as Washington Faulconer, so why should he not reward himself with a few civilized trappings from time to time?

Thus, when his Brigade was properly settled into its bivouac on the western flank of Jackson's army, General Faulconer soon found reason to visit Gordonsville for a night of comfort. He was not supposed to leave his Brigade without General Jackson's permission, but in the certain knowledge that such permission would not be forthcoming, Faulconer found his own justification. "I need spectacles," he told Swynyard airily. "Can't see the fine detail on maps these days," and upon that medical excuse he mounted his horse and, with Captain Moxey in attendance, rode eastward. The town was barely three hours' ride away, so the dereliction was hardly serious, and Swynyard had been left with the strictest instructions that nothing was to be done without Faulconer's permission and that, if any emergency did arise, a messenger must be sent to Gordonsville immediately. The General considered that even a fool could understand those simple commands, and Swynyard, in the General's opinion, was a fool. The man had made an idiot of himself with the bottle but was now making himself an even more conspicuous idiot with his ludicrous addiction to the Holy Spirit.

The General's own spirits began to soar the moment he rode away from the encampment. He always felt such an elation when he could leave behind the small-minded irritations of the Brigade, where nothing was ever straightforward and where the simplest order provoked a flurry of queries, obstructions, misunderstandings, and even downright disobedience, and the more he pondered those frustrations, the more convinced he became that the root cause of all his problems lay in the hostility of men like Thaddeus Bird, Colonel Swynyard, and Nathaniel Starbuck. Especially Captain Nathaniel Starbuck. Take the simple matter of the crescent patches. It had been no small achievement to have the cloth badges made, for such furbelows were a luxury in the war-straitened Confederacy, yet Faulconer had succeeded in having the insignia manufactured in France and then smuggled into Wilmington on a swift blockade-runner. The cost of the badges alone demanded respect! And certainly the proposed function of the badges was admirable, for the red crescent had been intended both to foster pride in the Faulconer Brigade and to serve as an identification mark in the smoky chaos of battle.

Yet what had happened? Grinning soldiers had employed the patches for gambling counters or given them to girlfriends. Others had cleaned their rifles with the badges or else used them to patch the seat of their pants, an insult that had driven the General to decree severe punishment for any man not displaying the red crescent insignia on his uniform jacket, whereupon there had been a religious outcry against the wearing of a Mohammedan symbol in a Christian country! Letters had been written to hometown newspapers, prayer meetings were held to intercede for Washington Faulconer's heathen soul, and seven army chaplains had carried their protests to the War Department itself, forcing Faulconer to explain that the crescent moon was not intended to be a religious symbol but was merely a part of his family's escutcheon, yet that explanation had only prompted new complaints about the restoration of aristocratic privileges in America. The campaign against the insignia had been an outrageous farrago of lies, and now the cause was utterly lost because any man who objected to wearing the red crescent could plausibly claim to have lost the badge in battle. Which all meant that Washington Faulconer had little choice but to accept defeat—a defeat made all the more odious because he was convinced it had been Nathaniel Starbuck who had orchestrated the whole controversy. Only Starbuck could have dreamed up the religious objection or have invented the fantastic claim that wearing the patch reduced the Brigade to the level of European serfs.

Yet even the memory of that humiliation receded as Washington Faulconer rode the summer roads toward Gordonsville. He was contemplating the pleasures of a long

178

bath, a clean bed, and a full table, and the anticipation was more than rewarded when he entered the public parlor of the Rapidan House Hotel to be surprised by the presence of four old friends from Richmond whose visit to the town happily coincided with his own. Two of the men were Confederate congressmen and the other two, like Faulconer himself, were directors of the Orange and Alexandria Railroad. The four men formed a commission that was supposed to be reporting to the War Department on how the army's supply system could be improved, but so far not one of the four commissioners had ventured further than the house of assignation that lay next door to the hotel. Happily all four men had read and admired the account in the *Richmond Examiner* that had described how the Faulconer Brigade had captured an enemy color at the recent battle, and now they insisted that the General and his aide join them and recount their version of the triumph.

Faulconer told the story modestly, claiming to have been momentarily unsighted when the enemy standard fell, though the modesty was beautifully calculated to encourage his listeners to draw the very opposite conclusion. "The standard-bearer was a great brute of a German, ain't that so, Mox'?" The General appealed for his aide's confirmation.

"He was indeed, sir," Moxey said, "and I was damned glad you were there to deal with the fellow and not me."

"The fellow took a half-dozen bullets"—the General lightly touched the ivory handle of his revolver—"and still he kept on coming. Some of these Northern fellows are remarkably brave, but of course there's not one of the rogues who can compare with our fine boys," and here the General paid a moving tribute to the Southern soldier, describing him as the salt of the earth, a rough diamond, and an honest warrior, each compliment being accompanied by a toast, so that it was soon necessary to order another bottle of whiskey.

"Not that it's very good whiskey," one of the congressman said, "but even the worst is better than water."

"Like the *nymphs du monde* next door," his fellow politician opined. "Gordonsville's whores are hardly enticing, but even the worst is preferable to a wife."

All six men laughed. "If you've nothing more pressing," one of the railroad men said to Faulconer, "maybe you'd like to saddle one or two of the ladies yourself?"

"I should be delighted," Faulconer said.

"It shall be our pleasure to pay," the other director said, then courteously included Captain Moxey in the invitation.

"Myself, I fancy the mulatto girl tonight," the fatter of the two congressmen said as he poured himself another glass of whiskey. "And we'd better enjoy ourselves this evening, because tomorrow we'll all have to look busy. Can't have Bobby Lee thinking we're idle."

"Lee?" Faulconer asked, hiding his consternation. "Is Lee here?"

"Arrives tomorrow," one of the railroad men said. "Train was ordered this morning."

"Not that any of us are supposed to know who the train's for," the other railroad man said, yawning, "but it's true. Lee's coming to take command."

"What do you make of Lee, Faulconer?" one of the congressmen asked casually.

"Hardly know the man," the General said, which was a transparent evasion, for the Faulconer family was as prominent in Virginian society as the Lees, and Washington Faulconer had been acquainted with Robert Lee almost all his life, yet even so Faulconer found himself puzzled by Lee's present eminence. Lee had started the war with a considerable reputation, but nothing he had achieved since had justified that good standing, yet, with an apparent effortlessness that Faulconer could only admire, Lee had risen to command the Army of Northern Virginia. Faulconer's only explanation for this phenomenon was that the leaders of the Confederacy were deceived by Lee's grave demeanor into believing that deep thoughts were being pondered behind the General's calm and trustworthy eyes, but he could hardly confess as much to two of those leaders. "I worry he's too cautious," Faulconer said instead, "though, of course, caution may be the right tactic to follow at the moment."

"Let the enemy come to us, you mean?" the fatter congressman suggested.

"For the moment, yes," Faulconer said, "because there's little point in maneuvering ourselves into trouble. Let them break themselves on our bastions, eh?" He smiled, sounding confident, but inside he was worrying that if Lee was arriving in Gordonsville next day, then the town would surely be filled with high-ranking Confederate officers who would look askance when they discovered Faulconer was absent from his Brigade without permission, and the very last thing Washington Faulconer needed was the enmity of Stonewall Jackson. Jackson was already suspicious of Faulconer because of his tardiness in joining the counterattack at Cedar Mountain, though happily the capture of the enemy color had gone a long way toward preserving Faulconer's reputation, but even so Jackson could prove a powerful enemy, especially as the *Richmond Examiner* was as supportive of Stonewall as it was of Washington Faulconer. All in all, Faulconer decided, this was a moment for a tactical withdrawal. "I think this news means that we should get back to camp tonight, Mox'," Faulconer said as he turned to his aide. "If Lee's coming there'll doubtless be orders for us and we need to be ready."

Captain Moxey concealed his surprise at so sudden a departure and his disappointment at being denied the pleasures of the house of assignation next door. "I'll order the horses, sir," Moxey said, and when the tired beasts were saddled, the two officers, without so much as taking a bath let alone partaking of the town's more exquisite recreations, retraced their steps west into the twilight. Back at the hotel one of the congressmen remarked that the country was fortunate indeed in having men as devoted and disciplined as Washington Faulconer at its service, and his three colleagues solemnly agreed before heaving themselves out of their chairs and ushering each other into the house next door.

It was black dark by the time Washington Faulconer reached the farm that was his Brigade's headquarters. Colonel Swynyard was still awake, sitting in candlelight beneath the crossed banners of the Faulconer Legion as he struggled to reconcile the Brigade's muddled accounts. He stood as Faulconer came in, hid his surprise at the General's sudden return, and offered a report on the day's happenings. Two men had been arrested for drunkenness at McComb's Tavern and were waiting for punishment in the morning. "I thought I put the tavern out of bounds," Faulconer said, stretching out his right leg so Moxey could tug off a riding boot.

"So you did, sir," Swynyard confirmed.

"But you can't keep a rogue away from his liquor, is that what you were going to say, Colonel?" Faulconer asked nastily.

"I was going to say, sir, that McComb keeps a pair of whores, and plenty of men will risk punishment for that."

"McComb keeps women?" Faulconer growled. "Then have the filthy creatures arrested! Goddamn it. I don't want half the Brigade felled by pox." He lit a cigar and half listened as Swynyard went on with his report, but while appearing to pay attention Faulconer was really thinking just how much he disliked this new manifestation of Swynyard's idiocy. The old, drunken Swynyard had been largely invisible, an embarrassment to be sure, but a predictable embarrassment and a small price to pay for the support of his cousin, the editor of the *Richmond Examiner*. Yet the new Swynyard was a man who flaunted his morality with an assiduity that Faulconer found grating. Where Swynyard had once been oblivious of the Brigade's affairs, he was now endlessly busy, and endless, too, in bringing complaints and suggestions to Faulconer's attention. Tonight there was a problem with a consignment of percussion caps from the Richmond Arsenal. At least half of the caps had proved defective. "Then send the damn things back!" Faulconer snapped.

"I need your signature," Swynyard pointed out.

"Can't you forge it?"

"I can, but would rather not."

"Damn your scruples, give it to me then," Faulconer said.

"And sadly there were three more desertions, sir," Swynyard said, placing the deserters' report sheets beside the document needing the General's signature. Swynyard's hand shook, not from nerves, but because sobriety had still not wholly calmed his alcohol-ravaged body.

"Who ran?" Faulconer asked in a dangerous voice. He hated desertions, translating the crime as a criticism of his leadership.

"Two are Haxall's men," Swynyard said, referring to the Arkansas battalion, "and Haxall suspects they're making for home, and the third is one of the new men from Richmond who reckons his wife is cheating on him. He's the same fellow who ran two weeks ago."

"So catch the bastard again and this time shoot him," Faulconer said, slapping at a moth that annoyed him. "And how the hell did they run? Aren't the pickets awake?"

"All three were part of a work party carrying ammunition to Starbuck's position, sir," Swynyard said.

Faulconer pulled his left boot back from Moxey's grasp, then looked up at the scarred, bearded Colonel. "Explain," Faulconer said in a very menacing voice.

Swynyard was well aware that the mention of Starbuck's name put him in a risky position, but the Colonel possessed both the courage of his military convictions and the strength of his newfound faith, and so he confidently explained the discovery of the unsuspected ford and told how Starbuck had suggested garrisoning the river crossing. "I gave him three companies, sir, and inspected him at dusk. He's well entrenched and can't be outflanked."

"Goddamn it!" Faulconer shouted, thumping the table beside his chair. "What orders did I give you?" He paused, but he was not waiting for any answer. Indeed the General could not have listened to any answer, for all the frustrations of his last few months had swollen into an abrupt explosion that was now unstoppable. Like a volcano's molten core that had been cribbed too long by a cap of cold, hard rock, Faulconer's temper erupted into an incandescent rage that had nothing whatever to do with the point at issue. Indeed, had Swynyard merely told Faulconer that an unguarded ford had been discovered on the Brigade's open flank, then the General would doubtless have ordered two or three companies of riflemen to watch the crossing, but the mention of Starbuck's name had tipped Washington Faulconer into instant fury.

For a few seconds it was a fury so profound that Faulconer was incapable of speaking, but then the words flowed and soldiers fifty yards from the farmhouse listened in awe, while men bivouacked further away hurried closer to hear the diatribe. Swynyard, Faulconer said, was a shadbellied weakling who if he was not sucking at his goddamned bottle was clasped to the tit of his new religion. "For Christ's sake, you fool, stand on your own goddamned feet!" This was unfair, for the apparent point of Faulconer's rage was that Swynyard had dared to take responsibility for moving part of the Brigade without Faulconer's express permission, but for these first few moments the flow of white-hot anger was not directed but simply went wherever Faulconer's frustrations let it fly, and so the General's anger encompassed Swynyard's breeding, his ugly appearance, and his family's involvement in the slave trade. Then Washington Faulconer raked over Swynyard's apparent conversion, scorning the Colonel's piety as fraudulent and his new-found efficiency as a pose.

It was a spectacular explosion. Washington Faulconer was already feeling cheated because his stay in Gordonsville had been cut short, but now all the bitterness over his traitor son and his resentments over Starbuck and the mulish manner in which the Brigade reacted to his simplest orders fed the bitter torrent. Two decades of being despised by his wife and scorned by his wife's damned schoolmaster brother poured in an ugly spew from Faulconer's mouth as he screamed his insults at Swynyard, and finally, when breathlessness alone made him drop his voice from a half scream into mere loudness, he suspended Swynyard from his duties. "You will consider yourself under arrest!" the General finished.

There was silence in the room. Moxey, his face white with fear, stood backed against the flags on the wall, while not a sound came from the astonished audience outside. The tic in Swynyard's cheek had begun to quiver, and he was clenching and unclenching his maimed left hand, but when at last he spoke, he used the mildest tone. "I have to protest, sir," he began.

"You can protest all you like, damn you, but it'll do no

good! I've endured too much! Too much! You're either drunk or praying, either flat on your back or down on your knees, and in either position you're no more damned good to me than a spavined bitch. You're under arrest, Swynyard, so get the hell out of my sight. Go!" Faulconer shouted the order, unable to bear the sight of the man for one instant longer. Then he stumped one-booted onto the veranda. "Major Hinton!" he shouted into the dark, confident that the summons would be passed on and obeyed swiftly. "Major Hinton! Come here!"

The General, at last, was taking command.

Starbuck took his supper in the bivouac, sitting beside a small fire with Truslow and Coffman. The night was warm and humid, darkening every moment as clouds heaped higher and higher above the Blue Ridge Mountains. For a time the moon silvered the trees; then the clouds misted and finally shrouded its light. Supper was a piece of corn bread and fat bacon. The corn had been badly milled, and Starbuck broke a tooth on a scrap of cob embedded in the grain. He swore. "Dentists' favorite bread," Truslow said as Starbuck spat out the cob and tooth fragment together; then the Sergeant offered a ghastly grin to show how many of his own teeth were missing. "Pulled half of them myself, the rest old McIlvanney yanked. He was a well-digger who doubled up as a dentist."

Starbuck flinched with pain when he took his next bite. "I don't know why God invented teeth," he said.

"I don't know why God invented Yankees," Truslow added.

"Because otherwise there'd only be Indians and Mexicans for Christians to shoot," Lieutenant Coffman unexpectedly observed.

"I know why God invented junior lieutenants," Truslow

observed. "For target practice." He climbed to his feet, stretched his arms, and picked up his rifle in readiness to relieve the pickets in the rifle pits above the river. "I wish it would rain," he said.

Starbuck led the relief party through the trees to where the river flickered white in the night. The far bank was utterly black and impenetrable, its only lights the tiny white and evanescent sparks of fireflies. Then, to the west, where the clouds were building, a spike of lightning shattered the dark above the mountains and shed a sudden blue-white light that silhouetted the half-ruined barn where the outlying picket guarded the riverside track. Sergeant Mallory was now in charge of that picket, and he sent Edward Hunt back along the riverbank to find Starbuck. "Captain! Captain!" Hunt called.

"What is it?"

"Bob reckons there's some son of a bitch on the track, Captain."

Starbuck climbed to his feet. "Truslow!" he called. "I'm down at the barn."

A grunt acknowledged the information; then Starbuck followed Hunt along the river. "It was that lightning," Hunt explained.

"You saw the man?"

"Man and a horse," Hunt said cheerfully. "Plain as a pair of planks."

Starbuck was skeptical. He had learned in the last year just how deceptive the night could be. A bush that would not attract a second glance in daylight could be transformed by darkness into a monstrous threat. A herd of cows could be changed into a rampaging troop of enemy cavalry while, just as easily, a whole battalion of enemy troops could resemble a field of standing corn. Night fed the imagination, and the imagination feared enemies or craved security and made the dark fit its desires. Now Starbuck groped his way to where the picket was positioned behind the barn's broken wall. Sergeant Mallory was nervous. "There's someone out there, sir," he said. "We all saw him."

Starbuck could see nothing except the darkness and the slight quivering sheen of the river. "Did you challenge?" he asked.

"No, sir," Mallory answered.

Starbuck placed his rifle on the makeshift parapet, then cupped his hands. "Who goes there?" he shouted as loud as he could.

Nothing answered except the small stir of the wind and the sound of the river running.

"We saw something, sir," Mallory insisted.

"We did, sir, truly," one of the men put in.

"Are you sure it isn't the old black fellow?" Starbuck asked.

"This was a man and a horse, sir," Mallory said.

Starbuck challenged again and again received no reply. "Maybe they got the hell out of here?" Starbuck suggested, and just as he spoke the far mountain range was raked with another stab of forked lightning, the streaks slashing down to silhouette the tree-lined crests with fire, but closer, much closer, the splinter of light touched a figure standing beside a horse not fifty paces away—or so it seemed to Starbuck, who had but a second to focus his eyes and make sense of the sudden stark contrasts of white night-fire and pitch-black dark. "Who are you?" he shouted as the light faded, leaving nothing behind but an imprinted image on his retinas that seemed to suggest that the man was wearing a saber scabbard and carrying a carbine.

No one answered. Starbuck cocked his rifle, taking satisfaction from the solid heft of the spring-loaded hammer. He felt with a finger to make certain a percussion cap was in place, then pointed the gun just above where he thought the man was standing. He pulled the trigger.

The explosion rebounded across the river valley, echoing back from the trees on the far bank, then fading like the crackle of the thunder in the distant mountains. The muzzle flash lit a few square yards of ground beyond the barn but could not reach as far as the solitary, silent, unmoving man whom Starbuck was now certain he had glimpsed in the lightning's glare.

"Hoofbeats, sir!" Mallory said excitedly. "Hear them?" And sure enough the sound of horses' hooves and the jingling of curb chains sounded above the endless river noise.

"Cavalry coming!" Starbuck shouted to warn the men in the rifle pits behind. He began to reload his rifle as Mallory's picket slid their guns across the wall. "We'll give the bastards a volley," Starbuck said, then checked his words because the hoofbeats were not coming from the west but from behind him, from the direction of the Brigade's lines. He turned to see a light moving among the trees above the ford, and after a few seconds he saw that the light was a lantern being carried by a horseman.

"Starbuck!" the horseman shouted. It was Major Hinton. "Starbuck!"

"Stand down," Starbuck told the picket. "Major?"

A second horseman appeared from the trees. "Starbuck!" the newcomer shouted, and in the lantern's light Starbuck saw it was General Washington Faulconer who had shouted. Moxey's ratlike face appeared next; then the three horsemen cantered down into the open ground beside the ruins of Mad Silas's cabin. "Starbuck!" Faulconer shouted again.

"Sir?" Starbuck shouldered his half-loaded rifle and walked to meet his Brigade commander.

Faulconer's horse was nervous of the distant storm and edged sideways as a volley of thunder roared in the mountains. Faulconer gave the beast a hard cut with his riding crop. "I gave orders, Mr. Starbuck, that no changes of disposition were to be made without my express permission. You disobeyed those orders!"

"Sir!" Major Hinton protested, wanting to point out that Starbuck had only been obeying Swynyard's instructions. Hinton himself had been busy at a neighboring brigade's court-martial all day, else he would have reinforced Colonel Swynyard's instructions himself. "Captain Starbuck received orders, sir," Hinton began.

"Quiet!" Faulconer rounded on Hinton. "There is a conspiracy, Major Hinton, to subvert authority in this Brigade. That conspiracy is now at an end. Major Hinton, you will take these three companies back to the Legion's lines immediately. Captain Moxey, you will escort Starbuck to headquarters. You are under arrest, Mr. Starbuck."

"Sir—" Starbuck began his own protest.

"Quiet!" Faulconer shouted. His horse pricked its ears back and tossed its head.

"There's a horseman down the path—" Starbuck tried again.

"I said quiet!" Faulconer shouted. "I do not give a damn, Mr. Starbuck, if the archangel Gabriel is on the goddamned path. You have disobeyed my orders and you are now under arrest. Give that rifle to Major Hinton and follow Captain Moxey." Faulconer waited for Starbuck to obey, but the Northerner remained stubbornly motionless. "Or do you intend to disobey those orders, too?" Faulconer asked, and underscored his implied threat by unbuttoning the flap of his revolver's holster. Truslow and Coffman, their faces dim in the lantern's small light, watched from the tree line.

Starbuck felt an insane urge to fight Faulconer, but then Paul Hinton leaned down from his saddle and took

190

Starbuck's rifle away. "It's all right, Nate," he murmured soothingly.

"It is not all right!" Faulconer was exultant. His evening, which had begun so ill with his precipitate flight from Gordonsville, had turned into a triumph. "Discipline is the first requisite of a soldier, Major," Faulconer went on, "and Starbuck's insolence has corrupted this regiment. There'll be no more of it, by God, none! There are going to be changes!" Lightning ripped the west, shattering the night over the mountains, and its sudden light betrayed the blissful happiness on Washington Faulconer's face. He had confronted his enemies and he had routed them both, and the General, for the first time since he had donned his country's uniform, felt like a soldier triumphant.

And Starbuck was under arrest.

Starbuck was put into Colonel Swynyard's tent. An embarrassed private from A Company stood guard outside, while inside the tent Starbuck discovered Swynyard sitting slumped on his camp bed and cradling what Starbuck supposed was a Bible. A wax taper burned on a folding table to shed a sickly and wan light. The Colonel's head was bowed, so that his hair fell lank across his bony face. Starbuck sat at the other end of the bed and announced his presence with an oath.

"A contagion," Swynyard responded mysteriously, without offering any more formal greeting to his fellow prisoner, "that's what I am, Starbuck, a contagion. A contamination. An infection. A plague. Unclean. Out of step. Do you ever feel out of step with all mankind?" The Colonel raised his head as he asked the question. His eyes were red. "I tell you, Starbuck, that the world would be a better place without me."

Starbuck, alarmed at the wild words, looked more closely

at the object in the Colonel's hands. He had presumed it was a Bible and now feared to see a revolver, but instead he saw it was an uncorked bottle. "Oh, no," Starbuck said, astonished at his own disappointment. "Are you getting drunk?"

Swynyard did not answer. He just stared at the bottle, turning it in his hands as though he had never seen such an object before. "What did Faulconer say to you?" the Colonel asked finally.

"Nothing much," Starbuck said, using a tone of indifference to show defiance. "He said I'd disobeyed orders."

"You obeyed my orders, but that won't make any difference with Faulconer. He hates you. He hates me, too, but he hates you more. He thinks you took his son away." The Colonel went on staring at the bottle, then shook his head wearily. "I'm not drinking. I took a sip and spat it out. But I was going to drink it. Then you came in." He held the bottle close to the dripping, spluttering taper, so that the feeble light refracted through the green glass and amber liquid. "Faulconer gave it to me. He says I deserve it. It's the best whiskey in America, he says, from Bourbon County, Kentucky. None of your bust-head tonight, Starbuck. No rotgut or pop-skull, no red-line special, no brain-buster, no skull-splitter, no tanglefoot tonight." The mention of tanglefoot whiskey evidently prompted some memory that made the Colonel close his eyes in sudden pain. "No, sir," he went on sadly, "only the best of Bourbon County whiskey for Griffin Swynyard. Clear as a dewdrop, do you see?" He again held the bottle to the taper's light. "Isn't that beautiful?"

"You don't need it, Colonel," Starbuck said softly.

"But I do, Starbuck. I need either God or whiskey, and whiskey, I have to tell you, is a great deal more convenient than God. It is more available than God and it is more predictable than God. Whiskey, Starbuck, does not make demands like God, and the salvation it offers is every bit as certain as God's, and even if that salvation is not as long in duration as God's salvation it is still a true and tried remedy for the miseries of life. Whiskey is a consolation, Starbuck, and a very present help in times of trouble, and never more so than when it comes from Bourbon County, Kentucky." He swirled the bottle slowly, gazing reverently at its contents. "Are you going to preach to me, Starbuck?"

"No, sir. I've been preached at all my damned life and it didn't do neither me nor the preacher one damned bit of good."

Swynyard lifted the bottle to his nose and sniffed. He closed his eyes at the smell of the liquor, then touched the bottle's rim to his lips. For a second Starbuck was sure that the Colonel was going to tip the whiskey down his throat; then Swynyard lowered the bottle again. "I guess preaching didn't do you any good, Starbuck, because you're a preacher's son. Probably hurt you rather than helped. If a man tells you all your born days to keep away from the women and the whiskey, then what else will you look for when they let go of the leash?"

"Is that why you looked for them?" Starbuck asked.

The Colonel shook his head. "My father was no preacher. He went to church, sure, but he was no preacher. He was a dealer in slaves, Starbuck. That's what it said on our housefront. Said it in scarlet letters three feet high: 'Jos Swynyard, Dealer in Slaves.'" The Colonel shrugged at the memory. "Respectable people didn't come near us, Starbuck, not near a dealer in slaves. They sent their overseers and managers to buy the human flesh. Not that my father minded; he reckoned he was as respectable as any man in Charles City County. He kept a respectable household, I'll say that for him. None of us dared cross him. He was a flogger, you see. He flogged his slaves, his women, and his children." Swynyard went silent, staring down at the bottle. The sentry

193

shifted his feet outside the tent, and pots clattered in the farmhouse kitchen as the servants cleaned up after Washington Faulconer's late supper. Swynyard shook his head sadly. "I treated my slaves bad."

"Yes, you did," Starbuck said.

"But he never flogged his dogs." Swynyard was thinking of his father again. "Never once, not in all his years." He smiled ruefully, then lifted the bottle to his nose and smelt it again. "It really ain't a bad kind of whiskey, judging by its smell," he said. "Have you ever drunk Scottish whiskey?"

"Once or twice."

"Me, too." Swynyard was silent for a few heartbeats. "I reckon I drunk just about everything a man can pour down his throat, but I once knew a man who called himself a connoisseur of whiskeys. A real connoisseur"—Swynyard rolled the word round his tongue—"and this connoisseur told me there wasn't nothing in the whole wide world he didn't know about whiskeys, and do you know which whiskey he reckoned was the best?"

"Tanglefoot?" Starbuck guessed.

Swynyard laughed. "Tanglefoot! Well, it works, I'll say that for tanglefoot. It works like a mule kick to the head, tanglefoot does, but it ain't the best liquor in the world, not if you want your mule kick to taste better than horse liniment. No, this man reckoned he'd drunk every kind of whiskey that this vale of tears has to offer us, and the best, the very best, the absolute real stuff, Starbuck, was whiskey from Ireland. Ain't that the strangest thing?"

"Maybe he was drunk when he tasted it?" Starbuck suggested.

Swynyard thought about that for a second, then shook his head. "No, I reckon he knew what he was saying. He was a rich man and rich folks don't get rich by being fools. At least they might, but they sure don't stay rich by being fools, and this man stayed rich. And he didn't drink much either. He just liked the taste, you see. He liked his whiskey, and he'd pay a rich man's price for Irish whiskey, but the guzzle he liked most of all was the widow's champagne. *Clicquot!*" He raised the whiskey bottle in a tribute to Madame Clicquot's champagne. "Have you ever drunk *Veuve Clicquot?*"

"Yes."

"Good for you. Be a sad thing to die without tasting the widow's champagne. But sadder still to die without salvation, eh?" Swynyard asked, but he seemed confused by the question. He stared at the bottle and again seemed about to drink from it, then, at the very last second, relented. "There was a time, Starbuck, when I could afford the widow's champagne morning, noon, and night. Could have watered my horse in it! Could have watered all my horses in it! I was rich."

Starbuck smiled but said nothing.

"You don't believe me, do you?" Swynyard said. "But there was a time, Starbuck, when I could have purchased Faulconer."

"Truly?"

"Truly," Swynyard said, gently mocking Starbuck's accent with the repetition. "I wasn't always a soldier. I left West Point, class of '29, forty-sixth in my class. You want to guess how many there were in West Point's class of '29?"

"Forty-six?"

Swynyard extended a pistollike finger at Starbuck and made a clicking noise of affirmation. "Forty-sixth out of forty-six. I didn't exactly distinguish myself. Fact is, twenty years later I was still no more than a captain, and I knew I wasn't going to rise any higher than a captain, and I wasn't ever going to kill anything more dangerous to the Republic than a Comanche or a Mexican. I always reckoned I might be a good soldier, but the whiskey made sure I never was. Then one night in '50 I got drunk and offered my resignation and that was the end of my career."

"What did you do?"

"I did what every sensible soldier wanted to do. I went to the Feather River. Ever heard of the Feather?"

"No."

"California," Swynyard said. "The gold fields. Feather River and Goodyear's Bar and Three Snake Run. That's where I struck it rich. I found a lump of gold the size of a dog. Gold," the Colonel said, staring into the heart of the whiskey, "real thick gold, soft as butter, pure as love, and big as a coon dog. In just one day, Starbuck, I made thirty thousand bucks, and all of it before breakfast. That was before they made gold-digging mechanical. Nowadays, Starbuck, they sluice that gold out of the gravels with water jets. That water flies so hard you could kill a regiment of Yankees with that hose, except it takes a regiment to build all the flumes and dams, and not even the Yankees are stupid enough to stand still while you construct it. But I was lucky. I got there early when all a man had to do was climb high and start rolling the rocks aside." He fell silent.

"And you lost it all?"

Swynyard nodded. "Every last cent of it. It all went down the gullet or across the barrelhead. Poker. Women. Whiskey. Stupidity. I lost these fingers, too." He held up his left hand with its three missing fingers.

"I thought those went to a Mexican saber cut," Starbuck said.

"That's what I tell people," Swynyard said, "or what I did tell them before I met the Lord Jesus Christ, but it ain't true. The truth is, Starbuck, that I had them blown away when me and a German miner were using black powder up above Shirt Tail Creek. Otto, his name was, and he was mad as a

196

snake. He reckoned there was a load of nuggets at the top of Shirt Tail and it took us a week to carry all our gear up there, and then we blew the thing wide open and there wasn't nothing up there but dirt and quartz. Only Otto blew it early, see, thinking he'd blow me to hell and get to keep all the gold to himself."

"And what happened to Otto?" Starbuck asked gently.

Swynyard blinked rapidly. His hands were gripping the whiskey bottle so hard that Starbuck feared he might break the glass. "I have many sins on my conscience," Swynyard said after a while, "many. I killed Otto. Took a long time a-dying and I mocked him all that while. God forgive me."

Starbuck waited a few seconds, praying desperately that the Colonel would not suck on the bottle. "And when the war started?" Starbuck finally asked.

"I came back east. Reckoned I could have a new beginning. I kind of persuaded myself I could do without the whiskey so long as I could be a proper soldier again. I wanted to redeem myself, you see? A new country, a new army, a new beginning. But I was wrong."

"No," Starbuck said, "you weren't. You've been off the whiskey for days now."

Swynyard did not answer but just stared into the golden depths of the expensive Kentucky whiskey.

"You don't want it, Colonel," Starbuck said.

"But I do, Starbuck, and that's the plain hard truth of it. I want a drink so bad that it hurts."

"Put the bottle down," Starbuck said.

Swynyard ignored him. "I never thought I could give up the drink, never, and then God helps me to do it at last and just as things are starting to be all right again, Faulconer does this to us. What was I supposed to do? Leave the ford unguarded?"

"Colonel," Starbuck said, reaching for the whiskey bottle.

"You did the right thing. You know that. And do you know why Faulconer gave you that bottle tonight?"

Swynyard would not relinquish the whiskey, but instead held the bottle just beyond Starbuck's reach. "He gave it to me," the Colonel said, "because he wants to humiliate me. That's why."

"No," Starbuck said. "He did it so you won't be in a fit state to testify at a court-martial. He wants you drunk, Colonel, because the son of a bitch knows he's in the wrong, but he also knows that no court will exonerate a staggering drunkard. But if you stay sober, Colonel, he's going to back down and there won't be any court-martial."

Swynyard thought about Starbuck's words, then shook his head. "But I did disobey his orders. Not that it matters, because Faulconer don't care one way or another about Dead Mary's Ford. He just wants to be rid of me. Don't you understand? It isn't what I did or didn't do, it's because I made an enemy. You too. We're being purse-whipped by a rich man, Starbuck, and there ain't nothing we can do about it."

"Goddamn it, there is!" Starbuck insisted. "Faulconer doesn't run this damned army, Jackson does, and if Jackson says you're right and Faulconer's wrong then it won't matter if you and I disobeyed George Washington's orders. Not all of Faulconer's money can change that, but I tell you one thing: If you go in front of Old Mad Jack with a hangover, or with whiskey on your breath, or looking like you used to look before you let Christ into your heart, then Old Mad Jack will have you out of this army faster than you can spit." Starbuck paused and held out his hand. "Now goddamn it, Colonel, give me the whiskey."

Swynyard frowned. "Why would Jackson care what happens to us?"

"Because we'll make him care. We'll tell him the truth.

198

So give me the bottle." He still held his hand outstretched. "Come on! I'm thirsty!"

Swynyard held the bottle out, but instead of handing it to Starbuck he tipped it upside down so that the liquor gurgled and slurped onto the tent's pine floorboards and there trickled between the cracks into the dirt. When the bottle was empty, Swynyard let it fall. "We've got a battle to fight, Starbuck," the Colonel said, "so let's both be sober."

"Son of a bitch," Starbuck said. The smell of the whiskey was tantalizing in the tent. "I was thirsty."

"And tomorrow you'll be sober," Swynyard said. Far in the distance the thunder grumbled. The sentry sneezed, and the Colonel closed his eyes in prayer. He had resisted temptation and endured despair. And now, like the soldier he knew he could be, he would fight.

Mad Silas began pulling the felled trees off the road that led north through the woods. It was hard work, especially as he had his darling Mary's skull in a sack hanging from his neck and he did not like to bump the skull too hard in case it hurt her. He talked to her as he worked, saying how he was keeping the road clear because the man in the blue coat had asked him to, and the man in the blue coat had said as how all the black folk would be better off if the blue ones beat the gray ones, and even though the white men in the gray coats had been polite to Mad Silas and had even given him some cigars, he still believed the blue horse soldier because the blue man had been young Master Harlan Kemp, the son of old Master Kemp who had given Silas his freedom.

By first light Silas had cleared the whole path. Then, very cautiously, he crept down to the riverbank and saw to his surprise that the gray soldiers were all gone. Their fires had cooled to ashes and their rifle pits were empty. He clutched the scorched skull in his arms and debated with it what the soldiers' absence might mean, but he could not really make any sense of it. Yet their absence made him feel safe again, and so he put his Mary back in the hole in the ruined chimney breast where she now lived. Then, glad to be home with her, he walked down beside the river, past the ruined barn, to the tree and bush that, at night, looked so like a man and a horse. He had a snare here, set to trap rabbits going down to the river.

Then, just as he was parting the leaves of the bush, he heard the hoofbeats. He rolled down the bank into the long grass and lay very still. The sun was not yet up, so the light was gray and flat and the river water had no sparkle, yet Silas could clearly see the far bank, and, after a time, he saw the men appear there. They were white men in blue coats. There were three of them, each on foot and each carrying a long rifle, a saber, and a revolver. They spent a long time staring across the river; then one of them ran through the ford, splashing the water high with his long boots and bright spurs. Silas lost sight of that man, but after a minute or two the man called back over the river. "The bastards were here, right enough, Major, but they've gone."

Then a whole column of blue horse soldiers appeared at the ford. Their spurs, scabbards, and curb chains jingled as they urged their horses through the river. The three men who had scouted the ford seized their reins and heaved themselves up into their saddles. Silas watched them go out of sight, then listened as their hoofbeats faded away to the south, and then he went on listening until there was nothing more to hear but the run of the river and the song of the birds.

Then, with a dead rabbit in his hand, he went back to tell his Mary just what excitements were happening at her ford this morning, while far to the south, unsuspected and unseen, the Yankee raiders went to ground and waited.

THE YANKEES' SPRING OFFENSIVE might have failed, stranding McClellan's Army of the Potomac on the muddy shore of the James River below Richmond, but now John Pope's Army of Virginia gathered its strength in Virginia's northern counties. More and more supplies crossed the Potomac's bridges to be piled high in the gaunt warehouses at Manassas Junction while, on the sun-ruffled water of Virginia's tidal rivers, boat after boat carried McClellan's veterans north from the James River to Aquia Creek on the Potomac. The two Northern armies were joining forces, and though that process of union was excruciatingly slow, once the Army of Virginia and the Army of the Potomac were united, then they would far outnumber Robert Lee's rebel Army of Northern Virginia.

"So we have to strike first," Lee said in a murmur that was intended only for his own ears. The General was staring northward in the dawn, scrying his enemies from the high vantage point of Clark Mountain, which lay on the southern bank of the Rapidan River. Lee's own veterans, who had first stopped and then chased McClellan away from Richmond, had all now come north to face Pope's threatened attack. Stonewall Jackson had served to deter Pope's belligerence for the best part of a month, but now the rebel army was once again united with Robert Lee at its head, and so the time had come to drive Pope back in utter defeat.

To which purpose Lee had come to Clark Mountain. He

was surrounded by mounted aides, but Lee himself was on foot and using the back of his placid gray horse, Traveller, as a rest for his telescope. The morning light was pearly soft. Great swathes of rain smoked across the western countryside, but it was dry to the north, where Lee could see folds of hills, small fields, white-painted farms, long dark woods, and, everywhere he looked, Yankees. The enemy's white-hooded wagons filled the meadows, their guns were parked on every road and farm track, and their tents dotted the fields, while above it all, like strands of tenuous mist, the smoke of their cooking fires mingled to make a blue-gray haze. In another ten days, two weeks at the most, that army would be doubled in size, and Lee knew there would be small chance of ever beating it out of his native Virginia.

But now, while McClellan's men still thumped north in their requisitioned river steamers and sleek transatlantic packets, there was a chance of victory. That chance arose because John Pope had placed himself in a trap. He had brought the bulk of his army close to the Rapidan so that it was ready to strike south, but behind Pope's new position ran the Rapidan's wide tributary, the Rappahannock, and if Lee could turn Pope's right flank, he stood a chance of driving the Northern army hard toward the rivers' junction, where Pope would be trapped between a horde of screaming rebels and the deep, fast-running confluence of the two rivers. But to make that maneuver Lee needed cavalry to screen his march and still more cavalry to mislead the enemy and more cavalry still to ride into the enemy's rear and capture the Rappahannock bridges and thus give the Yankees no way out from their water-bound slaughter yard.

"General Stuart says he's real sorry, sir, but the horses just ain't ready," an aide now told Lee in the dawn on Clark Mountain.

Lee nodded abruptly to show he had heard the gloomy report, but otherwise he showed no reaction. Instead he stared for a long last moment at the encamped enemy. Lee was not a vengeful man—indeed, he had long learned to school his emotions to prevent passion from misleading common sense—but in the last few weeks he had contracted a deep desire to humiliate Major General John Pope. The Northern general had come to Virginia and ordered his men to live off the land and to burn the houses of loyal Virginians, and Lee despised such barbarism. He more than despised it, he hated it. Carrying war to civilians was the way of savages and heathens, not of professional soldiers, but if John Pope chose to fight against women and children, Robert Lee would fight against John Pope, and if God permitted it, Lee would ruin his enemy's career. But the spring to snap the trap's lid shut was not quite ready, and Lee resisted the temptation to close that lid without the help of his horsemen. "How long before the cavalry will be ready?" Lee asked the aide as he collapsed the telescope.

"One day, sir." Most of the rebel cavalry had only just come north from its duty of screening McClellan's army beyond Richmond, and the horses were bone tired after the long march on dry, hard roads.

"By tomorrow's dawn?" Lee sought the clarification.

The aide nodded. "General Stuart says for certain, sir."

Lee showed no evident disappointment at the enforced delay but just stared at the long strands of smoke that laced the far woods and fields. He felt a twinge of regret that he could not attack this morning, but he knew it would take him the best part of a day to move his cumbersome guns and long lines of infantry over the Rapidan, and Jeb Stuart's horsemen would have to entertain and deceive the Yankees while those men and cannon moved into position. So he must wait one full day and hope that John Pope did not wake to his danger. "We'll attack tomorrow," Lee said as he climbed onto Traveller's back.

And prayed that the Yankees went on sleeping.

Major Galloway arrived just after dawn, guided by Corporal Harlan Kemp to where Adam's men waited in a stand of thick trees two miles south of the Rapidan. Galloway's troop was accompanied by Captain Billy Blythe and his men, who had returned from their frustrating reconnaissance. Blythe claimed the enemy held all the high passes through the Blue Ridge Mountains and had thus prevented him from crossing into the Shenandoah Valley, but Galloway's own foray beyond the Rapidan had convinced him that the rebels were not using the Shenandoah Valley to threaten Pope's army. Instead their regiments were bivouacking all along the Rapidan's southern bank, and it was there, in the heart of Virginia, that the threat existed, and it was there, thanks to Adam's timely message, that Galloway could both strike at the enemy and establish a rakish, hell-raising reputation for his fledgling regiment of cavalry. Which was why all Galloway's sixty-eight troopers were now concealed in a thicket just three miles from the western flank of Lee's army. Sixty-eight men against an army sounded like long odds, even to an optimist like Galloway, but he had surprise and the weather both on his side.

The weather had turned that same morning when, just one hour after dawn, a rainstorm had come from the mountains to hammer at the western rebel encampments. The roads had been turned into instant red mud. The rain poured off roofs and streamed down gutters and flooded gullies and overflowed ditches and spread along the plowed furrows of low-lying fields. Thunder bellowed overhead, and sometimes, way off in the rain-silvered distance, a slash of lightning sliced groundward. "Perfect," Galloway said as he stood at the edge of the trees and watched the rain claw and beat at the empty fields. "Just perfect. There's nothing like a good hard rain to keep a sentry's head down." He crouched under his cloak to light a cigar, then, because his own horse needed rest, asked to borrow one of Adam's newly acquired mares. "Let's look at your father's rebels," he told Adam.

Galloway left Blythe in charge of the concealed horsemen while he and Adam rode east. Adam was concerned about the danger of Major Galloway making the reconnaissance in person, but Galloway dismissed the risks of capture. "If something goes amiss tonight, then I don't want to think it was because of something I left undone," the Major said, then rode in silence for a few moments before giving Adam a shrewd look. "What happened between you and Blythe?" Adam, taken aback by the question, stammered an inadequate answer about incompatible personalities, but Major Galloway was in no mood for evasions. "You accused him of attempted rape?"

Adam wondered how Galloway knew, then decided that either Sergeant Huxtable or Corporal Kemp must have complained about Blythe. "I didn't accuse Blythe of anything," Adam said. "I just stopped him from mistreating a woman, if that's what you mean."

Galloway sucked on what was left of his rain-soaked cigar. He ducked under a low branch, then checked his horse so he could search the rain-soaked land ahead. "Billy tells me the woman was merely offering herself because she wanted Northern dollars," the Major said when he was satisfied that no rebel picket waited in the far trees, "and because she wanted to save her house. Sergeant Kelley told me the same thing."

"They're lying!" Adam said indignantly.

Galloway shrugged. "Billy's a good enough fellow, Adam. I ain't saying he's the straightest man as was ever born, I mean he sure isn't no George Washington, but we're a troop of soldiers, not a passel of churchmen."

"Does that justify rape?" Adam asked.

"Hell, that's your tale, Adam, not his," Galloway said tiredly, "and when it comes to telling tales, then you should know that Billy's telling a few on you too." The Major was riding ahead of Adam on a waterlogged path that ran beside a wood. The rain had finally extinguished his cigar, which he tossed into a puddle. "Blythe claims you're a Southern sympathizer, a gray wolf in blue clothing. In fact he says you're a spy." Galloway held up a hand. "Don't protest, Adam. I don't believe a word of it, but what else do you expect him to say about a man accusing him of rape?"

"Maybe he could tell the truth," Adam proclaimed indignantly.

"The truth!" Galloway barked a laugh at the very thought of such a notion. "The truth in war, Adam, is whatever the winner decides it is, and the best way for you to prove that Blythe is a liar is to make some rebel heads bleed tonight."

"Major," Adam said firmly, "all my men saw that woman. She didn't tear her own clothes, Blythe did, and—"

"Adam! Adam!" There was a note of pleading in Galloway's voice. The Major was a decent and honest man who had a vision of how his irregular regiment of horse could shorten this war, and now that vision was being threatened by rancorous dissension within his ranks. Nor did Galloway really want to believe Adam's accusations, for the Major liked Blythe. Blythe made him laugh and enlivened his dull evenings, and for those reasons, as well as a desire to avoid confrontation, Galloway tried to find extenuating circumstances. "Who's to say the woman didn't attack Billy when he tried to burn the barn? We don't know what happened, but I do know that we've got a battle to fight and a war to win and we're better employed fighting the enemy than each other. Now trust me. I'll keep an eye on Billy, that much I promise, but I want you to leave him to me. His behavior isn't your responsibility, Adam, but mine. You agree?"

Adam could hardly disagree with such a reasoned and earnest promise, and so he nodded. "Yes, sir."

"Good man," Galloway said enthusiastically, then slowed his horse as the two men approached the crest of a shallow rise. Their blue uniforms were smothered by black oilcloth cloaks that hung down to their boots, but each knew their disguise would serve small purpose if they were intercepted by a rebel patrol.

Yet the weather seemed to have damped down all rebel watchfulness, for Galloway and Adam were able to spy out the positions of the Faulconer Brigade without any sentry or picket challenging their presence. They mapped the Legion's turf-covered bivouacs, which were studded with pyramids of stacked arms and sifted with the smoke of the few campfires that still struggled against the windblown rain, then noted the substantial farmhouse standing among the tents that Adam knew belonged to the Faulconer Brigade's headquarters. From time to time a soldier would run between the shelters or slouch dejectedly away from the farmhouse, but otherwise the encampment appeared deserted. Further south still was a meadow where the Brigade's supply wagons were parked and where picketed horses stood in disconsolate rows. Adam showed Galloway the white-painted ammunition carts, then trained his binoculars on some unfamiliar vehicles and saw that they belonged to an artillery battery that had camped alongside his father's Brigade. "How many sentries would you expect on the wagons?" Galloway asked, peering through his own binoculars.

"There's usually a dozen men," Adam said, "but I can only see one."

"There must be more."

"Sheltering in the wagons?" Adam suggested.

"I guess so, which means the sumbitches won't see us coming." Galloway sounded enthused at the prospect of fighting. He knew he could not seriously hurt Jackson's army—indeed, this night's attack would be but the feeblest of pinpricks—but Galloway was not trying to cause grievous damage. Instead he was hoping to inflict on the South the same kind of insult that Jeb Stuart had thrust on the North when he had led his cavalry clean about McClellan's army. Few men had died in that ride, but it had nevertheless made the North into the laughingstock of the whole world. Galloway now hoped to provide proof that Northern horsemen could ride as defiantly and effectively as any Southern cavalier.

Adam was fighting a different battle: a battle with his own conscience. He had obeyed that stern conscience when he had abandoned the South to fight for the North, but the logic of that choice meant not just fighting against fellow Southerners but against his own father, and a lifetime of love and filial obedience struggled against the inevitability of that logic. Yet, he asked himself as he followed Galloway further south along the woodland tracks, what else had he expected when he crossed the lines and pledged his allegiance to the United States? Adam had agonized for months about the war's moral choices, and at the end of all that worry and self-doubt he had reached a certainty that was weakened only by the duty he owed to his father. But this night, under a rain-lashed sky, Adam would cut that filial duty out of his life and so free himself to the higher duty of the nation's union.

Galloway stopped, dismounted, and again stared southward through his field glasses. Adam joined him and saw the Major was examining a half-dozen cabins, a plank-wall church, and a ramshackle two-story house that all stood around a small crossroads. "'McComb's Tavern,'" Galloway said, reading the sign that was painted in tar on the house wall. "'Good Licker, Clean Beds and Plenty Food.' But bad spelling. Do you see any troops there?"

"Not one."

"Off limits, I'd guess," Galloway said. He wiped the lenses of his field glasses, stared a few seconds longer at the tavern, then came back to where his horse was tethered and hauled himself into the saddle. "Let's go."

By early afternoon the wind had died and the rain had settled into a persistent and dispiriting drizzle. Galloway's men sat or lay under what small shelter they could find while their horses stood motionless between the trees. The pickets watched from the edges of the wood but saw no movement. In the late afternoon, when the light was fading to a sullen, leaden gloom, Galloway gave his last briefing, describing what the troopers would find when they attacked and stressing that their main target was the park of supply wagons. "The rebels are always short of ammunition," he said, "and of rifles, so burn everything you can find."

Galloway divided his force into three. Adam's troop would serve as a screen between the raiders and the bulk of the Faulconer Brigade while Galloway's troop, reinforced with half of Blythe's men, would attack the supply wagons. Billy Blythe would wait with the other half of his troop near McComb's Tavern, where they would serve as a rear guard to cover the raiders' withdrawal. "It'll all be over quickly," Galloway warned his men, "only as long as it takes the sumbitches to get over their surprise." He had his bugler imitate the sound of the call that would order the retreat. "When you hear that played on a bugle, boys, you get the living hell out of there. Straight down the road to the crossroads where Captain Blythe will be waiting for us."

"With a jigger of rebel whiskey for every last man jack of you," Blythe added, and the nervous men laughed.

Galloway opened his watch. "Be another two hours before we leave, boys, so just be patient."

The day darkened toward evening. The troopers' clothes were clammy with a greasy, sweaty dampness. Galloway had forbidden fires so that the smoke would not betray their presence, and thus they simply had to endure the cloying dank as the minutes ticked by. Men prepared themselves obsessively for battle, believing that every small degree of painstaking care counted toward survival. They used cloaks and saddlecloths to keep the rain from their repeating rifles and revolvers as they loaded the weapons' chambers with powder, wadding, and minié bullets. On top of each bullet they put a plug of grease that was intended to prevent the flame in the firing chamber communicating with the neighboring charges and so exploding the whole cylinder. They sharpened their sabers, the sound of the stones harsh on the curved steel. Those men whose blades rattled in their metal sheaths dented the scabbards so that the weapons were held tight and silent by the compressed metal. Corporal Harlan Kemp then led a score of men in prayer. He put one knee on the wet ground, one hand on the hilt of his sword, and raised his free hand toward God as he prayed that the Lord would bless this evening's work with a mighty success and keep His servants free from all harm from the enemy.

Adam joined the circle of prayer. He felt very close to his men as he knelt with them, and the very act of praying imbued the night's action with a sacred quality that lifted it above mere adventure into the realm of duty. "I do not want to be here," Adam prayed silently, "but as I am here, Lord, then be here with me and let me help this war to a quick and just ending." When Harlan Kemp's blessing was finished,

Adam climbed to his feet and saw Billy Blythe standing beside the mare Adam had taken from the Faulconer stud. Blythe ran his hand down the mare's legs, then slapped her rump. "You got yourself some good horses, Faulconer," Blythe said as Adam approached.

"You're in my way," Adam said brusquely, then pushed the tall Blythe aside so he could throw a saddlecloth over the mare's back.

"Real nice piece of horseflesh." Blythe peeled back the mare's lips to examine her teeth, then stood a pace away to give the horse an admiring look. "Bet she runs like a bitch in heat. Specially with a touch of the whip. Don't you find the whip tickles a female up real nice, Faulconer?" Blythe chuckled when Adam made no answer. "Reckon a horse like this would suit me real well," he went on.

"She's not for sale," Adam said coldly. He heaved the saddle onto the mare's back, then stooped to gather the girth strap.

"Wasn't reckoning on buying her from you," Blythe said, then spat a stream of tobacco spittle close to Adam's face, "because there ain't no point in buying things in war, not when they have a habit of dropping into a man's lap. That's what I like about war, Faulconer, the way things come without payment. That's real convenient to my way of thinking. I figure it takes the sweat out of a man's life." He smiled at the thought, then touched a finger to the dripping brim of his hat. "You sure mind yourself now," he said, then ambled away, grinning at his intimates and leaving Adam feeling tawdry.

Major Galloway was the first to mount up. He settled his feet in his stirrups, pushed his repeating rifle into its saddle holster, eased his saber an inch or two from its scabbard, then made sure his two revolvers were in easy reach. "Smoke your last cigars and pipes now, boys," the Major said, "because once we're out of this wood there'll be no more lit tobacco till we wake the sumbitches." His incendiarists checked their supplies: lucifers, flints, steels, tinder, and fuses. Their job was to burn the ammunition, while others of his men carried axes to splinter wheel spokes and hammers and nails to spike the rebels' cannon.

One by one the men pulled themselves into their saddles. A horse whinnied softly while another skittered nervously sideways. Water dripped from the leaves, but Adam sensed that above the darkening canopy of trees the rain had stopped. The evening was young, but the clouds made the sky seem like night.

"For the Union, boys," Galloway said, and the more idealistic of the men repeated the phrase and added God's blessing. They were fighting for their beloved country, for God's country, for the best of all countries.

"Forward, boys," Galloway said, and the column lurched on its way.

To battle.

Captain Medlicott and Captain Moxey sat on the veranda of the farmhouse that served as General Washington Faulconer's headquarters and stared at the evening rain. On the western horizon, Medlicott noted, where it should have been darkest at this time of day, the sky was showing a pale strip of lighter cloud where the rainstorm had stalled, but that evidence of dry weather showed no sign of wanting to move east. "But it'll be a fine day tomorrow," Medlicott grunted. The sweat dripped off his beard. "I know these summer storms." He twisted in his chair and looked through the open parlor door to where the General was sitting at the claw-footed table. "It'll be a fine day tomorrow, General!"

Faulconer did not respond to Medlicott's optimism. The

evening was sweltering, and the General was in his shirt-sleeves. His uniform coat with its heavy epaulets and expensive braid trimming was hanging in the farmhouse hall along with his fine English revolver and the elegant saber that General Lafayette had presented to his grandfather. The General was staring at some papers on the table. He had been contemplating these papers for much of the day, and now, instead of signing them, he pushed them to one side. "I must be sure to do the right thing," Faulconer said, by which he meant that he must be sure not to make a mistake that could recoil onto his own career. "Goddamn it, but they should be court-martialed!"

Captain Moxey spat tobacco juice over the veranda's railing. "They should be in prison for disobeying orders, sir," Moxey said, emboldened by the privilege of being asked to give advice about the fate of Colonel Swynyard and Captain Starbuck.

"But they'll plead they were merely doing their duty," Faulconer said, worrying at the problem like a dog at a bone. "Our orders are to guard the river crossings, aren't they? And what were they doing? Just guarding a ford. How do we persuade a court otherwise?"

Captain Medlicott waved the objection away. "It ain't a proper ford, sir, not really. Not on the maps, anyway. It's just that the river's running uncommon shallow this year." He sounded very unconvincing, even to himself.

"But if I just dismiss them"—Faulconer now contemplated the alternative to a court-martial—"what's to stop them appealing? My God, you know their facilities for telling lies!"

"Who'd believe them?" Moxey asked. "One pious drunk and a Yankee troublemaker?"

Too many people would believe them, Faulconer thought, that was the trouble. Swynyard's cousin was

213

influential, and Starbuck had friends, and consequently Faulconer felt as trapped as a man who has made a wonderful attack deep into enemy lines only to find that he cannot extricate his forces. Last night he had been triumphant, but a single day's reflection on the night's achievements had thrown up a score of obstacles to the completion of that triumph, not the least of which was that Swynyard had obstinately refused to get drunk. A drunken colonel would have been much easier to court-martial than a sober and repentant colonel, and it was Faulconer's deepest wish to see both Swynyard and Starbuck dragged in front of a court-martial, then marched at rifle point to the Confederate army prison in Richmond, but he did not see how he could make the prosecution case irrefutable. "The trouble is," he said, changing his argument yet again, "that there are too many people in this Brigade who'll give evidence on Starbuck's side."

Medlicott sipped brandy. "Popularity comes and goes," he said vaguely. "Get rid of the sons of bitches and everyone'll forget what they looked like in a couple of weeks." In truth Medlicott was wondering why Faulconer did not simply march the two men down to the river and put a pair of bullets into their heads.

"Rain's slackening," Moxey said.

Medlicott turned to look at the General. He was even more aware than Moxey of the privileges of being one of the General's advisers. Moxey, after all, had pretensions of gentility; his family kept horses and hunted with Faulconer's hounds, but Medlicott had never been anything except a hired man, albeit a skilled one, and he liked being in the General's confidence and wanted to keep the privilege by making sure the General did indeed rid himself of the troublemakers. "Why don't you just return the two sons of bitches to Richmond," he suggested, "with a report saying they're unfit for field duty? Then recommend that they're sent to the coast defenses in South Carolina?"

Faulconer smoothed the papers on his table. "South Carolina?"

"Because by this time next year," Medlicott said grimly, "they'll both be dead of malaria."

Faulconer unscrewed the silver cap of his traveling inkwell. "Unfit for field duty?" he asked tentatively.

"One's a drunk, the other's a Northerner! Hell, I'd say they were unfit." Medlicott had been emboldened by the General's fine brandy and now, somewhat obliquely, offered his preferred solution. "But why be formal at all, sir? Why not just get rid of the bastards? Shoot them."

Moxey frowned at the suggestion while Faulconer chose to ignore it, not because he disapproved, but because he could not imagine getting away with murder. "You don't think I need to give a reason for their dismissal?" the General asked.

"What reason do you need beyond general unfitness for duty? Hell, add indiscipline and dereliction." Medlicott waved each word into the night with a careless gesture. "The War Department must be desperate to find men for the swamp stations in the Carolinas."

Faulconer dipped his pen into the ink, then carefully drained the surplus off the nib onto the inkwell's rim. He hesitated for a second, still worried whether his action might have unforeseen repercussions, then summoned his courage and signed the two papers that simply dismissed Swynyard and Starbuck from the Brigade. He regretted not recommending them for courts-martial, but expedience and good sense dictated the lesser punishment. The weather had made everything clammy, so that the ink ran thick in the paper's fibers as Faulconer scratched his name. He noted his rank beneath his name, then laid down the pen, capped the inkwell, and blew on the wet signatures to dry them. "Fetch Hinton," he ordered Moxey.

Moxey grimaced at the thought of walking a quarter-mile through the mud, but then pulled himself out of his chair and set off through the dusk toward the Legion's lines. The rain had stopped, and campfires pricked the gloom as men emerged from their shelters and blew kindling into life.

Faulconer admired the two dismissal orders. "And I give them passes for Richmond?"

"Good for tomorrow only," Medlicott suggested slyly. "That way if the bastards linger you can have them arrested again."

Faulconer filled in the two passes, then, his work done, walked across the veranda and down to the stretch of muddy grass that lay between the house and a peach orchard. He stretched his cramped arms. The clouds had made the dusk premature, casting night's pall over what should have been a sweet summer evening. "You'd have thought the rain would have broken this humidity," Medlicott said as he followed Faulconer down the steps.

"Another storm might do it," Faulconer said. He offered Medlicott a cigar, and for a few moments the two men smoked in silence. It was hardly a companionable silence, but Medlicott had nothing to say, and the General was evidently thinking hard. Faulconer finally cleared his throat. "You know, of course, that I've friends in Richmond?"

"Of course," Medlicott said gruffly.

Faulconer was silent for a few seconds more. "I've been thinking, you see," he eventually said, "and it occurs to me that we've done more than our fair share of fighting since the war began. Wouldn't you agree?"

"Hell, yes," Medlicott said fervently.

"So I was hoping we could have the Brigade assigned to

Richmond," Faulconer said. "Maybe we could become the experts on the city's defenses?"

Medlicott nodded gravely. He was not sure just how expert a brigade needed to be in order to garrison the star forts and trenches that ringed Richmond, but anything that took a man away from the slaughterfields of open battle and closer to hot baths, decent food, and regular hours seemed pretty inviting. "Experts," Medlicott said, "indeed."

"And some of my friends in the capital are convinced it's a good idea," Faulconer said. "You think the men will like it?" He added the question disingenuously.

"I'm sure, I'm sure," Medlicott said.

Faulconer examined the glowing tip of his cigar. "Politically, of course, we mustn't look too eager. We can't have people saying we shirked the burden, which means I'll probably have to make a show of refusing the job, but it would help me if my regimental commanders pressed me to accept."

"Of course, of course," Medlicott said. The miller did not really understand the prevarication but was quite happy to agree to anything that might get the Brigade back to the comparative comforts of the Richmond defenses.

"And I was thinking that I might make Paul Hinton my second-in-command," Faulconer went on, "which means that the Legion will need a new commanding officer."

Medlicott's heart gave a leap of anticipation, but he had the sense to show neither surprise nor delight. "Surely your brother-in-law will be back soon?" he said instead.

"Pecker might not want to return," Faulconer said, meaning that he hoped he could persuade Bird not to return, "but even if he does it won't be for a long time and the Legion can't manage without a new commanding officer, can it?"

"Indeed not, sir," Medlicott said.

"Some people, of course, would say the job ought to go to

a professional soldier," Faulconer said, teasing the eager Medlicott, "but I think this war needs fresh eyes and ideas."

"Very true, sir, very true."

"And you managed a fair number of men at the mill, didn't you?"

Medlicott's gristmill had never employed more than two free men at any one time, and one of those was usually a half-wit, but the miller now nodded sagely as though he was accustomed to giving orders to hundreds of employees. "A good few," he said cautiously, then frowned because Captain Moxey, muddied to his knees, was returning. Just a few seconds more, Medlicott thought, and he would have been the Legion's new commanding officer, but now an excited Moxey was demanding Faulconer's attention.

"Moxey?" Faulconer turned to greet his aide.

"Major Hinton's not here, sir. Not in the lines," Moxey said eagerly.

"What do you mean, not in the lines?"

Moxey was clearly enjoying making his revelations. "He's gone to McComb's Tavern, sir," he said. "It seems it's his fiftieth birthday, sir, and most of the Legion's officers went with him."

"God damn them!" Faulconer said. They were plotting. That was what they were doing, plotting! He did not believe the story about a birthday for one moment; they were conspiring behind his back! "Don't they know the tavern's off limits?"

"They know it's off limits," Captain Medlicott intervened. "Of course they know. It's downright disobedience, sir," he added to Faulconer, wondering whether he might not end up second-in-command to the whole Brigade after all.

"Fetch them, Captain," Faulconer ordered Moxey. Goddamn it, Faulconer thought, but Major Hinton would have to learn that there was a new tight discipline in the Faulconer Brigade. "Tell them to come here immediately," Faulconer said, then paused because Captain Medlicott had raised a warning hand, and the General turned to see a horseman approaching. The General recognized the rider as Captain Talliser, one of Stonewall Jackson's aides.

Talliser saluted Faulconer by touching a gloved hand to his hat brim, then fetched a packet of papers from his saddlebag. "Marching orders, General. Reckon you'll be busy packing up tonight."

"Marching orders?" Faulconer repeated the words as though he did not understand their meaning.

Talliser held on to the orders, offering a scrap of paper and a pencil instead. "I need your signature first, General. Or someone's signature."

Faulconer took the proffered paper and scribbled his name to confirm that General Jackson's orders had indeed been received. "Where are we going?" he asked as he took the orders.

"North, sir, over the river," Talliser said, tucking the receipt into a pouch on his belt.

"You'll eat with us, Talliser?" Faulconer asked, gesturing toward the farmhouse, where his cooks were busy preparing supper.

"Real kind of you, General," Talliser said, "but I should be getting back."

"You'll surely take a glass of something before you go?"

"A glass of water would be real kind." Talliser was not one of Jackson's favorite aides for nothing. He swung himself out of his saddle and winced at the soreness in his legs. "Been a long day, sir, a real long day."

Faulconer turned and was about to shout for Nelson, his servant, then remembered that the wretched man had not yet returned from his errand to Faulconer Court House.

"Moxey," he said instead, "before you go to McComb's Tavern, be kind enough to fetch a glass of water for Captain Talliser."

But Moxey was no longer paying attention. Moxey was instead staring slack-jawed and wide-eyed past the farm-house. Slowly Moxey's hand began to point; then he tried to speak, but the only sound he could make was an incoherent stammer.

"What the hell?" Medlicott frowned at Moxey's pathetic display; then he, too, turned and looked south. "Oh, dear Christ!" he blasphemed; then he began to run away.

Just as the Yankees opened fire.

It all started so much more easily than Major Galloway had dared to hope. The raiders, riding in column of pairs, stole through the dank twilight to the empty road that stretched between the rebel encampment and the crossroads, where dim candlelights gleamed behind the tavern's windows. No one saw the cavalrymen move through the half-light, and no one challenged them as they urged their horses up the small embankment that edged the road. Galloway chuckled as he heard singing coming from the tavern. "Someone's sure having a good time," the Major said, then turned to Captain Blythe. "Billy? Take your men south a little. Just make sure no one from the tavern interferes with us. And listen for our bugle."

Blythe touched his hat and turned his horse southward. "You take care now, Major," he called softly as he led his men away.

The rest of Galloway's Horse rode north. The horses' hooves sank into the mud, but the going was not nearly as difficult as Galloway had feared. In winter, once the snow and ice had thawed, Virginia's unmacadamed roads could become impassable strips of filthy mud while in summer they

220

could be baked hard enough to lame a well-shod horse, but this day's rain had merely served to turn the top few inches glutinous. A small and smoky fire burned under some trees fifty yards ahead, and Galloway guessed it marked the southernmost picket of the Faulconer Brigade. The Major eased his saber in its scabbard, licked his lips, and noted how the clouds were already reflecting the great swath of campfires that burned to the east and north. Those to the east were rebel fires, while the ones across the river were the lights of Pope's army. Only a few hours more, Galloway thought, and his men would be safe back in those Northern lines.

"Who the hell's there?" a voice challenged from the shadows some yards short of the fire.

Galloway, his heart thumping, reined in his horse. "Can't see a damned thing," he answered as unconventionally as the picket had challenged him. "Who in tarnation are you?"

There was the unmistakable sound of a rifle being cocked; then a man in rebel gray stepped out from the cover of the trees. "Who are you, mister?" the man returned Galloway's question. The sentry looked scarce a day over sixteen. His coat hung loose on his shoulders, his trousers were held up by a frayed length of rope, and the soles of his boots had separated from their uppers.

"Name's Major Hearn, Second Georgia Horse," Galloway said, plucking a regiment's name from his imagination, "and I'm sure glad you boys are Southerners else we'd have been in something wicked close to trouble." He chuckled. "You got a light, son? My cigar's plumb cold."

"You got business here, sir?" the nervous sentry asked.

"Forgive me, son, but I should have told you. We're carrying dispatches for General Faulconer. Is he anywhere about?"

"Another man just came with dispatches," the sentry said suspiciously.

221

Galloway laughed. "You know the army, son. Never send one man to do a job properly when twenty men can do it worse. Hell, wouldn't surprise me if our orders countermanded his orders. We'll have you boys marching in circles all week long. Now, how do I find the General, son?"

"He's just up the road, sir." The sentry's suspicions had been entirely allayed by Galloway's friendliness. There was a pause while he made his rifle safe and slung the weapon on his shoulder. "Did you ride with Jeb Stuart, sir?" The picket's voice was touched with awe.

"I just guess we did, son," Galloway said, "clean round the Yankees. Now have you got that light for my cigar?"

"Sure have, sir." The picket ran back to the fire and snatched a piece of wood out of the flames. The fire flared up, revealing two other men huddled in the shadows beyond.

"Sergeant Darrow?" Galloway called softly.

"Sir?"

"Take care of them when we're past. No noise now."

"Yes, sir."

The picket brought the flame back to Galloway, who bent toward it to light his cigar. Like all his men Galloway had a cloak drawn tight around his uniform. "Thank you, son," he said when the cigar was drawing. "Straight on up the road, you say?"

"Yes, sir. There's a farmhouse there."

"You keep dry tonight, son, you hear me?" Galloway said, then rode on. He did not look back as Darrow and his men disabled the picket. There was no gunfire, just a sickening series of thumps followed by silence. To Galloway's right was the wagon park where the Faulconer Brigade's ammunition was stored, while ahead, beyond a stand of dripping trees, he could see the farmhouse and tents that marked the Faulconer Brigade's headquarters. Galloway curbed his horse to let Adam's troop catch up with him. "You go on now," he told Adam, "and burn the farmhouse."

"Must I?" Adam asked.

Galloway sighed. "If it's being used by the enemy, Adam, yes. If it's full of women and children, no. Hell, man, we're at war!"

"Yes, sir," Adam said and rode on.

Galloway drew on his cigar and walked his horse in among the supply wagons, where a dozen black teamsters sat beneath a crude shelter made from a tarpaulin stretched between two pairs of wagon shafts. A small fire flickered in the shelter's opening. "How are you in there, boys?" Galloway asked as he peered past the fire's smoke, "and where do I find the ammunition?"

"The white carts, master, over there." The man who answered was whittling a piece of wood into the shape of a woman's head. "You got an order from the quartermaster, sir?"

"Fine carving that, real fine. Me, I never could whittle. Guess I don't keep the blade sharp enough. Sure I got orders, boy, all the orders you'll ever want. My sergeant will give 'em to you." Galloway waved at the teamsters, then walked his horse on toward the nearest ammunition cart that was painted white and had a hooped cover of dirty canvas. As Galloway rode he took a length of fuse from his saddlebag and a linen bag of gunpowder from a pouch. He pushed one end of the fuse into the gunpowder, then drew aside the wet canvas flap at the back of the cart to reveal a pile of ammunition boxes. He rammed the bag between two of the wooden boxes, then touched the glowing tip of his cigar to the fuse's end. He waited a second to make sure the fuse was burning, then let the canvas curtain drop.

The fire sputtered down the fuse's powder-packed tube to leave a small trickle of gray-white smoke. Galloway

223

was already assembling another small charge to place in the next wagon while more of his men were heading toward the artillery park, which was guarded by a handful of unsuspecting gunners armed with carbines. Galloway placed his second charge, then pulled his cloak back to reveal his blue uniform. He tugged his saber free and turned back to the sheltering teamsters. "Make yourselves scarce, boys," he told them. "Go on, now. Run! We're Yankees!"

The first bag of powder exploded. It was not a loud explosion, merely a dull thump that momentarily lit up the interior of the wagon's hooped canvas cover with a lurid red glow. The canvas swelled for a second or two; then a fire began to flicker deep inside the stacked boxes. The teamsters were running. One of Galloway's men leaned from his saddle and plucked a burning brand from the remains of their fire and tossed the burning wood into a third ammunition cart. The first load of ammunition began to explode in a series of short sharp cracks that sounded as close together as the snaps of a Fourth of July firecracker string, and then the whole wagon seemed to evaporate in sudden flame. The wet canvas cover flew into the air, flapping like a monstrous bat with wings dripping sparks. One of Galloway's men whooped in delight and tossed a firebrand into a stack of muskets.

"Keep 'em burning, boys!" Galloway shouted at those of his men who had been detailed as incendiarists; then he led the rest of his troop in a charge toward the startled gunners. The Major's saber reflected the flamelight. An artillery sergeant was still trying to prime his carbine as the saber sliced across his face. The man screamed, but all Galloway knew of the blow was a slight jar up his right arm and the juddering friction of steel scraping on bone; then the saber was free and he swung it forward to spear its tip into the neck of a running man. Two of Galloway's troopers were already dismounted and starting to hammer soft nails into the cannons' touchholes, others were setting fire to limbers crammed with ammunition, while still more were cutting loose picketed team horses and stampeding them into the night. Saddle horses were being captured and led back to the road. A powder charge exploded, shooting sparks high into the night air. Men were shouting in the dark. A bullet screamed high over Galloway's head. "Bugler!" the Major shouted.

"Here, sir!" The man put his instrument to his lips.

"Not yet!" Galloway said. He only wanted to make sure the bugler was staying close, for he knew he must sound the retreat very soon. He sheathed his saber and drew out the repeating rifle, which he fired toward the shadows of men beyond the guns. The wagon park was an inferno, the sky above it bright with flame and writhing plumes of firelit smoke. A dog barked and a wounded horse screamed. In the light of the fires Galloway could see rebel gunners gathering in the darkness, and he knew that at any moment a counterattack would swarm across the artillery park. He turned to his bugler. "Now!" Galloway called, "now!" and the bugler's call rang clear in the night's fiery chaos. The Major backed his horse through the gunline, where the cannons were all spiked and the limbers burning.

"Back, lads! Back!" Galloway called his men. "Back!"

Adam was inside the farmhouse when he heard the bugle call. He had found the house empty except for two of his father's cooks, whom he had ordered to run away. Sergeant Huxtable had meanwhile chased away a group of officers standing on the lawn, killing a captain dressed in riding boots and spurs, and Huxtable now had Adam's troop lining the ditch at the end of the farm's garden from where they were blazing rifle fire into the shadowy lines of the Brigade. The repeater rifles made it seem as if a whole company of infantry was attacking across the ditch.

Corporal Kemp joined Adam in the farmhouse. "Burn the place, sir?" he asked.

"Not yet," Adam said. He has found his father's precious revolver and priceless saber hanging in the hall. Explosions sounded outside, then the ripping noise of gunfire.

"Sir!" Sergeant Huxtable shouted. "We can't hold here much longer, sir!" The Faulconer Brigade had begun to fight back, and the rifle bullets were whipping thick above the farm's yard and orchard. Adam seized his father's sword and revolver, then turned as Kemp called him from the parlor.

"Look here! Look at this!" Kemp had discovered the twin standards of the Faulconer Legion on the parlor wall.

Huxtable called again from the dark outside. "Hurry, sir! For God's sake, hurry!" The bugle sounded again from the artillery park, its call sweet and pure in the night's angry fusillades.

Adam and Kemp pulled the two crossed flagstaffs off their nails. "Come on!" Adam ordered.

"We're to burn the house, sir, you heard the Major," Kemp insisted. He saw Adam's reluctance. "Belongs to a family called Pearce, sir," Kemp went on, "rebels through and through."

Adam had forgotten that Corporal Kemp was a local man. A bullet smacked into the upper floor, splintering wood. "Go! Take the flags!" Adam told him, then snatched up some papers that lay on a claw-footed table and held their corners into a flickering candle flame. He held the papers there, letting the fire take a good hold, then dropped the burning documents among the slew of other papers. There was a brandy bottle open on the table, and Adam spilt it across the floor's rush matting, then threw a burning paper onto the floor. Flames leaped up.

Adam ran outside. A bullet whipped past his head to shatter a window. He jumped the veranda's rail. The pair of captured rebel flags trailed huge and bright across the flanks of Corporal Kemp's horse. Sergeant Huxtable had the bridle of Adam's mare. "Here, sir!"

"Back!" Adam shouted as he pulled himself into the saddle.

The horsemen retreated past the farmhouse, where a fiery glow was already suffusing the parlor windows. Kemp had managed to furl the captured flags and now handed them to one of the troopers, then drew his saber to slash at the guy ropes of the nearest tents. A voice was shouting for water. Another voice shouted Adam's name, but Adam ignored the summons as he galloped toward the wagon park that now looked like a corner of hell. Flames were searing sixty feet high while the exploding ammunition spat trails of vivid smoke in every direction. The bugle sounded again, and Adam and his men spurred down the road toward Major Galloway's party. "Count!" Adam shouted.

"One!" That was Sergeant Huxtable.

"Two!" Corporal Kemp.

"Three!" the next man called, and so on through the whole troop. Every man was present.

"Anyone hurt?" Adam asked. Not one man was hurt, and Adam felt his heart leap with exultation.

"Well done, Adam!" Galloway greeted him just beyond the small stand of trees. "All well?"

"Everyone's present, sir! No one's hurt."

"And us!" Galloway sounded triumphant. Another limber of ammunition exploded, punching red fire across the wounded camp. Then, from the southern darkness, there sounded a crash of rifle fire so sudden and furious that Galloway looked momentarily alarmed. He feared his men were being cut off, then realized the noise was coming from the tavern at the crossroads, which meant that Billy Blythe

227

and his men were in a fight. "Come on!" he shouted, dug in his spurs, and galloped to the rescue.

"I don't feel fifty," Major Hinton told Captain Murphy. "I don't even feel like forty. But I'm fifty! An old man!"

"Nonsense!" Murphy said. "Fifty's not old."

"Ancient," Hinton lamented. "I can't believe I'm fifty."

"You will tomorrow morning, God willing," Murphy answered. "Have another drink."

A dozen officers had walked to McComb's Tavern to celebrate the Major's half-century. It was not much of a tavern, merely a cavernous house where ale and home-distilled whiskey were sold and where two whores worked upstairs and two kitchen slaves served huge plates of dumplings, bacon, and corn bread downstairs. Major Hinton's private supper party was held in a back room, where the day's menu, such as it was, was crudely chalked on the plank wall. Not that the Major needed to read the bill of fare, for his officers had generously subscribed to buy a rare and expensive ham that Liam McComb's cooks had boiled especially for the dinner. Captain Murphy asked for Irish potatoes to accompany the ham, but McComb had refused the request by saying that he would be happy if he never saw another damned potato in all his born days. "Unless it's been liquidated, if you follow my meaning, Captain," he said. McComb was a giant man, more than sixty years old and with a belly on him like one of his own beer barrels.

"You mean *poteen?*" Murphy asked. "Christ, and I haven't tasted *poteen* in seven years."

"You'll find it will have been worth the wait, Captain," McComb said, and when the supper was finished and the shirtsleeved officers were sharing a bottle of fine French brandy taken at Cedar Mountain, the tavern keeper brought a gallon stone jug downstairs. "A few sips of that,

228

Captain," he told Murphy, "and you'll swear you're back in Ballinalea."

"If only I was," Murphy said wistfully.

"The wife made it," McComb said as he placed the stone jug on the table, "before she was taken bad."

"Not fatally, I trust?" Hinton asked politely.

"God bless you, no, Major. She's lying upstairs with a fever, so she is. It's the heat that does it to her. They're not natural, these summers, not natural at all."

"We'll pay for the *poteen*, sure we will," Murphy said, sounding more Irish than he had for many a long year.

"You'll not pay me a ha'penny, Captain," McComb said. "Roisin and I have two boys serving in the 6th Virginia, and they'd want you to be having a taste of it for nothing. So enjoy it now! But not too much now, not if you want to enjoy the upstairs pleasures later!" A cheer greeted this remark, for part of the night's entertainment would doubtless be afforded by the two rooms upstairs.

"But not me!" Hinton said when McComb had gone. "I'm a married man. I can't afford the pox."

"Starbuck hasn't got the pox," Murphy said, "and he must have sneaked down here at least a dozen times."

"He never did!" Hinton said, shocked at the news.

"Starbuck and women?" Murphy asked. "My God, Major, it's like whiskey and priests, you couldn't keep the two apart with a pry bar. God knows what they fed him up in Boston to give him the energy, but I wouldn't mind a bottle or two of it myself. Now try the *poteen*."

The *poteen* was passed around the table. Every captain from the Legion was there except for Daniel Medlicott, who had been summoned to Faulconer's headquarters, and Starbuck, who was under guard in Colonel Swynyard's tent. No one, not even Major Hinton, was entirely sure what fate the General planned for Starbuck, but Lieutenant Davies was certain Faulconer wanted a court-martial. Hinton averred that a court-martial was impossible. "Maybe Swynyard disobeyed Faulconer, but Nate only did what Swynyard ordered him to do." Hinton lifted the *poteen* jug to his nose and smelt it suspiciously. "It'll all blow over," he said, speaking of Starbuck's predicament rather than the liquor. "Faulconer will sleep on it, then forget all about it. He's not a man for confrontation, not like his father was. Do I drink this stuff or use it as a liniment?"

"Drink that," Murphy said, "and you'll feel fifteen instead of fifty."

"What in God's name is it?" Hinton asked as he poured a few drops of the spirit into a tin mug.

"Potato whiskey," Murphy told him, "from Ireland. If you get the recipe right, Major, it's a drink from heaven, but get it wrong and it'll blind you for life and tear your guts into tatters for good measure."

Hinton shrugged, hesitated, then decided that at fifty years old he had nothing to lose and so downed the colorless liquor in one gulp. He took a deep breath, shook his head, then let out a hoarse sound that seemed to indicate approval. He poured himself some more.

"What was that?" Captain Pirie, the Legion's quartermaster, was seated beside a window.

"That was amazing," Hinton said. "It takes your breath clean away!"

"Gunfire," Pirie said and pulled aside the gauze curtain that kept the insects away from the candlelight.

The sound of an explosion thumped across the damp landscape, followed by the splintering noise of rifles firing. A great red suffusion of light blossomed to the north, silhouetting the trees that lay between the crossroads and the Brigade's lines. "Jesus," Murphy said softly, then pulled his revolver from the holster that he had hung from a nail on the wall and went through into the tavern's main room, which, in turn, opened onto a rickety porch. The other officers followed him, joining McComb and three of his customers under the porch's wooden roof from which hung two lanterns. A second explosion spread its sheet of light across the northern sky, and this time the great flame outlined a group of cloaked horsemen on the road. "Who's there?" Hinton called.

"Fourth Louisiana Horse!" a Southern voice called back. The skyline was red with flame, and more rifle shots cracked in the camp.

"It's a raid!" Hinton called as he ran down the porch steps, revolver in hand.

"Fire!" the Southern voice shouted, and a volley of rifles slammed at the tavern from the reddened dark. Hinton was thrown to the ground by a monstrous blow to his shoulder. He rolled in the mud toward the shadows under the porch as a bullet shattered one of the lanterns and rained glass fragments down onto the startled officers. Captain Murphy fired his revolver twice, but the sheer volume of return fire made him duck into the tavern for cover. Lieutenant Davies had followed Hinton down the steps and somehow made it safe across the road to the protection of the small church, but none of the other officers succeeded in leaving the tavern's veranda. Pirie was draped over the railings, blood dripping from his dangling hands. More blood was seeping between the planks onto Major Hinton, who was gasping with pain. Liam McComb had a shotgun that he fired up the road; then a bullet smacked into the tavern keeper's great belly, and he folded onto the porch with an astonished look on his face. His breath came in huge shuddering gasps as blood spread across his shirt and pants.

Murphy ran to a side window, but a second before he reached his objective a bullet slapped the gauze curtain aside, then a second bullet ripped clean through the wall to strike a splinter out of the tavern's counter. The slaves were wailing in the kitchen, while McComb's bedridden wife was calling pathetically for her husband. The other women upstairs were screaming in terror. Murphy cupped his hands. "There are women in here! Stop your firing! Stop firing!"

Another voice took up the cry from the porch. "Cease fire! Cease fire! There are women here!"

"Keep firing!" a man shouted from the fire-rent dark. "Bastards are lying! Keep firing!"

Murphy ducked as more bullets riddled the wall. The heaviness of the rifle fire suggested there had to be scores of enemy outside. John Torrance, C Company's Captain, was lying in the porch doorway, apparently dead. One of the Legion's lieutenants was crawling across the floor, his beard dripping with blood; then he collapsed onto a full spittoon and spilt its rancid contents across the floor. A fire had started in the kitchen, and its flames roared hungrily as they fed on the old building's dry wood. Two of McComb's customers ran upstairs to try and take the women to safety as Murphy hurried into the back room, where the remains of the celebratory supper lay on the table. He snatched his coat from the nail, grabbed his cartridge pouch, and leaped straight through a gauze curtain into the night. The curtain wrapped itself round him, tripping him so that he rolled helplessly in the mud for a few seconds. He had an idea he might be able to drive the horsemen away from the front of the tavern if he could just fire at them from the darkness at the building's rear, but as he struggled to extricate himself from the muslin curtain, he heard the click of a gun being cocked and looked up to see the dark shape of a horseman. Murphy tried to raise his revolver, but the horseman fired first, then fired again. Murphy felt something hit him with a blow like the kick of a horse; then a terrible pain whipped

232

up from his thigh. He heard himself scream, then lost consciousness as the rider fired again.

The fire spread from the kitchen. Mrs. McComb screamed as the flames licked up the stairs and the bedrooms filled with a thick smoke. The two men who had tried to rescue the women abandoned their attempt, instead stepping out of a bedroom window onto the porch roof in an effort to save themselves from the flames. "Shoot them down!" Billy Blythe ordered excitedly. "Shoot the bastards down!" A half-dozen bullets struck the two men, who collapsed, rolled twitching down the shingled roof, then dropped to the ground. Blythe whooped with victory while his men kept pouring their withering fire into the burning building.

A bugle called to the north, summoning the raiders to their retreat, but Blythe had his enemy trapped like rats in a burning barrel, and like rats, he decided, they would die. He fired again and again while the flames spread through the tavern, leaping up the gauze curtains, devouring the ancient wooden floors, exploding barrels of liquor, and hissing where it met the blood that was spilt so thick across the planks.

A man with burning clothes crawled across the porch, then fell shuddering as bullets ripped at him. A roof beam collapsed, showering sparks into the night, and Billy Blythe, his mouth open and eyes bright, watched enthralled.

Major Galloway arrived at the head of his raiders. "Come on, Billy! Didn't you hear the bugle?"

"Too busy," Blythe said, his eyes wide and fixed on the glorious destruction. Flames writhed out of collapsing liquor barrels and flared fierce and brief when they caught a dead man's hair. Ammunition crackled in the flames, each cartridge flashing white like a miniature firecracker.

"What happened?" Galloway stared in awe at the burning house.

233

"Sons of bitches fired on us," Blythe said, still gazing enraptured at the horror he had engendered, "so we taught the sons of bitches a lesson."

"Let's go, Billy," Galloway said, then seized Blythe's bridle and dragged his second-in-command away from the fire. "Come on, Billy!"

A figure stirred under the porch, and two horsemen emptied their rifles' revolving cylinders into the man. A woman screamed at the tavern's rear; then the kitchen roof collapsed and the scream was cut sharply off. "It was a horse," Blythe assured Galloway, who had frowned when he heard the woman's distress, "just a dying horse, Joe, and dying horses can sound uncommon like women."

"Let's go," Galloway said. There was a smell of roasting meat from the tavern, and horrid things twitching in the furnace heat, and Galloway turned away, not wanting to know what horrors he abandoned.

The horsemen rode west, leaving the sparks whirling cloudward and a whole brigade whipped.

Starbuck had wanted to challenge the raiders, but Swynyard stopped him from leaving the tent. "They'll slash you down like a dog. Ever been chased by a cavalryman?"

"No."

"You'll end up saber-cut to ribbons. Keep quiet."

"We must do something!"

"Sometimes it's best to do nothing. They won't stay long."

Yet the wait seemed forever to Starbuck as he crouched in the tent; then at last he heard a bugle call and voices shouting orders to retreat. Hooves thumped close by the tent, which suddenly twitched and half collapsed as its guy ropes were cut. Starbuck squirmed out of the sagging wet canvas and saw Adam on horseback not five paces away.

234

"Adam!" Starbuck shouted, not really believing his own eyes.

But Adam was already spurring south, his horse's hooves throwing up great gobs of mud and water as he went. Starbuck saw the headquarters house burning and more fires flaring skyward among the supply wagons. The sentry guarding Swynyard's tent had vanished.

"So how did they cross the river?" Colonel Swynyard asked as he crawled out from the tent's wreckage.

"The same way they'll go back," Starbuck said. The horsemen might have withdrawn southward, but he had no doubt they would be riding a half-circle to get back to the unguarded ford, which meant a man on foot might just be able to cut them off. General Faulconer was shouting for water, but Starbuck ignored the orders. He leaped over the ditch that separated the headquarters from the bivouac lines and shouted for Sergeant Truslow. "Turn out! Fast now!"

H Company fell into ranks. "Load!" Starbuck ordered.

Truslow had rescued Starbuck's rifle and now threw it to him with an ammunition pouch. "The General says we're not to take orders from you," the Sergeant said.

"The General can go to hell." Starbuck bit a cartridge and poured powder down the barrel.

"That's what I reckoned too," Truslow said.

Swynyard arrived, panting. "Where are you going?"

Starbuck spat the bullet into the muzzle. "We're going to Dead Mary's Ford," he said, then rammed the bullet hard down, slotted the ramrod back into place, and slung the rifle from his shoulder.

"Why Dead Mary's Ford?" Swynyard asked, puzzled.

"Because, damn it, we saw one of the bastards there last night. Ain't that right, Mallory?"

"Saw him plain as daylight," Sergeant Mallory confirmed.

"Besides," Starbuck went on, "where else would they cross the river? Every other ford's guarded. Follow me!" Starbuck shouted, and the men ran through a darkness made livid by the great fires that burned uncontrollably in the Brigade lines. The farmhouse roof collapsed to spew a gout of flames skyward, but that inflagration was dwarfed by the huge fires in the ammunition park. Every few seconds another powder cask would explode to send a ball of fire soaring up into the low clouds. Shells cracked apart, rifle ammunition stuttered, and dogs howled in terror. The inferno lit Starbuck's path across the waterlogged meadow and into the trees, but the deeper he ran into the woods the darker it became and the harder it was to find the path. He had to slow down and feel his way forward.

Sergeant Truslow wanted to know just what had happened at headquarters. Colonel Swynyard told him about the Northern raiders, and Starbuck added that he had seen Adam Faulconer among the enemy horsemen. "Are you sure?" Colonel Swynyard asked.

"Pretty damn sure, yes."

Truslow spat into the dark. "I said we should have shot the bastard when he crossed the lines. This way."

They stumbled on through the woods; then, when they were still a quarter-mile short of the river, Starbuck heard hoofbeats and saw a glimmer of flamelight showing through the black tangled silhouette of the trees. "Run!" he shouted. He feared his company would arrive too late and that the Northern horsemen would escape before he could reach the line of rifle pits at the wood's edge.

Then he saw the riders milling at the river's nearer bank. Someone had made a torch by strapping dead twigs to a length of timber, and the torch lit the horsemen's passage through a ford made dangerously deep by storm water. Starbuck guessed most of the riders had long crossed the river, but a dozen cavalrymen were still waiting on the southern bank as he slipped and skidded into a flooded rifle pit. He held his weapon up high to keep it dry and saw the nearest horsemen turn in alarm as they heard the splash of his fall. "Spread out!" Starbuck shouted to his men, "and open fire!" Three horses were in the middle of the ford with the river up past their bellies. One of the cavalrymen cut with a whip to urge his horse on. "Fire!" Starbuck shouted again, then aimed his own rifle at the nearest enemy. He pulled the trigger and felt a surge of relief that at last they were fighting back.

Someone fired from Starbuck's right. The woods were full of trampling feet, and the edge of the meadow was suddenly black with rebel infantry. The ruined house where Mad Silas lived was a dark shadow in the meadow's center, beyond which the Yankee carried his flaming torch high; then the man suddenly realized that he was illuminating the target, and so he hurled the brand into the river to plunge the night into instant and utter blackness. A horse was screaming in the dark. More rifles cracked, their flames stabbing the sudden dark.

The Yankees returned the fire. Rifles flared on the far bank. Men were shouting in panic, calling on each other to get the hell across the water. Northern bullets whipped through the leaves over Starbuck's head. He was up to his thighs in the flooded rifle pit. He rammed a new bullet down the rifle's barrel, then fired again. He could not see his targets because the muzzle flashes were dazzling him. The night was a chaos of gun flames, screams, and splashes. Something or someone floundered in the water, and Starbuck could hear desperate shouts as the horsemen tried to rescue their comrade. "Cease fire!" he shouted, not because he wanted to help the rescuers, but because it was time to take prisoners. "Cease fire!" he shouted again and heard Sergeant Truslow take up the call. "H Company!" Starbuck called when the rifles had fallen silent. "Forward!"

The company advanced out of the trees and ran down the grassy slope. A few Yankee shots came over the river, but in the dark the enemy's aim was much too high, and the bullets simply ripped their way through the black canopy of leaves. Starbuck ran past the ruined house, where Mad Silas was cradling his dead Mary. The company began screaming the rebel yell, wanting to scare the men who were still trying to rescue their wounded comrade from the river. Starbuck reached the ford first, dropped his rifle, and threw himself into the water. He gasped at the storm-given strength of the current, then grabbed at the shadows in front and found himself clasping a wet handful of uniform. A gun exploded a foot from his face, but the bullet went wide; then a man screamed as Starbuck dragged him back toward the southern bank. More rebels splashed into the river to help Starbuck. One of them fired at the Yankees, and the flash of his rifle's muzzle showed a group of Northerners wading to the far bank and a horse and rider being swept downstream.

Starbuck's prisoner gasped for breath while the drowning horse smashed the river's surface with its flailing hooves. "Give them a goodbye shot, boys!" Colonel Swynyard called, and a handful of Starbuck's men fired across the water.

"Come on, you bastard," Starbuck grunted. His prisoner was struggling like a fiend and throwing wild fists at Starbuck's face. Starbuck hammered the man hard with his right hand, kicked him, and finally dragged him back to the southern bank, where a rush of men overpowered the Yankee.

"Rest of the bastards got away," Truslow panted ruefully as the hoofbeats receded across the river.

"We got all we needed," Starbuck said. He was soaked through, bruised, and winded, but he had won the victory he wanted. He had proof that the ford had needed guarding, and it had been Washington Faulconer who had removed the guard and so let the Northern raiders cross the river. "Just let that son of a bitch put us on trial now," he told Swynyard, "just let that son of a goddamned bitch try."

GENERAL STUART'S AIDE reached Lee's headquarters before dawn and found the army's commander standing outside his tent in contemplation of a crude map scratched in the dirt. The map showed the rivers Rapidan and Rappahannock, while the fords across the further river were marked by scraps of twig. It was those fords that the cavalry needed to capture if Pope was to be trapped at the rivers' confluence, but it seemed there was to be no chance of success this day, for the aide brought only a repetition of the previous day's bad news. "The cavalry just aren't ready, sir. General Stuart's real sorry, sir." The aide was very sheepish, half expecting a tirade from an angry Lee. "It's the horses, sir," he went on lamely, "they ain't recovered. The roads are wicked hard, sir, and General Stuart was expecting to find more forage up here, and . . ." The aide let his hopeless explanations trail away.

Lee's grave face scarce registered his disappointment; indeed, he seemed much more disappointed in the taste of the coffee than in the failure of his cavalry. "Is this really the best coffee we have, Hudson?" he asked one of his younger staff officers.

"Until we can capture more from the Yankees, sir, yes."

"Which we can't do without our cavalry. Upon my soul, we can't." He sipped the coffee again, grimaced, then laid the tin mug on a washstand that was set with his aides' shaving tackle. On the General's own washstand, inside his tent, there lay a dispatch that reported that 108 Federal ships had steamed up the Potomac River in the previous twenty-four hours, and what that figure meant, Lee knew, was that McClellan's forces were well on their way to reinforcing Pope's army. The ships' sidewheels and screws were churning the Potomac white in their efforts to combine the enemy armies, and meanwhile the Confederate cavalry was not ready. Which meant Pope's army would be safe for one more day. The frustration rose in Lee, only to be instantly suppressed. There was no profit in displaying temperament, none at all, and so the General looked placidly back at the crude map scratched in the dirt. There was still time, he told himself, still time. It was one thing for the Northern generals to move an army by boat, but quite another to land the troops and reunite them with their wagons and guns and tents and ammunition. And McClellan was a cautious man, much too cautious, which would give the rebels even more time to teach John Pope a lesson in civilized warfare. Lee ruefully obliterated the map with the toe of a riding boot and gave orders that the army would not, after all, be marching that morning. He retrieved his coffee. "What exactly do they do to this coffee?" he asked.

"Mix it with ground goober peas, sir," Captain Hudson answered.

"Mashed peanuts!" Lee sipped again. "Good Lord."

"It makes the coffee go farther, sir."

"It surely does, it surely does."

"Of course, sir, we can always get some real beans from Richmond," Hudson said. "If we say they're for you, I'm sure they'll find some."

"No, no. We must drink what the soldiers drink. At least when it comes to coffee we must." The General forced himself to swallow more of the sour liquid. "The horses will be ready tomorrow, you think?" he asked Stuart's messenger very courteously, almost as though he regretted pressing the cavalryman for a decision.

"General Stuart's confident of that, sir. Very confident."

Lee forbore to remark that twenty-four hours earlier Stuart had been equally confident that the cavalry would be ready in this dawn, but nothing would be achieved by recrimination, and so Lee offered the discomfited aide a grave smile. "My respects to General Stuart," he said, "and I look forward to marching tomorrow instead."

Later that morning Lee returned to Clark's Mountain to examine the enemy on the river's far bank. As he climbed the wooded slope, he saw a pyre of dirty smoke smearing the western sky, but no one on his staff knew what the smoke meant. It came from Jackson's lines, and doubtless Jackson would deal with whatever had caused the fire. Lee was more concerned with what was happening across the river, and so, once at the summit, he dismounted and rested his telescope on Traveller's patient back.

And once again the Yankee presence in the Virginia hills was denoted by a myriad of smoking fires that hazed the green land like a winter mist, but then Lee saw that something was missing beneath that mist. There were fires aplenty, but no tents. He moved the glass. No wagons, no horses, and no guns. There was nothing but the remains of campfires that the Yankees had lit in the night, stacked high with wood, then left to burn as they crept away. "They've gone," Lee said.

"Sir?" One of his aides stepped forward to hear better.

"They've gone." Lee collapsed his telescope but still stared northward. "They've gone," he said again, almost as if he did not believe his own eyes.

Pope had taken his men out of the trap. He had retreated across the Rappahannock. He had seen his danger and abandoned the land between the rivers, which meant, Lee thought, that in a week's time Pope would have been reinforced by McClellan and then it would all be finished. Blue-coated Yankees would be rampaging all across Virginia, and John Pope, the wretched John Pope who so passionately hated Southerners, would be the tyrant of all he surveyed.

Unless, that is, the Confederacy risked everything on a daring and desperate chance. Not a maneuver from the rule book, but something from the devil's box of tricks instead. Lee sensed the idea like a temptation. He suddenly saw how he could tip John Pope off balance and then savage him, and the idea burgeoned in his mind even as the well-schooled and conventional part of his training attempted to reject the notion as too risky. But another part of Lee was tantalized by the beauty and symmetry of the outrageous idea. It was a maneuver that would humiliate John Pope and drive the Yankees clean out of Virginia, and as Lee considered the rewards and risks of his maneuver, he felt the excitement of a gambler staking everything on a single run of cards. The thing could be done! Yet his face betrayed no hint of that excitement as he climbed into his saddle and settled his boots into his stirrups. "My compliments to General Jackson," he said calmly, pushing his telescope back into its case and gathering Traveller's reins into his hands, "and I would be much obliged if he would call on me at his earliest convenience."

And then, Lee thought, he would let Old Mad Jack off his leash.

And God help John Pope then.

It was not convenient for Major General Thomas Jackson to call on General Robert Lee. It would be convenient soon, but not yet, for General Jackson had two urgent duties to perform. They were not pleasant duties—indeed, lesser men might have shrunk from them altogether—but Thomas

Jackson considered them simple responsibilities, and so he performed them with his customary dogged diligence.

Men had to be shot. Southern men. Except to the General they were not men, but curs and trash who had deserted their duties and thus placed themselves beneath contempt. Their commanding officers had pleaded for the condemned men's lives, but Jackson had answered that men who desert their comrades deserve to be shot and officers who pleaded for such men deserved to be hung, and after that curt response there had been no more pleas for clemency. Now, beneath a clearing sky and on a meadow still damp from the previous day's rains, Jackson had assembled his whole corps. Three divisions of soldiers, twenty-four thousand men, were paraded in rank after shabby gray rank to form three sides of an open square. The morning was hot and the air stifling.

Drums beat slow as a band played a ragged funeral dirge. The band was paraded a few paces behind Jackson, who sat on his small, rawboned horse and stared morosely at three wooden stakes that had been plunged into the dirt beside three rough-sawn pine coffins and three freshly dug graves. Behind him his staff sat silent in their saddles, some of them more nervous of this morning's killings than they had ever been of battle. Captain Hudson, Lee's aide, who was waiting to escort General Jackson back to meet the army's commander in Gordonsville, watched the gaunt, famous figure and wondered if ever, in all the history of warfare, any commander had appeared so unprepossessing. The General's beard was unkempt, and his clothes looked in worse condition than any of his soldiers' uniforms. He had an old blue coat that was vaguely military in cut but threadbare and faded, while for a hat Jackson favored a shabby cadet's cap with a creased brim that was pulled low over his eyes. His horse was a big-headed, knock-kneed, clumsy beast with a patchy chestnut pelt, while the General's enormous boots were thrust into rusted stirrups that hung from mended leather straps. The most impressive military aspect of the General, apart from his reputation, was his rigid pose, for he sat his horse straight-backed and with his head held high, but then, as if to spoil that martial stance, he slowly and inexplicably raised his left hand until it was poised higher than his scruffy, creased cap. He then held the hand motionless, as though he was beseeching the Almighty for blessing.

The three doomed men were marched onto the field, each man escorted by his own company. The General had insisted that the criminals must be shot by their own comrades, for those comrades were the men most immediately betrayed by each deserter. An army chaplain waited for the condemned men, who, on reaching the stakes, were ordered onto their knees. The chaplain stepped forward and began to pray.

A small wind stirred the sullen air. To the west a sifting plume of smoke showed where the Yankee raiders had struck in the night, and Jackson, reminded of that impudent raid, looked toward the Faulconer Brigade to see the regiment that paraded without its colors. They had lost their colors, just as they had lost most of their officers, and Jackson, brooding on the Yankee coup, felt a spasm of anger.

The prayer seemed unending. The chaplain's eyes were screwed tight shut, and his hands clenched hard about a battered Bible as he commended the three sinners' souls to the God they were about to meet. The chaplain reminded God of the two thieves who had shared His Son's death on Calvary and implored the Almighty to look as charitably upon these three sinners as Christ had looked upon the repentant thief. One of the three men was unable to check his tears. He was a beardless youth who had deserted because his sixteen-year-old wife had run away with his uncle, and now he was to die in a green field because he had loved her so much. He looked up at his Captain and tried to make a last-minute plea, but the chaplain simply raised his voice so that the useless request could not be heard. The other two men showed no emotion, not even when the band finished its funereal music and went suddenly silent after a last uneven flurry on the drums.

The chaplain also finished. He stumbled as he stepped backward from the victims. A staff officer took the chaplain's place and in a loud, slow voice that almost carried to the rearmost ranks of the twenty-four thousand witnesses, read aloud the charges against the three men and the verdicts of their courts-martial. The bleak sentences finished, he stepped back and looked at the three company officers. "Carry on."

"No, for the love of God, no! Please, no!" The young man tried to resist, but two of his comrades dragged him to the stake and there pinioned him with rope. The three men wore shirts, pants, and ragged boots. A sergeant blindfolded the weeping youth and told him to stop his noise and die like a man. The other two deserters refused their blindfolds.

"Ready!" the staff officer shouted, and over a hundred rifles were raised to the firing position. Some men aimed wide, some blatantly had their rifles uncocked, but most of the men obeyed the order.

"Aim!" the staff officer called, and two nervous men pulled their triggers instead. Both bullets flew wide.

"Wait for it!" a sergeant snarled. A company officer had his eyes closed, and his lips were moving in silent prayer as he waited for the order to fire. One of the doomed men spat onto the grass. To Lee's aide, who had not expected to witness death this morning, it seemed as though three whole divisions of troops were holding their collective breath, while Jackson, his left hand held high, seemed carved from stone.

"No, please! No!" the young man called. His blindfolded head was thrashing from side to side. "Nancy!" he shouted desperately, "my Nancy!"

The staff officer took a deep breath. "Fire!"

The smoke jetted suddenly. The volley's huge sound rolled across the fields to explode birds from far-off trees.

The three men jerked in sudden spasms as their shirts erupted with blood. The companies' commanding officers walked to the three stakes with their revolvers drawn, but only one of the men was still alive. The man's breath bubbled in the wreckage of his ribs, and his bearded head twitched. His company officer cocked his revolver, held his breath, and tried to stop his hand shaking. For a second or two it looked as though he would be unable to give the *coup de grace*; then he managed to pull the trigger, and the living man's head was shattered by the bullet. The Captain turned away and vomited into the open grave as the band jerked into the tune of "Old Dan Tucker." Lee's aide let out a long slow breath.

"Put 'em in their boxes!" a sergeant called, and men ran forward to cut the dead men away from their stakes and lift them into the open-topped coffins, which were then ramped up on the red earth mounds so that a passer-by could see the corpses clearly. "Take the wrap off the young lad," the sergeant ordered and waited as the cuckolded youth's blindfold was removed.

Then, one by one the regiments were marched past the dead. Men from Virginia and Georgia, from the Carolinas and Tennessee, from Alabama and Louisiana, were all shown the three corpses, and after the infantry came the artillery and the engineers, all made to look into the eyes of the fly-infested dead, so that they would understand what fate awaited a deserter. General Jackson had been the first man to inspect the three corpses, and he had stared intently into the faces as though trying to understand the impulse that could drive a man to the unforgivable sin of desertion. As a Christian the General had to believe that such sinners could be redeemed, but as a soldier he could not imagine any of the three men knowing a moment's peace throughout eternity, and his face showed nothing but disgust as he twitched his horse's reins and headed toward the farm that served as his headquarters.

It was there, in a parlor that was hung with an ancient portrait of President George Washington and a newer one of President Jefferson Davis, that the General undertook his second unpleasant duty of the day. He stood with his ramrod-straight back to the portrait of Washington and, flanked by three senior staff officers, summoned General Washington Faulconer into his presence.

The parlor was a small room made even smaller by a map table that almost filled the space between its lime-washed walls. Washington Faulconer entered the room to find himself cribbed in a narrow space and faced by four men behind the map table, all standing and all looking uncomfortably like judges. He had half expected to be seated opposite the General, but instead this meeting was evidently to be conducted formally, and Washington Faulconer felt even more uncomfortable at that daunting prospect. He was wearing a borrowed sword and a borrowed jacket that was at least one size too big for him. Sweat was trickling into his golden beard. The small parlor stank of unwashed bodies and dirty clothes. "General," Faulconer said in cautious greeting as he stood opposite his commanding general.

Jackson said nothing at first but just stared at the fair-haired Faulconer. The General's face showed the exact same expression as when he had stared down at the three slack-jawed, chest-shattered deserters in their cheap pine coffins, and Faulconer, unable to meet the intensity of that blue-eyed gaze, looked guiltily away. "I gave orders," Jackson spoke at last in his clipped, high voice, "that all the crossings of the Rapidan were to be guarded."

"I—" Faulconer began, but was instantly silenced.

"Quiet!" Even Jackson's three staff officers felt a frisson of terror at the intensity of that command, while Washington Faulconer visibly shook. "I gave orders," Jackson began again, "that all the crossings of the Rapidan were to be guarded. Men of your brigade, General, discovered an unmapped ford and were intelligent enough to obey my orders. While you"—and here the General paused just long enough for a rictus to shiver his body—"countermanded them."

"I—" Faulconer began, and this time was stopped not by a word of command but simply by the look in the General's blue eyes.

"The damage?" Jackson turned abruptly to one of his most trusted aides, Major Hotchkiss, a scholarly and painstaking man who had been deputed to discover the truth about the night's incursion. Hotchkiss had arrived at the remnants of the Faulconer Brigade's headquarters at dawn and had spent the next two hours questioning survivors, and now, in a dry, neutral voice, he offered his horrid list.

"Fourteen dead, sir," Hotchkiss said, "and twenty-four seriously hurt. Those are soldiers, but there were at least six civilians killed, and three of those, maybe more, were women. We won't know for sure till the tavern ruins are cool enough to be searched." Hotchkiss's news was all the more damning for being announced in a placid voice. Major Hinton was among the dead, while Captain Murphy was wounded so grievously that no one was certain that his name would not soon be added to the grim tally.

"And among the dead is Captain Talliser, my aide," Jackson added in a dangerous voice.

No one responded.

"Captain Talliser was the son of a good friend," Jackson delivered his aide's obituary, "and was himself a loyal servant of Christ. He deserved better than to be mauled to death by night raiders."

In the back of the house a man's voice suddenly began singing "How sweet the name of Jesus sounds." Pots clattered in that distant room; then the hymn was interrupted by laughter. The sound of the pots woke a tabby cat that had been sleeping on the parlor's windowsill. The cat arched its back, yawned, delicately stretched out each front paw, then began to wash its face. Major Hotchkiss looked back to his list. "Of material losses, sir," he said, "my preliminary estimate is that sixteen thousand rifle cartridges were lost in the fire, plus eighty-six charges of powder and thirty-eight rounds of common shell. Two limbers, four caissons, and three wagons were burned out and at least six horses taken." Hotchkiss folded the list, then raised scornful eyes to Washington Faulconer. "Two battle flags were also carried away by the enemy."

Another pained silence ensued. It seemed to stretch forever before, at last, Jackson spoke again. "And how did the raiders cross the river?"

"At a place called Dead Mary's Ford," Hotchkiss answered, "which had been properly guarded until the previous night. The raiders were intercepted during their withdrawal and a prisoner taken. The raiders also lost one horse." Hotchkiss, a dry, stern man who had once taught school, added the fact of the horse's death in a sarcastic voice. Faulconer colored.

"And it was by your orders, General," Jackson said, ignoring Hotchkiss's sarcasm, "that the ford was uncovered."

This time Faulconer tried no defense. He looked up briefly, but he still could not meet Jackson's gaze, and so he looked down again. He wanted to say that he had only been trying to instill discipline into his Brigade and that he had lost his precious saber in the night and, worst of all, that the whole humiliation had been at the hands of his own son. And not just one humiliation, for his servant Nelson had returned that same morning with the dreadful tale of Adam's raid on Seven Springs, which meant that Adam had attacked both his mother and his father, and the realization of those two awful betrayals filled Faulconer's eyes with tears.

"You must have something to say, Faulconer," Jackson said.

Faulconer cleared his throat. "Accidents happen," he suggested feebly. "The ford," he shrugged, "it wasn't on the map, sir, merely a shallow spot. Lack of rain, really." He knew he was stammering like a fool and tried to pull himself together. Goddamn it! Was he not one of Virginia's wealthiest men? A landowner who could buy this Tom Fool general a million times over? And Faulconer tried to remember all the risible stories about Jackson: how the General taught in a Negro Sunday school and how he gave a tenth of his income to the church and how he took a cold bath at six o'clock every morning, summer and winter alike, and how he held his left hand in the air so the blood would not collect and turn an old wound rancid, but somehow the catalog of Jackson's eccentricities and imbecilities did not make Faulconer feel any more confident. "I deemed that the ford was not important," he managed to say.

"And what did you deem my orders to be?"

Faulconer frowned, not understanding the question.

"I ordered all fords, regardless of their importance, to be guarded," Jackson said. "You thought I was amusing myself by delivering such a command?"

Faulconer, defeated, could only shrug.

Jackson paused a second, then delivered his verdict. "You are dismissed from your command, General." Jackson's voice was harsher than ever, prompted not just by Faulconer's dereliction of duty but also by the tears he saw in Faulconer's eyes. General Jackson did not mind tears in their proper place: at a deathbed, say, or in contemplation of Christ's miraculous atonement, but not here where men spoke of duty. "You will leave this army forthwith," Jackson continued, "and report to the War Department in Richmond for further orders. If there are any further orders for you, which it is my fervent hope there are not. Dismissed!"

Faulconer looked up. He blinked back his tears. For a second it seemed he might try and protest the hard sentence, but then he turned without any acknowledgment and left the room.

Jackson waited for the door to close. "Political generals," he said bitterly, "are as fit for soldiering as lapdogs for hunting." He reached for Major Hotchkiss's list and read its depressing statistics without showing any sign of regret or surprise. "Make the arrangements for Faulconer's replacement," he said as he handed the paper back to the staff officer. Then he picked up his shabby hat in readiness for his visit to Lee's headquarters. A final thought struck him as he reached the door and he paused there, frowning. "The enemy did well," Jackson said, apparently to himself, "so we shall just have to do better."

It was midday before the ruins of McComb's Tavern were cool enough to let a work party retrieve the bodies from the heart of the wreckage, and even then the salvage work had to be done by men wearing protective strips of water-soaked sacking around their boots and hands. The corpses had been shrunk by the fierce heat into black, brittle manikins that smelt disturbingly of roasted pork. Starbuck supervised the work. He was still officially under arrest, but no one else seemed willing to take charge of the salvage, and so, while the Brigade marched off to witness the executions and while General Washington Faulconer waited at General Jackson's headquarters, Starbuck took a dozen men from his own company and set them to work.

"So what's happening?" Truslow had asked Starbuck at dawn when the early light revealed the blackened and smoking wreckage.

"Don't know."

"Are you under arrest?"

"Don't know."

"Who's commanding the Legion?"

"Medlicott," Starbuck said. Faulconer had made the appointment during the night.

"Dan Medlicott!" Truslow said disgustedly. "Why in hell's name appoint him?"

Starbuck did not answer. He felt slighted by the appointment, for he had been a captain long before Daniel Medlicott had bribed his way to the rank in the spring election, but Starbuck also understood that Washington Faulconer would never have appointed him to command the Legion. "I've got a job for you," Starbuck told Truslow instead. "The prisoner's being unhelpful." The man they had captured was called Sparrow and came from Virginia's Pendleton County, one of the fractious western counties that had declared themselves to be a new state loyal to the Union.

"I'll make the sumbitch squeal," Truslow said happily.

The morning wore on. Most of the Legion witnessed the three executions, but even when they returned to their encampment, they still seemed dazed and stupefied by the night's disasters. Of the Legion's captains only Medlicott, Moxey, and Starbuck remained alive and unwounded, and of the officers who had attended Major Hinton's birthday supper only Lieutenant Davies had survived serious harm. Davies had received a bullet slash on his left forearm but had escaped the worst of the massacre by taking cover behind the small church. "I could have done more," he kept telling Starbuck.

"And died? Don't be a fool. If you'd have opened fire they'd have hunted you down and killed you like a dog."

Davies shook at the memory. He was a tall, thin, bespectacled man, three years older than Starbuck and with a perpetually worried expression. He had been reading law in his uncle's office before the war began and had often confided in Starbuck his fears that he might never master the intricacies of that profession. "They knew there were women in the house," he now said to Starbuck.

"I know. You've told me." Starbuck's tone was callous and peremptory. In his view there was little point in endlessly discussing the night's tragedy in the vain hope of finding some consolation. The mess had to be cleaned up, avenged, and forgotten, which was why he was employing his company in retrieving the bodies from the burned-out tavern. Davies had come to watch the salvage, perhaps to remind himself how narrowly he had escaped being one of the shrunken, charred bodies.

"Murphy told them there were women inside," Davies said indignantly. "I heard him!"

"It doesn't matter," Starbuck said. He was watching the Cobb twins, who were rummaging among the ashes in the center of the burned building. Izard Cobb had found some coins and an ivory cribbage board that had somehow survived the fire undamaged. "Those go to Sergeant Waggoner!" Starbuck called across the ruins. The newly promoted Waggoner had been charged with collecting what few pitiable valuables might be rescued from the burned tavern.

"But it does matter!" Davies protested. "They killed women!"

"For Christ's sake"—Starbuck turned on the pale, bespectacled Davies—"you're about to get a captaincy, which means your men don't want to hear what went wrong last night. They want to hear how you intend to find the son of a damned bitch who did it to us and how you're going to kill him."

Davies looked shocked. "Captaincy?"

"I guess," Starbuck said. The night's disasters had virtually beheaded the Faulconer Legion, which meant there would either have to be wholesale promotions or else new people drafted in from other regiments.

"Maybe Pecker will come back?" Davies said wistfully, as though Colonel Bird could make everything in the Legion better.

"Pecker'll be back when he's mended," Starbuck said, "and that won't be for a few weeks yet." He suddenly whipped around to look at the wreckage again. "Cobb! If you've pocketed that silver I'll hang you!"

"I ain't pocketed nothing! You want to search me?"

"I'll search your brother," Starbuck said, and saw his suspicion that Izard Cobb would palm the coins to his brother Ethan had been plumb right. "Give the money to Sergeant Waggoner," he told Ethan Cobb, then watched as his orders were obeyed. "Now pick up that body." He pointed to the blackened figure of one of McComb's cooks.

Izard Cobb made a great display of horror. "She's a nigger, Captain!" he protested.

"If she was alive you'd have been happy enough to bed her, so now you can carry her to the grave. And do it respectfully!" Starbuck waited until the Cobb brothers had stooped to their work, then turned back to Davies. "They're lazy sons of bitches."

"All the Cobbs are lazy," Davies said, "always were. The family ruined some prime bottom land off Hankey's Run, just let it go to rack and ruin. A shame." His knowledge of such matters was a reminder that the Legion was still largely composed of men who came from within a day's walk of the town of Faulconer Court House; men who knew each other and each other's families and each other's business. Men like Starbuck, an outsider, were the exception. It was that close-knit family feeling that had added to the regiment's pain; when Major Hinton was killed, the Legion lost not just a commanding officer but a friend, a sidesman of the church, a brother-in-law, a creditor, a hunting companion, and above all, a neighbor, and if Murphy died they would lose another. "Still," Davies said, "Dan Medlicott is a decent man."

Starbuck believed Daniel Medlicott was a sly, ponderous, and cowardly fool, but he also knew better than to criticize one local man to another. Instead he turned away to watch as Izard and Ethan Cobb carried the distorted body free of the ashes. Truslow's inquisition of the captured cavalryman had revealed that it was not Adam who had been responsible for this massacre but a man called Blythe, yet Starbuck still felt an extraordinary bitterness toward his erstwhile friend. Adam had ridden the high moral horse for so long, preaching about the sanctity of the North's cause, and now he rode with men who slaughtered women.

"Starbuck!" Colonel Swynyard called from the road beside the burned wagon park.

Starbuck shouted at Truslow to take charge, then went to join Swynyard. "Five dead women." Starbuck delivered the final tally in a harsh voice. "Two cooks, McComb's wife, and the upstairs girls."

"The whores?"

"They were decent enough girls," Starbuck said. "One of them, anyway."

"I thought the tavern was out of bounds?"

"It was," Starbuck said.

"And I didn't think you had any money?"

"I don't, but she was a sweet girl."

"Sweet on you, you mean," Swynyard said tartly, then sighed. "I do pray for you, Starbuck, I do indeed."

"Fitzgerald, her name was," Starbuck said, "from Ireland. Her husband ran off and left her with a pile of debts, and she was just trying to pay them off." He stopped, suddenly overwhelmed with the misery of such a life and death. "Poor Kath," he said. He had been hoping Sally Truslow might help the girl, maybe by finding her a more lucrative job in Richmond, but now Kath Fitzgerald was a shrunken corpse waiting for a shallow grave. "I need a goddamned drink," Starbuck said bitterly.

"No, you don't," Swynyard said, "because you and I are summoned to headquarters. To see Jackson, and he's not a man to visit if you're stinking with whiskey."

"Oh, Christ," Starbuck blasphemed. He had hoped that the night's raid would have finished his troubles, but now it seemed Jackson himself had taken an interest in his derelictions. "What does Mad Jack want?"

"How would I know?" Swynyard said. He scuffed a foot in the road, which was still imprinted with the hoofmarks of the night's raiders. "He's seeing Faulconer now."

"Who'll be bitching about us."

"But we were right about Dead Mary's Ford," Swynyard said in a hopeful voice. "Maybe Jackson will acknowledge that?"

"Maybe," Starbuck said, but without any real hope that justice might be done. General Washington Faulconer would doubtless have his wrist slapped, but colonels and captains, especially poverty-stricken colonels and captains, made far more convenient scapegoats for disasters. Last night, when he had captured the prisoner at the ford, Starbuck had been sure that he could defeat Faulconer's malevolence, but in his interview with Major Hotchkiss, Jackson's aide, Starbuck had not felt a flicker of understanding or sympathy, just a dry disapproval. Justice, he reckoned, was a rare commodity. He swore at life's unfairness, then changed the subject by fishing a scrap of paper from his pocket. "Did you ever hear of a fellow named Joe Galloway?" he asked the Colonel.

Swynyard thought for a second, then nodded. "Cavalryman. Regular army. Never met him, but I've heard the name. Why?"

"He led last night's raid." Starbuck described what he had learned about Galloway's Horse; how it was composed of renegade Southerners who could ride the paths of Dixie with the same familiarity as rebel horsemen, and how a Captain Billy Blythe had led the detachment that had surrounded and savaged the tavern with their repeating rifles.

"How did you find all this out?" Swynyard asked.

"Prisoner talked," Starbuck said.

"I'm surprised he told you so much," Swynyard said, staring disconsolate at the scorched field where the remnants of the burned-out ammunition wagons stood.

"He struck up a kind of rapport with Truslow," Starbuck said. "It seems Galloway has a farm near Manassas that he's using as his depot, and I was kind of hoping we might get back there one day."

"To do what?"

"That," Starbuck said, pointing to the ruins of the tavern.

Swynyard shrugged. "I doubt we'll get the chance. Young Moxey says we're both to be posted to coastal defenses in the Carolinas."

"Moxey's a poxed piece of ratshit," Starbuck said.

"No doubt you once said that about me," the Colonel said.

"Oh no, sir," Starbuck grinned, "I was never that complimentary about you."

Swynyard smiled, then shook his head ruefully. "Be ready to leave in an hour, Starbuck. I'll arrange a horse for you. And stay sober, you hear me? That's an order."

"I'll stay sober, sir, I promise," for he had a whore to bury and a general to see.

Major Galloway's raiders did not survive entirely unscathed. The unfortunate Sparrow was captured, a Marylander was missing, while Corporal Harlan Kemp, the Virginian whose local knowledge had led the raiders to Dead Mary's Ford, had been shot in the belly. All those casualties had been caused during the brief and unexpected fight at the river, which had left Kemp in terrible pain. He spent the homeward journey drifting in and out of consciousness, and every few minutes he would beg one of the men supporting him in his saddle to do him the same favor they would render to a badly wounded horse. "Just shoot me, for the love of Christ, please shoot me."

Adam carried Kemp's rifle and one of the captured flags. He was continually looking for any sign of pursuit, but no rebel pursuers appeared as the raiders crossed the Robertson River, then the Hazel and the Aestham, each waterway more swollen with storm water than the last, until just after midday they came to the flooded Rappahannock and were forced to ride six miles upstream to find a passable ford. Then, safe at last on the northern bank, they rode east toward the rail depot at Bealeton.

Two miles outside the town a shell screamed overhead to explode in a gout of mud and smoke just a hundred paces behind the horsemen. Galloway ordered the Stars and

Stripes unfurled. A second shell howled past to smash into a pine tree, splitting the wood with a smoky crack that startled the tired horses, so that the troopers had to struggle with their reins and slash back with spurs. They could see the roofs of Bealeton beyond the trees and see the smoke of the artillery edging one of those patches of woodland. More smoke, this time from a locomotive, plumed up from the town itself. "The rebels can't have captured the place!" Galloway said and told the standard-bearer to wave the flag more vigorously.

The field gun did not fire again. Instead an apologetic Northern artillery officer rode out to investigate the horsemen and to explain that General Pope was nervous of rebel cavalry who might be probing the Federal army's new positions on the Rappahannock's north bank. "We've seen no secesh horse," Galloway told the artilleryman, then spurred on into a town crammed with confused soldiery. Troops that had embarked in Alexandria and Manassas expecting to arrive in Culpeper Court House now waited for new orders, and meanwhile the rails south of Bealeton were being torn up and carried north for safekeeping, and the trains employed on that task were blocked by the stalled troop trains that had been heading south, so that now there were no fewer than eight trains marooned at the depot. The town's roads were equally clogged. There were men who had lost their regiments, regiments that had lost their brigades, and brigades that had lost their divisions. Staff officers sweated and shouted contradictory orders, while the townspeople, most of whom were rebel sympathizers, watched with amusement. Galloway and Adam added to the noise as they demanded a doctor for Corporal Kemp, while every few moments a nervous Northern gunner on the outskirts of the town would contribute to the chaos by loosing a shell into the steaming heat of the countryside in an attempt to see off some nonexistent Southern horsemen.

"Makes you proud to be a Yankee, don't it?" Galloway said sourly as he forced a path through the chaos. "I thought these boys were supposed to be marching down Richmond's Main Street, not running away?"

A doctor was found, and Harlan Kemp could at last be lifted from his horse. His pants were stuck to the saddle's leather by a mass of dried blood and had to be cut away before the moaning man could be carried into the Presbyterian church lecture hall that was serving as a hospital. A doctor gave the Corporal ether, then extracted the bullet from his guts, but claimed there was little more that could be done for him in Bealeton. "There's a hospital car on one of the trains," the harried doctor said, "and the sooner he's back in Washington the better." He did not sound hopeful.

Adam helped carry Kemp on a stretcher to the depot, where nurses of the Christian Sanitary Commission took the sweating and shivering Corporal under their care. The hospital car was a sleeping car requisitioned from the New York Central and still possessed its peacetime cuspidors, fringed curtains, and engraved lamp shades, though now the luxurious bunks were attended by four nurses and two army doctors, who were protected by a pair of faded red flags that hung at either end of the car's roof to proclaim that the vehicle was a hospital. Perforated zinc screens in the car's roof were supposed to provide ventilation, but there was no wind, and so the car stank of castor oil, urine, blood, and excreta. Major Galloway attached a label to Kemp's collar that gave his name, rank, and unit, put a few coins into a pocket of the Corporal's uniform coat, then he and Adam climbed down from the pustulant car to walk slowly past a heap of coffins carrying stenciled labels directing their contents homeward. There were corpses going to Pottstown, Pennsylvania; Goshen, Connecticut; Watervliet, New York; Biddeford, Maine; Three Lakes, Wisconsin; Springfield, Massachusetts; Allentown, Pennsylvania; Lima, Ohio; and Adam, reading the roll call of town names and knowing that each represented a family distraught and a town in mourning, winced.

"Faulconer! Major Galloway!" An imperious voice broke into Adam's reflections. At first neither he nor Major Galloway could see who had summoned them; then they saw a white-haired man waving vigorously from a window further up the train. "Wait there!" the man shouted. "Wait there!"

It was the Reverend Elial Starbuck, who, in deference to the oppressive heat, was wearing a linen jacket over his shirt and Geneva bands. Having attracted their attention, he worked his way out of the crowded passenger car and jumped down to the trackside, where he pulled on a ragged straw hat that had replaced his lost top hat. "You have news?" he demanded. "Good news, I trust? We need good news. You observe we are retreating again?" The preacher made this speech as he plunged toward the two cavalrymen, dividing the crowds with the aid of his ebony cane. "I fail to understand these things, I truly do. We have raised an army, the largest that God has seen fit to put upon the face of the earth, yet whenever a rebel scowls at us we scuttle backward like trespassing children fleeing a householder." The Reverend Elial Starbuck made this trenchant criticism despite the presence of a number of senior Federal officers who scowled at his words, but there was an authority in the Reverend Starbuck's presence that subdued any attempt to contradict his opinions. "No one is sure, anymore, if they can capture Richmond or whether they will simply defend the Rappahannock. There is confusion." The Reverend Starbuck made the accusation darkly. "If I administered a church the way this government runs an army, then I daresay Satan would turn Boston into an outpost of hell without so much as a bleat of opposition. It's too bad, too bad! I had hoped to return home with better news than this."

"To Boston? You're returning so soon?" Major Galloway asked politely.

"I undertook to be back in my pulpit by month's end. If I believed the capture of Richmond was imminent, then I would beg my congregation's indulgence and stay with the army, but I can no longer believe any such thing. I had hoped your horsemen might inspire the army. I recall some talk of making raids on Richmond?" This accusation was accompanied by a scowl from the preacher. "We shilly-shally, Major. We linger. We tremble at the slightest sign of the enemy. We leave the Lord's work undone, preferring timidity to boldness. It grieves me, Major, it truly grieves me. But I am making notes, and I shall report my findings to the Northern people!"

Major Galloway tried to reassure the preacher that Pope's retreat was merely a temporary precaution intended to give the North time to build its army into an irresistible force, but the Reverend Starbuck would have none of such reasoning. He had learned from one of Pope's aides that the retreat behind the Rappahannock had been calculated to take advantage of the defensive capability of the river's steep northern bank. "We have gone on the defensive!" the Reverend Starbuck exclaimed in a disgusted voice. "Would there have been an Israel if Joshua had merely defended the river Jordan? Or a United States if George Washington had done nothing but dig ditches behind the Delaware? The Lord's work, Major, is not done by digging and tarrying, but by smiting the enemy! 'And it shall be, when thou shalt hear a sound of going in the tops of the mulberry trees, then shalt thou go out to battle: for God is gone forth before thee to smite the host of the Philistines.' Does not the First Book of Chronicles promise us as much? Then why are we not hearkening to the mulberries and going forth!" The Reverend Starbuck asked the question magisterially.

"I'm certain we shall be advancing soon," Galloway said, wondering what mulberries had to do with the prosecution of war.

"Then, alas, I must read about your advance in the *Journal* rather than witness it for myself. If, indeed, I ever reach Boston again." This last sentence was uttered in savage reproof of the chaos in Bealeton's small depot. The Reverend Starbuck had been waiting a full day to leave for Manassas Junction, but his train was trapped in the town by three supply trains that were being unloaded. No one knew how long that unloading would take, nor even if the offloaded supplies might not need to be reloaded in preparation for a further retreat. "Still, we are not without our comforts," the preacher said sarcastically, "so follow me," and he led the two cavalrymen to the end of the depot, where volunteer ladies from the Christian Sanitary Commission were serving reconstituted lemonade, buckwheat bread, and ginger cakes. The Reverend Starbuck wiped the sweat from his face with an enormous handkerchief, then used his cane to force a way to the trestle table, where he demanded three servings of the refreshments. One of the ladies timidly pointed to a hand-lettered sign proclaiming that the comestibles were for the consumption of uniformed men only, but one ferocious glance from the preacher quelled her small protest.

Once the ginger cakes and lemonade were secured and a suitable spot found for their consumption, Major Galloway gave the Reverend Starbuck the splendid news. John Pope's army might be retreating, but Galloway's Horse had stung the enemy. The Major forgivably exaggerated the damage his raiders had inflicted on the rebels, multiplying the wagons and ammunition destroyed at least fourfold, and while admitting to his own casualties, he claimed his men must have killed at least two score of rebels. "We left their camp smoking with fire, sir," Galloway said, "and reeking of blood."

The Reverend Starbuck put down his mug of lemonade so he could join his hands in a prayerful clasp. "'Bless the Lord,'" he said, "'who smote great nations and slew mighty kings!'"

"The news is better still, sir," Adam said, for while Kemp had been under the doctor's knife, Adam had found paper and string and made a parcel addressed to the Reverend Elial Starbuck on Walnut Street in Boston. He had been planning to send the parcel from the depot, but now he could deliver the prize personally.

It was obvious from the consistency of the package that it contained cloth, and the Reverend Starbuck, prodding with his finger, was scarce able to believe what he suspected. "It isn't . . ." he began, then without waiting to finish his question he tore the paper and string greedily away to reveal a bundle of folded scarlet silk slashed with white and blue. The preacher sighed as he held up a golden fringe of the rebel battle flag. "God bless you, my dear boy," he told Adam, "God bless you."

Adam intended to keep the Faulconer standard for himself, just as he intended to use his father's saber and revolver, but the battle flag, the red silk flag with the eleven white stars on the blue Saint Andrew's cross, was a gift for the Reverend Elial Starbuck: a trophy dragged from the filthy heart of secession that the preacher could use to show his subscribers that their donations were not being wasted. "I'm not sure if you want to know this, sir," Adam continued diffidently as the preacher gazed entranced at the beautiful silk, "but that flag comes from Nate's battalion."

But the mention of his son's name only enhanced the preacher's pleasure. "You took Nate's tawdry rag away, did you? Well done!"

"You'll take it to Boston, sir?" Major Galloway asked.

"I surely will. We shall put it on display, Major. We shall hang it for all to see, and maybe we shall invite people to throw mud at it on payment of a small sum toward the war effort. Then we shall burn it next July fourth." He gazed at the rich red silk, and a shudder mixed of lust and loathing racked his body. "'And your altars shall be desolate,'" he said in his marvelous voice, "'and your images shall be broken: and I will cast down your slain men before your idols. He that is far off shall die of the pestilence; and he that is near shall fall by the sword, and he that remaineth and is besieged shall die by the famine: thus will I accomplish my fury upon them. Then shall ye know that I am the Lord.'" There were a few seconds of awed silence from the dozens of people who had turned to listen to the preacher, who now, to show that his peroration was done, picked up his mug of lemonade. "The prophet Ezekiel," he added helpfully.

"Amen," Major Galloway said weakly. "Amen."

"So what becomes of you now, Major?" the Reverend Starbuck asked as he bundled the flag together. He had ripped the wrapping paper into useless shreds, but he managed to salvage enough string to tie the big silk folds into an approximation of neatness.

"We'll look to do some work here, sir. Hurt the enemy again, I hope."

"It's the Lord's work you're engaged in," the preacher said, "so do it well! Lay their land waste, Major, strike them down! And God give your arm the strength of ten while you do it. You'll write a full account of your raid? So I might publish it to our subscribers?"

"Of course, sir."

"Then on to victory! On to victory!" The Reverend Doctor Starbuck thrust his empty lemonade mug into Adam's hand, and then, carrying the rebel flag as proudly as though he had captured it himself, went back to wait in his car.

Galloway sighed, shook his head in marvel at such energy, then went to find someone, anyone, who might have orders for his cavalry.

Colonel Swynyard and a nervous Captain Starbuck waited all afternoon to see General Thomas Jackson, and they were still waiting as dusk fell and as one of the General's aides brought a pair of lanterns out to the veranda of the house where Jackson had his headquarters. "Not that he sleeps in the house," the aide said, stopping to gossip. "He prefers the open air."

"Even when it's raining?" Starbuck forced himself to make conversation. He did not feel like socializing, not when he was facing an unpleasant interview, but the aide seemed friendly enough.

"Just so long as it ain't storming." The aide clearly relished retailing stories of his master's eccentricities. "And he's up every morning at six to take a cold dip. Jaybird naked and shoulders under. Out here he uses that old horse trough and on a summer morning that might be pleasant enough, but in winter I've seen Old Jack skim the ice off a tub before baptizing himself." The aide smiled, then turned as a black man appeared around the side of the house. "Jim!" he called. "Tell these gentlemen what the General likes to eat."

"He don't like to eat nothing!" the black man grumbled. "He eats worse than a heathen. It's like cooking for a fighting cock."

"Mr. Lewis is the General's servant," the aide said. "Not his slave, his servant."

"And he's a great man." Jim Lewis's admiration for the eccentric Jackson was every bit as heartfelt as the uniformed aide's. "There ain't more than a dozen men like the General in all the world, and that's a straight fact, and there ain't any man in the wide world like the General for the whippin' of Yankees, and that's a straighter fact, but he still eats worse than a goat."

"Nothing but stale bread, dirt-plain meat, egg yolk, and buttermilk," the aide said, "and fruit in the morning, but only in the morning. He reckons that fruit ingested in the afternoon is bad for the blood, you see."

"While the General's real bad for Yankee blood!" Lewis said with a laugh. "He sure is lethal for Yankee blood!" Lewis dipped a pail in the General's bathtub, then carried the water toward the kitchen at the back of the house, while the aide carried his second lantern to the far end of the porch. Voices sounded inside the house where candlelight shone at a muslin-curtained window.

"Win battles, Starbuck, and you can be whatever it pleases you to be," Swynyard said bitterly. "You can be mad, you can be eccentric, you can even be rich and privileged like Faulconer." The Colonel paused, watching the dark fall over the far woods and fields where the host of campfires glimmered. "You know what Faulconer's fault is?"

"Being alive," Starbuck said sourly.

"He wants to be liked." Swynyard ignored Starbuck's venom. "He really believes he can make the men like him by treating them leniently, but it won't ever work. Men don't like an officer for being easy. They don't mind being treated like dogs, like slaves even, so long as you give them victory. But treat them soft and give them defeats and they'll despise you forever. It don't matter what kind of man you are, what kind of rogue you are, just so long as you lead the men to victory." He paused, and Starbuck guessed the Colonel was reflecting on his own career rather than Faulconer's.

"Colonel Swynyard? Captain Starbuck?" Another aide appeared in the doorway. His voice was peremptory and his manner that of a man who wants to discharge an unpleasant duty quickly. "This way."

Starbuck plucked his coat straight, then followed Swynyard through the hall and into a candlelit parlor that was much too small for the trestle table that served as a stand for the General's maps. Not that Starbuck had time to take in the room's furnishings, for as soon as he entered he felt himself come under the fierce and off-putting gaze of the extraordinary figure who glared at the two visitors from the table's far side.

Jackson said nothing as the two men were shown in. The General was flanked by Major Hotchkiss and another staff officer. Swynyard, hat in hand, gave a short, sharp nod in salute, while Starbuck just stood to attention and stared at the gaunt, rough-bearded face with its bright wild eyes and malevolent frown; a face, Starbuck suddenly realized, that was uncommonly like Colonel Swynyard's own ravaged visage. "Swynyard"—Jackson finally acknowledged his visitors— "once of the 4th U.S. Infantry. But not a good record. Accused of drunkenness, I see." He had a sheaf of papers that he glanced at continually. "You were court-martialed and acquitted."

"Wrongly," Swynyard said, causing Jackson to look up from the papers in surprise.

"Wrongly?" the General asked. Like many artillery officers he was notoriously hard of hearing, his eardrums having been hammered by too many cannon blasts. "Did you say you were wrongly acquitted?"

"Wrongly, sir!" Swynyard spoke louder. "I should have been cashiered, sir, for I truly was drunk, sir, frequently drunk, sir, helplessly drunk, sir, unforgivably drunk, sir, but thanks to the saving grace of our Lord Jesus Christ, sir, I shall be drunk no more."

Jackson, confronted with this ready admission of guilt, seemed rather taken aback. He drew another sheet of paper from the sheaf and frowned as he read it. "Brigadier General Faulconer"—he said the name with a wry tone of distaste— "talked with me this morning. Afterwards he saw fit to write me this letter. In it, Swynyard, he says that you are a drunkard, while you, young man, are described as an immoral, womanizing, and ungrateful liar." The hard blue-gray eyes looked up at Starbuck.

"He's also a fine soldier, General," Swynyard put in.

"Also?" The General pounced on the word.

Starbuck suddenly resented the inquisition. He had been trying to win a damn war, not run a Sunday school. "Also," he said flatly and then, after a very long pause, "sir."

Hotchkiss looked intently down at his feet. Two of the candles on the map table were guttering badly, sending streams of sooty smoke to the yellowed ceiling. In the back of the house a voice began singing "How Sweet the Name of Jesus Sounds." Jackson looked momentarily annoyed by the sound; then he slowly lowered himself into a straight-backed chair, or rather he perched on the edge of the cane seat with his spine held rigidly parallel to, but not touching, the back. Starbuck supposed that his stupid belligerence had just destroyed any chance of receiving lenience, but it was too late to back down now.

Jackson turned his gaze back to Swynyard. "When did you find Christ, Colonel?" he asked, and Swynyard answered with a passionate testimony of seeing the light on the battlefield of Cedar Mountain. For a moment he ceased to be a soldier talking to his superior, but became just a simple man talking to his brother in Christ. He told of his former sinfulness and of his continual drunkenness, and he contrasted that fallen condition with his newfound state of grace. It was a testimony of salvation like the thousands of others that Starbuck had heard, the same kind of transforming story that had comprised the bulk of his youthful reading, and he supposed that the General, too, must have heard a myriad of such tales, but Jackson was plainly enthralled by Swynyard's tale.

"And now, Colonel," Jackson asked when the testimony was done, "do you still crave ardent spirits?"

"Every day, sir," Swynyard said fervently, "every minute of every day, but with the help of our Lord Jesus Christ I shall abstain."

"The great danger of temptation," Jackson said in a rather puzzled voice, "is how very tempting it is." He turned his gaze on Starbuck. "And you, young man, were brought up in a Christian household, were you not?"

"Yes, sir." A tabby cat had started to wind itself around Starbuck's ankles, rubbing its flanks on his frayed trouser ends and playing with the tags of his bootlaces.

"This letter claims you're a Northerner?" Jackson said, gesturing at Faulconer's letter, which now lay on the table.

"From Boston, sir."

"So why then are you fighting for the South?" Jackson frowned.

"That was the womanizing, sir," Starbuck said defiantly. He sensed Swynyard stir beside him, and he guessed the Colonel was trying to convey the message that Starbuck should quell his combativeness, but Starbuck was annoyed by the implication that he needed to prove his loyalty to these Southerners. The cat was purring loudly.

"Go on," Jackson said in a dangerously toneless voice.

Starbuck shrugged. "I followed a woman south, sir, then stayed on here because I liked it."

271

Jackson stared into Starbuck's face for a few seconds. He seemed to dislike what he saw and looked down at the papers instead. "We have to decide what to do with the Brigade. It isn't in a good state, eh, Hotchkiss?"

Hotchkiss gave a very small shrug. "No reserve ammunition, no transport, and one regiment virtually officerless."

Jackson looked at Swynyard. "Well?"

"We'll just have to take the ammunition from the enemy, sir," Swynyard said.

Jackson liked that answer. He turned his gaze back to Starbuck, who was suddenly and belatedly realizing that this interview was not a disciplinary affair but something altogether different. "What is this army's greatest failing?" Jackson asked Starbuck.

Starbuck's mind whirled in panic. Its greatest failing? For a second, remembering the morning's executions, he was tempted to say desertion, but before his tongue could frame the word a previous thought blurted itself out. "Straggling, sir." Some regiments lost a quarter of their number through men falling out of the ranks during long marches, and though a good number of those stragglers reappeared within a day or two, some went missing forever. He had given the General a good answer, but even so Starbuck wished he had thought for a moment longer and given a more considered response.

Then, astonishingly, he saw he had answered correctly, for Jackson was nodding his approval. "And how have you prevented straggling in your unit, Starbuck?"

"I just tell the sons of bitches they're free to go, sir," Starbuck said.

"You do what?" Jackson barked in his high voice. Hotchkiss looked alarmed, and the other staff officer shook his head as though he pitied Starbuck's stupidity.

"I just tell them they can leave the regiment, sir, but I

272

also tell them that they ain't allowed to leave with any property of the Confederate government just in case they straggle all the way home or into the enemy's arms. So I tell them they're free to go, but first I strip the sons of bitches stark naked and confiscate their guns. Then I kick them out."

Jackson stared at him. "You do that? Truly?"

It was hard to tell whether the General approved or not, but Starbuck could not back out of the tale now. "I did it once, sir," he admitted, "just the once. But I only needed to do it the once, sir, because we haven't had another straggler since. Except for the sick, sir, and they're different."

Starbuck's voice tailed away as the General began to behave in the strangest fashion. First he brought up a bony knee, then he clasped the raised knee in both his huge hands, and after that he rocked his body back as far as the stiff chair would allow. Then he put his head back and opened his mouth as wide as it would go though without uttering any sound at all. Starbuck wondered if the General was suffering a seizure, but then he saw the two staff officers grinning, and he realized that this odd display was Jackson's peculiar method of displaying amusement.

The General stayed in the weird pose for a few seconds, then rocked forward again, let his knee go, and shook his head. He was silent for a few more seconds, then turned to Swynyard. "How old are you, Colonel?"

"Fifty-four, sir," Swynyard said, sounding rather ashamed. Fifty-four was old for a soldier unless, like Lee, he was the commander in chief. Jackson himself was thirty-eight, while most of the fighting was done by boys yet to see their twenty-first birthday.

But Jackson's point was not about the optimum age for a soldier, but was instead a theological comment. "I was myself of mature years before I found Christ, Colonel. I do not say

273

one should be of ripe age before conversion, but nor should we blame the young for failing to do what we ourselves did not do. As for your womanizing"—he looked at Starbuck—"marriage will cure that if self-discipline fails. I find that daily immersion in cold water and regular exercise helps. Chop wood, young man, or swing from a branch. You can leap fences. But exercise! Exercise!" He suddenly stood and snatched up Washington Faulconer's letter, which he held into a candle flame. He held the paper in the flame until it was well alight, then moved it gently and safely into the empty fireplace, where he watched it burn into ash. "War brings change," he said as he turned back to his visitors. "It changed me, it will change you. I confirm your appointments. You, Colonel Swynyard, will take over Faulconer's Brigade and you, Major Starbuck, will take command of his Legion. In return you will fight for me, and fight harder than you have ever fought in your lives. We are not here to defeat the enemy, but with God's help to destroy him, and I look for your help in that ambition. If I receive that help I will accept it as your duty, but if you fail then I shall send you both after Faulconer. Good night to you."

Starbuck could not move. He had entered the room expecting punishment and had instead received promotion, and not just promotion, but command of his own regiment. My God! He had command of the Legion, and suddenly he felt terrified of the responsibility. He was only twenty-two, surely much too young to command a regiment; then he remembered Micah Jenkins, the Georgian who had led his whole brigade hard and deep into the Yankee army at Seven Pines, and Jenkins was not much older than Starbuck himself. There were other officers in their twenties who were leading regiments and brigades, so why should Starbuck not be ready?

"Good night, gentlemen!" Jackson said pointedly.

Starbuck and Swynyard were both startled from their

astonishment. They allowed themselves to be led outside by an aide, who offered his own congratulations on the lantern-lit porch. "Major Hotchkiss," the aide said, "recommended you both. He felt that the Brigade had suffered enough without having outsiders thrust on it."

"Give him our thanks," Swynyard said.

"And if I might give some advice, gentlemen," the aide said, "you should have your men cook as many rations as they possess and have them ready for a very early march in the morning." He smiled and walked back into the house.

"My God," Swynyard said faintly, "a brigade." The Colonel seemed moved nearer to tears than to exultation. He was silent for a few seconds, and Starbuck guessed he was praying; then Swynyard led the way to where their horses were picketed. "I wasn't altogether honest with you earlier," the Colonel said as he untied his horse. "I knew Hotchkiss was sounding me out about the Legion's new commanding officer, but I dared not raise your hopes. Or mine, I confess."

Starbuck clumsily mounted the borrowed horse. "Medlicott won't be happy."

"The object of this war," Colonel Swynyard said tartly, "is to correct Abraham Lincoln's political misconceptions, not to make Captain Medlicott happy." He waited until Starbuck had settled himself in the saddle. "I thought you were going to upset Jackson."

Starbuck grinned. "Old Jack can hardly be expected to approve of womanizing, can he?"

Swynyard looked up at the sky. The last clouds had gone, and there was a splendor of stars arching over their heads. "I suppose I shouldn't pass on rumor," the Colonel said, "but there are stories that Old Jack had a love child once. Long ago. The stories are probably untrue, but who knows? Maybe you have to know sin before you can hate it. Maybe the best of Christians are made from the worst of sinners?"

"So there's hope for me yet?" Starbuck asked teasingly.

"Only if you win battles, Starbuck, only if you win battles." The Colonel looked at the younger man. "The Legion won't be an easy job, Starbuck."

"No, sir, but I'm the best man for it." Starbuck smiled at the Colonel. "I'm an arrogant son of a bitch, but by God I can fight." And now he had a whole regiment to fight for him, and he could not wait to start.

General Thomas Jackson put the interview with Swynyard and Starbuck out of his mind the very second that they left the room, concentrating instead on the maps that Major Hotchkiss had painstakingly drawn for him. Those hand-made maps, spread edge to edge on the trestle table where their corners were weighted down by candlesticks, showed the country north of the Rappahannock, the country where Robert Lee's impudent and daring idea would be put to the test. It was an idea that Jackson liked because it was challenging, and because it held immense possibilities.

Which meant it also held enormous risks.

The enemy was digging in beyond the steep northern bank of the Rappahannock, inviting the rebels to throw away their lives in vain attacks across the deep river. The enemy doubtless planned to stay behind the river while more and more of McClellan's regiments joined their ranks until, at last, their numbers were overpowering and they felt confident of sweeping Lee's ragged army clean out of history.

So Lee, in response, was proposing to break one of the fundamental rules of war. Lee was planning to split his already outnumbered army into two smaller armies, each one horribly vulnerable to attack. That vulnerability was the risk, but it was a risk predicated on the likelihood that John Pope would not attack but would instead sit tight behind his steep riverbank and wait for McClellan's regiments to swell his ranks.

So Lee planned to divert Pope's attention by making threatening movements on the Rappahannock's southern bank, and while Pope watched that diversion, Thomas Jackson would march westward with the smaller rebel army. Jackson would march with just twenty-four thousand men, who would go west, then north, and then, with God's help, eastward until they had hooked far and deep into the enemy's rear, and once behind Pope's lines that small rebel army would cut and slash and burn and destroy until John Pope would be forced to turn back to destroy it. Then the small army, the vulnerable army, would have to fight like the devil itself to give Lee time to come to its aid, but at least the rebels would be fighting on ground of their own choosing and not attacking across a blood-dyed river. Jackson's small army was the anvil, and Lee's bigger army the hammer, and by God's good grace John Pope's army would be caught between the two.

But if the hammer and anvil failed to come together, then the history books would say that Lee and Jackson had thrown away a country by breaking the basic rules of war. By mere tomfoolery.

But tomfoolery was the only weapon the rebels had left. And it might just work.

So tomorrow, in the dawn, Tom Fool Jackson would march.

THEY MARCHED

They marched like they had never marched in their lives before and like they hoped they would never have to march again.

They marched like no troops had ever marched, and they did it through a day as hot as hell and as dry as hell's bones, and through a thick dust kicked up by the men and horses who marched in front; a dust that coated their tongues and thickened their throats and stung their eyes.

They marched on broken boots or with no boots at all. They marched because Old Mad Jack had told them he expected them to march, but no one knew why they were marching or where. First they marched west into a plump country unvisited by forage parties from either army, where the folk greeted the leading regiments with crackers, cheese, and milk, but there was not enough food to serve all the men who trudged past: regiment after regiment, brigade after brigade, the long hurting line of Jackson's foot cavalry heading west into America with dust on their faces and blood in their boots and sweat in their beards. "Where are you going, boys?" an old man shouted at the troops.

"Going to lick the Yankees, Pa!" one man found the energy to call back, but no one except the General really knew their destination.

"Lick 'em good, boys! Lick the sumbitches good and hard!"

The Legion had been woken at three in the morning by bugles that had stirred weary men from a shallow sleep. The soldiers grumbled and cursed at Old Jack, then blew their fires alive to boil their foul-tasting coffee.

Starbuck issued all the ammunition the Legion possessed. Each man would carry thirty rounds, half the usual issue, but that was all the cartridges that were left him. The men would carry their thirty rounds, their weapons, their bedroll, and a haversack with as much hardtack and boiled beef as they could carry, but they could carry nothing else. All knapsacks and heavy baggage were to be left south of the Rappahannock under a corporal's guard of wounded and sick men too weak to march.

Daniel Medlicott, whose promotion to major had been Washington Faulconer's final gift to the Legion, came with Sergeant Major Tolliver to make a formal protest at Starbuck's orders. If the Legion met an enemy, they said, then the men could not fight properly with only half an issue of ammunition. Starbuck, nervous at this first challenge to his authority, had delayed the confrontation by stooping to his campfire and lighting himself a cigar. "We'll just have to fight twice as hard then," he said, trying to turn away their unhappiness with levity.

"It isn't a joke, Starbuck," Medlicott said.

"Of course it isn't a joke!" Starbuck snapped the rejoinder louder than he had intended. "It's war! You don't give up fighting just because you don't have everything you want. The Yankees do that, not us. Besides, we ain't fighting alone. All of Jackson's men are marching with us."

The Sergeant Major looked unhappy but did not press the argument. Starbuck suspected Medlicott had talked the Sergeant Major into joining a protest that arose more from Medlicott's pique than from a genuine concern, and Medlicott, Starbuck conceded, did have cause to feel misused. For one day the miller had thought himself the commander of the Faulconer Legion, and then, out of the blue, the man he most disliked in the regiment had been promoted over his head. Medlicott maintained his protest had a more noble aim than salving his hurt pride. "You don't understand," he told Starbuck, "because you're not a local man. But I am, and these are my neighbors"—he waved a hand at the Legion—"and it's my duty to get them home to their wives and little ones."

"Makes you wonder why we're fighting a war at all," Starbuck said.

Medlicott blinked at the Bostonian, unsure how to understand the remark. "I don't think we should march," he reiterated his protest heavily. "And it won't be my fault if there's disaster."

"Of course it won't be your fault," Starbuck spoke caustically. "It'll be my fault, just as it'll be my fault if there ain't a disaster." A year before, he thought, his pride in being grammatical would never have allowed him to say "ain't," but now, to his private amusement, his Boston accent was following his allegiance south. "And your duty, Major," he went on, "is not to make sure your neighbors get home, but to make damn sure the Yankees get home, and if the sumbitches don't have the sense to go of their own accord, then your duty is to send them back to their wives and little ones inside boxes. That's your duty. Good morning to you both." He turned away from the two unhappy men. "Captain Truslow!"

Truslow shambled over. "Just Truslow's good enough," he said.

"Your company's at the rear," Starbuck said, "and you know what to do if you find stragglers." He paused. "And that includes straggling officers." Truslow nodded his bleak assent. In addition to commanding Company H Truslow also had command of the regiment's eight surviving draught horses that had once pulled the ammunition wagons and supply carts. Now, without any vehicles to drag, they would serve as ambulances for the men who genuinely could not keep up the pace.

The Legion marched at dawn. The order to leave their heavy baggage behind had alerted the men to the fact that this was to be no ordinary march, no stroll through the countryside from one bivouac to another, but no one had been prepared for a march as hard as this. Thomas Jackson usually allowed his men a ten-minute rest every hour, but not today. Today they marched without any rest stops, and there were staff officers beside the road to make sure no one dawdled, and there were more staff officers waiting at the first ford to make certain no man paused to take off his boots or roll up his pants. "Just keep marching!" the staff officers shouted. "Keep going! Come on!" The troops obeyed, squelching out of the ford to leave wet footprints that dried swiftly under the hot August sun.

The sun rose still higher. It had been one of the hottest summers in living memory, yet today it seemed as though the heat would reach new heights of discomfort. Sweat drove trickles through the layers of dust that caked men's faces. Sometimes, when the road ran across the summit of a shallow crest, they would see the line of infantry stretching far ahead and far behind, and they guessed that a whole corps was on the march, but where it was going only God and Old Jack knew. They did not march in step but loped along in the gait of experienced infantrymen who knew they would have to endure this agony a whole day through. "Close up!" the sergeants shouted whenever a gap appeared in a company's files, and the call would echo up and down the long shambling line. "Close up! Close up!" They passed parched fields, dried ponds, and empty barns. Farm dogs growled from the road's verges and sometimes started fights with the soldiers' pet dogs; such fights were usually popular diversions, but today the sergeants kicked the beasts apart and beat the country dogs away with rifle butts. "Keep going! Close up!" Every hour or so one of the cavalry patrols that were screening the march from the enemy's horsemen would canter past the Legion on its way to take up new positions far ahead of the long column, and the horsemen would answer the infantrymen's questions by saying they had seen no enemy. So far, it seemed, the Yankees were oblivious to Jackson's men as they moved across the hot summer landscape.

Men hobbled as muscles first tightened and then seized with cramp. The pain began in the calves, then spread to the thighs. Some men, like Starbuck, wore boots they had taken at Cedar Mountain, and within a few miles those new boots had worn men's heels and toes to bloody blisters. Starbuck took his boots off and tied them round his neck, then marched barefoot. For a few hundred yards he left small bloody footprints in the dust; then the blisters dried but went on hurting. His feet hurt, his legs ached, there was a stitch in his side, his throat burned, his bad tooth throbbed, his lips were cracked, his eyes stung with the sweat and dust, and this was just the start of the march.

Some officers rode horses. Swynyard was mounted, as were Major Medlicott and Captain Moxey. Moxey was now back with the Legion. Starbuck had not wanted him, but nor did Swynyard want him to stay as an aide, and so Moxey was now the Captain of Company B. The newly promoted Major Medlicott had gone to Company A with the consolatory honor of commanding the Legion's four right-flank companies. Moxey had the next company, Sergeant Patterson, now Lieutenant Patterson, had command of C, while Murphy's old Lieutenant, Ezra Pine, was now the

Captain of D Company. The left four companies had Sergeant Howes, now a Lieutenant, in command of E, a Captain Leighton, who had been borrowed from Haxall's Arkansas regiment to command Company F, Captain Davies took over Medlicott's old Company G, and Truslow, whom Starbuck had insisted on promoting into a full Captain, was in charge of Company H.

It was a ramshackle list of officers, cobbled together from disaster, and the men in the Legion knew it was makeshift and did not like it. Starbuck understood the disquiet. Most men did not want to be soldiers. They did not want to be torn away from home and women and familiarity, and even the most reckless young man's sense of adventure could be quickly eroded by minié bullets and Parrott gun shells. What held these reluctant warriors to their duty were discipline, friendship, and victory. Give them those things, Starbuck knew, and the men of the Faulconer Legion would believe they were the best damn soldiers in all the damned world and that there was not a man alive or dead, in any uniform in any country of any era, who could lick them in a fight.

But the Legion had no such belief now. Its sense of comradeship had been shattered by Galloway's raid and by the disappearance of Washington Faulconer. Most of the Legion's men had known Faulconer since childhood; he had dominated their civilian lives as he had their military existence, and, whatever his faults, unkindness had never been among them. Faulconer had been an easy master because he had wanted to be liked, and his disappearance had unsettled the ranks. They were ashamed, too, because the Legion was the only regiment that marched without colors. Every other unit marched with flying banners, but the Legion, to its disgrace, had none.

So, as they marched, Starbuck spent time with each company. He did not force himself on them but instead began by ordering them to close up and march faster, and then he would just march alongside and endure the embarrassed or unfriendly looks that told him most of his men believed he was too young to be their commanding officer. He knew those looks did not mean he was unpopular, for in the spring, when the Legion had held its final election for field officers, nearly two-thirds of the men had written Starbuck's name on their ballots despite Washington Faulconer's opposition, but that springtime defiance had not meant they wanted the young Northern rebel to be their commanding officer. Not at twenty-two, and not at the expense of men from their own Virginian community. And so Starbuck marched with them and waited for someone to throw the first question. The conversation he had with Company G was typical enough. "Where are we going?" Billy Sutton, newly made up to Sergeant, wanted to know.

"Old Jack knows and he ain't saying."

"Are we going to see General Faulconer again?" That question came from a man who had once worked on Washington Faulconer's land and who doubtless wanted to know that his old job would be waiting for him at the war's end.

"Reckon you will," Starbuck answered. "He's just gone on to higher things. Can't keep a man like General Faulconer down, you should know that."

"So where's he gone?" The question was hostile.

"Richmond."

There was another silence, except for the sound of boots slapping the road, rifle stocks knocking against tin canteens, and the hoarse rasp of men breathing. Dust drifted off the road to coat the bushes a reddish gray. "Story is that Old Jack gave Faulconer the back of his hand," Sergeant Berrigan asked. "Is that what you hear, Major?"

Starbuck noted the use of his new rank and guessed that

Berrigan was a supporter. He shook his head. "Way I hear it is that Old Jack just reckoned General Faulconer could be more use in Richmond. Faulconer weren't never happy with all this marching and sleeping rough, you all know that. He wasn't reared to it and he never got a taste for it, and Old Jack just agreed with him." That was a shrewd enough reply, intimating that Faulconer was not as tough as his men. Most of the Legion did not really want to believe that their General had been dismissed, for that truth reflected on themselves, and so they were ready enough to embrace Starbuck's kinder version of Faulconer's sudden disappearance.

"What about Colonel Bird?" a man asked.

"Pecker'll be back soon," Starbuck assured them. "And he'll have his old job back."

"And Captain Murphy?" another man called.

"Last I heard he was doing real well. He'll be back, too."

The company trudged on. "Are we still the Faulconer Legion?" a corporal asked.

"I reckon," Starbuck said. "Most of us come from there." The answer was an evasion, for given time Starbuck intended to change the regiment's name, just as Swynyard planned to change the Brigade's name.

"They going to make Tony Murphy a major? Like you?" That surly question came from a tall, scowling man called Abram Trent, who sounded deliberately unfriendly. Trent's question suggested that Starbuck's promotion had come too quickly and at the expense of men who were native to Faulconer County.

Starbuck met the question head-on. "Ain't my decision, Trent, but if you reckon I shouldn't be a major then I'll be real happy to discuss it with you just as soon as we stop walking. You and me together, no one else."

The men liked an officer who was ready to use his fists,

and Starbuck's offer to fight made them respect him, while the reluctance of any man to take up the offer only increased that respect. Starbuck knew that men like Abram Trent were the centers of resistance to his new and fragile authority, and by facing them down he helped make their defiance impotent. He finished by telling Company G what little he knew about their destination. "Old Jack doesn't march us like dogs for the hell of it, boys. We're on our way to give the Yankees a whipping, so save your breath and keep marching." Battle, he thought, and specifically victory in battle, was the elixir that would restore the Legion's confidence.

But not every man was eager for battle. Late in the morning, when few men had any breath left for questions or answers, Captain Moxey caught up with Starbuck. Moxey had been riding his horse, but now he led the beast by its reins. "I can't go on," he said.

Starbuck gave the sallow Moxey an unfriendly glance. "You look fresh enough to me, Mox'."

"It ain't me, Starbuck, but the horse."

Starbuck edged the sling of his rifle away from the spot on his right shoulder that was being chafed to rawness, though he knew that within seconds the sling would work its way back to the sore spot again. "Your horse ain't in command of a company, Mox', you are."

"She's lame," Moxey insisted.

Starbuck looked at the mare, which was indeed limping slightly on her right rear leg. "So let her loose," he said.

"It ain't probably nothing more than a bad shoeing job," Moxey said, "so if you give me a pass, Starbuck, I'll find a blacksmith in a village near here and catch you up."

Starbuck shook his head. "Can't do that, Mox'. Old Jack's orders. No one's to leave the march."

"I won't be long!" Moxey insisted. "Hell, it's what we've

always done on a march." He tried to sound offhand, but only succeeded in being petulant. His family had money, but, as Pecker Bird had always maintained, not quite enough money for its pretensions, just as Moxey did not possess quite enough grace to be a gentleman. There was a perpetual air of grievance in Moxey, as though he resented a world that had inexplicably denied his family the last few thousand dollars that would have made its existence free of all financial worry, while Moxey, the eldest son, lived in terror that one day he might have to work for a living.

Starbuck grimaced as he trod on a sharp-edged stone. He was marching barefoot, and for a pace or two the pain stopped him from speaking. Then the brief agony subsided. "So what is it, Mox'?" Starbuck asked. "You don't want to fight?"

Moxey bristled. "Are you accusing me of cowardice?"

"I'm asking you a goddamned question," Starbuck snapped.

Moxey immediately backed down. "My horse is lame! That's all!"

Starbuck shifted the rifle onto his left shoulder, though immediately the sore spot on that shoulder began to chafe. "The orders are clear, Mox'. If your horse can't keep up, then you're to leave it behind. Put her in a field where some farmer can find her."

"She's a valuable mare!" Moxey protested. "From Faulconer's stud."

"I don't care if she's a goddamned unicorn from the stables of the sun," Starbuck said coldly. "If she can't keep up then she stays behind."

Moxey's anger flared raw. "She ain't a Boston coal hauler's nag, Starbuck. She's real horseflesh. Worth near a thousand bucks."

Starbuck changed his rifle back to his right shoulder. "Just keep up with us, Mox', horse or no horse."

"You can boil your son of a bitch brains," Moxey said and turned angrily away.

Starbuck felt a sudden rush of fresh energy. He turned after Moxey, took him by his elbow, and steered the smaller man forcefully into some trees that grew beside the road. Starbuck made himself smile so that the watching men would not construe the scene as a fight between two officers, but as soon as he had Moxey and his horse safe out of the column's sight, he turned the smile off. "Now listen here, you son of a goddamned bitch. You may not like it, but I'm in charge of this goddamned regiment and you're nothing but a captain in it, and you're going to do what every other man in this regiment has to do. I don't care if you ride your damned horse till she's broke, and I don't care if you leave her here to starve, but I do care that you're leading Company B when we face the damned Yankees. So what are you going to do, Mox'? March or ride?"

Moxey had gone pale. "I ain't going to leave my horse. She's too valuable."

Starbuck pulled his revolver from its holster. "I tell you, Mox'," he said as he thumbed a percussion cap onto one of the cones, "they should have drowned you at birth and saved the rest of us a heap of trouble." He spun the cylinder so that the primed chamber would be the next under the hammer, then placed the revolver at the tired mare's drooping head with the muzzle just above her eyes.

"What the hell . . ." Moxey began.

Starbuck thumbed back the hammer as the mare stared at him with her soft brown eyes. "You're a leprous piece of ratshit, Mox'," Starbuck said in a calm voice, "but it just happens that I need you despite that, and if this here mare's the obstacle to you doing your job, why then, the mare'll just have to go to heaven." He tightened his finger on the trigger.

"No!" Moxey dragged the mare away from the revolver. "She'll make it!"

Starbuck lowered the hammer. "Just be sure you make it, too, Mox'."

"Goddamn it! You're mad!"

"And I'm your commanding officer too, Mox', and I reckon it's a wise thing not to upset commanding officers, especially mad commanding officers. Next time it'll be your brains, not the mare's." Starbuck lowered the revolver's hammer, then jerked his head toward the road. "Get back to your company."

Starbuck followed Moxey back to the road. Company H was just passing, and Truslow spat toward Moxey's disconsolate figure. "What was that about?" he asked Starbuck.

"Mox' and me were just looking at his horse. Deciding whether it could make the distance."

"It could go on forever," Truslow said scathingly, "so long as he takes the damn stone out of its hoof."

"Is that all it is?"

"What the hell did you think it was?" Truslow seemed not to be affected by either the day's heat or the speed of the march. He was one of the oldest men in the Legion, but also the toughest. He did not much care for being made into an officer, because rank had always been a matter of indifference to Truslow, but he did care about Starbuck, whom he perceived as being a clever man and a cunning soldier. "You need to watch Moxey," he said.

"I guessed as much," Starbuck said.

"I mean really watch him." Truslow moved a wad of chewing tobacco from one cheek to the other. "He's Faulconer's pet, and Faulconer won't want us to succeed."

Starbuck shrugged. "What can Moxey do about that? He

289

doesn't even want to be here, he just wants to run away."

"He's a sly one," Truslow said. "He's like a dog. He needs a master, see? And now that Faulconer's gone he'll like as not shove his nose into Medlicott's pocket." Truslow sniffed. "You hear the rumor that Medlicott is putting around? He says that if he'd kept command of the Legion we wouldn't be fighting with Jackson, but sitting in the trenches at Richmond. Says it's a fact."

"Like hell it is," Starbuck said, wincing as the weight of the rifle dug into his shoulder.

"But it's the kind of rumor men believe if they get unhappy," Truslow said, "and it ain't any good pretending that everyone in the Legion wants you to be in charge. You forget how many men in this regiment depend on Washington Faulconer for a living. They cut his trees, fish his streams, take his wages, keep their money at his bank, and live in his houses. Look at Will Patterson." Truslow was referring to the newly promoted commander of C Company.

"Patterson's been trying to become an officer ever since the fighting began," Starbuck said. "He should be grateful to me!"

"That family ain't grateful for nothing!" Truslow said. Sergeant Patterson, the son of a stonemason in Faulconer Court House, had twice tried to win election to officer but had failed both times. Starbuck was not certain Patterson would make a good officer, but there had been no one else he could promote. "And a good half of the Patterson business comes from Washington Faulconer," Truslow went on, "so do you think Will Patterson can afford to be your supporter?"

"So long as he fights," Starbuck said, "that's all that matters."

"But Medlicott, Moxey, and Patterson," Truslow said pointedly, "are in charge of your three right-hand companies. So just how hard do you think those boys will fight when matters get bloody?"

Starbuck thought about that observation and did not like what he was thinking. He kept his conclusion to himself, grinning at Truslow instead. "Some people like me," he said.

"Who?"

"Coffman."

"He's a boy, too young to know better."

"Swynyard?"

"Madder than a rabid bat."

"Pecker?"

"Madder than two rabid bats."

"Murphy."

"Murphy likes everyone. Besides, he's Irish."

"You?"

"I like you," Truslow said scornfully, "but just what kind of recommendation do you think that is?"

Starbuck laughed. "Anyway," he said after a few paces, "we're not here to be liked. We're here to win battles."

"So make sure you do," Truslow said, "make goddamn sure you do."

The tired, hot men received a respite when they came close to the Rappahannock. So far the army had marched well to the south of the river, but now they were turning north to march past the Yankees' flank. The river's northern bank was a bluff up which the road climbed steeply, and one of Jackson's eighty guns had stuck on the slippery bank. The teamsters used their whips, and the nearest infantry were summoned to put their shoulders to the gun wheels, but the delay inevitably backed the column up, and the grateful men collapsed beside the road to rest their aching legs and catch their breath. Some men slept, their faces given a corpselike look by the dust coated on their skin. Moxey surreptitiously removed the stone from his mare's hoof, then sat beside a glum-looking Major Medlicott. Most of the Legion's other officers gathered around Starbuck, hoping to glean more information than he had given to their men, but Starbuck insisted he did not know where they were going.

"It'll be the Shenandoah Valley," Captain Davies opined, and when no one contradicted him or even asked why he held the opinion, he explained it anyway. "That's Old Jack's backyard, right? He's a terror in the Shenandoah. Once the Yankees know we're in the Shenandoah, then they'll have to split their army in two."

"Not if they decide to let us rot in the Shenandoah," the newly promoted Lieutenant Howes commented.

"So we won't rot there, but cross into Maryland," Davies suggested. "Up the Shenandoah, straight across the Potomac and over to Baltimore. Once we've got Baltimore we can attack Washington. I reckon a month from now we could be running Abe Lincoln out of the White House on one of his own fence rails."

Davies's confidence was greeted with silence. Someone spat in the road, while another man tilted his canteen to his mouth and held it there in hope of finding one last trickle of tepid water. "Down the Shenandoah," Truslow finally said, "not up."

"Down?" Davies asked, puzzled by the contradiction. "Why should we march south?"

"Down's north and up's south," Truslow said, "always has been and always will be. You go to the valley and ask the way up and they'll send you south. So we'll be going down the Shenandoah, not up."

"Up or down," Davies said, offended by the correction, "who cares? We're still going north. It'll be a two-day march to the Shenandoah, another two to the Potomac, and then a week to Baltimore."

"I was in Baltimore once," Captain Pine said dreamily. Everyone waited to hear more, but it seemed Pine had nothing to add to his brief announcement.

"Up!" Starbuck saw the battalion in front being ordered to their feet. "Get your lads ready."

They crossed the river and headed north. They did not follow the road, which here tended westward, but marched over fields and through woods, across shallow streams and wide paddocks, following a shortcut that at last brought the column to a dirt road leading northward. Starbuck held a hazy map of Virginia in his head, and he sensed how they were now marching parallel to the Blue Ridge Mountains, which meant that just as soon as they reached the Manassas Gap Railroad they could turn west and follow the rails through the pass into the Shenandoah Valley. And that valley was aimed like a gun at the hinterland of Washington, so maybe the excitable Davies had it right. Starbuck tried to imagine the fall of Washington. He saw the ragged rebel legions marching through the conquered ring of forts that surrounded the Yankee capital and then, under the eyes of the silent, shocked spectators who lined the streets, parading past the captured White House. He heard the victory music and saw in his mind's vivid eye the starcrossed battle flag flying high above the white, plump, and self-satisfied buildings, and when the victory parade was finished, the soldiers would take over the captured city and celebrate their triumph. Colonel Lassan, the Frenchman, had spent a week in the North's capital and had described the city to Starbuck. It was a place, Lassan had said, devoid of hard sinews. There was no industry in Washington, no wharves, no factories, no steam-driven mills to scream their whistles and shroud the sun with their filth. It was, Lassan said, a small city with no purpose but to manufacture laws and regulations; an artificial city where slyness passed for intelligence and venality replaced industry. It was peopled by pale lawyers, plump politicians, rich whores, and faceless hordes of black servants, and when the rebels marched in, the lawyers and politicians would doubtless be long gone, which meant that only the good souls would be left behind.

That tantalizing prospect served to keep Starbuck's mind off his blistered feet and burning muscles. He dreamed of a soft city, of captured champagne, of wide beds and starched white sheets. He dreamed of fried oysters and turtle soup and roast beef and tenderloin steaks and peach tarts, all of it eaten in the company of the lawyers' rich Washington whores, and that tantalizing thought suddenly reminded him of the golden-haired woman he had glimpsed in her husband's open carriage behind the Yankee lines at the battle of Bull Run. She lived in Washington and had invited Starbuck to visit her, but now, for the life of him, he could not remember her name. Her husband had been a Northern congressman, a pompous and dim-witted man, but the wife had been golden and beautiful, a vision whose memory was lovely enough to console a weary man marching through the small Virginia towns where excited people applauded as their soldier boys went by. Year-old rebel flags, hoarded through the months when the Yankees had been the nearest troops, were hung from balconies and eaves, while small boys brought the troops buckets of tepid well water to drink.

Starbuck's pains seemed almost numb by the time the sun began to sink behind the serrated peaks of the Blue Ridge Mountains. Ahead of him he saw the soldiers taking off their hats, and he wondered why so many would make that gesture, and then a staff officer cantered back along the line of march calling out that the men were not to cheer. "We don't want any Yankee cavalry scouts to hear us," the staff officer said, "so no cheering."

Cheering? Why no cheering? Starbuck, his thoughts wrenched back from imagined Washington luxuries to his wretched, sweating reality, suddenly saw a poker-backed figure standing atop a house-sized rock beside the road. It was Jackson, hat in hand, watching his troops march by. Starbuck instinctively straightened his shoulders and tried to put some spirit into his step. He snatched the ragged, sweat-stained hat off his long black hair and stared at the hard-faced man, who, seeing Starbuck, gave the smallest nod of recognition. Behind Starbuck the Legion pulled off their hats and fell into step to march past the legendary General. No one cheered, no one said a word, but for the next mile it seemed to Starbuck that there was an extra spring in every man's pace.

They marched on into the evening. The western sky was a livid crimson streaked with gold, a blaze of color that slowly shrank and faded into a gray twilight. The marching pains came back, relieved now by the slow fall in the day's fierce temperature. The men looked for signs of bivouacs that would tell them they had arrived at their destination, but no troops were camped beside the road and no campfires drifted smoke into the evening; instead the march went on and on into the darkness. The moon rose to whiten the dust that coated the Legion's rifles and clung to the men's skin. No one sang, no one spoke, they just marched on and on, mile after damned mile under a gibbous moon. To their right, far off, a great red glow showed where the smear of Yankee cooking fires covered the northern Virginia counties, and Starbuck, trying to keep himself alert, realized that Jackson's army was already north of most of that glow, which surely meant that the enemy was outflanked, and for the first time he wondered if they were indeed planning to turn west into the Shenandoah. Maybe, he thought, they would turn east instead, to plunge like a dagger into the Yankee rear.

"In here! In here! No fires!" A voice startled Starbuck out of his reverie, and he saw a horseman gesturing toward a night-dark meadow. "Get some rest." The horseman was evidently a staff officer. "We'll be marching at dawn. No fires! There's a stream at the bottom of the hill for water. No fires!"

Starbuck acknowledged the orders, then stood in the meadow's gate to watch the Legion shamble past. "Well done!" he called out to each company. "Well done." The men scarcely acknowledged his presence, but just limped into the meadow that lay at the crest of a small hill. Moxey kept on the far side of his company so he would not even have to acknowledge Starbuck's existence.

Truslow's company went past last. "Any stragglers?" Starbuck asked.

"None that you need know of."

Starbuck walked beside Truslow into the meadow. "A hell of a march," he said tiredly.

"And tomorrow we probably do it again," Truslow said. "You want me to set a guard?"

Starbuck was tempted to accept the offer, but he knew the men of Company H would think he had picked on them because they were his old company, and so he deliberately chose Company A instead. Major Medlicott was too tired to complain.

Starbuck limped round his men's bivouac. He wanted to make certain that they had water to drink, but most had already fallen asleep. They had simply lain down on the grass and closed their eyes, so that now they lay like the dead collected for burial at battle's end. A few walked to the stream to fill their canteens, a few smoked, a few gnawed at hardtack, but most of the men just lay sprawled in the moonlight.

Starbuck stayed awake with the pickets. To the south the moon shone on yet more men tramping up the road, but one by one the regiments turned into the fields to snatch their brief rest. The regiments were still coming when Starbuck woke Medlicott to relieve him, and still marching when he lay down to sleep. He dreamed of marching, of pain, of a sun-bitten day spent sweating northward on a stone-hard road that led, not to whores on white sheets in a fattened city, but to battle.

On the morning that Jackson's army marched west Major Galloway received orders to report to General McDowell, whose troops formed the right wing of Pope's army. An odd and disquieting report had come from that western flank. One of General Banks's staff officers had been spying the enemy positions from a hill north of the Rappahannock and had spotted a distant column of mixed infantry and artillery marching westward on the river's far bank. The road the rebels were following snaked up and down through hilly country, so that the staff officer could only glimpse scattered parts of the column, but he had estimated the number of regiments by counting their flags and reported that the rebel force must have numbered at least twenty thousand men. The column had eventually disappeared in the heat haze that shimmered over the distant farmland and woods.

General Banks forwarded the report to General McDowell, who in turn sent it on to General Pope with an added comment that the column was probably aiming to cross the Blue Ridge Mountains and then advance north through the Shenandoah Valley. Maybe, McDowell surmised, the rebel force planned to attack the Federal garrison at Harpers Ferry, then cross the river and threaten Washington?

Pope added the report to all the other disquieting evidence of rebel activity. Jeb Stuart's horsemen had raided one of the army's forward supply depots at Catlett's Station. The rebel horse had swarmed out of a rainswept night like fiends from hell, and though the raid had done little real damage, it had made everyone nervous. There were more reports of rebel activity on Pope's eastward flank near Fredericksburg, while other observers saw clear signs that the rebels were planning a direct assault across the Rappahannock River. General Pope felt like a juggler given one Indian club too many, and so he sent a stream of peremptory telegrams to the War Department in Washington demanding to know when he might expect McClellan's forces to join his own, then rattled off a series of orders designed to repel all the threatened attacks at once. Union troops marched and countermarched under the hot sun, none of them knowing quite what they were doing or where the enemy was supposed to be.

It was the cavalry's job to determine the enemy's position, and so Major Galloway was ordered to report to General McDowell, who in turn instructed him to lead his men into the swathe of empty country that lay between the Northern army and the Blue Ridge Mountains. It was into that hazy spread of land that the mysterious enemy column had been seen marching, and McDowell wanted Galloway to find it, but just as Galloway was ready to leave, a new order arrived from General Pope's headquarters. It seemed a party of rebel horsemen had recently crossed Kelly's Ford, and Galloway was ordered to find out where that enemy was headed.

The Major demanded a map. It took him a long time to discover Kelly's Ford. He had somehow expected it to be near Warrenton, where McDowell's forces were anchored, but instead he found it to be fifteen miles away on the army's eastern flank. He protested the stupidity of one cavalry regiment being required to be in two places at once, but was told that most of the army's cavalry was either immobilized through lack of fodder or else was busy. Galloway stared down at the map. "Which job's the most important?" he asked.

Pope's staff officer, a Colonel, scratched in his beard. "I reckon that if the Johnnies are crossing Kelly's Ford, then they'll be planning to cut us off from McClellan's boys." He ran a nicotine-stained finger up from the ford to show how a rebel force could cut Pope's men off from Aquia Creek, where McClellan's army was coming ashore. "They'd split us up. And that'd be bad. Real bad."

"And this other column?" Galloway asked, gesturing toward the western landscape.

The Colonel squashed a louse between two nicotine-stained thumbnails. In truth he had no idea which threat was the greater, but nor did he want to consult his master, who was already in a furious mood because of the constant stream of conflicting intelligence reports that were confusing all his careful plans. "My guess," the Colonel ventured, "and it is only a guess, mark you, is that the seceshers are dragging a false trail. They probably want us to weaken ourselves by sending men to the Shenandoah Valley. But the war isn't going to be won in the Shenandoah, but here, on the river lines." He slapped the map across the band of rivers that barred the roads between Washington and Richmond. "But on the other hand, Major"—the Colonel was too canny not to qualify his judgment—"we sure would like to know just what in tarnation those twenty thousand Johnnies are doing. And everyone says your boys are the best for that kind of job. They say you can ride behind the enemy lines, isn't that right?"

So Galloway had no choice but to split his small force. If the threat at Kelly's Ford was the more dangerous, then that justified using two troops of men, and so Galloway decided to go there himself and to take Adam's troop with him, while Billy Blythe would take his men and investigate the mysterious western column. "You ain't to get in a fight, Billy," Galloway warned Blythe. "Just find out where in hell the rebs are headed and then get word back to McDowell."

Blythe seemed happy with his orders. His horses were tired and hungry, but he did not have so far to ride as Galloway, and once in the saddle, his men rode slowly. They headed into an empty countryside that was parched by an afternoon sun that burned like a furnace. Blythe led his troop a few miles west of the last Union pickets and then stopped at the summit of a small hill to stare into the empty landscape. "So just what in hell are we doing, Billy?" Sergeant Kelley asked Blythe.

"Chasin' our tails, Seth. Just chasin' our born-again tails."

Sergeant Kelley spat in disgust. "So what if the enemy are out here? Hell, Billy, our horses ain't been fed proper in three days and they ain't been rested proper neither. You reckon we can outrun Jeb Stuart's boys on these nags?" The men murmured their agreement.

Blythe waved at the serene, heat-hazed countryside. "What enemy, Sergeant? Do you see an enemy?"

Kelley frowned. There was a smear of dust way off to the northwest, but that was so far beyond the Rappahannock that it was surely being kicked up by Northern troops, while to the west, where the mysterious column had supposedly disappeared, there was nothing but trees and sun-glossed fields and gentle hills. "So what the hell are we doing here?" the Sergeant asked again.

Blythe smiled. "Like I told you, Seth, chasin' our tails. So why in hell's name don't we do something more useful instead? Like give our horses a proper feed." He tugged at his reins, turning his horse's head south. "I seem to remember a farm not so far away. A den of rebel vipers, it was, but there was fodder there and maybe it didn't all burn up to hell and I reckon you and I have got unfinished business there."

Kelley grinned. "You mean that Rothwell woman and her children?"

"I hate children," Blythe said, "I do so hate young children. But their mothers?" Blythe smiled. "Ah, I do so love a ripe young mother."

Twenty miles to the east Major Galloway found Kelly's Ford guarded by a strong rebel garrison on the southern bank. That garrison sniped ineffectually at Galloway's horsemen as they explored the northern side of the river, where they discovered no hoofprints nor any other evidence of a rebel force across the river. The local black population, always the best source of information for Northern scouts, said that no Confederates had crossed the river in two days, and those men had only come across to get fodder for their horses. Galloway dutifully searched the riverbank for five miles east and west, but neither he nor Adam found any rebels. The rumor had been false, and Galloway, knowing his day had been wasted, rode slowly home.

A dozen miles north of the ford was Warrenton Junction, where the branch rails from Warrenton joined the main Orange and Alexandria line. Confusion besieged the junction. Two trains loaded with guns and ammunition were trying to pass south to the Bealeton depot, while another was trying to haul twenty-four boxcars loaded with hardtack, uniforms, percussion caps, and artillery shells down to Warrenton. Meanwhile three empty trains and a hospital train waited in the pitiless sun for clearance northward. The sweet smell of pinewood lay over the depot, coming from the log stacks that waited to feed the locomotive furnaces.

The Reverend Elial Starbuck's passenger car was attached to the hospital train. The preacher escaped the heat in the car's stifling interior by walking up and down in the train's long shadow, where he was forced to watch as a succession of newly dead men were carried from the red-flagged cars. The men were not dying from their wounds but from heat prostration, and their fate angered the Reverend Elial Starbuck. These were good, decent young Americans who had gone to fight for their country, and their reward was to be dumped beside a rail track where their corpses crawled with flies. If the hospital train did not move soon, then every sick man in the cars would be dead, and so the Reverend Starbuck discovered an engineer colonel who appeared to possess some authority over the railroad and of whom he demanded to know when the trains would be cleared north. "In Boston," the Reverend Starbuck assured the Colonel, "we have such things as timetables. We find them useful."

"In Boston, sir," the Colonel retorted, "you don't have Jeb Stuart." The delay on the railroad was caused by the raid Stuart had made on Catlett's Station, the next depot on the line, where the rebel cavalry had taken scores of prisoners, captured a paychest, and even snaffled up General Pope's best uniform coat. A teeming rain had prevented the raiders from burning the bridge that carried the rails over Cedar Run, yet even with the bridge intact the raid had inflicted chaos on the rail schedule. "But your train will be the first one north tomorrow afternoon," the Colonel promised the Reverend Starbuck. "You'll be in Washington by Wednesday, sir."

"I had hoped to be in Richmond by then," the Reverend said caustically.

The Colonel bit back any retort, and instead arranged for the hospital cars to be moved into the shade of a warehouse and for water to be brought to the surviving wounded. Some fugitive slaves who were now employed as laborers on the railroad were ordered to dig graves for the dead.

The Reverend Starbuck wondered if he should witness for Christ to the laboring blacks but decided his mood was too bleak for effective evangelism. His opinion of the army had slipped all week but now reached fulminating bottom. In all his born days he had never witnessed any organization so chaotic, so incapable, or so sluggish. The smallest Boston grocery shop displayed more managerial acumen than these uniformed incompetents, and it was no wonder that the lumpen-skulled rebels were making such fools of the North's generals. The preacher sat on the open platform at one end of his passenger car, and as the sun sank huge in the west, he wiped the sweat from his forehead and took on the pleasurable chore of making notes in his diary for a pungent letter he planned to send to the Massachusetts congressional delegation.

Five miles away, in Warrenton itself, Major Galloway reported to the army headquarters. He found the same Colonel who had dispatched him that morning and who now seemed disappointed that no enemy had crossed Kelly's Ford. "You're sure," the Colonel asked.

"Certain. Absolutely certain."

The Colonel scratched at his beard, found a louse, and squashed it between his thumbnails. "What about the twenty thousand Johnnies in the west?" the Colonel asked.

"I sent my second-in-command that way, but he hasn't reported yet."

The Colonel yawned, then stretched his arms. "No news is good news, eh? If your fellow had found anything he'd have doubtless sent word. And no one else is squealing about twenty thousand rebels, so it's probably all moonshine, pure moonshine. Which reminds me." He turned in his chair and reached for two glasses and a whiskey bottle.

"You'll join me? Good." He poured the whiskey. "But even if there are twenty thousand Johnnies loose, what damage can they do?" He paused, thinking about his question, then laughed at the very thought of the whole United States Army being frightened of such a tiny force. "Twenty thousand men," he said disparagingly, "what harm can they do?"

Captain Davies woke Starbuck. "Reveille, sir."

Starbuck thought he had to be dreaming. No, worse, he thought he was not dreaming. His muscles were strips of pain, his bones were set solid.

"Starbuck! Up!" Davies said.

Starbuck groaned. "It's dark."

"They want us marching in twenty minutes."

"Oh, no, Jesus no," Starbuck muttered. He groaned again, then turned onto one side. The mere effort of rolling over hurt. Everything hurt. He could not bear to think of trying to stand on his blistered feet.

"Water." Davies, who had taken over picket duty from Medlicott, offered Starbuck a canteen. Starbuck drank, then felt for a cigar. He had two left, both preserved from harm by being wrapped in his hat. He borrowed Davies's cigar to light one of his own, then coughed some life into his lungs.

"Jesus," he said again, then remembered he had to set an example, and so he struggled to his feet. He blasphemed again.

"Stiff?" Davies asked.

"Why didn't I join the cavalry?" Starbuck asked, then tottered a few steps. It was night-dark still, without even a hint of dawn in the eastern sky. Stars were bright overhead, while the moon hung low above the Blue Ridge to mark its forested draws deep black and starkest white. He sat to pull on his boots. It hurt just to tug them over his raw feet.

"Awake?" Colonel Swynyard's voice asked.

"I think I died and went to hell," Starbuck said as he forced himself to stand again. "Maybe that's it, Colonel. Maybe none of this is real. We're all in hell."

"Nonsense! We're heavenbound, praise Him."

"Then I wish He'd hurry," Starbuck complained. Around him the field heaved and groaned as waking men realized the ordeal that waited for them. Starbuck scratched at a louse, transferred the one remaining cigar to his pocket, pulled the hat onto his head, slung his rolled blanket over his left shoulder and the rifle on his right, and thus was ready to start.

Breakfast was taken on the march. For Starbuck it was a slate-hard slab of hardtack that gnawed at his aching tooth. He tried to remember when he had last had a decent meal. His uniform trousers were belted with rope that gathered in at least five inches of material that had been well stretched before the war's first battle. Then the blisters on his feet began hurting again and the sore spot on his right shoulder began to chafe, and he forgot about food and just concentrated on walking through the pain.

The column still marched north. Once, when the road rose to offer a view of the moonlit western hills, Starbuck saw the notch that marked where the Manassas Gap carried the railroad through the Blue Ridge and into the fertile Shenandoah Valley. In the moonlight the gap looked a far way off, and Starbuck's spirits fell at the thought of marching all that long way. His muscles were slowly unknotting, but only to hurt even more. The Legion passed between two rows of houses, their windows dimly lit with candlelight. A tethered dog barked at the passing soldiers, and an unseen woman called from a window to offer the soldiers her blessings.

Then, abruptly, the road climbed a steep few feet, and Starbuck almost tripped on a steel rail. He recovered his footing and stepped safely over the metal to realize that the Legion had at last reached the Manassas Gap Railroad. The road divided here, one branch climbing west toward the Blue Ridge and the other going east toward the Yankees. A mounted staff officer dominated the junction, and he was pointing the troops east. So they were not going to the Shenandoah Valley after all but were instead to march toward the rising sun that climbed through the vast smear of smoke marking where a waking army's cooking fires burned. They were to march east toward battle.

The sun rose like hellfire in their eyes. It dazzled them and cast their shambling shadows long on the dusty road behind. Every now and then Starbuck would see the rails of the Manassas Gap Railroad lying alongside the road like twin streaks of reflected fire, but no trains ran on those strips of molten steel. All the locomotives and stock had been taken south or else commandeered by the Yankees to shuttle their supplies from Alexandria through Manassas Junction to their forces on the Rappahannock.

And now, Starbuck realized, Stonewall Jackson was behind those forces. And maybe, Starbuck thought, the Yankees knew he was coming, for how could twenty-four thousand men hope to avoid a hostile army's scouts? Ahead of the marching column lay a low range of hills, so low that in peacetime the hills would scarcely have been noticeable, but Starbuck could see that the apparently innocuous slopes were more than steep enough to check an infantry attack. And if the Federals had put guns in the dark trees at the crest of those hills, then Jackson's long march must end in bloody defeat.

The road and the empty railroad arrowed side by side toward a pass through the low hills. Jackson's cavalry advanced either side of the rail embankment, their carbines cocked as they nervously watched every fence and wood and house. The passage through the unregarded hills was called Thoroughfare Gap, and if the Yankees had been shadowing Jackson's march, then Thoroughfare Gap was the place to put their ambush, and as the steep walls of the pass narrowed, the horsemen advanced ever more slowly and cautiously. They tried not to think of hidden gunners waiting with taut lanyards or of lines of concealed infantry poised with loaded rifles. Every creak of a saddle or rustle of wind or clatter of a horseshoe on stone startled the scouting horsemen's nerves; then suddenly they reached the pass's summit and the whole eastern countryside lay open before them, and it was empty. There were no limbers, no guns, no caissons, no Federals at all. There was nothing but low hills and thick woods stretching into the long blue distance. Stonewall Jackson had hooked his small army clean and undetected into the Yankees' unprotected belly.

Now all he had to do was twist the hook and start the killing.

"Close up!" the officers shouted. "Close up!"

The men marched in silence, too tired to talk or sing. From time to time a man would break ranks to snatch a green apple or an ear of unripe corn from the farmlands on either side of the road, while other men broke ranks to be ill behind a hedge, but always they hurried on after their comrades and pushed themselves back into line. The horses pulling the guns labored under the whips, and their guns' wheels ripped the road's surface into broken ruts that turned men's ankles, but still they marched at the same cracking pace behind a cavalry vanguard that, late in the morning, rode into a small town where a Federal band was practicing in the main street. The band belonged to a regiment that had gone on a daylong route march, leaving their musicians to entertain the sullen Virginian townspeople. Those sullen people cheered up as the band fell slowly silent. The music ended with one last astonished and froglike grunt of a sax-horn tuba as the musicians realized that the horsemen in the street were pointing guns straight at their heads. The bands-men had been assured that they were at least twenty miles from any enemy forces, yet now they were faced by a gray-coated pack of grinning men on dusty, sweat-foamed horses. "Let's hear you play Dixie, boys," the cavalry leader ordered. Some of the bandsmen began to edge backward, but the cavalry officer cocked his rifle one-handed and the band-master hastily turned around, raised his hands to ready the musicians, and then led them in a ragged rendition of the rebel anthem.

In the middle of the afternoon, with the musicians now silent prisoners under guard, General Jackson's column struck southeast on a wide road that passed through har-vested fields and plundered orchards. The men could guess where they were going now, for ahead of them was a great moving plume of smoke that showed where the Orange and Alexandria Railroad carried the Northern army's supplies south to the Yankee troops. Every bullet, every cartridge, every slab of hardtack, every percussion cap, every shell, every pair of boots, every bayonet, every small and large thing that an army needed to fight was being carried down that single track, and Jackson's leading infantry was now within earshot of the wailing, whippoorwill cadence of the locomotives' whistles. They could even hear the distant and rhythmic clatter of car wheels crossing the rail joints.

The trains were running out from Manassas Junction, which lay only a few miles to the north. For a time Jackson had been tempted by the thought of marching directly on the Junction, but it seemed inconceivable that the largest Federal supply base in Virginia would not be guarded by earthworks and guns and regiments of prime infantry, so instead the General planned to cut the railroad at Bristoe

Station, which lay just four miles south of the depot. Local people said that Bristoe Station was guarded by a mere handful of cavalry and only three companies of Northern infantry.

Dusk was falling as the leading rebel infantry breasted a slight rise and started down the long slope to Bristoe. Rebel cavalry had ridden ahead of the infantry, but those horsemen were nowhere in sight, and all the leading infantry could see were the twin rails gleaming empty in the day's dying light and a scatter of clapboard houses from which kitchen smoke trickled skyward. The small garrison had no idea that danger threatened. A Northern cavalryman, stripped to the waist and with his suspenders dangling, carried a canvas pail of water from a well to a horse trough. Another man played a fiddle, assiduously practicing the same phrase over and over again. Men smoked pipes in the small warm breeze or read hometown newspapers in the last light of the setting sun. A few men saw the infantry on the western road, but they assumed the approaching soldiers must be Federal troops. The infantry's flags were flying, but the sinking sun was huge and red behind the rebel column, and so the Yankees could make out no details of the approaching banners or uniforms.

The leading rebel regiment was from Louisiana. Its Colonel gave the order for his men to put percussion caps on the cones of their loaded rifles. Till now they had marched with their guns unprimed in case a stumbling man set off a cartridge and so alerted the enemy. "I guess we arrived here before the cavalry," the Colonel said to his adjutant as he scraped his sword clear of its scabbard.

The sound of the steel on its scabbard's throat seemed to release the village to hell. For just as the Colonel pulled his sword into the sun's scarlet light, so the hidden rebel horsemen launched their charge from a belt of trees north of the settlement. Bugles ripped the sky and hooves pounded the earth as a screaming line of rebel cavalry broke from cover and stormed down on the village.

The man with the pail of water stood frozen for a second. Then he dropped the pail and ran toward a house. Halfway there he changed his mind and ran back toward his tethered horse. More Northerners mounted up and, abandoning everything except their weapons, fled eastward. A few of the Yankee horsemen were too late and were trapped in the small village as the rebel cavalry thundered into the single street. A Northerner wheeled his horse and cut with his saber, but before his stroke was half completed, a Southern blade was in his belly. The Southerner rode on, dragging his saber free from the clinging flesh.

Rifles crashed and smoked from the houses where the Northern infantry had taken cover. A horse and man went down, their blood splashing together across the dusty road. The Southern cavalry fired back with revolvers until their Colonel shouted at them to forget the sheltering infantry and capture the rail depot instead.

Another volley splintered from the houses, and a horseman was snatched back from the saddle. His comrades spurred on to the depot, where scattered groups of Northern infantry gathered under the water tower and alongside the fuel bunkers where the pine logs were stacked. The largest group of Yankees rallied around the green-painted shed where a terrified telegrapher was sheltering under the table rather than sending a message. The man was still cowering with his head in his arms when the victorious Southern horsemen scattered the infantry and threw open the shed's door and ordered the telegrapher out. "I ain't done nothing!" the telegrapher called desperately. He had been too frightened to send any message, so that no Northerner yet knew that the army's vital rail line was severed.

"Come on, Billy!" The horseman pulled the telegrapher

out into the dusk, where the victorious Southern horsemen were chasing the last of the Northern garrison out into the fields.

Behind them a cheer sounded as the Louisiana infantry swept into Bristoe's single street. A volley of shots crashed and splintered into a house where a group of Yankee infantry still tried to defy the attackers, but then the village's other defenders began to call out their surrender. The Louisiana men ran from house to house, yanking blue-coated soldiers out into the street. One last stubborn Yankee fired at the attackers from a shed behind a general store and received a full company volley for his pains, and then the firing in the village died away. A few shots still sounded in the field beyond the railroad, but otherwise the fighting had ended, and Stonewall Jackson had hooked clean behind John Pope and cut his eighty thousand men off from their supplies.

It was a feat that had been achieved by just twenty-four thousand men, who, on bloodied feet and with aching muscles and dry mouths and empty bellies, now marched into Bristoe. It was a summer's evening, and the light was fading into a warm soft darkness. They had marched more than fifty miles across country to sever the Yankees' supply line, and soon, Jackson knew, the stung Northerners would turn on him like fiends. Which was exactly what Lee wanted the Northerners to do. Lee wanted Pope's army to abandon its well-dug earthworks behind the Rappahannock's steep northern bank, and Jackson's job was to lure them out. Jackson's men were now the bait: twenty-four thousand vulnerable men isolated among a sea of Northern troops.

Which all added up, Jackson reckoned, to the probability of a pretty rare fight.

To the south of the depot a train whistle offered its mournful sound to the falling night. Smoke misted the sky;

then a locomotive's lamp appeared around a bend to glimmer its shivering reflections on rails that had begun to quiver from the thunder of the approaching wheels. The train, unsuspecting, steamed north to where a rebel army and a Yankee nightmare waited.

THE LEGION MARCHED INTO BRISTOE just as the train rounded the bend south of the depot. The doors of the locomotive's firebox were open so that the flames were reflecting bright on the underside of the long, rolling plume of smoke. The train was traveling so slowly that Starbuck's first thought was that it planned to make a stop at the depot; then a fountain of sparks whirled from the tall stack as the locomotive accelerated. There was just enough light remaining in the day for the engineer to have seen troops milling about the station, and, suspecting trouble, he pulled his whistle cord in warning and threw the regulator hard across to put all the locomotive's power into the great driving wheels. The reflected glow of the furnace disappeared as the firebox doors were slammed shut. The locomotive was hauling a light load: just two sleeper cars showing red flags to denote they were carrying wounded men, a passenger car that was routed through to Alexandria, and a mixture of unladen gondolas and boxcars that would be unhitched in Manassas Junction to be loaded with guns and ammunition for the next day's southward run.

There was a disorganized flurry of activity in the depot as rebel infantry seized whatever obstacles lay close to the track and hurled them across the rails. The most substantial blockage was formed from a pile of ties and rails that had been stacked ready for repair work and that were now hurriedly thrown into the locomotive's path.

The whistle sounded again. The bell was clanging incessantly, a tocsin of alarm in the darkness, while the rails were shaking with the weight of the approaching train. "Get back! Get back!" officers shouted, and the rebel soldiers scurried away from the tracks that were now bright with the reflected light cast by the locomotive's huge kerosene lamp. The windows of the passenger car flickered washes of yellow light over the fuel bunkers and water tower. Two rebels dropped a last length of rail over the track, then scrambled for their lives as the train thundered into the depot. The gilded and scarlet-painted locomotive plowed through the smaller barricades, splintered a heap of barrels and fence rails, scattered a cord of firewood as though the pine logs were mere twigs; then the engine flashed through the lamplit depot with its pistons pounding and its tall stack churning out a torrent of spark-ridden smoke. The engineer hauled on the whistle's chain as the kerosene lamp illuminated the ominous barricade of steel rails and massive timber ties that lay just beyond the depot. The train was still accelerating. Watching rebels held their breath in anticipation of spectacular disaster, then cheered as the locomotive's wooden cowcatcher struck the barrier, but the heavy barricade simply disintegrated in the face of the speeding train. There was a cascade of sparks from the front wheels, a tumbling of wooden baulks and clanging rails, a crash as the locomotive's lantern shattered into scraps of glass and metal, then the defiant whistle sounded once again as the train buffaloed its way through the remnants of the makeshift barrier and sped on northeast toward Manassas.

Passengers had peered anxiously out of the car windows as the train swayed and rattled through the depot, but the faces vanished when a handful of rebel soldiers opened fire. A bullet clanged off the locomotive, another severed a steam line, while a dozen windows in the hospital and passenger cars were shattered. Most of the bullets were fired at the boxcars, which the rebels fondly imagined contained a fortune in plunder that was being denied them. The train, safe through the obstacles, was sounding its whistle continually as a warning to the Federal troops ahead, though to the rebels the whistle sounded more like a mocking call of victory. The locomotive rumbled over the bridge that crossed the Broad Run stream just north of the depot, then disappeared into woods, and the caboose's twin red lanterns were the last things the rebels saw as the train hurried away. Men began firing at those lamps until officers shouted at them to cease fire.

The rumble of the rails died, then, mysteriously, swelled again. A staff officer had ridden a hundred yards south to where a small hillock offered a view, and now he cupped his hands and shouted back to the station. "Another train coming!"

"Pull up the track!" a second staff officer ordered. Just north of the depot, where the rails ran on top of an embankment toward the stream, an officer had discovered the trunklike box where the repair crews kept their tools, and suddenly the embankment was swarming with men carrying sledgehammers and crowbars.

The second train was still a mile away, but its rhythmic noise swelled drumlike in the night as the first lengths of rail were lifted and thrown aside. The work became more effective as it was organized; some troops were detailed to knock aside the chairs that held the rails to the ties, while others heaved the loosened rails off the track and down the embankment's slopes. Staff officers ordered the men not employed in lifting rails to hold their fire so that the approaching train would not be warned of danger.

"You'll get a passel of them through now," an elderly

315

civilian observed to Starbuck. The Legion's help was not needed to destroy the line, so its men were standing in the village street, from where they hoped to get a prime view of the destruction. "They run 'em up empty this time of evening," the old man went on. "Then they start hauling 'em back again all night and day. One-way traffic, see? Empty this way, full that. You boys come far?"

"Far enough."

"Right glad to see you. Yankees are too high and mighty for my taste." The old man grinned as the new train sounded its whistle to warn the depot of its approach. "That first one'll be pulling into Manassas right now. Guess those Northern boys there will be pissing themselves with worry. They told us we'd never see you boys again! Leastwise not till they marched you through as prisoners."

The locomotive whistle sounded again. Men scattered away from the embankment as staff officers cleared the milling soldiers from the depot so that the engineer of the approaching train would not be alerted to his danger by the sight of a waiting crowd. The locomotive thudded into sight. It was hauling a train of boxcars that rattled and swayed under the moonlit smoke.

Starbuck looked down at the old fellow who had spoken to him. "Are you saying that first train will be in Manassas by now?" he asked.

"It's only an hour's walk that way." The old man pointed northeast. "Train does it in ten minutes!"

Ten minutes, Starbuck thought. He was that close to where Galloway's Horse had its lair? My God, he thought, but what pleasure there would be in doing to Galloway's house what Galloway's men had done to McComb's Tavern. Then he pushed that apprehension of revenge aside as the train thundered into the village. "Hold your fire!" an officer shouted from somewhere down the line. "Hold your fire!"

Starbuck saw some of his own men level their rifles. "No firing!" he shouted: "Guns down!"

But the target was irresistible. The men nearest Starbuck lowered their guns, but a score of others fired, and suddenly the whole village crackled with rifle fire. On board the locomotive the fireman's first reaction was to jump to the tender and haul on the hand brake, and for a second there was a shower of sparks from the protesting machinery, but then the engineer realized his danger and shouted for the brakes to be released as he poured more steam into the driving wheels. The train lurched forward with gouts of steam hissing from a score of bullet holes that surrounded the locomotive with a lamplit halo of vapor through which the boxcars were dragged toward the embankment.

The engineer ducked to shelter from the rifle fire and so never saw the missing track ahead of his train. His locomotive was still accelerating as it plowed off the end of the rails. For a few seconds the whole train kept going in a straight line as dirt and stones spewed in a dark wave beneath the locomotive's churning wheels, but then the boxcars began to concertina and tumble, and the locomotive rolled slowly over, spilling fire as it slid down the embankment. The boxcars piled into a heap of twisted frames and shattered planks. Jackson's men cheered as the destruction continued, and still cheered as the commotion ended. The engine had stopped a few yards short of the bridge over Broad Run, while, fifty yards behind, the last dozen boxcars still stood upright on the undamaged track. The wrecked train had no caboose; instead a pair of red-lensed oil lamps glowed at the back of the last boxcar. Some men began to tear open the undamaged cars, hoping to find Yankee luxuries to replace the stone-hard biscuit, hard green apples, and unripe scavenged corn they had eaten in the last two days. Rightly or wrongly every Southerner believed that no Yankee could go to war without a larder of delicacies on his back, and so the rebels splintered the cars open in hopes of finding a lavish supper, but the wagons were all empty.

A whistle sounded in the dark. "Another train!" The staff officer watching from the hillock to the south of the station shouted the warning.

"Get back! Back!" Officers and sergeants pushed the disappointed plunderers away from the wrecked train, while other men stamped out the fires that had been sparked when the locomotive spilt down the embankment. Cavalry helped clear the scene so that the crew of the oncoming train would suspect nothing.

"Hold your fire this time!" A bearded officer rode along the line of grinning soldiers. "Hold your fire!"

"Son of a bitch won't keep coming with those lights burning." Truslow appeared beside Starbuck and nodded toward the stalled boxcars, where the twin red lamps still glowed to reflect on the steel rails. Truslow waited for someone to realize the fact, but no one seemed to have noticed the lamps, so he took matters into his own hands by running across the strip of waste ground that separated the rail line from the nearest houses. A cavalryman saw the running figure and wheeled his horse to intercept.

"Let him be!" Starbuck shouted.

Truslow reached the train, unhitched his rifle, and swung its brass-hilted butt into the two lanterns. There was a tinkle of glass, and the twin lights vanished just seconds before the new train rocked around the western bend. A hush fell over the watching men as the train steamed past the hillock, clattered over some switchgear that led to an unused siding, vented smoke around the water tower, and then hurtled into the dim yellow light cast from the lanterns hanging in the depot. No one fired a rifle. The engineer leaned from his cab to wave a greeting to anyone

318

who might be in the depot but saw no one and so sounded his whistle instead. The engineer was anticipating the comforts of Manassas, where he and his fireman would cook their supper by grilling two steaks on a greased shovel held in the locomotive's firebox. Afterwards they would play cards and drink some liquor in the engineer's shed before hauling a heavy train of ammunition south in the early morning. Both men were professional Pennsylvanian trainmen who had volunteered to serve in the U.S. Military Railroad, where the money was good, the liquor plentiful, the whores cheap, and the danger, they told each other constantly, pretty much minimal.

The engineer was still thinking of shovel-grilled steaks as his locomotive struck the remnants of the first train. The cowcatcher lifted up the rearmost boxcar, catapulting the vehicle high enough to scrape along the top of the boiler and shear the lamp, smokestack, steam dome, and bell clean off the locomotive. The impact of the third train collapsed the remaining cars of the second; then the deadweight of the moving boxcars piled into the crash and drove the locomotive deeper into the wreckage. The wheels finally jumped the rails, and the locomotive slid sideways to a halt. There was a passenger car behind the tender, and screams sounded from the chaos as the boxcars crashed in behind. The last boxcars stopped upright in the depot itself, while deep among the wreckage at the front of the train a fierce fire started to burn. On either side of the track, well out of danger's range, men were whooping with joy.

"Another train!" the staff officer called from the hillock, and once again a whistle sounded from the darkness.

"We'll do this all night!" Truslow was unusually animated. There was a brute joy in such freedom from all the customary and careful regulations of normal life.

A squad ran to the depot to extinguish the rear lamps of

the stalled train. Other men doused the depot's own lights so that the oncoming train would not glimpse the boxcars standing among the buildings. Deep among the burning wreckage smoke hissed from the locomotive. Men were trying to extricate the crew and passengers as well as extinguish the fires as the fourth train of the night rocked into sight with its lantern flaring yellow-white in the ever-blackening darkness.

"Come on, you son of a bitch!" Truslow growled.

But instead of a third crash there was a scream of brakes as the engineer scented trouble ahead. Maybe it was the darkened depot, or perhaps it was the unextinguished fires that still flickered in the wreckage, but something made the engineer apply his brakes. The wheels locked to skid down the rails through a fountain of flowing sparks. The locomotive stopped just short of the hillock, and the engineer rammed it into reverse gear and released the steam. Smoke poured from the stack as the machinery labored to push the great train backward. The staff officer on the hillock dragged his revolver free and spurred toward the locomotive that was now spinning its wheels. The officer's horse reared away from a jet of steam; then the wheels began to bite and the tons of steel and iron and wood began to crawl away southward. The staff officer fired at the cab and shouted at the engineer to halt, but the engineer kept the regulator fully open, and the protesting cars gathered speed and the rhythm of the locomotive became faster and faster as the train backed safely away. The staff officer fired again, but the train was now moving quicker than his horse could gallop, and so he abandoned the chase and just watched as the train disappeared into the dark with its whistle screaming shrilly.

It was clear no more trains would come this night, and so Jackson ordered his men back into the depot. There was work to do. The survivors had to be brought out of the two wrecked trains, the bridge north of the village had to be destroyed, and the prisoners had to be interrogated. The lanterns in the depot were lit once more, and the General paced up and down beneath their feeble light as he gave his orders.

The survivors of the train wrecks were brought to the depot. Confederate surgeons worked on the wounded while food and water were fetched from the houses. One Northerner, a burly and white-haired civilian dressed in an expensive suit and with a seal-hung gold watch chain stretched across his ample vest, heaved himself onto an elbow to stare across the track at the rebel officers in the depot. The civilian had a new bandage around his head and a splint on his left leg. He stared for a long time, seemingly unable to take his eyes from the skinny, bearded, unkempt, and plain-uniformed man who snapped his orders in a high-pitched voice. The Northerner finally beckoned one of the rebel soldiers to his side. "Son, who is that?"

"That's Stonewall, sir," the soldier said, and then, seeing that the civilian was weak and in pain, he knelt and supported the man's head. "That's Old Jack, sir, large as life."

The wounded man stared at the ragged figure who carried no insignia of rank and whose headgear was nothing but a cadet's shabby cap. The Northerner was a bureaucrat from Washington who was returning from a visit to discuss General Pope's supply problems. He was a man accustomed to the high, imperious style of officers like John Pope or George McClellan, which was why he found it so hard to believe that this unprepossessing figure with its tangled beard and threadbare coat and torn boots was the bogeyman who gave waking nightmares to the whole United States Army. "Are you sure that's Jackson, son?" the bureaucrat asked.

"I'm sure, sir, dead sure. That's him."

The civilian shook his head sadly. "Oh, my God," he said, "just lay me down." A gust of laughter echoed from the nearby soldiers.

Jackson, across the tracks, frowned at the laughter. The General was listening to a brigadier who was assuring him that the Yankees had tons of ammunition, a treasure-house of equipment, and a cornucopia of food stuffed into the warehouses at Manassas Junction. "But they ain't got nothing more than a corporal's guard to watch over it all," the brigadier asserted, "and by morning, General, they'll have a ton of boys out of Washington to keep us at bay. And the sons of bitches, excuse my language, General, are only four miles away. Let me take my two regiments, General, and I'll give you Manassas by dawn."

"With just two regiments?" Jackson asked skeptically.

"With my two regiments, General, I could take hell by storm, let alone a supply depot." The brigadier paused. "You want to talk to the man?" He jerked his head toward the captured engineer who had revealed just how small was the garrison and great the prize at Manassas Junction.

Jackson shook his head, then paused a second. "Go," he finally said, "go."

Because the night was still young, and the mischief merely beginning.

The Reverend Elial Starbuck had been an impatient passenger on the first train that left Warrenton Junction for the North. The rails were supposedly clear, yet even so the train made miserably slow progress. In New England, as the preacher proudly informed his traveling companions, the rails were capable of continuous high-speed travel, but he supposed army railroad management combined with Southern construction techniques had rendered the Orange and Alexandria Road incapable of matching the unsurpassed efficiency of the Boston and Albany. "Sixty miles an hour is not unusual in New England," the Reverend Starbuck declared.

A civilian engineer spat into a cuspidor and declared that a coal-burning locomotive of the Illinois Central had been timed at over seventy miles an hour. "Long way from New England, too," he added pointedly.

"Doubtless it was going downhill," the preacher responded, "or perhaps the timing watch was manufactured in Richmond!" He was pleased with that riposte and could not resist laughing aloud. Night was falling, glossing the car's windows with reflected lamplight. The preacher settled the bundled rebel flag more comfortably on his lap and tried to see some detail of the countryside, but just as he put his face to the glass, the train gave a sudden jerk and began to speed up.

The engineer pulled out his watch. "Just ten minutes to Manassas Junction," he said. The rhythm of the steam engine quickened as the car rattled faster and faster over the jointed rails to shake the brass cuspidors and vibrate the gas-jet flames behind their misted lamp globes. "I suppose you'd call this a snail's pace in New England, Reverend?" the engineer called across the car. The lanterns of a depot flashed by in the half-darkness; then, just as the Reverend Starbuck was about to respond to the engineer's taunt, the window beside him collapsed in a shower of broken glass. For a terrifying few seconds the preacher was certain the train was derailed and crashing. Eternity seemed suddenly imminent; then he heard men whooping outside, and there was the alarming sight of gray uniforms and a heart-stopping glimpse of rifle flames flashing in the dark. The train gave a violent lurch, but somehow kept going. A woman passenger screamed in fear.

"Keep down!" an artillery officer shouted from the front

of the car. Another window was smashed and a bullet ripped into the stuffing of the empty seat opposite the preacher, but then the train was running free into the welcome darkness beyond the depot. The wheels thundered over a bridge as the locomotive's whistle and bell sounded their warning.

"Is anyone hurt?" the artillery officer called as passengers' heads cautiously surfaced above the seat backs. The rush of air through the broken windows guttered the lamp flames and scattered the pages of a newspaper along the central aisle. "Anyone hurt?" the officer demanded again. "Sing out now!"

"By God's grace, no," the Reverend Starbuck answered as he shook spicules of broken glass from the folds of the flag. He was still picking the scraps from the precious silk as the wounded locomotive panted and groaned into Manassas Junction.

"All off now!" an imperious voice commanded the passengers. "Everyone off! Bring your luggage! Everyone off!" The ambushed car had been bound for the Alexandria depot, hard across the river from Washington, and the Reverend Starbuck had been looking forward to an early departure from the capital on the cars of the Baltimore and Ohio. At Baltimore he planned to take a horse-drawn tram across town to the depot of the Philadelphia, Wilmington, and Baltimore Road, where he would find a car bound for New York. Once in New York he would abandon the railroads for a cabin on one of the fast and comfortable Boston steamships, but now it seemed his journey was again to be delayed. "Take your luggage, folks!" the man ordering everyone off the train called.

The Reverend Starbuck's carpetbag was now considerably heavier than when he had first come south. It was true that he had distributed all his abolitionist tracts, but in their place he had gathered some valued souvenirs of battle. None, to be sure, was as precious as the great silken banner, but nevertheless he had discovered some objects with which he expected to excite Boston's curiosity. Packed in his carpetbag were two gray rebel caps, one with a bullet hole and the other satisfyingly stained with blood, a zinc plug from an unexploded shell, a revolver with a barrel shattered by a cannonball, the knucklebone of a dead rebel, and a rusting belt buckle with the initials CSA stamped clearly on its face. The heaviest of his souvenirs were copies of Southern newspapers: ill-printed on crudely made paper and containing editorials of an evil that even the Reverend Doctor Starbuck found breathtaking. It all added up to a considerable weight that he lugged off the train before accosting the young Captain who had so peremptorily ordered the passengers off the car. "You're preparing another train?" the preacher demanded.

"For what?" the Captain retorted, turning around from the open window of the telegraph office.

"For Washington, of course!"

"For Washington? My God, uncle, you'll be lucky! Don't suppose anything will move now till first light. If there are bushwhackers at Bristoe then God knows where else they might be."

"I have to be in Washington by morning!" the preacher protested.

"You can walk," the Captain said rudely. "It isn't a step more than twenty-five miles, but there won't be any more trains tonight, uncle. And in the morning I daresay they'll be sending troops down from Washington." He paused. "I guess you can wait for one of those trains to go back? But this train isn't moving anyplace, not till it's been in the workshops for repairs." He turned back to the telegrapher. "What do they say?"

The telegrapher eased back from his machinery, which

was still stuttering tinnily. "They want to know how many raiders, sir."

"Well?" the Captain demanded of the train's engineer, who was standing behind the telegraphers. "How many bushwhackers did you see?"

"Two or three hundred?" the engineer suggested uneasily.

The Reverend Elial Starbuck cleared his throat. "They were not bushwhackers," he said sternly, "but rebel soldiers. I saw them clearly."

The Captain gave the elderly minister a tired look. "If they were troops, uncle, they'd have cut the telegraph. But they haven't, which makes me think they're amateurs. But we've told the army what's happening, so there's no need to worry."

"They've cut the wire now, sir," the telegrapher broke in. "Just this second, sir." He jiggled his key, but nothing came back. "Line's still open to Alexandria, but everything's dead to the south of us, sir."

"So what are we to do?" one of the dispossessed travelers demanded plaintively.

The Captain grimaced. "You might get rooms at Micklewhite's Tavern here, but if Mick's full you'll have to leg it into Manassas town. It's not far up the track, or there's a road beyond the wagon park."

If the Reverend Elial had wanted rest and shelter, he would have used Major Galloway's house, which lay not far beyond the town, but he had no mind for creature comforts this night. Instead, with his ebony cane clutched firmly in his right hand, and with the flag and carpetbag clasped awkwardly in his left, he set out in search of some officer who might pay him more attention than the glib young Captain. The depot itself hardly encouraged his hopes, for it consisted of nothing but great, dark buildings hastily thrown up on the foundations of the warehouses burned by the rebels when they had abandoned the depot earlier in the year, while here and there among the dark monstrosities a sentry's brazier fought the night with a small red glow. Between the huge warehouses were weed-strewn rail spurs where more materials were stored in boxcars and where long, low gondola cars carried brand-new field guns. The moon silvered the cannons' long barrels, and the Reverend Starbuck wondered why the guns were here instead of pounding the rebels into submission. The war, he decided, was being prosecuted by half-wits.

He left the warehouses behind and stumped through a wagon park toward the lights of the nearby town. A lesser man than the Reverend Elial Starbuck might have hesitated before entering the town's main street, for the place was raucous with drunks. Most of the drinkers were railmen, but there were plenty of black folk among them, and the sight of the Negroes angered the Reverend Starbuck. Where, he wondered, were the missions? And where the Christian teachers? The town had been declared an official refuge for escaped slaves, but by the evidence before his eyes it seemed that the Negroes would have been better off in servitude than being thus exposed to debauchery, uncleanness, and liquor. There would need to be changes!

He asked a soldier where the commander of the garrison might be found and was directed to a guardroom attached to the post office. A lieutenant scrambled to his feet as the Reverend Starbuck entered, then answered the preacher's query by saying that Captain Craig was absent. "He's gone to look to our defenses, sir. It seems there are bandits on the rail line south, sir."

"More than bandits, Lieutenant. The raiders are rebel troops. I saw them with my own eyes. Infantry, definitely rebel infantry. I saw the same scum at Cedar Mountain, so I know of what I speak."

327

"I'll make sure Captain Craig hears what you have to say, sir." The Lieutenant spoke respectfully, though he was privately dubious about the preacher's report. There had been rumors of rebel raiders near Manassas every night for the last two weeks, but none of the rumors had proved true, and the Lieutenant doubted whether a minister of the gospel could tell the difference between rebel soldiers and bushwhackers, especially as even the best-dressed rebels looked little better than cutthroat outlaws. "But not to worry, sir," the Lieutenant continued, "Captain Craig ordered our artillery and cavalry to deploy, and he put all our infantry on alert." The Lieutenant decided it might be wiser not to add that there were only eight cannon in the defenses, aided by a mere hundred cavalrymen and a single company of infantry. Manassas was supposed to be a safe posting, as safe as garrison duty in Maine or California. "I don't think our sleep will be disturbed, sir," the Lieutenant said soothingly.

The Reverend Starbuck was pleasantly surprised to discover that at least one officer seemed to have performed his proper duty this night. "Captain Craig? Is that his name?" The Reverend Starbuck had taken out his diary and was now penciling a note. "He's done well, Lieutenant, and I like to report commendable behavior when I encounter it."

"His name is Captain Samuel Craig, sir, of the 105th Pennsylvania," the Lieutenant said, wondering just how important this authoritative minister was. "You report to the government, perhaps, sir?"

"I report to the greatest government that ever ruled on this earth, Lieutenant, or on any other," the Reverend Starbuck said as he finished writing his note.

"Then maybe you'd like to add my name, sir?" the Lieutenant said eagerly. "It's Gilray, Lieutenant Ethan Gilray of the Provost Guard. Just the one *L*, sir, and thank you for asking." Gilray waited as the minister penciled his name. "And will you be wanting quarters for the night, sir? There's a Mrs. Moss in Main Street, a most Christian woman who keeps a very clean house. For a Virginian."

The Reverend Starbuck closed his diary. "I shall wait in the passenger depot, Lieutenant." Much as he was tempted by a clean bed, he dared not miss the chance of a north-bound train, yet before he returned to the depot he still had one Christian obligation to discharge. "The Provost Guard is responsible, is it not, for discipline?" the Reverend Starbuck asked.

"Indeed it is, sir."

"Then I shall have no alternative but to report you for the grossest dereliction of duty, Lieutenant, a duty that is Christian before it is military. There are Negroes in town, Lieutenant Gilray, who have been permitted access to in-ebriating liquor. Would a loving parent put ardent spirits in the way of his children? Of course he would not! Yet the Negroes came to Manassas on just such a promise of protec-tion, a promise made by our government that you, as that government's representative, have broken by allowing them to fall prey to the temptation of strong drink. It is a disgrace, sir, a shameful disgrace, and I shall make certain that our authorities in Washington are made fully aware of it. Good day to you." The Reverend Starbuck left the speechless Gilray and went back into the night. He felt better for that discharge of his duty, for he was a fervent believer that each man, every day, should leave the world a better place than he found it.

He walked back through the town, listening to the drunken songs and seeing the scarlet women who lifted their skirts in the stinking alleys. He fended a drunk off with his cane. Somewhere in the dark a dog whined, a child cried, a man vomited, and a woman screamed, and the sad sounds made the Reverend Starbuck reflect on how much sin was souring God's good world. Satan, he thought, was much abroad in these dark days, and he began to plan a sermon that likened the Christian life to a military campaign. Maybe, he thought, there was more than a sermon in that idea, but a whole book, and that pleasant thought kept him company as he strode down the moonlit road toward the depot. Such a book would be timely, he decided, and might even earn him enough to add a new scullery to the house on Walnut Street.

He had already planned his chapter headings and was beginning to anticipate the book's adulatory notices when suddenly, shockingly, the sky ahead of him flashed red as a cannon fired. The sound wave crashed past him just as a second cannon belched flame that briefly illuminated a rolling cloud of gunsmoke; then the Reverend Starbuck heard the chilling and ululating sound that he had mistaken at Cedar Mountain for Aristophanes' *paean*. He stopped, knowing now how the devil's noise denoted a rebel attack, and he watched in disgust as a scatter of blue-coated soldiers fled from the depot's shadows. Northern cavalrymen were galloping between the dark buildings, and fleeing infantrymen were running along the rail lines. The Reverend Starbuck listened as the rebels' foul *paean* turned into cheers, and then, to his chagrin, he saw gray coats in the moonlight and knew that the devil was scoring yet another terrible victory in this summer's night. A brazier was tipped over, causing fire to flare bright between two warehouses, and in the sudden flamelight the Reverend Starbuck saw the satanic banner of the Southern rebels coming toward him. He gaped in horror, then thought of the greater horror of being captured by such fiends, and so he hid the captured flag under his coat and, stick and bag in hand, turned and fled. He would seek shelter in Galloway's house, where, hidden from this rampaging and seemingly unstoppable enemy, he would pray for a miracle.

The Legion marched at dawn. They were hungry and tired, but their steps were lightened by rumors that the warehouses at Manassas had been captured and that all the hungry men in the world could be fed from their contents.

Starbuck had last seen the Manassas depot wreathed in smoke when the Confederates had destroyed the junction. The Legion, indeed, had been the very last rebel infantry regiment to abandon Manassas, leaving the warehouses nothing but ashes, yet as the depot came into view, Starbuck saw that the great spread of buildings was now more extensive than ever. The Northern government had not just replaced the burned warehouses but had added new ones and built fresh rail spurs for the hundreds of freight wagons that waited to be hauled south, but even those new facilities were not enough to hold all the Northern supplies, and so thousands of tons of food and materiel had to be stored in hooded wagons parked wheel-to-wheel in the fields beyond the warehouses.

A staff officer spurred back down the marching column. "Go get your rations, boys! It's all yours. A present from Uncle Abe. All yours!"

The men, invigorated by the thought of plunder, quickened their pace. "Slow down!" Starbuck shouted as the leading companies began to break away from the rest. "Major Medlicott!"

The commander of A Company turned in his saddle and offered Starbuck a lugubrious expression.

"We'll take the end warehouse!" Starbuck pointed to the easternmost part of the depot, which was still clear of rebel troops. He feared the chaos that would result if his regiment was scattered among a score of warehouses and mixed with revelers from a dozen other brigades. "Captain Truslow!" he shouted toward the rear of the column. "I'm relying on you to find ammunition! Lieutenant Howes! I want pickets around the warehouse! Keep our men inside! Coffman? I want you to find some local people and discover where the Galloway farm is."

Yet for the moment there was no time to consider revenge on Galloway's Horse, only to plunge into the stacks of boxes and barrels and crates that were piled in the vast, dim warehouse and inside the adjacent boxcars and wagons. It was a hoard that the hard-pressed Confederate army could only dream of possessing. There were uniforms, rifles, ammunition, haversacks, belts, blankets, tents, saddles, boots, bridles, percussion caps, gum rubber groundsheets, picket pins, telegraph wire, signal flags, and lucifer matches. There were candles, lanterns, camp furniture, drums, sheet music, Bibles, buckets, oilcloth capes, jars of quinine, bottles of camphor, folding flagpoles, bugles, replacement pay books, friction fuses, and artillery shells. There were spades, axes, augurs, saws, bayonets, cooking pots, sabers, swords, and canteens.

Then there was food. Not just army-issue hardtack in boxes and desiccated soup in canvas bags, but luxuries from the wagons of the Northern army's sutlers, who made their money by selling delicacies to the troops. There were barrels of dried oysters and casks of pickles, cakes of white sugar, boxes of loose tea, slabs of salt beef, sacks of rice, cans of fruit, sides of bacon, jars of peaches, combs of honey, bottles of catsup, and flasks of powdered lemon. Best of all there was coffee, real coffee; ready-sweetened coffee, baked, ground, mixed with sugar and packed into sacks. There were also bottles of liquor: rum and brandy, champagne and wine, cases and cases of wine and spirits packed in sawdust and all disappearing fast into thirsty men's haversacks. A few conscientious officers fired revolvers into the cases of liquor in an effort to keep their men from drunkenness, but there were simply too many bottles for the precaution to be of any effect.

"Lobster salad, sir!" Private Hunt, his dirty face smeared from ear to ear with a pink confection, offered Starbuck a knife blade loaded with the delicacy from a newly opened can. "Came from a sutler's wagon."

"You'll make yourself sick, Hunt," Starbuck said.

"I hope so, sir," Hunt said. Starbuck tried the proffered salad and found it delicious.

Starbuck wandered in a daze from one store bay to the next. The supplies seemed to have been stacked without any system, but just crammed into the warehouse in whatever order they had arrived from the North. There were cartridges from Britain, tinned food from France, and salt cod from Portugal. There was lamp oil from Nantucket, cheese from Vermont, and dried apples from New York. There was kerosene, medical sulfur, calcined magnesia, sugar of lead, and laxatives made of powdered rhubarb. There was so much material that if two armies the size of Jackson's force had plundered the depot for a month, they could not have opened every box or explored every dusty stack of crates.

"What you can't carry away, we'll have to burn," a staff officer called to Starbuck, "so search it well!" and the Legion, like small boys released to a toyshop, splintered open the crates and whooped with glee at every fresh discovery. Patrick Hogan of C Company was distributing officers' shoulder boards, while Cyrus Matthews was cramming his face with a nauseating mix of dried apple and chipped beef. One man had discovered a cabin trunk that seemed to contain nothing but chess sets, and he was now disgustedly scattering knights, rooks, and bishops as he dug down in search of greater treasures. Bandmaster Little had found a box of sheet music, while Robert Decker, one of the best men in Truslow's company, had discovered a cased match rifle, precision-made for a marksman and equipped with a barrel-length telescopic sight, a hair trigger, a separate cocking trigger, and a small pair of legs at the barrel's muzzle to support the weapon's huge weight. "It'll kill a mule at five hundred paces, sir!" Decker boasted to Starbuck.

"It'll be heavy to carry, Bob," Starbuck warned him.

"But it'll even things against the sharpshooters, sir," Decker answered. Every rebel hated the Yankee sharpshooters, who were lethally equipped with similar long-range target rifles.

Captain Truslow had commandeered two brand-new seven-ton wagons that both carried small brass plates proclaiming them to be the products of Levergood's Carriage Factory of Pittsburgh, Pennsylvania. There were boxes attached to the wagon sides that were filled with repair tools, lanterns, and cans of axle grease, and Truslow, always reluctant to concede that anything could be well made in the hated North, nevertheless admitted that the Levergood's Company built a half-decent vehicle. The two gray-painted wagons would replace the old ammunition carts burned in Galloway's raid, and Truslow had his men busy stacking the wagon beds with boxes of rifle ammunition and crates of percussion caps. The draught horses were fitted with brand-new collars, hames, and traces, then backed into the shafts.

Captain Pine's men were distributing boots, while Lieutenant Patterson's company was handing out sacks of coffee. Captain Davies's company was employed in taking down the barn doors from a warehouse; the doors were needed as ramps so that a Georgian artillery battery could maneuver some brand-new Northern cannons off their gondola cars. The Georgians were presently equipped with Napoleon twelve-pounders that were, in their commander's word, "tired," but now they would be armed with a half-dozen Parrott twenty-pound rifles so new that the packing grease from the foundry was still sticky on their barrels. The artillerymen wrecked the wheels and spiked the vents of their old guns, then dragged away their new weapons, each of which displayed a neatly stenciled legend on its trail: PROPERTY OF THE USA.

Colonel Swynyard watched the plunder from horseback. He had helped himself to a brand-new saddle and was sucking on a strip of beef jerky. "Sixteen men," he said gnomically to Starbuck.

"Sir?"

"That's all we lost to straggling. Out of the whole Brigade! And most of them will turn up, I don't doubt. Some other brigades lost hundreds." Swynyard grimaced as the strip of beef aggravated a sore tooth. "I don't suppose you came across any false teeth, did you?"

"No, sir, but I'll keep a lookout."

"I think I'll have Doc Billy take all mine out. They're nothing but trouble. I confess, Starbuck, that my new faith in Almighty God is shaken by the existence of teeth. Do your teeth hurt?"

"One does."

"You probably smoke too much," Swynyard said. "Tobacco smoke might be good for keeping the lungs open, but I've long believed that the juice of the weed rots the teeth." He frowned, not for the thought of tobacco juice, but because a train whistle had sounded in the warm morning wind. Swynyard gazed toward the northern horizon, where a billow of smoke showed above distant trees. "We've got company, I guess," Swynyard said.

The thought of Northerners reminded Starbuck that Stonewall Jackson would not have marched fifty miles in two days just to replenish his army's stock of ammunition and food. "Does anyone know what's happening?" Starbuck asked the perennial soldier's question.

"I'm told that General Jackson is not given to confiding in his inferiors," Swynyard said, "or in his superiors either, for that matter, so I can only guess, and my guess is that we've been sent here as bait."

"Bait." Starbuck repeated the word flatly. It did not sound good.

"I'm guessing that we've been sent up here to pull the Yankees out of their defenses on the Rappahannock," Swynyard said, then paused to watch a soldier shake loose yards and yards of mosquito netting, "which could mean that in a few hours we'll have every blessed Yankee in Virginia trying to kill us." He finished, then stared northward to where a brisk rattle of rifle fire had sounded. The volley was followed by the heavier sound of artillery. "Someone's getting thumped," Swynyard said with a blood-thirsty relish, then twisted in his saddle to watch a sad procession come into sight beside the warehouse. A group of rebel soldiers were escorting a long line of black men and women, some crying but most walking with a stiff dignity. "Escaped slaves," Swynyard explained curtly.

A woman tried to break away from the column but was shoved back into place by a soldier. Starbuck counted almost two hundred of the slaves, who were now ordered to form a line close beside a captured portable forge. "What they should have done," Swynyard said, "is keep running north of the Potomac."

"Why didn't they?"

"Because the Yankees declared Manassas a safe refuge for contrabands. They want to keep the darkies down here, you see, south of the Mason-Dixon line. It's one thing to preach emancipation, but quite another to have them living in your street, ain't that the case?"

"I don't know, sir." Starbuck grimaced as he saw a leather-aproned blacksmith test the heat of the forge's furnace. The portable forge was a traveling blacksmith's shop mounted on the back of a heavy wagon that could travel with the army and shoe horses or provide instant repairs to broken metal. The smith dragged a length of chain out of a barrel, and Starbuck immediately understood what was about to happen to the recaptured slaves.

"So how many blacks live in your father's street?" Swynyard demanded.

"None, except for a couple of servants."

"And has your father ever had a black at his dinner table?"

"Not that I know of," Starbuck said. A hammer clanged on the anvil. The smith was fashioning manacles out of barrel hoops, then brazing the open manacles onto the chain. Heat shimmered over the small open furnace, which was being fanned by two soldiers pumping a leather bellows. Every minute or so a recaptured slave was forced to the forge to have one of the newly made manacles closed around an ankle. A huge-bellied captain with a bristling black beard was supervising the operation, cuffing the slaves if they showed any resistance and boasting how they would suffer now they had been recaptured. "What happens to them?" Starbuck asked.

"You can never trust a black that's run away," Swynyard said, speaking with the authority of a man born into one of Virginia's oldest slave-trading families. "It don't matter how valuable he is, he's been spoilt for good if he's tasted a bit of liberty, so they'll all get sold down the river."

"Women too?"

The Colonel nodded. "Women too. And children."

"So they'll all be dead in a year?"

"Unless they're real lucky," Swynyard said, "and die sooner." Being sold down the river meant going to the

337

sweated chain gangs on the cotton plantations of the deep South. Swynyard looked away. "I guess my two boys had the good sense to keep on running. They ain't here, anyway, I looked for them." He paused as the gunfire to the north reached a crackling crescendo. Powder smoke was whitening the sky, indicating that a skirmish of some severity was taking place, but the fact that no staff officers were demanding reinforcements from the troops rifling the depot suggested that the enemy was well in hand. "Right now," Swynyard said, "I'd guess that we've just got a few odds and ends coming to attack us. The real attack won't hit till tomorrow."

"Something to look forward to," Starbuck said dryly. The Colonel grinned and rode on, leaving Starbuck to stroll among his happy men. There was no grumbling now about missing a chance to join the Richmond garrison; instead the Legion was reveling in its chance of loot. Captain Moxey had found some frilled shirts and was pulling them on one above another to save himself the trouble of cramming them into a haversack already stuffed with tins of chicken in aspic. Sergeant Major Tolliver had unpacked a whole case of long-barreled Whitney revolvers and was attempting to stow as many as possible in his clothing, while Lieutenant Coffman had discovered a handsome black cloak edged with blue silk braid that he swirled dramatically around his body. At least two men were already blind drunk.

Starbuck dragged one of the drunken men off a case marked "Massachusetts Arms Co. Chicopee Falls." The man groaned and protested, but Starbuck snarled at him to shut up, then levered the case open to find a shipment of Adams .36-caliber revolvers. The guns, with their blued barrels and cross-hatched black-walnut grips, looked deadly and beautiful. Starbuck discarded the clumsier long-

338

barreled Colt he had taken from a dead New Yorker at Gaines Mill and helped himself to one of the new revolvers. He was just loading the last of the Adams's five chambers when a chorus of shouts erupted from further down the warehouse. Starbuck turned to see an excited mob of his men chasing an agile black figure, who swerved around an astonished Coffman, leaped over an opened crate of canteens, and would have got clean away had not the drunk beside Starbuck reached out an oblivious hand that inadvertently tripped the fugitive. The boy—he was hardly more than a boy—sprawled in the mud, where he was pounced on by his cheering pursuers.

"Bring the bastard here!" Major Medlicott strode down the warehouse carrying a teamster's whip.

The prisoner yelped as Abram Trent cuffed him around the head. "Goddamned nigger thief!" Trent had the boy by one ear and was hitting him with his free hand. "Thieving black bastard."

"Enough!" Starbuck pushed a man aside. "Let go of him."

"He's a thieving—"

"I said let go of him!"

Trent reluctantly let go of the boy's ear, but not without giving the captured fugitive a last savage blow. The boy staggered but managed to stay on his feet. He looked around for an escape, realized he was trapped, and so adopted a defiant air. He had a thin face, long black hair, a straight nose, and high cheekbones. He was dressed in a sailor's bell-bottom pants and a billowing striped shirt that gave him an exotic look. Starbuck had once spent a few weeks with a traveling troupe of actors, and there was something in the boy's flamboyance that reminded him of those distant times. "What's your name?" Starbuck asked him.

The boy looked up at his savior, but instead of showing gratitude, he spat. "Ain't got a name."

"What's your name?" Starbuck insisted again, but only received a truculent glare for answer.

Medlicott pushed through the ring of men. "Stay out of this, Starbuck!" he said, raising the whip against the black lad.

Starbuck stepped in front of Major Medlicott. He kept a smile on his face as he put his mouth close to Medlicott's right ear, and he kept smiling as he spoke softly, so softly that only Medlicott could hear him. "Listen, you lily-livered son of a bitch, you give me orders one more time and I'll pistol-whip you down to corporal." Starbuck was still smiling as he stepped a pace backward. "Don't you agree that's the best way to proceed, Major?"

Medlicott was not certain at first that he had heard right and just blinked at Starbuck. Then he took a backward pace and flicked the whip toward the captured boy. "He stole my watch," Medlicott said. "The little black bastard lifted it out of my pocket when I laid my coat down. It was a present from my wife, too," he added indignantly, "from Edna!"

Starbuck looked at the boy. "Give the Major his watch."

"Don't have it."

Starbuck sighed and stepped forward. The boy tried to twist aside, but Starbuck was too quick for him. He grabbed a handful of long dirty hair and held the squirming boy still. "Search him, Coffman," he said.

Lieutenant Coffman nervously began searching the boy's pockets. At first he found nothing; then it became apparent that the pants pockets had been elongated into long, capacious, sausage-shaped sacks specially strengthened to hold and conceal plunder, and the men watched in amazement as the evidence of the boy's thefts was dragged into the light. Coffman produced two hunter watches, a gilt picture frame, a collapsible silver cup, a folding mirror, two razors, a brass match case, a carved pipe, a signet ring, an ivory-handled shaving brush, a comb, a pack of cards, and a handful of coins. The men stared in awe at the hoard. "Oh, my God," one of them said, "just lay me down," and a bellow of laughter swept through the crowd.

Coffman stepped away from the boy. "That's all, sir," he said.

"They're all my property!" the boy insisted, trying to retrieve one of the watches, and the ring of men laughed and cheered at his insolence. They had been baying for his blood just a minute before, but there was something irresistible about the young man's unrepentant face and impressive haul of thefts.

Medlicott retrieved his watch. "He's a goddamn thief. He should be whipped."

"But I thought we were all thieves today," Starbuck said, and he was about to kick the boy on his way when a stentorian voice shouted from outside the ring of Legionnaires.

"Hold on to that nigger!" the voice shouted, and the men slowly parted to make way for the big, bearded Captain who had been supervising the manacling of the recaptured slaves. "Another damn runaway," the man said, reaching for the boy.

"I'm a free man!" the boy insisted.

"And I'm Abraham Lincoln," the Captain said as he grabbed the boy's striped shirt. He cuffed the long black hair aside and displayed one of the boy's earlobes to Starbuck. "Took his earring out, didn't he? First thing a runaway does, take off the earring." Earrings denoted slave status. "So if you're free, lad," the Captain went on, "why don't you show us your papers?"

The boy plainly had no papers. For a second or two he looked defiant; then he was overwhelmed by despair and tried to twist out of the Captain's grip. The Captain slapped him hard around the head. "You'll be picking cotton now, lad."

"He belongs to me," Starbuck said suddenly. He had not intended to speak, and certainly he had never intended to claim ownership of the boy, but there was something appealing about the young man's spirit that reminded Starbuck of his own desperate attempts to remake himself in an image of his own devising, and he knew that if he did not speak up, then the boy would be hammered and burned into the chains and then sold down the river to the living hell of the cotton plantations.

The Captain gave Starbuck a long, hard look, then spat a viscous brown stream of tobacco juice. "Out my way, boy."

"You call me 'sir,'" Starbuck said, "or I'll have you arrested and charged for rank insubordination. Now, boy, get the hell out of my regiment."

The Captain laughed at Starbuck's presumption, then twitched the fugitive slave toward the forge. Starbuck kicked the man hard between the legs, then rammed a flat palm into the bearded face. The Captain let go of the escaped slave and staggered backward. He was in terrible pain, but he succeeded in keeping his footing and was just starting forward with his fists clenched when there was the unmistakable click of a gun being cocked. "You heard the Major," Truslow's voice said, "so git."

The Captain put a hand to his face to wipe blood away from his mustache. He looked askance at Starbuck, wondering if the youngster really was a major, then decided that anything might be true in wartime. He pointed a blood-smeared finger at the cowering boy. "He's a contraband. The law says he's got to be returned—"

"You heard the Captain," Starbuck said, "so git."

Starbuck waited till the man had gone, then turned and took hold of the boy's ear. "Come here, you son of a bitch," he said, dragging the boy away from the crowd and into the warehouse, where he threw the lad hard onto a pile of grain

342

sacks. "Listen, you little bastard, I've just saved you from a whipping, and better still, I've just saved you from being sold down the river. So what's your name?"

The boy rubbed his ear. "You really a major?"

"No, I'm the goddamn archangel Gabriel. Who are you?"

"Whoever I want to be," the boy said defiantly. Starbuck guessed he was fourteen or fifteen, an urchin who had learned to live by his wits.

"So who do you want to be?" Starbuck asked.

The boy was surprised by the question, but he thought about it, then grinned and shrugged. "Lucifer," he said at last.

"You can't be Lucifer," Starbuck said, shocked, "that's the devil's name!"

"Only name I'm giving you, master," the boy insisted.

Starbuck guessed that was true, so he settled for the satanic name. "So listen to me, Lucifer, my name's Major Starbuck, and I need a servant real bad and you just got the job. Are you hearing me?"

"Yes, sir." There was something cheeky and mocking in the response.

"And I need a comb, a toothbrush, field glasses, a razor that'll hold an edge, and something to eat other than hardtack and shoe leather. Are you hearing me?"

"I got ears, master! See?" Lucifer insolently plucked back his long ringlets. "One on each side, see?"

"So you go and get those things, Lucifer," Starbuck said. "I don't care how, and you be back here within the hour. Can you cook?"

The boy pretended to think about the question, drawing out his silence just beyond the edge of rudeness. "Sure, I can cook."

"Good. So get whatever you need for cooking utensils." Starbuck stood aside. "And bring me as many cigars as you can carry."

The boy sauntered into the sunlit doorway, where he stopped, plucked his disarrayed clothing into shape, then turned to look at Starbuck. "Suppose I don't come back?"

"Just make sure you aren't sent down the river, Lucifer."

The boy stared at Starbuck, then nodded at the wisdom of that advice. "Are you making me into a soldier?" he asked.

"I'm making you my cook."

The boy grinned. "How much are you paying me, Major?"

"I just saved your worthless life and that's all the wages you're getting from me."

"You mean I'm your slave?" The boy sounded disgusted.

"I mean you're a goddamn servant to the best goddamn officer in this goddamn army, so get the goddamn out of here and stop wasting my goddamn time before I goddamn kick you out."

The boy grinned. "Do I get a goddamn gun?"

"You don't need a gun," Starbuck said.

"In case I have to protect myself from the Yankees who want to make me into a free man," Lucifer said, then laughed. "Can't be a soldier without a gun."

"You ain't a soldier," Starbuck said. "You're a cook."

"You said I can be whatever I want to be," the boy said, "remember?" Then he ran off.

"That's one nigger you won't see again," Truslow said from just outside the door.

"I don't really want to see him again."

"Then you shouldn't have risked a fight for him," Truslow said. "That Captain would have murdered you."

"So thank you," Starbuck said.

"I didn't run him off to save your good looks," Truslow said sarcastically, "but because it don't do the boys no good to see their Major having the shit thumped out of him. You want a pickled oyster?" He held out a jar of the delicacies;

344

then, as Starbuck helped himself, Truslow turned and watched as a disconsolate herd of blue-coated prisoners limped past. The men were smartly uniformed but looked utterly whipped. Some of their heads showed livid saber slashes, wounds that had cut so deep that the blood had soaked their tunics down to their waists. The Northerners limped past, going to their long imprisonment, and Truslow grinned. "Just ain't their day, is it?" he said. "Just ain't their goddamn day."

Colonel Patrick Lassan of His French Majesty's Imperial Guard, who was officially a foreign military observer attached to the rebel army but who preferred to do his observing from the front ranks of the rebel cavalry, took a handful of his horse's mane and slowly drew his long straight sword through the coarse hair to scrub the blade clean of blood. He needed to clean the steel three times before it was fit to slide back into the scabbard; then, lighting a cigar, he trotted slowly back along the path of the cavalry charge.

A brigade of New Jersey troops had come from the defenses of Washington to evict what they believed was a band of rebel cavalry raiders from the depot at Manassas Junction. Only instead of encountering a handful of ragged cavalrymen, they had marched straight into the depot's old defensive earthworks manned by Stonewall Jackson's veteran infantry and artillery. Whipped by rifle fire and flayed by cannons, the New Jerseymen had retreated. It was then that Jackson had unleashed the cavalry, who had turned their retreat into a rout.

Dazed Northerners still reeled blindly about the field where the horsemen had charged. The Northerners were mostly wounded in the head or shoulders, the bloody wounds of men caught in the open by cavalrymen carrying sabers. Their comrades were either lying dead where the volleys of the entrenched defenders had ambushed them, or else were struggling to safety across the rain-swollen Bull Run, where, a year before, so many of their countrymen had drowned in the defeat of the first invasion of the Confederate States of America.

Lassan watched the rebels round up the living and loot the dead. The Confederates were joking about the ease of their victory, claiming it was further proof that a half-dozen Northerners were no match for a single Southerner, but Lassan was both more experienced and more sanguine and knew that the attack of the New Jersey brigade had been a blunder by an inexperienced general. The New Jersey officers had been so new to war that they had attacked with drawn swords, oblivious that they were thus making themselves targets for Southern marksmen. The Northern officers had led their men to horror, but Lassan knew that this slaughter of the innocents was an aberration and that soon the real fighting would begin. The North had been surprised by Jackson's march, but it would not be long before the Yankee veterans arrived to snap at the bait that hung so temptingly at Manassas Junction. For the North now had Stonewall Jackson outnumbered, they had him isolated, and, so they must surely believe, they had him doomed.

ALL DAY THE YANKEES tried to make sense of the storm that had broken behind their backs. The first confused reports merely spoke of bushwhackers, then it was claimed the raiding party was a large band of Jeb Stuart's horsemen, and finally there were worrying reports of rebel infantry and artillery inside the defenses of Manassas Junction, but no one could tell John Pope precisely what was happening at his supply depot. He knew that no trains were coming from Manassas and that the telegraph to Washington had been cut, but neither of these events was uncommon, and for much of the day Pope regarded all reports from Manassas as mere alarmist rumors spread by panicking men frightened by a handful of Confederate cavalry raiders. John Pope was unwilling to abandon his conviction that Lee must do what John Pope had planned for Lee to do, which was to launch a grand yet suicidal attack across the swirling Rappahannock, but slowly, grudgingly, like a man refusing to admit that the heavy clouds above his parade had begun to rain, Pope began to understand that the commotion at Manassas amounted to a great deal more than a raid. It was the opening move of a campaign he had not planned to fight but to which he was now forced to react.

"We'll be riding north tonight, you mark my words," Major Galloway observed. "Did you hear me, Adam?" But Adam Faulconer was not listening to his commanding officer. Instead he was staring at a recent copy of the *Richmond*

Examiner that had been exchanged for a *New York Times* by one of the Northern pickets, then brought to John Pope's headquarters, where Major Galloway and Adam had been peremptorily summoned. The Major had scanned the ill-printed sheets, snorted in disgust at the editor's secessionist distortions, then relinquished the rag to Adam. Now Galloway was kicking his heels in the hallway and waiting while a succession of flustered aides carried maps into the parlor, where the General was trying to comprehend the day's events.

"Did you read this?" Adam suddenly demanded of Galloway.

Galloway did not need to be told what item in the newspaper had offended Adam. "I read it," the Major said, "but I don't necessarily believe it."

"Five women dead!" Adam protested.

"It's a rebel newspaper," Galloway pointed out.

The story was headlined "Outrage in Orange County." Yankee raiders, the newspaper reported, seeking to emulate the exploits of Jeb Stuart, had crossed the Rapidan to raid Lee's forces, but had instead burned down a country tavern and killed everyone inside. There was no mention of the raid on the Faulconer Brigade, nor of the guns and wagons that Galloway's men had destroyed, but only a pitiful description of the innocent civilians dying inside the inferno that had engulfed what the newspaper described as "McComb's Hotel," presumably because a goodly number of the *Examiner*'s readers might well approve of taverns being destroyed, even if their destroyers were the hated Yankees. Hotels, on the other hand, were not necessarily the devil's way stations, and so Liam McComb's establishment had been appropriately elevated. "The reader can only imagine the terror of the women as they beseeched their attackers to spare their lives," the *Examiner* trumpeted, and a paragraph later, "It seems Northern cavaliers can be brave enough when their foes are women and children, but they display nothing but clean heels and horses' tails when faced by Southern soldiers."

"They're beating the patriotic drum," Galloway said wearily, "by telling half-truths and outright lies. There were soldiers in that so-called hotel, Adam, even the newspaper admits as much."

"And it says here, sir, that those soldiers called on the enemy to cease fire."

"What else would it say?" Galloway asked, and then, in grudging acknowledgment of Adam's anger, he went on, "When Billy gets back we'll ask him the truth."

"And you think he'll tell you the truth?" Adam asked hotly.

Galloway sighed. "I think maybe Billy has an excess of zeal, Adam, but I don't reckon Billy murdered any woman that night. I ain't saying no woman died, but only that it was an accident. Tragedy happens in wartime, Adam. It's why we're trying to end the war quickly."

Adam threw the newspaper down in disgust. His disgust was not so much with the *Examiner* but with Galloway's refusal to face the truth that Billy Blythe was a man who used warfare as an excuse for criminality. Blythe even boasted about using the war as a means of enrichment, and the more Adam reflected on Blythe the angrier he became, so that he was forced to calm himself down by taking a deep breath. He listened to the angry voices coming from the General's parlor, and it struck him that war was a dreadful instrument that stirred a whole society into turmoil, bringing the worst to the top and driving the best down.

Galloway saw the anger on the younger man's face and wondered whether Adam was too tender for war; maybe a man needed Billy Blythe's callous carapace to be a good soldier, yet it was undeniable that it had been Adam and not Blythe who had provided Galloway with his one victory. Galloway now wondered where Blythe was, for his second-in-command had never returned from his patrol into the west. Maybe he had followed the strange column to its destination and would be waiting at Galloway's farm, or maybe, more disastrously, Blythe's troop had been ambushed and cut to pieces by the rebels. Beyond the town a train whistle hooted mournfully, while further away, where the Federal army was dug in on the Rappahannock's northern bank, the thunder of cannon fire rumbled incessantly. The Southern gunners had started an artillery duel that had been raging all day, probably, Galloway now realized, as a means of diverting John Pope from what was happening behind his back.

"When this war's over"—Adam broke his silence after a long pause—"we shall have to live in this community. We shall have to make our peace with neighbors and family, but we'll never have peace if we condone murder." The North's virtue, he wanted to add, lay in its moral rectitude, but the sentiment sounded too pompous for utterance.

Galloway privately doubted whether any Southerner who had fought for the North could ever hope to make a home south of Washington again, but he nodded anyway. "I'll make inquiries, Adam, I promise you," he said, and Adam had to be content with that promise, for suddenly the parlor door was thrown open and John Pope himself strode into the hallway.

The Northern commander checked when he saw the waiting cavalry officers. "You're Galloway, right?"

"Yes, sir."

"A Manassas man, aren't I right?"

"Yes, sir," Galloway acknowledged.

Pope snapped his fingers. "The very man! You're to take

your fellows home, Galloway. Jackson's there. One of our fellows saw the wretch in person and escaped to tell the tale. There's no doubt about it, Jackson's in Manassas, and you know what that means? It means we've got him in the bag! You understand me?" The General was suddenly exultant. He might have been reluctant to accept that his battle lay at Manassas and not across the Rappahannock, but a few hours of reflection had convinced him of the advantages of accepting Jackson's foolhardy challenge. "The damned fool has marched halfway round our army to maroon himself in Manassas, and tomorrow we're going to snap him up! My God, Jeb Stuart might make a fool of George Brinton McClellan by riding clean around his army, but no Stonewall Jackson will march clean round John Pope! No, sir! So, Galloway"—Pope jabbed a finger at the Major—"take your fellows north and find out just where the wretched man is, and report to me when you know. We're going to Bristoe tonight. If you want to put your horses on our train, then come now, hurry!" The commander strode into the street, followed by flustered aides clutching luggage and maps.

"So where's Lee?" Galloway asked faintly, but no one responded, perhaps because no one heard him or perhaps because no one thought the question important. All that mattered was that Stonewall Jackson had marched himself into a trap and that John Pope was about to destroy him once and for all. "We've got the fool in the bag!" Pope boasted as he hurried toward the train he believed would carry him northward to victory. "Right in the bag!"

Lucifer did return. He returned with a leather grip that had been put in store by a Northern officer but that now held Starbuck's new possessions. "Every damn thing you wanted," Lucifer said proudly, "and a silver hairbrush, too. See? Make

you look real good. And I got you cigars. Good ones."
Lucifer had also discarded his flamboyant clothes and
replaced them with a Northern cavalryman's pants over
which he was wearing a gray jacket, a leather belt, and a
button-flapped holster, yet somehow his natural elegance
imbued even that humdrum uniform with flair.

"Is there anything in that holster?" Starbuck demanded.

"I got myself a cooking implement," Lucifer said, "made
by Mr. Colt of Hartford in Connecticut."

"You mean you've got a gun," Starbuck said flatly.

"It is not a gun," Lucifer protested. "It is a utensil for
killing the food you want me to cook for you, and if I can't
have a utensil I can't get meat, and I can't cook the meat I
can't get, and you can't eat the meat I can't cook, and then
you'll starve and I'll be so hungry I won't even have the
strength left to bury you."

Starbuck sighed. "If you're caught with a gun, Lucifer,
then someone will take the skin off your back."

"If I have got myself a Colt cooking utensil, Major, then
there ain't no son of a stinking bitch alive who can take the
skin off any one little part of me."

Starbuck gave in. He sent the boy to find some food but
warned him to be ready to leave at any minute. The daylight
was fading, its twilight obscured by the myriad of fires that
burned among the wagons and boxcars, and Starbuck
expected imminent orders to move away from the fiery
smoke pillars that were surely serving as beacons to draw
every Northern soldier within twenty miles. Not that the
rebel army was in a fit state to move; some men snored in
alcoholic stupors, while others, gorged with rich food, slept,
oblivious of the incendiary parties who went from warehouse to warehouse burning what could not be carried away.

In the last of the light Starbuck shaved himself, using a
new mirror and razor that Lucifer had found; then he feasted

on pickled oysters and fresh bread and butter. Dark came and there were still no orders to move. Starbuck assumed Jackson had decided to run the risk of spending the night in the captured, burning depot, and so he made himself a bed from a pile of brand-new Northern overcoats, but the softness of the makeshift mattress was disconcertingly comfortable, and so he rolled off the pile onto the familiar dirt. And there slept well.

And woke to inferno.

He opened his eyes to see a sky lancing with red fire and to hear a thunderous roll of monstrous noise filling the night. He started up, reaching for his rifle, while all around him the men of the Legion woke to the same terrifying cacophony. A burning fragment fell from the sky to thump into the dirt beside Starbuck. "What the hell's happening?" Starbuck asked of no one in particular.

Then he realized that the North's great supply of ammunition was being destroyed. Boxcar after boxcar of cartridges, percussion caps, shells, and artillery propellant was being torched. The explosions thumped across the depot, each one flashing a bright illumination that pulsed its brilliance high into the sky. Monstrous flames boiled hundreds of feet into the air, where hissing missiles spat through churning smoke. "Oh, my God," a man said after one particularly sharp and bright explosion, "just lay me down." The phrase, which was spreading throughout Jackson's army, prompted an immediate burst of laughter.

"Major Starbuck! Major Starbuck!" Captain Pryor, now Swynyard's aide, searched among the startled men.

"I'm here!"

"We're to march now."

"What time is it?"

"Midnight, sir. A little after."

Starbuck shouted for Sergeant Major Tolliver. A warehouse crammed with shrapnel disintegrated in flame to make the night momentarily as bright and red as hell's deep at noon. The explosion was followed by a tantalizing smell as barrels of cured bacon caught the flames and fried. A loose horse galloped in terror past a gang of sweating demons who were destroying the last locomotives in the depot by stuffing their fireboxes with gunpowder and mangling the condenser tubes with bullets.

"Ready?" Colonel Swynyard shouted. He was already on horseback, and his gelding's eyes reflected the night's fires like some mythical beast. "March!"

They went north, blindly following the brigade in front and leaving behind a writhing pit of red horror. Explosion after explosion ripped through the burning depot as flames climbed yet higher into the night. The North had labored mightily to amass the supplies necessary to subdue the South, and now all that labor was evaporating into flame, smoke, and ash.

Starbuck's men trudged wearily, burdened by their plunder and hardly refreshed by the few hours of sleep they had snatched at the day's end. Some of the men's heaviest loot was abandoned early, joining the other trophies thrown aside by tired soldiers. In the flickering, unnatural light Starbuck saw a discarded snare drum beside the road, then two swords with chased gilt handles, a pair of post office scales, and a fine saddle. There were piles of food, candlesticks, greatcoats—whatever treasures a man had fancied, taken, then abandoned as his muscles cramped again.

No one knew where they were going, or why. Their progress was slow, and never slower than when it was discovered that the column was on the wrong road and local guides had to be stirred from their beds to guide the heavily laden soldiers across the country toward dark woods. The gun teams were whipped bloody as they hauled their heavy cannon through entangling hedges and across fields of growing wheat.

Lieutenant Coffman, still swathed in his handsome cloak, fell in beside Starbuck. "I found out what you wanted, sir," he said.

Starbuck could not even remember what he had asked Coffman to discover. "So?" he asked.

"It's just off the Sudley road, sir. There's a farm track near the fords and you go north a quarter-mile and there it is. There's meant to be a lime-washed pillar at the gate of the track, though the fellow I spoke to says it needs repainting."

Starbuck frowned down at the young Lieutenant. "What in hell's name are you talking about?"

"The Galloway farm, sir." Coffman sounded aggrieved.

"Yes, of course. Sorry." Yet now the information seemed very trivial. Starbuck would dearly have liked to visit the Galloway farm, but he realized the wish was quixotic in this night of fire and tumult. Jackson was withdrawing from Manassas, so the Legion's revenge on Galloway must wait. "Thank you, Coffman," he said, "and well done," he added, trying to soothe the young man's ruffled feathers.

Just before dawn the Legion stumbled across a road, climbed a hill, and so came to a stretch of deep woods. Behind the soldiers, beyond a fold of night-black land, the depot's fires roared like the stokehold of hell. The glow of the destruction was furnace fierce, and the smoke a gigantic pyre, so that to Starbuck, standing at the wood's edge and looking back, it seemed as though a great section of the earth itself was burning. The fires had been set four hours before, yet still the bright explosions pulsed the night and churned their smoke skyward. Beyond the fire, and dimmed by its brightness, the world's edge just showed the first cold silver line of dawn.

"Back now, back now." A mounted staff officer was

pushing men away from the open meadow and into the cover of the woods. "And no fires! No fires!"

"What's happening?" Starbuck asked.

"Get some rest," the man said, "and stay hidden. And no one's to light a fire unless they want to be burned alive by Old Jack himself."

"We're not marching any further?" Captain Davies asked the staff officer.

"Not for the moment. Just stay in hiding. Get some rest. And no fires!" The staff officer rode on, repeating his message.

Starbuck pulled his men back into the wood. Jackson had come to Manassas, turned the place to hell, and gone to ground.

The Reverend Elial Starbuck hardly slept that night. At times his eyes closed out of sheer weariness, and he would lean his aquiline head against the chair's high back and begin to snore gently, but almost immediately another great explosion would rattle the windows of Major Galloway's parlor, and the preacher would wake with a start to see yet another ball of fire climbing up from the incandescent glow that marked where the great depot was now a furnace. The devil was at his work, the preacher thought grimly, then tried to sleep again. He had decided against using one of the bedrooms in case he needed to make a quick escape from marauding rebels, and so he spent the night in the half-furnished library parlor with his stick, his heavy bag, and his precious flag beside him. The only weapon to hand was Major Galloway's decorative guidon on its lance-tipped staff that the preacher leaned against the chair in the fond hope that its spear point might be useful to skewer a godless rebel.

He had spent the whole of the previous day in the same parlor. His frustrations had twice driven him from the house in search of an escape from the rebel forces, but each time he had glimpsed gray-clad horsemen in the distance and so had scurried back to the dubious safety of the farm. Before the preacher's arrival there had been a guard of four cavalry troopers in residence, their job to protect Galloway's depot against the depredations of the Major's sullen Southern neighbors, but the men had fled when Jackson's troops had arrived. The farm's three black servants had stayed, and they had fed the preacher and prayed with him, but none of the servants was convinced by the Reverend Starbuck's optimism that John Pope would surely come to punish the men who had dared put Manassas to the torch.

The preacher did manage to sleep a little toward dawn. He lay slumped in the wing chair with the rebel banner clasped to his lean belly until a final massive explosion woke him to the wan light of early morning. He felt stiff and cold and tired as he climbed to his feet. From the parlor window he could see an enormous pillar of smoke climbing heavenward, but he could see no enemy cavalrymen in rat gray coats disturbing the landscape.

It seemed too early to expect breakfast, and so, leaving his luggage in the house and taking only his cane and the precious flag, he ventured timidly into the morning. There was dew on the grass and mist in the folds of land. Two white-tailed deer bounded away from him and crashed through a thicket. Just to the north he could see the glint of the Bull Run through a gap between trees, but he could still see no soldiers. He walked past the servants' cabins to the end of Galloway's yard and searched for enemies, but all that moved in the pearl gray landscape was the pillar of smoke churning from the depot. There was a sense of lonely desolation in the landscape, almost as though the preacher was the last man left on earth. He walked slowly up the farm path, ever watchful, but he saw nothing that threatened him, and when he reached the road, he turned to his left and climbed to the crest of the gentle rise so he could see across the long valley that lay to the east. There was still no enemy in sight. The fields were stripped of livestock, the farms seemed deserted, and the land lay barren.

He walked on. He kept meaning to turn back to the farm and roust the servants to their morning duties in the kitchen, yet curiosity kept him walking just a few paces more, and every few paces he would determine to go just a little bit further still, until at last he decided he would explore as far as the crest at the valley's far side, and if he had still seen no sign of the enemy, then he would return to the farm, take his breakfast, and carry his luggage northward. So resolved, he walked doggedly on, following the pillar of smoke as Moses had followed the pillar of cloud across the wilderness. He climbed the valley's eastern side, following, though he did not know it, the course of the first Northern attack in the battle that had opened the fighting in Virginia and passing, though he would not have wanted to know it, the place where his son had first stood in the rebel battle line. This was the ground where the North's first invasion of the South had been turned back, and the fields on either side of the road still showed white where fragments of bones had been unearthed from shallow graves by scavenging animals. Someone had placed a skull atop a tree stump at the entrance to a farm road, and the macabre face grinned yellow teeth at the preacher as he passed by.

He reached the wooded crest. He had now walked a mile from Galloway's farm, and in front of him he could see the Warrenton Turnpike running empty through a valley, while, on the valley's far side, at the crest of a steep green hill, the ruins of a burned-out house stood gaunt and black against the great smear of dirty smoke that hideously obscured the dawn. The house had been destroyed in the battle fought across these Manassas fields a year before, but the preacher assumed the dwelling had been burned by the rebels on the previous day. It did not occur to him that a Southern army would hardly torch a Virginia farm; he simply saw new evidence of the devil's work and knew it had to be the responsibility of the forces of Slavocracy. "Barbarians!" he said aloud into the empty country. "Barbarians!"

Something thumped on the road behind, and the preacher turned to see the grinning skull had been tipped from its tree stump and was now rolling across the road. Beyond the skull was a horseman holding a rifle that was aimed straight at the Reverend Starbuck. To his surprise the preacher discovered he was not really frightened at thus facing one of the devils who had scourged this land. "Barbarian!" the preacher shouted angrily, waving his stick at the horseman. "Heathen!"

"Doctor Starbuck?" the horseman responded politely. "Is it you, sir?"

The preacher gaped at the cavalryman. "Major Galloway?"

"You're hardly the person I expected to meet here, sir," Major Galloway said as he spurred toward the preacher. A whole troop of horsemen followed the Major from the trees as Galloway explained to the Reverend Starbuck how he and his men had taken a train north to Bristoe during the previous night and were now trying to establish the whereabouts of Stonewall Jackson's army.

"I haven't seen any rebels this morning," the preacher said, and he told how he had spent the night at Galloway's farm. He confirmed that the property was unscathed and reported that although he had seen a handful of Southern horsemen the day before, he had seen none in this dawn. "They appear to have vanished," the Reverend Starbuck said darkly, as though the rebels possessed satanic powers.

"So has Captain Blythe," Galloway said, "unless, perhaps, he's at the farm?"

"Alas, no."

"I'm sure he'll turn up in his own good time," Galloway said wanly, then turned in his saddle and called on Adam to bring one of the spare horses for the preacher's convenience. "We were on our way to the farm," Galloway told the Reverend, "and after that we're ordered to search the country north of the Bull Run."

"I was hoping to go north," the preacher announced. "I have to reach Washington."

"I'm not sure you've much hope of doing that today, sir," Galloway said respectfully. "There's some evidence that Jackson took his troops north. Maybe they're planning to attack the Centreville defenses? He might have vanished, but he's certainly not far away." The Major peered round the empty landscape as though he half expected the rebels to appear like stage villains springing from a trapdoor.

"I can't tarry here!" the preacher protested vigorously. "I have a church to administer, responsibilities I cannot escape!"

"You'll certainly be safer here, sir," Galloway suggested calmly, "seeing as how General Pope's here now and the rest of his army is on its way." He leaned out of his saddle to hold the spare horse while the preacher clambered into its saddle. The rebel flag almost fell from the Reverend Starbuck's grip, but he managed to hold on to the bundled silk as he settled himself on the horse's back. A trooper handed up the preacher's stick, then gave him the reins. "In fact if you do stay here, sir," Major Galloway went on, "I reckon you might even see a scrap of history being made."

"History! I have been promised nothing but history all month, Major! I was promised a pulpit in Richmond, but for all those fine promises I might just as well have planned on preaching God's word in Japan!"

"But the rebels have blundered now, sir," Galloway explained patiently, "leastwise, General Pope reckons they have. Jackson's stranded here, sir, miles from his own lines, and General Pope plans to cut him off and destroy him. That's why Pope's here, sir. We're going to finish Jackson once and for all."

"You really think Pope can do that, Major?" The preacher's question was caustic.

Galloway's reply was emollient. "I reckon General Pope means to try, sir, and none of us really know just what the General can do in battle. I mean he was pretty successful in the west, sir, but he ain't fought here, and that was why he was brought to Virginia, so I guess he might astonish us all yet. Yes, sir, I reckon we might see a fair battle before the day's out, and I even reckon we might win it, too."

The prospect tempted the Reverend Starbuck. He had come to Virginia with such high hopes and had seen those hopes crumble to nothing, but now it seemed there was a chance of victory after all. Besides, it was now Thursday morning, and he knew he could never reach Boston in time for Sunday worship, which meant he might just as well stay here and see the North's nemesis beaten in battle. And what a fine subject for a sermon that would make, he thought. Like Satan plunging into the abyss, Jackson would be brought low, and the Reverend Starbuck would be a witness to the demon's shattering fall. He nodded assent. He would stay and fight.

All day long Jackson's troops waited in the woods. Most slept like the dead, so that Starbuck, setting his sentries just inside the tree line, could hear the murmur of the sleeping army like a swarm of bees. Twenty-four thousand rebel

361

soldiers were snoring not six miles from Manassas, yet the Northern army was oblivious of their presence.

Lucifer brought Starbuck an early dinner of cold pork, apples, and walnuts. "Still eating off the Yankees," he explained the luxury foodstuffs; then he squatted beside Starbuck and stared down the hill toward the empty turnpike in search of Yankees. There were none in sight. "So where are the black folks' friends?" Lucifer asked.

"God knows. Let's hope they don't find us." The sun was low in the sky, and with any luck night would fall before the enemy found Jackson's hiding place.

"You don't want to fight?" Lucifer asked sarcastically.

"I don't want to die."

"You won't die. You were born under a lucky star. Like me. I can tell."

Starbuck scoffed at the boy's confidence. "And I tell you, Lucifer, that just about every poor son of a bitch who's died in this war thought he was too lucky to get killed."

"But I really am lucky," Lucifer insisted, "and you'd better be just as lucky as me, because you know what I was hearing back there among the other humble servant folk? That there are men in this regiment who don't like you."

"I know that," Starbuck said. The pork was tender and the apples fresh. He wondered how long it would be before he was back on hardtack and salted offal.

"But did you know they've written a letter about you?" Lucifer offered a sly sideways glance, then lit himself one of the cigars he had acquired for Starbuck. "The bald fellow wrote the letter, you know? The man you made me give his watch to, Meddlesome, is that his name? And I hear some three or four officers have signed it, and at least forty or fifty soldiers, and they're sending the letter to a congressman. They say you're too young and that you should be sent down the river just as fast as the army can get itself rid of you." The boy grinned, then drew his finger across his throat. "They got nothing but trouble for you, Major."

Starbuck told Lucifer what the letter writers could do with their damned letter. "No one's sending me down the river," he added, "not if I win battles."

"But suppose they don't let you win?" Lucifer asked.

Starbuck acknowledged the question with a deprecating shrug, then stole the boy's cigar. "You know what I've learned about soldiering?"

"To take another man's smoke away?"

"That the worst enemy is never the fellow in the other uniform, that's what." He paused with the cigar halfway to his lips because a sudden fusillade had sounded in the west. The shots were from far away, but they ripped and crackled angrily in the late afternoon. "Here we go again," Starbuck said and sucked on the cigar as his heart lurched. He wondered if fear ever decreased, or whether it got worse and worse until a man could no longer make himself stand upright in battle.

Men woke among the trees and listened uneasily to the sound of firing. All but the newest conscript had learned to judge a fight's intensity from the sound of its guns, and this fight was hard and furious, and so they expected orders that would send them to join in, but no such orders came. The fight continued into the dusk, and no one knew who was fighting or who was winning, only that a skim of powder smoke showed white above the tree line in the west.

Colonel Swynyard finally brought the Legion news. It seemed that a column of Yankee troops had been marching on the turnpike and that Jackson had ordered his own Stonewall Brigade to intercept and destroy the column. "Except the Yankees are too stubborn to run," Swynyard said. "They're standing toe-to-toe and fighting like demons."

"I thought we were supposed to be hiding from the Yankees?" Starbuck said.

"I guess we've hid long enough. Maybe Old Mad Jack reckons it's time to draw the Yankees on to us," Swynyard suggested. He looked up at the darkening sky and grimaced. "Not that they'll come tonight, but tomorrow?" He glanced over at Lucifer, who was crouched beside Starbuck's few possessions. "How's your darkie?" the Colonel asked gruffly.

"He seems willing enough."

"He looks a sly one to me. He's got soft hands, Starbuck, which like as not means he's been someone's house pet. And those pants he was wearing when you found him, the long-pocket ones, they ain't the pants of an honest man. If you want a good slave get yourself a bone-brained field hand who ain't afraid of a bit of work, but your boy looks more like the dangerous type of slave to me."

"What is the dangerous type?"

"The clever type. Not all the darkies have brains like mules, you know. Some of them are real sharp, and my father always reckoned it was the clever ones who needed breaking first. Whip 'em bloody, he'd say, then work them to death because if there's trouble among the people then you can be sure it's the clever ones who started it, so get rid of the clever ones and that way you'll have no trouble. That's the first and last rule of keeping slaves, Starbuck, and you're probably breaking it. I don't suppose it's Christian to beat a darkie without cause, so I won't suggest you do it, but I'd still advise you to send the boy away."

"I won't do that. I like Lucifer," Starbuck said.

"Lucifer? Is that what he calls himself? Dear Lord," Swynyard said, shocked by the name's impiety. "Find out what he's really called, Starbuck. Don't put up with that kind of nonsense! And have him cut his hair off. You don't want a black dandy. And for the Lord's sake take that gun off him! For a start it's illegal, but more important if you encourage him to think he's a cut above the other darkies he'll soon think he's a cut above you. Give a clever slave an inch and he'll take you for everything you've got." The Colonel checked this stream of advice to listen to the firing, which had reached a new intensity, almost as if the two sides were equally desperate to reach a victory before the sun dipped beneath the horizon. "Not our business, thank God. Get some sleep tonight, Starbuck, because I daresay we'll be neck deep in Yankees tomorrow."

The long-haired, gun-toting Lucifer watched the Colonel go. "What did he say about me?" he asked Starbuck.

"He gave me good advice," Starbuck said. "He told me to whip you bloody then work you to death."

Lucifer grinned. "You don't want to do that. I'm your good luck, Major." He turned back toward Swynyard's retreating figure and made a deliberately formal gesture with his clenched right fist, which, at the last moment, he uncurled to let fall a few scraps of fragile bone and powdery white dust.

Starbuck thought he recognized the ribs of a small bird among the litter Lucifer had let drop, but he did not like to ask what the strange gesture meant. He was afraid to know, so instead he looked out from the trees and saw, at last, Yankees. Horsemen were galloping across distant fields, spurring toward the firefight that still crackled in the west. The enemy was gathering like storm clouds heaping. And tomorrow they would fight.

The Reverend Elial Starbuck's hopes, which had plunged so low during the inconveniences of the rail journey, now soared again, and once again it was the acrid smoke of battle that filled him with that fierce exaltation. He had breakfasted with Major Galloway, and afterward, leaving his luggage in the farm, the preacher had ridden to Manassas Junction to see the damage done to the depot and to introduce himself to General Pope's headquarters. The General had been affability itself and had willingly given his permission for the famous preacher to stay with the army, even inviting him to share the headquarters' potluck suppers for the next few nights. Thus honored, the Reverend Starbuck had ridden south to Bristoe to commiserate with his old friend Nathaniel Banks, who had been given the undemanding task of guarding the rail depot. Banks, who still considered his action at Cedar Mountain a victory, complained bitterly about his present duties, but the Reverend Starbuck was in no mood to encourage such backbiting. His spirits were being revived by the arrival of train after train from Warrenton Junction, each train crammed with troops fetched from the Rappahannock defenses. The damage to the rail line north of Bristoe meant that the trains had to disgorge their passengers in the open country, and soon the line of parked locomotives and cars stretched for more than two miles. The men marched in from the fields where they had alighted and boasted that they had come to knock Stonewall down once and for all. The preacher liked their spirit. His own spirits rose even higher when, late in the afternoon, he heard the sound of gunfire coming from the north.

He took his tired horse toward the sound of the guns, passing through quiet fields and deserted woods until at last he came to the valley where the Warrenton Turnpike ran and where a rill of smoke showed where men fought in the valley's bottom. He rode toward the fighting, arriving just as an enemy regiment made an attack on the Yankees' open right flank.

The gray-coated attackers advanced in a line two ranks deep. Their rifles were tipped with bayonets that reflected the dying sun's scarlet light. They came in good order, kicking down a snake fence and then advancing across a pasture. The attack was silent, suggesting that these rebels planned to save their famous yell for the last few yards of their charge. Some rebels were screaming that weird sound off to the preacher's left, but that larger battle seemed stalemated between two opposing lines of riflemen.

The Northerners had seen the threat to their right flank and hurried three regiments to meet it. Two of the regiments were from Wisconsin and the third from New York. The Northerners formed their ranks in a fold of land where they crouched behind a fence. The attackers, oblivious to the number of Yankees facing their charge, began to hurry, and their first shrill yells yipped in the dusk. The defiant sound prompted the Northern line to stand behind their fence and fire a shattering volley across the pasture. The volley's noise ripped over the valley and rolled back. Rifle flames glittered in the failing light, while the layered cloud of powder smoke drifted across the meadow to where the Confederates had been brought to a sudden, astonished halt. The Reverend Starbuck, oblivious of the bullets that whipsawed around his horse, cheered his Northerners on. Their first volley had stopped the rebel attack dead, their second turned it into a bloody mess, and their third began to drive the gray-clad regiment backward. The rebel fire became ever more feeble as the Northern fire increased. One of the rebel's banners toppled, was plucked up, and immediately fell again as the new standard-bearer was thrown back by a dozen bullets. "That's the way to deal with devils, boys!" the Reverend Starbuck shouted. A heaped line of dead and injured men showed where the tide of the Confederate attack had stalled, and now the survivors grudgingly abandoned that writhing, bloody heap as they edged backward. Earlier in the day the preacher had equipped himself with a Colt revolver from among Galloway's stores, and now he remembered the weapon and drew it from his saddle pouch. He fired at the stubborn rebels who, though their line had been broken and bloodied, still tried to return the overwhelming Northern fire.

"By the left oblique! Forward!" a stentorian voice shouted, and the New York regiment swung forward like a gate that threatened to close on the remnants of the rebel attackers.

"Halt!" the New Yorkers' commanding officer called. "Aim!"

The preacher hurried his horse after the advancing New Yorkers.

"Fire!"

The New York volley slashed into the rebels' tattered flank. It was a killing volley, a massive blow that seemed to twitch the surviving rebels bodily backward. Blood misted the evening air as the bullets smacked home. Gray coats were splattered with red, and the field littered with still more dead and dying bodies. A man reeled out of the rebel line, blood pouring from an eye socket. He collapsed to his knees, looking as if he was praying, and the Reverend Starbuck cried in triumph as he fired his revolver at the man.

"Doing God's work?" The New Yorkers' Colonel rode across to the preacher's side.

"'Think not that I am come to send peace on earth: I came not to send peace, but a sword.'" The Reverend Starbuck trumpeted the text, then fired at a rebel who seemed to be giving orders. "Our Lord's own words," he added to the Colonel.

"We're certainly doing His work well this time!" the Colonel shouted over the sound of his men's volleys.

"I pray as much!" The Reverend Starbuck fired his gun's last cylinder and hoped he had slaughtered at least one rebel with his efforts. His wrist hurt from the gun's massive kick. It was a long time since he had fired a gun, and he was not sure he could remember quite how to load a revolver.

"I suppose you wouldn't know where Pope is?" the Colonel asked the preacher.

"I last saw him in Manassas."

"Would you be going back there, sir? And if so, can you take a message?"

"Willingly."

The Colonel scribbled on a page of his notebook. "Lord knows where Jackson's main body is, but it can't be far away. We need to bring everyone here tomorrow morning to flush the mudsill out and finish him off." He tore the page out of his book and handed it to the preacher. "Just like we've finished off these rogues," the Colonel said, gesturing at the rebel regiment that had been beaten back with terrible loss. The field writhed with bodies, while a sorry handful of survivors limped back toward the far woods. "Poor fellows," the Colonel said.

"Poor fellows? The scum of creation!" the preacher averred. "Devils in cretinous shape, Colonel, as even a casual glance at their skull shapes might reveal. They are Southerners: half-witted, morally infantile, and criminal. Don't feel sorry for them. Expend your pity on the Negroes they enslaved."

"Indeed," the New Yorker muttered, taken aback by the vehemence of the preacher's words. "You'll deliver my message to Pope, sir?"

"With pleasure, Colonel, with pleasure," the Reverend Starbuck said, and then, feeling as though he was at last making a real contribution toward the destruction of the Slavocracy, he turned his tired horse and headed back across the hills.

He arrived in the day's last light at the smoking ruins of the depot, where lines of twisted, scorched boxcar frames stood on blackened wheels amidst great drifts of smoking ashes. There was acre upon acre of ruin, of desolation, of destruction. Indeed, to the preacher's heightened senses, there was something biblical in the awful sight, almost as though he witnessed the results of a visitation of God's wrath upon a people who had been lax in their duty. The Reverend Starbuck did not doubt that God could use even the hated Slavocracy to scourge the North for its sins, but the time would surely come when the North would repent, and on that happy day the armies of the godly would inflict a destruction similar to this horror upon all the rebels' habitations and towns and farms. And perhaps, the Reverend Starbuck fervently prayed, that great revival and consequent victory was starting here and now.

He discovered the army's commanding general in a farm just north of the depot. A score of senior officers surrounded Pope; among them and outranked by all of them was Major Galloway, his face coated with dust and his uniform soaked with sweat. Pope snatched at the message the Reverend Starbuck carried. "It's from Wainwright," he announced. The General read the scribbled note quickly and was so pleased by what he read that he slapped the table. "We've got him! We've got him! He's on the Warrenton road, but he's been blocked there. He's trapped. He was at Centreville, now he's retreating toward Warrenton." Pope made a fine, slashing pencil mark on one of the maps that lay on the table.

"I saw no sign of him at Centreville, sir," Galloway said nervously.

"No wonder! The fellow was going backwards!" Pope laughed. "But who minds whether you saw him or not, Galloway? It doesn't matter where he was, but where he is now! And he's right here!" He made another pencil slash, forming a cross on the Warrenton Turnpike at the place where the Reverend Starbuck had seen the rebel attack trounced. "So tomorrow we'll bag the whole crowd!" The General could not hide his elation. For almost a year the North had shuddered at the name of Stonewall Jackson, and tomorrow Pope would end the fear and destroy the bogeyman.

Major Galloway, though outranked by the bearded men around him, stuck to his guns. "But what about the fellows my officer saw at Salem, sir?" He was speaking of Billy Blythe, who had at last reappeared with a convoluted and not wholly convincing story of being chased by Southern horsemen and of being forced to take shelter for two days and nights in a draw of the Blue Ridge Mountains, but however false the tale rang, the final part seemed true enough. Blythe claimed he had returned to the North's lines by following the foothills of the Blue Ridge until he reached the deserted rails of the Manassas Gap Railroad, but that when he had tried to follow that rail line east, he had almost been captured by Southern cavalry pickets who had been guarding an immense column of troops hurrying toward Thoroughfare Gap. Blythe's men had confirmed that part of their Captain's story, and Galloway had brought the grim news to Pope.

"But how reliable is this fellow?" Pope asked Galloway. The Northern General did not want to believe that yet more rebels were marching toward Manassas; he preferred his own theory that Jackson's panicked retreat had been intercepted on the turnpike.

"Captain Blythe is . . ." Galloway began, then could not continue. "Billy can be wild at times, sir," he admitted truthfully, "but his men are telling the same tale."

"And so they should. Men ought to support their officers," Pope said dismissively. "So what exactly did they see?"

"Men approaching the Thoroughfare Gap, sir. Wagons, guns, and infantry."

Pope chuckled. "What your fellows saw, Galloway, was Jackson's supply train slipping off to the west. Stands to reason, Major! If Jackson's retreating this way"—he slashed the pencil from east to west—"then his wagons and guns won't be going in the opposite direction, not unless he's a good deal more stupid than we suppose. No, Major, your fellow saw the rebels retreating, not advancing, and tomorrow we'll turn that retreat into a rout!" His aides murmured agreement. Tomorrow the North would turn the war around. Tomorrow the North would begin the utter destruction of rebellion in Virginia.

Only one of Pope's senior officers demurred. He was an elderly artillery officer wearing the star of a brigadier general on his collar, and he seemed worried enough by Galloway's report to ask whether it was worth running any risks. "If we pull back behind the Centreville defenses, sir, we can wait for McClellan's troops to join us. In a week, sir, with respect, we can overwhelm every rebel in Virginia."

"You want me to retreat?" John Pope asked scathingly. "This army, sir, is far too accustomed to retreat. It has been led by men who know nothing except how to retreat! No, it's time we advanced, time we fought, and time we won."

"Hallelujah!" the Reverend Starbuck interjected.

"But where's Lee?" Galloway asked, but no one had heard the question. General Pope and his staff had gone to their potluck supper, taking the generals and the visiting preacher with them, and leaving Galloway alone.

The fighting died as darkness swamped the turnpike. The North, assuming that Jackson had tried to force his way past them, claimed victory, while Jackson, whose object had been to draw the Northerners into a full attack, kept his silence. The wounded cried in the dark, while all around them, rustling in the night, an army gathered for the kill.

AT MANASSAS, ON FRIDAY AUGUST 29, 1862, the first light showed a few moments after half past four. It was a gray wolfish light, at first little more than a cold thinning of the eastern darkness, yet it was sufficient to rouse Jackson's army. The men rolled their blankets and, for the first time since they had left the burning depot, were allowed to light fires. "The sons of bitches know we're here now, so we don't have to hide," Starbuck told his men, then sighed with content as he smelt the wondrous aroma of real coffee being brewed on dozens of fires.

At a quarter past five, a mug of the coffee clasped in his hands, he watched the scenery take shape across the turnpike. There were troops now where there had been none the night before. The brown smear of smoke that still rose from the depot had drawn an army to Manassas, and Starbuck could see lines of bivouacked infantry, parks of guns, and rows of tethered cavalry horses. The enemy, like his own men, were brewing coffee or shaving, while curious Yankee officers trained their field glasses and telescopes toward the silent western woods where the mingling plumes of smoke at last revealed the true extent of Jackson's position.

"We'll fight here, you reckon?" Captain Ethan Davies asked Starbuck. Davies was cleaning his spectacle lenses on the skirt of his coat. "It ain't a bad place to defend," Davies added, hooking the spectacles back onto his ears. The land fell away from the woods toward the turnpike, and Starbuck, like Davies, reckoned it was not a bad place to stand and fight, because the Yankees would have to attack uphill while the rebels would have the concealing woods at their back.

Yet, as the sun rose, Jackson abandoned the position and ordered his army to retreat westward. They did not go far, just a half-mile across untilled fields into another ragged stretch of blackjack oaks, maples, and birch trees. This new wood was interrupted by small patches of rough meadowland and cut by two streams and a railbed that had been graded but never finished with ties and rails. The railbed had been intended to carry a line that would bypass Manassas Junction and so keep the trains of the Manassas Gap Railroad from paying the exorbitant fees required to use the rails of the Orange and Alexandria Railroad, but the investors had run out of cash and abandoned the work, leaving only a smooth, wide, grassy roadway that ran through deep cuttings and along high embankments as it curved, always level, through the undulating woods. It was on the railbed that Jackson stopped with his twenty-four thousand men.

Colonel Swynyard's brigade would defend a stretch of the unfinished railroad that ran through a deep cutting. The eastward-facing bank of the cutting provided a firestep for riflemen, who could, if overwhelmed, retreat across the wide entrenchment into the woods on the western side. A hundred paces behind the cutting the ground rose steeply, though to the right of Swynyard's line, where the Faulconer Legion was posted, that hill faded away so that Starbuck's right-hand companies had no natural barrier behind them, only a flat stretch of young woodland and dense shrub. That change in topography also meant that the cutting became shallow as the railbed rose toward an embankment, while the existence of a deep spoil pit behind the line only made the defense line even more confusing. The spoil pit, only half filled, was where the railroad men had dumped the dirt and rocks they had not needed to build up their embankments.

The spoil pit marked the dividing line between Swynyard's brigade and their neighbors to the south, and Starbuck, once his men were in position, walked to meet those neighbors, a regiment from North Carolina. Their Colonel was a very tall, very thin, very fair-haired man in his early middle age with an elaborately drooping mustache, amused eyes, and a weather-beaten face. He had very long and studiedly old-fashioned hair that flowed past the faded blue collar of his gray frock coat. "Colonel Elijah Hudson," he introduced himself to Starbuck, "of Stanly County, and uncommon proud of it."

"Major Starbuck, of Boston, Massachusetts."

Colonel Hudson pushed back a lock of his curled hair to uncover one ear. "I do believe my hearing has been quite obliterated by the artillery, Major, for I could swear you said Boston."

"So I did, Colonel, so I did, but my boys are all Virginians."

"The good Lord alone knows why you came here from Massachusetts, Major, but I sure am glad to make your acquaintance. Your boys up to hum, are they?"

"I reckon."

"Mine are rogues, each and every one of them. Not a man of them's worth a wooden nickel, but Lord above, how I do love the wretches. Ain't that so, boys?" Colonel Hudson had spoken loud enough for his nearest men to hear, and those men grinned broadly at his words. "And this here Major," Hudson went on to introduce Starbuck to his men, "is a poor lost Northerner fighting for us miserable rebels, but you all be nice to him, boys, because if his lads give way then we'll all be so many dead ducks waiting for John Pope to

375

pluck us. And I don't have a fancy to be plucked by a cleric this day."

Starbuck led Hudson past the spoil pit to the Legion and introduced him to Major Medlicott, explaining that Medlicott not only commanded the company immediately adjacent to the North Carolinians but was also responsible for the whole right wing of the Legion. "Sure pleased to meet you, Major," Hudson said, putting out a hand. "My name's Elijah Hudson and I'm from Stanly County, the best county in all the Carolinas even though my dear wife does come from Catawba County, God bless her, and how are you?"

Medlicott seemed disconcerted by the tall man's friendliness but managed to make a civil response.

"We've got ourselves a killing patch," Hudson said, gesturing across the rail cutting to where the ground ran bare to the closest stretch of woods. It was a killing patch because any Yankees attacking out of the woods would be forced to cross those fifty paces of open land under constant fire. "I can't say it was ever my burning ambition to kill Yankees," Hudson said, "but if the dear good Lord above wants me to do it, then he sure does make it easy in a place like this. Mind you, if the Northern gentlemen do manage to get past the railbed, then we're all going to be in a heap of trouble. If that happens we might as well all pack it in and go back to our jobs. What is your job, Major?" he inquired of Starbuck.

"Soldiering, I guess. I was a student before the war."

"I'm a miller," Medlicott answered to a similar inquiry.

"And what better job could a man have," Hudson asked, "than to grind the Lord's corn into our daily bread? That sure is a privilege, Major, a genuine privilege, and I'm proud to know you for it."

"And your profession, sir?" Starbuck asked the tall Hudson.

"Can't rightly say I've got any profession, Starbuck, other than a love of God and Stanly County. I guess you could say I do a little of everything and a fair heap of nothing, but if I was pushed to the scratch I'd have to confess to being a farmer. Just one of America's toil-laden farmers, but proud as heck of it." Hudson smiled broadly, then offered his hand again to both men. "I guess I should go and make sure my rogues aren't running away out of sheer boredom. I count it a real privilege to fight beside you gentlemen and I wish you much happiness of the day." With a wave of his hand the lanky Hudson strode away.

"A nice fellow," Starbuck said.

"Grasping folk, North Carolinians," Medlicott said dourly. "I never did trust a North Carolinian."

"Well, he's trusting you," Starbuck said tartly, "because if we give way here then he'll be outflanked." He stared at Medlicott's riflemen, who were making themselves comfortable in the shallow stretch of the railbed cutting, then turned to look at the remains of the construction crew's spoil pit, which was now an overgrown hollow stretching for thirty yards behind the makeshift entrenchment. The hollow's stony, overgrown bed could serve as a hidden path into the rear of the rebel defenses. "I guess we ought to barricade the pit," Starbuck said.

"I don't need you to teach me my business," Medlicott answered.

Starbuck's temper whiplashed uncontrollably. "Listen, you son of a damned bitch," he said, "I ain't losing this damned battle because you don't like me. If the Yankees use that pit to get behind my line I'm going to use your damned skull for regimental target practice. You understanding me?"

Medlicott, unable to compete with the intensity of Starbuck's anger, backed away two paces. "I know how to fight," he said uneasily.

Starbuck resisted the temptation to remind Medlicott of his cowardice at Cedar Mountain. "Then make sure you do fight," he said instead, "and to help you, put an abatis across the pit." An abatis was a barrier of branches that would entangle an attacker and offer a breastwork to a defender. Starbuck saw the hurt in the miller's face and regretted the fierceness of his tone. "I know you don't like me, Medlicott," he said, trying to make amends, "but our quarrel ain't with each other, it's with the Yankees."

"And you're a Yankee," the miller said sullenly.

Starbuck resisted the impulse to tongue-lash the wretched man a second time. "Get your fellows to build the abatis"—he forced himself to speak calmly—"and I'll be back soon to look at it."

"Don't trust me, is that it?"

"I hear you write a good letter," Starbuck said, "but I just don't know how good an abatis you can build." With that parting shot he walked away, blowing the frustration from his lungs in a plume of cigar smoke. He wondered if he should have reversed the Legion's usual order of battle by putting Truslow's men on the right and Medlicott's on the left, but such an act would have been construed as a deep insult to the right-flank companies, and Starbuck wanted to demonstrate to the men of those companies, if not to their officers, how he trusted them. He walked on to the northern end of his line, where Truslow's company was entrenched in the deepest section of the railbed's cutting. On their left was one of the Brigade's small Florida battalions. Truslow had paced the open land in front of the cutting to make certain his men knew the exact range of the woods.

"It's seventy-five yards from here to the timberline," Truslow told Starbuck, "and even a blind son of a bitch can hit a Yankee at seventy-five yards. The bullet will hardly have started to drop." He raised his voice so that the nearest

Floridans could hear him. "Aim straight at the bastards' hearts and at worse you'll puncture their bellies. This is infant-school killing, not the hard stuff." The hard stuff was open-field fighting, where a bullet's long-range trajectory was so pronounced that a shot properly sighted at a man standing three hundred yards away would sail high over the cap of a soldier a hundred paces nearer. Starbuck had seen a full regimental volley fired at a line of skirmishers without a single bullet finding its mark.

There was a constant coming and going of staff officers probing the woods beyond the killing patch to watch for the Yankee advance. Colonel Swynyard made a similar reconnaissance and returned to give Starbuck what news he could. "They ain't advancing yet," he said.

"You think they'll come?"

"If they do what they're supposed to do, yes." He confirmed that the previous evening's action on the turnpike had indeed been designed to draw the Yankees to the attack. "I guess our job is to hold them here while Lee brings up the rest of the army."

Swynyard's mention of Lee was the first mention Starbuck had heard of the army's commander since they had arrived in Manassas. "Where is Lee?" he asked.

"Just the other side of Thoroughfare Gap," Swynyard said.

"He's that close?" Starbuck was surprised.

"I guess that's where he always intended to be," Swynyard said with undisguised admiration. "He sent us on ahead to draw the Yankees away from the river, and now he's following on behind, which means that if we can just hold the Yankees all morning, then Lee should hog-tie the lot of them this afternoon. If the good Lord wills it, that is," the Colonel added piously. The tic in his right cheek, which had slowly subsided after his abandonment of liquor, had

379

mysteriously returned to full force. For a second Starbuck wondered if Swynyard had been at the bottle, then realized the tic must be a symptom of nervousness; this was the Colonel's first battle as a brigade commander, and he desperately wanted it to be a success. "How are your boys?" Swynyard asked.

"Good enough," Starbuck said, wondering what symptoms of nervousness he was displaying. Shortness of temper, maybe?

Swynyard turned and pointed to the hill behind the Legion's line. "I've got Haxall's Arkansas boys up there. If things get hard I'll send them down to help, but once they've gone we don't have any reserves."

"Artillery?" Starbuck asked.

"None that I've seen," Swynyard said. "None at all, I guess, but if Lee gets here fast then maybe we won't need none."

The Colonel climbed back to his command post. The sun rose higher, promising to bring another stifling day. Off to the south, muffled by distance, rifle shots sounded, but it was hard to tell whether they were being fired in anger or were merely the sound of men trying to provoke distant pickets. Some of Starbuck's men slept as they waited. A few pinned paper labels to their jackets to identify their bodies in case they died, others wrote letters or read or played cards. In the spoil pit the abatis was now breast high. "Tall enough for you?" Medlicott asked Starbuck.

"Is it tall enough for you?" Starbuck retorted. "It's your life it might save, not mine."

"If they attack at all," Medlicott said in a tone of voice suggesting that Starbuck's expectation of battle was merely alarmist.

By late morning Starbuck was himself wondering if the Northern army would ever attack.

Maybe the Northerners had detected Lee's approach and slipped away to fight another day, for this day had become somnolent, its peace broken by nothing more threatening than an occasional and distant rifle shot. Then, just as Starbuck had convinced himself that he was safe from battle this day, the woods to the left erupted with furious rifle fire. Startled men woke and pushed their rifles over the cutting's crude parapet. All along the line hammers clicked as men cocked their guns, but no Yankees appeared in the killing patch, only a frightened deer that ducked in and out of the sunlight before any man could squeeze off a shot.

Then a staff officer from the brigade to the north rode up the line, shouting for men to advance into the woods.

"To do what?" Starbuck shouted back.

The staff officer was excited and sweating, a drawn sword in his hand. "Yankees are over there. You can hit them in the flank."

"Do it, Starbuck!" Colonel Swynyard had arrived just in time to hear the officer. "Go for them!"

Starbuck sent Coffman to tell Colonel Hudson what was happening. He wanted to keep the North Carolinian well informed, just as Hudson had promised to keep Starbuck apprised of any threats on his southern flank. Then Starbuck scrambled up the cutting's face. "Legion!"

The men climbed from the cutting and formed in two ranks. There were no battle flags to be raised in the Legion's center, where Starbuck took his place. "Forward!" he shouted. The fighting was crackling and spitting in the woods, punctuated by rebel yells. It was hard to tell just what had provoked the fight, but plainly some rebel troops had crossed the railbed to intercept some Yankees among the trees, where Starbuck now led the Legion. He went fast, knowing that his careful battle line would be shredded by the oaks, but also knowing that any chance of finding

381

an open Yankee flank was too compelling to be ignored.

The men panted behind him, crashing through under-growth and splintering dry fallen branches as they ran. Starbuck was leading the Legion to his left, going slantwise across the rebels' front line. He could see gunsmoke sifting through the leaves ahead; then he glimpsed flashes of blue where a handful of Northern soldiers ran through the woods. He ran toward those enemy, but the blue coats disappeared in the trees. Somewhere a rifle fired, and Starbuck heard the bullet ripping through the leaves overhead, but he could not see the gunsmoke or tell whether it was a friend or foe who had fired. He slowed down to catch his breath. The Legion had long lost its cohesion as the companies broke apart in the woodland, so that now they were streaming through the trees like packs of hunters on a quick scent. A volley crashed to Starbuck's left, but no bullets came his way. A riderless horse foaming with sweat and with white eyes flashing plunged through the brush and galloped unchecked between two of Starbuck's companies. The wood suddenly seemed empty of enemy. Starbuck could hear shouted orders and sporadic rifle fire, but he could see no one, and he feared he had led his men far astray; then a sudden warning shout turned him to his left.

And there, suddenly, was an enemy. A huddle of Yankees were kneeling and firing, loading and aiming, but their tar-gets were not the men of the Legion but other Southerners way off to the Legion's left, which suggested that Starbuck had indeed discovered the North's open flank. "Legion, halt! Aim!" He was giving his men precious little time. They skidded to a halt and raised their guns.

"Fire!"

The small group of Yankees were swept cruelly away. Over two hundred bullets had been fired at a score of men, and only one of them was able to stand when the volley was done, and that man was staggering and bleeding.

"Charge!" Starbuck shouted. "And let me hear you scream!"

The Legion began to sound the rebel yell. Starbuck remembered that he had not ordered the men to fix bayonets, but it was too late to remedy the lack now. The Legion had been unleashed, and nothing could stop the ragged charge that screamed through the wood to take the enemy's open flank. The trees ahead were filled with fleeing Yankees. More rebels were coming from the left, and Starbuck shouted at his men to wheel right. "This way! This way!" The breath was pounding in his lungs. Somewhere a man screamed again and again, the sound terrible and pathetic until it was blissfully cut short by a rifle shot.

Starbuck leaped a dead man, stumbled on a fallen log, pushed through a laurel screen, then saw he had blundered into an open field covered with running men. "Halt!" he shouted. "Stop here! Reload!"

The Legion made a rough line at the wood's edge and fired at the horde of retreating Yankees. The men were too breathless and too excited to shoot well, but their rifle fire did serve to hasten the Yankees' panicked retreat. Another rebel regiment appeared to the Legion's left and pursued the enemy into the open meadow, but when Company H began to follow, Captain Truslow pulled them back just a second before a Northern battery unmasked itself in a stand of trees on the meadow's far side. The first cannon whipped a barrelload of canister through the exposed rebel pursuers. A second gun fired, this gun aiming shell at Starbuck's men. The missile cracked overhead and exploded in the trees just as a ragged Northern volley whistled over the pasture.

"Back!" Colonel Swynyard had advanced with the Legion. "Back to the railbed, lads! Well done!"

"Lieutenant Howes?" Starbuck shouted. "A party to collect guns and ammunition!"

"We've got some prisoners here, sir," Howes called back.

Starbuck had not been aware of any prisoners being taken, but sure enough there was a disconsolate group of a dozen men under a corporal's guard who had to be escorted back to the Brigade headquarters. Howe's men found a score of usable rifles and several hundred cartridges that they carried back through the woods.

"A nice beginning," Colonel Swynyard said to Starbuck when the Legion was back in its cutting.

"Easy pickings." Starbuck was dismissive. He could not recall a single bullet coming near him. He knew the Legion had not needed to be involved in the fight, but he was glad that his regiment had been given such a swift and simple victory. It was, as Swynyard had told him, a good beginning.

"But your man Meddlesome didn't move." Lucifer waited till Swynyard was gone before talking to Starbuck. "I watched him. He took his men into the woods and stopped there. You went on, he stayed back."

Starbuck grunted, not wanting to encourage Lucifer's indiscretion. "How old are you?" he asked the runaway slave instead.

Lucifer blinked with surprise at the unexpected question. "Seventeen," he said after a while. "Why?"

Starbuck suspected Lucifer had added at least a year to his age. "Because you're too young to die, that's why, so take yourself back to the wagon park."

"I ain't going to die. I'm charmed!" Lucifer said.

"Charmed?" Starbuck asked. "How?" He was remembering the crushed bird bones.

"Just charmed," Lucifer said. "Like I never got caught as a thief. Till your men trapped me, and there you were!" He grinned. "See? Charmed."

"But you were a thief," Starbuck said, not with disapproval, but simply to pin down the first piece of information about his past that Lucifer had so far offered.

"You think I'd wear those pants with long pockets otherwise? Mick gave them to me."

"Mick?"

"Mr. Micklewhite," Lucifer said. "He owns the big tavern at Manassas Junction and I worked for him."

"You were his slave?"

"I was his thief," Lucifer said. "But he wanted me to do other things. Because he said I'm young and good-looking." He laughed in self-mockery, but Starbuck detected an anxiety behind the words.

"What sort of things?" Starbuck asked.

"You need to be told? You don't know about appetite?"

"Appetite?"

But before Lucifer could answer there was a loud snap of a breaking twig in the woods beyond the killing patch. The Legion went still, fingers poised on triggers, but nothing more sounded from the trees. Off to the right the firing began again, but that far-off battle belonged to someone else. Starbuck looked for his servant again, but Lucifer had vanished, taking his past with him. Ahead of Starbuck the green woods were silent. Somewhere beyond the silence eighty thousand Yankees gathered, but here, for the moment, there was peace.

Starbuck had chosen not to put skirmishers into the woods. The killing patch between the railbed's cutting and the tree line was too wide, so that by the time his own skirmishers would have returned to the Legion's lines the pursuing Yankees would already have been halfway across the open space. The North Carolinians on the Legion's right, however, were faced by an ever-narrowing strip of open land and had taken the precaution of putting a skirmish line among the trees, and it was those men who alerted Starbuck to the day's second Yankee attack, an assault much better organized than the North's first motley advance.

The battle between the skirmishers did not take long. The Yankees were advancing in too much force, and the woods were no place for scattered men to fight against a horde. Hudson's skirmishers fired a single round each, then ran for their lives, yet that scattered volley was sufficient to warn the Legion that the attack was coming.

Starbuck was in the cutting with Company C, which was now commanded by the excitable, quick-tempered William Patterson, who was a stonemason and thus the unwilling butt of too many jokes about gravestones. Patterson had pretensions of gentility and had greeted his unexpected promotion by adorning himself with a red waist sash, a plumed hat, and a sword. He had discarded the sword and plumed hat for this day's fight, but the sash still marked him as an officer. "Ready, boys, ready!" he shouted, and his men licked dry lips and watched the trees anxiously. "They're coming, boys, they're coming!" Patterson called, yet still the green woods were empty, the trees dappled by sunlight alone and the humid air unsullied by powder smoke.

Then, suddenly, the Northerners were in sight. A mass of men ran soundlessly into view. Flags and bayonets were bright. For a second, a split heartbeat, Starbuck watched the rare sight of a whole army attacking straight into his face, then bellowed the order to open fire.

"Fire!" Patterson echoed the shout, and his company's front vanished in a cloud of powder smoke.

"Fire!" Moxey screamed at the company next door. Patterson's men were spitting bullets into rifles, shoving ramrods down barrels, and scrabbling for percussion caps in the upturned hats placed conveniently beside the firestep.

"Fire!" Company D's Captain Pine shouted.

"Fire!" Lieutenant Howes called from Company E. The Yankee attack was oblique, emerging from the trees first to the south, then to the north.

And suddenly, like a great tide bursting on a beach, the sound of the attack overwhelmed Starbuck. It was the sound of a great infantry charge: the noise of cheering, screaming, swearing men, and the noise of drums and bugles behind them, and the noise of his own men's bullets whacking into rifle stocks, and the noise of minié bullets thumping into flesh, and the noise of the first wounded men screaming and gasping, and the noise of ramrods rattling metallic in rifles, and the whistling whip-quick noise of hollow-tailed minié bullets, and the noise of thousands of heavy boots, and the noise of screaming orders, and the noise of men cursing their clumsiness as they fumbled to tear open cartridges.

It was an unending crescendo of noise, a tumult of battering sound waves that obliterated senses already swamped by powder smoke. All a man could do now was fight, and fighting meant pouring lead into the gunsmoke to drive away the pounding, cursing enemy. And the enemy still came forward, rank after rank of blue-coated men beneath their high striped banners. "Fire!" a Yankee shouted.

"Fire!" Truslow's voice answered from the Legion's left flank.

"They're firing high," Private Matthews exulted just five paces from Starbuck, then Matthews was flicked backward by a bullet to the head that took away a saucer-sized piece of his skull and spattered his neighbor with blood and brains. Lieutenant Patterson stood transfixed as Matthews's body slid to a halt at his feet. The body twitched, blood pouring from the shattered cranium.

"Fire!" Starbuck shouted. He saw a boy pull the trigger; nothing happened, yet the boy started to ram another charge

387

down a barrel probably stuffed with unfired charges. Starbuck picked up Matthews's blood-sticky rifle and ran to the boy. "Fire the damn thing before you load it!" he snapped, handing the frightened lad the new gun. Starbuck took the boy's rifle and tossed it back out of the cutting. He fired his own rifle into the gray mist of smoke, then ran along the cutting past Moxey's company to where Medlicott guarded the vulnerable right flank. The miller was fighting well enough, firing his revolver into the smoke that was now being fed by the volleys of both sides to create a single filthy-smelling leprous yellow cloudbank. The Yankee charge seemed to have stalled, though it had not been defeated. Instead the Northerners were holding their ground in the killing patch and trying to overwhelm the rebel line with volley fire.

"We're still here, Starbuck, still here!" The speaker was the genial Colonel Hudson, who had come to his own left flank on an errand not dissimilar to Starbuck's own. "Mr. Lincoln's Republican party is noisy today, is it not?" the Colonel said, gesturing toward the Yankees with a switch of hazel that was apparently his weapon of choice. A bullet slapped past Hudson's long hair. "Rotten shot," the Colonel lamented, "terrible shooting! They really should look to their musket training."

Then a second great cheer sounded from beyond the smoke, and there was a resurgence of that first terrible sound that had swollen to burst against the rebels' defenses. "Dear Lord," Hudson said, "I do believe a second line is coming. Hold hard, boys! Hold hard!" He strode back along his line.

"Oh, Christ, oh, Christ!" Major Medlicott was fumbling percussion caps onto his revolver. "Oh, Christ!" He raised the gun, only half primed, and shot blindly into the smoke. Beyond that smoke the Yankee fire had slackened as the first wave of attackers made way for the second. The rebels fired on into the gloom, seeing their targets only as dark shadows

388

in the luminous smoke cloud; then a screaming mass of men with fixed bayonets materialized in that fogbank.

"Back!" Medlicott shouted, and his men scrambled away from the shallow cutting.

"Stay and fight, damn it!" Starbuck bellowed, but the panic was infectious, and the company streamed past him. For a second Starbuck was alone in the wide ditch; then he saw the open mouths of Yankee attackers not ten paces away, and he ran for his life. He expected a bullet in the back at any second as he scrambled up the western bank and followed Medlicott's company into the tangle of saplings and bushes.

The Yankees scented victory. They cheered as they jumped down into the cutting and as they scrambled up its further bank. Their flags streamed forward. A gap had opened between the Legion and Hudson's North Carolinians, and the Northern infantry poured into the gap, where they discovered the unguarded spoil pit. Like a wave of water released by a broken dam they swarmed into the hollow, only to surge up against the abatis. They recoiled for a second as the tangle of branches checked their headlong charge; then they flowed around the barrier's flanks to swarm up to the spoil pit's edge.

"Fire!" Colonel Swynyard had brought Haxall's Arkansas battalion down the hill to meet the Yankee charge where it tried to climb out of the spoil pit. Rifles slashed fire into the pit. The rebels could not miss, for the Yankees were crammed tighter than rats in a terrier pit. "Fire!" Major Haxall called, and a second volley whipped down and the Yankee mass seemed to quiver like a great wounded beast.

"Get your men formed, and fight!" Swynyard shouted angrily at Starbuck. "Goddamn it, fight!"

"Damn!" Starbuck was lost, confused. The attackers in the pit were being slaughtered, but more Yankees had crossed the ditch and were charging through the scrub, where handfuls of dogged rebels resisted them. Starbuck blundered through the trees, seeking men, any men, finding nothing but chaos, and then he saw Peter Waggoner, the giant, Bible-thumping Sergeant from Company D. Sweet Jesus, Starbuck thought, but if Company D had been thrown out of the railbed, then the Legion must be unraveling all along its length. "Waggoner!"

"Sir?"

"Where's your company?"

"Here, sir! Here!" And there, crouching frightened behind the big Sergeant, was most of Company D. Captain Pine was pushing men into line, screaming at them to stand and fight.

"Fix bayonets," Starbuck called, "and follow me! And scream! For God's sake, scream!"

The ululating, blood-chilling sound of the rebel yell whipsawed in the air as the company followed Starbuck back toward the railbed. Goddamn it, but he would not be beaten! A Yankee appeared in front of Starbuck, and he fired his revolver straight into the man's face, which seemed to vanish in a spray of red as the shock of the gun's recoil jarred up to Starbuck's shoulder. He half slipped in a slick of blood, then fired into a mass of blue uniforms in front. "Charge!" he screamed. "Charge!" And Waggoner's men came with him, screaming like devils released to mischief, and the disordered Yankees went backward. The desperate charge through the brush had collected more groups of scattered Legionnaires, so that Starbuck was now leading almost a third of his regiment in a blood-crazed, desperate, vicious counterattack. The Northerners had been on the brink of victory but were suddenly confused by this unexpected opposition. The Yankees retreated.

Starbuck leaped back into the railbed. A Northerner

slipped on the far bank, turned, and swung his rifle. Starbuck fired at the man, heard him scream, then jumped over the falling body to sprawl and trip at the top of the embankment. A rifle shot cracked over his head, then a wave of his own men went past him and a giant hand plucked him onto his feet. "Come on, sir!" It was Sergeant Peter Waggoner. A cannon fired somewhere, adding its new noise to the din of battle. Behind Starbuck, at the rim of the spoil pit, the rifle volleys still flailed down to turn the hollow into a charnel house. The Yankees were retreating, stunned by the violence of the rebel backlash. Starbuck ran past the heap of bodies killed in the rifle duel that had preceded the second Yankee surge forward. He knew he had lost command of his men and that now they were fighting from instinct and without proper guidance, and so he sprinted forward to try and get ahead of them and somehow bring them under control.

The Yankees had brought a small cannon forward to the edge of the trees. The gun was scarcely four feet high and had a short, wide-muzzled barrel. They had managed to fire one shot with the gun, and now its four-man crew was desperately trying to haul the weapon back through the trees to save it from being captured by the screaming, battle-maddened gray wave. In their haste the gunners rammed one of the gunwheels into a tree and thus stalled their retreat. "The gun!" Starbuck shouted. "The gun!" If he could concentrate his men at the gun, then he had a chance of regaining control of the Legion. "Go for the gun!" he shouted and ran toward the cannon himself. Something hit him hard on the left thigh, spinning him and almost knocking him down. He limped for a pace, waiting for the delayed agony to sear through his body. He took a breath ready to scream and almost sobbed instead as he felt wetness spill down his leg, then realized the enemy bullet had merely smashed his

391

canteen. It was not blood, but water. His hip was bruised, but he was unwounded, and his self-pitying scream turned into a defiant yelp of relief. All around him the rebel yell filled the air. One of the Yankee gunners, knowing that the trapped weapon was lost, leaned across a wheel to tug the lanyard of the cannon's primer, and Starbuck, realizing with horror that the cannon was still loaded and that a storm of canister was about to be unleashed on his men, fired the last shots of his revolver. He saw a slash of bright metal show on the cannon's barrel as a round ricocheted off the bronze; then his last bullet whipped the enemy gunner backward onto the ground.

"Legion!" Starbuck screamed. "To me!" He was among the trees now, just yards from the gun. The Yankees had fled into the broken, smoking wood, where the trunks were bitten by rifle fire. "Legion! Legion! Legion!" Starbuck shouted. He reached the cannon and put a proprietorial hand on its bullet-flecked barrel. "Legion! Form line! Form line! Fire! Legion! Legion!" He was screaming like a mad thing, as though he could impose his will on the excited men by sheer force of mind and voice. "Form!" He shouted the word desperately.

And men at last heard him and at last obeyed him. Companies were mixed together, officers were missing, sergeants and corporals were dead, but the maddened charge somehow shook itself into a crude firing line that slammed a volley into the wood. The volley was matched by one from the enemy. The Yankees, retreating into the trees, had turned and formed their own battle line. One of Starbuck's men screamed as he was hit in the leg, another staggered back into the smoky sunlight with blood seeping between fingers that were clutched to his belly. A bullet smacked hollowly into one of the captured cannon's ammunition chests. Somewhere a man gasped the name Jesus over and over.

God Almighty, Starbuck thought, but somehow they had

survived. He felt sick to his stomach. He felt ashamed, and his hands were shaking as he reloaded his revolver. He had failed. He had felt the Legion disintegrate around him like a crumbling dam, and there had been nothing he could do. There were tears on his face, tears of shame at having failed. He pressed the percussion caps onto the revolver's cones and fired it into the shadowed smoke beneath the trees.

"Sir!" Captain Pine of D Company, his lips blackened by powder and his eyes red from the smoke, appeared beside him. "Do we take the gun, sir?" He gestured at the captured cannon.

"Yes!" Starbuck said, then forced himself to calm down, to think. "Keep firing!" he shouted at the Legion's ragged line; then he looked more carefully at the gun. A dead horse lay nearby, just one horse, and there was no limber, but only wooden chests of ammunition, and Starbuck remembered Swynyard telling him about the mountain howitzers of the old U.S. Army, and he realized that this twelve-pounder cannon was one of those old rough-country guns that were transported on the backs of single packhorses. This captured howitzer was not a heavy gun, but even so it would need a half-dozen men to drag it through the trees and back to the railbed, and Starbuck knew that the absence of even a half-dozen men would weaken his line enough to let the Yankees surge back. Maybe, he thought, he should just spike the gun and abandon it; then he saw a mass of blue uniforms behind his fragile line and panic soared in him.

He was about to scream at his men to turn and drive this new enemy away, then realized that the blue coats belonged to prisoners. They were Yankees who had survived the horror in the spoil pit and who had now climbed out into the open ground. "Get some of those Yankees," Starbuck said to Pine, "and have them drag the gun back. And be careful, it's loaded!"

"Use prisoners, sir?" Pine asked, apparently shocked at the idea.

"Do it!" Starbuck turned back to the east to see that his men were doggedly firing and loading, firing and loading. Most were sheltering behind trees, just as the Yankees were, which meant that the firefight was settling into a stalemate, but soon the Legion must withdraw to its railbed trench, and Starbuck was determined that the retreat should be made in good order. He would not lose control as he had before.

Lieutenant Pine was arguing with a captured Yankee officer. Starbuck stooped to the gun's trail and picked up a length of one-inch rope with iron prolonge hooks spliced into its ends. He threw the rope to Pine. "Shoot the bastard if he won't do as he's told!" he shouted.

Pine finally organized a morose work party of a dozen prisoners, who were given the rope to hold. Pine himself attached one of the hooks to the lunette, the ring at the tip of the gun's trail, then shouted at his unwilling team to haul away. The trail swung around, and the gun eased itself away from the tree, so that its short, black-mouthed muzzle was turned to face back toward its erstwhile owners. "Stop!" Starbuck shouted.

The astonished prisoners dropped the rope. "Clear me! Clear me!" Starbuck bellowed at those of his men who were firing at the enemy from in front of the cannon. "Clear me!" Two men looked around, saw the gun facing them, and ran hastily to one side. Starbuck, when he was sure the field of fire was clear of his own men, leaned across the wheel and grasped the primer's lanyard. He waited a handful of seconds until he could see some Northerners stepping from behind trees to aim their rifles, then pulled the lanyard.

The gun cracked like the shattering hammer blow of doom. Smoke jetted thirty yards forward, while the gun itself recoiled clear out of the trees and almost ran down its blue-coated haulers. The tin canister had split apart at the muzzle to scatter its balls like giant buckshot. Starbuck's ears were ringing from the explosion. "Take it away! Hurry!" Starbuck shouted at the scared Yankee prisoners. "Whip them if they won't work," Starbuck shouted at Pine. "We slavers know how to whip!" The startled Yankee prisoners began to haul as though their lives depended on it, and the smoking gun trundled away across the rough ground so fast that it bounced two feet in the air when its wheels struck a sprawling corpse. In the trees the cannon smoke cleared to reveal a patch of woodland ripped and scarred by canister. "Keep firing!" Starbuck shouted at his men; then, as Pine's team dragged the gun back across the shallowest part of the cutting and so up to the sparse woodland beyond, Starbuck ran to his right to determine where his men's line ended.

He found Lieutenant Patterson. "Where's Medlicott?" Starbuck shouted over the rifle fire.

"Haven't seen him, sir."

"Have your men load, then go back to the railbed and be ready to fire when the rest of us come back!" Starbuck had to shout over the splintering rifle fire. Patterson nodded. He was wild-eyed and frenetic, firing a revolver again and again at the Yankees. Even when the revolver's hammer began clicking on exploded percussion caps, Patterson kept cocking and firing, cocking and firing. Starbuck slapped the unprimed gun down and made the Lieutenant repeat the orders he had been given. "Do it now!" Starbuck ordered, then ran northward to find Lieutenant Howes, Sergeant Tyndale, and Captain Leighton. He told them to pull their men back to the railbed. "One last volley to keep the Yankees busy," he ordered, "then run like hell, understand?" Starbuck was beginning to understand the Legion's ragged dispositions now. Medlicott and Moxey were missing, the four center companies were either in the trees or gone back with Lieutenant Patterson, while presumably Truslow and Davies had never moved from the railbed.

"Fire!" Captain Leighton shouted, and the rifle flames speared bright in the trees.

"Back!" Starbuck shouted. "Back!"

They ran back, leaping the tideline of blue-coated bodies and then jumping over their own dead into the railbed. The Northerners were slow to realize that the rebels were gone, and it was a long moment before their first skirmishers appeared at the tree line. "Had enough, Johnny?" one Northerner shouted.

"Go back, Billy, before we send you home in a box!" a rebel called back.

"Oh, my God," another man said, panting from the exertions of the last few minutes, "just lay me down."

Starbuck ran down the railbed until he came to Captain Davies's company, which, as he had suspected, had never moved from its position. Truslow had seen to that, barricading the railbed with a fallen tree so that the threatening disaster to the South had been given no chance of spreading as far as his company. There were dead Yankees all along the front of Truslow and Davies's men, but none of the enemy had come closer than fifteen yards from the parapet. "So what were you doing up there?" Truslow asked calmly.

"Not very well," Starbuck confessed.

"The Legion's still in place," Truslow said in a voice so grim that it was a moment or two before Starbuck realized the words were probably meant as a compliment.

"God knows if we can take another attack," he said.

"Ain't none of God's business," Truslow said, "but if the bastards do come again, then we'll just have to drive them off again. Well done!" This rare enthusiastic praise was not directed at Starbuck but at Sergeant Bailey, who had brought replacement ammunition to the railbed. Two other men were tending a fire so that Truslow's company would have boiling water to scour the powder deposits from their rifles.

Starbuck walked back along his defense line. The Yankees had settled at the tree line, from where they were directing a constant and harassing rifle fire at the railbed. Starbuck's men kept their heads down, sometimes raising themselves to fire a shot or sometimes just lifting a rifle over the makeshift parapet and squeezing the trigger blindly. "Don't waste ammunition!" Starbuck snarled at one man who had thus fired without sighting first. "If you're going to shoot, aim, and if you're not, keep low."

There were bodies in the railbed. Some were the Legion's own dead, lying on their backs, mouths open and hands curled. Starbuck recognized a few men with sadness, some without any regret, and a handful with satisfaction. One or two of the rebel dead were strangers. He should have known them, but he had not had time to learn the names and faces of every new conscript. The Yankee dead had mostly been hoisted onto the parapet to help protect the rebel living, while the Legion's white-faced wounded lay breathing shallowly against the rear slope of the cutting.

Starbuck resisted the urge to crouch as the cutting became shallower. An officer was supposed to show his men an example of fearlessness, and Starbuck kept his pace steady even as his mind screamed and his pulse raced with fear. Bullets slapped the air around him for the few seconds that he was exposed to the Yankees; then he was able to jump down into the spoil pit, which was grotesque with enemy dead. The smell of blood was thick, and the first flies already swarming on the bloodied wounds. It was the spoil pit, Starbuck reckoned, that had saved the Legion. The hollow had drawn the attackers away from the rest of the line because of its promise of a safe, covered route into the rebel rear. But once in the pit the Northerners had been trapped, first by the abatis and then by the fire of Haxall's battalion, which Swynyard had brought down from the hill.

"We're thin on the ground, sir," Lieutenant Patterson greeted Starbuck.

"Thin?"

Patterson shrugged. "Half A and B companies are missing."

"Medlicott? Moxey?" Starbuck need not have asked. Both men were absent, and no one knew where they might be. Coffman was safe, crouching under the railbed's shallow parapet with a rifle he had taken from a dead man, and Captain Pine's mountain howitzer was also safe. It had been parked at the back crest of the spoil pit, where it was attracting Yankee bullets.

Patterson saw Starbuck glance at the gun. "We forgot to bring the ammunition, sir."

Starbuck swore. Nothing was going right this day, nothing, except, as Truslow had said, the Legion was still in place. Which meant the battle was not lost. And happily, except for the one hapless mountain howitzer, the Yankees had not deployed any artillery against the Legion. The woods were too thick to let the gunners of either side deploy their weapons, though just as that thought occurred to Starbuck, some shells began to explode. They were rebel shells, and they burst in the woods over the Yankees, who, astonished by the shrapnel, crept back from the tree line. The gunfire seemed to be coming from far to the south, but it stopped abruptly as a surge of cheering and rifle fire sounded further down Jackson's line. Starbuck, listening to the sound of battle, guessed he was hearing a Yankee attack like the one the Legion had just, though barely, survived. The gunners had shortened their range to enfilade the attackers, and the Yankees close to the Legion crept back to the tree line to begin their harassing fire again.

Haxall's men had returned to the hill, from where they were now sharpshooting across the railbed, while Hudson's North Carolinians were also back in place. The tall Colonel Hudson saw Starbuck and strode toward him. "A hot place, Starbuck!" He meant the railbed hard by the spoil pit.

"I'm sorry my fellows ran."

"My dear man, mine went as well! Scattered like barn-yard fowls!" Hudson decently refrained from pointing out that his men had no choice but to run once Medlicott had exposed their flank. "Have you the time?" the Colonel now asked. "A Yankee shot my watch, see?" He showed Starbuck the torn pocket where the watch had been stored. "Bullet went straight through without touching me, but it rather mangled the watch. Pity. It belonged to my grandfather. It kept terrible time, but I was fond of it and hoped to pass it on to my son."

"You've got a son?" Starbuck asked, somehow surprised by the information.

"Three altogether, and a brace of daughters. Tom's my oldest boy. He's twenty-four now and serves as one of Lee's aides."

"Lee!" Starbuck was impressed. "The Lee?"

"Bobby himself. Nice fellow. Still, pity about the watch." The Colonel picked a piece of shattered watch glass from the remnants of his pocket.

"Coffman!" Starbuck shouted. "What time is it?"

Coffman had inherited an ancient timepiece from his father, and now he fished its bulbous case from an inner pocket and clicked open the lid. "It says thirty minutes after four, sir."

"It must have stopped this morning," Starbuck said. "It can't be that late."

"But look at the sun!" Hudson said, intimating that it truly was that late in the afternoon.

"Then where's Lee?" Starbuck asked. "I thought he was coming to relieve us."

"I find it best to plan military affairs on the twin principles that whatever I am told is certain will never occur, and that whatever is proclaimed impossible is disastrously imminent. There is no good news in war," Hudson pronounced grandly, "only less bad news. Dear, oh dear." The mild oath had been caused by a resurgence of enemy rifle fire from the tree line. "I do believe, my dear Starbuck, that the Republican party claims our attention again. Ah, well, to our toil, to our toil."

And the storm broke again.

The Reverend Elial Starbuck was trying to understand what was happening. Comprehension, he thought, was not much to ask. War was as rational an activity as any other human endeavor and must, he presumed, yield to analysis, yet whenever he inquired of a general officer what exactly was occurring in the western woods, he received a different answer.

The North was attacking, one general said, yet the general's own men were sprawling in the meadows playing cards and smoking pipes. "All in good time, all in good time," the General said when the preacher asked him why his men were not supporting the attack. One of the General's staff officers, a superior young man who made clear his disapproval of a civilian intruding on a battlefield, informed the Reverend Starbuck that Jackson was retreating, the Yankees were pursuing, and that the commotion in the woods was nothing but a noisy rear guard.

Major Galloway also tried to reassure the preacher. Galloway had been ordered to wait until the attacking infantry broke through Jackson's line, after which his men would join the Northern cavalry in their pursuit of the shattered enemy. The Reverend Starbuck waited on horseback for that promised breakthrough and tried to convince himself that the Major's explanation made sense. "Jackson's attempting to retreat southward, sir," Galloway told the preacher, "and our fellows have him pinned against the woods over there," but even Galloway was unhappy with that analysis. The Major, after all, had failed to find any evidence that Jackson had ever gone to Centreville, so it did not make sense that he would now be retreating from that town, which raised the mystery of what exactly the Southern general was doing. And that mystery was made even more worrying by Billy Blythe's repeated assertions that he had seen a second rebel army marching toward Manassas from the west. Galloway was unwilling to share his anxiety with the Reverend Doctor Starbuck, but the Major had the distinct impression that perhaps General Pope had utterly misunderstood what was truly happening.

Galloway's unhappiness was compounded by the acrid mood that prevailed within his small regiment. Blythe's return had stirred Adam Faulconer's anger, an anger that had come to a head the night before when the Virginian had accused Blythe of murdering civilians at McComb's Tavern. Blythe had denied the accusation. "We was fired on by soldiers," Blythe maintained.

"And the soldiers begged you to stop firing because there were women there!" Adam insisted.

"If a man had done that," Blythe said, "I would have ceased fire instantly. Instantly! Upon my word, Faulconer, but what kind of a man do you take me for?"

"A liar," Adam had said, and before Galloway could intervene, the challenge had been made.

But the duel had not yet been fought, and perhaps, Galloway dared hope, the duel would never be fought, to which end he now enlisted the Reverend Starbuck's aid. The preacher, happy to have a purpose while the infantry battle still raged, spoke first to Captain Blythe and afterward brought a report of the conversation back to Galloway. "Blythe admits there might have been women in the tavern," the Reverend Starbuck said, "and the thought distresses him greatly, but he plainly wasn't aware of them at the time and he promises me that he heard no calls for any cease-fire." The preacher paused for a moment to watch the smoke trails of artillery shells arching across the distant woods, then frowned at the Major. "What kind of women would be in a tavern anyway?"

Galloway hoped the question was rhetorical, but the preacher's expression suggested he wanted an answer. The Major cast around for a suitable evasion and found none. "Whores, sir," he finally said, coloring with embarrassment for having used such a word to a man of God.

"Precisely," the preacher said. "Women of no virtue. So why is Faulconer making this commotion?"

"Adam has a tender conscience, sir."

"He is also in your regiment, Major, by courtesy of my money," the preacher said sharply, conveniently overlooking that the money for Galloway's Horse had actually been subscribed by hundreds of humble, well-meaning folk throughout New England, "and I will not have the Lord's work hampered by a misplaced sympathy for fallen women. Captain Faulconer must learn that he cannot afford a tender conscience, not on my money!"

"You'll talk to him, sir?" Galloway asked.

"Directly," the preacher said and immediately beckoned Adam to one side. The two men rode far enough for their conversation to be private; then the preacher demanded to

402

know exactly what evidence Adam had for his accusation of murder.

"The evidence of a newspaper, sir," Adam said, "and my own apprehension of Captain Blythe's character."

"It was a Southern newspaper." The Reverend Starbuck easily demolished the first part of Adam's evidence.

"So it was, sir."

"And your other evidence is merely founded upon your dislike of Captain Blythe's character? You think we can afford the luxuries of such self-indulgent judgments in wartime?"

"I have grounds for that dislike, sir."

"Grounds! Grounds!" The Reverend Starbuck spat the two words out. "We are at war, young man, we cannot indulge in petty squabbles!"

Adam stiffened. "It was Captain Blythe who issued the duel challenge, sir, not me."

"You called him a liar!" the Reverend Starbuck said.

"Yes, sir, I did."

The Reverend Starbuck shook his head sadly. "I have talked with Blythe. He assures me, on his word as a gentleman, that he had no idea any women were present in the tavern, and he still maintains there were none present, but he accepts he might be mistaken, and all he asks of you is your acceptance that he would never have continued the battle had he known that his actions were risking the lives of women. I believe him." The Reverend Starbuck paused, offering Adam a chance to utter agreement, but Adam remained obstinately silent. "For the love of God, man," the preacher protested, "do you really believe that a man of honor, an officer of the United States Army, a Christian, would persecute women?"

"No, sir, I don't believe that," Adam said pointedly.

It took a few seconds for the Reverend Starbuck to

appreciate the debating point Adam had made, and the appreciation did not improve the preacher's temper. "I'll thank you not to be clever with me, young man. I have investigated this matter. I know the wickedness of mankind better than you, Faulconer. I have wrestled with iniquity all my life and my judgments are not based on Southern newspapers, but on hard experience tempered, I trust, with prayerful charity, and I am telling you now that Captain Blythe is no murderer and that his actions that night were chivalrous. It is unspeakable that a man could behave in the way you describe! Unthinkable! Manifestly impossible!"

Adam shook his head. "I could tell you of another occasion, sir," he said, and was about to tell the tale of the woman he had discovered in the barn with Blythe, but the preacher gave him no chance to tell the story.

"I will not listen to rumor!" the Reverend Starbuck insisted. "My God, I will not listen to rumor. We are engaged upon a crusade, Faulconer, a great crusade to forge God's chosen nation. We are purging that nation of sin, burning the iniquity from its heart with a fierce and righteous fire, and there is no room, no merit, no satisfaction, no justification for any man to put his personal whims ahead of that great cause. As our Lord and Savior Himself said, 'He that is not with Me is against Me,' and upon my soul, Faulconer, if you oppose Major Galloway in this matter then you will find that Christ and I are both become your enemies."

Adam began to feel a sympathy for his onetime friend, Nathaniel Starbuck. "I would have no one doubt my loyalty to the cause of the United States, sir," he said in feeble protest to the preacher.

"Then shake Blythe's hand and admit you were wrong," the Reverend Starbuck said.

"Me? That I was wrong?" Adam could not help asking the astonished question aloud.

"He admits you might be right, and that perhaps there were women there, so can you not do the same and admit that he would have behaved differently had he known?"

Adam's head was awhirl. Somehow, he was not sure how, he had been maneuvered into the wrong. He was also painfully aware that he was in the preacher's debt, and so, though it cut hard against a stubborn grain, he nodded his head. "If you insist, sir," he said unhappily.

"It's your conscience that should insist, but I am glad all the same. Come!" And the Reverend Starbuck thumped his horse's flanks to lead Adam across to where the grinning Billy Blythe waited. "Mr. Faulconer has something to say to you, Captain," the Reverend Starbuck announced.

Adam made his admission that he might have misjudged Captain Blythe, then apologized for that misjudgment. He hated himself for making the apology, but he nevertheless tried to make it sound heartfelt. He even held out his hand afterward.

Blythe shook the offered hand. "I guess we Southern gentlemen are just too hotheaded, ain't that right, Faulconer? So we'll say no more about it."

Adam felt demeaned and belittled. He put a brave face on the defeat, but it was still a defeat and it hurt. Major Galloway, though, was touchingly pleased by the apparent reconciliation. "We should be friends," Galloway said. "We have enemies enough without making them from our own side."

"Amen to that," Blythe said, "amen to that."

"Amen indeed," the Reverend Starbuck echoed, "and hallelujah."

Adam said nothing but just stared at the woods where the smoke rose from the guns.

While to the south, unseen by any Northern troops, regiment after regiment of rebel infantry was marching on a country road that led to the open flank of John Pope's army. Lee's reinforcements were arriving just as the Yankees' last great charge of the day was hurled against the railbed in the woods.

Above the Blue Ridge Mountains the sun sank slowly into a summer's evening. The Reverend Starbuck saw the imminence of nightfall and clenched his fists as he prayed that God would grant John Pope the same miracle that He had granted unto Joshua when He had made the sun stand still above Gibeon so that the armies of Israel would have the time to strike down the Amorites. The preacher prayed, bugles sounded in the woods, a loud cheer echoed among the trees, and the last great onslaught of the day charged on.

THE LAST NORTHERN ATTACK of the day was by far the strongest and most dangerous, for instead of being launched in line it came in an old-fashioned column that struck like a hammer blow at the shallowest section of the railbed. It also struck at the vulnerable junction between Starbuck's men and Elijah Hudson's North Carolinians, and Starbuck, watching from the lip of the spoil pit at the back of the railbed, instinctively understood that his men would never stand against this tidal wave that streamed from the woods. The attacking battalions were so close together that their flags made a bright phalanx above the dark ranks. The flags showed the crests and badges of New York and Indiana, of Pennsylvania, Maine, and of Michigan, and beneath the flags the shouts of the attackers drowned the snapping sound of the Legion's rifles.

"Ten paces back!" Starbuck shouted. He would not wait to be overrun. He heard Hudson shouting a similar command; then all sound from the rebel side was momentarily obliterated by the vast Northern cheer that greeted the retreat of the defenders. "Back," Starbuck shouted again when the Northern cheer faded. "Back! Keep in line! Keep in line!" He strode along the Legion's ranks, watching his men rather than looking at the surging enemy. "Backwards! Steady now! Steady!" He was suddenly so proud of the Legion. They were watching blue-coated death come at them in a massive rush, yet they retreated in good steady order as he took them back another ten paces into the thin woodland behind the railbed. He halted them among the saplings. "Reload!" he shouted. "Reload!"

Men bit cartridges, poured powder, and spat bullets. They rammed the charges hard down, then upended the rifles and pressed percussion caps onto fire-blackened cones.

"Aim!" Starbuck shouted. "But wait! Wait for my order!" All along the Legion's line the heavy rifle hammers clicked into place. "Wait for my order and aim low!" Starbuck called. He turned to watch the charge just as the Northerners reached the railbed's cutting. The triumphant Yankee troops poured down the trench's sloping outer wall and then, still cheering, swarmed up its rearward slope straight into the sights of the waiting Legion.

"Fire!" Starbuck shouted.

The volley exploded along the line, hurling Northerners back into the trench. At twenty paces such a volley was mere slaughter work, but it did no more than check the onrushing attack for the few seconds necessary for the unwounded attackers to push aside their encumbering dead and dying. Then, urged on by officers and inflamed with the prospect of victory, the Yankees came forward for their revenge.

But Starbuck had already taken his men back to the hill, where Haxall's Arkansas battalion waited in support. The Legion's retreat had again opened a gap in front of the spoil pit, and again that gap enticed the Yankee attackers. It was the place of least resistance, and so the attacking column poured into the inviting open space. A few of the Northerners found themselves among the stinking bodies in the spoil pit, but most ran around the pit's rim and then charged on toward the open country beyond. They left behind a litter of wounded men, a trail of crushed saplings, and Starbuck's forlorn, captured howitzer, which had been thrown off its carriage.

Haxall's men helped seal the gap by firing one blistering volley, and by the time the smoke of that volley had cleared, the Legion's rifles were loaded again. "Fire!" Starbuck shouted and heard the command echoed toward the regiment's left flank. The Northern attack was slowing, not because it was being outfought, but simply because too many Yankees were trying to push through the narrow gaps either side of the spoil pit and were meeting a stiffening resistance as Starbuck's right flank and Hudson's left closed on each other. Haxall's men extended Starbuck's line and, when at last the gap was closed, turned back to hunt down the Yankees who had broken through. The junction of Starbuck's Virginians and Hudson's North Carolinians was now some fifty paces behind the spoil pit, and it was there that the line steadied and began a murderous fight with the Yankees who had not succeeded in breaking through Jackson's line.

The fight started with the two sides just thirty paces apart; close enough for men to see their enemies' faces, close enough to hear an enemy's voice, close enough for a bullet to mangle a man's flesh with undiminished horror. This was an infantry fight, rifle against rifle, the ordeal for which both sides had trained incessantly. Starbuck had to forget those Yankees who had broken through and were now loose at his rear; his sole duty was to stand and fight and trust someone else to worry about the Yankees who had breached the line, just as someone else must worry about the possibility of more Yankees crossing the railbed to join this duel of rifles. If those enemy reinforcements arrived, Starbuck knew, then the Legion must be overwhelmed, but for the moment the Northerners were being held. They were being held by men who knew their survival depended on being able to load their rifles faster than the enemy. There was no need for any officers or sergeants to give commands. The men knew what to do. They did it.

Lieutenant Patterson was dead, killed by his red sash that had attracted too many Yankee bullets. It was a miracle to Starbuck that any man survived the maelstrom of close-range rifle fire, but the sulfurous powder smoke served as a screen, and the Yankee fire slackened as the Northerners edged back toward the railbed. No regiment, however brave, could long survive a rifle duel at close range, and the instinct for both sides was to retreat, but Starbuck's men were standing hard against the hill's base, and the slope inhibited their natural instinct to shuffle a few inches backward every time they reloaded their rifles, but the open land behind the Yankee line tempted the Northerners to yield their ground inch by bloody inch, then yard by smoldering yard.

Starbuck lost count of the bullets he fired. His rifle was now so fouled with powder that it was painful to ram each new bullet down the barrel. He fired and fired again, his shoulder bruising from the recoil, his eyes smarting from the smoke, and his voice hoarse from the day's shouting. He heard the distinctive meat-ax sound as bullets struck men around him and was dimly conscious of bodies falling backward from the line. He was also conscious that rank gave him the freedom to leave the battle line, except that the responsibility of command perversely decreed that he could not take that voluntary backward step.

And so he fought. Sometimes he shouted at the line to close up, but mostly he just rammed and fired, rammed and fired, consumed by the conviction shared by every man in the line that his were the bullets that were pushing the enemy back. He flinched each time the heavy gun slammed back into his shoulder, and he choked each time he bit open a cartridge and so tasted the acrid, salt-rich, mouth-drying gunpowder. Sweat stung his eyes. Somewhere in the back of his mind was the terror of being injured, but he was too busy loading and firing to let that terror overwhelm him. An occasional bullet slicing close by left him momentarily shaking, but then he would ram another round into the recalcitrant rifle and crash another shoulder-bruising shot toward the Yankees and fish for another cartridge in his haversack as he let the rifle's heavy stock fall to the ground. Once, pouring powder into the barrel, the new charge caught fire and exploded a bright gash of flame into his face. He recoiled from the pain, his eyeballs seared raw, then angrily rammed the embers dead in the barrel with his ramrod. Minutes later another sharp pain shot hard through his right arm, and he almost dropped the rifle from the sudden agony; then he saw he had been struck not by a bullet but only by a sharp-tipped splinter of bone that had been ripped from his neighbor's ribcage by a Yankee bullet. The man was on the ground, twitching as the blood flooded from his shattered chest. He looked up at Starbuck, tried so hard to speak, then choked on blood and died.

Starbuck stooped to feel in the man's haversack for more cartridges and found just two. He was down to the bottom layer of his own rounds now. "Close up!" he shouted. "Close up!" And a momentary lull in the fighting gave him an opportunity to back out of the line, where men were asking friends and neighbors for any extra ammunition. Starbuck handed out what few rounds he had left and then climbed the steep hill in search of the Legion's spare ammunition supply. A score of wounded men had taken refuge on the hill. One of Haxall's Arkansas men, his left arm hanging bloody, tried to load his rifle one-handed. "Goddamned sons of bitches," the man muttered over and over, "Goddamned sons of Yankee bitches." A shell burst overhead to slap hot scraps of smoking metal into the hill.

"Yankees have brought up two more howitzers!" Colonel Swynyard was seated halfway up the hill, field glasses in hand. He sounded very calm.

"We need ammunition!" Starbuck said, trying to sound as collected as the Colonel but unable to keep a note of panic out of his voice.

"None left!" The Colonel shrugged helplessly. "I have to apologize to you, Starbuck."

"Me?"

"I swore at you earlier. I apologize."

"You did? Christ!" Starbuck spat out the blasphemy as another shell screamed low overhead to ricochet up from the slope and explode somewhere beyond the summit. Had Swynyard sworn at him? Starbuck did not remember, nor did he much care. He was suddenly worrying far more about what had happened to the mass of Yankees who had streamed through the gap into the army's rear and there disappeared. Suppose those men were about to counterattack? "We must have ammunition!" he shouted to Swynyard.

"Used it all. Long day's fighting." The Colonel seemed remarkably calm as he aimed his revolver at the Northern battle line and methodically pulled the trigger. "They're slackening! When they're gone we'll pillage the dead for ammunition."

Starbuck ran downhill and pulled two of Captain Davies's men out of the ranks. "You're to search the dead and wounded," he told them, "and find ammunition. Hand it out! Hurry!" He sent one man to the left, the other to the right, then took their place in the ranks and drew his revolver.

Starbuck found himself standing alongside the bespectacled Captain Ethan Davies, who was fighting with a rifle. "They're from Indiana," Davies said, as though Starbuck would be interested in the news.

"What? Who?" Starbuck had not been listening. Instead he had been searching the smoke-smeared enemy line for any sign of a man giving commands.

"These fellows." Davies indicated the nearest Yankees with a jerk of his chin. "They're from Indiana."

"How do you know?"

"I asked them, of course. Shouted at them." He fired, flinching from the painful impact of the rifle's heavy recoil against his bruised shoulder. "I almost married a girl from Indiana once," Davies added as he dropped the rifle's butt onto the ground and pulled out a paper-wrapped cartridge.

"What stopped you?" Starbuck was priming his revolver with percussion caps.

"She was Catholic and my parents disapproved." Davies spoke mildly. He bit off a bullet, poured the gritty powder down the hot barrel, then spat the bullet into the muzzle with powder-blackened lips. His spectacles were smeared into opaqueness with dust and sweat. "I often think of her," he said wistfully, then rammed the bullet down hard, swung the rifle up, capped it, and pulled the trigger. "She came from Terre Haute. Don't you think that's a wonderful name for a town?"

Starbuck cocked his revolver. "How did a Virginian happen to meet a Catholic girl from Terre Haute?" He had to shout the question over the splintering noise of gunfire.

"She's some kind of distant cousin. I met her when she came to Faulconer Court House for a family funeral." Davies cursed, not because of the memory of his lost love, but because the cone of his rifle had become brittle from the heat and shattered. He threw the gun down and took another from a dead man. Somewhere in the battle smoke a young man screamed horribly. The scream went on and on, punctuated by short gasps of breath. Davies shuddered at the awful sound. "Oh, my God," he said callously when the screaming ended suddenly, "just lay me down."

"I wish people would stop saying that," Starbuck said, "it's getting on my nerves."

"You'd prefer biblical quotes?" Davies asked. "Lambs to the slaughter," he offered, misquoting Isaiah.

"'The sword of the Lord is filled with blood.'" Starbuck offered another quotation from the same prophet as he fired two rounds of the revolver. "'It is made fat with fatness and with the blood of lambs.'"

Davies shuddered at the sentiment. "I keep forgetting you were a theology student."

"There's nothing like a course of Old Testament studies to make a soldier ready for battle," Starbuck said with relish. He lowered his revolver and listened to the sound of the fighting. The Yankee fire was definitely slackening. "They won't last long now," he said. His mouth was so dry that talking was difficult. He had replaced his shattered canteen with another but had long drained its tepid contents. Now he stooped and unlooped a dead man's canteen.

"Her name was Louisa," Davies said.

"Who?" Starbuck said. He tipped the canteen to his mouth and was rewarded by a trickle of lukewarm water. "Who?" he asked again.

"My distant Catholic relative from Indiana," Davies said as he primed his new rifle, "and two years ago she married a corn chandler."

"With any luck you're about to kill the bastard," Starbuck said, "and that'll make the lovely Louisa into a respectable young widow and you can marry her when the war's over." He emptied the rest of his revolver's chambers into the smoke. "Keep firing!" he shouted at the company, then slapped Davies on the shoulder as he left the company to walk back along the Legion's rear. "Bastards are giving way,

414

boys! Keep firing! Keep firing!" He reloaded his revolver as he walked, doing the job without needing to look down at the weapon. Starbuck remembered his first day of battle, not a mile or two from this very spot, when he had been unable to load his revolver because his hands had been trembling and his vision blurred, while now he did it without thinking or looking.

The Legion kept firing but were taking very little return fire except for an occasional shell lobbed by the small howitzers at the edge of the trees, and those shells were mostly fused too long and so exploded harmlessly among the shattered saplings behind the battle line. The Yankee line, splintered into groups by the steady rebel firing, was stumbling back across their own dead toward the railbed. There was a danger they might go to ground there, and Starbuck reckoned his dazed and bloodied men would have to charge with fixed bayonets to keep the Northern retreat moving, but just a second before he shouted the order, so a great backwash of attackers surged from the west.

The Northerners who had passed clean through the rebel line into the open land beyond were now streaming back. They had been harried by Haxall's Arkansas battalion, then intercepted by a brigade sent by Lee to reinforce Jackson's hard-pressed men, and now the Northerners were in full retreat. "Let 'em through?" Hudson shouted at Starbuck. The choice was either to open ranks and let the Northerners go back beyond the railbed or else to turn and fight, but Hudson's implied choice was to give the enemy a free pass home. There were simply too many Yankees for the battle-weary rebel line to take on, especially as there were still plenty of Northerners firing from the railbed. A decision to fight would have meant firing both east and west, so Starbuck gratefully shouted his assent to Hudson and then pulled the Legion's right wing clear of the retreating Yankees. The fleeing enemy surged past the spoil pit.

Starbuck watched the disorganized enemy run past; then another flicker of movement closer to the hill made him look right to see a small group of gray-clad men running parallel with the enemy but keeping well away from danger. Major Medlicott and Captain Moxey were in the lead of a score of men who now tried to rejoin the Legion's ranks without their arrival being noted. Starbuck ran toward the fugitives. "Where were you?" he asked Medlicott.

"What do you mean?" Medlicott demanded. He turned away from Starbuck and aimed his rifle at the Yankees running past fifty paces away.

Starbuck slapped the rifle down. "Where were you?"

"The Yankees pushed us back," Medlicott said, his tone daring Starbuck to contradict him. "We tried to rejoin."

Starbuck knew the man was lying. He could see from the state of Medlicott's soldiers that none of them had been fighting. Their eyes were not reddened by smoke, their lips were not blackened by powder, and their faces did not have the feral, half-scared, half-savage look of men pushed to the edge of endurance. All still wore the red crescent badge denoting their loyalty to Washington Faulconer, and all of them, Starbuck was sure, had skulked for the best part of the day. Yet he could prove nothing, and so he settled for a feeble acceptance of Medlicott's lie. "Keep fighting," he said. He knew he had handled the confrontation badly, a suspicion confirmed when Moxey laughed aloud. The laughter was drowned by a sudden ear-hurting roar as a flight of shells crashed into the killing patch beyond the railbed. The rebel artillery, which had been preoccupied these last long minutes with Yankee attackers further south, had switched their fire back to the ground opposite Swynyard's brigade, and the effect of the shrieking, bursting, smoke-riven shells was to drive the enemy's howitzers away from the tree line and the retreating Yankees into the shelter of the railbed cutting.

"You've got to get them out of there, Starbuck!" Swynyard immediately shouted from the hillside.

The Yankees had suddenly learned the value of the railbed and were using its protection to start a galling rifle fire on the Legion. The men returned the fire, but the rebels were getting by far the worst of it. Starbuck, still standing beside the recalcitrant right-hand companies, cupped his hands. "Fix bayonets!" He watched as his men crouched behind the thin cover of the fire-blasted saplings and slotted long blades onto the black, hot muzzles of their rifles. He turned and saw Moxey's resentful men doing the same. Moxey was wearing one of the frilled shirts he had looted at Manassas Junction, and somehow the finery made Starbuck hate the man even more. He pushed that hatred out of his mind as he capped the five chambers of his new Adams revolver. "Ready?" he called to Medlicott's men. One or two nodded, but most ignored him. He looked to his left and saw the strained, anxious faces of the other companies. "Charge!" he shouted. "Charge!"

The Legion rose from its crouch like men snapping from nightmare. The Yankees in the railbed responded with a volley that billowed smoke along the lip of their makeshift parapet. A shell cracked overhead to make an instant black cloud. Men were falling, bleeding, calling in pain, but most of the Legion were still running through the blackened scrub and reeking smoke. They screamed their war scream. The smoke of the Yankee volley cleared, and the Northerners, armed now with unloaded rifles, saw a glitter of bayonets fast approaching, and so they scrambled hurriedly out the railbed's far side.

Just as a salvo of rebel-fired shells crashed into the dirt and exploded shrapnel into their faces. Most of the Northerners instinctively shied away from that high-explosive death just as the rebel line leaped into the trench.

"Kill them!" Truslow shouted and rammed forward with a bayonet that he abandoned in his first victim so that he could unsheath his bowie knife. Most of the Yankees decided that fleeing through the shells offered a better chance of survival than being disemboweled in a blood-sodden trench, and so a horde of Northerners scrambled out of the railbed and ran across the open ground. Others stayed and surrendered. A handful tried to fight the rebel counter-attack and were killed. Starbuck saw Peter Waggoner leading a squad of men against a stubborn group of Northerners; there was a volley, a scream, then Waggoner swung his rifle by the muzzle to smash its stock against a man's head, and the other Northerners began to shout their surrender. Out in the open ground another salvo of shells ripped smoke, flame, and metal shards through the fugitives. Starbuck, a smoking revolver in his hand, saw a man's head bowling along the ground like a spent cannonball. He gaped at it, not sure that his eyes were really seeing what his brain was registering.

"No, no, no, no, please!" A Northerner was staring up at Starbuck with horror on his face. The man's hands were raised. He was shaking in terror, thinking that he was about to be executed by the tall Southern officer with the bitter eyes and smoking gun.

"You're safe," Starbuck told the man, then turned to see that neither Medlicott's men nor Moxey's company had charged with the Legion. Instead they were in the spoil pit, where they were attempting to look busy by rounding up prisoners. There was unfinished business there, and business that had to be settled soon or else there would be no Legion left to command. "Major Medlicott?" he shouted across to the spoil pit.

"Yes?" Medlicott's tone was cautious.

"I want the Legion's ammunition pooled, then redistributed. And search the dead for cartridges." He looked up at the sky. It would be dark soon. "Your men have first picket duty. And keep a careful watch."

"They always do," Medlicott said defiantly. He had been half expecting a reprimand for disobeying the order to charge the railbed, and his tone suggested the scorn in which he now held Starbuck for not daring to impose discipline.

Starbuck ignored him. He had other things to do. He had the dead to count, the wounded to rescue, and ammunition to find. So he could be ready to fight again. Tomorrow.

"A good day's work, gentlemen, an excellent day's work." John Pope was ebullient about his army's achievement as he strode into the farm that was his field headquarters. A dozen men awaited his arrival, and so infectious was the General's pleasure that they actually burst into applause as he came through the door. Most of those who had been waiting for Pope were general officers, but there was also a congressman from Washington and the Reverend Elial Starbuck from Boston carrying, inevitably, the bundled rebel flag that was his precious trophy and souvenir. The Reverend Starbuck had spent the day on the field and was as dusty, dirty, and tired as any of the soldiers, though Pope himself looked very fresh as he lifted the lid of one of the supper tureens on the long dining table. He sniffed its contents appreciatively. "Venison steak? Good! Good! I hope there's some cranberry jelly to go with it?"

"Alas, sir," one of the aides murmured.

"Never mind." Pope was in a forgiving mood. The railroad bridge at Bristoe had been repaired, so that trains could now run the length of the Orange and Alexandria, which meant that the last regiments being carried north from

419

Warrenton could be transported all the way into the smoking ruins of Manassas Junction, from where it was a short step to tomorrow's battlefield. Or rather to tomorrow's victory, for John Pope was now convinced that he was on the brink of a historic triumph.

General McDowell, who had lost the first battle fought at Manassas but who now led Pope's Third Corps, was similarly confident of victory, especially as more troops were arriving hourly. Those reinforcements were coming not just from Pope's own Army of Virginia but also from McClellan's Army of the Potomac. "Though I doubt we'll see the young Napoleon here tomorrow," McDowell said heavily.

"I doubt it, too," Pope said, sitting at the table and helping himself to a piece of venison. "George won't want to witness another man winning a victory. That would take far too much shine off his buttons, eh?" He laughed, inviting the table to laugh with him. "Whereas I don't mind who gets the credit so long as the U.S.A. gets the victory, ain't that a fact?" Pope threw this outrageous statement at one of his aides, who blandly confirmed its truth. "You know what George wants me to do?" Pope went on as he helped himself to buttered beans. "George wants me to pull the army back to Centreville and wait there! Here we are with Stonewall Jackson skewered to the wall, and I'm supposed to walk away to Centreville! And why? So the young Napoleon can take command!"

"He doesn't want you to win the victory he couldn't win," McDowell suggested loyally.

"And I've no doubt that if I did pull back to Centreville," Pope went on without actually disagreeing with McDowell's statement, "then the very first thing our young Napoleon would do is hold a parade. I hear George is uncommon fond of parades."

"Very fond," the visiting congressman said, "and why not? Parades are very good for the public's confidence."

"A victory might be better for their confidence," McDowell suggested. The Third Corps's commander had piled his plate with venison steaks and sweet potatoes.

"Well, damn George's parades," Pope said, wondering like everyone else about the table whether McDowell could possibly add another spoonful of supper to his heaped plate. "I shall not retreat to Centreville. I shall win a victory instead. That'll astonish Washington, isn't that so, Congressman? You're not used to generals who fight and win!" Pope laughed, and his laughter was echoed about the supper table, though the General noticed that the famous Boston preacher alone seemed unamused. "You look tired, Doctor Starbuck," the General observed genially.

"A day in the saddle, General," the preacher said. "I'm most unaccustomed to such exertions."

"No doubt I'd be weary if I spent a day in your pulpit," Pope responded gallantly, but the preacher did not even smile at the response. Instead he put a notebook on the table, pulled a candle close to its open pages, and expressed a polite puzzlement at some of the events he had witnessed that day. "Such as what?" John Pope asked.

"Men attacking, other men doing nothing to help them," the preacher said succinctly. It seemed to the Reverend Starbuck that the Federal attacks had come so close to success, yet the survivors complained that the reinforcements who might have guaranteed Northern victory had never stirred from their bivouacs.

John Pope felt an impulse of anger. He had no need to explain himself to meddlesome priests, yet Pope knew that he possessed few allies in the army's highest reaches, and fewer still in Washington. John Pope was an abolitionist, while most of his rivals, like McClellan, were fighting not for the slaves but for the Union, and John Pope knew that he needed public opinion to be on his side if he was to prevail against his many political enemies. The Reverend Starbuck was a powerful persuader of the Northern public, and so the General subdued his irritation and patiently explained his day's achievements. He spoke between mouthfuls, gesturing with a fork. What the Army of Virginia had done, he said, was to pen Stonewall Jackson up against the western hills and woods. Pope glanced at the congressman to make sure that he was listening, then went on to explain how Jackson had wanted to escape down the Warrenton Turnpike but had instead been corralled.

The preacher nodded impatiently. He understood all this. "But why do we need wait till tomorrow to kill the snake? We had him trapped today, surely?"

Pope, mindful of what the pencil in the preacher's hand could achieve, smiled. "We've pinned Jackson into some rough country, Doctor, but we haven't quite cut off all his escape routes. What you were witnessing today was a gallant fight to keep Jackson staring in this direction while our other fellows curled around his flanks." The General demonstrated the strategy by surrounding a gravy boat with cruets. "And tomorrow, Doctor, we can attack again with the absolute assurance that this time the wretches have no escape." He dropped a salt cellar into the gravy, splashing the tablecloth. "No escape at all!"

"Amen!" McDowell said through a mouthful of venison and butter beans.

"You only saw a small part of a greater design," Pope explained to the preacher. "Does not the good book have something to say about there being more things in heaven and earth than we can dream of?"

"Shakespeare said it," the preacher remarked stiffly, still penciling his notes. "'There are more things in heaven and

earth, Horatio, than are dreamt of in your philosophy.'
Hamlet, Act One, Scene Five." He closed the book and
slipped it into his pocket. "So tomorrow, General, we might
expect a victory to rank with Cannae? Or with Yorktown?"

Pope hesitated to claim ground quite that high, especially
in front of a congressman, yet he had raised the expectation
himself. "So long as McClellan's men fight as they should,"
he answered, neatly shifting the responsibility onto his rival.
No one responded. Indeed, no one liked to stir that can of
worms. McClellan's men were famously loyal to their general, and many of them resented being under the orders of
John Pope, and there was a fear that resentment might be
translated into a reluctance to fight.

"I wonder what Lee's doing?" an artillery officer at the
table's far end asked.

"Robert Lee is doing what Robert Lee always does best,"
Pope declared, "which is sitting on his hands and letting
someone else do the scrapping. Lee's waiting south of the
Rappahannock, digging in. He sent Jackson to disrupt our
preparations, but he reckoned without the swiftness of our
response. He underestimated us, gentlemen, and that will be
his undoing. Is that a plate of pears? Might I trouble you for
a serving? Thank you." An orderly brought a jug of lemonade for the teetotalers and a decanter of wine for the others.
Beyond the farm windows there was a pretty sprinkling of
firelight where the nearest battalions were bivouacking on a
hillside. A band was playing in the distance, the music sweet
and plangent in the warm summer darkness.

"Did anyone discover what those rebel troops were doing
beyond Groveton?" one of McDowell's officers asked as he
spooned thick cream onto his pears. There had been a handful of reports about rebel troops arriving on the open western
flank of Pope's army.

"Alarmist rumors," Pope said confidently. "All they saw

were enemy cavalry scouts. The last throes of a dying army, gentlemen, are always the sight of its cavalry scouts looking for a way out. But not tomorrow, not anymore. From now on this army marches forward. To Richmond!"

"To Richmond," the assembled officers murmured, "and to victory."

"To Richmond," the congressman said, "and reelection."

"To Richmond," the Reverend Starbuck said, "and emancipation."

All in the morning.

During the night Hudson's North Carolinians made a new abatis in front of the railbed, where neither the cutting nor its adjacent embankment offered a real obstacle to the Yankee attackers. "I should have thought of it before," Hudson admitted.

"So should I," Starbuck said. He paused. "Except I thought Lee was coming. I never reckoned we'd have to fight alone all day."

"I told you," Hudson said in a kindly voice, "always to expect the worst."

"But where is Lee?" Starbuck insisted on the question despite the older man's advice.

"The Lord only knows," Hudson said softly, "and I guess we'll just have to go on fighting till the good Lord lets us into the secret."

"I guess so, too," Starbuck said bleakly. He was morose, aware that his first day in command of a fighting regiment had not been a success. The Legion had twice been driven from its position, and though it had twice regained the railbed, it had suffered cruelly in the process. Worse, two whole companies of the regiment were in virtual mutiny. Starbuck remembered Moxey's laughter, and he knew as certainly as he knew anything in all his life that the mocking laughter had been his opportunity to crush the defiant right-hand companies once and for all. Starbuck knew he should have pulled out his revolver and put a bullet smack between Moxey's eyes, but instead he had pretended not to hear, and so had given his enemies a victory.

The construction of the new abatis was harassed by Yankee sharpshooters, whose fire did not end at nightfall. In the dark the sharpshooters fired wherever they saw movement beside a distant fire, and that constant danger drove men to take cover in the railbed or else to seek the safety of the hill's rearward slope, where the Brigade's surgeons worked by candlelight. The Brigade's own sharpshooters replied to the Yankee fire, the flames of their heavy-barreled rifles spitting long and whip-thin in the darkness. The marksmen held their fire only when a shout requested that they respect the movements of a stretcher party, but whenever the stretcher bearers had finished their task and had called their thanks for the enemy's courtesy, the firing would begin again.

The only good news of the night was the arrival of a mailbag that had been brought from Gordonsville with Lee's advancing troops. Sergeant Tyndale distributed the letters and parcels, making a sad pile of mail addressed to dead men. One of the parcels had come from the Richmond Arsenal and was addressed to the officer commanding the Faulconer Legion. The big package proved to contain a standard-issue battle flag: a four-foot-square banner woven from common cloth that was intended to replace the captured silk standard. There was no flagstaff, so Starbuck sent Lucifer to cut down a straight, ten-foot sapling.

Then, in the light of a campfire at the rear of the hill, he opened his two letters. The first came from Thaddeus Bird, who reported that he was recovering remarkably well and hoped to return to the Legion very soon. "Priscilla does not share this hope and constantly discovers new symptoms that might require a further period of convalescence, yet I feel my absence from the Legion keenly." The letter went on to say that Anthony Murphy had safely reached Faulconer Court House and was also recuperating, though he was not expected to be on his feet for a week or two yet. "Is it true," Bird then asked, "that Swynyard has seen the divine light? If so then it proves Christianity must be of some use in this world, but I confess I find it hard to comprehend such a conversion. Does the dragon purr? Does he pray before he beats his slaves, or after? You must write to me with all the malicious details." The letter finished with the news that Washington Faulconer had not been seen in Faulconer Court House but was rumored to be stirring up political trouble in Richmond.

Starbuck's second letter had come from the Confederate capital. To his surprise and pleasure the letter was from Julia Gordon, Adam's erstwhile fiancée, who now regarded Starbuck as her friend. She wrote with good news. "My mother has yielded to my wish and allowed me to become a nurse in Chimborazo Hospital. She did not yield graciously, but under the pressure of poverty and to the hospital's solemn undertaking to pay me a wage, though I have yet to see that promise fulfilled. I am being tutored, they say, and so must abjure all hopes of payment until I can distinguish a bandage from a bottle of calomel. I learn, I learn, and at night I weep for the poor boys here, but doubtless I shall learn not to do so." She made no mention of Adam, nor was there anything personal in the letter; it was simply the words of a friend seeking a sympathetic ear. "You would not recognize the hospital now," Julia concluded. "It daily spreads fresh buildings across the park, and each new ward is filled with wounded before the builders' sawhorses are even moved out. I pray daily that you will be spared seeing it from one of the cots."

Starbuck stared at the letter and tried to recall Julia's face, but somehow the picture would not form in his head. Dark hair and good bones, he remembered, and a quick intelligence in the eyes, but still he could not see her image in his mind's eye. "You're looking homesick," Colonel Swynyard interrupted Starbuck's thoughts.

"Letter from a friend," Starbuck explained.

"A girl?" Swynyard asked as he sat opposite Starbuck.

"Yes," Starbuck said, then, after a pause, "a Christian girl, Colonel. A good, virtuous, and Christian girl."

Swynyard laughed. "How you do yearn for respectable citizenship in the Kingdom of God, Starbuck. Maybe you should repent now? Maybe this is the hour for you to put your trust in Him?"

"You're trying to convert me, Colonel." Starbuck made the accusation sourly.

"What greater favor could I do you?"

Starbuck stared into the fire. "Maybe," he said slowly, "you could replace me as commander of the Legion?"

Swynyard chuckled. "Suppose, Starbuck, that after one day of abandoning alcohol I had told you I was finding the whole thing too hard. Would you have approved?"

Starbuck managed a rueful grin. "Back then, Colonel, I'd have told you to wait a day, then go back to the bottle. That way I might have won the bet I had on you."

Swynyard was not altogether pleased with the reply, but he managed a smile. "So I'll give you the same advice. Wait a day, see how you feel tomorrow."

Starbuck shrugged. "I didn't do well today. I panicked. I was shouting and running around like a scalded cat."

Swynyard smiled. "None of us did well today. I'm not real sure Jackson did well today, and the good Lord alone knows

427

what happened to Lee, but the enemy didn't do well either. We're still here, Starbuck, and they ain't beat us yet. See how you feel tomorrow." The Colonel stood up. Sparks whirled past his lean face. "Maybe you should turn your companies around tomorrow?" he suggested. "Put Truslow on the right and Medlicott on the left?"

"I did think about doing just that," Starbuck admitted.

"And?"

Starbuck plucked a burning brand from the fire and used it to light a cigar. "I think I've got a better idea, Colonel." He tossed the brand back onto the flames and looked up at Swynyard. "You remember what you said about Old Mad Jack? That it didn't matter how eccentric a man was, so long as he won?"

"I remember. So?"

Starbuck grinned. "So you won't approve of what I'm going to do. Which means I won't tell you what it is, but it'll work."

Swynyard thought about that answer. "So you didn't really want to be replaced?"

"I'll let you know tomorrow, Colonel."

Starbuck spent the night in the railbed, where he slept for a few precious moments, but it seemed he was woken every time a sharpshooter let a bullet fly across the ground separating the armies. In the morning, before the mist lifted to make him into an easy target, he climbed the hill to watch the land emerge from the vapor. In the distance, beyond the trees, a swarm of smoke tendrils marked the enemy's cooking fires, while off to the left, and much closer than he had expected, a bright gleam between two stands of trees briefly showed beneath the shifting skeins of mist. He borrowed a rifle from one of Haxall's sharpshooters and used its telescopic sight to inspect the gleam. "I guess that's the Bull Run," he said to the sharpshooter.

The man shrugged. "Can't think there's another river that big 'round here. Sure ain't the Big Muddy though."

Nearer at hand Starbuck could see a stretch of road running between two pastures. He suspected it was the Sudley road, which meant the Legion was less than half a mile from the twin fords across the Catharpin and Bull runs. He had crossed those fords a year before on the day that Washington Faulconer had tried to eject him from the Legion, and if that far gleam was indeed the run and the road really was the highway leading from Manassas to Sudley, then it meant that the Legion was close, tantalizingly close, to the Galloway farm.

With nothing but an army between the Legion and its vengeance.

Starbuck handed the sharpshooter's rifle back, then went downhill to where the surgeons still worked on the previous day's wounded. He talked with the Legion's casualties, and then, with a dead man's rifle on his shoulder and a handful of salvaged cartridges in his haversack, he ran back to the railbed. A sharpshooter tried to kill him as he crossed the scrubland, but the Yankee's bullet whipped a foot wide to thump into a bloated corpse and startle a swarm of flies into the warm morning air. Then Starbuck leaped the parapet and slid down into the railbed's cutting to begin his new day's work.

THE FIRST ATTACK OF the Saturday morning was an advance by two companies of Northern infantry who emerged from the trees in skirmish order. They walked gingerly and with bayonets fixed, almost as if they suspected that their orders to advance on the railbed were a mistake. "Oh, my God." Captain Davies began the idiotic refrain that had the mysterious power to convulse Jackson's army.

"Don't," Starbuck growled, but he could have saved his breath.

"Just lay me down." A half-dozen of Davies's men finished the sentence and immediately began laughing.

"Imbeciles," Starbuck said, though no one could tell whether he referred to the Legionnaires or to the handful of Yankees who were crossing the open ground where hundreds had died the day before.

"Some idiot got his orders confused," Davies commented with an indecent relish. "Lambs to the slaughter, march!" He eased his rifle over the parapet.

"Hold your fire!" Starbuck called. He was waiting for the enemy's main body to appear at the edge of the trees, but it seemed the handful of Northern skirmishers was expected to capture the railbed on their own. Such suicidal behavior suggested Davies was right and that some poor Northern officer had misunderstood his orders, or perhaps the enemy believed the rebels had abandoned the railbed during the night. Starbuck disabused them of the notion. He used just two of his companies. He wanted the other companies to conserve their ammunition, but the fire of F and G Companies was sufficient to send the Northern soldiers scuttling ignominiously back to the tree line. Two skirmishers were left on the ground and another half-dozen limped as they fled. One of the wounded men repeatedly flapped an arm as though gesturing at the rebels not to fire again. None did.

"I suspect our Northern neighbors were feeling us out, Starbuck. Taking our pulse to see if any life remains in us. Good morning to you!" The speaker was the exuberant Colonel Elijah Hudson, who was ambling down the railbed as though he were merely taking a morning stroll. "I trust you slept well?"

"Half well," Starbuck said. "It was a noisy night."

"So it was, so it was. I confess I abandoned my efforts to sleep and retired into the woods to read Homer by lantern light. I was struck by the line about arrows rattling in their quivers as the archers advanced to battle. You remember it? He must have heard the noise to have described it. Those were the days, Starbuck. None of this loitering in a trench, but up with the sun, a quick sacrifice to all-seeing Zeus, and then a chariot ride to glory. Or to death, I suppose. You breakfasted?"

"Cold chicken and hot coffee," Starbuck said. Lucifer was proving adept at feeding Starbuck, though admittedly the boy still had the supplies taken from the Manassas depot as his larder. Lucifer's real test would come when all he had was weevil-ridden hardtack, rancid bacon grease, and rotting salt beef. If the boy even stayed long enough to face such a culinary test. So far the fugitive slave seemed amused at being a part of the Confederate army, but doubtless he would run whenever the whim took him.

"My son came to see me last night," Hudson now told Starbuck, who had to think for a second before remembering that Hudson's eldest son was an aide of Robert Lee. "Tom told me that Lee arrived yesterday," the Colonel went on, "but Pete Longstreet declined the order to attack. Our Mr. Longstreet is a meticulous fellow. He likes to make certain he has a sufficiency of mud and water before he makes his pies. Let us hope the Yankees stay long enough to be attacked. Or maybe I shouldn't hope that. My boys are wicked low on cartridges."

"Mine too," Starbuck said.

"Well, if all else fails," Hudson said, "we shall just have to throw rocks at them!" He smiled to show he was jesting, then prodded his stick into the cutting's bank like a farmer testing the dirt at planting season. "Did your fellows suffer badly yesterday?" He asked the question in a deceptively casual tone.

"Badly enough. Twenty-three killed and fifty-six with the doctors."

"Much the same, much the same," Hudson said, shaking his head at the news. "A bad business, Starbuck, a bad business. But can't be helped. What fools we mortals be. I have some coffee on the boil if you want to make a neighborly call." Hudson gave a wave with his stick and strode back to his own regiment.

Lieutenant Coffman had resumed his role as Starbuck's aide. He had been slightly wounded the day before by a bullet that had cut a ragged, dirty groove in the flesh of his upper left arm. Truslow had cleaned and dressed the wound, and Coffman kept touching the makeshift bandage as if to make certain that the badge of his courage was still in place. He bore no other badges; indeed, it was now impossible to tell that the ragged Coffman was an officer, for he carried a rifle, had a haversack and cap box on his belt, and had the half-starved, half-fearful, dirty face of a common soldier. "What happens now, sir?" he asked Starbuck.

432

"That's up to the Yankees, Coffman," Starbuck said. He was watching Sergeant Peter Waggoner lead a small prayer group and remembering how another group of men had willingly followed the big Sergeant into the railbed's cutting, where Waggoner had swung his rifle like a club to break apart a knot of Yankee resistance. It was not so much the Sergeant's bravery that now impressed Starbuck as the fact that men had so willingly followed Waggoner into the fight. "Captain Pine!" Starbuck shouted at Company D's commanding officer.

"Six cartridges apiece," Pine said, leaping to the conclusion that Starbuck needed to know the bad news of how many rounds his men had left.

"Who's your best sergeant after Waggoner?" Starbuck asked instead.

Pine thought about it for a second. "Tom Darke."

"You might have to lose Waggoner, that's why."

Pine flinched at that news, then shrugged. "To replace poor Patterson?"

"Maybe," Starbuck said vaguely. "But don't say anything to Waggoner yet." He walked back to the south, passing the remnants of Patterson's Company C, now under the command of Sergeant Malachi Williams, who offered a curt nod as Starbuck passed. None of Company C had joined Medlicott's retreat the day before, nor indeed had every man in A and B Company. The rot, Starbuck decided, was confined to a stubborn handful who doubtless assumed that Washington Faulconer still wielded more power in the Legion than Nathaniel Starbuck.

Starbuck resisted the temptation to crouch as the trench became shallower. "Keep your head down," he told Coffman.

"You're not keeping yours down," the Lieutenant replied.

"I'm a Yankee. I lack your valuable blood," Starbuck said

433

just as a sharpshooter in the Northern-held woods tried for him. The bullet struck a branch in the new abatis and ricocheted up into the air while the sound of the gun echoed back from the hillside. Starbuck gave a derisive wave to his unseen assailant, then jumped down into the spoil pit, where Medlicott and Moxey were standing beside a small fire over which a coffeepot was suspended. A half-dozen of their men were lounging near the fire and looked up suspiciously as Starbuck and Coffman arrived. "Is that coffee fresh?" Starbuck asked cheerfully.

"There isn't much left," Moxey said guardedly.

Starbuck peered into the pot. "Plenty enough for Lieutenant Coffman and me," he said, then gave his tin mug to Coffman. "Pour away, Lieutenant." Starbuck turned to Medlicott. "I had a letter from Pecker. You'll doubtless be pleased that he expects to be back soon."

"Good," Medlicott said forcefully.

"And Murphy's well. Thank you, Lieutenant." Starbuck took the proffered mug and blew across the steaming coffee. "Is it sweetened?" he asked Medlicott.

Medlicott said nothing but just watched as Starbuck sipped the coffee. "We heard from General Faulconer," Moxey blurted out, unable to keep the news to himself.

"Did you now?" Starbuck asked. "And how is the General?"

For a moment neither man answered. Indeed Medlicott seemed annoyed that Moxey had even mentioned the letter, but now that its existence was known the Major decided to take responsibility for its contents. "He's offered Captain Moxey and I jobs," he said with as much dignity as he could muster.

"I am glad," Starbuck said feelingly. "What sort of jobs? In his stables, perhaps? Serving at table? Kitchen hands, maybe?" Somewhere a cannon barked flat and hard. The

434

noise of the shot rolled and faded across the countryside; then a train whistle sounded in the far-off depot. The whistle was a very homely sound, a reminder that a world existed where men did not wake to sharpshooters and bloated corpses. "The General needs a pair of boot-cleaners, maybe?" Starbuck asked. He sipped the coffee again. It was very good, but he made a disgusted face and poured the liquid onto the spoil pit's stones so that it splashed onto Medlicott's boots. "What sort of a job, Major?" Starbuck asked.

Medlicott was silent for a few seconds as he controlled his temper; then he managed a grim smile. "General Faulconer says there are vacancies in the Provost Guard at the Capitol."

Starbuck pretended to be impressed. "You'll be guarding the President and Congress! And all those Richmond politicians and their whores! Is it just the pair of you who are needed? Or can you take the rest of us with you, too?"

"We can take enough men, Starbuck," Medlicott said, "but only the right kind of men." He added the childish insult, and there was a murmur of agreement from the nearby soldiers, who had clearly been invited to share Medlicott's supposed good fortune.

"And that explains why you're avoiding all the fighting!" Starbuck said as though the idea had only just dawned on him. "Dear Lord above! And I thought you were simply being cowards! Now you tell me you're keeping yourselves safe for higher and better duties. Why didn't you tell me before?" Starbuck waited, but neither man answered. Starbuck spat at their feet. "Listen, you sons of bitches, I've served in the Richmond provosts, and General Winder runs that crew of spavined leprous bastards, not General Faulconer. General Faulconer has about as much influence in Richmond as I do. He's promising you an easy berth just to make you unhappy here, but I ain't going to let you play that game. You're here to fight, not dream, so this morning you sons of bitches are fighting with the rest of us. Is that clear?"

Moxey looked apprehensive, but Medlicott had more faith in Washington Faulconer than Moxey. "We'll do what we have to do," he said stubbornly.

"Good," Starbuck said, "because what you have to do is fight." He walked to the edge of the spoil pit and leaned with pretended nonchalance on its slope. He propped his rifle against the bank and started cleaning his fingernails with the bodkin he used for reaming out the cones of his revolver. "I forgot to shave this morning," he said to Coffman.

"You should grow a beard, sir," Coffman said nervously.

"I don't like beards," Starbuck said, "and I hate cowards." He was watching the men around Medlicott, seeing their hatred and wondering if any dared threaten him with violence. That was a risk he would have to take when the moment came, and until it came he would wait in the spoil pit that he turned into a temporary regimental headquarters. Bandmaster Little, who served as the battalion's chief clerk as well as its fussy maker of music, brought him a bagful of tedious paperwork, and Starbuck passed the time filling in the lists of dead, indenting for rations, and sending urgent pleas for ammunition.

No ammunition came, but nor did the Yankees. The sun rose to its height and still no attack came. Once in a while a rattle of gunfire would crackle across the country, but otherwise there was silence. Two armies were poised side by side, yet neither moved, and the peace of the day frustrated Starbuck. He needed a fight to bring his confrontation with Medlicott to fruition.

"Maybe the bastards have gone home," he told Lucifer

when the boy brought him a midday meal of bread, cheese, and apples.

"They're still over there. I can smell them," Lucifer said. The boy glanced at the brooding Medlicott, then looked back to the cheerful Starbuck. "You've been tugging on his chains," Lucifer said with amusement.

"It's none of your business, Lucy."

"Lucy!" The boy was offended.

Starbuck smiled. "I can't call you Lucifer, it isn't proper. So I shall call you Lucy."

The boy bridled, but before he could think of a response, there was a sudden shout from one of Colonel Hudson's pickets, and then a great rushing and trampling noise in the woods beyond the killing patch. Starbuck abandoned the bread and cheese, snatched up his rifle, and ran to the pit's forward edge, where a squad from Moxey's company was lying on their bellies with their rifles trained under the abatis. "See anything?" Starbuck asked.

"Nothing."

Yet the noise was getting louder. It was the noise, Starbuck reckoned, of hundreds if not thousands of boots trampling down the undergrowth. It was the noise of an infantry attack designed to break through Jackson's line once and for all. It was the noise that foretold battle, and all along the railbed men pushed rifles over the parapet and cocked hammers.

"Sumbitches don't give up," the man next to Starbuck said. He was one of those who had stayed and fought the day before.

"What's your name?" Starbuck asked him.

"Sam Norton."

"From Faulconer Court House?"

"Rosskill," Norton answered. Rosskill was the nearest railhead to the Legion's hometown.

437

"What did you do there?"

Norton grinned. "Last job I had in Rosskill was sweeping out the county jail."

Starbuck grinned back. "Unwillingly, I guess?"

"Never minded sweeping it out, Major, 'cos once you'd swept out the jail you had to sweep out the sheriff's house and Sheriff Simms had two daughters sweeter than honey on a comb. Hell, I know men who robbed stores and stood rock still just begging to be locked up for a chance at Emily and Sue."

Starbuck laughed, then went silent as the trampling of feet was translated into a sudden rush of men, hundreds of men who shouted their hoarse war cry and charged across the narrow strip of open land toward the embankment where Elijah Hudson's North Carolinians waited.

"Fire!" Hudson shouted, and the embankment was rimmed with smoke.

"Fire!" Starbuck shouted, and the Legion gave what flanking fire they could, but for most of the men the angle was too acute for their rifles to help the beleaguered Hudson.

The Yankee charge reached the embankment's foot and surged up its face. Hudson's men stood up. For a second Starbuck thought the Carolinians had merely stood to run away, but instead they advanced across the flat railbed and met the Yankee charge head-on. They swung rifles, slashed with bowie knives, and rammed forward with bayonets.

Starbuck stared into the woods directly opposite the Legion and saw no threat there. The noise of the hand-to-hand fighting to his right was terrible, an echo from the medieval days of men being butchered by steel and crushed by clubs. The bestiality of the sound was a temptation to leave well alone and stay in the railbed's cutting on the excuse that a second Yankee attack might come straight for the Legion's position, but Starbuck knew that assumption was merely an excuse for cowardice, and so he slung his rifle and jumped down to the spoil pit's floor. "Major Medlicott! We're going to help."

Major Medlicott did not move. The men with him stared sullenly at Starbuck.

"You heard me?" Starbuck asked.

"It ain't our fight, Starbuck." Medlicott summoned his courage to articulate his defiance of Starbuck. "Besides, if we leave here the Yankees could attack straight into the pit again and then where would we be?"

Starbuck did not answer. Instead he looked sideways at Coffman. "Go and send Sergeant Waggoner to me," he said softly so that only Coffman could hear, "then tell Truslow that he's got to hold the railbed with Companies G and H. He's to ignore my order to charge. Understand?"

"Yes, sir." Coffman ran off on his errand. Medlicott had not heard the orders Starbuck gave but sneered anyway. "Sending for Swynyard?"

Starbuck could feel his heart beating flabbily in his chest. "Major Medlicott," he said very slowly and distinctly, "I'm ordering you to fix bayonets and go to Colonel Hudson's assistance."

Medlicott's big red face seemed to twist in a spasm of loathing, but he managed to make his answer sound respectful. "It's my judgment we should guard our own position," he said just as formally as Starbuck.

"You're disobeying an order?" Starbuck asked.

"I'm staying here," the miller said stubbornly, and when Starbuck did not respond immediately, Medlicott grinned in anticipation of victory. "No one's to move!" he called to his men. "Our job's to stay here and—"

He stopped speaking because Starbuck had shot him.

Starbuck did not really believe he was doing it. He was aware that the act would either seal the Legion as his regiment or else condemn him to a court-martial or a lynching. He drew the heavy Adams revolver and straightened his right arm while his thumb clicked the hammer smoothly back; then his finger took the trigger's pressure so fast that the look of triumph on Medlicott's face had scarcely started to change when the bullet struck him just beneath his right eye. Blood and bone made a cloud of droplets about the Major's shattering skull as he was thrown backward. His hat went straight up in the air while his body flew back three yards, twitching as it flew, then flapping like a landed fish as it thumped heavily onto the dirt. There the body lay utterly still with its arms outstretched. "Oh, my God," Starbuck heard himself saying, "just lay me down." He began to laugh.

Medlicott's ashen-faced men watched him. None of them moved. Medlicott's dead fingers slowly curled.

Starbuck pushed the revolver into its holster. "Captain Moxey?" he said very calmly.

Moxey did not wait for the rest of the sentence. "Company!" he shouted. "Fix bayonets!"

Moxey's men ran south along the railbed to help Hudson's left-hand company. Medlicott's men still stared dumbly at the body of their officer, then up at Starbuck. This was the moment that Starbuck had half expected to turn mutinous, but none of the company made any move to avenge the dead miller. "Anyone else want to disobey my orders?" Starbuck asked them.

No one spoke. The men seemed dazed; then Peter Waggoner ran up, panting. "Sir?"

"You're a Lieutenant now, Waggoner," Starbuck said, "in charge of A Company. Take over, follow Captain Moxey, and get rid of those Yankees."

"Sir?" Waggoner was slow to understand.

"Do it!" Starbuck snapped. Then he unslung his rifle and

pushed his bayonet into place. He turned toward the rest of the regiment. "Legion! Fix bayonets!" He waited a few seconds. "Follow me!"

It was a risk, because if the Yankees were waiting to attack the Legion's positions, then Starbuck was giving them victory, but if he did not help the North Carolinians, then the Yankees would probably break through into the woods, and so he took three-quarters of the Legion down the railbed to help Hudson's men. Some of those men were out of ammunition and were hurling rocks at the Yankees, throwing so hard that the heavy stones drew blood when they struck on sweat-streaked faces.

"Follow me!" Starbuck shouted again. Moxey and Waggoner were helping Hudson's left-hand companies, but the biggest threat was in the center of the Colonel's line, and Starbuck now led his reinforcements down the back of the embankment to where that Yankee pressure was fiercest. Some of the Northerners had gained the flat summit of the embankment, where they were struggling to take Hudson's two standards, and it was there that Starbuck intervened. "Come on!" he screamed, and he heard his men begin the terrible, shrill rebel yell as they scrambled up the slope and into the fight. Starbuck pulled his rifle's trigger as he neared the mêlée, then rammed the bayonet hard into a blue jacket. He was screaming like a banshee, suddenly feeling the extraordinary release of Medlicott's death. My God, but he had cut the rot clean out of the Legion's soul!

There was a rebel on the ground trying to fight off a Northern sergeant who had his hands around the rebel's throat. Starbuck kicked the Northerner's head up, then sliced his bayonet back and upward so that the blade slit the man's throat open. The sergeant collapsed, gushing blood over his intended victim. Starbuck clambered over both men and rammed the bayonet forward again. Men were grunting and cursing, tripping on the dying and slipping in blood, but the Yankees were giving ground. They had been trying to fight up the embankment's slope, and the rebels had managed to keep most of them on that forward slope and at a consequent disadvantage until the Legion's arrival tipped the balance. The Northerners retreated.

They went down the embankment, but they were not beaten yet. The woods here grew close to the railbed, so close that the Yankees could retreat to the tree line and still fire over open sights at the rebel position, and once back among the trees they poured an immense fire at the embankment. The storm of bullets drove the rebel defenders back from the crest and down into cover. The bullets whistled and hissed overhead; they thumped into the bodies of the dead or else ricocheted off the embankment to tear through the leaves behind. Every few moments a group of Yankees would charge the apparently empty parapet only to be met by a sparse rebel volley, a shower of stones, and the sight of waiting bayonets.

"They don't yield easily, do they? My God, Starbuck, but I owe you thanks. Upon my soul, I do." Colonel Hudson, his long hair matted with blood and his eyes wild, tried to shake Starbuck's hand.

Starbuck, encumbered with a rifle, ramrod, and cartridge, fumbled the handshake. "You're wounded, Colonel?"

"Dear me, no." Hudson pushed the long, blood-thick hair out of his face. "Other fellow's blood. You killed him, remember? Cut his throat. Dear me. But upon my soul, Starbuck, I'm grateful. Grateful, truly."

"Are you sure you're not hurt, sir?" Starbuck asked, for Hudson seemed unsteady on his feet.

"Just shocked, Starbuck, just shocked, and I shall be just dandy in a moment or two." The Colonel looked up at the railbed, where a rock had just landed. It seemed the Yankees were throwing the stones back now. Starbuck finished loading his rifle, wriggled up the bank, and pushed the gun between two bodies. He sighted on a blue jacket, pulled the trigger, and slid back to reload. He had five cartridges left, while most of his men were now reduced to just one or two. Elijah Hudson was similarly short of ammunition. "One more attack, Starbuck," the North Carolinian said, "and I suspect we're done for."

The attack came almost as he spoke. It was a frantic, desperate charge of tired, bloodied men who burst out of the woods to throw themselves up the embankment. For two days these Northerners had tried to break the rebel line, and for two days they had been frustrated, but now they were on the very brink of success, and they summoned their last reserves of strength as they scrambled up the scorched bank with fixed bayonets.

"Fire!" Hudson shouted, and the rebels' last guns flamed as a barrage of rocks hurtled overhead. "Now charge, my dears! Charge home!" the Colonel called, and the tired men threw themselves forward to meet the Yankee assault. Starbuck thrust with the bayonet, twisted the blade, and thrust again. Coffman was beside him, firing a revolver; then he glimpsed Lucifer, of all people, firing his Colt. Then Starbuck's bayonet stuck in a man's belly, and he tried to kick it free, then tried to twist it free, but nothing would loosen the flesh's grip on the steel. He cursed the dying man, then felt a gush of warm blood on his hands as he unslotted the blade and pulled the rifle away from the trapped blade. He reversed the rifle and swung it overhand like a club. He was keening a mad noise, half exultation, half lamentation, expecting death at any second, but determined not to give an inch against the mass of men who pushed into the rebels' blades and rifle stocks.

Then, suddenly, without any apparent reason, the pressure eased.

Suddenly the great charge was gone, and the Northerners were running back into the trees and leaving behind a tide-line of bodies heaped on bodies, some of the bodies moving slow beneath their pall of blood, others lying still. And there was silence except for the panting of the wild-eyed rebels who stood on the embankment they had held against the charge.

"Back now!" Starbuck broke the silence. "Back!" There might still be sharpshooters in the woods, and so he pulled his men back down the embankment into cover.

"Don't leave me, don't leave me!" a wounded man cried aloud, and another wept because he had been blinded. The stretcher bearers went across the railbed. No one shot at them. Starbuck cleaned the blood from his rifle's stock with a handful of oak leaves. Coffman was beside him, eyes gleaming with a maniacal delight. Lucifer was reloading his revolver. "You're not supposed to kill Northerners," Starbuck told him.

"I kill who I want," the boy said resentfully.

"But thank you anyway," Starbuck said, but Lucifer's only response was a look of hurt dignity. Starbuck sighed. "Thank you, Lucifer," he said.

Lucifer immediately grinned. "So I ain't Lucy?"

"Thank you, Lucifer," Starbuck said again.

A triumphant Lucifer kissed the muzzle of his gun. "A man can be whatever a man wants to be. Maybe next year I'll decide to be a rebel killer."

Starbuck spat on the rifle's lock to help clean the blood clotted there. Somewhere in the woods behind him a bird burst into song.

"It's quiet, isn't it?" Hudson said from a few paces away.

Starbuck looked up. "Is it?"

"It's quiet," the Colonel said, "so beautifully quiet. I do believe the Yankees are gone."

The line had held.

The Reverend Doctor Starbuck beheld a nightmare.

He had spent a second day with Major Galloway's horsemen in the hope that he would have a chance to join in the pursuit of a broken rebel army. He was aware that the next day would be the Lord's Day, and he whiled away the waiting hours planning the sermon he would give to the victorious troops, but as the hours passed and there was still no sign of a rebel collapse, the prospect of the sermon receded. Then, in the afternoon, just after the firing in the woods had died suddenly away, a message came ordering Galloway's men to investigate some strange troops seen marching to the southwest.

The preacher rode with Galloway. They passed trampled cornfields and orchards looted of their fruit. They crossed the turnpike where the battle had started two days before, splashed through a stream, then rode up a bare hillside to where two gaudily uniformed regiments of New York *Zouaves* were resting on the grassy crest with their rifles stacked.

"All quiet here," the young, dapper commander of the nearer regiment, the 5th New York, proclaimed, "and we've got a picket line in the woods"—he gestured downhill to where thick woods grew—"and they're not being disturbed, so I guess it will stay quiet."

Major Galloway decided he would ride as far as the New York picket line, but the preacher elected to stay with the infantry, for a moment's small talk had elicited the astonishing information that the 5th New York's commanding officer was the son of an old colleague, and that old colleague, the Reverend Doctor Winslow, was actually the chaplain to

445

his own son's regiment. Now the Reverend Winslow galloped across to greet his Boston friend. "I never thought to find you here, Starbuck!"

"I trust I shall always be found where the Lord's work needs doing, Winslow," the Boston preacher said, then shook hands.

Winslow looked proudly at his son, who had ridden back to his place at the head of the regiment. "Just twenty-six, Starbuck, but in charge of the finest volunteer regiment in our army. Even the regulars can't hold a candle to the New York 5th. They fought like Trojans in the peninsula. And your own sons? They're well, I pray?"

"James is with McClellan," the Reverend Starbuck said. "The others are too young to fight." Then, wanting to change the subject before Winslow remembered the existence of Nathaniel, the Boston preacher asked about the 5th New York's flamboyant uniform, which consisted of bright red baggy pantaloons, short blue collarless jackets with scarlet trim, a red waist sash, and a crimson cap rimmed with a white turban and crowned with a long golden tassel.

"It's a copy of a French uniform," Winslow explained. "*Zouaves* are reputedly the fiercest fighters in the French army, and our patron wanted us to emulate their dress as well as their *élan*."

"Patron?"

"We're paid for by a New York furniture manufacturer. He paid for everything you see here, Starbuck; paid for it lock, stock, and barrel. You're seeing the profits of mahogany and turned legs at war."

The Reverend Starbuck eyed his old friend's uniform and wished that he was able to wear such finery. He was about to inquire what arrangements Winslow had made to fill his pulpit while he served with the army but was distracted by a burst of gunfire in the woods. "Our skirmishers, I guess,"

Winslow said when the sound had faded. "They were probably attacking a regiment of wild turkey. We ate a couple last night, and very good eating they were, too." The resting regiment had stirred at the sudden fusillade, and some men retrieved their rifles from the stacks, but most just cursed for being half woken up, pulled the turbans over their eyes again, and tried to go back to sleep.

"Your son said there's been no sign of the enemy here?" the Reverend Starbuck inquired, wondering why the hairs on the back of his neck were suddenly prickling.

"None at all!" the chaplain said, staring toward the woods. "I think you might say we've drawn the short straw. Our part in the great victory is to be spectators. Or maybe not."

His last three words were prompted by the appearance of a group of *Zouaves* at the tree line on the regiment's left flank. They were evidently skirmishers returning to their parent regiment, and they were agitated. "Rebels!" one of the men shouted. "Rebels!"

"They're panicking!" the chaplain said scornfully.

More of the *Zouaves* snatched up their rifles. A captain mounted on a nervous black horse cantered past the two pastors and touched his hat respectfully. "I think they're imagining things, chaplain!" the Captain called good-naturedly to Winslow, then put his hand to his throat and started making a mewing sound as he struggled to breathe. Blood began to seep through his fingers, and while the Reverend Starbuck tried to make sense of this strange apparition, he was suddenly overwhelmed by the sound of firing that had somehow taken a second or two to register on his stunned senses. Stunned because the hilltop was being swept by a typhoon of fire, a whistling whipping terror of bullets that crashed from the tree line where, appallingly, regiment after regiment of rebels now appeared. One moment there had been a summer's peace prevailing on the warm hilltop, where bees had sucked at clover blossoms, then there was death and screaming and blood, and the transition had been too abrupt for the preacher's mind to comprehend.

The dying captain was jerked back from the saddle to be dragged along the ground by a foot trapped in a stirrup. He cried pathetically; then a great rush of blood silenced him forever. The chaplain began shouting encouragement to the dazed *Zouaves*, who seemed to shrink back from the weltering rifle fire. The Reverend Starbuck's horse bolted from the unending splintering crack of rifles that outflanked the two New York regiments. The horse ran north, fleeing the attack, and it was not till he reached the edge of the hill that the preacher was able to curb the scared animal and turn it just in time to see a line of rebel regiments appear from the far trees. These were Lee's men, who had marched one day after Stonewall Jackson and who were now being unleashed from the valleys and woods where they had hidden overnight. They all made their devilish, ululating scream as they attacked, and the preacher's blood ran chill as the terrible sound washed across the hilltop.

The Reverend Starbuck dragged his revolver out of its saddle holster but made no effort to fire it. He was faced by a nightmare. He was watching the death of two regiments.

The New Yorkers tried to fight. They stood in line and returned the rebel fire, but the gray lines overlapped and decimated the *Zouave* ranks with an overwhelming volume of rifle fire. Brightly uniformed men were plucked back from the New York ranks, and though the sergeants and corporals tried to close the gaps, the gaps kept coming faster than they could be filled. Men slipped away, running north and east. The Reverend Starbuck shouted at the fugitives to hold their ground, but they ignored his ravings and ran downhill toward the stream. The furniture maker's regiment was reduced to three groups of men who tried to hold off the overpowering assault, but three times their number could not have stopped this rebel surge.

The New Yorkers died. There was a spatter of final shots, a scream of defiance, then the flags toppled as the last stubborn defenders were overrun. The hill was suddenly swarming with rebel rat gray coats, and the preacher, startled from his shocked immobility, kicked his horse and let it run downhill among the scattered fugitives. The first rebels were already firing after the running men, and the Reverend Starbuck heard the bullets whiplash about him, but the preacher's horse kept running. It splashed through the stream and so up into the safety of the trees on the far side. The scream of the obscene rebel yell soured the preacher's ears as he slowed the sweating horse. All around him now he could hear that terrible scream, the noise of the devil on the march, and he sensed, even if he did not understand, that another Northern army was being ignominiously beaten. Tears ran down his cheeks as he tried to understand the unfathomable ways of God.

He crossed the turnpike, going back to where he had spent so long waiting to begin the pursuit of the beaten rebels, but there was no sign of Galloway's men there, nor, thank God, any rebels either. The preacher cuffed the tears from his cheeks as he rested his horse. To his right, where the smoke from the burning depot still made a brown smear in the sky, there was only a tangle of woods and steep valleys, and it was through that broken ground, he suspected, that the rebel advance was being made. To his left, across the wider fields, lay the woods where one Northern attack after another had been launched toward the railbed, but none of those attacks had succeeded, which surely meant that the rebels still lurked among those woods, while behind him the devil's troops had just made carrion out of Winslow's *Zouaves* on a Virginia hilltop, which left the preacher just one place to go.

He rode northeast, his grief turning into a rage fit to fill all heaven. What dolts led the armies of the North! What strutting turkey-cock fools! The preacher felt a duty being laid upon him, the duty to awaken the North to the poltroons who were leading its sons into one defeat after another. He would go to Galloway's house, fetch his luggage, then have one of the Major's servants show him an escape route north across the Bull Run. It was time to return to the sanity of Boston, where he would begin his campaign that would wake a nation to its sins.

Cannons fired in the hills, their sound echoing confusedly around the sky. Rifles cracked, the gunsmoke showing in rills above trees and streams. Robert Lee had brought twenty-five thousand men and placed them at right angles to Jackson's beleaguered line, and not one Yankee had known the rebels were there until the starry banners came forward above the gray lines. Now the rebels' flank attack advanced like a door swinging shut on John Pope's glory. And the Reverend Elial Starbuck carried his righteous anger back toward home.

The sun sank slow toward the western hills. Nothing stirred in the woods to the east. The noise of battle rolled like distant thunder, but what the noise meant or where the Yankees were no one knew. A patrol from Truslow's Company H was the first to cross the shell-scorched strip of land into the trees, but they found no Yankees there. The sharpshooters had gone, and the woods were empty except for the litter of the abandoned Northern bivouacs.

Ammunition arrived and was handed out among the weary men. Some troops slept, indistinguishable in their exhaustion from the dead around them. Starbuck tried to compile a list of the dead and the wounded, but the work was slow.

An hour before sundown Colonel Swynyard rode his horse up to the railbed. He was leading another horse by the reins. "It belonged to Major Medlicott," he told Starbuck. "I hear he died?"

"Shot by a Yankee, I hear," Starbuck said straight-faced.

Swynyard's mouth flickered in what might have been a smile. "We're ordered to advance, and I thought you might appreciate a horse."

Starbuck's initial reaction was to refuse, for he took pride in marching like his men, but then he remembered the house with the lime-washed stone pillar at its lane gate and thanked Swynyard for bringing him the animal. He pulled himself into the saddle just as the Legion was stirred from its rest. The tired men grumbled at being disturbed but shouldered their rifles and climbed from the railbed. The wounded, the surgeons, the servants, and a sergeant's guard stayed behind while the rest of the Legion formed ranks around the color guard, where Lieutenant Coffman carried the replacement battle flag on its sapling staff. Starbuck took his place at the head of the regiment on Medlicott's horse. "Forward!" he called.

Hudson's North Carolinians advanced to the Legion's right. Colonel Hudson was mounted on an expensive black mare and was now accoutred with a sword in a gold-mounted scabbard. Hudson waved in friendly greeting as the two regiments advanced in line, but once among the trees Starbuck deliberately led the Legion to the left and so opened a gap between himself and the Carolinians.

He crossed the small pasture where they had checked their pursuit of the first Yankee attack the day before. There were still unburied dead in the field. Beyond the pasture was a strip of woods, then a wider stretch of open farmland that was bisected by a road climbing to a far crest. Starbuck rode to the left of his line. "Remember this place?" Starbuck asked Truslow.

"Should I?"

"We fought our first battle here." Starbuck pointed to his left. "The Yankees came out of those trees and we waited up there"—he pointed right to the ridge—"and I was scareder than hell and you behaved like it had all happened before."

"It had. I was in Mexico, remember?"

Starbuck let the horse walk at its own pace across the old battlefield. There were yellowing bone fragments in the furrows, and he wondered for how many years the farmers would plow up men's bones and the bullets that put them there.

"So what happened with Medlicott?" Truslow asked. The two men were thirty paces ahead of the ranks.

"What do your men say happened?"

"That you picked a fight with him, then shot the son of a bitch."

Starbuck thought about it, then nodded. "Just about. Do they mind?"

Truslow twisted a piece of tobacco from a plug and put it in his mouth. "Some of them feel sorry for Edna."

"His wife?"

"She has children to feed. But hell, no, they don't mind about the miller. He was a mean son of a bitch."

"He's a hero now," Starbuck said. "He's going to get his name on a statue in Faulconer Court House. Dan Medlicott, hero of our War of Independence." He crossed the road, remembering when he had watched a Northern army attack across these fields. They were not much changed; the snake fences were long gone, burned to boil the coffeepots of soldiers, and flecks of bone disfigured the dirt, but otherwise it was just as Starbuck remembered. He led the Legion on across the farmland, angling still more to his left until, rather than heading toward the eastern ridge with the rest of the Brigade, he was heading toward a stand of timber that topped a small ridge that lay to the north.

Swynyard galloped up to Starbuck. "Wrong way! Up there!" He pointed eastward up the road.

Starbuck reined in. "There's a place I want to visit, Colonel, just over the hill. Not more than a quarter-mile now."

Swynyard frowned. "What place?"

"The house of the man who took our flags, Colonel, and the house of the man whose troops burned women in a tavern."

Swynyard's initial reaction was to shake his head; then he had second thoughts and looked at Truslow's company before turning back to the two officers. "What can you achieve?"

"I don't know. But then we didn't know what we were going to achieve when we ran to Dead Mary's Ford in the middle of the night." Starbuck deliberately reminded Swynyard of that night and the implicit favor that the Colonel owed him as a result.

The Colonel smiled. "You've got one hour. We'll be going up the road," he said, pointing to the right, "and I guess it would only be prudent for someone to take a patrol north, just in case any of the rascals are lurking. Do you think one company will be enough?"

"Plenty, sir," Starbuck said and touched the brim of his hat to the Colonel. "Company!" he called to his old company. "Follow me!"

He borrowed a lit cigar from John Bailey and lit one of his own with its glowing tip. He walked the horse slowly, pacing the beast beside Truslow. The rest of the Legion climbed the

453

gentle eastern slope toward the sound of battle that now seemed very far away—so far that none of the advancing battalions seemed in any hurry to join that distant fighting. Starbuck looked to his left and saw the white-painted pillar on the road at the end of the stand of trees. "Not far now," he told Truslow. "Through these woods and in the next fields."

"What happens if the place is full of Yankees?" Truslow asked.

"Then we'll go back," Starbuck said, but when the company emerged from the trees on the ridge, they saw that the place was not full of Yankees. Instead the Galloway homestead seemed deserted as the rebel soldiers walked slowly down the long slope toward the farm buildings that were set among a grove of leafy, mature trees. It looked a handsome house, Starbuck thought, a place where a man could settle and live a good life. It seemed to have good watered land, well-drained fields, and plenty of timber.

A black man met them at the yard gate. "There's no one here, massa," the man said nervously.

"Whose house is it?" Starbuck asked.

The man did not answer.

"You heard the officer!" Truslow growled.

The black man glanced at the approaching company, then licked his lips. "Belongs to a gentleman called Galloway, massa, but he's not here."

"He's with the army, is he?" Starbuck asked.

"Yes, massa." The man smiled ingratiatingly. "He's with the army."

Starbuck returned the smile. "But which army?"

The black man's smile vanished instantly. He said nothing, and Starbuck kicked his heels to ride past him. "Any slaves in the house?" he called over his shoulder to the black man.

"Three of us, massa, and we're not slaves. We're servants."

"You live in the house?"

"In the cabins, massa." The servant was running after Starbuck, while Truslow brought the company on behind.

"So the house is empty?" Starbuck asked.

The man paused, then nodded as Starbuck looked back at him. "It's empty, massa."

"What's your name?"

"Joseph, massa."

"Then listen, Joseph, if you've got any belongings in the house, get them out now, because I'm about to burn this goddamned house to the ground, and if your master wants to know why, tell him it's with the compliments of the whores he burned alive at McComb's Tavern. You got that message, Joseph?" Starbuck curbed the horse and swung himself out of the saddle. He jumped down, spurting dust from beneath his boots. "Did you hear me, Joseph?"

The black servant gazed in horror at Starbuck. "You can't burn it, sir!"

"Tell your master that he killed women. Tell him my name is Starbuck, you hear that? Let me hear you say it."

"Starbuck, sir."

"And don't you forget it, Joseph. I am Starbuck, avenger of whores!" Starbuck declaimed that final sentence as he climbed the veranda steps and threw open the house's front door.

To see his father.

Clouds heaped in the south, darkening a day already declining toward dusk. In the steep hills and valleys where the rebel flank attack surged forward, the fading light made the rifle flames stab brighter and the smoke look grayer. There was a sense that the weather must break soon, and indeed, far to the south, on the empty earthworks that the Yankees had abandoned by the Rappahannock River, the first drops of rain splashed heavy. Lightning flickered in the clouds.

At Manassas the rebel flank attack grew ragged. It had been launched across broken country, and the advancing brigades soon lost touch with each other as they detoured about thorn-choked gullies or around thick groves of trees. Some regiments forged ahead while others met Yankee troops, who put up unexpectedly stubborn resistance. Cannons cracked from hilltops, canister fire shredded woodlands, and rifle fire stuttered along a crooked three-mile front.

Behind the Yankees was the Bull Run, a stream deep and wide enough to be a river in any country other than America, and a stream deep and wide enough to drown a man encumbered with a pack, haversack, cartridge box, and boots, and if the rebels could just break the Yankees and hurl them back in panic, then eighty thousand men might be struggling to cross that killing stream, which boasted only one small bridge. The beaten army could drown in its thousands.

Except the Yankees did not panic. They streamed back across the bridge, and some men did drown as they tried to swim the run, but other men stood shoulder-to-shoulder on the hill where once a man called Thomas Jackson had earned the name of Stonewall. They stood and met the oncoming rebel troops with a cannonade that lit the hill's forward slope red with the flash of its gun flames and made the valley beyond crackle with the echo of rifle volleys; volley after killing volley, a stinging flail of lead that ripped the gray ranks apart and held the land west of the bridge long enough to let the bulk of John Pope's army escape. Only then did the stoic blue ranks yield Stonewall Jackson's hill to Stonewall Jackson's countrymen. It was a Northern defeat, but the Northerners had not been routed. Lines of blue-uniformed men trudged away from a battlefield where they had been promised victory but had been led to defeat, and where the victorious rebels began to count the captured weapons and captured men.

And at Joseph Galloway's farm, on the southern bank of the Bull Run, the Reverend Starbuck stared at his son, and his son stared back.

"Father?" Starbuck broke the silence.

For a second, a heartbeat, Starbuck thought his father would relent. For that one second he thought his father was about to hold out his arms in welcome, and there was indeed a sudden expression of pain and longing on the older man's face, and for that one second all the plans Starbuck had ever made for defying his father should they ever meet again vanished into thin air as he felt a swamping wave of guilt and love sweep through him, but then the vulnerable expression vanished from the preacher's face. "What are you doing here?" the Reverend Starbuck demanded gruffly.

"I've business here."

"What business?" The Reverend Starbuck barred the hallway. He was carrying his ebony stick, which he held out like a sword to prevent his son from stepping further into the house. "And don't you dare smoke in my presence!" he snapped, then tried to swat the cigar out of his son's hand with his ebony cane.

Starbuck easily evaded the blow. "Father," he said, trying to appeal to old ties of stern affection, but he was brusquely interrupted.

"I am not your father!"

"Then what kind of a son of a bitch are you to tell me not to smoke?" Starbuck's temper flared high and fierce. He welcomed the anger, knowing it was probably his best weapon in this confrontation, for the instant that he had seen his father's stern face a lifetime of filial obedience had made him cringe inside. At that moment when the door had swung open, he had suddenly felt eight years old again and utterly helpless in the face of his father's unforgiving certainty.

"Don't you swear at me, Nathaniel," the preacher said.

"I'll goddamn swear where I damn well want. Now move!" Starbuck's anger burned bright. He pushed past his father. "You want to pick a quarrel with me," he shouted over his shoulder, "then make up your mind whether it's a family quarrel or a fight between strangers. And get yourself out of this house, I'm burning the damn place down." Starbuck shouted these last words from the library. The shelves were empty, though a handful of account books were piled on a table.

"You propose to do what?" The Reverend Starbuck had followed his son into the big room.

"You heard me." Starbuck began tearing the account books into scraps that would burn easily. He piled the scraps at the edge of the table, where their flames would work on the empty shelving above.

The Reverend Starbuck's face showed a glimmer of pain. "You have become a whoremonger, a thief, a traitor, and now you will burn a good man's house?"

"Because he burned a tavern"—Starbuck started tearing apart another book—"and killed women. They pleaded with his soldiers to stop firing, but they wouldn't. They went on shooting and they burned the women alive."

The Reverend Starbuck swept the pile of paper scraps off the table with his cane. "They didn't know there were women in the tavern."

"They knew," Starbuck said, starting to make another pile of torn paper.

"You're a liar!" The Reverend Starbuck raised his cane and would have slashed it down on his son's hands had not a shot been fired inside the room. The sound of it echoed terribly inside the four walls, while the bullet ripped a scar into the empty shelves opposite the door.

"He ain't lying, preacher. I was there." Truslow had appeared in the open garden door. "I carried one of the women out of the ruins myself. Burned to a crisp, she was. Kind of shriveled to the size of a newborn calf. There were five women burned like that." He spat tobacco juice, then tossed a tin to Starbuck. "Found these in the kitchen," he said. Starbuck saw they were lucifers.

"This is my father," Starbuck said in curt introduction.

Truslow nodded. "Preacher," he said in brief acknowledgment.

The Reverend Starbuck said nothing but just watched as his son made another pile of broken paper. "We kind of got upset," Starbuck went on, "on account of not fighting against women ourselves. So we decided to burn this son of a bitch's house down to teach him that fighting against women ain't worth the price."

"They were whores!" the Reverend Starbuck snapped.

"So they're making me a bed in hell right now," Starbuck snarled back, "and you think they won't be better company than you saints in heaven?" He struck one of the lucifers and held its flame to the heap of paper scraps.

The cane struck again, scattering the new heap of paper and instantly extinguishing the small flame. "You have broken your mother's heart," the preacher said, "and brought shame on my house. You lied to your brother, you have cheated, you have stolen!" The catalog of sins was so great that the Reverend Starbuck was momentarily overcome and he was forced to hold his breath and shake his head.

"The son of a bitch drinks whiskey, too." Truslow used the silence to add his contribution from the doorway.

459

"Yet!" The preacher shouted the word, the shout intended to govern his temper. "And yet," he said, blinking back tears, "your Lord and Savior will forgive you, Nate. All He asks is that you go to Him on bended knee with a confession of faith. All our sins can be forgiven! All!" Tears ran down the preacher's cheeks. "Please?" he said. "I cannot bear to think that in heaven we must look down on your eternal torment."

Starbuck felt another great tidal surge of emotion. He might have rejected his father's house and his father's stern religion, but he could not deny that it had been a good house and an honest religion, nor could he claim that he did not fear the flames of eternal damnation. He felt the tears pricking at his own eyes. He stopped tearing paper and tried to summon up the anger that would let him face his father again, but instead he seemed to tremble on the brink of total surrender.

"Think of your younger brothers. Think of your sisters. They love you!" The Reverend Starbuck had found his theme now and pressed it hard. He had so often sworn to disown this child, to cast Nathaniel out from the fellowship of Christ as well as from the Starbuck family, but now the preacher saw what a victory over the devil his son's repentance and return would make. He imagined Nathaniel making a confession of his sins in the church, he saw himself as the father of the prodigal son, and he anticipated the joy in heaven at the repentance of this one sinner. Yet there was more than a spiritual victory at stake. The preacher's anger had flared just like his son's, but the father was also discovering that a year of angry denial had been destroyed by a moment's proximity. This son, after all, was the one most like himself, which was why, he supposed, this was always the son with whom he had fought the hardest. Now he had to win this son back, not just for Christ, but for the Starbuck family. "Think of Martha!" he urged Starbuck, naming Starbuck's favorite sister. "Think of Frederick and how he's always admired you!"

The preacher might have won the battle had he not spread his arms as he mentioned his son Frederick. He had intended the gesture as a reminder that Frederick, five years Starbuck's junior, had been born with a withered arm, but the gesture also released the battle flag that had been clasped under the preacher's left arm. The flag fell to the floor, where it sagged out of its fraying, abused string binding. Starbuck, glad not to have to meet his father's gaze, looked at the flag.

He saw the silk, the lavish fringe, and he looked up at his father's face and for an instant all memories of Martha and Frederick vanished. He looked back to the flag.

Truslow had also noticed the richness of the flag's material. "Is that a battle flag, preacher?" he asked.

The Reverend Starbuck stooped to snatch up the flag, but the violence of the motion only destroyed what was left of the string so that the banner spilt richly into the evening light. "It's none of your business," the preacher said to Truslow defiantly.

"That's our flag, goddamn it!" Truslow said.

"It's the devil's rag!" the preacher snapped back, bundling the silk into his arms. He had dropped the cane to make the task easier.

"I'll take the flag, mister," Truslow said grimly, stepping forward with an outstretched hand.

"You want this flag," the Reverend Starbuck said, "then you'll have to strike me down!"

"Hell if I care," Truslow said and reached for the banner. The preacher kicked at him, but Elial Starbuck was no match for Thomas Truslow. The soldier hit the preacher's arm once, but hard, then took the flag from the suddenly nerveless grip.

461

"You would let your father be hit?" The preacher turned to Starbuck.

But the moment when Starbuck's surrender was just a tremble of remembered emotion away had passed. He scraped another lucifer alight and put it to a page torn from an account book. "You said you weren't my father," he said brutally, then ripped more pages and piled them onto the tiny fire. He sprinkled the flames with powder from a revolver cartridge that he tore apart, so that the small fire flared violently. His father snatched up his cane and tried to sweep the burning papers off the table again, but this time Starbuck stood in his way. For a second the two stood face-to-face; then a voice called from the yard.

"Johnnies!" It was Sergeant Decker.

Truslow ran to the door. "Yankees," he confirmed.

Starbuck joined Truslow on the veranda. A quarter-mile to the east was a ragged band of men who were watching the house. They wore blue, and some were on horseback and some on foot. They had the look, Starbuck decided, of a cavalry troop that had been put through hell. One of the men had golden hair and a short square beard. "Is that Adam?" he asked Truslow.

"I guess."

Starbuck turned to see that his father was obliterating the last vestiges of his fire. "Truslow," he said, "burn this damn house down while I go and tell those Yankees to get the hell out of Virginia. And I'll take the flag."

There was a spear-tipped lance pole in a corner of the room. Starbuck took the lance, stripped it of its spearhead and swallow-tailed cavalry guidon, then slotted the silk flag onto the staff. Then, ignoring his father's angry voice, he jumped down into the yard and called for a man to bring his horse.

He rode eastward, carrying the flag.

Adam rode to meet him, and the two erstwhile friends met in the middle of the pasture next to the farmhouse. Adam looked ruefully at the flag. "So you got it back."

"Where's the other one?"

"I'm keeping it."

"We always used to share," Starbuck said.

Adam smiled at the remark. "How are you, Nate?"

"Alive. Just," Starbuck said.

"Me too," Adam said. He looked tired and sad, like a man whose hopes have taken a beating. He gestured at the ragged band of men and horses behind. "We got ambushed in some woods. Not many of us left."

"Good." Starbuck turned in the saddle to see a wisp of smoke showing at a window of the house. "I know it wasn't your fault, Adam, but some of us took badly to women being burned alive. So we thought we'd do the same to Galloway's house."

Adam nodded dully, as though he did not really care about the destruction of the farmhouse. "The Major's dead," he said.

Starbuck grimaced, for it seemed that he was burning the house for nothing. "And the son of a bitch who killed the women? Blythe?"

"God knows," Adam said. "Billy Blythe disappeared. Billy Blythe has a way of making himself scarce when there's trouble about." Adam leaned on his saddle's pommel and stared toward Galloway's farm, where more smoke was showing at a half-dozen windows. "I can't imagine Pecker giving you permission to do this," he said with an obvious distaste for the destruction.

Adam clearly had not heard about Bird's wound, nor any of the Legion's other news. "Pecker's back home wounded," Starbuck told him, "and I'm the new colonel."

Adam stared at his friend. "You?"

"Your father was thrown out."

Adam shook his head in apparent disbelief, or maybe denial. "You have the Legion?" he asked.

Starbuck twitched the reins to turn his horse. "So the next time you want to play games with a regiment, don't choose mine, Adam. I'll goddamn kill you next time."

Adam shook his head. "What's happening to us, Nate?"

Starbuck laughed at the question. "We're at war. And your side says that houses have to be burned and goods taken from civilians. I guess we're matching you stride for stride."

Adam did not even try to argue the point. He stared at the farmhouse, which was now gushing thick smoke from several windows. Truslow had clearly set about his incendiarism with an expertise that quite outstripped Starbuck's feeble efforts. "Is that your father?" Adam had seen the black-dressed figure come from the burning house.

"Send him safe home, will you?"

"Surely."

Starbuck clumsily turned his horse away. "Look after yourself now. And don't interfere with us. We'll be gone in five minutes."

Adam nodded his agreement; then, just as Starbuck was urging his horse forward, he spoke again. "Have you heard from Julia?"

Starbuck twisted in his saddle. "She's well. She's a nurse in Chimborazo."

"Remember me to her," Adam said, but his onetime friend had already ridden away.

Starbuck rode back to the house, where his old company had gathered outside the yard fence to watch the flames. His father shouted something at Starbuck, but the words were lost in the roar of the fire. "Let's go!" Starbuck called and turned away from the burning house. He did not say farewell to his father but just rode up the hill. He thought

464

how close he had come to a tearful reconciliation, then tried to convince himself that there were some roads that could never be revisited, no matter what lay at their ends. He stopped at the wooded ridge and looked back. A roof beam collapsed into the fire, spewing a fountain of sparks into the evening air. "Come on!" he called to the company.

They caught up with the Brigade a mile to the east. Swynyard was resting the men and waiting for orders. There were rain clouds in the south and a fresh wind gusting, but to the west, above the Blue Ridge Mountains, the sun flared bright as it dipped behind America's rim. In the North an army was in full retreat, while to the east and south, wherever a man looked, there were only rebel banners advancing in victory. And now a brighter banner joined the triumph as Starbuck kicked back his heels and let his borrowed horse run free, so that the shining colors of the recaptured flag streamed and rippled in the breeze. He rode in a curve, bringing the flag back to its Legion, and as he turned the horse toward their ranks, he raised the flag higher still, standing in the stirrups with his right arm braced aloft so that the battle flag's white stars and blue cross and crimson silk were made livid and brilliant by the last long rays of daylight. He was bringing the bright flag home, and in the sudden cheer that filled the sky Starbuck knew that he had made the Legion his. It was Starbuck's Legion.

HISTORICAL NOTE

ALL THE BATTLES AND SKIRMISHES in the novel are based on real actions that were fought in the summer of 1862, a campaign that ended Northern hopes for a swift victory in the east that year. McClellan had failed in his ambitious amphibious attack; now John Pope had been beaten back overland.

I simplified some of the events that took place in between Cedar Mountain and Jackson's epic march around the Northern flank. There was an extra week of fighting in between those two events, but it was very confused fighting, and so I took a fiction writer's liberty and simply pretended it never happened. Readers who would like to know the true story of the confrontation across the Rapidan and Rappahannock should read John Hennessy's splendid account of the campaign, *Return to Bull Run*, a book that was constantly at my elbow as I wrote *Battle Flag*.

Washington Faulconer's stupidity at Dead Mary's Ford is based on an exactly similar event at Raccoon Ford, when Robert Toombs, a Georgia politician turned soldier, stripped the ford of its guard on the grounds that he had not ordered the guard set and therefore the guard should not exist, and on that very night the ford was crossed by a force of Federal cavalry that raided the Confederate lines and very nearly succeeded in capturing Jeb Stuart. They had to settle for the famous man's hat instead. Stuart vowed to repay the insult, which he did by capturing John Pope's best uniform coat at

Catlett's Station. Stuart offered to exchange the hat for the coat, but Pope, a humorless man, refused the offer. The unfortunate Toombs, meanwhile, was placed under arrest.

Pope's notorious General Orders numbers Five and Seven were issued and, unsurprisingly, were regarded by many Northern soldiers as licenses to steal. They also offended Robert Lee grievously, which is why he was so intent on destroying Pope. He did. After the second battle of Manassas (Bull Run to Northerners) Pope was never to hold high command again.

The battle is not as well known as it deserves to be. Jackson's flank march was a fine achievement, and Lee's strategy thoroughly confused a pedantic Northern command. The train crashes at Bristoe Station and the sack of the Federal depot at Manassas all happened, and the wounded civilian's weary judgment on the improbable Jackson ("Oh, my God, lay me down") did become a catchphrase in Jackson's army. Lee's victory might have been more complete had Longstreet attacked on the day he arrived on Pope's unguarded flank rather than waiting a full twenty-four hours, but the battle was still a notable Southern victory and marked by at least one gruesome record. The casualty rate in the 5th New York *Zouaves* was the greatest in a single regiment on a single day in the whole war: 490 men entered the fight, 223 were wounded, and 124 killed, a casualty rate of 70 percent. The Reverend Doctor Winslow and his son both survived. Lee's overall casualty rate was 17 percent, which, to a country short of manpower, was an ominous loss.

The battlefield is well preserved and a short drive from Washington, D.C. Much of the ground is shared with the field of First Manassas, and the two share an informative visitor center, where a pamphlet outlining a driving tour of the second battle is available.

One reason why Second Manassas is not as well known as it might be is that it is inevitably overshadowed by the events that followed. The North has just seen its latest invasion of the Confederate States of America trounced, and now Lee will try to exploit that victory by leading the first Confederate invasion of the United States of America. His army will march to the banks of the Antietam Creek in Maryland, and there, not three weeks after fighting each other on the Bull Run, the two armies will contest the bloodiest day in all American history. It seems that Starbuck and his men must march again.